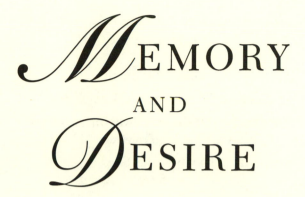

MEMORY AND DESIRE

LISA APPIGNANESI

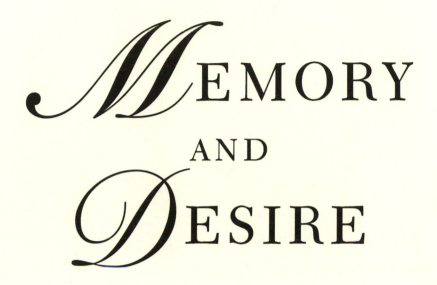

MEMORY

AND

DESIRE

A DUTTON BOOK

DUTTON
Published by the Penguin Group
Penguin Books USA Inc., 375 Hudson Street,
New York, New York 10014, U.S.A.
Penguin Books Ltd, 27 Wrights Lane,
London W8 5TZ, England
Penguin Books Australia Ltd, Ringwood,
Victoria, Australia
Penguin Books Canada Ltd, 10 Alcorn Avenue,
Toronto, Ontario, Canada M4V 3B2
Penguin Books (N.Z.) Ltd, 182–190 Wairau Road,
Auckland 10, New Zealand

Penguin Books Ltd, Registered Offices:
Harmondsworth, Middlesex, England

Published by Dutton, an imprint of New American Library,
a division of Penguin Books USA Inc.
Distributed in Canada by McClelland & Stewart Inc.
Originally published in Great Britain by HarperCollins Publishers.

First American Printing, February, 1992
10 9 8 7 6 5 4 3 2 1

 REGISTERED TRADEMARK—MARCA REGISTRADA

LIBRARY OF CONGRESS CATALOGING-IN-PUBLICATION DATA
Appignanesi, Lisa.
    Memory and desire / Lisa Appignanesi.
        p.   cm.
    ISBN 0-525-93403-0
    I. Title.
PR6051.P616M45 1992
823'.914—dc20   91-24920
                                                 CIP

Printed in the United States of America
Set in New Caledonia and Snell Roundhand Script
Designed by Julian Hamer

FIC

For John
who does

Memory is the past tense of desire

—WILFRED BION, 1967

PART I

CHAPTER
ONE

*T*here is nothing quite like spying to feed the erotic imagination.

Seeing and not being seen, gazing upon what thinks itself unob-
served, trembling on the brink of the secret. Hazarding discovery.

Alexei Gismondi, as he trailed through the wet Manhattan streets
on a day in early spring, was not unaware of the links between spy
and lover. And he had watched too many B movies in his youth for
his reflection amidst the bric-à-brac in a boutique window not to
bring a smile to his lips. There it was, the soft slouch to his hat, the
light belted coat which kept the persistent drizzle from his shoulders.
He had unthinkingly dressed for the part.

For a moment the irony of his situation dispersed the grimness
of his mood. Not a sleuth, yet for the last four days he had been
assiduously shadowing one particular woman.

And the cast she had taken on in his imagination did not altogether
please him. He had not come to New York to indulge in a lover's
overheated fantasies.

Perhaps it was this city which was doing it to him. This Manhattan
of dream and danger and celluloid. This week it seemed to him
like a medieval fortress full of dark corners and crevices and secret
underground passages. A perilous, moated medieval town, magnified
and transported into a future present of outsize spires and tunneled

windswept canyons. A mere individual could vanish here without a trace. Or a woman be snatched from the ramparts.

He moved on, keeping her slender form in view. Then abruptly he stopped. She had disappeared into the porticoed depths of a restaurant. He waited a few moments and then followed her in. Cool colors, hushed voices. A little enclave of peace in the ferocity of the city. He was beginning to know her tastes.

Alexei Gismondi rid himself of his hat and coat and slipped the hostess a twenty-dollar bill.

The woman looked at him curiously. Foreign. Definitely a foreigner. A determined and far too handsome foreigner in a pale cream-colored suit. She shrugged her shoulders imperceptibly and led him to a table no different from five others, except that it bore a reserved sign.

Except, too, that it gave him a clear view of Katherine Jardine.

Was she who he thought she might be? Was he?

Alexei leaned back in his chair, hid his restlessness, studied the menu unseeingly. Perhaps he ought to stop this farce of detective work now. That sense of vertigo which had hovered around him these last months threatened him again as he looked at her. That feeling that the solid ground of accepted truths was crumbling into a chasm of lies. The sense that history had cheated him.

Alexei puffed once on the acrid cigarette he had lit and then stubbed it out angrily. Perhaps he should never have come on this absurd, self-indulgent journey.

And yet he was here. He had taken the plane out of Rome the moment the film was finished. When he was frank with himself, he knew that he had thought of little else but coming here to New York over the last six months. Ever since he had seen that picture in the exhibition.

How strange it all was. This power of coincidence. This power of a picture. One moment the future had seemed empty, a cold, bleak, unpeopled horizon. Nothing propelled him forward. And his memories, the past, abutted in a series of brutal dead ends. As dead and brutal as the broken body of Aldo Moro, Italy's elder statesman shot eleven times and stuffed into the trunk of a car.

Then one day he had stumbled on that face. An extraordinary portrait in an exhibition which had borne the title *Paris Between the Wars*. Ranged amidst Picabia's mechanical monsters and Dali's surreal nightmares, that particular face had called out to him. A face that was childlike in its innocence, yet rampantly seductive. Troubled, too, as it sat atop the owlish feathers of a bird's body. The caption to the picture read: " 'Portrait of Sylvie Kowalska.' Collection—Katherine Jardine (New York)."

He had stared at the image for a long time. It moved him, drew him on. He had pondered the name. Remembered. It had been signatory to a letter he had received over ten years ago. A bizarre letter. There had also been a ring.

He returned to look at the picture every day for the length of the exhibition. The face of Sylvie Kowalska, vital, alive, mysterious, possessed him. And standing, gazing at that haunting image, Alexei had been filled with a rush of curiosity and excitement of an intensity he had not experienced since Rosa had died.

"Are you ready to order, sir?"

Alexei heard the hint of impatience in the waiter's voice which signaled that the question had already been asked a number of times. He named the first items on the menu his eyes lit on.

When he looked up he met Katherine Jardine's eyes for the first time. The directness of the contact was like a shock. Her eyes bore a trace of wry amusement. But it vanished as soon as he returned her gaze. Her expression then settled into that cool unblinking remoteness which he already recognized.

It was thus that he had first seen her through the glass of her gallery window. A slender, graceful woman with arresting gray eyes beneath a luxuriant sweep of dark burnished hair. She was standing completely still, yet watchful amidst that hive of activity which was the mounting of a new exhibition. Assistants were placing canvases large and small up on the gallery walls, waiting for her authoritative nod before completing their task. He recognized her from the photograph the agency he had hired had sent him. But seeing her in the flesh was an experience he had not sufficiently prepared himself for. She was beautiful, far more beautiful than Rosa. And she intrigued him, troubled him. That cool, musing poise which distinctly whispered, don't touch. And then, the sensuality of those wide lips, the wildness behind the eyes.

Alexei laughed at the direction of his thoughts. In another life, he might have trailed her, shadowed her movements for a far different purpose. Even now he wondered what he would have done had Katherine Jardine turned out to be a portly, substantial woman of middle years.

He had left Rome with the sense that he was on an urgent mission. Revelations had to be made. Truths uncovered. But in these last days in New York he had grown less sure. Perhaps his earlier certainty had merely been the fruit of need. The result of an obsession which had found the facts to sustain its existence. The face of Sylvie Kowalska had propelled him on a voyage of discovery, a search for a different history which would endow him with a new future.

And if he revealed all this to Katherine Jardine, might she not simply turn those cool gray eyes on him and see him as a burnt-out case in pursuit of the lives he might have led?

She had been joined now by an older man with thickly curling white hair. He kissed her on both cheeks in continental fashion. She smiled a warm slow smile, accepted apologies for lateness. Alexei watched. He could see only the man's back. Was he a friend? A lover? The thought disconcertingly distressed him. There was no husband. That much he had ascertained.

He listened intently, trying to distinguish their low voices from those of the diners now interposed between them.

Suddenly he saw her face cloud over, the gray eyes grow dark. Her voice now was distinct.

"No, I will not go to Italy. I will not set foot there again."

She was speaking French. He could make out only a phrase or two of what her partner said.

"But you must, Katherine . . . think of the damage . . ."

He thought she might cry. How vulnerable she suddenly looked. He felt like shaking the man.

Then she met Alexei's eyes again. This time he read a note of suspicion in them. Hastily he called for his check. It would spoil everything if he was found out. He pulled his hat low over his brow.

Soon. Soon, he would make direct contact. But he had learned something today. With Katherine, he sensed he would have to move slowly, by indirection, if he were to learn more about her. And more about Sylvie Kowalska.

Meanwhile there was his next appointment.

With a backward glance at Katherine, Alexei made his way out into the damp streets. The drizzle had hardened into rain, large drops of it, gathering and swirling in the gutters. On Madison Avenue, people hurtled by, their umbrellas a rainbow of mushrooms beneath the towering forest of the city.

Alexei took his time. He had over half an hour to cover the short distance to the Park Avenue address. Ample space in which to stroll by her house again. There it was. A gracious brownstone squeezed by the giant presence of its neighbors. Crocuses jutted purple and white from an ivy-strewn windowbox. Inside a light glowed, making plain the shining surface of a baby grand, a panoply of canvases on the wall. He was tempted to ring the bell, find an excuse, go in, examine, touch, sniff.

No. It would have to wait.

At the corner of the street, an old man, huddled against a building's concrete, stretched out a begging hand. On closer inspection, Alexei saw that the stoop, the gray face, had nothing to do with age. He pulled out a wad of bills and placed them in the shaking hand. Money. That wasn't his particular lack.

He turned the corner into Park Avenue and then hastened his steps. He mustn't be late. The appointment had been set up for him by a friend weeks ago. Famous psychoanalysts like Dr. Jacob Jardine were not instantly at one's beck and call.

Alexei announced himself to the porter, made his way over thickly carpeted floors to the lift. The doors were about to close when a man came rushing in. Thickly curling white hair, erect carriage. It was the man Alexei had seen in the restaurant with Katherine. He looked away guiltily. Tried to make himself small. To no avail.

"Sam tells me you are on your way to my office." The older man looked up at him with dark piercing eyes. "I am glad not to have kept you waiting." He thrust out a hand. "You must be Alexei Gismondi. I am Jacob Jardine." He chuckled as if he were caught in the midst of a joke.

Alexei hoped his surprise did not show too blatantly. The photographs on the Italian book jackets had prepared him for a far younger man.

Jardine was sizing him up with an intelligence born of years of quick assessments. Alexei, discomfited, mumbled something banal about the weather.

"This way." The older man ushered him into an outer office. "Mrs. Frampton will take your details and I shall be with you in a moment."

Mrs. Frampton did indeed take his details, as quickly and efficiently as Alexei's not altogether truthful responses allowed. Then a little buzz announced Dr. Jardine's readiness and Alexei was shown into a large airy room complete with the requisite couch, the works of Freud in a variety of languages and a splendid array of tomes amongst which he would happily have browsed. All this he took in at a glance before Dr. Jardine gestured him toward a comfortable chair positioned in front of a mahogany desk on which a number of antique figurines kept guard.

"Of what use can I be to you, Mr. Gismondi?" The older man placed a pair of spectacles on his nose and leaned back comfortably in his chair.

Alexei was aware of the French lilt to his speech.

"I had hoped you might be able to advise me on an analyst. I wish to begin an analysis. I have even hoped it might be with you," Alexei said, hearing the words reverberate strangely in his own ears.

"You *wish.* To *begin.*" Jardine took him up on his words, stressed them so that they acquired a new significance. "Do I take it then that you have not been driven here out of need, but by a whim? And that a *beginning* is perhaps all there might be? Analysis is not a pleasurable excursion, Mr. Gismondi, like a weekend trip to Paris, or like a brief tantalizing encounter with a beautiful woman." He chuckled again and looked at Alexei amiably. But it did not take the sting out of his words.

"My English may be at fault, Dr. Jardine. *Wish* in Italian is a very strong word," Alexei defended himself. He shifted in his chair. He would have to be on his guard with this man.

"Ah yes, of course. It is not your language. But then why do an analysis *here* in a foreign tongue? Tell me honestly, Mr. Gismondi. What brings you to analysis? On first judgment, I see nothing that tells me that you are not what you seem: a man in your prime."

The dark eyes bored into him.

It was Alexei's turn to laugh and he did so with sardonic zest.

"What brings me to analysis is the small question of my mother. My mothers." He was pleased to find himself honest at last.

"Now that interests me." Dr. Jardine scrutinized him closely. "Your mothers, you say?"

"Yes. They have given me a deep and abiding sense of unreality. Nothing I touch anymore seems to be real, have any meaning."

"Ah, meaning, Mr. Gismondi. We can deal with sex. We can deal with fear. We may even be able to deal with death. But meaning . . . I think you would be better served by a priest or a philosopher."

Alexei found himself angry. "And you, Dr. Jardine, why did you go into analysis? Was it because you were impotent? Or afraid of your own shadow?"

Dark eyes twinkled at him. "You are quite right of course. I plead guilty to intellectual curiosity. But then, Mr. Gismondi, I was training. I was already a psychiatrist. But we're not here to talk about me. Tell me, have you ever seen someone suffering from the many states we now loosely place under the categories of paranoia or schizophrenia or depression?"

Alexei nodded briefly.

"Then you will not tell me that you, as I see you here before me, are suffering from anything more than what Freud would have called 'ordinary everyday unhappiness.' And that, after all, is our common lot."

"So you won't help me?" Alexei surprised himself by his persistence.

Jacob Jardine shrugged. "If you wish to squander your money in order to satisfy your intellectual curiosity and to gaze in the presence of another into the navel of your memories and desires, I shall certainly not stop you." He scribbled a few lines on a piece of paper and handed it to Alexei. "I myself am now an old man and take on very few patients."

Alexei realized he was about to be dismissed. He rose to his full height. "I'm sorry to have wasted your time, Dr. Jardine." He spoke quietly. "I have read your books and they have forced me to think rather more than some others."

Jacob Jardine removed his glasses and smiled. "You flatter me."

Alexei stretched out his hand and the older man took it.

"Incidentally, Mr. Gismondi," he called Alexei back as he turned, "if you wish to discuss psychoanalysis, or even as you so mysteriously put it, your mothers, you have only to invite me to dinner. There is no need to come to my consulting room." There was a mischievous expression on his face. "And by the way, I have also seen two or three of your films and enjoyed them enormously. Goodbye."

The chuckle followed Alexei out of the room.

But Jacob Jardine looked after him a little more reflectively than its sound implied. There was something about this young man. Something that reminded him of . . . what was it? He tapped his pencil impatiently on his desk and then shrugged. He was growing old. And he was preoccupied. Preoccupied with that stubborn daughter of his who would not budge an inch. What had that ghastly Italian husband of hers done to her to keep her away from Italy so many years after his death? Katherine would never tell him, never confess. She was as silent as the tomb.

Two days later promptly at three, Alexei Gismondi strode purposefully into the Katherine Jardine Gallery. He had his opening remarks well rehearsed.

"I have an appointment with Ms. Jardine," he announced to an almond-eyed young man who was sitting behind an old-fashioned secretaire and lazily turning the pages of an art magazine.

"Oh yes, Mr. Gismondi." The youth smiled at him cheerfully. "I'll tell Kat you're here. Look round. It's a great show." He sped up a flight of stairs and was back before Alexei could so much as take in a single canvas.

"You can go straight up. She's ready for you. It's right at the top."

Alexei climbed two flights and found himself in front of a paneled door. He knocked and without waiting, walked in.

Katherine Jardine was standing by her desk, her back to him, the telephone balanced on her shoulder. She turned at the sound of his footsteps and as he walked toward her across the expanse of the room, he noticed the flicker of recognition in her eyes.

He looked at her intently and let his features register surprise. It wasn't altogether an act. At this distance of intimacy, with only a desk between them, he was startled again by her beauty. It was almost a physical sensation. There was nothing seductive about her. Indeed, her tailored gray dress had an austerity about it, echoed in the way she had pulled back the luxuriance of her hair in a simple clasp. But the fine-boned modeling of her face, the porcelain hue of her skin, the serious, slightly haughty cast of those wide gray eyes, the fluidity of her gestures, all gave him the sense that the particular quality of her beauty would continue to surprise him.

There was a catch in his throat as he spoke. "I believe we have seen each other before, if I am not mistaken. You *are* Katherine Jardine?"

She nodded, replaced the receiver carefully on the slab of glass which served as her desk. There was a hint of amusement in the eyes she focused on him.

"And you are the man whose ears even a persistent New York waiter cannot penetrate." She stretched out a slender hand. Wide lips curled into a smile.

"I'm afraid my attention had a more interesting object," Alexei found himself saying. Abruptly he dropped the hand he had held on to a second too long.

"Indeed." Katherine stiffened slightly. She sat back in her chair, putting the distance of the desk between them. "What can I do for you, Mr. Gismondi?"

Alexei told her.

"At an exhibition some months ago I saw a picture I am interested in acquiring. A beautiful portrait of Sylvie Kowalska by Michel St. Loup. It is in your possession?"

A series of emotions passed like lightning over her face, darkening her eyes. They settled themselves into a polite iciness.

"That portrait is not for sale." Her voice had a note of finality. But Alexei persisted.

"It's simply that I have a special admiration for St. Loup," Alexei lied, "and the picture seemed to me a particularly fine one. Money is no object . . ."

"Money is not *my* object either, Mr. Gismondi," she said coldly.

"Oh?" He was irritated by her coldness. "I thought that in New York art and money were inseparable partners." There was a sardonic emphasis to his words and he saw two red spots form in her cheeks. He had hit a nerve.

"I dare say that may sometimes be the case." She met him on it, her voice even. "But in this instance . . ." She lifted her face to him. Anger warred with pride. "Sylvie Kowalska was my mother, Mr. Gismondi. One does not sell one's mother." She stood up abruptly.

"But I could show you some other work," she added quickly. "We are not in the habit of turning away clients for whom money is no object."

She was parodying him, laughing at him. Alexei wouldn't be deflected from the intermediary goal he had set himself. "Of course, I'm sorry. I did not know Sylvie Kowalska was your mother. How silly of me." He looked at her intently, studied her.

"How could you know, Mr. Gismondi? We do not look alike. And we never had anything in common." The bitterness in her voice was only slightly veiled. Alexei wondered at it.

"Well, even if you won't sell," he added after a moment, "I would still dearly love to see that picture again."

Katherine considered. Before she could answer, a child rushed in and flung her arms round her.

"Natalie, I've told you not to dash in here without knocking," she scolded, but her face glowed as she embraced the girl.

"I just had to tell you that I got an A in my dreaded math test, Mommy."

"That's wonderful, darling." Katherine hugged the child to her again and then noticing Alexei's gaze, extricated herself.

"I'm afraid my time is up, Mr. Gismondi. Shall I ask one of my assistants to show you round this current exhibition? You may find something there which is to your taste."

Her arm still lingered round her daughter's shoulders and Alexei knew he was being summarily dismissed.

"But I did really want to see that portrait of Sylvie Kowalska again. I have traveled a long way for the sole purpose," he persisted.

"Surely not with that *sole* purpose, Mr. Gismondi? A man with your schedule." There was a tinge of irony in the gray eyes. It was the first indication Alexei had had that she knew anything about him. He stirred uncomfortably.

"Sylvie Kowalska," the girl intervened. "You mean my grand-mother? Does he mean the picture in your study, Mommy?"

Katherine nodded briefly and turned back to Alexei. "I'm afraid that's impossible, Mr. Gismondi," she said with a note of finality.

"I could show it to him, Mommy. I just popped in for a moment on my way home. Sandy's waiting for me downstairs. We could all go back together."

Alexei overrode Katherine's "but": "I would like that very much, Natalie." He smiled warmly at the girl. "My name's Alexei, by the way."

She shook his hand shyly. She had all the candid directness of a child, but her long limbs and delicate features already signaled the woman to come.

"You can hardly expect me to allow a stranger to go home with my daughter, Mr. Gismondi." There was wry amusement in Katherine's face. "This is New York, after all."

"Yes, no, of course," Alexei mumbled, then suddenly laughed. "Here" —he reached into his pocket and drew out wallet and passport, placed them on her desk—"I'll leave you all these as proof of my good intentions."

She gazed at him for a moment. "You know there are far better portraits of my mother, Mr. Gismondi. She was much painted at a particular point in time."

"Gramps has three great ones," Natalie contributed.

"But it is this particular one by St. Loup that interests me." Alexei smiled, raised his hands in an imploring gesture. "Please."

Katherine fingered wallet and passport and handed them back to him. "I shall ask my assistant, Joe, to take you round to the house. I would hate to see such rare dedication to a work of art disappointed."

She was mocking him again. He didn't mind. He would see the picture, see her home. He met her eyes seriously.

"Thank you."

*   *   *

The picture hung in Katherine's study, behind her desk. Perhaps it was Alexei's overheated imagination, but he felt it cast a particular aura over the place, filling it with ghosts. He understood why Katherine would have wanted to put it behind her when she was working. Yet its presence was inescapable. It shadowed the room, which was strangely spare: the neat desk, books, an armchair, behind it a curling, petaled lamp, the only feminine note in a space remarkably free of bric-à-brac. He sensed Katherine's imprint, contained, yet harmonious.

He gazed at the picture steadily. There was an imperfection in the bird's feathers. He touched it. A small tear in the canvas. Then he looked again at the face. The deep, blue eyes. He flinched and pondered the enigma again. She had a Polish name. But this picture had been painted in Paris in the thirties. How did the pieces fit?

"Would you like a chocolate milk shake?" Natalie's voice burst into his reverie. "Doreen's just making some for us. She's a whiz at it."

"Mmmm," Alexei smiled. He followed the girl down two flights of stairs to a well-appointed kitchen.

"Doreen, Doreen, I told you he'd want one," Natalie said excitedly.

"All right, all right. No need to shout. You just sit yourselves down at that table there and I'll rustle up another shake." A broad face of indeterminate age embraced them all in a smile. "And make sure you help your guests to those brownies, you hear?"

When Katherine came home, she found a replete Alexei sitting with two laughing girls and Joe round her kitchen table. There was a look of consternation in her eyes.

"I hope I haven't outstayed my welcome," Alexei began politely, "but the girls have plied me with chocolate. An irresistible inducement."

The girls giggled.

"Alexei's from Rome. Did you know that, Mommy? He's been telling us stories about it. Invited us to visit him."

"Yes, I knew that," Katherine said in a controlled voice, but her eyes blazed anger at him. "Natalie, have you done your homework? It's after six."

Natalie didn't answer. Instead she looked directly at Alexei. "I didn't tell you, but my father was from Rome." There was a challenge in her voice, as if she had been waiting precisely for her mother's entrance to mention this. "Did you know him, Alexei? He's dead now. His name was Carlo Negri della Buonaterra." She said it proudly and then turned to look directly at her mother.

"Natalie, that's enough now. Off with the two of you."

"I'll be off now too, if that's okay, Kat?" Joe rose and Katherine nodded him off, barely seeing him. She was staring at Alexei, waiting for his response.

"No, I don't believe I knew him," Alexei said softly. "I'm sorry he's dead."

Natalie turned dark eyes on him. "So am I," she murmured. Then with a change of mood, she tugged at her friend's arm. "Come on, Sandy, let's go up." She smiled innocently at her mother and the two girls bounded away.

Before Alexei could frame appropriate words, Sandy poked her face round the door. "Natalie dared me, so I'm going to say it. We think you're very handsome." She giggled loudly and rushed away again.

"Those girls," Doreen tsked from the other end of the room.

Alexei gazed at Katherine. She was trembling. He had an overpowering urge to take her in his arms.

Instead, he murmured, "I'm sorry. I didn't mean to interfere."

She wouldn't meet his eyes.

"I'm very grateful to you for letting me come here. Allowing me to look at the picture," he continued. "Perhaps you would let me repay you in some way? Let me take you out to dinner."

She turned to face him. Gray eyes tinged with pain. A tremor in the lips.

"I . . . I should like to very much. I should like to express my thanks in some way," Alexei urged her softly.

"Yes. Yes, why not, Mr. Gismondi." A hint of self-derision crept into her voice. "I'm sure it would make my daughter exceedingly happy."

Less than two weeks later, Alexei Gismondi stood in the departure lounge of Kennedy Airport, his boarding pass for Rome in his hand. He had spent three evenings with Katherine Jardine. Evenings which had moved him, filled him in turn with elation and fear. At the end of the second, he had held her in his arms. Breathed in her subtle fragrance. Kissed her. It was a kiss he felt himself powerless to prevent.

And then he had seen those drawings.

At dawn this morning, after a sleepless night, he had made his decision. He had to go. To flee. Katherine's face had replaced Sylvie Kowalska's in his imaginings. Mother given way to daughter. He would take steps to find out more about Sylvie Kowalska. But not in Katherine's presence. It was too dangerous.

Meanwhile, he had sent her a note. An inadequate note. For the moment he felt he could do nothing more.

The bell had rung just as Katherine emerged from a hasty morning shower. She had answered it herself and with a smile that lit her features taken the vast bouquet from the messenger's arms. Alexei. Who else could it be? She hummed a meaningless tune to herself and buried her face in the proliferation of spring blooms. How long had it been since she desired a man? Yes, desired, she acknowledged it with a sense of surprise and growing elation, hugging the flowers to herself.

A small box tumbled out of the bouquet as she unwrapped it, and a note. She tore open the latter first. The words were in Italian. She could still read it fluently.

"*Mia cara*," the note read. "Meeting you has been more than a delight. Thank you. But for now, I fear, it can only be a meeting. I must return to Rome urgently. Try to understand. Alexei."

Disappointment flooded through her. With clumsy fingers, Katherine opened the small velvet box. In it there was a ring, a single emerald, luminous in its finely crafted setting of white gold and tiny diamonds. She stared at it for a long time with a sense of growing disbelief. No, it couldn't be. She looked at the band and there, untarnished by time, were the initials, S. K. The jewel fell from her fingers, burning her.

S. K. Sylvie Kowalska. Her mother. Her mother's ring. The ring that had gone missing so many years back, the ring that had never been found amidst her mother's jewelery. How had this ring come into Alexei Gismondi's possession? Why did he want Sylvie's picture?

Katherine felt her mind growing blank and a deep sob rising in her, forcing its way from the pit of her stomach into her throat. Her mother. How she had hated her mother.

The slap stung Katherine's face and the force as well as the surprise of it almost knocked her over. She struggled to keep her balance, struggled, too, to keep the tears from flowing, to strangle the cry which came to her lips. She knew that any sound would only inflame her mother's anger further.

"What have you done with it?" Her mother's voice pitched high in rage echoed in her ear. Katherine stood rigidly still, her small body tense with fear. She had already twice protested her ignorance. She had no idea what had happened to her mother's ring. She knew only that she wanted to run away and hide in her room.

"I've seen you eyeing it, you little wretch. Now you've stolen it. Where is it?" Her mother's voice rose even higher.

Katherine twisted to evade the raised hand. She stumbled.

"Sylvie." Her father's voice, low as a hiss, intruded upon them. "I've asked you not to hit the child." Despite the quiet tone, it was an implacable command.

Katherine saw her mother's face grow an ugly red. She turned and ran from the sight. The voice behind her moved from shrillness to plaintive tears. "But you don't know what she's done. She stole my ring. You always take her side."

Katherine's short legs sped her to the quiet of her own room. Sobs began to shake her now and she climbed blindly onto the high bed where the white coverlet felt cool against her hot cheeks. Misery consumed her. Why wouldn't her mother believe her? Yes, she had looked at the ring. It was so pretty. But she hadn't taken it. Wanting wasn't the same as taking. She knew that. And it was her birthday today. Her fourth. She had been so looking forward to the party this afternoon. Princesse Mat was coming. And Leo would soon be back from school just for the occasion.

That morning at the *maternelle*, the nuns had been so kind. She had sat on the tall reading stool in the middle of the large room and everyone had sung "Joyeux Anniversaire" to her. It was only the second time she had ever sat on that stool, her legs dangling well above the floor. The first time had been last week when she had read out her favorite story to the children in the bigger class she had just been moved to. She had been frightened, but excited too. And the nuns had been full of praise.

She liked the nuns, their hushed voices, their faces so white and sweet against the black of their habits. So unlike her mother. She tried to please *her* too, but it was very hard. Today she had rushed home from school, waiting only for Madame Sarlat to help her across the *grand boulevard*, past the nice policeman who whistled for the cars to stop. Then she had raced along the street, up the steep stairs, which no longer seemed to be as big as she was, into their apartment.

She had scrubbed her hands and face till they were pinkly clean, pulled off her school smock and put on her best party dress, with its big blue velvet bow. She had even remembered to brush her hair, just as her mother always told her. But when she had knocked at the door of her mother's room to tell her she was all ready for the party. . .

Katherine buried her face in her pillow and pulled the coverlet up so that it hid all of her.

It was like this that Jacob Jardine found his daughter. His heart went out to his child. What could he do to stop his wife's frenzied rages? He stroked the small dark head and waited for the sobs to stop, for Katherine to turn to him when she was ready. The child had not had an easy life. For the first two years, Sylvie had pretended she didn't exist. Everything had been done by the nanny he had hired. It was pitiful to see Katherine seeking her mother's approval, her caresses, and finding nothing.

Then around the time of Katherine's third birthday, the sudden rages, the slaps, had begun, as if Katherine were responsible for everything that was wrong with Sylvie's life. The rages had grown less frequent of late, or so he had thought, though he was so little at home in the daytime that he had no way of knowing for certain. He had hoped. Hoped that with Leo away at Maison Lafitte and their plans for the long-awaited move to America almost finalized, Sylvie would grow less tense. The rages might disappear altogether. Then today . . . His fingers tightened into a fist.

"I didn't do it, Pappy. I didn't take her ring." Katherine turned her tear-stained face to him and looked up with earnest eyes.

"I know you didn't, *ma petite Kat*," Jacob consoled her.

Katherine liked being called Kat. She knew it meant cat in English and she liked cats. She threw her arms around her father and nestled against him.

"But why did Maman hit me then? I told her I hadn't taken it."

Jacob shrugged, at a loss for an answer which would satisfy the child without damning the mother. "She's just in a bad mood," he offered lamely. "But now, why don't you wash your face and you and I will go down to the café for a bite. And when we get back, everything will be ready for your party, and your mother won't be in a temper anymore," Jacob said with more optimism than he felt.

"Oh can we?" Katherine beamed.

Jacob nodded.

The Paris streets reflected something of Jacob's grimness as he strolled toward the local café with his small daughter. The immediate postwar years had not been kind to the city. Despite the handsome buildings of the *sixième arrondissement,* everything had an air of tarnished poverty: the shops with their meagre display of goods, the cafés with their peeling paint and shabby surfaces. Worst of all were the disgruntled faces of the passersby. A kind of sourness seemed to have descended over people. The euphoria of liberation, when German troops had finally left the occupied city, had been all too quickly replaced by the reality of recrimination. Who had been a collaborator? who an honest member of the resistance? People eyed each other with hostility or simply refused to meet each other's eyes. Suspicion, despite the passage of years, had become a habit it seemed impossible to shake. And amidst the material difficulty of everyday life, envy was rife.

True, in this last year or so, things had begun to improve, although Jacob still sensed the long fingers of suspicion everywhere. It was simply that the content of that suspicion had changed. Now the emphasis was on hunting would-be communists, rather than simply collaborators. The sour taste on one's tongue was much the same.

It was all a far cry from the prewar city Jacob remembered so vividly and with such affection. Many of his friends were gone now: some dead in the camps or in the resistance; others settled in distant climes. Soon he, too, would be leaving this blighted Europe. Even his own profession had become increasingly infected with savage quarrels and petty rivalries. The current battle raged between analysts who had medical training and so-called lay analysts who were now prevented from practicing. Like Freud, Jacob, despite his own medical training, placed himself firmly on the side of the lay analysts. Bitter arguments were part and parcel of every professional meeting. That irascibility, too, was part of the war's legacy. It wasn't easy to live with the guilt. The guilt of being alive. The professional guilt which accompanied the knowledge that a third of all asylum inmates in France had died under the Occupation. The Nazis and their French collaborators had hardly been tolerant of deviance however defined—racial, religious, or any of those countless conditions which were trapped under the catch-all of madness.

America promised a cleaner, more innocent terrain. Even Sylvie might find life there a little happier.

The war had taken it out of her. The war, the trip to Poland she refused to talk about, Caroline's death—they seemed to have changed her ineradicably. During the war, she had been a woman of extraordinary daring and courage. And then, it was as if she had gone into a state of limbo. Nothing held her attention for more than ten minutes. The cruelty was the worst of it. It left him helpless, despite his professional skills.

At the age of forty-five Jacob Jardine was a handsome prepossessing man in the prime of life. Widely acknowledged by his colleagues, considered by some to be the only genius France possessed in the developing field of psychoanalysis, and by others who knew little of this, as an unsung hero of the resistance, Jacob Jardine was nonetheless a troubled being. His intimate friends, and they were few, might be aware of his deep professional concerns, but they were only partially privy to the problems which ate at him daily. Amongst these, his wife Sylvie and his daughter Katherine were principal.

He glanced at Katherine's small perfect face now in one of the café's many mirrors. How much her own person she already was, her expression wiser than her years, a trace of wariness around the wide gray eyes. She smiled at him and he saw the redness of her cheek where her mother's hand had left its trace. He vowed to make more time for this child whose loneliness must be acute now that the brother she adored was away at school.

Eating her ice, Katherine was wholly happy. She loved being with Pappy, loved having him altogether to herself. It was too bad he had to be at work so much. That left her only Suzanne and her mother. Katherine's little hand shook. And Kazou, she mustn't forget Kazou. Kazou was her best friend and he was always there when she needed him, since he lived at the bottom of her cupboard. No one else could see him so he was there especially for her. He had come from a faraway place in the Arctic just when Leo had left for school. And he had come just for her, even though now his mamma missed him terribly. She was a nice mamma, Kazou always said in his quiet sort of voice.

But Pappy—Katherine focused her gray eyes on him—Pappy was the best. He always took time to explain things carefully to her so that she understood. Like now, when he was talking about America. A vast country he said, and drew its size compared to that of France in his small notebook. She liked maps. Those wavy lines which meant water. They were going to cross that water on a big boat. She had never been on a boat before. Would the nuns come, she asked him. She would miss them. But there would be Pappy, her handsome Pappy, and Leo.

❊   ❊   ❊

"Bonjour," Katherine's clear voice pealed out well in advance of her arrival in the sitting room. Suzanne, the maid, had told her that Princesse Mat and Leo had already arrived and she raced to greet them. She was met by an enthusiastic hug as Princesse Mathilde lifted her up to her own impressive height and smothered her against her generous form.

"Et comment va ma belle Katherine? How big and serious you're getting now that you're four."

Katherine kissed the Princesse on both cheeks and breathed in her rich perfume. *"Très bien,"* she answered and then instantly made a dash for Leo, who despite an initial gesture of boyish embarrassment let Katherine throw her arms around him. It was an endearment he would accept only from his sister and Katherine clung to him for a moment. She had missed her brother terribly and constantly. There was no one now to deflect her mother's moods when her father was out at work, no one to share the vast dinner table with as she swallowed the food under vigilant eyes. Except sometimes Kazou, when he was very hungry.

Katherine looked at her mother's stiff form, nodded a polite but almost inaudible *"Bonjour, maman"* before turning to greet Princesse Mat's daughter, Violette, who was even taller than Leo. Then Katherine returned to her brother's side, echoing his movements and gestures like a diminutive shadow.

Anyone who had entered the Jardine sitting room at that moment would have been easily forgiven for mistaking the scene in front of him for one which epitomized gracious postwar family life. Indeed graciousness combined with remarkable style. The large room with its high molded ceiling contained some flawless pieces of art nouveau furniture: a chaise-longue whose curves invited and imitated the female body; a pair of elegant high-backed chairs of the same period; two comfortable sofas covered in a cubist pattern which drew the eye and pleasured it with its intricate brightness. Walnut tables of a prior age were placed here and there with an eye for proportion and usefulness. On them stood lamps whose human or organic forms gave way to delicately tinted petals of glass. A baby grand graced a corner of the room.

Jacob's art collection, too, was more than enviable. A rakish Dali dreamscape hung next to one of Picabia's mechanical fantasies. Both bore Jacob's name and they were only two amongst many. A closer look revealed that the Picasso on the far wall did indeed bear a remarkable resemblance to the woman who now lounged in the chaise-longue.

At first glance, she had a singular beauty. Pale blonde hair pulled back from a delicate flowerlike face framed in its straying wisps; eyes of an exceptional blue which looked at you confidingly; slenderness of a touching fragility. She formed a picturesque contrast to the woman who sat opposite her, though sitting was hardly the word. With her bold, fluid gestures, her strong, energetic face across which expressions raced with lightning vivacity, this woman seemed to be moving even when she was sitting still. Her dark eyes shone with intelligence and wit, and if her clothes had something of the *outré* in their cut and color, she wore them with a daring which was completely in character.

The man who reached now to light the cigarette she had placed in a long holder was equally striking. The dark leonine head was held at a commanding angle. His bearing spoke of cultivation, though beneath the loose line of his suit, there seemed to be rather more muscle than urbanity demanded. A touch of whimsy in the mouth betrayed the strict correctness of his manner and made one want to hear his words. The deep laugh which boomed out of him as the dark woman paused in her tale had an engaging warmth.

It made the children who had been sitting in another corner of the room look up expectantly. Their shining faces completed the family idyll. The boy, it was immediately evident, was the son of the reclining woman. His blond fragility as yet bore no trace of the manhood to come, except perhaps in the length of his hands and feet and in the seriousness of his expression. The older girl was his mirror opposite in every way. There was mischief in her dark eyes, a robustness in her demeanor. Only in the care which she lavished on the smaller child was she kin to the boy.

The maid's entry into the room, her plump form preceded by a trolley loaded with enticing edibles, brought the children rapidly toward the adults.

"Chocolate cake," Katherine and Leo exclaimed in unison.

"Especially baked for your birthday, my sweet." Suzanne's smile spread. "And fruit and . . ."

"Oodles of presents," the Princesse announced, suddenly bringing boxes of varying shapes and sizes out from nowhere.

As cakes, tea and cocoa were passed round in elegant china and presents opened with increasing hilarity amidst the children, Jacob Jardine looked round the small gathering. He was acutely aware of the tensions beneath the gaiety. His wife's fixed expression was only momentarily broken by a tightening of the lips and an all but imperceptible flinch every time Katherine laughed in abandon. The small girl's eyes, if she accidentally met her mother's, widened in fear. Leo, always sensitive to atmosphere, beneath his boyish nonchalance, was overly protective of his sister. Thank heaven for the Princesse, who kept up a voluble patter, bringing them animated gossip from Switzerland, from Britain, and endless tales about the origins of Katherine's presents.

Jacob Jardine had good reason to feel grateful to Princesse Mathilde. She had acted as benevolent guardian of his family fortunes for years now and he was deeply aware of the debt he owed her. It was the Princesse who through one of her innumerable contacts had, after the war when they had nowhere to go, found them this spacious apartment. During the war, it had served as home to a German officer and its original owners had never returned. It was the Princesse, too, who had somehow managed to salvage his possessions and his treasured pictures, when Sylvie had fled south during the occupation. She who had kept his mother's fortune miraculously intact, invested it in America, so that the family now had a substantial income. And there was more, much more.

He felt her eyes on him now, read the veiled concern they registered. Jacob stirred himself into action. It was a family custom that any children present received gifts after the birthday child. With a great deal of ceremony, Jacob hushed the assembled group and brought out two large packages. Leo opened his first. He gasped in delight at what he found: an intricately inlaid box which unfolded into a chessboard. He fingered the carved pieces appreciatively.

"After dinner, tonight, we'll play," Jacob challenged him.

"And I'll beat you again," Leo beamed.

"And he will, too, Pappy," Katherine echoed her brother happily.

It was Violette's turn. The girl untied the ribbon with nervous anticipation. She loved receiving presents from Jacob, not because she was a child in whose life gifts were rare. Rather the contrary. But Jacob's presents were always special. They made her feel inordinately grown up. And they always seemed to answer a secret hankering. This time was no exception. Her package contained three beautifully bound volumes: Dickens's *Great Expectations* and *A Tale of Two Cities* with the original illustrations; and Thackeray's *Vanity Fair*.

Violette looked first at the books, then at Jacob lovingly. For the last four years, she had had an English governess, whom her mother had imported to their Swiss home so that Violette could learn what the Princesse called "the language of the future."

"How did you know, *Ton Ton,* that I was tired to death of reading all that baby rot Miss Beatrix always gives me? Why, if she had her way I'd still be going over *The Secret Garden.*"

Jacob winked mischievously at Violette.

"Thank you, kind uncle, thank you very much," Violette said in her best English.

Suddenly Sylvie, who had reclined listlessly throughout these proceedings, tensed into action like a cat who has just smelt danger. She strode over to Violette and tore the books out of the child's hand. "I thought so," she muttered. "I thought so." She turned venomously on Jacob. "You said you were going to buy those books for Leo."

Startled, Katherine dropped the cup and saucer she had been balancing precariously. The china smashed into a hundred pieces and the warm liquid splattered on to Sylvie's dress.

"You clumsy fool," her mother shouted at her. She lifted a hand to strike the girl and then remembering herself stopped it in mid-air. "Go straight to your room. I don't want to see you for the rest of the day," she said in a shrill cracked voice.

The Princesse and Jacob exchanged a mute look.

"Calm down, Sylvie. The child didn't mean to drop the cup," Jacob soothed.

Katherine looked down at the mess she had made and then fearfully up at her mother. Her eyes were filled with tears. Without making a sound, she walked stiffly from the room. Leo followed her and Violette was just a few paces behind. She picked up an armful of toys but when she got to the door of the room, she seemed to have second thoughts. She turned, a look of cold contempt on her normally vivacious face, and said, "You're silly, Aunt Sylvie, amazingly silly." With that she left them.

Jacob hid the smile which the girl's spunk had brought to his face.

"Now you've turned them all against me." Sylvie's fury directed itself at her husband. "How can I get any respect around here if you always counter what I say?"

"Calm yourself," Jacob said, his tone terse. "We're not alone."

"Oh yes," Sylvie shouted. "Of course, the great Princesse is here. We must all bow." She performed a mock curtsey in the older woman's direction, and then suddenly went limp. Listlessly, she returned to her chair, her face now as immobile as it had been before her outburst.

Jacob exchanged another look with the Princesse and then followed the children.

The Princesse sat quietly for a moment gazing at Sylvie. Though she must now be thirty-five, the woman still looked like a child. Only the slight dryness of skin, a few tense lines around the mouth and eyes, betrayed that she was no longer the girl of eighteen whom Jacob had fallen in love with. Did they still sleep together, she wondered, repressing a tingle of jealousy, surprised that she might still feel it. She knew that things were far from well between them and that Sylvie seemed to be sliding again, moving into a world where her grasp on reality grew more and more tenuous. Sylvie, whose brilliance and beauty and wildness had once compelled fascination. How unpredictable life was.

It had been too long since Jacob and she had talked. These last three years had been taken up with her ailing husband's death. Poor Frederick, he had dragged his enfeebled, shrinking body round Europe's remaining noble families, making what he called his official last visits, before settling into the precincts of their Swiss château and waiting for that final guest. He had long felt that he had outlived his time. And during his last years, Princesse Mathilde had perhaps been more in his company than ever before. Strangely, she had felt closer to him then than throughout the years of their long married life. During those she had forged other existences for herself, other personae than that of a royal princess. After a funeral replete with the pomp and glory befitting a Danish prince had come the official period of mourning, the complicated tying up of affairs, the countless visits to relatives in Copenhagen, Greece, Britain, France.

On these last, Violette usually accompanied her and they always saw Jacob and the family. She saw him, too, at professional gatherings at the Institute. But she had rarely seen him alone and she had not realized quite what a strain he was living under. Certainly the numerous letters which passed between them contained nothing of what she had garnered today. Not a word had been said of Sylvie's state.

Princesse Mathilde was rather more given to doing than to sighing. But she sighed now. If only all those years ago, other choices had been possible. She fingered the many strands of pearls which she had recently taken to wearing, put another cigarette into her long holder and decided on her tack. "Are you playing the piano again, Sylvie, and singing those wonderful songs of yours?"

Before Sylvie could stir in response, Suzanne announced a new arrival.

Jacques Brenner strode into the room with all the loquacious vitality which made of him one of Paris's most charming men. His long loose limbs clothed with a dandy's flair kept pace with his vivid tongue. In a trice, he had raised Sylvie from her couch, kissed her hand, paid tribute to the Princesse, asked after Jacob and the children, and told them that they shouldn't be sitting here but out in the Place de la Bastille where a magnificent demonstration was in full swing.

The Princesse saw Sylvie transformed. In answer to Brenner's rush of compliments, she was metamorphosed into an excited adolescent. She pouted and preened, held his gaze and when it strayed from her offered one of those outlandish comments which had once been her distinguishing mark, so that his attention returned to her.

"Oh yes, Jacques, let's go out and join the thick-skinned pachyderm, trumpeting their protest. I'm tired of my private zoo," she said beguilingly.

"But where is that genius of a husband of yours? He can't miss this."

"Right behind you, you old troublemaker." Jacob shook the other man's hand warmly. Jacques was his closest and oldest friend. "We've missed you here."

"And now that I'm here, I'm going to waft you all, and I mean all, straight out again. That's an order, oh most bohemian of princesses." He smiled broadly at Princesse Mathilde. "And those beautiful children. Where have they got to?"

"They're playing in Katherine's room," Sylvie said as if nothing was amiss.

"Right, on with your coats and I'm off to get them."

They all piled into Princesse Mathilde's mammoth Daimler and drove smoothly along the Boulevard Saint-Germain. They crossed the stone-gray waters of the Seine at the Pont Saint-Michel flanked on the left by the grandly buttressed Notre-Dame and made their way regally toward the Place de la Bastille.

Katherine loved the big car with its smell of leather, the sight of the Paris streets moving slowly before her eyes. It was nice to be perched on her father's knee. She snuggled against him. It had been a trying day, but a happy one too, what with Pappy and Leo and Violette and Princesse Mat all there, all with presents for her.

And now they were off on an adventure. The car came to a smooth stop. They all piled out and walked. Katherine held on tightly to Pappy and Leo's hands, one on each side. She felt safe between them, despite the sea of people they suddenly found themselves amidst. Legs, legs everywhere. Katherine tugged on Pappy's hand and he lifted her onto his shoulders. Now she could see over the heads, hundreds of them bobbing in this direction and that. In the distance there was a platform, a man's voice boomed out. It seemed to be coming from all directions. *"Français,"* he said, and then something she didn't understand. Someone pulled the microphone away from him. A policeman came up on the platform. There was a tussle and then a woman's voice sang. *"Allons enfants de la patrie-ie-e . . ."* A deep raucous voice. She knew that song. Her mother knew it, too. She could hear her singing just behind her. That was the nicest thing about Maman. Her voice and the sounds she made the piano make. Katherine couldn't do that and she liked it when Maman sang. But she didn't like the way Maman's body squirmed. Just the voice. If only Maman was just a voice singing.

She felt herself being lifted again and suddenly there she was on Uncle Jacques' shoulders. He had blond hair like her mother. Hers was dark, like Pappy's. She was glad of that. Though Leo had blond hair. Where was he? She called, "Leo." No one could hear her except Uncle Jacques and he pointed to where Leo stood. Then the crowd started to move and push. Uncle Jacques was being propelled away from the others. She couldn't see them anymore. Maybe if she were lost, Maman would miss her and cry.

But no, she wasn't lost. There was the Princesse's car. The others were already there. All except Pappy. Where was he? Katherine clambered down from Jacques' shoulders and clutched at Leo's hand. Pappy. In the swirl of legs none were his. Katherine was afraid. What would she do without Pappy? She shouted, "Pappy, Pappy, Pappy."

There he was at last. She held on to him tightly.

The big car started its gentle motion and Katherine leaned back against her father. They were all together again. She relaxed. She felt sleepy now. She would have to show Kazou all her lovely presents before going to bed.

Suddenly Katherine felt something sharp pressing against her stockinged leg. Her gaze focused on her mother's hand. "Oh Maman, you've found your ring." The diamonds sparkled around the deeper glow of the emerald. "I'm so glad," Katherine said. Now she could no longer be blamed for something that wasn't her fault. What a relief.

"Yes, I found it where you hid it, you little thief," her mother rasped. She pressed the ring harder into Katherine's thigh.

The little girl flinched away and muffled the cry that rose to her lips.

PART II

CHAPTER
TWO

$\mathcal{S}$ome marriages are made by
life. Others are made by ideas. In later years, Jacob Jardine would
recognize his as the latter. Like a Madame Bovary infected by penny
romances which told of glorious love affairs between simple girls
and wealthy noblemen, Jacob Jardine had been infected by that
constellation of ideas and art known as surrealism. It was this which
had led him to his bond with Sylvie Kowalska.

Despite the impressions left by artists' and writers' memoirs,
France in the 1930s was still a deeply conventional society. The
family was a sacred unit. Parents, particularly fathers, were figures
of authority, demanding respect and obedience. Girls of good family
went unsullied from the parental to the marital home. Thus, in the
autumn of 1933, when the case of Violette Nozière erupted upon
the public consciousness, it sent shock waves into all corners of the
nation.

On the evening of August 21, Violette Nozière, eighteen-year-old
daughter of a railway engineer, poisoned her parents with a drug of
her own concoction. Her father, Baptiste, died instantly; her mother,
Germaine, possibly wary of her daughter's intentions, had consumed
only half of the proffered potion, and survived. For some time, it
transpired, Violette Nozière had been living a double life. With her
parents, she was prim, studious, the perfect daughter. Freed of their
presence, she made herself up, dressed in slinky black, cavorted

31

round the Latin Quarter, and took lovers with the ease of the professional courtesan. It was thus that she met and fell passionately in love with the student Jean Dabin; for him, possibly, that she prostituted herself. For him, too, that she stole, one day offering him the ring she had taken from her father.

When Violette Nozière developed syphilis, she managed to convince her parents that the fault was theirs—the disease hereditary. Every night she prepared a medication for them, purportedly on doctor's orders. On the night of the murder, her father had grown suspicious. He had rushed to the chemist's to find out the contents of the potion he was being given. It was too late. The shop was closed. The fatal dose was swallowed.

In court, Violette Nozière testified that she had never intended to kill her mother, only her father, who she claimed had been raping her for months. Until she had met Jean Dabin, she had been frigid.

France was in an uproar. Family values, the stability of the nation, seemed to be at stake. Fueled by the press, sides were taken, heatedly argued in every café and on every street corner. The majority, conservative, patriotic, saw in Baptiste Nozière the flower of innocent French manhood, a kind paterfamilias, cruelly murdered by a vile, ungrateful daughter. They railed against the depraved Violette, this scandal of a daughter. Popular songs invoked her satanic figure and called for torture, hanging, the most brutal forms of punishment.

Jacob Jardine had just qualified as a psychiatrist. Daily he went to the Hôpital Sainte-Anne and daily he grew more exasperated with the existing practice of psychiatry, its often sadistic methods, its endless incarcerations. So much more needed to be understood, investigated about sexuality, about what was too easily seen as criminal behavior. His interest in psychoanalysis, the talking cure, was already well in place. He had had several years of a training analysis and though he often found himself at loggerheads with the traditionalists in the Paris Psychoanalytic Society, he had the year before traveled to Vienna and met the famous Dr. Freud.

Increasingly he found his friends amongst rebellious artists, poets, writers, members of an avant-garde who wanted to rid the world of prevailing hypocrisies. It was they who were exploring the territory which interested him. And they were doing it with far more prescience than his fellow doctors. At the Dôme, he would sit with André Breton, self-proclaimed head of the surrealist movement, the poets René Char and Paul Eluard and artists like Max Ernst, Giacometti, and Dali. They would all heatedly argue the case of Violette Nozière.

For them, Violette was a heroine, a modern Electra who had lived out the deepest and most terrifying aspects of the unconscious. Her sexuality and savagery provided a clue to the modern mind. She made visible the anarchic forces, the hidden desires at play beneath the thin layer of everyday respectability. Violette had killed off the dead order of hypocrisy.

In retrospect, Jacob Jardine realized that when he met Sylvie Kowalska he was already passionately in love with the idea of the girl revolutionary, this heroine of the new modernity who would enable him to probe the depths of the human psyche. The character of their first encounter determined all the rest.

It was Jacob's habit in those days to meander through the streets after he had finished his shift at the hospital. He would walk anywhere his feet led him and eventually, almost by accident, happen upon one of the cafés where he was certain to find some friends. Preoccupied with the patients he had seen during the day, he played over their respective cases. Sometimes a chance event in the streets, a glimpse of some occurrence would tie in with what he had heard or seen in the clinic and stimulate him to fresh insight. These hours of walking reverie were often his most productive.

One late afternoon in the autumn of 1934 he was strolling through one of those bustling markets which formed the center of any Paris quarter when he chanced upon a class of schoolgirls trailing in double file behind two nuns. He liked the way the girls' severe blue uniforms cut a swathe through the rampant color of the market. Lazily he followed them. They were big girls, he reflected, undoubtedly in their final year preparing for their baccalaureate. Almost women. Yet caught in the time trap of their uniforms, their black cotton stockings and school procession, they seemed inordinately young.

One of the girls caught his attention. She had fallen back behind her fellows. Her golden hair tied in a loose knot captured the fading gleams of the sun. Suddenly she turned. A delicately chiseled profile presented itself to him, a face from a child's story book, all innocence and susceptibility. Jacob stopped. He knew something was about to happen. With a quick, bold gesture, the girl reached out and in a trice she had taken a gleaming red apple from a stall and popped it into her pocket. Her features retained their guilelessness. Then abruptly she turned and looked him full in the face. An air of con-summate mischievousness spread over her features. The look made him complicit. But it was no sooner seen than it had vanished and Jacob would have thought he had imagined the whole thing, had she not in darting back to rejoin her file, provocatively lifted her skirt from behind and yes, he was sure of it, waggled her bottom at him.

Astonished, he stood his ground for a moment and then burst out laughing. From a safe distance he followed the little group to its destination, a convent school just a few minutes away. The girl did not turn back once. The doors of the school enveloped her safely. Without thinking, Jacob noted the street and looked at his watch. He had never engaged in this kind of adventure before, but he knew he wanted to see this girl again.

The next day at the same time he deliberately made his way to the very same market and waited. The file of girls did not appear. The depth of his disappointment shook him. He persisted and two days later was rewarded. There were the girls again, orderly in their double file amidst the noisy commotion of the marketplace. He waited and watched. Again the girl with the golden hair lagged behind her fellows. Just at the moment when she reached the stall which had marked the place of her previous crime, she turned. Jacob's breath caught. She gave him a bold look, almost as if to announce her act. Then with a minimum of furtiveness, she clasped two shining apples and put them unobtrusively in her pockets. The smile she gave him before turning back to her friends was a brazen challenge.

Jacob felt a rush of excitement such as he hadn't experienced since his early adolescence, when the merest flicker of a woman's eyes filled him with illicit longings. In confusion, he trailed behind the girls. Then, just as the vast convent doors were swallowing up the first of their number, he made up his mind. Rapidly he tore a sheet of paper from the small notebook he always carried. He scrib-bled on it: "Café du Dôme, Saturday, 5 p.m." and signed his name.

Purposefully, he strode down the street. In front of the wide con-vent doors, he let the thick tome he was carrying drop. He picked it up just as his girl, the last, walked past. In rising, he covertly dropped the note into her pocket, just where the apple bulged slightly. As he stood to his full height, he noticed a nun waiting sternly just inside the open door. With the air of a man impatient to reach a destination, Jacob Jardine walked away.

At four o'clock that Saturday, Jacob was already seated on the *terrasse* of the Café du Dôme. The newspaper he held in front of him served less as reading material than as a cover: should any acquaintance see him thus preoccupied, he would pass him by. For the last two days Jacob had been counting the hours. Would the girl come? He could think of nothing else. In the thirties, respectable girls, convent girls, did not take up assignations with strange men. It was a chance in a million.

Tense, Jacob hoped. Behind the screen of his paper, his eyes continually scanned the boulevard with its crowds. It was a bright day, despite the lateness of the season, and the faces of the passersby were alight with laughter and sunshine. When his watch showed a few minutes past five, Jacob began to berate himself for his idiocy. Ten minutes later, he had begun to create elaborate schemes by which he would identify the girl and present himself at the convent door with messages from absent parents.

Yet still he sat there, glued to his place, awaiting what he had ceased to expect. Half an hour later, she arrived. Jacob, man of words and trenchant intellect, found himself speechless. Her hair, wild and uncombed, flew around the perfect oval of her face, framing it in an aureole. She was wearing a wide full skirt, which accentuated her slenderness; a blouse with a demure lace collar, but which she had left unbuttoned at the top, so that Jacob without realizing it was aware of breasts too full for her childlike stance. It was a style which ran completely counter to the times, but which she made strikingly her own.

Her voice, when it came, surprised him with its deep contralto.

"Bonjour, je vous ai apporté ceci." From the folds of her skirt, she brought out a gleaming apple and placed it obtrusively in the center of the table. A wide, mischievous smile spread across her face.

Jacob laughed, picked up the apple and bit into it with delighted complicity.

"Good, isn't it?" She looked at him greedily.

"Very. Thank you." Jacob was bewitched. He looked into the blue of her eyes and then remembered himself. "I'm Jacob Jardine." He extended a hand. She took it with a formal grace which immediately changed her aspect.

"My name is Sylvie," she said, offering no other. "It is very bad of you to have me meet you here in this way." Jacob couldn't tell whether the flat tone of her comment reproved him or teased.

"Sylvie. A wood nymph. I should have known," he murmured.

"I would like a chocolate ice," she announced, once more a child. "A very large one."

"Of course." Jacob hailed the waiter. He wondered about the hint of an accent he couldn't trace in her voice.

No sooner had he placed her order than she said, "I am not a wood nymph at all, you know. I don't like the woods. I like cities, big cities, especially at night. What I hate most of all are convents." She shivered. "They only let me out for my music." She reached down for the large school satchel she had been carrying, opened it and took out a sheaf of music books. "Here, this is what I like." She flung aside a volume of Chopin, another of Liszt, and at last proffered some unbound sheets. "Gershwin. *Rhapsody in Blue*." She began to mimic the piano's deep percussive sounds. "What about you?"

"Mmm. Very much." Again Jacob found his intelligence deserting him. "I should like to hear you play," he said.

She considered him. "What do you do?" she asked.

"I'm a doctor," Jacob answered, deliberately not specifying.

She looked at him quizzically; then flinging back her long slender neck she laughed uproariously. "A doctor eating stolen apples." The thought filled her with evident glee. Then she stopped, suddenly serious. "You're very handsome for a doctor," she said.

Jacob was in turn embarrassed and elated. Young women in his circle didn't speak this way, act this way. A clear breath of freedom encircled him as he looked at her wide-eyed face, the way she spooned the ice cream lavishly into her mouth.

Then abruptly, with a touch of coltish clumsiness, she stood up. "I'm off," she said, and without turning back to say goodbye, she was gone.

"Wait," Jacob called after her. "I don't even know your name." His voice trailed off as the people at the table next to him paused in their conversation to watch the scene.

Frustrated, Jacob turned to order another Pernod. It was only when the waiter placed the colorless liquid on the table and paused to pour the water which turned it thickly yellow, that Jacob noticed a large square card on the table. He picked it up, turned it over and read: "*Les soeurs de Saint-Ange vous invitent à un concert . . .*" The date of the concert was two weeks away. Amidst the names of the performers he noticed Sylvie Kowalska. Polish, yes, that would account for the accent, the blond chiseled features.

Reflectively Jacob sipped his bittersweet drink. Had the enthralling Sylvie Kowalska left the card there deliberately, as an invitation to him? Or was it an oversight? Whatever the case, he would go. Of course he would go.

The intervening weeks passed all too slowly for Jacob Jardine. He was by nature not a man cut out for waiting. His impatience was as proverbial among his friends as his patience was lauded by his professional colleagues. When Sylvie didn't turn up at the Dôme, as he had hoped she might on the following Saturday, he decided to act. Amongst his acquaintances, he had remembered a woman with Polish connections. Promptly he went to see her.

Madame Eugénie de Troye (née Sokorska) was all too pleased to receive the young Dr. Jardine, despite the unexpectedness of his visit. He had once graced one of her receptions in the company of Princesse Mathilde and any friend of the Princesse's was a most welcome guest, as she was quick to make clear to her gathered visitors when Jacob made his entry.

"And how is Princesse Mathilde?" Eugénie de Troye asked as soon as a dainty black-skirted maid had placed a delicate cup of China tea in Jacob's hand.

"Very well, I believe," Jacob answered casually. "She's in Scotland at the moment." He looked round the room's gilded columns, the heavy Empire furniture; he refused to be drawn. "And you? I believe you spent some time this summer near Montpellier. My mother mentioned to me that she had bumped into you at the Beauchamps'." This piece of useless information from his mother's round-up of local gossip had just crystallized itself adroitly in Jacob's mind.

"Ah yes, your mother." Eugénie de Troye had forgotten the incident. But she noted the connection, noted too the way Jacob had skillfully diverted the conversation from Princesse Mathilde. She had often wondered about the nature of the Princesse's connection with Dr. Jardine. They were rather too frequently in each other's presence when the Princesse was in Paris. But then the Princesse allowed herself certain liberties which might blemish a lesser woman's reputation. Looking at Jardine, she thought she guessed what was unspoken.

Jacob knew too well what Eugénie de Troye was thinking. With a dexterity which spoke of years spent in salons of varying aspects, he flattered Eugénie while drawing her out. All the time, he was looking for a way to tackle the subject which he had come about without being too obvious. The teapot from which the maid replenished his cup gave him the opportunity.

"Ah, isn't that part of the famous Polish Ćmielów porcelain? How very fine. Of course, I had quite forgotten, your family is from Poland, isn't it?"

"Yes, indeed."

"I met a rather interesting young Polish woman not so long ago. Sylvie Kowalska." Jacob had to keep his tongue from stumbling over the name, so heavy had it grown with significance.

"Yes, the young Kowalska. Her godparents, Paul and Julie Ezard, are good friends of the Princesse's." This, in Eugénie de Troye's mind, accounted for any connection Sylvie might have with Jacob. Jacob, on the other hand, had to hide the confusion the link caused in him. His world seemed to be growing far too small. He could only trust himself to nod interrogatively.

He needn't have worried, however, for Eugénie de Troye was an adept at gossip. An energetic woman, she had resigned herself to the constrained activity her class imposed on her. All her animation and her aspirations now went into her social life. And if she could please this young friend of the Princesse's by entertaining him with what was by any standards a choice tale, she would have no hesitation in doing so.

"Poor Sylvie. It's a sad story. She was sent to school here at the age of thirteen by her parents. They used to come and visit her regularly. Good stock, you know, nobility, but a little wild, especially the mother, and a little impoverished. The Ezards looked after Sylvie, when she wasn't in the convent. Then, now let's see, when was it? Three or four years ago, there was a fatal flying accident. The mother and father were both killed and the little boy, Sylvie's brother. The father liked to fly, it seems. It was his passion. They were on their way here, I believe. Met a storm over the Alps and came straight down." Eugénie made a dramatic swooping gesture with her hand. "It was all over instantly. Poor Sylvie."

"I see," Jacob murmured.

"There's a grandfather left and uncles and aunts, of course. But the Ezards thought it would be better for Sylvie to finish her schooling here. I believe she wanted that as well. They've replaced her family. She's not an easy child, I'm told. Still with all that . . ." Eugénie threw her arms up in the air.

Jacob shook his head. "Tragic," he said quietly. The air of the room had become stifling. He simultaneously wanted to get up and go, and to barrage his hostess with questions about Sylvie. Politeness would allow neither. He searched his mind for other subjects and could find none. Luckily his hostess had no such difficulty. She was burning with interest about psychoanalysis, his *séjour* in Vienna. She had heard he had met the infamous Dr. Freud.

The following Saturday Jacob Jardine sat tensely in the large cool hall of the Couvent de Saint-Ange. Stone walls, bare but for pictures of the saints, hard wooden seats; an aura of austerity imposed itself on the gathered company. All eyes were on the raised platform at the front of the room. Here a grand piano and a harp stood, lit by the colors which filtered through two stained glass windows. The contrast between the vivid stage and the somber room could not have been more dramatic.

Jacob Jardine was a man who rarely worried about the impression he made on his fellows. Adored child of a doting mother and a father who treated him as an intelligent equal, he had always been far too preoccupied with whatever goal he was pursuing to give second thoughts to the figure he might cut in the course of that pursuit. Nonetheless on this occasion, society's mirror confronted him with unsparing severity. In the hushed atmosphere of the convent, amidst the soberly clad families, scrubbed children and the omnipresent white-faced nuns, he suddenly saw himself as a man bent on ludicrous folly. Surely it was visible to everyone that he was here on a passionate mission utterly antithetical to the whole atmosphere of the place. He almost turned round and went home. And then, remembering the obsessive anticipation with which he had looked forward to this day, he sat as inconspicuously as he could at the very back of the hall.

One by one the girls, dressed in virginal white, sat down at piano or harp. Their names, the music they were to play, were announced by a clear-voiced nun. Jacob waited and listened and waited. The playing was of varied skill, the girls of varying ages. His waiting took on a tactile quality. He could feel it in the muscles of his legs, in his taut shoulders. At last she was there. Her hair was tightly drawn back in a knot. Her face, with its pure lines, was luminous in the golden glow of the colored glass. She played. A rush of breath escaped Jacob's lips. Rich, sonorous, the music flowed effortlessly from her hands. They flew over the rapid arpeggios, the innumerable trills of a Liszt rhapsody. She played for effect, mustering drama, exaggerating fortissimi, dwelling on the rallentandi. The applause was raucous, felt. There were shouts of encore. Jacob joined them.

Sylvie stood and made a small, graceful bow to the audience. Her eyes scanned their numbers. At last, after what seemed a long moment, they fell on him. A wide smile spread over her features. And then—but he couldn't be sure, it all happened so quickly—she winked at him: the rakish gesture of a street urchin turned vamp. The audience's applause continued, the calls for an encore. The starched nun nodded at Sylvie. She sat down at the piano again, paused for a second, and then with a wildness which matched the throbbing rhythms of the music brought a new kind of life into the room. *Rhapsody in Blue.* Before Jacob lost himself to the music, he noticed a look of bewilderment spread over the nun's face.

The applause this time was more contained. There were some looks of incredulity. Jacob smiled. He had made up his mind. He wrote a hurried card to Sylvie, taking care that it could pass before the eyes of others with no undue repercussions. "Congratulations. You played wonderfully. Do come and see me as soon as you can. I shall be at home Monday and Thursday evening and over the weekend." He added, for the nuns: "We would all like to hear you play." He was pleased that the new cards bore both his hospital and home address. The word *doctor*, after all, was a sign of a certain reliability.

Before making a hurried exit, Jacob politely asked one of the nuns to give his note to Sylvie.

Despite the pressure of innumerable commitments, time now lay heavily on Jacob's hands. Though he felt increasingly certain that Sylvie would come to see him, he had no way of knowing when. It was fortunate that the case he was currently writing up fascinated him to the degree that few did. He had spent the last months working in the hospital with a certain Naomi, a woman of middle years who had spent a blameless life until one evening, she had attempted to knife a famous opera singer. Her attempt had failed and, since the singer had not brought a charge, Naomi had been sent to Sainte-Anne. Here Jacob had unearthed the intricate web of connections which had led this woman to attempt to kill a person she had never met, but whom she saw as her archrival in life, a persecuting presence who invaded her dreams and daily activities.

Sylvie did not turn up on the first of the appointed evenings, nor the second, nor the third. Restless, Jacob cursed his inactivity. He felt trapped in the momentum of waiting. He had not really expected her before the weekend. Convent regimes were strict. But he knew that girls often went home at the end of the week and this was Friday. By ten o'clock he was in a foul humor. He went out to lose himself in the crowds and make his way to the Coupole. It was a regular haunt for his friends.

He was not disappointed. No sooner had Jacob set foot in the vast, noisy interior of the famous restaurant than he heard his name called. He joined the group. There was the actress, Corinne, whose striking dark eyes and throaty voice could reduce an audience to tears in seconds. Jacob had had a brief affair with her some years back, which had ended amicably on both sides. Jean-Paul Sartre was there holding forth in his suasive tones, and his mistress, Simone, whose laugh came boomingly from her petite frame. He had met them once before with his painter friend, Michel St. Loup, who now introduced him to some others at the table.

Jacob ordered quickly. The group were discussing Germany, from where Sartre had just returned, horrified at the temper of the country, the mass rallies which had the power of transforming thousands of people into a single entity, all under the spell of a single man. With vivid detail, he evoked the image of a nation hypnotized by a voice which played on all its hidden fears and glorious hopes, a voice which was rapidly stripping the country of any constitutional controls, the voice of a dictator.

"I've had enough of this," the woman opposite Jacob suddenly said in an unmistakably American accent. "I didn't come all the way from North Carolina"—she drawled the words—"to spend my first weekend in Paris drowning in gloom."

They all burst out laughing. Jacob looked at the woman. Her blonde hair was cut boyishly short and accentuated her arresting features—chestnut eyes, a straight nose, full, generous lips, and with it all an impish expression.

"Why don't we all go dancing? We've been sitting here nattering for what seems like days."

It was while he was looking at the American that Jacob saw reflected in the mirror just behind her the person in the world he had least expected to see here. Sylvie. Yes, it was distinctly her. She was walking through the restaurant arm in arm with a dark youth, a student, he thought. Her mouth was painted a dazzling red.

"You've seen a ghost?" the American woman said in English.

Jacob pulled himself together. "No, no, just an unexpected friend," he answered her in kind. "Did I hear you say you wanted to go dancing?" Suddenly it seemed the best idea in the world.

"Mmm. Amy's my name. Dancing's my game," she drawled. "Particularly with a Frenchman who speaks some English." She seemed to be laughing at him.

Jacob didn't mind. All he wanted was to lose himself. "Amy"—he tasted the name—"shall we go?"

They said goodbye to the others. Jacob deliberately led Amy a roundabout way to the door. He had to ascertain that the woman he had seen was indeed Sylvie. Yes, it was she, despite the too red mouth, the sleek black dress. Jacob stiffened. To think that he had been worried about her innocence. He placed his arm loosely on Amy's shoulder. She was tall, almost as tall as he.

"So you've seen the unexpected person again," Amy said flatly.

"You're very observant."

"I've had to learn. You men aren't very easy to deal with, you know."

"Neither are you women." Jacob's look challenged her.

"Oh me, I'm as easy as apple pie," Amy drawled.

And she was, Jacob noted to himself some time in the course of that long night. Though the flavor was somewhat richer. They danced. They boogie-woogied in a black jazz club that had recently opened its doors to an avid Quartier Latin. They fox-trotted in another more decorous locale on the Rue de Seine. They were perfectly in step, perfectly matched. They danced as if there were no tomorrow and too many yesterdays needed to be forgotten.

"We're in the same boat, aren't we?" she said to him over a drink at some point in the evening.

He looked into her strong, intelligent face. "Yes, maybe we are."

"Perhaps we should be in the same bed." She said it calmly.

He held her hand, stroked it delicately. "If I liked you less . . ." he said.

"And desired me more," she finished his sentence for him.

He shrugged, nodded, admitting it.

"And you, supposedly an expert in the human psyche," she challenged him.

He pulled her up onto the dance floor and held her close. "A mere man," he whispered in her ear.

In the small hours of the morning, he took her home. In the courtyard, he kissed her lightly on the lips. "Thank you, Amy. Let's meet again soon." He said it with great seriousness.

She nodded.

Jacob walked. He walked through dark empty streets, hating himself. Almost, once or twice, he turned back toward Amy's flat. Her body would have been warm, lavish, welcoming. And here he was chilled, alone, with only the illusory heat of an obsession to warm him. He stopped on the small bridge leading to the Île Saint-Louis, where his apartment was, and looked down into the shadowy waters of the Seine. Why was it always the obscure, the unknown which drew him? He shrugged and saw the light reflected in the waters flicker over ripples and shape itself into Sylvie's enigmatic form.

The next day Jacob sat in his study overlooking the Seine and pondered the papers in front of him. They were filled with his own writing, pages and pages of it in a bold, strong hand. Now his pen lay open, but unused. He had slept fitfully and had risen late. A cup of cold coffee stood half drunk on the large mahogany desk. His mind wasn't on his work. He stood to his full height and passed a hand through already tousled hair. He had not bothered to get dressed yet and his woollen robe was loosely tied round his frame.

He walked over to the window and looked out. This wasn't like him. He was a man of regular and arduous habits, and Saturday was set aside for putting the thoughts of the week in order. It was a gray, somber day. Normally, he liked to see a slate sky, the slate-colored river beneath him. It served as the perfect, neutral background for his work, tempered its excitements. Today it depressed him.

He looked back at his laden desk and the large painting which hung over it. Picabia's melodramatic eye stared out at him. It cheered him a little. He picked up the cold coffee cup, walked barefooted over the profusion of Persian rugs which covered the large, highly polished living-room floor and made his way to the small kitchen.

Just as he was brewing fresh coffee, the doorbell startled him. Jacob wondered if the concierge might have some urgent post for him, or a package. He opened the door unthinkingly.

"Oh, it's you." The surprise was evident on his face. Sylvie Kowalska stood there, a flush rising in her pale cheeks. She was wearing a blue serge coat with a matching midi hat. Her hair was loosely tied into a tail with a blue ribbon. She looked more than ever like a slightly gawky schoolgirl.

"You weren't expecting me. I'm sorry." She looked meaningfully at his state of undress. "Your note didn't specify a time."

"No, no, come in. I was expecting you. I just didn't know when

you might come. I . . . I was just doing some work." Jacob's voice
trailed off. "Come in," he said more firmly, as she hesitated visibly.

He took her coat, her hat. Her dress matched her outward apparel
exactly: a low-waisted blue with a white-trimmed sailor collar.

"I was making coffee. Can I get you some?"

She nodded, her eyes skimming the ample room. "It's very pretty
here. And you can see all the lines of the roofs and the river. It's
beautiful. And you have a piano." Her eyes shone.

"Do play if you like." Jacob strode toward the kitchen. He needed
to compose himself. He couldn't believe that Sylvie was the same
woman he had seen with painted lips and garish dress the previous
evening. His eyes, his secret expectations must have been playing
hallucinatory tricks on him. He chided himself. His hand as he
poured the coffee was slightly unsteady.

When he came back into the sitting room, she was standing by
the piano, stroking its mellow wood with a slender hand.

"Did you like my playing the other day?" she asked.

"Very much," he replied. "Very very much."

"I was playing for you," she said, looking up at him. Her eyes
suddenly took on a taunting expression. "The Gershwin. Mother
Theresa was very very angry. It's not meant to be suitable, you see.
Would you like me to play for you now?"

Jacob nodded. "But tell me first. Was it you I saw yesterday at
La Coupole?"

She took the coffee from his outstretched hand. "Me?" she said,
her voice high. Then she shook her head vigorously and laughed.
"Not me, no." She drank the hot strong coffee down in one gulp,
sat down on the piano stool and with one smooth gesture, pulled
the ribbon from her hair and shook her head vigorously. The golden
cloud settled on her shoulders. Demurely, she attempted a few
chords, sped through a few scales and then without warning, a deep
raucous contralto issued from her.

Jacob sat down in the low armchair nearest the piano. Her profile
was clearly visible to him and he watched with fascination as Sylvie
the girl metamorphosed into Sylvie the woman. Not any woman, but
a bold blues singer. He recognized the style, but not the song. Her
voice wailed plaintively one moment and took on a seductive world-
weariness the next, beguiling him, exciting him.

Jacob sat transfixed. When she turned her eyes on him, they were
a deep, luminous blue. They trailed over him provocatively, languor-
ously. He felt a tugging at his loins. He could see the excitement in

her face, too, the wide, open mouth, the arching throat as she threw back her head. Suddenly she played a jarring chord and leapt up. Before he could move, she had placed herself on his lap. She took his hand, led it to her full breast.

Jacob tried to still himself.

"*J'aime ça*," she said, pouting a little, guiding his fingers over her firm nipple. "Yes, yes, I like it. Here and here." She led his hands.

Moaning, Jacob crushed her against him. He kissed her fiercely. Her hot dry tongue flicked over his. Her hands sought his bare taut skin. Sharp little animal cries issued from her.

"*Pas si vite, Sylvie*," Jacob whispered hoarsely through the cloud of her hair. His penis was throbbing dangerously. He felt like an inexperienced youth. His robe offered little protection. Gently he lifted her off him, stood up. She clung to him. Suddenly strong, she pulled him toward the sofa. Her eyes were wide open as she rubbed against him. She guided his hand beneath her thick skirt to the bare skin above her stockings. It was silken smooth, warm. She moved slightly so that his hand covered the arch of her mound. The heat burned him. She rocked against him. "Yes, yes, there." Her voice was muffled. He groaned, kissed her savagely. The restraining thought that she was a mere girl fled. He lifted her astride his leg, following her desires. A shudder of pleasure passed through her, again and again. Her head arched backward, her hair flowing. And then, before he could stop her, her hand reached inside his briefs. "Yes, that." Her eyes were blazing as they met his. She stroked, once, twice, firmly, and then she brought her mouth down over him, licking, sucking, hungrily, rhythmically. Her hair, electric, spilled over his loins. Jacob trembled. He was not a man of inconsiderable experience, but there was little he could do to stop himself now. From the base of his spine, he could feel the juices gathering in him, oozing, pulsing out violently.

Her face gave witness to a wild triumph as she looked up at him. He drew her toward him and cradled her in his arms, kissing her gently. But she drew away from him.

"This is what I like best of all," she said, like a cat licking her whiskers. Then in a flash she was up, her dress straightened, again the demure girl. "I have to go now or Tante Julie will wonder where I've got to. Can I come again next week? I usually meet my friend, Caroline, about this time and I've told her about you."

Jacob stood to his full height, looking down on her. He nodded, not trusting his voice.

"Goodbye, then." She pecked him on the cheek. "If you want to see me before then, I might be able to come by the Dôme on a Thursday."

Again, Jacob nodded. He wanted to grab her, shake her, make her speak to him. But before he could do anything, she was gone. Jacob looked out the window and watched her walking down the street, her step light, innocence in the swing of her shoulders.

As the days passed, Jacob realized that the unspeakable feeling that haunted him was that he had a sense of having been raped. That might not have been an accurate description of events, but it was nonetheless his sensation. Despite his initial invitation to Sylvie, he felt himself to have been utterly passive in their sexual encounter. Indeed, he felt humiliated. Yet still he was transfixed. Transfixed by the disparate images of her which floated unceasingly through his mind. Sylvie the good little girl; Sylvie flagrantly mischievous. And then the woman, wanton—as wanton as a prostitute in a brothel. And yet, unlike her, taking evident pleasure. Such pleasure. He had never encountered anything like it. He sensed that it would be wise to stop seeing her. But he could think of nothing but their next meeting.

Gradually over the next months, their relationship unfolded. The first few times she came to see him in his flat were like a replay of the original encounter. Except that he was more in control of himself, less surprised by the forthrightness of her desires. Gradually, she let him undress her. He was reverent over the beauty of her flawless body, the heavy breasts, the slender shanks, the golden skin. But she would never allow him inside her. He understood this, understood the fear, he thought. She was nineteen, ten years younger than he was. Soon she would trust him. But what he had never experienced with any woman before was her sheer excitability. He had only to touch her there, and she shuddered wildly. And she wanted him, wanted him in her mouth, as much as she could take, as much as he could give. It exhilarated him and depressed him, in turn.

He learned more about her. She told him of her studies, which were coming to an end with her baccalaureate this year, far too late as far as she was concerned. Told him, too, of her parents, their death, though she passed over all this blithely, as if it were long in the past and of little concern. What she preferred to talk about were what she called her adventures. These were intricate and varied and

Jacob was never too sure whether he altogether believed her. At times he felt sure she was spinning fantasies. This troubled him only a little. His training after all had taught him that fantasies were as telling as facts. Often these stories had to do with her childhood.

She told him how she and her brother hated being in the big house—which was what she called their country estate. "Everyone there was always dying of boredom or telling lies. They were horrible mean little lies and they had mean, horrible faces. Stiff and empty and pompous. Like cardboard cutouts depicting high seriousness." She pulled a grotesque face, then giggled. "Once Tadzio and I decided we would pee on the floor in unison, just to see what they would do. You should have seen their expressions. My father was apoplectic. We were sent to our rooms and had to live on bread and water for a day." Sylvie laughed hilariously.

"What we liked best was running wild in the grounds. The woods were so beautiful. And the summer before I was sent away we took to spying on the gamekeeper." Sylvie's eyes sparkled as she warmed to her subject. She was sitting on his bed, wearing only her shirt and knickers, while he lay back, an arm under his head, listening.

"It was always after he was out shooting. We'd follow him, very very quietly, back to his house and peek through the window. He'd drop the rabbits on the big wooden table and then shout for his wife. She'd come running, a big heavy woman, and he'd smack her, once, twice, across the face, really hard. Then he'd push her down on the floor by the shoulders so she'd be kneeling in front of him. He made her unbutton his trousers and his cock would come rushing out."

At this point Sylvie stopped, a little breathless, and looked at the region of his groin. Jacob kept himself very still, unwilling to feed her fantasies, though stirred into tumescence by her excitement, despite himself.

"Then, he'd lift her up onto the table, right on top of the dead rabbits, lift her skirts and ram into her." Sylvie giggled. It was obvious to Jacob that she identified with the gamekeeper.

"He caught us once. He looked up in the middle of it all and saw our heads at the window. He bounded out and shook me, just me," she added proudly. "He said if he caught us at it again, *I* had better watch out."

"And did you?" Jacob asked.

She answered by stroking him, so that he forgot his question, until the next time when the incident might be repeated with a slightly different twist.

"And your brother?" Jacob once asked. "How did he feel about all this?"

"Oh Tadzio, Tadzio was much braver than me," Sylvie answered proudly. Then her eyes clouded over and she changed the subject.

One day Sylvie told him how her father had had an affair with their governess, who was promptly sent back to France. Sylvie was miserable. She was attached to the woman, yet distressed at what she had learned about her and her father. She rarely mentioned her mother.

From time to time, she would also elaborate on her current life in the convent. There was one nun who particularly hated her, who watched her with an eagle eye. She loathed the woman, her spying, her utter ecstasy in prayer, and she had filled a notebook with the execrable punishments she would like to inflict on her. One day she looked at Jacob wildly and, with utter conviction, said if she didn't get out of that convent soon, she would wreak her vengeance on the woman.

The more Jacob saw her, the more intrigued he grew.

She started to bring him presents. One week, it was a painting she had done, which Jacob instantly framed and placed in his bedroom. She brought him another. She was talented, this Sylvie, and he liked the madcap animals with which she peopled her whimsical pictures. Then she started to bring him other kinds of gifts, a lighter, cologne, a watch. These worried him. He suspected she might have stolen them. When he asked her, she merely laughed in her mischievous way and when she next came to see him, she presented him with an apple.

Jacob had never been so excited by a woman, so enthralled and at the same time so frustrated. Sylvie's sheer lack of inhibition, the wickedness of her language, fascinated him. Where had she learned such things? Sexually, she aroused him to the point of frenzy; yet that final hold was barred. He waited, unable to do anything else, unwilling to force her.

By February, when they had been meeting regularly in his flat almost every Saturday afternoon for over four months, Jacob felt he had somehow to break out of what was quickly becoming a *folie à deux*. The preceding week she had failed to appear, as she had on only a few previous occasions, and he had been thrown into an agony exacerbated by his enforced passivity. He had no way of contacting her: he could only wait until the following week or trail her to the convent like a demeaned slave. Jacob resolved to act.

The following week when she arrived, offering no excuses for her previous breach, he sat her down and insisted that they talk. Despite the pain it caused him, he refused her kisses, her fervent hands. He said he wanted to meet her godparents. It would make things easier for her, put things on a slightly more normal footing. They could go out together. She could meet his friends. Sylvie sprang up from her chair, sat down on the piano stool and angrily bashed out some wild jazz improvisation. Then coolly, with demurely veiled eyes, she turned to him: "No, I don't want you to meet them," she said flatly.

He threw the book he was holding down on the floor with a thump and strode over to the window. He was rigid with anger. She came up behind him and embraced him. Her fingers toyed with his shirt. "But you can meet Caroline. We can all go out together. I'd like to know your friends. Next Saturday. I'll see you then." Before he could stop her, she was out the door.

Next week, when, more nervous than he would care to admit, he arrived at the Dôme, she was already sitting there, at her side a dark girl with a high forehead and sharp nose. They were both sipping hot chocolate and chatting away with such girlish vivacity that Jacob suddenly felt that his secret encounters with Sylvie had been wholly the fruit of his imagination. He sat down beside them and before any introductions were made, Sylvie giggled and said, "You see, I told you he was exceptional. A real Apollo."

The other girl flushed slightly and put out a hand to greet him. They talked, casually, pleasantly enough, though Jacob was too vigilant to relax. He watched Sylvie. The golden features, the wide blue guileless eyes. Had he built a mountain of mystery around a simple schoolgirl with a slightly risqué tongue? Then the sensation of that tongue as it flickered over his body presented itself to him. He stirred uneasily. He wondered how much Sylvie told her friend.

"Who is that?" Sylvie murmured, pointing to a remarkable-looking woman with glowing dark eyes and high cheekbones beneath a dazzling Schiaparelli hat.

Jacob smiled. "That's Gala Dali. If you haven't seen *her* before, you may have come across her eyes. Dali has immortalized them in a series of photographs in a wonderful little book, *La Femme Visible*. And there's the man himself. Would you like to meet them?"

Sylvie was irradiated. He could almost feel a feverish heat emanating from her. "That's how I would like to be," she murmured. She clutched Jacob's knee under the table, while he performed introductions. Others came to join them, artists, poets. Sylvie's excitement mounted and with it a wildness came into her beauty and the flow of her speech. Her outlandish commentary on the poet Hugo, her suggestive asides, had the assembled company hypnotized.

Sylvie lapped up their attention, becoming more audacious with each sign of appreciation. Caroline looked on with a wistful expression. Jacob had the increasing sensation of watching a virtuoso performance. He was at once appreciative and dismayed that the performance wasn't only for him.

When Sylvie announced that she wanted nothing more in the world than to be a nightclub singer, like Bessie Smith, one of the gathered number instantly suggested that he take her off to a club which had just opened its doors. Without looking at Jacob, Sylvie readily complied. She and Caroline would want to go home first and change. But there wouldn't be any problem. Her godparents were away for the weekend and old Nanou, the maid, slept heavily.

Jacob was taken aback. He had known nothing of all these household arrangements. Indeed, he realized, on one level he knew nothing at all of Sylvie's life. Perhaps there had been other weekends, other expeditions to dives and dance halls. He remembered the night he had been certain he had seen Sylvie at La Coupole with a young man. Jealousy seized him with unaccustomed ferocity.

By the time they met at The Harlem Bar, his imaginings had turned it into a low constant ache. Sylvie's demeanor, once he had lifted the girlish serge coat from her shoulders, did nothing to assuage it. She was wearing a short black velvet frock which without clinging to her body accentuated every curve. Her bare shoulders shone like porcelain against its darkness. Her legs in the silk stockings he had never seen her wear, gleamed dangerously long. *"Tu aimes?"* she asked him, throwing back her mane of hair with a challenge. "I borrowed it from Tante Julie." She laughed, her eyes glittering.

It was the only remark she was to address directly to him for the next few hours. While Jacob was left to take care of Caroline, whom he noted subliminally still looked, despite the addition of make-up, like a young woman of good family, Sylvie eagerly went off into the dark interior of the club with his friends. Caroline's attention followed her as carefully as did his own.

The room was throbbing with people, the sound of ragtime, the pulse of voices. Paris had been transformed into nighttime New

York. Sylvie was in her element. No sooner had they sat down at a table which bordered stage and dance floor, ordered a drink, than Sylvie was up, her hand in his friend Michel St. Loup's. She danced with a wild abandon, her hair swinging, her body a pliant instrument in the band's beat. Jacob watched transfixed.

A mellow voice insinuated itself into his consciousness.

"You, Dr. Jardine, have got it bad." Amy was sitting at his side. He had not noticed her come in. He smiled, slowly coming back to himself.

"Yes," he said, answering her in English. "I think I do."

She followed the line of his gaze. After a moment she said in a weary voice, "I think I can see why." Then her tone changed. "I can't bear all this good music going to waste," she challenged him.

Jacob laughed. "Will you do me the honor?" He had forgotten how good it was to be with this woman whose eyes looked directly into his, how sinuously her firm body moved against him. He forced his mind into emptiness, let the music drive them. They stopped only with its last throb.

Sylvie and the others were already back at the table. Her eyes shone with a strange agitation. There was a cigarette in her hand. "Who is that blonde witch you've been swooning over?" she said in a low voice. Her hand, as he sat down, clasped his leg under the table. She dug her nails into him. Jacob stopped her. How frail her hand seemed, despite her savagery, how cold. He held it firmly. He had not touched her for weeks and desire bounded through him.

"We must go home now, or the parents will complain. Jacob will take us," Sylvie suddenly announced in the tone of an obedient daughter.

They rose, bid everyone goodnight. Amy, he noticed, gave him a lingering look. He shrugged, all but imperceptibly, and followed after Sylvie and Caroline.

At the door, Sylvie suddenly stopped. "Oh I forgot." Jacob's eyes followed her as she went back into the room and planted a kiss full on Michel's lips.

In the taxi, Sylvie instructed the driver. Rue Saint-Honoré. He hadn't even known where she lived. She leapt in first, ordered Caroline to sit beside her. The two girls nestled against each other. Sylvie took Caroline's hand and held it, excluding him. His jealousy coiling within him leapt indiscriminately. He imagined the two girls in a narrow bed, wrapped in each other's arms, whispering secrets. His face grew grim. When they left him, Sylvie offered only a casual "*A bientôt.*"

In bed Jacob tossed and turned, enmeshed in fitful dreams and waking fantasies, the one indistinguishable from the other. At their center was always Sylvie, her hair tumbling wildly over his naked body. Or was it his? Was it Michel's or, his breath was dry, a woman's? The doorbell pealed so insistently that it finally penetrated his consciousness. He opened the door to see her standing there. He pinched himself, checking to see whether he was still dreaming.

"So you *are* here," she said, her eyes fiery.

"Where else might I be?" He held her fiercely in his arms. Her face was pale, cold; her hair moist in winter drizzle.

"I thought since I wouldn't, can't . . ."—she stumbled for words— "that you had gone. To her." She hissed the last words and raked her nails over his chest.

He smiled, strangely pleased. Gently he undressed her, his passion mounting as her golden skin emerged beneath the loosed dress. In the simple white shift she wore beneath it, she looked as if she had come fresh from a morning bath in some rippling stream. He carried her to his bed. She was unusually calm, almost passive, letting him take the lead. He caressed her slowly, searchingly, waiting for her response. None came. He reached for her full breast; his lips lingered over her nipples. She gasped and pulled away from him. "Just hold me," she said softly. "I feel so alone."

With greater forbearance than he knew he possessed, he cradled her in his arms. She snuggled into him, like a child. He realized she was crying. He held her gently until the evenness of her breath told him she was asleep.

Later that night, Jacob woke to the exquisite sensation of lips trailing over his body, of hands caressing him fervently. He was throbbingly erect. Sylvie. Her kisses came in hot little moans. She was sitting astride him, her head now arched back wildly like a Valkyrie. He pulled her down on him, kissed her achingly on the lips and then without thinking turned her over and pressed, pressed into her with the passion of a man who had held back his desires too long. Shudderingly her heat enveloped him. Seconds before it was too late, Jacob withdrew with a groan. His seed spilled over her golden mound. His voice was hoarse. "I won't let you be alone again, Sylvie. Never again." His arms entwined her.

When he woke, she was gone. It was only then in the cool gray light of a winter dawn that Jacob realized there was no telling stain on his sheets. And it was only then that he knew that either he must stop seeing Sylvie or he must link his life fully to hers. By the end of a restless day when he had paced the length and breadth of his flat over a hundred times like some caged beast and still mind and body, despite the dictates of common sense, cried out for her, he accepted the only course open to him.

The next day he went out and bought her an emerald ring surrounded by small diamonds. The way in which the lush underwater green and cold glitter mingled somehow reminded him of her. With the determination of a strong man finally bent on action, he also rang Paul Ezard.

CHAPTER
THREE

Jacob Jardine was a man who always pursued his goals to their end. If that end was sometimes bitter, he braced his shoulders, thought deeply about what he had felt and observed, and tried to salvage a small parcel of truth from the episode. He was not afraid of experience. His father had already pronounced about him, when he was five: "Watch our eldest, Marie. He has a hunger for truth. It will make him either a great man or a very disappointed one."

The episode which had provoked the comment had been Jacob's summer pursuit. At the age of five, he was obsessed by the phenomenon of flight. The spacious grounds of the family's summer home in the Alpes-Maritimes provided ample opportunity for him to pursue his interest. He would sit on the first spreading branch of an ancient beech and drop things—an apple, a small toy, a sheet of paper, a feather. Only the feather and the paper, if the wind were blowing, traveled anywhere but down. For hours he lay on the ground watching birds. Without moving, in an intensity of concentration, he would emulate in himself the sensation of their flight. One day he found a dead swallow in a copse of trees. He brought it home. Cook allowed him to spread it out on the large kitchen table. He measured the wings' spread, drew them on a sheet of paper, cut them out and fixed them somehow to an old rag which he felt was as light as the bird's frail body. It was thus that his father, who had come to take him for their afternoon walk, found him. Jacob led him to the beech tree, climbed up to his usual bough, and released his rag bird. When it flopped to the ground, the disappointment on the boy's face was acute.

"We shall have to wait for the wind," he said to his father.

Gently, patiently, Robert Jardine explained. He was impressed by his small son's observations and his ingenuity. From that time on, the tone he took with him was always that of a rational equal. Sometimes his wife would grow irritated with him:"You'll drive him mad with your explanations and your reasons," she would say. But Robert Jardine persisted. Even when Jacob had done something which necessitated punishment, Robert Jardine would always explain in full why the punishment was needed and why it took the particular form it did. By the time Jacob was an adolescent, he had a vast repertoire of whys and wherefores and an understanding of motive far beyond his years.

Jacob might have rebelled, but since he saw his father for extended periods of time only on summer holidays, his company was always both stimulating and respected. In any case, his mother, whom he saw far more often, provided such a marked contrast to his father that he was in no danger of suffocating from too much reason, too many words. She doted on her three children, watched over their welfare with a careful eye, and managed their country residence and Paris home with a perfectionist's grasp of detail. She spoke little and laughed a great deal, and when the children were small, she was quick to hug or occasionally to slap. Her only interests aside from her family were her porcelain figurines, her music and, latterly, her religion.

Marie Jardine was as pretty as the eighteenth-century porcelain figures she collected. Petite, blonde, curly-haired, with a mole on her left cheek, just above the dimple she frequently showed, she was the daughter of a wealthy Parisian banker. By an accident of circumstance, her mother's early death, she had been raised, a solitary child, by grandparents who lived in retirement in their country home in the Auvergne. It was a mining district and it was here that she had met Robert Jardine, already a campaigning doctor, who was investigating the prevalence of emphysema in miners. He was a friend of her older brother, had been with him to university. In Paris, their parents knew each other. The instant attraction Robert Jardine felt for this irresistible creature found its ready solution in a sanctioned courtship and marriage.

Robert Jardine was the third son of a wealthy Jewish banking family. As the youngest son, there was no pressure for him to go into the family firm and his early decision to study medicine was welcomed. Tall, dark, with piercing eyes and determined step, he quickly made a mark for himself, not only as a practitioner amongst the brightest and wealthiest of Parisian families, but increasingly as a crusader for medical reform. He was particularly interested in health in the workplace and he campaigned ceaselessly for safety measures and better conditions for workers, pointing out with indefatigable common sense that the funds spent in prevention would be more than recouped by the good health of the workforce.

The family home the young Marie and Robert established just after the turn of the century in the newly elegant sixteenth arrondissement, bordering on the greenery of the Bois de Boulogne, was a gracious and happy place. As Marie gave birth first to Jacob and then, at intervals of two years, to his brother, Marcel, and his sister, Nicolette, the house filled with the sounds of children's games and laughter. In the evenings, it echoed with the sterner tones of debate and argument as increasingly the Jardine home became a salon for reforming politicians eager to hear of Dr. Jardine's researches into social medicine. The two old bankers would occasionally come to these gatherings and shake their heads wryly, commenting to one another that their fortunes were at last buying them a seat in heaven.

In the summer, the family would remove itself to their retreat in the Alpes-Maritimes. The house, the extensive grounds where the children lost themselves in daylong uninterrupted adventure, was Marie's father's wedding gift to the young couple. The estate had belonged to a wealthy eccentric, who in the middle part of the nineteenth century had decided to re-create for himself an English country house in the style of John Nash. The porticoed entrance, the gleaming white columns, the gracious floor-to-ceiling windows and the twenty or so well-proportioned rooms sat happily in the blue Mediterranean light. It was a house which suited Marie, with her taste for the eighteenth century, perfectly. And Robert, as he beavered away the summer mornings in his book-lined library, could cast his eyes over a resplendent garden of English design, complete with sunken lake and distant folly.

It was the time he spent in this house which Jacob remembered as the happiest of his childhood. The constant presence of his father, the uncannily green grounds and the shady copses set against the brilliantly blue sky, the treasure trove of medical and physiological tomes, normally housed in his father's Paris *cabinet* but here accessible to his eager young mind, all combined to make the summers perfect. Even the miseries of the First World War cast only a scant shadow here. The flowers in the garden gave way to vegetables. His father, handsome in his blue uniform, visited them all too briefly, since his first duty was to his hospital on the front. But the Mediterranean sun continued to shine and the children played their carefree games and adventured up hills and down valleys.

It was also in the Alpes-Maritimes that Jacob's childhood ended. He was fourteen and had almost reached his full height, a tall youth with a shock of black hair that tumbled over intense dark eyes. His bronzed skin gave an added severity to his regular features and his chin already had that firm, determined set which was to characterize him in later years. He had noticed in the village that the market girls turned to look at him from beneath lowered lashes. His younger sister would giggle and tease him, and this, combined with the sensations the girls' looks produced in him, made him flush with embarrassment. His mother now had to look up to him to proffer the customary goodnight kiss which he began adamantly to refuse. At night his dreams were filled with limbs intertwined with his and he would wake in a hot sweat, guilty of crimes he had not committed. He pored over his father's medical textbooks, trying to transform their clinical two-dimensionality into a reality he could only half imagine.

Toward the middle of that summer, his mother introduced a new maid into the house. She was a small curly-headed young woman with a pert face and laughing dark eyes who moved with quick dancing steps through the house. When she served them at table, Jacob was intensely conscious of her presence and if she brushed against him, the blood would race to his cheeks. He could barely bring himself to mumble a thank you when she placed what was always an inordinately large portion on his plate.

One particularly hot afternoon when he had excused himself from table saying he felt unwell and was lying in the coolness of his shuttered room, she knocked at his door and came in. *"Votre mère m'a demandée de vous apporter ceci."* She placed a tall glass of lemonade on his night table. Startled out of secret thoughts, Jacob murmured incoherent thanks. She was wearing a light, flowered summer frock which exposed the curve of her full breasts. Jacob could feel the shaft of his penis filling. Embarrassment gnawed at him. He was lying naked but for white shorts atop rumpled sheets and as her eyes trailed over him, he knew that she could see the shaming bulge. Jacob gripped the sheets and kept himself very still. Their eyes met. A little smile fluttered around her full red lips. She bit them. The boy was beautiful, his legs already muscled and strong from the miles of cycling, his chest sinewy but still smooth.

It was that bite that gave Jacob courage. As she turned on her heel with a little *"C'est bien, monsieur,"* he called to her, "Wait." When she faced him again, speech deserted him. His hand fled to his crotch. He wanted to hide his visible tumescence.

Slowly, with a smile spreading over her lips, she unbuttoned her dress. Her breasts emerged pink-tipped from their confinement. "Is this what you want to see?" she asked in a teasing voice. She moved toward him, bent over his rigid body, and swung her breasts over his chest so that their hard nipples brushed against his skin provocatively. She bent lower and for a split second let them rest against his taut penis. Jacob gasped. "Oh yes, quite the man already," she said and then with a laugh and a little skip she was gone. Jacob hid his hot face under the sheets. He could easily have stayed there for the rest of the day and the night. And the summer, he thought shamefacedly; but he knew that if he didn't emerge for dinner, his mother would fuss, ask if he was ill, take his temperature.

So he sat down at the dinner table and kept his eyes firmly fixed on his plate whenever the maid came into the room. Somehow he managed to get through the innumerable courses and make his escape, mumbling that he needed some fresh air after the heat of the day. Just outside the door of the room, the little maid was waiting for him. "I can meet you later, by the lake, if you like," she said, her eyes taunting him. Jacob grabbed her wrist, almost making her drop the tray she was holding. "Will you?" He raced out of the house and threw himself down on the cool grass at the edge of the pond. The night sky seemed immeasurably bright as he gazed up at it and waited.

When she arrived, she bent over him and brushed his lips lightly with hers. Then she laughed, leapt up and whispered, "Catch me." She was off, with a merry tripping step, her flower-sprigged dress fluttering round her. Its colors led him through the dark to the far side of the lake, where the heavy pines scented the night air. Here she let him catch her. The perfume of her breath, her hair, the heave of her bosom against him gave Jacob such delight that he forgot all his embarrassment. His adolescent yearnings over the pages of his father's books had given him no glimmer of the sensation of skin, the silk of her thighs, the crisp triangle of hair to which she teasingly guided him. And when he poured his young manhood into her and she stroked him so that he grew full again inside her and this time thrust more surely, more deeply, he felt as she lapped and surged against him that he had entered a country he never again wanted to leave.

Every night that summer, except on Sundays when she went home to her family, Jacob and Mariette met somewhere in the spacious grounds of the house. They would make love on the cool grass or on ground springy with pale gray pine needles or, sometimes, in the secret recesses of the folly. They would plunge into the silvery water of the pond and embrace, their hair streaming, their bodies deliciously wet. For years after, the heavy scent of pine and the croaking of frogs would fill Jacob with a poignant joy.

In the daytime, Jacob would retrace the path of their nighttime encounters. He would stare for hours at a crushed campanula or a patch of grass to see whether he could elicit from it the sensation of that secret experience. He took to reading poetry. The lines committed to memory were one of the presents he would bring to Mariette. Amongst the cries of the cicadas, his voice would take on a serious sonority. Looking at his strong young face etched against the moonlight, Mariette would run her fingers gently along the back of his head, until he turned to crush his full lips against hers.

When Jacob's mother announced one day near the end of the summer that that Friday they would have a celebratory drink with Mariette, who was leaving them to get married, he was aghast. He waited for her with mounting impatience at the meeting place they had appointed the previous evening. When she arrived, he railed at her. Why hadn't she told him? In his imagination, he had never thought beyond the next meeting. She fondled him. Words were not her element. Wasn't it enough that they had had this much? She would never forget him. In the elegiac quality of their lovemaking that night, Jacob took another step toward manhood.

That Friday when Mariette's fiancé, a sturdy young peasant of thirty, came to collect her from the house, Jacob felt not so much betrayed as confused. He kept his distance and watched. What had this man to do with him? Would Mariette's hands move over him in the same way as they had fluttered over Jacob? He flushed. Her mystery grew for him. It set the conditions of his relationships with women.

When he returned to his room, he found a dried cornflower of the purest blue in his volume of poetry. It was folded in the page of the last poem he had spoken to her. He left it there for the rest of his life.

The summer of 1919 marked the end of an epoch in Jacob's life in other ways. Shortly after the family's return to Paris, Madame Jardine's brother succumbed to the last wave of the great influenza epidemic which spread across Europe, killing more people than the war itself. A week later, her adored father died. Marie moved through the darkened house, like a wraith. Everything was covered in black. There were no more smiles, no trills of laughter. She began to go to mass daily. At home, she sat for hours in a vast corner chair, a prayer book in her hand, her lips moving soundlessly. The children tiptoed through the house, their drawn faces echoing her shock.

It was around this time that Jacob began to distinguish a new tone in his parents' communications with each other. One night he heard them arguing behind the closed door of their bedroom. "It's my fault." His mother's shout was only slightly muffled. "It's because I transgressed, because I married a Jew."

"Stop it, Marie." His father's voice was angry in response. "You're being infected by priestly nonsense."

Jacob, upset, slipped away quietly to his room. The next morning his father was not at the breakfast table. His mother's face was strained. A few weeks later, she began to try to convince the children to go to mass with her. Jacob went once, was impressed by the cathedral's rich architecture, the ornate columns, but the priest's soft, pink cheeks, his fluttering hands and insinuating voice disgusted him. In any event, his loyalty to his father, together with the science and philosophy courses he was taking at the Lycée Henri IV, left little room for religion. Only Nicolette, his sister, dutifully continued to accompany his mother. The boys were relieved. It took some of the pressure off them.

A few months later, Marie determined to sell the house in the Alpes-Maritimes. It now seemed a brazen location to her, too lavish in its sensuousness, its fertility. Jacob was heartbroken. Throughout these autumn months, he had dreamt of Mariette, had tenderly caressed her memory. He had vowed to himself that he would see her again. What had a husband to do with their secret meetings? He appealed to his mother. When this failed, he tried to enlist his father's support. But Robert Jardine would not go against his wife's wishes. He felt that perhaps if she sacrificed the house they had all so loved, it would put her conscience at peace. He was only partly right. After the momentous sale had taken place, Marie did indeed seem to come back to something of her former self. But she never again relinquished her prayer books.

It was during this period, when life at home was blighted by mourning and contention, that Jacob grew close to one particular schoolmate. A year older than Jacob, Jacques Brenner was a tall, slim youth, with a swathe of golden hair which continually fell over his brow. He had a flair for mimicry and in the dark cold corridors of the Lycée Henri IV or the grim high-ceilinged classrooms, he would ape the masters with singular panache. One day Jacob could not hide his grin quickly enough, or offer any explanation for his smirk when their Latin master turned. He was forced to stay in after school and conjugate the verb *to laugh* in all its tenses in the negative twenty-five times. When he emerged from his detention, Jacques was waiting for him.

The two boys shared an interest in philosophy and they walked through drizzling streets together arguing, debating, laughing. Having learned the nature of Jacob's punishment, Jacques presented him the next day with a copy of Henri Bergson's *Le Rire*. They became firm friends—Jacob dark, serious, questing; Jacques blond, quick-witted, a master of the ready rhyme and scurrilous pastiche.

Jacob began to frequent Jacques' home, a grand iron-gated *hôtel particulier*, rich in baroque ornamentation on the outside, festooned on the inside with velvet and brocade. Rows of gilt-framed oils lined the walls like ancient presences. When they came in, Jacques' mother would come tripping down the elegantly curved staircase, a startling contrast in her loose-fitting trousers and casual manners to the formal home she inhabited. In a trice they were sat down to toast, muffins and tea, for Jacques' mother, Lady Leonore, was English, and had introduced into her French home certain of the habits and tastes of her own childhood. After Jacques had regaled her with a host of anecdotes garnered from the school day, she would leave them to their own devices, only warning them that enough time had to be set aside for work.

That summer, after the boys had vied for top place in their form, the Brenners invited Jacob to accompany them to their summer home in Brittany. He was only too pleased to go. Life at home had lost its easy merriment. His father was preoccupied and seemed to take little interest in him. His mother's company led only to arguments. His sister spent all her time in giggling complicity with her friends, while his younger brother was still a child, who no longer shared any of his interests. The thought of a summer with only last year's pleasures with Mariette to rehearse had depressed him.

The Brenners' vast country estate with its turreted façade and Gothic spires bordered the Atlantic. There were stables and sleek horses, which Lady Leonore tended with an expert and loving hand. On misty days, the boys galloped over windy headlands and, exhilarated, dropped onto moist ground to argue over Lenin's progress in Russia, the cause of internationalism, the pros and cons of pacifism. They talked about their futures: Jacob already more than half committed to medical studies; Jacques less sure, slightly cynical about the value of anything, humorously imagining himself as a posturing writer, a professor, a financier or wine-grower.

When the weather was bright, they would ride down to one of the many sandy coves which dotted the shore. Jacques' mother would often join them on these occasions. They would loll about on the beach and take the occasional dip in the icy waters of the Atlantic, the boys laughing as they raced out into the waves. For lunch a picnic might magically arrive with a servant: cold chicken with creamy mayonnaise, langoustine, crisp cucumbers, ripe tomatoes, and sweet, black cherries. Or sometimes, Jacques' mother would motor them over to a small hotel near the beach where they lunched on vichyssoise and oysters, while she regaled them with stories of England. With her long mobile hands, short straight-cut blonde hair and wide gray eyes, Jacob thought she was the loveliest woman he had ever seen.

Three weeks into their stay, they were joined by Jacques' father, an elegant gray-haired man far older than his wife. He brought with him Lady Leonore's sister and her daughter, Celia, a girl of seventeen. Jacob couldn't take his eyes off the girl: she was a younger replica of her aunt. The slightly crooked generous smile, the slender long legs, the short blonde hair—all were the same. Jacob found himself tongue-tied, and not only because the family were all conversing in fluent English, whereas he had still only half grasped the language. When the girl, Celia, addressed him, he flushed hotly, unable to find the simplest response. He sensed Jacques looking at him curiously and all he could find to say to extricate himself in his friend's eyes was, "I think I need some more English lessons."

After Celia's arrival in the house, the boys began to talk about women. Jacques' tone was that of a man of the world who had already tasted too much forbidden fruit. They were silly creatures— he was off on one of his comic flights—who had nothing worthwhile to say and, his mother apart, only interested in clothes and chit-chat. Jacob said nothing. He was remembering Mariette, her teasing eyes and hands, the sensations she had wrought in him. His image of women had nothing to do with Jacques'. He demurred.

One night that week, after a particularly chill day, the two boys were lying on the floor in Jacques' deeply carpeted room and watching the flames darting in the hearth. In his nervousness before Celia, Jacob had had an uncustomary glass of wine, and his tongue loosened, he now began hesitantly to tell Jacques about his experience of the previous summer. His face grew hot as he spoke. It was difficult to communicate the tenderness he had felt, still·felt; the excruciating pleasure of the senses. His voice was low. When he had finished, he was afraid that he had betrayed Mariette. Afraid that his friend might laugh.

There was silence between them. When Jacob finally dared to look at Jacques, he noticed that his friend's face bore an expression of pain. "Jacques, what is it?" Instantly Jacob was all contrition and worry.

Jacques shook his head. The blond swathe fell over his brow. "Jacob, will you touch me, hold me?" He was staring intently into the flames.

Jacob crouched by his friend and put his arm round his shoulders. "What is it, Jacques?" he repeated. His friend was trembling.

Jacques turned to face him. His eyes were burning. "I love you," he said simply. "Here, feel."

Before Jacob realized what Jacques was doing, the older boy had taken his hand and drawn it to the bulge in his trousers. He could feel the shafting penis within. His own swelled in response. Noticing, Jacques drew closer. "No!" Jacob leapt up and dashed from the room.

As he reached the safety of his own quarters, confusion raged in him. He was ashamed, deeply ashamed. He wasn't like that. He knew some of the boys were, but Jacques . . . not Jacques. His ears ringing, Jacob threw himself down on his bed and pulled the sheets high over his head. And him, what about him? He had been aroused by Jacques: that much had been clear to them both. His body hot, Jacob writhed in shame. Yet he had never before been stirred by a man. With his customary zeal for truth, Jacob examined himself. No, in all honesty he couldn't think of a single incident. It was always the women, the women in their finery on the trolley cars, the girls with their swift, secret glances, Mariette. Jacob exonerated himself.

And yet, tonight . . . Unable to come to terms with what had happened, Jacob was in torment.

The next morning at breakfast, Jacques was not there. Jacob prowled the grounds in solitary ferment. At lunch, when they met at last, Jacques held his head high and made brittle jokes. Jacob was sullen. For the next few days, they avoided each other, never meeting each other's eyes. As the time of Jacob's departure drew close, he grew more and more miserable. The days seemed unduly long, barren and a school year devoid of Jacques' companionship a desolate prospect.

The night before he was due to leave, Jacob took his courage in his hands and knocked at Jacques' door. When he met his friend's face, it was ashen. Jacob's throat felt parched. At last he blurted out, "I don't know what I want to say, but I . . . I want us to be friends."

Jacques motioned him to sit down in one of the fine leather armchairs which were paired by the window. He sat in the other and in the dim light they both looked out over the windswept landscape. Two boys, almost men, one dark, the other blond, sat nervously gazing out on the ghostly trees perpetually bowed by Atlantic gusts. After a moment, Jacques said, "I want us to be friends, too."

"But I'm not like that," Jacob said. "At least I think I'm not. I . . ." His face flushed.

"I know you're not." Jacques' voice was pained, but he intoned the words clearly.

Jacob turned to look at him. "And yet, I responded to you," he said quietly.

Jacques shrugged. He smiled a wide, warm smile. "Sometimes it happens."

"And you?" Jacob asked. "Are you . . . ?"

"Like that?" Jacques finished it for him flatly. Sorrow flashed across his face only to be quickly effaced. He held his head with dignity. "Yes, I probably am."

Jacob took it in. "I like you, Jacques," he said simply, after a moment.

Jacques felt it as a benediction.

"And you, Jacob, you have a great capacity for tenderness." He uttered it with the tone of a prophecy.

The next January, when Jacob was nearing his sixteenth year, his father invited him into his study. Robert Jardine looked up at his favorite son with approval and motioned him to a chair in front of his vast desk. The boy, the young man, he corrected his thoughts, was now taller than his father. A broad-shouldered youth with a clear gaze and a resonant voice, he played his part in the gatherings of friends which once again took place in the Jardine home, with dignity and a quick intelligence. Robert Jardine had seen the women's eyes on him.

It was the custom, amongst a certain class of free-thinking Parisians, for fathers to ascertain that their sons had an appropriate sexual education. There was no puritanism here, no shamefaced mumblings about the birds and the bees. From father to son, the sense that pleasure too had its school was passed down. And if girls were not privy to this form of schooling and were kept pure until marriage, it was somehow accepted that in due course they too would benefit from the male's prior knowledge.

Thus, when Robert Jardine called his son into his study, it was to tell him that he had arranged a particularly special birthday celebration for him this year. He didn't spell anything out. He simply said that he and Jacob were to dine together at the Ritz on the specified day. He didn't know whether his son understood him. But it was no matter. Surprise was no terrible thing.

On the evening in question, Jacob donned his black dinner-jacket, white bow tie and looked forward with excitement to his outing with his father. Their solitary moments were all too few. His father's reputation was at its peak and he was often away traveling the country, investigating conditions here, looking into high mortality figures there, so that when father and son met, there was always more than enough to talk about.

Then, too, Jacob had never been to the Ritz.

As they approached the Place Vendôme with its implacable obelisk, and gazed upon the rigorous beauty of the square, Jacob thought with glee of how he could on the morrow tell Jacques of the glitterati gathered in its bar and restaurant. For the Ritz was then the meeting place of *le tout Paris*. Here pearl-decked duchesses rubbed shoulders with American writers and visiting dignitaries and gossip rushed from mouth to mouth with the speed of an epidemic.

Robert Jardine told his son to watch the headwaiter with particular care. He was a genius at his profession, a tall distinguished man, who added to his tact as a diplomat the slightly sinister aspect of a chief of secret police. Several times a night he would murmur to his favorite clients, "I have given monsieur the best table."

Robert and Jacob Jardine sat in the resplendent interior of the

Ritz and sipped champagne. They ate in a leisurely fashion, plump white asparagus in a fragrant butter sauce, *ris de veau braisé villageois.* All around them faces were animated in conversation. Diamonds sparkled, catching the light, and loosely draped furs rivaled for attention with pale, bared shoulders. Waiters hovered like discreet spirits. Two or three people, a politician, a noted surgeon, a famous actress, stopped at their table to greet his father and exchange a few words. Jacob was proud of him, excited by the atmosphere.

When a striking woman approached them just as the waiter was serving Jacob's favorite dessert of *crêpes suzette flambées,* the youth thought nothing of it. But when Robert Jardine asked the woman to sit down with them, Jacob promptly forgot to eat. Germaine Bataille, beneath the thick auburn hair which she wore piled high, had features of an angelic refinement. Her blue-green eyes, shadowed by thick lashes, were as serene as the sea, but like it they also promised turbulence. Her short black silk dress with its full pannier skirt and flounces of white organdie revealed dancer's legs and smooth, flawless skin. She had just come from a special performance at the Champs-Elysées theater. With a certain acerbic wit, she recounted the spectacle of Cocteau's farce *Le Boeuf sur le Toit,* the characters in carnival costume, the grotesque masks, the charming music of Darius Milhaud; and also gave them a running commentary on the audience with its smiles and postures and whistles and hoots. Jacob was rapt.

Robert Jardine watched his son with a secret smile. Yes, he had been right to choose Germaine. She would see to everything now and do it discreetly. On his part, it would mean only a few generous presents, tactfully given. He waited his moment and when he saw that Jacob was well and truly hypnotized, he cleared his throat. "I'm afraid it's time we were off now," he said.

Jacob's face dropped. "But it's not late," he protested.

"I have some work I must complete by tomorrow, Jacob, but if you wish to stay, I . . ."

"Oh yes." Jacob looked from his father to Germaine.

"Just leave your son in my capable hands, Robert. We'll have a little more champagne in the bar, gossip a little . . ." She smiled a dazzling smile at the youth.

With a twinkle in his eye, Robert Jardine wished his son happy birthday again and them both a good evening. Jacob was oblivious to his going. Among the people who frequented his family circle, he had never encountered a woman like this before. His skin tingled with excitement as the champagne bubbled down his throat.

Germaine Bataille sat back in the deep cushions of the Ritz bar, an elegantly ringed hand over her long legs. She had not been looking forward to this evening with any particular relish. She was a woman who had had more than her fill of men and now that she was adequately established with her old count and her financier to look after her in style, she rarely engaged in escapades other than those of her own choosing. And these were usually with an eye to the eventual marriage which would see her into her old age.

Germaine Bataille had fled to Paris from Orléans at the age of seventeen, a mere few months after her marriage to an infantry captain had revealed to her the abuses men were capable of. Gifted with exceptional good looks, she had found herself a job at the famous Folies Bergères, where her flaming hair and extraordinary legs had won her a steady stream of courtiers. Their increasingly generous gifts, as her fame grew, allowed her to establish herself. She became that desirable asset of the *belle époque,* a courtesan of taste and wit, who was prized as much for her company as her beauty. Now at the age of thirty-four, though she admitted only to twenty-nine and could in the glow of evening pass for far less, she was occasionally gnawed by anxieties about the future. So she had taken on the task of this evening only out of special consideration for Robert Jardine. She owed him certain favors.

But now as she looked at the handsome youth with the dark sparkling eyes and slow smile, and gauged the effect she was having on him, her spirits rose emphatically. Too much time had passed since she had allowed herself an escapade for sheer pleasure. Casually, she suggested that Jacob see her home and they have another glass of champagne there. Her carriage was waiting in the square. It would be nice to chat in intimacy.

Wide-eyed, Jacob followed her. At once nervous and exhilarated, he sat by Germaine's fur-clad side and listened to her rippling voice punctuated by the clip-clop of horses' hooves on cobblestones. When she opened the door on her apartment, Jacob felt he had entered a magic lantern world. Germaine had a taste for the theatrical which verged on the vulgar, but managed to stay within the purview of mere extravagance as long as she was at the center of her surroundings. Her sitting room was heady with the fragrance of roses, an opulence of velvet and satin. She moved within it with the ease of a woman who has read her beauty in men's eyes over a surfeit of seasons.

What she read in Jacob's features was not quite that. Yes, he was appreciative, excited. She could see that. But the look he slowly cast around the room and over her also had curiosity in it, as if he were storing up impressions which he would later mull over. He was anything but overwhelmed. It intrigued her, this reflectiveness, challenged her. She sat down next to him on the sofa and with a little smile, pulled at his bow tie.

"You'll be more comfortable without that," she said. "It's warm in here." She ran a glossy nail down his starched shirt and then with a provocative tilt to her features, lingeringly opened first one button, then the next. As her fingers brushed his bare skin, Jacob caught at her wrist.

"Ah, you don't like to be touched, perhaps? Pity." Her small pointed tongue moved slowly over her lower lip. "Pity," she said again. Under the shadow of lowered lashes, her eyes trailed over him, stopping for a moment at his crotch.

That look jolted Jacob into action. He had been nervous, unsure of what was appropriate to him. Could this friend of his father's really be touching him like that? He had kept himself as still as he could. But now came that taunting look. He pulled her toward him and kissed her with fervency and the little skill that Mariette had given him.

"*Tiens, tiens, tiens,*" Germaine whispered as she drew back from him. "You're not quite the novice I imagined. Your father would be surprised."

Confused, Jacob flushed and turned away from her. He paced to the end of the room and restlessly fingered one of the many mementoes which decorated a corner table. Germaine came up to him from behind and wove slender arms round him. She found herself moved by this youth with his mixture of pride and uncertainty. "Come," she said gently, "let us see what you know about women."

Jacob followed her into her bedroom. She bade him unbutton her dress. Clumsily Jacob did so, marveling at the smooth skin. Her fragrance enveloped him. As she rustled out of the short silk dress, the movement of her hips sent the blood rushing through him. With a practiced eye, Germaine caught the bulging of his trousers. Dark pupils grew darker. She came close to him and with infinite care undressed him, easing him out of his shirt, slowly unbuckling his trousers. Her fingers trailed over him, deftly followed by pursed lips.

When she reached his shorts, she stopped for a moment and looked up at him with mocking eyes. Then she clasped his penis. It was agonizingly hard. Jacob moaned. In a second it would all be over. He threw her down on the bed and lunged into her with all the strength of his youth. He came almost at once.

Embarrassed then, he turned away from her, reached for his trousers. He had learned enough with Mariette to know that he had just made a fool of himself. But it had been so long ago. And this Germaine had tantalized him, touched him where Mariette's hands had never strayed. He couldn't meet her eyes.

Her voice reached his ringing ears. "Jacob," she said, a new low note in her tone, "Jacob, I would be honored if you were to stay and we played that scene again with just a little variation." He turned to face her. Her green eyes bore no trace of mockery. She smiled a small moue. The boy's face with its fine earnest eyes moved her. How difficult it must be to be constantly betrayed by that jutting flesh. And he was remarkably beautiful, with his long muscled limbs. She took his hand and brought it to her taut small breast. Jacob's penis filled almost at once. *"Doucement, mon ami,* slowly," she said. Germaine guided his hand into places he had never explored. His tongue followed, until she was moaning at his touch.

By the end of that night, Jacob knew a great deal more about women than he had ever imagined there was to know. And that, he felt with a rare certainty, was still only the beginning. Throughout that year, he visited Germaine as often as she would permit him. Each time he left, he counted the days until his return, reveling in the memory of her silken flesh, her limbs entwined around him in a ballet of positions.

As her hunger for him began to match his for her, Germaine started to worry. It was foolish of her to develop an involvement with a mere stripling who could do nothing for her. She should be spending her time wisely, finding a husband who would allow her comfort in her old age. But his youthful passion was such a relief after the saggy flounderings of her old count and her bullish financier that she allowed the time with Jacob to stretch. And stretch. Until she discovered that she could not do without him. His lovemaking had grown so subtle. He listened to her so attentively, ate up the stories she told him of her life with such appetite, that she found herself feeding his ardor with increasing invention, flowering in his presence.

Jacob listened and learned. He learned hungrily about the ways of a world which was not yet his. At first his mouth would fall open in disbelief when Germaine told him of the doings of a man who was a friend of the family or a great lady whom he had thought a perfect wife. Gradually he laughed, as she did, about these little vagaries. He did not feel disillusioned or aghast at what were evident hypocrisies and double standards. The world appeared to him as a place vast in foibles, full of curiosities. He was like a spectator in an incessant comedy—untouched, happy to smile wryly. Neither, after the first few months, did he have any false sense that Germaine could ever be his and only his. It was enough that each of their meetings should stretch into this time-caught infinity.

But one night, when he was sitting in her apartment waiting for her to come home from a date at the opera—something she would never give up even for him—Jacob happened to leaf through a pile of books he had not chanced on before. One of them he noticed was a tome of his father's. He opened it unthinkingly, wondering only how curious it was that Germaine should be interested in a medical treatise. On the title page, there was a hand-written inscription. *"A Germaine, qui m'a tant appris sur la vie."* The signature was his father's. Jacob stared at it. Stared at it hard. Germaine had taught his father about life, the inscription said. Jacob dropped the book as if it were a hot coal and rushed out of the apartment.

He had had a sudden vision of his father wrapped in Germaine's embrace. Shame pounded through him. He walked blindly through a labyrinth of streets. His father, his respected, indeed idealized father and Germaine, between whose legs he burrowed with such consummate delight; Germaine, who sat astride him and moaned, her bright hair tumbling over his chest. All at once all the men Germaine had talked about as she regaled him with her stories crystallized into his father. For the first time, he was stung by real jealousy which turned as quickly into rage. He suddenly remembered it was his father who had introduced him to Germaine. He hated them both. They had probably laughed over him as he had over others.

Oblivious to the rain which drenched his clothing, Jacob blundered on, his emotions askew. He wanted to hit Germaine, punish her as he would never be able to punish his father. He wanted to straddle her, pin her down with his penis until she begged him to stop. The violence of his imaginings made him pause. He realized he was perspiring profusely, despite the chill rain. He walked into a café and quickly downed a cup of bitter coffee. A woman strolled up to him. Her proposition was unmistakable. Jacob looked at her with distaste: she was old, almost as old as his mother. The angelic purity of Germaine's face flitted through his mind.

With fleet steps, Jacob raced back to Germaine's apartment. She was already there, perched on the sofa where they had originally kissed. She looked vulnerably small. There were tears running down her face. In her hands, she held Robert Jardine's book. Jacob met her eyes and held them for a long moment. It was in that moment which mingled anger, dismay, yearning, understanding, that Jacob suddenly felt he had crossed the border into manhood. He walked over to Germaine and kissed her gently where the tears had stained her cheeks. He lifted her in his arms and carried her lightly over to the bed which had seen so many of their ardors. Tenderly, lingeringly, they made love. They both knew it was for the last time.

Two years later, Germaine was dead, drowned in the Mediterranean, some said by her own doing. A mysterious package was delivered to Jacob. In it, together with a solicitor's letter, he found Germaine's journals. She had bequeathed them to him. He read them avidly over and over again, astounded at Germaine's mixture of cynicism and innocence, at her shrewd observations and ear for gossip, at her humor and eroticism. He always blushed when the entries were about him. He was also shadowed by a residue of guilt: had he contributed in any way to Germaine's death? For a long time he was haunted by the fact that at each reading the mystery of this woman who had overseen his journey into manhood seemed always and only to increase.

Afterward when he was in the midst of his training as an analyst, he would wonder whether it was his inability to understand Germaine and even Mariette which had spurred him to enter a profession intent on deciphering human actions.

CHAPTER
FOUR

In the autumn of 1929 the presence of a young dark-haired woman at the lectures of Gaétan Gaitan de Clérambault, chief of the Paris Special Infirmary, caused a stir amongst the medical students, almost equal to that occasioned by the Wall Street Crash. It was not simply that women were rarely to be seen amongst the ranks of psychiatric interns; nor that M. de Clérambault's utterances were often deeply misogynist; nor even that his manner of classifying madness led him to disquisitions on eroto-mania hardly thought suitable for the better class of female ear. What troubled the students was that this woman in their midst, who scribbled incessant notes during the course of the lectures, disappeared as mysteriously as she came. None of them knew who she was, even though several had taken steps to find out.

By Christmas, rumors were rife. One faction had it that she was M. de Clérambault's secret mistress, this despite the previously held belief that he was a consummate woman-hater. He had been seen in close private conversation with her. Moreover, one enterprising student had slipped out of the lecture hall early and followed her round the block. The elusive woman had vanished into the entrails of a vast silver-gray limousine and been sped away. They all knew of their maître's aristocratic lineage, a family tree which linked him to Descartes. What more appropriate than that he should keep his mistress in style?

Another faction, unable to imagine M. de Clérambault straying from his famed and rigid celibacy, had constructed a far more elaborate history for this evasive female. They determined that she was a former patient whom their teacher, in his haste to institutionalize all and sundry, had mistakenly confined years ago when he was in charge of the nightly police round-up of unclassifiable offenders. Her crime had been to smack a policeman. The story she had told to explain her act had borne enough relation to M. de Clérambault's understanding of a hallucinatory paranoia for him to have her locked up. It had however been true (and here the students gave endless examples of how close "normal" behavior and delusion could come to one another). Some weeks later, the young woman's family had unearthed her from a psychiatric ward. And now, she was attending M. de Clérambault's lectures in order to build up a case against him and expose the fallacy of his beliefs and methods.

Needless to say, the students who put round this latter version of affairs were a rebellious lot who had fantasies about displacing their teacher. Jacob Jardine was amongst them. He was intrigued by this woman, who, in her tailored suits of unostentatious gray, with her look of serious concentration as she took notes, bore so little resemblance to the women he knew. But then, at this stage of his life, he was intrigued by everything. His medical studies complete, he had opted to pursue a specialization in psychiatry, a field in which it seemed to him everything still needed to be done and which fed his ravenous curiosity about people and ideas.

Jacob's friend Jacques Brenner, who, after his philosophy studies, had moved in a dilettantish way into his father's firm, would laugh at Jacob. "Your ceaseless activity exhausts me," he would say. When Jacob would smile in turn and tell him to stop pretending to a laziness he didn't really have, Jacques, a veritable magpie, would regale him with a concise and witty résumé of the latest novel by Gide, a current philosophical treatise or archaeological foray, or the state of the stock market. As a result of their interchange, Jacob, when he was off-duty, would spend nights catching up with Jacques' reading. His interests were those of a polymath and he dreamt of somehow being able to unite the disparity of fields which interested him.

That New Year's Eve he had been invited by Jacques' mother to celebrate the *Reveillon* with them. They were having a little party. Jacques warned him that "little" in his mother's vocabulary had nothing, in this case, to do with small or intimate. Indeed, when Jacob

made his way through the trail of luxurious automobiles and uniformed chauffeurs lining the street which led to the Brenner house,
he chuckled at his friend's warning. A liveried servant announced his
arrival. The house shone with the brilliance of a hundred chandeliers.
Mirrors glowed with refracted crystal, the bare shoulders and dia-
mond-strewn throats of women. Voices trilled and galloped. Waiters
poured wine and champagne of unforgettable years. A vast table
bowed beneath the weight of delicacies decked with an eye to shape
and color. In retrospect, Jacob was to remember this eve of 1930 as
the last, glittering celebration of Europe's brief postwar holiday of
plenty. The air had an electric edge, as if the gathered guests knew
that for the next thirty years, nothing was to equal *this* for sheer
dazzle and ostentation.

Jacob paid his respects to Lady Leonore, who curled her long
lower lip into her customary wry smile.

"Thank you for coming to our little party," she said to him in
English. Resplendent in a long sheath of golden fabric, she waved
him in a particular direction. "Jacques was last seen somewhere over
there."

Jacob was happy to wander and observe, equally happy to stop
and exchange a few desultory words with the people he knew. He
made his way into a second, slightly quieter room and cast his eyes
over the assembled groups. In a far corner a woman caught his
attention. With a particularly animated gesture of braceleted arms,
she was addressing a small circle of friends. Jacob strolled in her
general direction and watched.

She was wearing a gown made out of two splendid lengths of
glitter, knotted at shoulder and waist. Her dark hair waved around
a face memorable as much for its expression of intelligence as for
its subtlety of brow and bone. The eyes were lacquered, intensely
dark, fine. Jacob stared and when, discomfited, she returned his look,
he turned away, only to renew his study of her after a moment. He
was almost certain he recognized in this striking figure the woman
who had caused him and his friends hours of intrigued speculation.

The woman in question noticed the young man staring at her with
particular intentness and identified him instantly. She had already
singled him out amidst M. de Clérambault's students for the distinctive way he posed questions, the polite but trenchant criticism he
occasionally leveled at the older man. After a moment, she walked
toward Jacob.

"So you have found me out," she said quietly. There was a rich vein of humor visible just beneath her haughty manner.

Jacob nodded briefly. He was unsure of his ground.

"But you won't break my cover," she continued tentatively, watching for his response.

"I wouldn't even if I could." Jacob smiled a slow smile. "I still have no idea who you are."

"Perhaps it would be easier if we kept it that way," she hesitated.

"It might be easier, but I would hardly find it desirable," Jacob said. Now that she was standing so close to him, he found her even more compelling. They examined each other carefully.

Suddenly Jacques was upon them. "So there you are. I should have known that I would find you with our most exquisite guest."

"Ah, but we haven't formally met," Jacob murmured.

Jacques chuckled. "Let me do the honors then. Princesse Mathilde of Denmark, may I present Jacob Jardine, my erstwhile friend and sometime doctor."

Jacob could do nothing to hide his startled expression. The last thing in the world he had expected was to find in this woman who haunted the Infirmerie a princess whose name was linked to that of Europe's principal royal houses. His tongue refused to formulate a sentence.

Princesse Mathilde gave him a ravishing smile. "Your friend seems none too pleased to learn my identity," she said to Jacques.

"Jacob is always, I'm afraid, unpredictable." Jacques tossed back the strand of heavy blond hair which still fell boyishly over his forehead. "Which is probably why we're still friends after all these years," he whispered with mock seriousness.

The Princesse watched them. Suddenly she seemed to reach a decision. "Perhaps the two of you might like to come to one of my Wednesday evenings. Monsieur Jardine might then find my name easier to bear." Irony played over her features and then with a parting nod, she went to rejoin her group.

Jacob continued to stare after her.

There are certain beings who are born with a radical sense that they are displaced in time or milieu. Princesse Mathilde de Polignesco was one such. Born into a family of expansive wealth and impeccable descent, she was the only child of a mother who had died a mere year after Mathilde's birth. Her father's interests had hardly been in the tiny infant and, parsimonious by nature, he had left her upbringing to a succession of nannies and governesses whom he paid little and who paid Mathilde back in kind. As a result, Mathilde had always felt that she was an unwelcome outsider in her own home. When she visited her baronial cousins, the feeling was exacerbated. She was always by comparison meanly dressed and as she grew into adolescence, it became clear that she had also been poorly educated. An intelligent little girl, Mathilde was intensely embarrassed by these comparisons. She was also intensely lonely and deeply affected by the evidence of lovelessness around her.

No sooner could she write than she began to escape from her immediate environment by inventing stories and poems peopled by characters who might be her friends. These friends were to save her from the death she was haunted by and which echoed her mother's. When she was twelve and she recognized the sheer scale of her ignorance, she took her courage in hand and approached her father with a request. She wanted either to be sent away to school—which was instantly denied—or to be permitted free access to his extensive library and to be given a governess and tutors of some intelligence. The latter wish was granted.

Mathilde put all her youthful energy and her loneliness into her studies. She read voraciously and at random. She demanded to be taught mathematics, Greek, Latin, botany. She learned to write in English and German as well as French. When she turned eighteen, her father suddenly developed an interest in her. It was time to find an appropriate match for his daughter, one which would enhance the family line. The year was 1919. The war was over. Europe's royal families were reconcerting the interests left to them. Mathilde's aunt was asked to prepare the young woman. The best couturiers were called in, their wares paraded before the discerning aunt. With their help, she transformed the clumsy girl her father had never troubled to look at into a striking young woman his eyes could not leave.

Discreet gatherings were arranged. The word was put out that a rich and noble heiress was in the offing. Suitors began to make themselves known from amongst Europe's leading aristocracy. Mathilde frequented balls and select parties. Under the watchful eye of a chaperone, she conversed with men, several of whom were at least as old as her father. Through all this Mathilde conducted herself with dignity. But she remained unmoved. None of it seemed to have anything to do with her. Yes, she was pleased, even deeply touched, that her father seemed at last to take notice of her. But the charade of suitors left her cold. They were far more interested in her father than in her. Nor did their behavior in any way correspond to what in the books or in her governesses' reminiscences was called love. Nonetheless, she knew that she would do her father's bidding and marry the man of his choosing. There were no other options open to her.

At the end of Mathilde's eighteenth year, her father announced that the appropriate man had been found: a Danish prince whose wealth and position matched theirs. The fact that he was twenty-five years older than she was of no moment. Prince Frederick was duly met; the engagement announced. Until her wedding night, Mathilde saw her future husband only twice on his own. On both occasions, he talked to her of his guiding interests—the military and fishing. She stole swift glances at him from under discreetly lowered lashes. He was tall, broad-shouldered, well made; he had sandy-colored hair and a benign smile. Her pulse raced a little. She tried to mold him into the roles her reading had given her.

The wedding, a grand affair, took place in Paris. The couple, with their retinue, then traveled to the site of their month-long honeymoon, a Scottish castle which had been loaned to them by a member of the extended family. Mathilde was at once excited and full of trepidation. Sir Walter Scott had given her a taste for the wilder aspects of nature, for abbeys and lochs, mountain and meadow, moss and moor and in none of this was she disappointed. The castle was a regal Jacobean pile, its high walls lined with tapestries and the glow of wainscoting. Outside, the wind blew over purple hillside. Stallions, their manes flowing, challenged the slopes. Streams rushed in a burble of sound over sleek pebbles and weathered rocks.

Mathilde's disappointments were reserved for the indoors. She and Frederick had adjoining rooms in the castle's west wing. In the midst of hers stood a vast four-poster bed. From the moment in which she had been ushered into the room, it was this object which claimed her imagination. She knew that something momentous was intended for this site, though she had no clear idea what it was. Her reading, the very few intimate conversations she had had with her governess, had led her only as far as the excitement of a kiss. Once or twice, while she was reading she had felt a tremor at the base of her stomach which she associated with such scenes. But on the two occasions when Frederick had kissed her, she had been aware only of the not altogether pleasant bristle of his moustache and the moonlike vastness of his face as it approached hers.

After dinner on their first night in the castle, Mathilde slipped up to her room while the men were sipping brandy in front of a blazing fire. Her maid helped her out of her dress and into a white satin nightgown with an appliqué of lace. It was the garment her aunt had instructed her, with a meaningful inflection of her voice, to reserve for her wedding night. As its cool length slipped over her head, Mathilde thought of her dead mother. If only the pretty young woman the photographs showed were here to counsel her. She almost engaged the maid in conversation: surely this girl with her winning ways knew more than she did. But she couldn't bring herself to it. Instead, her toilette over, she lay down on the vast bed and stared at the intricate pattern of its curtaining.

By the time Frederick knocked at her door and she murmured a low "Come in," she was tense with anticipation. The gas lamp by the bedside threw ghostly shadows round the room. She couldn't read the expression with which he looked at her, but she sensed a note of hostility in his terse "My wife awaits me." Or perhaps it was simply the note of her own anxiety. Unceremoniously, he took off his jacket and trousers. Mathilde closed her eyes. The bed creaked slightly as his broad boxer's form lowered itself. She could smell the brandy on his breath. Bristles scratched her face, rough lips met hers. A hand skimmed the length of her torso, then pushed her legs apart. The weight of a body descended on hers taking her breath away. She felt her buttocks being kneaded and then something jabbed into the center of her. She cried out in pain. She heard an answering grunt, then another jab and another. Then nothing. Only the harsh sound of his breathing and the hot hurt. She lay very still.

After a few moments, he got up, pecked her perfunctorily on the cheek, put on his shoes, almost, Mathilde thought, clicked his heels as he nodded and wished her goodnight. Then he was gone through the side door, his shirt tails trailing behind him.

From somewhere deep inside Mathilde, a laugh rose catching at her throat, strangling her. So this was what she had been waiting for. The laugh mingled with her tears.

For the next two nights, it was much the same, only that the hot pain was somewhat less. She tried to talk to Frederick, but there were no words with which to engage him. And polite and kind as he was to her during the days, at night communication was minimal, abrupt. On the fourth night, he did not appear. Nor on the fifth. She had not yet seen the instrument which jabbed at her center. Mathilde took to her bed. She developed a rasping cough. She was suddenly oppressed with the fear of dying. She imagined that her mother must have perished of that hot pain between her legs, of that heavy, suffocating body. The doctor was called.

When he arrived and was examining her alone in her room, Mathilde took her not inconsiderable courage in her hands.

"Doctor." She cleared her throat. "This is perhaps an indelicate question, but is it right that when my husband and I are together"—she pointed toward the bed—"all I should feel is pain?"

The doctor, an old Scotsman who had an animosity toward language, looked at her as if she had reached the summit of impudence. "Woman's lot is pain," he said as if he were quoting from an ancient text. "Be grateful you have all this"—he gestured dramatically around the room while his "r"s rolled. "And there is nothing wrong with you that a little less bone idleness won't cure," he added for good measure as he closed his bag.

Mathilde repressed the anger which boiled within her and took him at his word. Every morning she began to ride with a vengeance. Trailed by a young groom, she explored the vicinity of the castle, and then ventured further afield, past small huddled villages to where the sea pounded vociferously against vertiginous cliffs. In the afternoon, if the weather permitted, she explored the castle grounds and systematically executed botanical drawings of the vegetation. If the rain was too heavy, she stayed indoors and embroidered, an activity she had abandoned, but now took up again with an increasing delight in complexity of pattern. She gave up reading novels; their contents had misled her. The evenings were devoted to her notebooks: one French, another German, another English. These she filled with reflections and increasingly with fablelike stories and poems. She was left much to her own devices.

Only at mealtimes did she regularly see her husband and engage in conversation. Their company was small. Frederick was regularly attended by two friends who were also advisers and the talk moved desultorily from the subtleties of angling to the comparative excellence of different streams and rivers, and sometimes to politics. Only the latter interested Mathilde at all, but the occasional sharpness of her interventions brought a frown to her husband's face.

Halfway through the month, they were joined by a cousin of Frederick's and his young wife. The two women became friendly. Mathilde asked the latter to give her some elementary lessons in Danish. It filled the afternoons. But when Mathilde tried to share with her new friend her feelings about the boredom of their lives, the latter looked at her with utter incomprehension.

After a month they traveled to Denmark. A large wing of the family home just outside Copenhagen had been prepared for the new couple. Again Frederick paid three consecutive and abrupt visits to Mathilde's bedroom. She was confronted with the realization that there was nothing more to expect in that domain. In other ways, her life took on a fuller shape. Here in Denmark, the house hummed with the bustle of guests accompanied by numerous children, of grand weekly dinner parties. There were occasional expeditions to the ballet and the theater. Mathilde took a liking to Frederick's aunt, whose store of memories was rich and which she recounted in a vivacious and unhindered fashion. She learned of court intrigues across Europe, of her husband's hitherto unmentioned military prowess. As her Danish improved and as her quick wits began to make their mark amidst the entourage, Mathilde realized that she was not particularly unhappy.

There was another reason for her newfound confidence. In the fourth month of her marriage, Mathilde found that she was pregnant. Frederick grew tender, solicitous, proud. It became clear to her that this had been the sole object of his brief nighttime visits. They had been as unpleasant for him as for her. She stored the fact away for further perusal.

In quick succession and with relative ease, Mathilde gave birth to two boys. She loved their milky smell, their tiny clasping hands; loved too, as they grew, their clumsy running gait across the carpetlike lawns, the clear peal of their too-loud voices. But the boys were cared for by a succession of nurses and servants. By the time the younger one was four, Mathilde had grown restless, dissatisfied. Time lay heavily on her hands and as she looked into the future, all she could see was the endless unfolding of routine domesticity, punctuated by the occasional flurry of trips abroad. She hungered for the sharper air of Paris, for the crisp sound and wit of her own language, for study, for she didn't know quite what. She had taken to reading novels again. French newspapers and magazines arrived daily on her table. Avidly she pored over a feature about Marie Curie and wished that she too could dedicate herself to some great task.

Mathilde confronted Frederick. At twenty-five, she was a tall, striking young woman, whose youthful angularity had rounded into a graceful slenderness. Her nose under the dark eyes was a little too long, her mouth a little too wide for picturely perfection, but the mobile vivacity of her features captured the gaze. And when she spoke, the sheer concentrated power of her presence was vividly apparent. Frederick was a little afraid of her.

"I should like to spend part of every year in Paris, Frederick." Mathilde spoke slowly and distinctly so that he would take in the seriousness of her statement.

He looked at her in astonishment and said nothing. The wives of Danish princes did not suddenly pick up and leave the courtly circle.

Mathilde read his mind. "I know it is an unusual request. But my father is growing old and I should like to be near him in his last years. The children can come with me, if you allow it. It will do them no harm to taste a little of France." Mathilde paused and chose her words carefully. "I would like it if you too could be with us, at least part of the time, when your affairs permit."

Frederick thought as rapidly as his painstaking mind permitted. Mathilde had fed him the appropriate cues. It was true that no one could object to a daughter going to her father's side in his last years. It was true that his children were part French and of a family which prided itself on its origins. But he would miss them. He had no taste for Paris, with its quick-witted ways. Still, he might join them for a month at a time.

Frederick looked cautiously at his wife. "Perhaps we could try it for a year or two. Only four months at a stretch, mind."

Mathilde planted an uncustomary kiss on his cheek. She was euphoric and as Frederick listened to the fluent stream of her plans, he grew increasingly pleased with himself. He had obviously granted his wife a long-desired wish and he had also exercised his authority by setting a limit on it. He had made her happy; and as he gradually admitted to himself, he was also making himself happy. He never felt quite at ease with Mathilde. She challenged his peace of mind with her constant queries and endless activities. And he always felt just a little bit guilty about his increasingly infrequent visits to her bedroom. This new scheme might prove satisfactory to everyone.

Frederick's sanction obtained, Mathilde buzzed with new energy. She made a preliminary journey to Paris, reorganized the family house in Neuilly so that it was ready to receive her and her children. With the ample private inheritance she had from her mother, she also bought an apartment in the center of Paris, near the Champs-Elysées. It was this site which was to serve as the true birthplace of her new and independent identity.

Mathilde threw herself into her Paris life with the zest of a woman who had been restrained too long. No sooner had the news of her return made the rounds than she was besieged by invitations from every quarter. In addition to her rank, her personal charm ensured that these invitations recurred. Mathilde could be seen at the opera, at the theater, at salons where politics, or literature, or music were the focus of affairs. For the first time, she developed an interest in her appearance and in clothes. Paris was not the outskirts of Copenhagen. Top couturiers came to her home in Neuilly and the models paraded their latest designs. She indulged herself, developed a taste for high style and on occasion for the slightly *outré*.

Mathilde's married status gave her far more freedom than she had enjoyed as a girl. She could talk to anyone and everyone about almost anything within the magic circle of the gatherings she attended. In the daytime she could, though with a little more difficulty, walk through the Paris streets alone, sit in cafés in unfashionable quarters and observe the life around her. Her predilection for these anonymous outings grew and she ventured further and further afield. What she observed both horrified and fascinated her. In the sheltered life she had led, she had always been oblivious to poverty. Now, in her wanderings, without the distance of car or carriage to shield her, its brutality confronted her daily. She took to talking to the grubby street urchins who begged centimes from her. She bought them hot chocolate and listened to their accounts of their lives. Feeling helpless, she gave away everything in her purse.

After two seasons like this, Mathilde began once again to suffer from what she perceived as the constraints of her life. She would have liked, she thought, to train for some profession, to study at the university, to fight cases in the law courts, even to work like one of those female stenographers in solicitors' offices. Her status, her position as Princesse Mathilde, Prince Frederick's wife, barred her from any real activity. She began to despise her idleness, the uselessness of the chit-chat she engaged in daily in her own and others' salons. She determined to do something.

The first thing she did was to fund a residential school for her street urchins. It wasn't, for Mathilde, a simple act of charity, performed at a distance paved by finance. She did her own research, traveled to England and Germany, consulted experts, talked to children themselves to see what it was they would prefer, and then brought in the talent she considered most progressive. It took three years to bring things to a point of readiness and she found the undertaking exhilarating. At last she was stretching herself, accomplishing something of use; even, she was prepared to admit it, taking advantage of the privileges she had so long thought did no more than confine her range of possibilities.

In the corridors of her school, Mathilde fell in love with the part she was playing. No longer the grand Princesse, she was by turns the compassionate or stern headmistress. Her staff adored her and bowed to the trenchancy of her quick decisions, her infallible instinct for what would be best for individual children. Visitors from the Ministry of Education or the courts were quick to jeer behind her back at the progressive ideas of this eccentric aristocrat. But faced by Mathilde they quailed in their boots and gave in to all her demands.

The second thing Mathilde did was quite different and it involved a greater obliteration of her identity. In the quiet of her own apartment, she began regularly and systematically to write. Several men in her circle had commented that Mathilde had a particular genius for listening. She now put this to some benefit. Every day from ten to twelve, she sat at her desk and wove the things that she had heard and seen and felt into stories. They were crisp little tales told with a mordant wit which exposed the vagaries of high life. When she had written twelve of these stories, Mathilde sent them off pseudonymously to a publisher. With an excitement she had not experienced since her wedding night, she waited for the response. It came. M. Roland Duby, for this was the name she had chosen, was congratulated on his brilliant stories, which the Editions de Blais would be delighted to publish. Mathilde clapped her hands in glee. She reveled in this newfound secret existence; and even when Paris was agog to unmask the identity of a writer who seemed to know its corrupt core, yet whom no one had met, she revealed herself only to a single person.

It was during the time when she was writing her first stories that Mathilde's father's health began seriously to fail. Albert de Polignesco had suffered a stroke just before Mathilde had determined to move to Paris. He had recovered. Now complications of various kinds had set in and he was quickly losing his grip on reality. During the daytime, he would lie on a chaise-longue in the vast Neuilly conservatory where he was attended by two nurses. At night, once the children were in bed, Mathilde cared for him. Sometimes she read to him and her voice seemed to soothe his pain. At other times, they would talk in a desultory way. It was clear that he wanted her near him and she took to sleeping in a small bed at the far corner of his room.

This unaccustomed proximity had a strange effect on Mathilde. In all her years, she had never been so close to her father. During her lonely childhood she had sought his love and approval, even simply his attention, and rarely received it. Now his dependence on her gave her an uncomfortable power that she both relished and despised. It was deeply troubling to get to know the person, who for years had been an unreachable superior, only in the guise of this pathetic old man.

One night she was woken from light sleep by the sound of a shrill curse. Instantly she was by her father's bedside. Though his eyes were wide open, he seemed not to see her. Nor did he respond to her words. The voice that emerged from him was one she had never heard her father use: it was rampant with hostility.

"Filthy slut. So you've been at it again. I told you what I would do to you, if I found you out." He flailed a thin fist. "Come here, Claire, come here, you impudent hussy." The voice had changed now. It was wheedling, cajoling. "There, what do you think of that? It's bigger than his, isn't it? It belongs to a prince of the realm. Yes, stroke it, suck it."

A thin stream of spittle emerged from her father's mouth. Mathilde trembled. She felt nausea rising in her stomach. Claire, that had been the name of the English governess she had had at the age of eight. She had stayed longer than some of the others. Her father's eyes were closed now. He was quiet. Mathilde watched him for a long time, her mind in turmoil.

The next night, it happened again. But the scene his delirious words evoked was different. This time the woman's name was unknown to Mathilde, but he was evidently in bed with her. "It's beautiful. With you, it's beautiful. Your pussy is beautiful. Everything moves." His expression changed, grew sour. "Not like that cold tight little cunt I'm married to." He stared straight at Mathilde, his luminous eyes unseeing.

Mathilde lurched away from him. She didn't want to hear any more, know any more. She drew her blanket over her ears. The next day, like the previous one, her father seemed to remember nothing. He was as always, passive, slightly absent, grateful when things were done for him. As for Mathilde, she was racked by his revelations. The shock of hearing her mother referred to in that way; the horror of what must have been their marriage. Inevitably, she thought of her own. Was she like her mother? Did Frederick think of her like that? And what were these wonders of women that her father referred to? Mathilde's thoughts could focus on nothing else. She was terrified of facing any more of his delirious memories, yet simultaneously she wanted to hear them. She steeled herself to return to his room, rationalizing her fascination with the excuse that she did not want her father to feel she was withdrawing from him. Nor did she want any strange nurse to hear his delirious wanderings.

For one long week, Mathilde listened to the old man and learned and cried, as much over herself as over her mother and him. At the end of that time, her emotions in turmoil, she spoke shamefacedly to her father's physician.

"At night, he's delirious. He talks. He doesn't recognize me." Mathilde gazed at the elderly doctor beseechingly.

Dr. Picard patted her hand. "It is not unusual at this stage," he comforted her.

"But the content of his delirium . . ." Mathilde couldn't bring herself to go on. She had known Dr. Picard since her earliest childhood.

"The mind is a strange apparatus and not always a noble one." He accepted the cup of tea the maid brought in and looked at it reflectively. "You're overwrought, tired. We shall bring a night nurse in."

Mathilde shook her head emphatically.

"He is nearing his end, you know," Dr. Picard said gently.

"But I need to understand." Again, Mathilde couldn't go on. What was it exactly that she wanted to know? Was it to do with the content of her father's deliria or the fact that they occurred? She looked into herself and realized that it was both. She took her courage in her hands. "I want to know why it is that he talks about his sexual life." There, she had brought it out at last, and she rushed on, "And why, how, this delirium takes hold of him."

The old man shrugged. "I am neither a philosopher nor one of these newfangled psychoanalysts. But if you must take advice, here." He wrote two names on a slip of paper. Mathilde took the piece of paper. In her heart of hearts, she sensed that it was neither doctors nor philosophers who would help her understand what she sought. But she read the names in any case. One of them would, in a circuitous way, eventually change the course of her life.

CHAPTER
FIVE

$\mathcal{M}$y father said some very strange things before he died."

"Strange things?" Prince Frederick savored the full flavor of his pouilly-fumé, before swallowing and looking at his wife.

It was early summer and the golden glow of the setting sun warmed the terrace of their Neuilly residence. Roses, clambering profusely round ornate railings, gave off a heady perfume.

"Yes." Mathilde paused. She stroked the sleek head of her father's prize borzoi, who now trailed her everywhere. "Yes," she murmured again, "very strange things." Ever since her father's death the month before, she had wanted to talk to Frederick about her fears, question him. The desire had become an obsession. But amidst the endless funeral arrangements, the pomp and circumstance of the event itself, amidst the array of family and visiting dignitaries, the moment had never presented itself. Now they would be leaving the Neuilly house in two days' time to return to Denmark, and Mathilde felt that if she didn't seize the occasion, another would not easily present itself.

"He talked about my mother in his delirium, talked about intimate matters." Mathilde couldn't find the appropriate expression. She met Frederick's eyes. He was looking at her expectantly. "Yes, he seemed to suggest there was something wrong with her . . . well, in her female parts." She blurted it out clumsily. Frederick stiffened. His face closed, he looked away from her. Mathilde hurtled on, "Frederick, are you happy with me in that way? Am I properly formed?"

He stood up, almost dropping his glass. "I cannot talk about these things, Mathilde." His normally ruddy complexion had grown white. He looked at once angry and helpless. "I am not French, you know." It was his parting shot. He bowed to her briefly and turned away.

Mathilde, looking after his lumbering form, felt contrite, sorry for him. Yet the feeling did nothing to ease her own sense of frustration. She knew that he would now go off with his preferred secretary, a rotund young man given to leather coats and boots, and sit for hours discussing the intricacies of the next week's fishing expedition.

Had Princesse Mathilde been born fifty years later the whys, hows and wherefores of what she was feeling would have been paraded for her daily in the pages of the women's magazines. Indeed, she might even have had prescribed for her a little dialogue with which to confront her husband. As it was, the limited circle of her experience, her class, the lack of a common language in which to talk about sexuality, all conspired to make her feel that she was somehow, like her mother, at fault. Throughout the long succeeding months, no matter how much she buried herself in activity, this subterranean fear oppressed her. Was she sexually misshapen? Was something wrong with her? The fear was accompanied by a vague longing. Despite her new enterprises, despite the strong young limbs of her growing children, the Princesse again felt dissatisfied with herself and the world. Without telling her husband, she arranged to attend lectures at the Paris Special Infirmary, lectures which she hoped would rid her of her ignorance and her fear.

Princesse Mathilde sped lightly from Gaitan de Clérambault's lecture hall just before the professor terminated his opening gambit of the season. Then, in the dim gloom of the corridor, she hesitated. Yes, why not wait? True, Jacob Jardine had not taken up her invitation to attend one of her Wednesday evenings, but he had nodded to her from across the room and it would be rude to vanish without exchanging some form of greeting. She made herself small as the young doctors emerged from the room and by the time Jacob appeared, she had made up her mind.

"Would you do me the honor of accompanying me home? I should very much like to discuss some of the points M. de Clérambault raised today."

Jacob detached himself from his group. His friends' curious eyes were on his back. He hesitated. He had thought about Princesse Mathilde after having met her some four weeks back at the Brenners'. But he had deliberately not taken up her earlier invitation. Indeed he and Jacques had argued over it. "I will not be paraded in front of society people to titillate them with stories about madness. I will not be party to their gawping and tut-tutting over others' suffering," he had said then.

His suspicion about Princesse Mathilde was unabated. Yet he had no other immediate engagement, no excuse to offer and the woman with the straightforward gaze and charming smile who stood before him now in a tailored gray suit seemed a distant cousin of the gilded and bejeweled creature he had met on the eve of the new year.

Jacob nodded his assent. He had another momentary misgiving as they approached the Princesse's silver Daimler and a stern liveried chauffeur bowed a greeting. But when he had been ushered into the book-lined comfort of her study, where afternoon light poured through large windows, he began to relax. He liked the unostentatious elegance of the room; he liked, too, the way the Princesse sank into a deep chair, crossed long, slender legs, and looked at him intently, without a trace of coyness, as they talked.

She questioned him about his work, about his interest in psychiatry and Jacob found himself answering her with a fluency normally reserved for Jacques and his other male friends. It was to do with the quality of her listening, the wide arch of her eyes, the spirited irony which lit up her features. He knew from her lively responses that she followed him in everything he said and understood the intent beneath the words.

When they had moved from their second cup of coffee to wine, the Princesse asked, "And M. de Clérambault. What do you think of him?"

Jacob grinned. "He's madder than the patients he pretends to diagnose. Completely and rigorously systematic. He's a pigeonhole man. He doesn't listen to a jot of what patients say. He simply peers at them with his eagle eye, classifies them into one of his categories and happily locks them away in perpetuity. Because, of course, if their illness is organic, as he insists it is, there is nothing to be done." He shook his head in disgust, earnest now.

"So you have found masters more to your taste, Henri Claude, perhaps?" Princesse Mathilde pressed him.

Jacob shrugged. "Don't get me wrong. Clérambault is a genius.

With all his faults, at least he understands the propulsion of the erotic."

The Princesse's dark eyes grew darker. She looked away for a moment, straightened her skirt.

Jacob noticed her discomfort. "But you, how did you come to be interested in all this?" he asked, suddenly burning to know more about her.

The Princesse laughed. "If you want the truth, it's all to do with my father." She had never said this to anyone but old Dr. Picard before and she was surprised at the facility with which the statement had tripped off her tongue.

Jacob pressed her. "Your father?"

The Princesse reached for one of the cigarettes she had taken to smoking and waited for Jacob to light it. She inhaled deeply. With Jacob the words seemed to flow out of her with relative ease. "Yes, in his delirium, just before he died, he talked only of sex." She flushed slightly. "It was something, as you can imagine, which he normally didn't mention. I wanted to know why . . ."

He seemed not in the least surprised. "When the censors of the conscious mind are at bay, all kinds of repressed thoughts, hidden wishes make themselves known. It is only natural." Jacob examined her face acutely and read the anxiety there. "But, of course, it is not usually something we would choose to reveal to our children. You must have been deeply distressed."

It was all so simple the way Jacob put it, so clean, almost scientific. The Princesse felt one layer of shame lifted from her. There was more, but that was not something she wanted to broach now. After all, they hardly knew each other. Instead she asked, "But the things that are revealed in this kind of state, are they true?"

A twinkle lit up Jacob's dark eyes. "What is truth?" he intoned with mock solemnity. "For the unconscious, for human beings, for us, can there ever be a *single* truth?"

The Princesse took it and remained silent for an extended moment.

Jacob continued, "Have you ever read Freud?"

Mathilde shook her head. "I have heard his name, though not always mentioned with great respect."

"I shall bring you one or two of his books. You must judge for yourself. He makes it clear how we are propelled by forces within us which are beyond our knowledge; and that these forces are to a large extent sexual." With that he rose. "I ought to get back to the hospital now. Thank you for a most enjoyable few hours."

"The pleasure has been all mine," Mathilde responded, meaning it. Then she restrained him for a moment. "The problem is I want to *know;* I want desperately to know."

"Yes." Jacob considered. "In that I fear we may be alike."

From her window, she watched his back receding along the street. She had a mounting sense of exhilaration.

Over the next weeks, Jacob and Princesse Mathilde met with growing regularity after M. de Clérambault's lectures. In the quiet of her large airy study, they talked, hungrily exchanging ideas and impressions. Since she read German, he had brought her Freud's *Studies on Hysteria* and *The Interpretation of Dreams.* She read them avidly and he was impressed by the acuity of her response. They often argued, sometimes agreed. Occasionally, too, they offered up little fragments of their own lives, small gem-like distillations of their experience, a revealing anecdote, a pointed aside. But rarely did they mention the matter-of-fact substance of their day-to-day existences. Jacob knew little more than when he had begun seeing the Princesse about how she spent her days and all she knew of him was his passion for his work.

Nonetheless, Mathilde felt that for the first time in her life, she was truly awake. A film of what she now thought of as boredom seemed to have lifted from her eyes. She was alive to everything: to the pace of the March clouds across the sky, to the shoots pushing through the ground of the garden at Neuilly, to her boys' scamperings and tears. She found herself hugging them a great deal and when she held their taut little resisting bodies, tears would suddenly come to her eyes. But no matter how busy she was, no matter how numerous the run of her activities and duties, her inner clock was set by her meetings with Jacob. Without thinking about it, she anticipated and drew her energies from those brief weekly hours in the confines of her study when the whole workings of the human world seemed to inform the agility of their two-handed conversation.

One afternoon, late in March, Jacob grew particularly heated in his description of a scene he had witnessed earlier that day between a head psychiatrist and a young female patient. He was pacing the room, his face stormy. Mathilde rose to ring for the maid. It was time for a drink. Unwittingly, Jacob brushed against her. They both stopped in their tracks. A palpable current of electricity had passed between them. Their eyes met and suddenly Jacob's arms were round her. He kissed her fiercely on the lips and then as quickly let her go. "I'm sorry," he murmured. "I've been wanting to do that for some time."

Before Mathilde could gather her thoughts, he was abruptly gone.

The next evening Jacob was due to dine with the Brenners. As usual the sitting room of their sumptuous home was aglow with soft lights, discreetly positioned flowers. The old master portraits, the solid Empire furniture, everything was in its customary place. Yet as soon as Jacob entered, he sensed something ominous in the air.

Lady Leonore was in strangely extravagant garb. She was bedecked with jewelry, row upon row of pearls, rings on most of her fingers, jangling bracelets, a tight sheath-like dress in luminous green, which obliterated the grace of her features. When she embraced Jacob, it was with unusual ardor. "Ah, the most handsome man in Paris has arrived at last. My son's best friend. And my son could use some best friends."

"Mother." Jacob could hear the warning note in Jacques' voice.

There were two bright spots on Lady Leonore's cheeks. "What is it, Jacques? Would you rather kiss him on the lips yourself?"

Jacob realized she was drunk. He sat down quietly in a corner of the room next to Jacques and observed M. Brenner trying not to pay any attention to his wife. The man looked ill. Jacob cast a questioning glance at Jacques and the latter shrugged. "The market. The money. It's all gone." He made a despairing gesture.

Before Jacob could respond, there was a little flurry of excitement as all eyes turned on the new arrival in the room. Jacob drew in his breath. For some reason he had lost all sense of the Princesse having a life distinct from their meetings. And here she was in the full splendor of what he suddenly realized was her real life. She was clothed in a deep burgundy gown of some fluid material which moved with her and admirably set off the warm tones of her skin, the luminous texture of her hair. She was, Jacob thought, regally beautiful.

"And now that our guest of honor has arrived, we can all go to table," Lady Leonore announced in a voice too shrill. "You know everyone, of course, Princesse. In any case, everyone knows you," she giggled oddly at her own rudeness.

Princesse Mathilde looked round the room graciously and smiled. Her fine eyes rested on Jacob fractionally longer. Perhaps he imagined it. He bowed formally in response, as did every man there.

They moved into the dining room, where the long rectangular

table was laid with lace, ornate silver and gleaming candelabra. Jacob was too far from the Princesse to be able to engage her directly and he did his best to keep up a polite conversation with the women on either side of him. But he could see Mathilde clearly and also hear the barbed comments Lady Leonore continued to address to her. The rest of the table gradually grew breathlessly still.

"And are those two darling boys of yours safely tucked up in Neuilly? It must be very convenient to have two houses so close to one another."

"Yes, very." Princesse Mathilde responded in a neutral voice.

"And particularly convenient to have one's husband a good thousand kilometers away."

Jacob thought he detected a flush in the Princesse's cheeks.

"Frederick is not particularly fond of Paris," she murmured.

"No. They are boring, those Danes, aren't they?" Lady Leonore continued as she took another sip of wine. "I don't know why you married him. Guess you had to, didn't you. Poor thing. Poor little Princesse."

"Come, come, Lady Leonore," the man at the Princesse's side, whom Jacob had just begun to notice, intervened. "Surely your own Shakespeare found the Danes a particularly interesting people." He tried to change the course of the conversation. Princesse Mathilde looked at him gratefully.

"Dear dotty old Hamlet was the exception." Lady Leonore laughed too loudly. "But the rest of them are cold"—she stressed the word—"and orderly, boringly cold, dismally orderly, wouldn't you say, Princesse?"

"It depends what one's tastes are," Princesse Mathilde said evenly. "I personally like a little order."

"But not coldness, surely. Not with your father's waggish genes in your blood. He was quite the ladykiller in his youth, I'm told."

This time the flush was evident in Mathilde's face.

Lady Leonore seemed to be pleased by its appearance. She turned the direction of her assault. "Yes, but then so was my François in his youth." She looked pointedly at the other end of the table where M. Brenner was quietly picking at his *canard aux cerises*. Lady Leonore shook her blonde head balefully. "Not now. Not anymore. Nor my son, of course. No, no, certainly not my son."

"Mother!" This time Jacques' voice was harsh. He pushed his chair back loudly. "You will all excuse my mother, please, but we have had a hard day." With that he took Lady Leonore's arm and all but pulled her from her chair. They vanished through the room's double doors.

"Please, my friends, be patient with us." François Brenner broke the resounding hush which had spread round the table. "Leonore is distressed. It may be the last time we are able to entertain you in this house which she has so loved." His voice had a quiet dignity. "Please, let us try to enjoy the rest of this dinner."

Random talk sprang up, but everyone was relieved to be able to move on to coffee in the dimmer light of the sitting room. Jacob hoped he might be able to exchange a few words with the Princesse now. He felt her embarrassment acutely. But the opportunity didn't arise. She was talking intently to the man she had sat next to at dinner, and soon with the briefest of nods to Jacob, the two of them left together.

Suddenly Jacob was struck with the thought that Lady Leonore's comments might have had a deeper intent than he had supposed. Could she have been suggesting that this man and Mathilde were engaged in an affair? Jacob's hand twisted into a tight fist. He felt an overwhelming urge to dash out and confirm whether they were getting into Mathilde's silver Daimler together.

Jacques chose this moment to come back into the room. One look at his friend and Jacob knew that he couldn't leave without first comforting him.

An hour later, however, he found himself hailing a taxi and ordering the driver to take the route to the Princesse's apartment. He had an excuse ready. He simply wanted to make sure that Mathilde wasn't too distressed by Lady Leonore's onslaught. When he arrived and looked up at the darkened windows, he had a moment of trepidation. He had never come here without being awaited, expected. The Princesse's everyday life was an unexplored terrain. He almost turned back. But then the feeling which had flooded through him as he watched the Princesse leave with her companion came back to him. He rang the bell, tried to sidle past the concierge's all-seeing window invisibly, and raced up the stairs. When, after a long pause, the maid opened the door and looked at him with great perplexity, he sought uncomfortably for a pretext.

"No, no, of course Madame la Princesse isn't in. Perhaps you can tell me when you expect her? I need . . . I need urgently to retrieve an article I lent her."

"Madame is not expected until Monday, Docteur Jardine."

At least she recognized him, Jacob thought. He hadn't been sure.

She looked at his crestfallen face. "Would you like to come in and retrieve the article yourself? I am sure Madame would not mind."

Jacob was a little taken aback; but now he couldn't extricate himself gracefully. He nodded. She led him to the study and waited at the door. Jacob was at a loss. He felt like a thief though he didn't know what it was he had come to steal. Dismayed, he looked at the Princesse's neat desk and sheepishly rifled through some notepads and sheets of paper stacked on its right hand side. In his clumsiness, part of the pile slipped off the desk. Jacob reached to pick it up. Letters fluttered out of a bound notebook. Despite himself, Jacob read, *"Ma adorable Princesse."* Hastily, he returned the letter to the notebook. In doing so, he scanned the contents. Stories, vignettes, journal entries in the Princesse's unmistakable hand. Furtively and with an increasing sense of malaise, he replaced the papers.

"No. I'm sorry. I can't find the piece. I have no idea where to begin to look." A salutary notion came to him. "Perhaps you could mention to the Princesse on Monday that I shall come round. The article I need is one of my own which I gave her a few weeks back." Luckily that much at least was true. Quickly, Jacob made his escape.

Over the next few days, Jacob was tormented as much by his perfidy as by his musings about the Princesse, her husband, and the man she had left the Brenners' with. At the age of twenty-five, he was a relatively inexperienced young man. Not sexually or even altogether emotionally: Mariette and Germaine, whom he numbered as his *loves,* had been succeeded by a number of demi-mondaines with whom he had had attachments of varying brevity and pleasure. But unlike many young men of his background, he had stayed away from intrigues with married women, though several had made their availability known. He simply wasn't interested. Life was already too full. And the young unmarried women he met, his sister's friends, though he was dearly attached to her, seemed to him vapid, full of endless, empty twitterings. Of course, he had read widely and in his imagination he was a man of consummate experience. But the lived reality was somewhat different.

On Monday, as soon as he could free himself, Jacob went to Princesse Mathilde's. The maid ushered him into the salon. "Madame is receiving today," she said.

Jacob had rarely set foot in the Princesse's more formal salon. Here a classical harmony reigned, a formal symmetry of elements which defied the existence of private turmoil. The graceful chairs, upholstered with Aubusson tapestries; the curved splendor of a tête-à-tête; the fine Louis XVI cabinets with their intricate Boulle marquetry and engraved coat of arms; the elegantly carved walnut secretaire; the inlaid Renaissance cabinet, with its richly painted panels—all spoke of a world where public and social relations took pride of place over any inner sphere. Jacob suddenly felt daunted, like an adolescent going to his first party. His prepared speech fled from his mind.

"Jacob, I was told you might be dropping by. How very nice." The Princesse looked at him with a gracious smile.

"Yes, yes. I needed to retrieve that article I had given you. I hope it's not an imposition," he added, as an afterthought. He was embarrassed by the presence of the other people in the room.

"Not at all. I shall fetch it for you in a moment. But do join us for a cup of tea first. These are my friends, Madame Ezard and Princesse Soutzo. We were just bemoaning the fact that a mere 3.5 percent of boys in France receive a secondary school education from the state. It's a scandalously small number."

Jacob murmured his agreement. He was surprised by the subject of conversation. It sat so oddly in this room which spoke of an older epoch of privilege. He contributed little and was relieved when after a few moments the women, in a flurry of hats and gloves, began to take their leave.

"I've chased them away. I'm sorry," Jacob said stiffly, once they were alone.

The Princesse shook her brown curls. "Not at all," she responded politely. But the look she gave him was a quizzical one.

An unusual and uncomfortable silence descended upon them, covered by the mutual sipping of tea. They broke it simultaneously. "I shall get that article now."

"I wanted to see you after the other night . . ." Jacob followed her into the study, watched as she opened a drawer and pulled out a sheaf of papers. He was at a loss for words. He could only stare at the fluidity of her movements, the fine texture of her skin where the black dress met her slender neck. Hot unreason poured through him. Rashly, he walked over to her, took her hands in his. He looked down at them. They were beautiful, like her. Slim, gracious, yet somehow vital. He traced the outline of her fingertips. Then he kissed her. She didn't resist, didn't resist the growing strength of his embrace as he drew her to him. Only when his tongue probed her soft mouth did she murmur. Jacob withdrew a little. His breath came fast as he looked into her eyes. "I only realized over these last few days how much you mean to me," he said, feeling the words were somehow extraneous, and then to hide his emotion, he drew her face to his shoulder. He stroked her hair. She trembled.

Commotion reigned in Princesse Mathilde's senses as thoroughly as in her mind and emotions. Despite her thirty years, her two children, she was in many respects a complete novice. Prince Frederick's cursory kisses had never moved her in any way. Isolated from her peers, she had never had a childhood friend steal an excited embrace. She was more insulated by privilege from the advances of men than any Victorian spinster might have been by the armor of morality. Now, suddenly, for the first time in her life her pulses raced dangerously. She lifted her face to him. "Kiss me again," she said, surprised at her naked, abrupt voice.

Jacob moved his mouth lingeringly along the fine line of her chin where it met her ear until their lips found each other. From that kiss they emerged on the other side of an invisible barrier. Mathilde felt shy, vulnerable, and at the same time supremely powerful— powerful in the desire which she evoked in him; powerful, too, in the sensations which coursed through her own body. She looked into the smoldering darkness of Jacob's eyes. "Come," she said, taking his hand. She led him into her bedroom, closing the door softly behind them.

He kissed her again, more harshly now, his desire growing surer, keener. His hands strayed over her, cupping her breasts. Then with one easy movement he unclasped her dress, letting it slide down her silk slip. In a moment he was as naked as she. Mathilde drew in a rapid breath. She had never seen a man fully nude before, not in the flesh, not outside museums. She was enthralled by Jacob's beauty, the strong neck, the agile torso, the firm elasticity of skin over muscle. Her eyes traveled lower, then stopped in momentary fear. No, there would never be room inside her. She remembered the hot dry pain, the disappointment, her father's words, the humiliation.

Jacob was awake to her sudden fear. It excited him. Hungrily he stroked the slender outline of her body, his lips following his fingers. He touched her there, rubbed softly. Her cry of surprise fueled his passion. She was strangely innocent. The thought crystallized in him and filled him with awe. He drew her gently on to the bed, guided her quivering hands, urged her to explore until she found his penis. Cool fingers on jutting warmth. He gasped, buried his face in her breasts. Something in Mathilde was released by that sound, by the feel of that strong quivering animal in her hand; sensation rippled through her from unknown quarters; she could feel the wetness between her legs. She arched against him, called his name in small moans. Suddenly she wanted him inside her as she had never wanted anything before.

Later they lay side by side, a little breathless, on the rumpled silk sheets. She stroked his body wonderingly, perched her face on the roughness of his chest and looked into his eyes. Her own were luminous. "I never knew," she said, "I had no idea it could be like this." Jacob smiled lingeringly. He drew her on top of him and kissed her eyes, her nose, her lips. She could feel his penis beneath her filling again, and she wondered at this too. Again, could it happen again, now? Jacob grasped her hips and pulled her down on him, thrusting into her so that she cried out at the infinite pleasure of it.

"And like this," he said with a glimmer of irony when she had stopped rippling against him and their bodies lay entwined in moisture.

She sat up and looked away from him. "You mustn't laugh at me," she said softly. There were tears in her eyes. "For all your brilliance, you can't understand what it's like not to know, to think there is something uniquely wrong with you, to imagine it's a congenital doom, to feel humiliated and yet helpless at the hands of a man."

Then Mathilde began to talk as she had never talked before. She told him about herself, about Frederick, about her father, not in any particular consecutive order, but in small capsules of interrelated pain. Jacob stroked her, stroked the small frightened girl in her. He wanted somehow to make it all up to her. He held her tightly in his arms and let her cry. The tears streamed over his bare shoulders.

They slept. Mathilde dreamt Frederick was on top of her, his bulky form constricting her chest. She pushed him away, then realized it was her father. He cursed her vilely and she clung to him, moaning, "I love you." She woke, bathed in perspiration, to find her arms around Jacob's back. He turned and kissed her, quieting her with his love.

Over the next weeks, Jacob and Mathilde met whenever it was possible. Between meetings, they floated, wrapped in thoughts of each other. Jacob had never been with a woman whose whole being excited him and satisfied him so much. The Princesse had simply never been in love and she reveled in it. Sexually awakened, suddenly free of years of a gnawing unspecified anxiety, she found unknown resources in herself. She was witty, teasing, always generous. Her apartment became their world. In it the accumulated matter of their lives thronged. They interspersed their lovemaking with ardent discussions about sex, psychiatry, politics, education and Jacob's growing interest in psychoanalysis. They gossiped endlessly about friends and acquaintances.

One day Jacob confided in her his deep worry about Jacques and his parents. M. Brenner's financial plight was destroying the family. Lady Leonore was suicidal; her husband, caught in a tide of hopelessness, seemed utterly paralyzed. Jacques, at his wits' end, simply sat and watched his mother embalm herself in alcohol.

A few days after he had spoken of this to the Princesse, Jacob received a telephone call from Jacques. A miracle had occurred. An unknown had underwritten his father's company, halting the bankruptcy proceedings. Jacques was going to make sure that they made good that mysterious confidence.

When Jacob related all this to Mathilde, he watched her face closely.

"What wonderful news," she said to him, her face brilliant with her smile. "I'm so pleased."

"Was it you?" Jacob asked.

"Me?" She looked at him, eyes wide in innocence. "What makes you think that?" She laughed teasingly and stroked his hair. "And here I thought it was all your doing."

Jacob kissed her passionately, recognizing the truth.

The Princesse grew bold with his embraces. She wanted to shout her bliss to the world. Instead, she cultivated the pleasures of secrecy. She would turn up in a salon or café that Jacob frequented and brazenly pretend he was a mere passing acquaintance. She asked him the most innocuous and maddening questions. Coolly, Jacob matched her at her game, deriving a similar delight from its elaboration. Later, in her apartment overlooking the Champs-Elysées, they would laugh hilariously at the masked interludes they enacted.

On one of the rare evenings when they were to have the whole of a night together, Jacob arrived at the Princesse's flat in a state of peculiar excitement. His dark eyes gleamed. No sooner had the Princesse's servants left them alone, than he lifted Mathilde in his arms.

"I have a very particular pleasure in store for you this evening."

"Oh?" She fluttered thick lashes at him playfully. "I do hope it's not dinner at the Ritz, because I was so looking forward to being alone with you tonight." Her long fingers grazed the roughness of his face and insinuated themselves beneath his shirt.

Jacob stopped her hand. "The terrible brazenness of royalty!" He shook his head in mock disbelief.

A shadow passed over Mathilde's face. She turned away from him and walked to the end of the long room. Pensively, she looked out of the window.

"Am I being brazen, Jacob? Are you tiring of me?" With his words, it had suddenly occurred to her that Jacob might be growing weary of her, growing weary of their enforced seclusion. It was she after all who imposed constraints. She who could not allow herself to be seen with him. Other women would be free. They would behave differently. How would they behave? She had so little experience. Perhaps even the lovemaking which she found so utterly wonderful was something he was growing weary of.

Jacob watched her. In the long brocade gown with its softly glowing colors, she looked as if she were indeed ready for a night at the Ritz. Or perhaps more accurately for an evening at the court of some Renaissance prince. He didn't understand her sudden change of mood, but he knew that he had wounded her.

Gently he took her hand and led it to precisely where it had previously rested. "I love your brazenness, Mathilde," he said softly. At her hesitation, he gathered her in his arms and kissed her softly. There was a tremulous quality in her which roused his passion. "You see how I love it," he murmured in her ear, pressing her to him, guiding her hands so that she could feel the hardness of his penis. The small moans she made as he caressed her breasts, the musky scent which issued from her, all fed his ardor.

Usually, they waited until after dinner to begin their lovemaking in earnest. The clothes of the day needed to be shed, the material of their other lives negotiated, until the magic of the twosome took them over utterly. Tonight, he made love to her instantly, there on the sofa of the grand room. He sensed her need, met it fervently.

Later, they laughed as they looked round the room and saw their tumbled clothes, lying askew like witnesses to an adolescent hunger.

"And now, Madame la Princesse," Jacob said, caressing her nakedness, "the very special pleasure I referred to earlier. Let me reveal to you in what the true brazenness of royalty lies." He laughed wickedly, strode to where his jacket lay in disarray and drew a book from its pocket. With playful grandeur, he opened it and began to read. "In the salon of a certain Madame R., a bizarre event took place . . ."

An uncustomary flush rose in Mathilde's face.

"Have I found you out, Roland Duby? Have I?" Jacob kissed her passionately. "And isn't it of a terrible brazenness to write like this secretly under a male name? Who else would dare?"

"Shh," Mathilde put a finger to her lips. "The world will hear you." But she was pleased that he had found her out.

Some weeks later the Princesse announced to Jacob that her boys were going off to see their father. She suggested they spend a little time together, away from Paris. He managed to free himself for five days. It was Easter. On a crisp bright morning, they set off in Jacob's white Mercedes convertible. The long tails of Mathilde's scarf blew in the wind as tree-lined roads and softly rolling countryside sinuously unfolded before them. It was the first time they had driven any distance alone together. Mathilde studied Jacob's profile, the concentrated strength of his face intent on the car's movement. Her hand, despite herself, reached out to rest on his thigh. He flashed her a smile. "Later," he mouthed and then returned his attention to the road.

Jacob loved driving, loved the feel of the engine roaring in front of him, the dream state the endless *route nationale* engendered in him. Every time he glanced at Mathilde in her sky-blue suit, her hair and scarf tumbling in the breeze, a thrill went through him. He couldn't quite believe they were here, together.

When the sun grew hot, they stopped to picnic in a meadow beneath some splendid elms. Mathilde had provided a gourmet's feast. Quail's eggs, caviar, a sumptuous pâté, crisp baguette, tomatoes, fruit, white wine. As she spread the bright food with an artist's eye on the immaculate cloth, she brushed against Jacob. He clasped her hand. A surge of pure happiness washed over her. She looked into his eyes, flecked golden by the sun. Desire, reckless, uncaring, coursed through her. It surprised her how her desire for him seemed to have grown rather than abated since the time of their first encounter. She recognized the signs of it in him too, in the slightly pursed lips, the tilt of mockery in his face. "Now, please," she said.

He teased her for a moment. "A Princesse. Here. On the grass." Mathilde smiled achingly. Nodded. Her hand fumbled to loose his shirt. He pulled her up and drew her into a shaded copse. She snuggled against him, reached for his crotch. He was hard. Clumsily in her excitement, she unbuttoned his trousers, freed his penis. There was a pearly drop at its end. She licked it. He shuddered and threw her down on the ground, pulling at her panties. They were wet. With deep wild jabs, he thrust into her. They both came almost instantly.

When their breathing had quieted, Jacob examined her vivid face wryly. "And this is the woman who thought she was frigid." He shook his head in dramatized wonder.

Mathilde laughed, a deep throaty sound. "I guess I needed an expert doctor," she teased him.

"Well, the expert doctor now recommends some food. I wouldn't want you to acquire the reputation of a Princesse who starves her lovers."

"Lovers?" she queried the plural. "You mean, you're two, three, four in one? Let's not exaggerate." Mathilde skimmed his body tauntingly.

"Enough." He pulled her up. "Give me food. And a little food for thought. Have you read that last bit of Freud I gave you? The case of Dora?"

Mathilde nodded. "Yes. And I decided your dear master understood very little of women." Before Jacob could answer, she forced a piece of baguette into his mouth. "Listen, before you refute me, you mere man. You need to learn."

And so it went on over four glorious days. They traveled to Orléans, visited the cool depths of the ancient cathedral, went west to the Loire Valley. Avoiding the luxurious châteaux where Mathilde might be recognized, they stayed in small hotels under the name of Mr. and Mrs. Jardine, where the beds creaked under their love. They meandered along winding trails, hand in hand, stopping when passion overtook them on a shady bend in the river or on the crest of a rolling hill. They were blissfully, ecstatically happy. Mathilde was haunted by the sense that she might never be so happy again.

On the night before their return to Paris, they were having dinner on the terrace of a small restaurant overlooking the river when Mathilde suddenly announced, "I'm leaving for Denmark next week."

Jacob looked at her openmouthed. "But why? You didn't tell me. You never said anything . . ." He felt betrayed, cheated, angry.

"I didn't want to spoil everything. I was afraid." Mathilde looked down at her plate and played with her food. She found it difficult to speak. She didn't want it to end, but in her mind she had no choice. She had already stretched out her allotment of time in Paris to its utmost limit.

"But you intimated Frederick meant nothing to you. It was simply a case of the children, of social forms." Jacob gripped the ends of the table. He wanted to hit her. She had lied to him. She had never said anything about leaving.

"I thought you understood." Mathilde paused. She tried to meet his eyes so that he would read her feelings.

Jacob looked away, his face set in somberness.

"He's my husband," Mathilde said flatly. "In my world, that carries a certain meaning. There are forms I have to comply with. And that includes spending a part of the year with him. And in his own way, he's good to me. He cares. He's tried to understand me, given me certain freedoms which are already well beyond the range of what his family thinks is acceptable. I stay in Paris part of the year. That's the arrangement. I can't break it. I can't," she emphasized. "I have to go back to him." Mathilde thought her heart would break as she said it.

Jacob stood up brusquely, almost upsetting the table. He strode away. Despite Mathilde's soft call, he didn't turn back. He jumped into the Mercedes, revved the engine and drove recklessly away. Wildly, he maneuvered roads which grew teacherous through speed. He had no idea where he was heading. One thought pounded through his mind: How dare she? How dare she spring this on him? How dare she treat him like some lackey to be called and then dismissed?

His headlights picked out a man on the narrow road. Jacob veered round him, barely missing him. He screeched to a halt. His heart was pounding. His head dropped into his hands. He could feel that his eyes were wet though he hadn't known he was crying. Nor did he know how long he stayed like that.

Eventually, he made his way back to their small hotel. It was late. He asked for a separate room so as not to wake his wife. The word made him pause. No, she would never be his wife. Had he ever really thought she would be? Jacob stumbled into bed without bothering to undress.

Early next morning, Mathilde woke him from restless sleep. Her eyes were red.

"May I come in?" she asked hesitantly.

He stepped back for her.

"Jacob . . ." She paused, looked at him. She moved toward him, trying to nestle into his arms. But he stood there, stiff against her, resisting her.

"Jacob, I love you," she said in a low voice. "I love you more than I have ever loved anyone. I will always love you. Please believe that. I'm sorry I didn't prepare you. But I thought it would be better. Better like this." She looked round helplessly.

Still he didn't answer her, made no move.

"I can't break the terms of my marriage with Frederick. I can't make an innocent man, the father of my children, suffer. He knows nothing of all this." Her tone was imploring. After a moment, she turned away from him. "I will make my own arrangements to get back to Paris," she said with quiet dignity.

Jacob caught hold of her just as she was reaching for the door. He folded her into his arms and held her, held her for a long time.

"Please wait for me, darling, please." Mathilde looked up into his ruggedly somber face. "It won't be so very long. I'll come back to you as soon as I can." The sadness in her was intolerable.

Jacob nodded. Then he smiled into her eyes and kissed her lips lightly. "One can only obey one's Princesse," he said. With a grim certainty he knew that his feelings would not allow him to do otherwise. Not now. Not in the springtime of their love.

CHAPTER
SIX

Thwack—the ball left Sylvie Kowalska's racket with a clean strong sound and landed just where she had intended. Gérard slipped trying to return it and tumbled. Sylvie laughed gleefully. "Thirty–love," she called. "One more game and it'll be my set if you're not careful. Wake up." He was clumsy in his tennis, this Gérard; though quite sweet otherwise with his puppy-dog expression.

In this early summer of 1935 the sun shone brightly on Paul and Julie Ezard's Fontainebleau residence. The tennis courts and flower-strewn gardens, the dappled woods and growing circle of weekend guests were all warmed by its rays and apparently oblivious to the storm clouds in the atmosphere. Around the tennis court, a small white-clad group had lazily gathered. Sylvie's closest friend, Caroline, and Gérard's father, the bulky Emile Talleyrand, newspaper magnate of some fame, chatted, while Julie Ezard explained to Madame Talleyrand the changes that she planned for her garden. Only Jacob Jardine sat tensely silent as he watched the unfolding spectacle of the tennis match.

Sylvie aimed her serve, waited for the return, ran, hit it, and again and again. Her short white skirt swished over shapely legs. Her unbound hair flew lavishly. She could feel Jacob's eyes on her, with the peculiar bright intensity they had borne in the past few weeks. She didn't meet them. It was his fault if she didn't. She had begged

104

him not to get in touch with the Ezards and he had. Now, he would have to suffer the consequence of his action. He could hardly expect to have her come and visit his room here with her godparents in attendance. Not that she had been to his apartment in Paris much either after that night, after he had given her that ring. True, it was beautiful. She kept it in a locked drawer in her room and went to look at it occasionally. But she wouldn't wear it. It made her feel trapped.

Sylvie leapt and gave the ball a resounding smack.

"Game," Gérard shouted. "I'll never beat you, Sylvie."

Sylvie looked toward Jacob triumphantly. He was gone. She grimaced. She wanted to play with him again, even if he consistently beat her. Watching him move, leap, thrust the ball cleanly to her—it created a magnetic intimacy between them which aroused her. Why had he abandoned her?

"Where is Jacob?" Sylvie ran toward her friend Caroline, who was now stretched out on the grass. "I want to get another game in before dinner." Caroline pointed in the opposite direction. Swinging her racket, Sylvie sauntered down a path thick with the scent of flowering hawthorn. It led past a short stretch of wooded ground. Little clumps of moss, newly unfolding ferns, wild flowers nestled under the trees. Sylvie left her path. Something in the softness of the ground underfoot, the way the light played through the trees, the tender fragrance of moist greenery reminded her . . . What was it? Babushka's house. In Poland. Sylvie frowned, thwacked a fern with her racket and wiped her mind clean.

There were voices coming from the summer house. Jacob? Yes, it was his baritone. He was speaking quickly. Sylvie edged up to the paneless window prepared to call out and surprise him. But now there was another voice. She stopped and listened. Princesse Mathilde, yes, of course, Tante Julie had said she might be joining them. Sylvie liked Princesse Mathilde, rather more than she liked many others. The Princesse had style. That proud bearing, those extraordinary clothes. And her comments were never bland, like those she always knew she would hear from her godmother's friends.

Sylvie peeped through the window and then drew back rapidly, pressing herself against the wooden slats. Jacob and Princesse Mathilde's hands were clasped together. They were looking into each other's eyes. Sylvie held her breath and listened.

"I didn't know you were back in Paris." This from Jacob.

"Yes, just a few days ago. And only for another short while."

"It's been a long time. I've missed you, missed your company."

Sylvie had heard enough. She stepped a few paces back from the window, raised her racket and with all her strength pounded a ball directly at the Princesse. Then she turned and ran. Ran as fast as she could toward the shelter of the little wood. Her breath raucous, she flung herself on the ground. The moss was soft. The ferns tickled her bare legs. Sylvie cradled her head in her arms and examined the earth. They wouldn't find her here. No one ever stepped off the path. No one could *ever* find her. That's what Babushka had said was most naughty about her. The fact that even when they all went out across the woods and meadows and called her name, no one ever found her. She had her secret places, this Sylvie.

Sylvie never knew whether Babushka was pleased or angered by the fact. But then there was a lot that Babushka said that she never altogether understood. She talked such a lot. Sylvie loved Babushka, liked it when she combed her hair and sat her on her lap to tell her stories, scary stories. She liked her almost as much as she liked Tadzio, her brother, and often a lot more than mother and father and governesses all put together. But Babushka was growing old. She only came to the big house sometimes. To cook special dinners. Sylvie would help her knead the pastry and the dumplings. Babushka would give her thick slices of bread rich with her own cherry jam. She could taste it now, sweet with a tang of bitterness.

Best of all, Sylvie liked running across the meadow to the little house that Babushka lived in. It smelled of wood and ashes from the fire and raisins cooked with cabbage. They would sit on the terrace, Babushka on her old rocking-chair, Sylvie on the little step. Babushka would darn and talk. She told her a tale about a game-keeper, a lord and a rabbit.

"I like gamekeepers," Sylvie said.

"Baaa. Men," Babushka said. "They're not worth a cock's crow. First they're all sweetness and fine words. Then they poison you, give you babies and leave you. It's the boy babies, especially. They can't stand the boy babies."

"Papush loves Tadzio," Sylvie interjected.

"Your Papush is different. He's a special man. He's a Lord."

Sylvie was silent and Babushka continued, "Five children I had. One girl. He didn't mind her. And then the boys came, four of them, one after another. Then he left." She jabbed the darning needle into the big ball of cotton. "Two of the boys died. You hear that, Sylvie, two of them, dead."

Sylvie cried.

❖   ❖   ❖

The Ezards' summer salon mingled cane and chinoiserie. Black lacquer tables replete with flowers and birds, ebony cabinets, fluted cloisonné vases played through the room amidst Jamaican palms and cushioned cane armchairs. Tall French doors opened onto a patio fragrant with honeysuckle. The sounds of Debussy wafted through the mellow evening air from some point beyond the gathered guests.

Suddenly in the middle of a bar the music stopped. The voices now seemed too loud, and abruptly they died out as well. Princesse Mathilde and Jacob looked at each other from across the room.

"I think we'll be able to eat now." Julie Ezard rose in cloaked embarrassment and addressed the assembled company. "I know we're a little late, but I didn't want to start without Sylvie. She seems to be finished her playing now." She smiled, a little tremulously. Only she knew that she had been trying to coax Sylvie downstairs for the last hour and a half, though she was certain that the others suspected. Why *was* the girl proving so difficult just when Jacob Jardine was here?

She led her guests through to the dining room and showed them to their respective places. Sylvie walked in just as the last one was sitting down. "Oh, I'm sorry. Am I late?" she asked innocently. In a black dress with a little lace collar, her hair pulled back with a black ribbon which yet allowed the tendrils to play round the fine clear lines of her face, she looked at once ravishing and vulnerable. Every male eye, old and young, turned.

"Oh no, Tante Julie, I told you I wanted to sit next to Gérard, not here with Jacob. I have to explain to Gérard how he can improve his tennis. Don't I, Gérard?" Sylvie pouted a little. "Caroline will change places with me." The switch was made with a minimum of fuss.

Only the Princesse intercepted the blazing look that passed between Jacob and the young woman. Her nails dug into her hands. Something was going on there. She knew Jacob's face so well and beneath the polite smile he leveled at his neighbor, his expression was grim. Princesse Mathilde shuddered. There it was again. That look. Desire, yes, and pain. Why hadn't he said anything, written? She rubbed her arm where the tennis ball had accidentally hit her. So strange, so sudden, out of the blue. And now there was that ugly welt, hidden under her sleeve. Almost like a sign.

It was always so difficult when she came back to Paris after a long absence. And this one had been particularly long. There had been an extended round of weddings, official family visits which she had had to take part in—Greece, Spain, England, the royal roll-call. She had written to Jacob as she always did, those carefully worded letters which didn't dare to speak her love except in a code which she trusted he would understand. His answers had been regular, but increasingly bland, filled with reports of her school where he now acted as a consultant. Not like in those first two years of their passion, when absence was only a tantalizingly prolonged anticipation of being together. And even in the third, though she had recognized then that his desire for her was abating. The lightly poached salmon tasted like sawdust in the Princesse's throat. She swallowed with difficulty. She had no idea what her friend Julie was saying to her. She pleaded tiredness. Her eyes flew to Jacob's face across the table. He had grown even more ruggedly attractive with the years, his face leaner, the dark eyes deeper. A knot coiled in her stomach.

"Sylvie grows more and more beautiful every year, don't you think?" Julie addressed her in a low voice as the maid filled their glasses.

Mathilde observed the profile at the other end of the table. Those vast blue eyes, the arch of the immaculate throat as Sylvie emptied her glass in a gulp. Yes, the girl was stunning. Not a girl now. Not the little tearful orphan of fourteen she had first met at Julie's. But a woman. A *young* woman, the Princesse thought bitterly. Jealousy cut through her with the force of a butcher's knife.

Just then, as if Sylvie had read her thoughts, she heard her say to her neighbor, "And would you believe, Princesse Mathilde's boys are as tall as me now." Perhaps she had imagined it. But no, that stiff Maître Darieux had distinctly turned to stare at her.

She had to speak to Jacob, get him to acknowledge her somehow. She couldn't bear the pained look on his face. She searched for a subject.

"I read that poor Gaitan de Clérambault, your old teacher, committed suicide in rather bizarre circumstances," the Princesse said.

"Yes." Jacob looked at her a little wildly. "On the morning of November seventeenth in his house in Montrouge." Jacob remembered every detail reported about the event. It had coincided almost exactly with his meeting Sylvie. He was sometimes haunted by the sense that his teacher had left him an uncanny legacy.

"Didn't they say something about finding hundreds of wax mannequins, intricately draped dolls, in his home? Strange, when you think of Clérambault's reputation as a fierce celibate, a woman-hater."

All eyes at the table had focused on the Princesse and Jacob. He shifted uncomfortably in his chair and spoke quietly.

"He had an outlandish, a fetishistic love for drapery. It started when he lived in North Africa. The intricate folds and pleats and materials of the Arab women's robes and veils fascinated him. They became an obsessive passion. A secret and abiding, inescapable one. That's probably why he was such a genius at describing erotic obsession. Mad and single-minded love. What our surrealist friends have called *l'amour fou.*"

Jacob paused to sip his wine. There was silence the length of the table. "Clérambault killed himself after he was blinded. He couldn't study the detail of his draped dolls anymore. Things became too much for him." Jacob shrugged. He looked up to find Sylvie staring at him. There was a taunting set to her features. He met her gaze painfully.

The Princesse recalled his attention. "Poor man. To lose his sight must have been to lose everything. I have read that he had a singular talent for observation. A rigorous and impeccable vigilance. Almost a disease, an imbalance of the seeing faculty. Like a police detective. It distorted everything else in him."

Jacob flinched and studied the Princesse's calm features, her perfect composure. She was quoting his own words back at him, words they had exchanged at the height of their affair. Yet there was no trace of any emotion, of any memory in her face.

Women all wore veils which draped and shrouded them in mystery. What had Freud said of them—the last mysterious continent. More than ever Jacob felt as if he were a cartographer who had only recently learned the art of mapping.

He met the Princesse's eyes and allowed himself a little complicit smile.

She returned it.

Yes, she knew what she was doing. She had not chanced on the subject of Clérambault accidentally. She was reminding him and warning him, perhaps. Had she already guessed his obsession with Sylvie? They knew each other so well.

He wished he had been told Mathilde was coming to the Ezards' this weekend. He might have stayed away. It wasn't right meeting here, like this, now. He hadn't prepared her.

And yet he couldn't have stayed away. Sylvie had been proving so elusive, it drove him to frenzy. And now look at her, flirting outrageously with Gérard so that the boy was tied up in knots. No wonder he couldn't play tennis with her. Even that Maître Darieux, who reeked of celibacy, had a hectic flush about him. Yet Jacob felt certain her gestures were all somehow for his benefit. She had seen him with Mathilde. That tennis ball had been her message. He was sure of it.

Sylvie's voice suddenly rang round the table. "What I'd like most in the world now is a swim. Before the moon vanishes. Who's game?" She cut Jacob, avoided his eyes. "Gérard, Caroline?"

"Not me," Caroline answered. "It's too cold."

"Come on, you coward. You know Tante Julie will fuss if I'm left alone with a man," Sylvie announced in a girlish voice intended for everyone's ears.

"And quite right she would be, too," Paul Ezard intervened, looking significantly at Jacob.

"All right, I'll come. Will you join us, Jacob?" Caroline asked, politely. She wished she knew him better, could speak to him. Sylvie's fitful moodiness of late worried her. Jacob would understand, she felt sure.

"No, no, not this evening." Jacob shook his head, met Mathilde's secret smile. He wasn't going to fall in with Sylvie's pranks. He couldn't bear the teasing game she played with him socially. He needed to see her alone.

"Perhaps a little coffee for those of us who prefer a different sort of liquid refreshment," Paul Ezard said amiably. "And then a stroll. It is a lovely evening."

Sylvie, her skin still coolly moist from the pool, draped herself in a long robe and stole out of her room. She slipped silently down the length of the long corridor to Jacob's door. She lifted her hand to knock and then stopped herself. No, it would be better to go straight in. He might be asleep and she didn't want to wake anyone with her knocking. Gently, she twisted the knob. The bedside lamp threw a soft light on the bed. There was no one in it.

So, she had been right. Her hand trembled. He was with Princesse Mat. Never let a man in *there*, Babushka had warned. Sylvie raced out of the house to lose herself in the shelter of the small wood. The stars were bright now that the moon had gone. In Poland you could never see the stars in the woods. The forest was vast, gnarled, thick, an ancient world of trees ripe with boar and deer. Clearings were a little miracle of light. The gamekeeper's house was in one of those clearings. Sylvie shivered and drew her robe more tightly round her. The scene she had so often evaded came back to her now with a frightening urgency.

Tadzio had been ill and she was left to her own devices, irritable, slightly bored. In the late afternoon she wandered, found herself near the gamekeeper's cottage and with a sullen sense of repetition perched herself at the small kitchen window. She peered in. The room was empty. Even here there was no entertainment today. Suddenly she heard a twig crack behind her. She turned. The gamekeeper. His eyes two black coals, beneath the lank overlong hair. Sylvie whipped away. She could hear the heavy thud of his boots just behind her as she raced into the twilight of the woods. Her heart pounded. She stumbled.

In a moment his fingers bit into her arm, forcing her to turn toward him. "I warned you. Warned you if I caught you here spying again . . ." The low menace of his words was succeeded by the lash of his hand across her bottom. Sylvie bit her lip to restrain her cry. She never liked anyone to see her cry. As he hit her again, her eyes focused on his trouser buttons. They were undone. For some reason they were undone. She could see dark, curling hair. Something in there was moving.

With his third slap, she moaned, but her eyes did not move. He followed her gaze. "So that's what you're interested in. *Curva,*" he hissed at her, "slut." With his free hand, he brought out the hooded creature. She watched in fascination as it grew under her gaze. Her legs felt wobbly. She had a momentary sense of power. It increased when she heard his breathing change. "That's what you want, is it? Stroke it." His words were half command, half plea.

Sylvie stroked. A bone. Smooth. But warm, alive. It leapt to the power of her fingers. She sucked in her breath. *"Curva,"* he repeated. And again, forcing her fingers to the rhythm of his imprecation, wrapping her hand round his bone with the greater strength of his own. She looked up and met his eyes. They were blind to her. His face was a grotesque of exaltation and punitive disgust. Cold fear enveloped her for the first time. She lurched her hand away, escaped. The gesture startled him. But only for a moment. In the next, he leapt after her, tumbled her to the ground. His weight covered her. Suffocated her. Sylvie struggled, screamed, a high shrill shriek which pierced the stillness of the forest world. A large hand muffled her mouth and simultaneously a vast object tore at the secret places of her body. The last thing she remembered before the world went dark was the hiss of his voice in her ear, "If you tell anyone, I shall string you up like one of my rabbits."

When she woke, she was being carried. A murmur of low voices, her mother's, her father's. She was in her father's arms. She could smell that particular mixture of lemon and tobacco which she loved. She snuggled close to him. He stiffened, holding her away from him like a suspect parcel. Through lowered lids Sylvie stole a glance at him. In the half-light of the long corridor, he was gazing down at her body with barely concealed disgust. She closed her eyes again quickly. The back of her head throbbed.

"You wash her yourself," Papush said. "Don't let the servants see the blood."

"Stasek said he found her like that in the forest?" Her mother's voice was angry, suspicious. "I've never trusted that gamekeeper of yours."

"He wouldn't have brought her back himself, would he, if it had been him? Not like this. All bloody." Her father, her beloved Papush, seemed to recoil even further away from her. He let her fall unceremoniously onto a bed.

Soon after, she was sent to Paris. Banished. Expelled. The big pink stuccoed house with its rounded turrets receded into the still distance as she gazed out of the window of the large, lumbering car. Only Tadzio waved and waved, a tiny, solitary figure etched against a vastness. Papush, with his clean white shirts, his manicured fingernails, hadn't even held her to say goodbye. He never held her again.

Sylvie clasped her bathrobe more firmly around her. She was cold, cold with memory more than with the chill of the night air. "Never let a man in *there*," Babushka had said. How right she had been. A man had forced his way in and Papush had been lost to her forever. She had wanted to explain to him in those weeks that it wasn't her fault, but she had been afraid, afraid of the memory, afraid of the gamekeeper, most afraid of Papush's eyes, which now never met hers though she could feel them secretly burning into her with contempt, distaste, as if she were irrevocably sullied, unclean. That was the effect of letting a man in there. She had lost her power. Before that Papush's eyes used to dance over her. He would hold her close. She could do anything with him she wanted.

And now Jacob. Secret tears gathered in Sylvie's eyes. She had *let* him in. He hadn't forced his way. He didn't look at her with contempt. No, never that. But he was lost to her, too. Her hold over him had gone. Heavily, Sylvie lifted herself from the stump where she had been sitting and made her way back to the house. The tears streamed down her face, as she silently opened the door to Caroline's room. She curled round her sleeping form. Caroline. Her friend.

It had been Caroline who had come into her small hard bed that night many years ago in the cold, dark convent dormitory. The nuns had made a fuss of Sylvie all week, because her parents had died. Every night at evening mass the girls were urged to pray for Sylvie's parents to ease the passage of their souls into heaven. Sylvie didn't cry. She tried to imagine her parents and brother with wings making their way past the archangels. Her prayers were propelling them on, giving lightness to their bodies. But the harder she prayed, the funnier the image seemed and she would break into giggles. The nuns gave her stern looks. She tried praying alone. She went to the small chapel and threw herself prostrate before the pretty virgin who looked a little like her mother. The only image that came to her mind was that of a large rat that she and Tadzio had found in the barn one day. The rat's eyes were wide open, but it lay motionless, its head severed from its body. Tadzio prodded it with a stick. "It's dead," he announced importantly. "It can't move. It won't move ever again."

That night Sylvie started to cry. Tadzio was dead. He wouldn't move ever again, not even if she prodded him with her prayers. Nothing would make him quicken. Nothing. Sylvie sobbed into her pillow and beat it with her fists. She wished she had been the one to die. She *should* have been the one to die. She hated her life here, hated the grim cold corridors, the constant surveillance. I will die, she thought, and then the girls can pray for me to go to heaven. Suddenly she felt a cold hand on her shoulder. She started.

"Shh," Caroline, the girl who slept in the bed next to hers, enjoined her. "Move over." She crawled in next to Sylvie and pulled the blanket over their heads. "I'll be your friend," she whispered. She cradled Sylvie, stroked her hair. Gradually the tears stopped. Caroline's body was warm round her. Her hands were nestling her breasts. One of them dropped to her stomach. Sylvie drew in her breath. There was a pulling at her loins, a sensation she sometimes had when she listened to particular music, a stirring which had always accompanied her secret escapades to the gamekeeper's house. Caroline's breathing was different now too. The girl rubbed against her, pressed her hand against her mound. Suddenly Sylvie was engulfed in waves of pleasure. Caroline kissed her lightly on the head and snuck back to her own bed.

Now Sylvie wrapped herself round Caroline and held her close. Her hands strayed over her friend's firm, rounded body. Caroline woke.

"No," Caroline said adamantly. "I told you that was all finished. We're too old now."

"Why? Just because we've left the nuns? You think because we're not forced to pray every day, we won't be forgiven our sins?" Sylvie laughed maliciously. She knew that Caroline took this taunt seriously, as if somehow the ritual of school prayer, the little penances they imposed on themselves, had absolved them of their nighttime guilt— for they had carried on loving each other, well past that first night, their games growing more refined. They knew the schedule of the nuns' nightly rounds so well that they had been caught only after some six months, when one particular nun had broken the routine. Then, they had been moved to separate dormitories, punished. All that this meant was that now they spent the weekends at one or the other's home and paradoxically, once it had been dared, they enjoyed far greater freedom.

No one suspected the closeness of their friendship. Indeed, the Ezards were relieved that Sylvie finally had a friend, a serious, responsible girl like Caroline Berger. But in the quiet of their large rooms, the girls invented elaborate games. Sylvie, more adventurous, had begun to take the lead, and when one night Caroline wouldn't accede to her wishes, she had threatened that she would find a man. She had. For three weeks, Caroline in a flush of jealous pique refused to speak to her. Sylvie had vowed that she loved Caroline far more than any man and it had begun again. Then Sylvie began to add extra spice to their relationship by occasionally making illicit little forays into the world of men. She would dress herself up well beyond her years, go out to a dance hall and dance with strangers. If their advances grew too bold, she ran away. Though once or twice it had grown unpleasant. And once, she had succumbed rather more than she might wish. The stories which she told Caroline of these encounters fueled their lovemaking. And so it had gone on until Sylvie had met Jacob, introduced Caroline to him. Then Caroline had announced it had to stop between them. "Finished"—Caroline had slapped her hands together in a definitive gesture—"otherwise I refuse to see you at all anymore."

Sylvie had agreed. Since she had met Jacob, her nights with Caroline had in any case lost their luster and begun to seem like mere child's play. But tonight she needed to elicit her friend's desire, her focused attention.

"I've told you. It's finished. Put your clothes back on and stop behaving like a slut," Caroline said vehemently. It was one of the words they had habitually used to increase their ardor.

"Me, the slut?" Sylvie taunted her. "Who was it who first seduced little innocent me? Was it this that tempted you?" She arched a golden leg on the bed. "Or this?" She cupped her full breasts with her hand. "Or perhaps it was this?" She waggled a pointed tongue at Caroline. Sylvie had adopted all the gestures of the elaborate games they had invented over the years.

Jacob heard the commotion coming from the room as he was making his way quietly back to his own. He stopped despite himself to listen. He had no way of knowing that he was hearing a repeated ritual now at its end. The black cloud he had been living under during the last weeks suddenly threatened to engulf him. Had Sylvie's interest in him been but a momentary affair? Not that he was surprised to learn of her relationship with Caroline. He had half-suspected as much. But the reality of the scene he was hearing now, his imaginings of what he didn't see, served at once to heighten the enigma of Sylvie and to cut across him with the force of despair. Pain lashed through him. It contorted his face.

It contorted Caroline's too, as she looked at Sylvie, who grew more wildly beautiful with each taunt. "Stop it, Sylvie. Stop it. Go, please go." Caroline turned a stubborn back on Sylvie and stared blindly out of the window.

"All right, I'll go." It had the force of finality. Sylvie rushed from the room.

Jacob heard her from the other end of the corridor and in the momentary glimmer of light he thought she looked straight into his eyes.

The next day, when they all gathered for lunch, Julie Ezard announced in a slightly shaky voice that Sylvie was gone.

"Where?" Gérard looked crestfallen. "She didn't tell me she was going anywhere."

"Women, my son," Emile Talleyrand pronounced in stentorian tones, "are not known for their advance warnings. It is something you will learn in life." He patted his stomach comfortably.

Gérard flushed. His father carried on regardless. "Why only the other day one of my papers carried a story about a woman who disappeared right in the middle of dinner—purportedly to bring in the dessert—only to turn up again as if nothing had ever happened, three years later just as dessert was being served." He stopped himself in the middle of a guffaw as he took in the faces around him. "But of course that was just a story . . ." he added belatedly.

"Did Sylvie say where she was going?" Caroline asked, trying to keep her tone steady. She was shrouded in guilt. Her sharp, honest face had a sallow tinge.

"To Paris, I imagine." Julie Ezard put more assurance into the statement than she felt. She turned to Jacob with an explanation which was also a plea. "She had said to me she didn't want to be here this week. There was a particular concert she wanted to catch."

Paul Ezard put a steadying arm round his wife's shoulders. "We'll phone Paris after lunch. I'm sure she'll be at home."

"I've already done that," Julie said softly. "She's not there. The servants haven't seen her."

"She's undoubtedly staying with a friend," Princesse Mathide said forcefully. She couldn't prevent a small tremor of glee rising in her. Sylvie's absence would give her time.

But when she saw Jacob's face, she realized that time might not be on her side.

Sylvie knew exactly where she was going. She sat back in the train's cushioned seats and let its rhythmic motion hypnotize her. Nothing mattered but that sound and the countryside changing before her eyes. Green fields gave way to sun-dried earth and rocky escarpments. Orchards of peach and orange appeared, their trees heavy with fruit. Dusk fell, instantly followed by dark southern night. She closed her eyes. Freedom. No one knew where she was. No one. Elation filled her just as it had done in those days when as a little girl she escaped into the forest, fleeing the sharp nails and slaps of an overzealous governess or the stifling hollow rituals of an afternoon party.

She left the train at Apt. The small station was eerily still. A single ticket collector stood outlined in yellow light. She was suddenly a little afraid.

"I need to get to Roussillon," Sylvie announced to him.

He looked at her suspiciously from under bushy brows and shrugged, pointing toward a solitary taxi. The driver was dozing. Sylvie knocked at the window. She repeated her destination. "*Ah non, c'est trop tard,*" the man muttered. "It's too late. Tomorrow."

"But what am I to do?" Sylvie was desolate.

"There's the hotel." He signaled down the street. "Someone might still be up." Sylvie followed the line of his hand and saw a dismal two-story building with a rusty shingle announcing "Hôtel des Voyageurs."

Sylvie did some quick mental calculations. If she spent the night in a hotel and then took a taxi, most of her money would be gone. She stiffened her back.

"I'll wait there." She pointed toward a wooden bench. "Tell me when you're ready." The driver looked at her oddly as she arranged herself on the bench, then shook his head sourly. *"Ces Parisiennes,"* he muttered, loud enough for Sylvie to hear.

When the first glimmers of morning sun lightened the sky, Sylvie approached the taxi again. The driver was gone. She was suddenly in despair. Her body ached from the hard bench. She felt dirty. More waiting. She hated waiting. A scraping sound caught her attention. Down the road, the little hotel seemed to be in motion. Tables, chairs, gaily colored parasols were making their way on to the pavement. Coffee, Sylvie thought, brightening. With long-legged strides, she entered the little bar.

"Ah, here is my first customer already." Her driver stood there, peacefully sipping a vast bowl of café au lait.

In the morning light, Sylvie saw a small robust man. His arms against his blue shirt were strong, deeply browned. White teeth accentuated a friendly smile. She bit into a flaky croissant, still warm from the oven. Yes, she had after all been right to come.

They traveled over a narrow dusty road in growing heat, past tiny villages. In the distance, the abrupt shapes of the Provence hills broke the still air. As the earth turned from sandy yellow to rich ochre red, the driver announced, *"Voilà,* we're approaching Roussillon." Houses hewn out of the red stone clustered over a hilltop, at its peak ramparts and a spire. The road rose sharply into the town, wound through it, and came down the other side into vineyards, miles of them, stretching sea green as far as the next sudden escarpment.

Sylvie's destination was a large old ramshackle farmhouse in the midst of the vines. Its windows were shuttered. Everything had an ominous quiet about it. Sylvie looked to the driver for reassurance. "Perhaps everyone is still asleep."

He shrugged disdainfully. "They're artists, aren't they? Parisians.

I heard about them in town. They probably don't wake up until the best of the day is over."

"Come in and have a drink." Sylvie, reassured, was generous. She knocked at the vast wooden door, while he looked at her skeptically.

"Sylvie?" Michel, short, bronzed, with the muscled arms of a workingman, looked at her with astonishment. "I never thought you would make your way here." He pulled her to him and embraced her delightedly.

"Neither did I, Michel." She clung to him for a moment. "Neither did I."

Jacob stepped out of the taxi in front of the Hotel Crillon, glanced at his watch and then waited for the driver to pull away before heading off in the opposite direction. Evening traffic hummed round the obelisk of the stately Place de la Concorde. Millions of lights glittered, emphasizing the darkness of the small tree-lined *allée* which bordered the Champs-Elysées. He headed for the darkness and walked. The Princesse had summoned him. The message had arrived at the hospital. Le Crillon: eight thirty. He had no choice but to come and he needed to arrange his thoughts before meeting her. He realized it must be all but her last day in Paris and that he had behaved badly. Since that dismal weekend in Fontainebleau, he had made no attempt to get in touch with her. It was cowardly of him, he knew. But he also knew that there was nothing he could say to her, nothing she would want to hear. He couldn't pour out his agonies about Sylvie, who had still made no sign. And apart from that, he seemed to have no feelings. Only an intensity of work kept him going.

There is nothing so difficult, Jacob reflected, as telling a woman you respect that your passion for her has died. When hers so evidently hasn't. It would have been so much simpler if the Princesse's inner clock had been tuned to his or vice versa. On impulse he made a dash back to the Crillon, found the boutique he remembered and selected a fine but simple platinum watch which he thought the Princesse amongst all her riches might not despise. He wrote out a card, "Always, with us, a question of time and timing. My love, Jacob." He paused next at the florist's and chose a vast bouquet of roses, velvet red and iceberg white. He asked that these, together with the watch, be delivered immediately to the Princesse's room. Fifteen minutes later, Jacob followed.

"I thought you might not come." Princesse Mathilde opened the door herself.

"I always come when you call for me. I shall always come," Jacob said simply. "You mean a great deal to me. I think you know."

She looked at him hesitantly for a moment. "Yes," she said. Then, "I think I do. Thank you for this." She lifted her slender wrist and allowed her gift to catch the light. "I shall treasure it."

"Yes, time needs treasuring."

"We have tonight. A whole night. It is a great deal to treasure," she murmured. She had the look of a woman struggling to reconcile her fate and her desires. Her composure imbued him with awe.

They stood by the windows and looked out on the splendor of the Place de la Concorde and the long swathe of the Champs-Elysées leading to the triumphal arch. "Our city," the Princesse said.

Jacob had the sudden urge to take her in his arms and hold her slender form. Her face above the warm peach tones of her swirling summer dress held such sadness and yet was so contained in its emotion. It was like this splendid room, rich in the memory of history, and yet discreet.

She led him to a softly lit corner where a small round table had been intimately set. She gestured toward a silver bucket which held two bottles of champagne.

"For the rest, tonight, I shall serve you myself. I thought you wouldn't mind a cold dinner." A teasing smile flew over her expressive features. "Like on our picnics, but with great gleams of silver."

Jacob poured and they lifted their glasses to each other.

"So, my friend," the Princesse said, once they were seated. "It is over between us."

Jacob shrugged. "So it would seem." He suddenly felt in this room which floated above Paris that he had moved out of time. A muted ache, somewhere in the region of the heart, reminded him of Sylvie, of the agonies of the past months. They seemed strangely distant. He held the Princesse's eyes. "But you are weaving a spell around me."

She caught his mood. "Only for tonight. Tomorrow I shall be gone."

Jacob didn't contradict her. They were silent for a moment. She lifted silver lids to expose an array of seafood, oysters, lobster, arranged on a fairy-tale landscape of ice.

"I know I have always asked the impossible of you," Mathilde said after a pause. "It was selfish of me."

Jacob shook his head adamantly. "No, I accepted the conditions. It is not because of anything you have done or said that . . ." He threw his hands up, unwilling to finish his sentence. "It is simply in the way of things," he finished lamely.

"And this child you have taken up with. Will she make you happy?" As soon as she had said it, Mathilde realized it had been the wrong thing to say. Jacob had made no confessions to her, named no names. He had simply intimated and she had surmised the rest. His face was dark now, brooding. He avoided the specificity of her question.

"We all carry a child within us," he said, his tone abrupt. "Sometimes that child's needs may seem peculiar, even to ourselves."

"I'm sorry." Mathilde let it go. "I didn't invite you here to pry."

He answered her now. "Yes, Sylvie is a child. But she is also a woman. I want both. And no, I don't know whether she will make me happy."

The name was now between them, a stumbling block. The Princesse leapt over it. "I've known her for years, you realize. I knew her parents."

"And you don't approve," Jacob taunted her. "Say it."

The Princesse paused for a moment. Then she gave him one of those ravishing smiles which lit her face with intelligence. "If I were a man, I might approve. She is exceedingly beautiful. But I am a woman . . ." She lifted her hands in the air with a little helpless gesture.

Jacob laughed. "Something I'm presumably supposed to have forgotten." He stood to his full height and stretched his arms out to her. "Come here, Madame la Princesse, and let us see if I can revive the memory."

He kissed her with leisurely relish and something in the slow voluptuousness of her hands in his hair, the little moans, reminded him. He lifted her in his arms. "If Madame la Princesse would not feel her dignity was at stake in directing me to the bedroom, I might just rise to the occasion of memory . . ." He bathed them both in his irony.

"My dignity," she smiled, meeting him, "has rarely been an issue between us."

"No," Jacob said lightly, "there has always been far too much else."

He left her in the early hours of the morning, sorry to be away from the glow of her warmth. But they both knew it was over.

"Our last night has perhaps been worthy of us," she said, looking him directly in the eyes.

Jacob nodded, squeezing her hand. "Thank you, my friend," he said.

Two weeks later, Caroline rang Jacob. "I've got to see you right away." Her normally soft voice was fraught. "It's about Sylvie."

"Where is she?"

"I can't talk now. I'll meet you at the Café de la Paix in half an hour." She rang off.

"You've got to go and get her." Caroline looked at him earnestly, from across the table. She wrung her serviette with stocky fingers. "You've got to."

"Tell me again what Michel St. Loup said to you." Jacob lit a cigarette and inhaled deeply.

"That he was worried about her. That she was behaving strangely. That he didn't know what to do."

"Why didn't he ring the Ezards?" Jacob interrogated her.

Caroline shrugged impatiently. "Presumably he didn't want to worry them. He said he'd found my number in her notebook."

"Why didn't he ring me?"

Caroline looked away. "I don't know. I . . ." She wrung her hands, lit one of his cigarettes nervously and started to cough. "She told him she didn't want to see you. You were the last person in the world she wanted to see."

Jacob flinched. "But you think *I* should go," he said after a moment. "Rather than you?" He looked at the girl with the sharp, serious face with a glimmer of suspicion. Did she realize that he had found her and Sylvie out?

"She doesn't mean half of what she says," Caroline said bluntly. Her eyes stirred with memory. "I know she doesn't. She's always saying things she doesn't mean." They gazed at each other for a moment, both suddenly acutely aware of the bond their shared love for Sylvie created between them.

"Look, I'll go with you if you insist," Caroline offered, "but I think from what Michel says, I may be out of my depth. And I suspect this has something to do with you. Please."

"Yes, of course I'll go." Jacob rose. He knew, as he spoke, that he couldn't in any case have stayed away.

Within an hour, he had rung his assistant, explained that he would have to be away for a few days, given detailed explanations of what needed to be done in his absence, packed a small bag and set off into the night. He drove relentlessly until his eyes threatened to close. Then he pulled up on the side of the road and dozed restlessly for a few hours. By midmorning he was in Roussillon.

The picture that met his eyes when he approached Michel's farmhouse through the sun-warmed courtyard was one that stayed engraved on his mind for the rest of his life. The sitting-room windows were flung open to the morning air and white tulle curtains moved lazily in the breeze. Michel, darkly brooding, was sitting by his easel. He jabbed at a large canvas where thick dabs of paint had half-formed an image. In front of him, half-reclining in a cane chair, Sylvie sat. She was bare to the waist; a long loose skirt trailed round her legs. Her head was flung back in abandon, her long hair reaching almost to the floor. Her eyes were half-closed and Jacob could just glimpse their stark blueness. The atmosphere reeked of intimacy.

Jealousy hovered over him and settled in a scowl on his face. Caroline had misinformed him. There was no need for him here.

"Hello, Michel. Hello, Sylvie," he said in a voice too loud. "I trust I'm not disturbing you *too* much."

"Jacob." His friend dropped his brush and rushed over to him. "How good to see you." He shook Jacob's hand with apparent warmth. "Sylvie, Jacob is here." He enunciated the words with care as if speaking to a small child. "Jacob," he repeated.

Sylvie didn't stir. Only her eyes opened a little wider.

Michel walked over to her and shook her.

"Leave her," Jacob commanded, his tone threateningly low.

"Leave her be." The second order bore no trace of the jealous lover but had the distinct authority of the doctor. Sylvie, Jacob recognized, was in a bad way.

At the sound of his voice, Sylvie now moved her head in his direction. Her lips curled into a sudden ravishing smile and then she lapsed back into her previous position.

Jacob's fists clenched. He gestured Michel into another room. On the walls, amidst a variety of canvases, a series of photographs was pinned. They were recent. One of them showed Michel leaning over Sylvie, his hands proprietorially covering her bare breasts. Jacob steeled himself.

"What's been happening?" he asked as soon as they were out of Sylvie's hearing.

Michel shrugged. His brow was furrowed in worry. "I don't know. Everything was fine until about a week ago. She was glorious." His eyes glowed with the memory. "A little wild, but that's the Sylvie we love. We both painted her, Max and I. Nastasie was here, too, and she and Sylvie drew. We swam, drank, went for walks together, did a little automatic writing. Hers was extraordinary, full of the most erotic images, tangled vines and unicorns." He flushed a little.

"Did you sleep with her?" Jacob asked in a low voice. "Are you sleeping with her?" He thought he could easily punch his friend in the face. He fought to separate the clinician from the lover.

"I . . . She . . ." Michel hesitated, turning away from the force of Jacob's eyes. He threw his hands up in the air. "She teased me outrageously. She was always brushing against me, playing with my hair, looking at me with those seductive eyes. I know you and her . . . But I thought when she turned up here alone and . . . well, she aroused me." He looked at his friend helplessly. "Anyhow, it was a fiasco. I'd rather not go into it."

"I need to know," Jacob said in a steely voice.

Michel put a bottle of wine on the table, uncorked it, poured out two glasses and downed his in one. "Nothing happened, Jacob. When it came to it nothing happened, not for my lack of trying. I don't want to talk about it anymore." He paused for a moment then went on, "Maybe it was because of the picture. That's when things started to go wrong."

"What picture?" Jacob urged him on.

"I painted her. Painted her as a bird. I'll show you. I think it's good."

"Later. Tell me what went wrong."

"The bird. I think it got to her."

"And . . ."

"Well, somehow she decided she was that bird. She found a dead mouse, a large one, in the shed over there," he gestured nervously, "and she brought it to me. 'See,' she said. She was gleeful. 'I've caught a mouse for you. Look at its neck. It's got my mark.'" Michel shivered. "Then she brought another and another. She just sat and looked at them all lined up in a row. I told her to stop. It was enough of that game. 'Don't you like birds?' she asked me. 'My brother liked birds, but he's dead, like these. I killed him. I flew away.'

"I didn't know what to say. I took the mice and threw them all out. She hasn't spoken to me since. Hasn't spoken at all. She just sits there or prowls around." He shivered again.

"Why didn't you get in touch with me straight away?"

"I wanted to. I said to her, right when she started to play this bird game, I said to her, 'Why don't we invite Jacob down?' And do you know what she did? She slapped me hard, right across the face and then drew her nails down my cheek. Look."

Jacob saw the trace of red welts on Michel's face. "And so you rang Caroline?"

Michel nodded. "I was at my wits' end. I rummaged through her bag, found a notebook with a few addresses. I rang the one person I knew." He paused. "Jacob, I'm very glad you're here. Can you do anything?"

Jacob shrugged. "We'll see. It would probably be better if you stayed out of the way."

Michel breathed a visible sigh of relief. "There's nothing I'd like better. I'll go into Gordes for the day." He got up with alacrity.

"There's just one more thing," Jacob detained him. "How attached are you to your picture?"

"Why?"

"It might be necessary to get rid of it."

Michel looked confused. "But it's one of my best. I ..." He stopped as he took in the grim cast of Jacob's features. "I leave it to you," he said finally and turned to leave. "But you should have a look at hers, if you're interested. You might want to destroy those too." It was a parting shot, which Jacob didn't answer. He went back to Sylvie.

She was reclining where they had left her, immobile in her chair. Jacob sat down on the sofa behind her and waited. A long time passed before she stirred. Then she got up and draped a shirt loosely over her. She didn't look at Jacob but he knew she was aware of him. She walked over to Michel's easel and stared at it intently. Then she sat down at the desk, took a pencil and did a quick sketch. She brought it toward Jacob and let it fall near his feet, before turning abruptly away. He picked up the drawing, saw a bird in a cage, its human face blackened, its beak tied with a thick rope.

Sylvie was watching him. He played into her logic. He walked toward the wall where Michel's canvases were racked, turned them round one by one. Yes, this was the one. Michel was right. It was very good. His Sylvie had a frenzied reality, a vast magical birdlike creature whose feathers were like heavy fur. Not a bird who could fly, Jacob reflected. He rummaged in the desk and found a pair of scissors. It was one chance in a thousand, but it might stir her to an action. He put the scissors in a prominent position and returned to his place on the sofa. He waited. In the heavy warmth of midday, the waiting took on trancelike proportions. A fly buzzed at the window. Its sound invaded the room's hush. Suddenly Sylvie leapt up. With a swift sure animal gesture, she trapped the fly in her fist.

She's going to swallow it, Jacob thought. And indeed, Sylvie raised her hand to her mouth. Then a look of confusion spread over her features. She looked at her hand intently and strode determinedly over to the canvas which leaned against the wall. With an aggressive thrust, she squashed the fly against the face of Michel's bird-girl.

A feeling of relief pervaded Jacob. It wasn't as bad as he had feared. Yes, Sylvie's guilt over her brother's, her parents' death had taken on a palpable embodiment. She was the bird who had flown away, escaped. But she could still separate a part of herself off from that. She wasn't altogether Michel's image of her.

A malevolent smile had now lodged itself on Sylvie's face. With a rapid gesture, she picked the scissors up from the table, headed back toward the canvas, jabbed once lightly and then, as if she had changed her mind, she marched toward Jacob. She pointed the scissors at him threateningly. Jacob met her eyes and held them. Otherwise he didn't stir. For a breathless moment they looked at each other, the man contained, his strong face a study in neutrality; the girl, wildly beautiful, menace in every inch of her stance.

"Go away. Run," Sylvie hissed, her voice erupting with the force of a loudspeaker. She wielded the scissors blindly. Jacob kept very still. Her use of words was a cue. Instinctively he realized that if he didn't move, she wouldn't harm him. Sylvie thrashed the air and then with a clatter let the scissors drop on the bare tiles.

"Go away," she repeated. "Go away." She flew to the other end of the room and hid her face in her hands.

Jacob ached to go over to her and hold her in his arms. Her suffering was grittily tangible. Instead he rose and said in his neutral doctor's voice, "Sylvie. I am doing as you bid. But I am not going far. If you want me I shall be outside in the courtyard."

"Go away." She was crying now. "You killed him. It was you, you, with your flying. You deserve to be dead." All this in a pained, muffled voice.

Jacob moved slowly toward the door. For a moment he was baffled by her utterance, but then he remembered. Her father, of course. Her father had been flying the plane. A small smile dented his somberness. The unconscious had its cunning. Sylvie had now shifted some of her guilt onto her father. It was an easier place for it to rest for the moment, than on her own burdened shoulders.

Jacob paced round the courtyard. He was worried about leaving Sylvie on her own. She might in this state do something dangerous to herself. But if he countered her wishes, he knew she would become more violent or simply resist him by retreating into greater silence, deeper isolation. In his pacing, he looked surreptitiously into the room. She was kneeling on the floor, her back to him. He couldn't see what she was doing. He sat down on one of the deck chairs a short distance from the windows and tried to think what it was that had made Sylvie run away, what it was in her that had occasioned this breakdown.

Caroline had rejected her: he had overheard the scene. That was obviously part of it. It must have brought back to her older, deeply buried rejections. Her mother. Sylvie never spoke of her. There must have been problems there—a flighty woman, he had been told, who probably paid little attention to her child, then sent her far away to school. Nothing terribly unusual in that, except that she had died before Sylvie had a chance to come to terms with her or with her mother in herself. He wondered for a moment what role Sylvie took on in her relationship with Caroline. Odds on, it was the man's. Jacob rose again and paced. All that was too painful to think about. As was the thought of Michel in bed with Sylvie. Obviously he had tried to force her. Jacob gripped the arms of his chair. He felt again the impossibility of his position. He was too involved with Sylvie to think clearly, perhaps too involved to help.

The sun beat down on the paved courtyard. Heat rose from the stones in response. Jacob realized his shirt was soaked through. He took it off and wiped his brow with it. A small gray lizard whisked along the ochre wall and trapped a fly with its flickering tongue, then disappeared into a trellis. The cicadas hummed in the heavy air. Jacob pulled his chair into a single patch of shade and again glanced into the room. He couldn't see Sylvie. Anxiety pulsed through him. He stepped over the threshold and looked around. She had gone. Strewn all over the floor were pieces of paper. Drawings, cut up in a thousand pieces. Jacob picked some up. They were her own; he recognized the style. Then, in the distance, he heard a resounding splash. Sylvie, where was she? He ran in the direction of the sound, his fear now palpable.

A small path led along the edge of ancient vines thick with clumps of purple grape. Jacob raced blindly down it and found himself at a dead end. Lush rampant greenery spread before him, blocking his way. He looked round him with mounting despair. He was certain the sound had come from the direction he had followed. Now he would be too late. He was about to turn and rush back when he identified what he was certain was a watery trickle very close by. He gazed at the wall of greenery. It was impenetrable. Then to one side he noticed the breeze lifted some trailing branches. He pushed them aside. Sure enough, there was an opening here, a kind of shoulder-high tunnel. He made his way quickly through it and then stopped abruptly. An old *bassin* had been converted into a swimming pool. In the middle of the pool, Sylvie floated. She was naked, motionless, her eyes closed. His heart pounded. He had come too late. Only Sylvie's hair fanning out luxuriantly on the water seemed to have life.

"Sylvie—" the cry bounded into his throat. He strangled it just in time. He had seen her eyelids flutter. It was his fear that had imposed death on her. Jacob crouched in the shade of the leafy tunnel and watched. A sigh inadvertently escaped him. She was so beautiful, floating there on the glistening water, only the shadows of the vegetation wrapping her golden skin in intricate and changing garb. A nymph clothed in innocence. Despite himself, his body stirred. How easy it would be to dive in beside her, take those full breasts in his hands, kiss her.

Sylvie's sudden movement shattered Jacob's daydream. With wild, vigorous strokes, she now pounded the water and swam back and forth, back and forth, back and forth, like a caged animal. Then, exhausted, she lifted herself out of the pool. Jacob shrouded himself in bushes. Her harsh breath broke the afternoon's stillness as she ran, hair and body streaming, blindly past him toward the house. Slowly, Jacob followed.

Later, Sylvie lay on the rumpled bed in the dusky room. Strips of light played through the shuttered windows and fell on her like prison bars. She tossed and turned and struggled with the sheets. "It's all right," Babushka said. "He'll be home tonight. He promised. Your father never breaks his word."

"But why did he go away? Just when I was ill? He missed my fourth birthday. Mama must have made him go." A small, strangled voice came from Sylvie. She felt hot, dizzy, as if she were waking from a long sleep filled with terrible dreams.

Babushka's calm tones comforted her. Her cool hand was on her brow. "He had to go away. With your mother. And when they come back, they'll have a lovely new baby brother for you to play with."

"I didn't want him to go away. I don't want a baby brother. I don't want Mama. She's smelly," Sylvie wailed plaintively.

"There, there. You're getting much better now. Soon, you can get up and have some bread and jam and put on your pretty white dress. Then Papush will be back."

"Papush, Papush, are you there?" Sylvie's eyes fluttered open. In the half-light she studied the form sitting on the bath chair by her bed. Dark, curly hair, furrowed brow, strangely worried eyes, broad shoulders, long legs stretching, stretching almost up to her bed. This wasn't Papush. She shivered. Her body felt coldly clammy. She looked down at her legs. They were too big. Where was she? Then with a shudder she remembered.

"What are you doing here?" she asked in a cold voice. She looked Jacob directly in the eyes. "What have you done with her? Is she here with you?"

Jacob met the hostility of her gaze. He didn't know which Sylvie was addressing him so directly. The little girl he had begun to piece together from her dream mutterings or the troubled woman who lay there so poignantly naked.

"Who?" he asked quietly.

Sylvie sat bolt upright. "Who?" she repeated in a high piercing voice. "Who, he asks," she addressed an invisible audience. "Why Madame la Princesse de Polignesco. Your mistress, that's who," she shrieked.

With the speed of a tigress, she leapt off the bed and struck him across the face. Jacob caught her wrist and held it. Sylvie glowered at him. Then with a savage look, she sat astride him, wrapping long legs round his, pressing her taut breasts against him. "Does she do this to you? Or this?" She ran her nails under his shirt, nibbled his ears. Jacob's mouth crushed down on her with all the force of weeks of pent-up passion and worry. He held her tightly. Held both the frightened little girl and the ardent woman who aroused him unbearably.

"No one does this to me, Sylvie. Only you," he whispered to her. "There is no one else. No one." Then, with a force which he thought would tear him in two, he lifted her away from him. He held her at arm's length and looked deeply into the blue ocean of her eyes.

"I love you, Sylvie," he said, his voice aching. "I want to be with you. Always." He waited, watching her face, the confusion of mistrust, of pain, the glimmerings of a smile tugging at her wide lips. Then the large, silent tears. He shielded her in his arms and let her cry for the length of the night.

By the end of that week, Sylvie Kowalska, with little fuss and less bother, had brought her two suitcases of possessions to Jacob Jardine's apartment. They began their life together.

CHAPTER
SEVEN

ven for those Europeans not addicted to pessimism, 1937 could hardly have been called a promising year. True, the electoral victory of the Popular Front in France in May of the previous year had been the cause of celebration. Conditions for workers were looking up: a forty-hour week had been instituted and for the first time paid holidays were ensured. But the Popular Front had come to power on the back of Hitler's occupation of the Rhineland. And for those, like Princesse Mathilde, who had observed the increasingly violent regimentation of the German dictatorship at first hand, who had heard Hitler's bloated, hate-filled rhetoric conjuring up a purified Germany at the helm of Europe, it seemed that more than tough words from Léon Blum, the Popular Front's leader, would be needed to stop Germany's advance and the spread of Fascism. Why, even the League of Nations with its fifty-two member states had not been able to summon up the muscle to stop Mussolini's invasion of Ethiopia.

There was more. What had started as a small-scale mutiny in Spanish Morocco against the young Spanish Republic had gained the momentum of a full-scale civil war. After Franco's forces, aided and abetted by Germany and Italy, had held Madrid under siege for several months and still the French and British governments did nothing, the Princesse began to despair. Everywhere, the very fabric of the civilization she had known seemed to be at the mercy of irrational and destructive forces. And no government did anything about it.

Princesse Mathilde knew herself well enough to recognize that her despair was not only political. It had a personal component. Her friends, her family, seemed increasingly alien to her. They cocooned themselves from realities. They didn't share her fears. The one person she felt she could talk to honestly, Jacob Jardine, was hopelessly estranged from her. She was carrying the burden of a secret which she now feared might follow her to the grave. The dishonest weight of it tormented her more with each passing day.

Whereas on the political front the Princesse felt she was impotent to do more than bend the ear of any politician or journalist who would listen to her views, on the personal front she could take action. It was simply a question of building herself up to the moment.

Late one afternoon toward the end of February, after a downpour had washed the Paris streets clean and the houses glowed anew in the setting sun, the Princesse made her decision. She had just seen Charlie Chaplin's *Modern Times* yet again and his invented nonsense language kept pace with her footsteps as she walked toward the Quai Voltaire:

> La spinach or la tacho
> Cigaretto torlo totto

Her destination was Jacob Jardine's new consulting room.

She had not seen Jacob alone since that evening over two years back which had marked their parting. Oh yes, they had bumped into each other two or three times at social gatherings and exchanged a few polite, if strained, words. There had even been the occasional note: when her last pseudonymous book appeared, Jacob had sent a carefully worded congratulatory letter. She had returned the gesture when his book was published. True, she had not been in Paris as much as had been her wont previously. But she had hoped, particularly in those first months after their last meeting, that he would make some sign. There had been none. And on her side, she had been too proud to make any. She was pregnant.

When she had first discovered her pregnancy, the Princesse had longed for Jacob, ached for him. His loss created a void which threatened to engulf her. Then, as her body swelled and burgeoned, she partly succeeded in putting him out of her mind. This pregnancy, unlike her earlier ones, took her over fully, perhaps because she was more at ease with her womanliness. She relaxed into her body, watched its changes in wonder. Luckily, Frederick was always at his most attentive during her pregnancies and his comfortable presence reassured her. He had no doubt but that the child was his. The Princesse knew that it was otherwise. However, she did nothing to dissuade him. The ignominy of discovering that he was fathering another man's child would have been too great for Frederick. And the Princesse had no desire to hurt him. Sometimes, too, in those early days, she relished her secret. It replaced that other joyful secret—the affair with Jacob.

She must have, she realized in retrospect, unconsciously foreseen her pregnancy, for on her return to Denmark after her last meeting with Jacob, she had done everything in her power to lure Frederick into her bedroom. She had succeeded. As a result, there was no reason for Frederick to suspect anything. Only the Princesse when she had seen Violette for the first time had been confirmed in her knowledge. The child's large, dark eyes, the shape of her brow, were unmistakably Jacob's. The Princesse had kept her counsel. She had made no sign of Violette's arrival to Jacob. She was, in any case, so enthralled by her little girl, so immersed in her dainty movements and her ready show of affection, that she felt at first no desire to do otherwise. This baby, she told herself, was entirely hers—the embodiment of *her* love, not the product of another's desire for succession.

Violette had been born Elizabeth Marie, after Mathilde's own mother. The second of the Princesse's sons had nicknamed her Violette, claiming that the baby's vast dark eyes and darker pupils were just like the flower. The name had stuck.

It was only as the little girl grew out of her tiniest infancy and her total dependence on her mother that the Princesse began to have twinges of a desire to share her with Jacob. In the last year, this desire had taken on a new and troubling momentum. It was fueled by the Princesse's sense of an impending cataclysm. Thoughts of death brought in their train memories of her father and a troubling focus on the question of Violette's paternity. After Mathilde had visited Germany and experienced life under Hitler, the need to see Jacob and reveal her secret became imperative. She had to speak to the one person whom this matter intimately concerned.

The bronze shingle at the side of the wide double door confronted Mathilde. *"Dr. Jacob Jardine, Psychanalyste."* Taking a deep breath, she rang the consulting-room bell. As she did so, she realized that she should have made an appointment. Jacob would almost certainly be with a patient and would have no time to see her. But it was too late to turn back; nor did she wish to, now that she had taken the most difficult step.

A small neat woman of middle years answered her ring and looked at her sternly. Before Mathilde could speak, she said, "Dr. Jardine is with a patient. You will need to telephone for an appointment."

"I prefer to wait till he is free," Mathilde said evenly.

"He will not be free for another two hours," the woman said emphatically.

Mathilde had the impression the woman was about to close the door in her face. She drew herself up to her full height and said authoritatively, "Please tell him that Princesse Mathilde de Polignesco wishes to see him." She watched the woman hesitate, saw the consternation on her face, the tug between her duty to consulting-room regulations and the impact of her name. Yes, Mathilde smiled inwardly, despite the democratic tenor of the times, the word *Princesse* still carried some weight. As did Mathilde's not inconsiderable demeanor. With the years, she had acquired a formidable presence—a tall, statuesque woman, whose strong features bore down on any challenger with shriveling authority. The Princesse, it was immediately clear, had a character to be reckoned with.

Jacob's assistant ushered her into a small antechamber, turned away and then as if to prove that duty still held the upper hand, looked back to say, "I will not be able to speak to Dr. Jardine until his present patient has left, of course."

"Of course," Mathilde murmured. She sat down in one of the two armchairs the space held and waited. There was a stillness about the room with its sparse furnishings and muted colors. The rush of traffic seemed far away. It was as if she had stepped into a neutral terrain designed only to take on whatever flavor its occupants wished to give it. There wasn't a newspaper in sight. Mathilde looked out of the window to remind herself of her bearings, the impetus which had brought her here. At a depth of three floors below her, the Quai Voltaire bustled with life. The *bouquinistes* displayed their wares: hoary old volumes, sheets of music, cards. Beyond them, the River Seine's gray waters curled round a passing boat. The sight reassured the Princesse.

She didn't know how much time had passed before the receptionist came back into the room. Her manner had visibly changed. "Would Madame la Princesse like to come and wait more comfortably next door? Dr. Jardine says he will see you as soon as he has finished with his next patient."

The Princesse followed the woman. She had a better sense of the lay-out of the apartment now. Opposite the room in which she had been sitting, a door stood slightly ajar to reveal a similar space in which she glimpsed a seated figure. Between them, a closed door signaled what she surmised must be Jacob's consulting room. Down the corridor, to the right, she was ushered into a room she instantly knew must be Jacob's study. It bore his stamp. Books lined the walls, a shelf full of Freud in German, French and English; surrealist manifestoes; novels, medical tomes; journals. The large desk with its sheaves of papers must have held his gaze just hours before. In the far corner of the room a striped divan and chairs provided a lounging space.

It was here the Princesse sat breathing in Jacob's atmosphere, remembering what she might have preferred to forget. No one had come into her life to fill the void Jacob had left. In retrospect now, the void appeared to be as much one of companionship as anything else. While Jacob had remained in her life, there had been a whole series of thoughts that she had stored only in order to share them with him. Now there was no one with whom to argue those perceptions, indeed to quicken them. She felt as if a part of her had gone into long hibernation.

When the receptionist brought in a tray of tea and biscuits, Mathilde quickly picked up a newspaper and pretended to be immersed in the day's headlines. What did Jacob make of Europe's current plight? Would he share her sense of despair, understand why she had come to him now? As she stared into the middle distance, her eyes suddenly focused on a series of photographs: Sylvie, artfully posed by a photographer whose style she recognized. The Princesse wrenched her gaze away. Somehow in the course of this afternoon, she had forgotten about Sylvie's existence. Now, as the mixed innocence and archness of that face confronted her, she shivered. Perhaps it would be better to let secrets lie undisclosed. The Princesse gathered the folds of her coat round her. She wasn't after all an abandoned parlormaid who needed to sue for love. The whole thing might prove too demeaning.

"I see I have kept you waiting almost too long. I'm sorry." Jacob's deep voice resonated across the room. He walked toward her. "If only you had let me know you were coming . . ." He paused to look at her—the theatrically wide-brimmed hat, the mobile expressiveness of her features—and then took her hands in his. "I have missed you," he said softly.

As he spoke them, Jacob realized how true the words were. It was not that over these last few years he had consciously thought of Princesse Mathilde with any regularity. Nor had he made any attempts to see her. Between work and the peculiarly obsessive nature of his relationship with Sylvie, his life was full. Sometimes, he thought, overfull. But seeing her now in all her dramatic vividness, he was acutely aware of what had gone out of his life.

"I am glad you have come," he said.

"You may not be so glad by the time I have left." The Princesse's tone was wry, light. What she felt was altogether different. Somehow, she had not prepared herself for the impact of Jacob's physical presence. The passing of the years had left their mark, but they had only served to increase his attraction. They looked at each other for a long moment.

At last Jacob dropped her hands. He took the full, richly colored coat from her shoulders and placed it carefully on a chair.

"And now you see where I spend my hours outside the hospital." He gestured round him. "My father in his wisdom decided to retire to the South, where he keeps fit by running a clinic for workers." Jacob smiled ironically. "He insisted I take over his consulting rooms, though personally he has little patience with psychic ills, particularly of the more expensive variety."

"I wish someone had seen to the expense of Herr Hitler's psychic ills a decade ago. Had I had the foresight, I would have done so myself. Then perhaps we would have been spared the sight of his unconscious unleashed on the rest of us." The Princesse's face grew grim as she spoke, though she kept her voice light.

There was a pause between them as they studied each other. In it they recognized how, despite their separation, their minds had followed a similar track.

Jacob poured her a drink from an old crystal decanter, and then as he handed it to her, asked, "Why have you come, Mathilde?"

She was startled by the directness of his question and she blurted out what she would have preferred to keep back for some moments yet.

"To tell you that you are the father of a very lovely girl—my daughter." Her voice was low, direct. Dark eyes challenged him.

Jacob stood very still, so still for what seemed so long that Mathilde was acutely aware of the tapping of a typewriter in the next room, of a bell ringing somewhere, of the sound of her own heart. She looked away from him.

"Why didn't you tell me before, Mathilde? Contact me?" He sat down heavily. He looked sad, dejected. "Why, Mathilde? Have I become such a stranger? Is it not something in your world to be a father?"

He understood nothing, Mathilde thought. She shivered, held her shoulders proudly high.

"Oh, of course." Jacob stood, paced. "It's my doing, isn't it? I should have made some sign." He exhaled a ragged breath. "I'm sorry, Mathilde. All those months without a word." He took her hand now, brought it to his lips, examined her features urgently. "It must have been difficult for you, very difficult." He paused. "But . . . what can I say?" He turned away from her with a gesture of self-exasperation. "Had I known, I would have come to you. Somehow. Instantly." His voice was muffled.

A weight lifted from Mathilde's heart. "Thank you for saying that, Jacob," she murmured. Now she could make light of it all, repeat the words she had endlessly repeated to herself, when her pain was at its worst. "And it wasn't so very difficult." Mathilde raised a rueful eyebrow. "After all, I am hardly a helpless, impoverished little girl. The waif hasn't been sent out for adoption, you'll be pleased to hear." She paused, met his eyes. "But I have missed you, wanted to tell you . . ."

"I should like to see her," Jacob said softly. His face was raw with emotion, as defenseless as a youth's. "More than anything, I should like to see her. Please, Mathilde. When can I see her?"

The Princesse was surprised by the fierceness of the longing she read in him. She smiled a little wistfully. "Given the times we live in, there is perhaps no better moment than the present."

"Tonight then." Jacob's features shone with relief. He had had a momentary fear that no sooner announced would his daughter be taken away from him. A child. A daughter. The thought thrilled him. "Yes, straight away." He looked at the Princesse with an air of wonder. "Did I tell you often enough in those distant days, what a remarkable woman you are?"

Mathilde smiled as with buoyant alacrity he picked up the telephone and dialed his home number.

"No, I do not want to go to Neuilly for the weekend to visit Princesse Mathilde. I have already said so. You know I'm singing at the Razzma on Saturday." Sylvie raged around the bedroom and flung the silk stockings she was holding onto the floor. "If you must see your former mistresses, then you can very well do so without my company."

"Sylvie, I've told you that all that is over. Has been over for many years. And that the Princesse specifically invited both of us." Jacob restrained his temper and spoke evenly.

Sylvie's eyes blazed. "You know what you can do with your damned Princesse." She jerked her fingers lewdly in his face. "That's how much I care about her. Now get out of here."

"All right, I will." Jacob could see the sudden consternation on Sylvie's face as he left the room. He hesitated and then, refusing to have the row escalate, marched out of the house. He needed some time to himself, needed to think. It was a dark, cold night and the Île Saint-Louis was cloaked in the shadows cast by its hooded lamps. Jacob walked rapidly along the embankment in the direction of the Quartier Latin. Here he lost himself in the milling crowds.

Sylvie had made exactly the same scene the previous week when the Princesse's prior invitation had come. He had felt trapped then and continued to do so. After all, Sylvie had good reasons not to wish to see the Princesse. On the other hand, ever since he had spent his first few hours with little Violette just over ten days ago, the desire to be with her had been constant in him. He was enraptured by her plump toddler's body, her alert dark eyes, her surprising speech patterns and comments. He was also perplexed by the strength of the emotions she elicited in him. Fatherhood, for him, had always been something of an intellectual construct: the experience was altogether different.

The force which had impelled Jacob through the thirty-two years of his life had always been a desire to grasp and grapple with the unknown. That which was veiled, mysterious, called out for understanding. It was that which had drawn him to his work as a psychoanalyst. It was that which had initially propelled him toward the Princesse, with her code of values and mores which hearkened back and forward to another time. It was what kept him fixed by Sylvie's side despite, or perhaps because of, all their difficulties.

Now he found that force driving him toward his daughter. Yet he knew for all the rational social reasons that he could not allow himself—nor would he be allowed—to grow too close to Violette. It was tacitly understood between the Princesse and himself, that the matter of Violette's paternity was only between them. She was, as far as the world and Frederick understood it, Frederick's daughter. It could not be otherwise: too many people stood to suffer. The Princesse had made it clear that she was in Paris for only six weeks. After his second meeting with his daughter, she had pointedly invited him *and Sylvie* to spend the weekend in Neuilly. Sylvie had refused and Jacob had gone down for the day by himself. He would, he knew, do the same this weekend.

But the situation was fraught with danger. There was a look he had caught on a number of occasions in the Princesse's eyes while he was playing with Violette. It spoke of a yearning he no longer reciprocated. The look served as a warning. If he spent too much time alone with the Princesse and their daughter, he knew that sooner or later that look would have to be confronted. Whatever his response, the situation it would engender would be intolerable.

Jacob reached the Place Saint-Michel and walked into a café. He sat down beneath an expanse of mirror and ordered a pastis. The locale had a soothing effect on him: the constant movement; the raised yet muffled voices; the clang of dishes; the dramas being lived out at separate tables, all rendered him at once part of a crowd, yet anonymous. Cafés, he thought to himself, provided the perfect place of repose for modern urban man. He didn't know what he would do without them.

Certainly his life at home with Sylvie provided no still center. But that was hardly why he was with her. Not married, no. She had initially refused him again and again and now he had ceased asking. It angered his mother and troubled the Ezards, but they had learned to live with it. Sylvie was, after all, no ordinary bourgeoise.

She had become the toast of his surrealist friends, who painted her and photographed her and made her the muse of a hundred verses. He never knew when he walked through that door, made up of a man and woman conjoined, into the Gradiva Gallery how many variations on the figure of Sylvie he might meet.

There had been no recurrence of the breakdown which had preceded her coming to live with him. Yet the sense of her vulnerability, the precariousness of her emotional balance, never left him. Sometimes it made him retreat into the safety of his professional guise.

Without ever speaking of it, Sylvie knew that her "case" hovered around them and occasionally positioned itself squarely and emphatically between them like an insurmountable concrete barrier. His retreat into a calculating professionalism, when it occurred, irritated her and made her goad him with a vengeful sadism. On one occasion, she had succeeded in tearing away his professional mask, and the results had not been pretty. He had been guiltily ashamed of himself. Yet even as Sylvie had lain on the bed crying softly and trembling like a wounded defenseless sparrow, he had seen the glint of triumph in her eye. Jacob didn't want a repetition of that scene.

He sometimes felt they were trapped in a frenzied mortal dance which propelled them forward with no volition of their own. Yet he was still enthralled by her: he continued to desire her with a passion which seemed unquenchable. It made him wonder about his own balance.

Shortly after their life together had begun, she had taken to singing and playing the piano in a variety of clubs, mostly on weekends. He had not been averse to it. It was so exactly what she wanted to do. Initially, he had shared her excitement, accompanied her to a variety of haunts and watched her perform. The whole process made her glow with a feverish pleasure. Sylvie with a spotlight on her, her eyes and hair alight, her body sheathed in a tight dress, belting out a song, was an irresistible force. The hundred eyes focused on her, desiring her, gave her a palpable strength.

In the small hours of the morning, it was Jacob who was the sole recipient of her excitement. Their lovemaking had a frenzy which made everything else pale beside it. On some of those rare nights, she forgot herself so completely that she even allowed him to come inside her. Usually, it was the one prohibition. It troubled him that after all their months together, the prohibition still existed. He now thought he knew something about its conscious source, her fear of having children, her greater anxiety about being abandoned. But that was only half the picture. Knowledge did little to abate his gnawing sense of inadequacy. Sylvie still preferred to initiate their sexual encounters. He had never known a woman who could burn so hot and within twenty-four hours freeze him with her iciness.

Over the last months, the situation had been exacerbated. Instead of performing to a massed crowd, Sylvie had taken to singling out men in the audience and flirting with them outrageously, sitting down with them to have drinks, exciting their expectations. At the end of it all, she would come back to him as if nothing had happened. He felt increasingly like a pimp, a whoremaster. It was not a feeling he relished and he had begun to refuse to accompany her. She always came home, though the hours grew later and later. And it was on one such night that they had the tumultuous scene he was so ashamed of. His self-control destroyed, he had hit her, not hard, but hard enough. She had crouched in the corner, whimpering like an infant.

He never knew whether Sylvie slept with any of the men she tantalized. She was too consummate an actress for that, provoking his fantasies, then behaving like an innocent. As she herself told him when he confronted her coolly with his suspicions, whatever she said would not make one iota of difference to the truth of things or to his jealousy. He could as easily believe that she slept with all of the men she met as with none. In any case, he did not own her just because he put his cock into her. Sylvie's language, when roused, was hardly restrained.

But it was Jacob's restraint which always elicited her greatest wrath. If he asked her nothing about her movements, pretended sleep or indifference, she goaded him blithely. It was clear he cared nothing about her now. He enjoyed being a pimp, a lazy one to boot who couldn't even bother to simulate arousal. She would throw her earnings from the club onto the bed and stomp off to sleep on the sofa.

Jacob drained his pastis and shrugged inwardly. Where all this would lead to he had no idea. In any event, now something new and overridingly important had moved into his horizon: his child. His step light, he donned his coat and made his way to his consulting room. He would sleep there this evening. It would be best. And tomorrow he would go to see Violette.

At dawn the next morning, Jacob was woken from restless sleep by the insistent pealing of the doorbell. He gazed blindly at his watch, stumbled across the study, pulling his trousers on in the process. His first thought was that some desperate patient had decided to seek him out at this unearthly hour. His second that something had happened to Sylvie.

She stood at the door and gazed at him angrily. Then without any greeting, she strode past him and one by one threw open the doors of all the rooms in the apartment.

"There is no one here but me, Sylvie," Jacob said firmly.

She turned toward him, her face now childishly defenseless. "I've decided to come to Neuilly, after all." She swung her overnight bag ostentatiously to emphasize her point.

"I'm glad." Jacob took her bag and lifted her coat from her shoulders. Beneath it, she was wearing one of the glittering dresses she preferred for her club performances. It sat on her now like a costume, plundered from another woman's wardrobe. On her bare arms

Jacob noticed a series of bruises, like a man's fingerprints. He winced.

"Have you been to sleep yet?"

She shook her head. "When I didn't find you at home, I came here." Tears gathered in her eyes. He read her fear in them. She rushed toward him and buried her face in his bare chest. Her arms clasped him tightly. He held her, stroking the wild tumble of her hair.

Jacob was surprised after a moment to feel his arousal. It confused him. He lifted her gently in his arms and carried her to the divan. "You need some rest before we head off," he said gently.

She looked up at him, a question on her face. He unbuttoned her dress and eased it down over her hips. Her beauty as he gazed at her nudity struck him again forcibly. But he tucked her in like a child and merely brushed her forehead with his lips. He could hear her soft crying as he closed the door behind him.

Sylvie looked at Princesse Mathilde curiously and bristled faintly at her words.

"I don't know whether you realize how lucky you are to have a man like Jacob by your side."

There was no trace of wistfulness in the Princesse's words. She spoke matter-of-factly. "I have never had the chance to say this to you before, but I hope you will be, are, very happy together."

Sylvie didn't respond. But suddenly and strangely, she felt as if she had been given a benediction.

They were sitting on the marble terrace at the back of the Princesse's Neuilly house. A vast, beautifully tended lawn stretched out in front of them and their eyes focused on the group in the distance who were playing a version of football. Jacob, the Princesse's two lanky teenage sons who had arrived that morning, Violette and her nanny. Violette romped amongst the others occasionally grasping the large ball with hoots of laughter and to the delight of everyone.

The other guests had dispersed after the copious Sunday lunch and Sylvie had found herself alone with the Princesse. The day was unseasonably warm and they had installed themselves on the terrace where the sun shone most brightly.

Although Sylvie had arrived at Neuilly the day before in a hostile frame of mind, ready to locate faults in everyone and everything, she had found herself peculiarly charmed by Princesse Mathilde. Nothing the older woman said could in the least be construed as insidious or offensive. Indeed, the Princesse had introduced Sylvie to her other guests as a longtime friend and a talented pianist and singer. Her tone was the same as she had always used with her in those distant days when Sylvie had admired the older woman, except now it had a note of greater equality. No matter how hard Sylvie tried to intercept secret glances between the Princesse and Jacob she had not been able to. The fact of the matter was that the Princesse had given her far more attention than him. It had perplexed Sylvie initially, but she had now given way to the Princesse's charm and decided that despite her doubts the only link between her and Jacob was that of old friends.

At first, too, when Sylvie had met Violette and seen Jacob's evident affection for the little girl, she had prickled with suspicion. Could this toddler so akin to Jacob in coloring be his daughter? The thought had hounded her. And then after lunch yesterday when Jacob had tossed the little girl into the air to her hilarious delight, the Princesse had suddenly laughed gaily and said in everyone's presence, "Looking at the two of them, like this, one might suspect she was his daughter." She had turned to Sylvie and said pointedly, "Very soon now you must give him one of his own." All Sylvie's suspicions had vanished.

Now, as she watched Jacob tossing the little girl in the air again and running across the lawn with her in his arms, Sylvie felt a peculiar longing. Perhaps the Princesse was right. Perhaps she should give Jacob a daughter, like those presents she used to bring to him in the early days of their courtship. Sylvie glanced down at the ring he had given her. She had chosen to wear it this weekend. She fingered it tentatively.

The Princesse glanced surreptitiously at Sylvie and then settled back in her chair with an inward sigh. She felt as if she had been walking a precarious tightrope and had only now begun to ease herself down the pole which led to the safety of the ground. Ever since that momentous night which now seemed so distant when Jacob had driven down with her to Neuilly to meet Violette, she had realized that if she wanted Jacob to remain a part of her and Violette's life without disastrous consequences, then Sylvie was the key stumbling block.

She had not counted on the strength of Jacob's instant interest in Violette. It both moved her and troubled her. He had been unable to take his eyes off the child and played with her with joyous delight. After Violette's bedtime, he had made the Princesse recount to him

with great detail all aspects of her life and character. He had wanted
to return the following evening and the one after that.

"But what about Sylvie?" the Princesse had asked. "Won't she
wonder where you are, grow suspicious?"

Jacob had clenched his fists and shrugged.

"Well, you can come tomorrow. But after that, I suggest you bring
Sylvie along," she had said with determined clarity.

From days past, the Princesse knew Sylvie was unpredictable. She
could be emphatically selfish, wild, could pronounce from the roof-
tops her belief that Jacob and Mathilde were having an affair. Jacob's
demeanor betrayed that things were in any case not altogether easy
between them.

The Princesse also realized that if she found herself alone with
Jacob too much, her own feelings would be in an even greater state
of turmoil. So she set herself the task of wooing Sylvie, making her
a friend, taking her into her confidence. It was the only way of
preventing disaster. Now she felt she had all but succeeded. There
was only one more step to be taken to consolidate her position.

As ultimately honorable as the Princesse's intentions were, she
had planned her campaign with Napoleonic shrewdness. It was not
for nothing that she numbered him amongst her ancestors. After
a few moments of silence between them, the Princesse turned to
Sylvie.

"There is something I have been wanting to give you for some
time. Would you come up to my room with me while the others are
busy with their football?"

Sylvie followed the Princesse's stately form through the house.
The furnishings were so gilded and heavy that they oppressed her.
She felt small, insignificant, an ungainly child. Only once they had
made their way up the grand, curved staircase with its sweep of
royal blue carpet and finely grained marble did she feel that she had
regained her usual stature. The Princesse led her into an intimate
room—her boudoir. From an ornate inlaid chest, she took a wine-
red velvet box.

"This came to me when my father died," the Princesse said.
"When I studied it, I realized that the crest was that of your mother's
family. I have always wanted to give it to you." She handed Sylvie
the box.

Sylvie opened it and found a large pendant strung on a heavy old
gold chain. Emblazoned on the crest was a unicorn and a strange
bird, a phoenix perhaps. Sylvie traced the image with her fingertip.

Dimly she remembered her mother saying something about fire and purity and new lives. With trembling hands, she took the pendant out of its box and lifted it over her head. It felt substantial, weighty. It anchored her.

"Thank you," she said in a small voice.

The Princesse looked at the young woman with the vast troubled eyes. "I knew your mother, Sylvie. You are not unlike her. She was exceedingly beautiful."

Sylvie recoiled. Her lips trembled under the Princesse's insistent gaze. A small, unfamiliar, querulous voice leapt up in her. "She sent me away. She didn't want me with them. At home."

The Princesse was silent for a moment. At last she said quietly, "Your mother was very young when she had you. Perhaps having a child was difficult for her. But I know she cared for you very much."

"She sent me away," Sylvie repeated stubbornly. "Banished me so I couldn't make it up with Papush." Sylvie fingered the heavy pendant nervously. The gesture carried her back.

There had been a cross in the pendant's place then, a simple cross of old ruddy gold. Her fingers had traced its form, tugged at it as she lingered in her white cotton nightie by the great oak door of her parents' room. Her mother had ordered her out, back to her own bed. She had had a nightmare and come running to them and her mother had ordered her away. They were arguing now, her father's angry baritone against her mother's lilting contralto.

"I don't want her running in here at every opportunity." Her father's voice. Sylvie pulled at the cross.

"She's your daughter. What happened wasn't her doing. She's just a child." Her mother, appeasing, low.

"I can't stand her pawing at me, wanting me, needing me. It makes me feel ill. Anyhow, in your condition, it's better if she's away. The burden will fall on me." Papush's voice rose. It was met by silence. Sylvie listened, tensed.

Then her mother's voice, exasperated. "All right. I'll send her away to school."

"Do it soon." The muffled sound of her father. "Otherwise every-one will find out." Sylvie yanked the chain off her neck and let it fall tinkling to the floor.

"Is that pendant too heavy for you?" The Princesse's even tones brought her back.

Sylvie's hand dropped stiffly to her side. She shook her head. "No, no, it's fine. It's exquisite. Thank you. Thank you."

The Princesse's steady gaze assessed her. "Remember, Sylvie," she said slowly, quietly, "our families have known each other through generations. If you ever need a friend, need help, you can count on me."

The Princesse meant it.

Next to Jacob, in the front seat of the Citroën on the drive home, Sylvie felt the memories clawing at her, forcing her to make little adjustments to her sense of the past, her sense of herself. Her mother was emerging in a new light, less enemy than protectress. If only she could talk to somebody from that time. Babushka. Babushka could tell her more about her mother. But they hadn't let her see Babushka after it had happened. Babushka would have known, would have read it in her. They wanted to hush the whole thing up.

With an effort Sylvie forced the past away. She gazed at Jacob: in the dusky light, he looked huge, strong, a bulwark against the world. He had that air of intense inner concentration which made him oblivious to her. It had almost become a habitual state when they were together.

She touched his arm. He flinched. The car swerved slightly. "Jacob, Jacob, let's not go back to Paris tonight. Let's drive off into the country, go somewhere different, anywhere."

Jacob glanced at her wrapped in the folds of the leopard-skin coat which so perfectly matched the golden aureole of her hair. Her eyes were alight with an expression he couldn't decipher. He slowed the car and in two swift movements reversed their direction.

The night darkened. Grand houses gave way to wooded country-side, dense with oak and elm. Sylvie's hand rested lightly on his thigh, played with the wool of his trousers. Her face in the blaze of a passing car emerged nakedly white. He lifted her fingers to his lips. She twisted her hand away.

"Jacob, let's stop here. In the woods. Please." He caught the sudden note of urgency in her tone and he pulled up on the soft verge of the road. She leapt out of the car with the grace of a cat and ran amidst the bare trees, finding her footing with a surprising sureness. Jacob following a moment later thought he had lost her. Then he saw her form flickering golden in the moonlight, the sound of her light footsteps on the crisp carpet of fallen leaves. Just when he thought he had caught up with her, she disappeared again.

He heard the sound of her breath and turned to find her behind him. She was leaning against the vast trunk of an ancient elm looking in her leopard coat as if she were far more at home here than in the jungle of the cities which she normally inhabited. She moved sinuously against the bark, as if to evade him again.

Desire flared in him. He caught her in his arms and kissed her fiercely, his hands moving through the open coat to embrace her slim form. Her breasts were taut against him.

Sylvie could feel him hard against her belly, her thighs, his tongue hot in her mouth. Her body felt alight. Rough bark pressed into her. Yes, tonight, here. Here under the stars. She would exorcise the past. She hitched her dress up above her hips and fumbled with the buttons of his fly.

Jacob paused as he always did at this juncture, unsure whether she would push him away from her in order to take him into her mouth. But no, tonight her hand guided him with unmistakable intent between her thighs. He thrilled to her, his penis hard, his desire now sure of its aim. Her little gasps urged him on. With one sure movement, he lifted her off the ground and arched into the folds of her. They came together almost instantly and with a violence so unexpected that it ruptured the silence of the night air.

Sylvie kissed him lingeringly. There were tears on her cheeks. He held her close, rocking her gently, and together they tumbled onto the carpet of leaves. "Again, please," she whispered to him. "Again, I want you inside me." Jacob trembled. Her words devastated him. He realized that he had conditioned himself to never hearing them on her lips and now that they were spoken, he was filled with an overarching joy.

"I love you, Sylvie," he said simply.

Then, he made love to her, slowly, intently and with a tenderness which was beyond excitement. As he moved inside her, Sylvie felt herself lulled, transported into another place. Her body arched against him with a rhythm she didn't recognize. Her consciousness receded. She was floating. In a distant clearing she heard the harsh lashing double syllable of *Curva, curva,* sniffed Papush, with his lemon scent, glimpsed a pink stucco house, and the receding figure of a small waving boy. The images jostled, bobbed, merged. Another made its way toward her. What was it? What was it? She couldn't quite grasp it. It vanished and in its place the tangible shape of the man who now held her, moved with her, gently, firmly, carrying her to a space where she felt washed clean, fresh. Like a newborn child.

When she opened her eyes she seemed to be emerging from a deep sleep. Jacob was looking at her, his face, strangely beautiful, outlined in the moonlight. She could feel his penis resting inside her. She smiled.

Years later, when he had to lie on a cold leafy bed from necessity and not from choice, Jacob would remember that night with a poignant melancholy.

A bare month after the Princesse and Violette had left Paris for Denmark, Sylvie woke unusually early. Jacob, shaving in the bathroom, was startled to see her reflected in the mirror. He was equally startled by her words.

"I have a surprise for you," Sylvie said mysteriously. Her hands were folded behind her back as if she were about to give him something. Her hair, tumbled from sleep, spread across the shoulders of the white girlish nightie she had taken to wearing. She looked again like the slightly gawky schoolgirl Jacob had traced to the convent all those years back.

"I'm pregnant. Soon I'll have a little girl to give to you."

Jacob looked at her in disbelief and then folded her in his arms, forgetting the soap which covered his face. Sylvie giggled. He carried her into the living room and twirled her round and round, before pulling her, protesting, into the bedroom.

That very afternoon, Jacob set about making the arrangements for the wedding. They were married a month later and held a party for a small circle of friends in a *pavillon* at the Bois de Boulogne. The setting was Jacob's tribute to the magic the woods had held.

Sylvie was resplendent in a creamy white suit trimmed with old lace, her sensuality somehow more potent in the demureness of her clothes. Madame Jardine was so pleased at the fact that her favorite son was at last to be wed, that she stilled her disapproval of his choice and behaved with impeccable graciousness. Monsieur Jardine, too, was pleased and aware, where his wife was not, of Sylvie's magic. The Ezards were there, relieved that Sylvie was settling down at last and no longer their responsibility even nominally. Jacques Brenner, trim and witty as ever, acted as best man and Caroline, appropriately tearful, as bridesmaid. The presence of Princesse Mathilde, statuesquely elegant in a shimmering dark blue frock, was noted by all. She had come to Paris specially for the occasion. Jacob and Sylvie were pleased in equal measure.

She drew Jacob aside in a quiet moment and looking him straight in the eyes said in a throaty voice, "I hope you will be happy, my friend." He wanted to embrace her in front of everyone and only her slightly stern look held him back.

The chandeliers shone; flowers perfumed the atmosphere; the women's gowns twirled and lifted rhythmically; laughter and the babble of voices could be heard above the music of the jazz band Jacob had chosen as a special tribute to Sylvie. It was a joyously festive occasion. And one that did not go unnoted in the Paris press. The list of Jacob's friends and colleagues could have kept any name-dropping cultural columnist happy.

Jacob too was happy, but his happiness was tinged by foreboding. As he looked round the assembled ranks of his friends and family, he saw dotted amongst them a few strained, less familiar faces. Colleagues from Germany, refugees from Hitler's Nazi state, which was bent on the elimination of a people he counted amongst his own. Even Sylvie's throbbing song—for there she was now, radiant on the small stage, flanked by the eloquent musicians—could do nothing to erase the haunted expression of those eyes which focused only on memories of violence and destruction.

CHAPTER EIGHT

Some women bloom with pregnancy, rapt by the secret life their body enfolds. Sylvie Kowalska, as she still insisted on calling herself, was not one of these. As her body swelled and grew, so did her revulsion for it. The sight of her veined, pendulous breasts, the mound of her belly in her wardrobe mirror filled her with a disgust so acute that it threatened with each passing day to overwhelm her. She studied the signs of change in herself for hours with a fascinated loathing. This heavy, ungainly beast had nothing to do with Sylvie. If a stranger's eyes happened to fall upon her in the street, she rushed away certain that their disgust trailed her vile form. She hid herself in darkened cinemas and sat mesmerized while sylphlike movie queens enacted rapturous scenes.

With Jacob, the whole matter was exacerbated. If he so much as touched her or attempted an endearment, nausea engulfed her. How could he love this loathsome creature and still love Sylvie?

She had long since insisted on a separate bedroom. By the time she entered the seventh month of her pregnancy, she barred him from her room altogether. Her condition seemed to have taken on an unending quality. There was no thought of a child at the climax of the process, only the constant presence of this horrendous other which was herself. Jacob was at the root of all this, the perpetrator of the evil which had overtaken her. He embodied all her self-loathing. She couldn't bear the sight of him.

Feeling trapped, Jacob confided his worries to his friend Jacques Brenner. They were having dinner in the restaurant on the second floor of the Tour Eiffel. Below them Paris floated in a sea of twinkling lights as if it were still a world capital of pleasure. But the rival pavilions of the great world exhibition of 1937, ominously visible, were a reminder of something else. Atop the German pavilion a giant eagle proclaimed the glories of National Socialism. Directly opposite it, a bulky statue of a heroic pair vaunted the glories of Communism. The sight of these vying presences did nothing to ease Jacob's mood.

"I'm at my wits' end, Jacques. I really don't know what to do."

Jacques shook his head in mock dismay. "And I had hoped that by bringing you up here, I'd raise you above your cares."

"It's not a joke, Jacques." Jacob pushed his plate away brusquely and reached for a cigarette. "I sense things might be better if I weren't with her. But I'm afraid to leave, afraid she might do something to herself."

"If only you had been like me, you need never have confronted all these problems of female fecundity." Jacques smiled wickedly, refusing to be drawn into his friend's gloom.

"We can't all be like you," Jacob said with a touch of venom. "Otherwise humankind would soon be extinct. Either by sexual or political proclivity." He had still not forgiven Jacques his brief flirtation with fascism some years back. Jacques had then been enthralled by the image of strong blond youths marching in unison toward a superhuman future.

"*Touché,* oh venerable Dr. Jardine." Jacques drained his glass. "So, what is to be done about this grotesque Sylvie who hates you, hates herself and will probably hate the bouncing baby who pops out of her? If it ever does."

"Jacques!" The single syllable tumbled out reproachfully from Jacob's lips, just as the stiff moustachioed waiter came to clear their plates. Jacob pushed back his chair and asked for the bill. "Remind me to have dinner with you again some time when I'm faced by a crisis."

"Sit down, old chap. I'm sorry. It's just that you're so damnably gloomy of late, so serious, so full of insoluble dilemmas. It's this reek of humanity. I can't bear it. Sit down." Jacques suddenly turned intent, unlaughing eyes on him. "I'm probably just jealous, you know." He puffed reflectively on his cigarette for a moment.

Jacob sat back in his chair and gazed down on the sinuous river, the flicker of lights it reflected. Jacques was right. Over these last months he had turned into an old bore. He felt oppressed. Oppressed as much by the general situation as the one at home.

Jacques interrupted his thoughts. "You know, I can put myself in Sylvie's skin." He shuddered. "It's not a very happy place. One minute, you're the glamorous Gloria Swanson. No one can keep their hands or eyes off you. The next you're this bloated pouch. It makes you think you've died."

"It's not like that. It's wonderful, natural . . ." Jacob stopped himself.

"Natural?" Jacques caught him up on it. "Did I hear Jacob Jardine, psychoanalyst extraordinaire, correctly? Natural? Next you'll be saying normal. What's natural about any of us? Have you examined your dreams lately? Been to your hospital?"

"Yes, yes, of course, you're right," Jacob conceded, and wondered whether he had been trying to fit Sylvie into an unsuitable mold.

"Wait a minute, I've got an idea. You know how we've always agreed that Sylvie is a consummate actress, never so much herself as when she's playing a grand part? Never so happy as when she's in front of a transfixed audience?"

Jacob nodded, vaguely remembering a distant conversation.

"Well, all we have to do is coach her into a new part. That's it. I should have thought of it before." Jacques leapt up with all the alacrity of a man bent on a racing hunch. He took a set of keys from his pocket and dropped them on the table. "You stay at my place for the next few days. Otherwise you'll just be in the way. Use my clothes. And only come when I call you."

Before Jacob could stop him, he was off. Halfway across the crowded room, he called back, "If any of my undesirable friends turn up, just send them away." Then to the delight of the assembled diners, he added, "And get yourself a woman."

Jacob found a mass of curious eyes focused on him. He was tempted to laugh.

Jacques' apartment on the Rue des Saints Pères just a short distance from the bustle of Saint-Germain-des-Prés suited Jacob's mood perfectly. The rooms had a surprising austerity. What furniture there was had been selected and placed with a connoisseur's eye, but the overall impression was of strict sobriety. Only the Oriental prints which hung here and there spoke of Jacques' love of the fantastical. Jacob breathed freely in this atmosphere of serene order.

Jacob had recently given over his consulting-room apartment to three German refugees. That, together with the fact that in the last months, Sylvie had all but made his home uninhabitable for him, meant there was no place he could call distinctly his own. In Jacques' apartment, he gave himself up to the thoughts which had been pre-occupying him. He was disturbed only once. A young man in naval uniform appeared at the door, looked at him curiously, timidly asked for Jacques and then dashed away.

On his third morning in Jacques' flat, Jacob woke with a clear sense of purpose. He rapidly donned a borrowed shirt, his dark suit, and set off for the hospital. Once there he marched straight to his chief's office and waited to see him.

"What can I do for you, Dr. Jardine?" Old Vaillancourt wiped his spectacles carefully before placing them on his eyes and peering at the younger man.

"I have come to give my notice," Jacob stated flatly.

"Just like that, no reasons?" Lusterless eyes suddenly held a twinkle.

"I wish to move to another hospital, a general neurological ward. Of course, I shall wait until you have found a replacement."

"Of course," the old man said dryly. "And may I so much as ask for a reason?"

"Let's just call it the times." Jacob looked at his watch, nodded brusquely and turned away. He was not prepared to be engaged in a long argumentative conversation. He had made up his mind.

With determined strides, he walked down the long gray-green corridor toward his first ward. The women's long-term ward. As the doors swung open he was, for a moment, overwhelmed by the cacophony of pained sound which burst upon him. Murmurs, shrieks, irascible mutterings, groans, unstoppable monologues, an inferno of competing instruments in an out-of-tune orchestra. Gray faces in indistinguishable gray gowns, some unmoving, their eyes fixed on a minuscule speck of dirt in a barred window or wall; others rocking, prancing, moving hands, feet, heads in abruptly repeated gestures.

As always Jacob took a deep breath and focused his gaze on a single individual. With *that* one, *any* one in perspective, the picture fell into place, the orchestra took on its own atonal harmony. The ward nurse came up to him. They exchanged a few words. His rounds had begun.

There were over fifty women in the ward. As he made his way amongst the beds where the patients lay in their variable states of insulin-induced catatonia, others tugged at him, tried to hug him, kiss him. One vilified him continually, accusing him of having abused her, impregnated her. Another complained of the noise her five invisible children were making and smacked him hard.

The three nurses who surrounded him tried to make the patients keep their distance. Jacob went to the end of the ward and sat down in his customary chair. Every day he sat here for an hour, sometimes two, and as the patients got used to his presence, they lost their fear of him. Some of the manic behavior would quiet down. A few would come to talk to him in the coded riddles he gradually came to understand.

Eighteen months ago he had fought hard to establish a smaller special space in which ten of the more withdrawn patients could convene daily with two nurses and himself. He had noticed that these patients were acutely aware of the smallest details of their environment and responded to it. To go to the new room, they dressed in ordinary clothes, wore stockings, even make-up. In this smaller, less hostile, therapeutic space, as he called it, they placed magazines, a small cooker, paints. The women began to talk to one another, to the nurses, to him. They were seen as individuals and became such. Within a year, six of the patients had left the hospital. Five of them were now back. The new chief had closed the space. It required too high a concentration of staff. He preferred insulin treatment. Jacob was deeply suspicious of it.

But this disagreement was not, he reminded himself now as he left the ward, why he had decided to change tack. It was what was going on outside the psychiatric world, not inside it, that had determined him. Everywhere, in the press, in countless pamphlets and books, in cafés, salons and over family dinner tables, the polemical battle was being waged. Strident anti-Semitic voices proclaimed the need for cleansing France, called in militaristic fervor for the rule of the strong, invoked the Nazi example, a narrow patriotism and a narrower moral rectitude. The liberal premises of the Republic were under attack as well as the toleration and freedoms it enshrined. Jacob's nightmares told him it was but a short step from the peak of polemic to the pitched battle.

He made his way downstairs to the short-stay ward, that shifting sand where the city night had deposited its array of human flotsam and jetsam. There they were, the police force's pickings, a few unmanageable prostitutes, old clochards suffering from alcoholic dementia, a woman clutching a bundle to her breast and weeping inchoately.

Three of the ward's staff were clustered around a young soldier who was retching violently. Jacob walked over to them and listened to the medical student's terse report. The youth had been brought in by a fellow soldier who had stopped him from ramming himself repeatedly against a brick wall. He had purportedly been eating iron filings, nuts, bolts for the last weeks. X-rays confirmed the fact.

"Before he started retching," the student murmured to Jacob, "he told us quite calmly that he had turned himself into the strong soldier the army required. He was going to be a man of iron."

A grim smile hovered over Jacob's lips. "To be a man of iron." The words played through him. The perfect case for this day of decision. Why else was he leaving the slow and long-term battles of his chosen profession? Why else was he reimmersing himself in the flesh and bone of physical medicine, but to prepare himself for the men of iron? To cope with the wounds the men of iron made and suffered. It was what the times demanded.

That night under some obscure impulse Jacob wrote of his decision to Princesse Mathilde. He also wrote to his father. He, at least, would be pleased by Jacob's change of course.

The next morning the telephone rang early. "Jacob." Jacques' voice at the other end of the line was excited. "Tonight's the night. Nine o'clock. Not before. See you." He rang off, enjoying the drama of his terse announcement.

Jacob arrived at his apartment on the Île Saint-Louis with all the trepidation of a stranger making his first visit. Reaching for his keys he hesitated and instead rang the doorbell. Jacques opened the door and welcomed him in, excitement visible in every movement of his long, loose frame.

"Come in, come in. Everyone's already here."

Before Jacob could question him, Jacques ushered him into the living room where a small, lively party of some ten people was gathered. There were two or three of Sylvie's friends from her club circle, two black men he didn't recognize, the painter Michel, and Caroline, who with Sylvie's pregnancy had been increasingly at her side and now greeted him a trifle nervously. Amy, the American woman he hadn't seen for some time, was there too, and he wondered whether she had come with Michel. He went to speak to her. A maid he didn't recognize poured wine liberally into proffered glasses and passed round a tray of tiny canapés. Sylvie was nowhere to be seen.

No sooner was Jacob served than Jacques called for everyone's attention. "As some of you know, we've invited you here tonight for a rather special occasion. Sylvie Kowalska is, shall we say, trying on a new voice." Jacques smiled endearingly.

Caroline started to clap loudly and the others followed.

From the end of the hall, Jacob heard the sound of a trumpet and a cornet. All eyes turned to watch two black tuxedoed men emerge, their horns wailing. After a moment Sylvie followed. Jacob was riveted. She was almost unrecognizable. From top to toe, she was clothed in a voluminous sequined gown which exaggerated her girth, but somehow cloaked the cause of it. Her hair was all but covered in a theatrical tiara from which pearl droplets hung.

It was, Jacob thought, in the most execrably garish taste. It repelled him. But the drama was undeniable. Sylvie's stance was heavy, solid, each foot planted firmly on the floor. A devouring shade of lipstick exaggerated her mouth. And when she opened her lips, a contralto more deeply pitched than anything he had ever heard from her emerged. Her voice, raucous, bitter, moving, complained, merged with the moan of the trumpet, in a song which was also speech.

As she bowed statuesquely to the assembled clapping, Jacques whispered in Jacob's ear, "You have before you an incarnation of Ma Rainey."

"Who?" Jacob murmured.

"It doesn't matter. Some earth mother or other, but nothing so messy as a specific one."

Sylvie sang again, "Goodbye daddy goodbye. I don't want you no more . . ." A contempt for all men merged in her voice with a mournful regret.

Jacob watched spellbound. It was extraordinary. It was not the song which was so different from some of her usual repertoire. It was Sylvie herself. Gone was the seductive temptress whose hips flicked rhythmically. Gone was the plodding pale-faced frightened girl, obliterated beneath the weight of her pregnancy. In her place a solid, powerful presence, an icon of the maternal.

During the next round of clapping, Jacques whispered, "She's bloody good. You ought to be congratulating me."

"I am. You have a future as a latter-day Diaghilev. But what happens when the show is over?"

Jacques shrugged. "I'm not sure. But I have a feeling you may not altogether like it. My concern was Sylvie. *You* can cope."

Jacob didn't like it. The spectacle over, Sylvie sat down heavily, but regally. Kisses flew. Congratulations were general. Jacob awaited his opportunity. When the small circle around Sylvie had unwound, he approached her.

"You were superb, Sylvie," he said softly. Sensing Jacques' eyes on him, he bent to kiss her lightly on the cheek. She didn't recoil as she would have just a few days back. She simply dismissed him with an austere thank you as if he were one of a numerous crowd and turned to Caroline.

"By the way," Sylvie said a moment later, "I've invited Caroline to stay. Jacques' place is quite comfortable for you, isn't it?"

Jacob looked at her uncomprehendingly.

There was a vengeful glimmer in Sylvie's eye. "I'll be much happier with her here. These things should be kept among women, really."

Jacob strode off to his study, which until a few days ago had also served as his bedroom. He could barely contain his rage. Wildly, he threw some clothes and books into a case. Jacques came in and watched him for a moment. His eyes were amused.

"So she's kicking you out. I thought she might."

"And you find the sight entertaining. What on earth did you do to her?"

"I simply freed her of her self-loathing. Told her the big mamas of this world, the Ma Raineys, were proud of their girth, proud of their babies, proud of their sex. I thought that was the point of the exercise. She looks better, doesn't she? She's not moping around in a suicidal daze."

Jacob looked at his friend with undisguised hostility. "No, that's quite true. On the other hand, she's hardly reconciled to me."

"No." Jacques smiled reflectively. "In order to prove my point, I had to make it evident to her that men were irrelevant. Both dispensable and replaceable. I should say it wasn't too difficult to do, really. Once I'd got through to her, she seemed quite ready to turn her self-hatred into a murderous contempt, passing, I'm sure, for you."

Jacob snapped his suitcase shut noisily. He looked Jacques steadily in the eyes. "I don't know what enrages me more, Sylvie's histrionics or your obvious relish in the spectacle of my misery."

"Come come, old chap. You can drown your misery in my best brandy."

"While you crow with delight. No thank you."

Jacob stormed from the room and out of the apartment. At the bottom of the stairs, he bumped into Amy, who was coming out of the lift.

"Running away from home?" She looked meaningfully at his case and turned softly mocking brown eyes on him.

"*Running* is not the operative word," Jacob said with more bitterness than he had intended.

Amy swung her short sheaf of corn-blonde hair away from her face. "She's given you the push, has she?" She broke into English as she always did with him.

"You might call it that." He looked at her intently.

Then he laughed. A tie, a pair of socks peeked disreputably from the crack in his case. Jacob was suddenly struck by the picture he must cut in the bedraggled suit he had worn for several days, the shirt which didn't fit. "You have before you the very image of a man who has, as you say, been given the push."

Amy shook her head. "Brave woman, that Sylvie of yours."

"I guess she is," Jacob murmured. "But what about you? Can I buy you a drink?"

"So that you can weep on my shoulder?" She eyed him wryly.

"A distinctly strange posture for a man of my profession, don't you think?" He met her mockery.

"Well, since I've always liked you and I'm leaving for the States in a few weeks' time . . ." She gave him her arm. "I've had enough of this old world of yours." She looked round her with general distaste.

"I'm not surprised," Jacob said as he opened his car door for her. "I'm not at all surprised."

Later that night he drove her to her door and turned to kiss her goodnight. He was surprised by the rush of passion her cool wide lips elicited in him. He pulled back and gazed at her.

"Would you like to come up?" she asked, without a trace of coquetry.

Jacob nodded. "Very much." His voice was hoarse. Months had passed since he had held a woman.

She led him up four long flights of stairs to her small studio flat. No sooner were they inside the door than he embraced her. Her body was long, supple. It curved to him with a languorous energy. She threw her neck back to receive his kisses. Her flesh smelled of the freshness of apples. When he moved heavily inside her, she dug her fingers into his shoulders and gasped softly. He felt as if he had come home.

"We should have done this before," she said to him afterward.

They were lying naked on the large mattress which served as her bed. Amy lifted her head from where it had nestled on his chest and searched his eyes.

Jacob stroked the heavy sheen of her hair. He remembered his first meeting with Amy, her wry wit, the straightforward honesty of her eyes. If only on that night his desires had not already been fixed on Sylvie. Sylvie, the fugitive, the ungraspable. Pain streaked across him. He found refuge in Amy's mouth.

"We should in any event do it again," he murmured.

"Yes." Her eyes played lazily over him and rested humorously on his jutting penis. "Yes, perhaps we should," she teased him.

Wonderingly, he traced her smile with his fingers. His lips lingered over her taut nipples, the long smooth expanse of her belly, the blonde mound. She gasped. Then with an urgency which was sure of its goal, he thrust into her with hard certain strokes.

Jacob stayed with Amy. The delight of being with a woman who shared his uncomplicated desire was like a new world. Nights grew into weeks. He lived in a state of limbo. Both of them knew he would not, could not, abandon Sylvie. Yet Amy postponed her departure for America. She shared his life more than Sylvie had ever done. He showered her with presents. He was grateful and guilty.

Every evening or two, Caroline rang him to report on Sylvie's welfare. They had agreed this between them. Should Sylvie wish to see him, then he would be available. But from Sylvie herself there was no sign. Jacob did not allow himself to think beyond the baby's birth.

One Saturday evening just before Christmas Jacob and Amy were leaving the flat when loud voices echoed through the inner courtyard from the concierge's rooms.

A broad, darkly clothed form turned as they approached.

"I knew he was here," Sylvie hissed as she spied Jacob.

Before he could altogether take in her presence, he felt a hard slap ringing across his face.

"You swine." She gave him and Amy a withering look and then, her shoulders high, strode out of the building.

A moment passed before Jacob rushed after her. He put a staying hand on her arm. Sylvie shrugged it off. The eyes she turned on him were coldly contemptuous.

"It hardly matters what cesspit you put your cock into, does it?"

Jacob held back and watched her receding form.

Amy put her arm through his and followed the line of his gaze.

"From one cesspit to another, I have to hand it to her. She's got style." There was a bitterness in her voice which played havoc with her words.

Jacob squeezed her arm.

Christmas arrived in gray drizzle. In the recognition that his situation was hardly one of the worst, Jacob held a dinner for his new-found refugee friends from Germany and Austria in the Bois de Vincennes. The generous quantities of drink consumed lightened the atmosphere only slightly.

Two days later, Amy booked her passage to New York.

"Come with me," she said to Jacob, a note of challenge in her eyes. "It's all over, here." She gestured randomly, diffusely, implicating the room, the streets beyond.

Jacob held her close. The sheen of her hair, her skin had a buoyant health, which made the small attic room seem tawdry.

"You know I can't," he said softly. He searched for her lips.

Amy turned away. "I know." There was a hardness in her tone.

"I shall miss you." Jacob forced her to face him. "You know I shall miss you."

She nodded, her eyes filling with tears. He held her for a long time. Then they made love slowly, lingeringly, with the sense that each gesture would become a memory to be traced over and over again.

He drove her to Le Havre. The white bow of the liner shimmered in the winter light. A city on water, its decks had a far more festive air than the town beneath. In the plush bar, they shared a bottle of champagne.

"It would all be a lot simpler if I despised you," Amy said, "if I didn't think you were a *good* man."

Jacob laughed hoarsely. "One woman's good is another woman's evil." He was suddenly tempted to break loose, to stay enclosed in the ship's festive world, to set sail to unknown lands. The whiff of freedom elated him. He emptied his glass. A sardonic expression crept over his face. "But Amy, just think, if I were to stay here, escape to the brave new world with you, I would cease in your eyes to be a good man." He kissed her brusquely. "We'll meet again, I hope."

With long even strides, Jacob left the ship. Amy's tears followed him.

Jacob had arranged to stay on in Amy's flat. No sooner had he returned there than the concierge gave him an urgent message. He was to go straight to the Hôpital Sainte-Marie. Jacob flew. Sylvie. The baby. He suddenly thought hungrily of Violette, her plump arms around his neck, her joyous chatter. And now a second child, one which might again be kept from him.

He marched purposefully through the hospital corridors toward the maternity ward. In the nurse's office, he asked for Madame Jardine.

"There is no one here by that name," the duty nurse informed him. Jacob looked baffled. He insisted. He couldn't have mistaken Caroline's message. The nurse cast increasingly suspicious eyes on him. There was a wild air to this man. His hair was uncombed. His eyes were dangerous.

Jacob took on the crisp tone of hospital authority. "I am Dr. Jardine, Miss . . ." He looked down on the desk where he recognized a rota book and read her name upside down, "Miss Brabant. My wife has perhaps registered here under her maiden name, Sylvie Kowalska," he said, the idea having just come to him. Trust Sylvie to try to exclude him, even at this point.

The nurse hesitated for a moment and then led him to a small room. To his right, he could hear the cries of infants, the comforting mews of mothers, voices. But now, as the nurse opened the door of the labor room, a more piercing sound confronted him: Sylvie's cries. Mingled amongst them was his name.

She was lying on a narrow bed. From where Jacob stood, her high bared stomach obscured her face. Between her raised legs, he could see the soft bloodied down of an infant's head beginning to emerge. His heart pounded and he stepped forward. One of the midwives stopped him sternly and gestured for the nurse to take him away. "It won't be long now," she added.

In the waiting room, he found Caroline. "At last you're here." She masked her nervousness in anger. "It's been going on for over twelve hours."

Jacob put a consoling arm round her shoulders. "Don't be so reproachful. I would have been here all the time if I'd been wanted. I know it's hard on you."

"What do you mean, 'if you'd been wanted'?" Two pink spots burned in her pale cheeks. "She went to get you and said you wouldn't come home."

"What?" Jacob stared at her in some perplexity.

But there was no time for explanations. The nurse came to fetch them. "You've got a beautiful boy, Dr. Jardine. Do come through. No, no, one of you at a time please."

Jacob hurtled after her.

The sheets were now drawn neatly round Sylvie's waist, as she rested against plumped pillows. In her arms lay a tightly swaddled infant, its blind, fistlike face bright pink beneath a shock of dark hair. Her face drawn and perplexed, Sylvie looked down at the baby with an air of shocked disbelief.

"Sylvie, oh Sylvie." Jacob forgot the ordeal of the last months and moved to kiss her.

She seemed to have some difficulty in focusing on him. At last, she picked up the baby and handed it to him as if she were holding an inanimate parcel. "Here. Your present. I promised you a present. But it's not a girl." She diverted her eyes and twisted away from him, muffling her face in the pillow. "It's a boy," he heard her say in a strange voice, shrouded by sobs.

Jacob barely had time to look at his child before the nurse lifted the bundle from his arms. "A handsome little fellow," she said reassuringly, as if she had just witnessed the most ordinary scene in the world. Then with a brisk gesture, she effectively dismissed Jacob. He was being banished from a woman's world.

A boy. The words rebounded in Sylvie's mind. The gypsy had said it would be a boy. There. In the crowded street under the gothic window of Notre-Dame, the gypsy had singled her out. Crushed a sprig of dried lavender in her hand. "For luck," she had said. "For your son." The grimy, reddened hand, freed of its lavender, was thrust at Sylvie. Payment was due. Sylvie had clumsily searched out some coins.

As the gypsy woman turned away, Sylvie had caught at her tattered coat. "Wait."

The woman had looked up at her slyly.

"My son, you said my son." Sylvie's voice broke.

"Yes." A smile which was half sneer spread over the woman's face. She patted Sylvie's stomach. "Very soon, now. A boy." She clutched at Sylvie's hand. "You want me to tell your fortune?"

Sylvie twisted away, shaking her head.

She walked off in a daze. Babushka. Babushka had warned her about boys. Her husband had left her. Two boys had died. Tadzio, her brother, had died. Sylvie's eyes clouded with tears. She tripped on a cobblestone and only a passing woman saved her from falling.

That evening, she had taken a taxi to the address she had extracted from Caroline. Jacob needed to be told. She had intended a girl. She had told him she would give him a girl. Like Violette. Confusion poured through her, catapulting the months. No time intervened between her promise to Jacob and the present. Perhaps Jacob already knew there was a boy. That was why he wasn't with her now. Babushka had warned her. The men. First they poisoned you with their cocks; then the sons came and they left you.

Sylvie sobbed into the starched hospital pillow. The gas, the overarching pain between her legs had blurred her mind. The midwives had had sneering faces like the gypsy.

A boy, one of them had said. Jacob had come. A vast frightening shadow. She had given him the bundle they said was a boy. He could keep him. She wanted nothing to do with him. With any of it.

Sylvie slept.

For the next three weeks, Sylvie lay in a private flower-bedecked room in a maternity clinic. Jacob, seeing her state, had arranged for it. On the surface, everything was as it should be. The attentive father spent as many hours a day as possible with his wife and stared contentedly at his child or held the tiny form cautiously in his arms. Friends came to visit. The baby was docile and cried little. Every few hours he was brought to his mother's breast and fed.

But Sylvie spoke almost not at all and cried and slept a great deal. She paid no attention to the child and less to her husband. While the infant lay in her arms, sucking at her breast, she stared abstractedly into space. It was her only contact with him.

Meanwhile, with an eye to the future, Jacob organized. He rented a vast house in the quiet of Fontenay overlooking the leafy Bois de Vincennes. In the converted coachhouse at the end of the garden, he installed a penniless Austrian couple, the composer Erich Breuer and Anita, his Jewish wife. They had fled Vienna with only two suitcases between them and they were only too happy to look after the house, Sylvie and the child's needs. Madame Jardine, ever vigilant about her grandchildren, and particularly the firstborn of her favorite son, oversaw the establishment of a nursery and herself interviewed potential nannies. Jacob set aside two rooms for Caroline's use. As yet he had no idea whether he and Sylvie would be able to live side by side.

On the day before she was due to leave the clinic, Jacob sat with Sylvie and described all these new arrangements. She seemed not to be listening, but he persisted. In his arms he held his small son and rocked him gently. Suddenly the baby started to cry. Jacob paced the room with him, trying to quiet his shouts.

All at once Sylvie leapt from her bed.

"Give him to me," she said adamantly.

Startled by the first direct words she had spoken to him in weeks, he hesitated for a moment.

"Give Tadzio to me," Sylvie repeated in a tone of command.

Smiling, Jacob handed her the small bundle. She stared at the baby for a moment, then crushed him to her breast. With swift assurance, she sat down on the edge of the bed and bared her nipple to the child's searching lips.

Jacob looked on silently. Sylvie's expression was one of intent concentration. The trace of a smile seemed to hover over her lips. After a while, he asked quietly, "Is that the name you want to give him, then, Tadzio, like your brother?"

Sylvie nodded vigorously.

Jacob waited. Then, he said, "Perhaps we could give him another name as well, one all for himself?" He was acutely aware that Sylvie was in some shadowy way reliving an aspect of her relationship with her brother. The identification seemed to have some positive benefits. But she also needed to recognize the baby's separate existence. He didn't want to press her. He waited.

She was studying the infant. The tip of her finger played over his face, then his hand. The baby's tiny fist closed round her finger. After a while Sylvie said, "Leo. Leo Tadzio Kowalski."

"Leo Tadzio Kowalski," Jacob murmured, imitating her pronunciation and giving the middle name its long *ooo* sound.

Sylvie suddenly looked up at him as if at last taking cognizance of his existence. "Leo Tadzio Kowalski . . . Jardine." Her eyes met Jacob's for a fleeting instant. Then she returned her attention to the baby.

Life in the big house at Fontenay took on its own orderly pace. Sylvie had not blinked when Jacob, masking his anxiety, had simply settled into the bedroom next to hers. Her concerns were all directed at Leo.

Anita supervised the house's running with a controlled precision which belied her soft tones and demure bearing. Meals were served punctually and were copious. When Jacob returned from the hospital not a speck of dust nor an item out of place could be seen anywhere.

Only the nursery and Jacob's desk were permitted their own comfortable chaos.

Sylvie's time was dedicated to the baby. She was totally immersed in his small life. Jacob wondered at the concentration which she brought to the task. As soon as the clouds lifted, Sylvie was out with the large pram, airing Leo, walking the width and length of the woods. Indoors, she would sit by his side for hours, playing with him, watching the flow of his expressions, his tiny hands grasping at air. At night, his little cot was placed by her bedside and the smallest cry stirred her awake. The nanny became a mere shadow.

When Jacob so much as lifted his son into his arms, he would see fear invading her eyes. She watched him jealously, jumping in nervousness if he attempted any mildly boisterous games and snatching Leo from him. Her anxiety was so palpable that he sadly refrained from touching the child. He began to feel like a stranger, excluded from the magic circle which was mother and child. They did not talk about this. They did not in the ordinary course of things talk very much at all. They lived side by side, but not together.

In early spring, when the trees in the Bois de Vincennes had donned their fresh green coats and daffodils and bluebells carpeted the woods, Princesse Mathilde and Violette came to visit. Jacob spent an entire Sunday romping with the little girl. She shrieked in delight over elaborate games of hide-and-seek, clung to him as they chased invented monsters through the trees, presented him with a haphazard bouquet of drooping flowers. All the love he was unable to lavish on his son Jacob poured out on Violette, while Sylvie and the Princesse paraded slowly through leafy lanes, Leo's pram in front of them.

When they returned to the house in late afternoon, they gathered in the spacious room which looked over the garden. A fire crackled merrily in the hearth. Anita served them creamy coffee and her own freshly baked cakes, rich with the memory of Vienna. Violette, taking a sudden interest in Leo, while the adults chatted, tried to lift him.

"No." Sylvie's shout punctured the atmosphere. She leapt up and grabbed Leo away from Violette and followed her action with a swift slap.

"Sylvie." Jacob was angry. "There's no need for that," he chastised her severely and lifted Violette protectively into his arms.

Sylvie, cradling Leo, made no response for a moment. Then she looked venomously at Jacob. "You don't care about him at all. You're not interested in him. All you care about is her. That little girl." She strode out of the room, carrying a now wailing Leo with her.

Jacob looked helplessly at a pensive Princesse Mathilde and shrugged.

In the summer of 1939, when Leo was eighteen months old and his dark hair had been transformed into a blond mop, Sylvie got it into her head that she would take him to Poland. She wanted Babushka and her grandparents to see him. Perhaps she could even bring Babushka back to Paris with her so that she could look after Leo as she had looked after her and her brother. No amount of argument from Jacob—no considered analysis of a Europe marching inexorably into the arms of war, no tirade about the fact that Poland stood directly in the path of Hitler's call for *Lebensraum,* living space— could deflect her from her aim.

Poland would stand up heroically to Hitler, Sylvie felt. And in any case didn't her native land now have the backing of the British, who had promised to keep her safe against German aggression?

"But it's ludicrous, Sylvie. You don't even know if the woman, this Babushka, is alive," Jacob said for the umpteenth time.

"She's alive. I know," Sylvie said firmly.

Over the months, as her figure had returned, Sylvie had grown even more beautiful than she had been before the pregnancy. Her eyes had a peculiarly deep luster as if their light came from some stormy ethereal place. Her movements were slow, languorous and her skin glowed with an inner fire. On a number of occasions, Jacob had not been able to prevent himself from touching her, from stroking the golden blaze of her tumbled hair. Normally she paid no attention. Once she had looked at him as if he were a stranger and offered him her lips. There was a nascent hunger in them and Jacob kindled it. They had begun wildly to make love. At the last moment, she had stopped herself and walked abruptly away from him. He had driven dangerously fast to the Rue Saint-Denis and for the first time obliterated his desires in the arms of a prostitute.

But Jacob's thoughts these days were decidedly not with women. The British Prime Minister, Neville Chamberlain, together with France's own Daladier might have thought they had appeased Hitler at Munich in October 1938 by sacrificing Czechoslovakia to Germany. But Chamberlain's proclamation of "peace in our time" had an increasingly hollow ring as 1939 unfolded. Jacob, in any case, had never believed in it. The appeasing forces were merely deluding themselves, happy to turn their eyes from what to nearly all now seemed inevitable. Hitler would go to war to impose his dream of a Nazi New Order.

Refugees from Germany, Austria, Czechoslovakia crowded into Paris in ever-growing numbers. Jacob listened to their tales of concentration camps, of hideous brutality, with barely containable rage. European civilization, he sensed, was nearing its end. He did his best to help in the only way he could. He found jobs, housing, funds, pulled intricate strings to engineer visas and official papers.

The workers' clinic his father had established on the outskirts of Marseilles became, by the summer of 1939, a haven for a group of refugee medics and psychoanalysts.

"Who would have thought," old Dr. Jardine mused ironically, "that I would spend my declining days immersed in the one branch of medicine I feel is utterly alien to me."

Jacob patted his shoulder affectionately. He, Sylvie and Leo spent as much time as they could in the parental home set in the pine-strewn hills above the city. "You may yet change your colors."

Dr. Jardine grimaced as he looked out on the blue of the Mediterranean spread at a distance of miles beneath them. "Never," he said.

But he had given over not only part of his clinic, but much of his capacious home to these colleagues from the East. Leo, toddling in its grounds amidst refugee children, had already spoken his first words of German. Meanwhile Madame Jardine organized the increasingly complex running of what was an ever-expanding household. Her face, despite her years, still had the delicacy of the porcelain dolls she so loved, but as the July days rolled on, it took on an increasingly preoccupied air.

"Your father is not well, Jacob. He's working too hard. I'm worried about him. I want him to come to Portugal with me next week. I wish you would all come. Speak to him, please."

"I will, Maman." Jacob looked at his mother and for the first time noticed the strain in her features, her sudden frailty. He hugged her. "You know how grateful I am to you for all you've done here."

She shrugged and met his eyes. "We must all help in these hard times."

Ever since Jacob had at last married Sylvie, and Madame Jardine's Catholic conscience could be put to rest, an easy understanding had once again developed between mother and son. Jacob had realized that his mother's religious conversion had transformed itself into a frenzy of good works which ran parallel to his father's interests.

Madame Jardine was active in the *Equipes sociales*. She read the Christian Democratic press and if she opened her house to refugees from the East, it was as much in keeping with the dictates of her mentors as in accord with her husband's and son's wishes.

But now, she longed to see her daughter, Nicolette, and her grandchildren. Her son-in-law's business had taken their family to Portugal in the early part of the year. It had always been intended that Dr. and Madame Jardine would join them there for the summer. Madame Jardine had hoped to convince her other children to come along as well. It had been so long since they had all been together. Marcel, her younger son, had agreed, and was already in the house on the Algarve. She and her husband would have been there already too, but Dr. Jardine had postponed and postponed.

"You'll speak to your father, Jacob," Madame Jardine entreated him again.

Jacob nodded. "Straight away."

Early that Friday morning, Jacob drove his parents to the station in Marseilles. A second car followed with their cases. Old Dr. Jardine did not cease listing the things Jacob would have to take care of in his absence until the jostling station crowds made it impossible for him to continue. Jacob boarded the train with his parents and settled them into their compartment.

It was only after he had kissed his mother goodbye and was shaking his father's hand that he was filled with a sudden premonition. His "Don't worry about anything" rang hollow in his own ears. He met his father's eyes and the older man drew Jacob to him.

"I don't worry with you in charge." Dr. Jardine gripped his son's shoulders. "Oh here, I almost forgot. I found this in the library the other day and thought you might want to have it." He reached into his jacket pocket and drew out a small tattered notebook.

Jacob looked at it, opened it. A child's clumsy hand. His own. Drawings of birds. The spread of wings. Then, more sophisticated patterns. His father's.

"Thank you," he said. There were tears in his voice. He saw them reflected in his father's eyes as he waved to his parents through the open window. The train lumbered into action, shivered and chugged slowly away.

"If you can't join us, then try and convince Sylvie to bring Leo." His mother waved, called after him, her voice barely audible in the din.

But Sylvie was wrapped in her own dreams of a return to childhood haunts. She made elaborate plans for her trip to Poland. Caroline would come with her. They would take the nanny. There would be so many bags to carry. She booked their tickets for September. Autumn in the Polish woods. The trees would be russet.

Before Sylvie could make her trip, Hitler's troops had invaded Poland. Their rapid march obliterated much more than Sylvie's plans.

ude!" The word slipped from the nurse's starched lips with the force of an expletive.

Jacob Jardine followed the line of her gaze and saw it rest, as if transfixed, on his penis. He almost grinned. There it was: his telltale mark, plain for all to see. His circumcised penis. His father's concession to his grandmother. Jacob's insignia as a Jew. He might well think of himself as a Frenchman. But the Nazis summarily classified him otherwise, identified him with a category they considered subhuman. The world in a foreskin.

"Fräulein Kalb"—Dr. Schrader's tone was the closest Jacob had yet heard it to a bark—"you will see to the patients in the infirmary now." The German doctor ordered the nurse from the room and himself quickly administered the tetanus injection to Jacob. With swift, sure movements, he cleaned the surface wound on Jacob's leg and bandaged it. "You should have shown me this before."

Jacob shrugged. "There were more pressing cases."

He looked at Lieutenant Schrader. They were of a height, of an age. For three days they had worked nonstop side by side in the infirmary of the POW camp and Jacob knew, whatever the color of Schrader's uniform, that he was not the enemy. He was simply a harassed doctor trying to cope with too many patients under difficult conditions. In another life, they would have been friends. Fräulein Kalb was a different matter: she was severely put out to find that the interpreter she had been rubbing shoulders with, the interpreter who was so helpful and knew so much about medicine, was a despicable *Jude*. This time, as Jacob remembered the nurse's astonished face, the grin spread over his features.

Schrader half met him on it. "Ja, ja, it is also funny. A woman looks down at your manhood and all she can say is *Jude*. I know, I know. But these are not ordinary times." He clenched his lips. "If I were you, Dr. Jardine, I would try to be as far away from *us* as possible." He nodded curtly and left the room.

No, not ordinary times, Jacob thought as he donned the prisoner's garb which had been left out for him.

The endless stretch of absurd waiting, that phony war, which had been the French condition for the last nine months, had not been ordinary. France's farcical defensive strategy—which consisted in waiting for the Germans to attack across the supposedly impregnable Maginot Line—was not ordinary. Playing football in order not to go mad—a therapy he had instituted for the demoralized soldiers in his army camp—had not been ordinary. Listening to German loudspeaker exhortations floating across the waters of the Rhône telling you that the Germans were friends, that the French needn't die for Poland or Britain, all while you were playing football was also not ordinary.

Even less ordinary was the unexpected suddenness and unimagined strength with which the Germans had finally advanced. Belgium, Luxembourg, and now France, all toppling in a matter of weeks. Never mind the expensive Maginot Line. Never mind the Rhône. Only that blind bulk of armored cars, lumbering vehicles of destruction.

And bombs. And blood. Blood and dust everywhere. It pervaded his nostrils.

Jacob grasped the set of identity papers and the small gold cross he had taken from Jules Lemaître's pocket. He held them in his clenched fist for a moment and nursed that knot of anger which had been coiling in the pit of his stomach for weeks. With a savage gesture he transferred the papers into his new uniform. Jules was dead, gratuitously killed in that first battle. A waste. He blotted the image from his mind and looked instead at the small picture of Sylvie and Leo he always carried.

His thoughts flew to Sylvie. She had been so shy and then so ardent when she had last come to see him at the camp in February. Like the Sylvie of old, the Sylvie he had fallen in love with. Her voice like quicksilver. Recounting stories: stories about Leo and his most recent pranks; embroidered stories in which the difficulties of everyday life—the search for Leo's favorite bread and pastries, the treks through the piles of snow which gathered in the Paris streets now that there were no men available for cleaning, the heroic attempts to cope with the boiler in this coldest of French winters— emerged as so many hilarious adventures.

One name he didn't know kept recurring in these stories: Andrzej.

"Andrzej? Who is this Andrzej?" he had asked her at one point.

"Oh, you know, Andrzej Potacki. He's a relative of sorts," she had replied casually. She had then turned to finger the bright buttons of his uniform, trace the major's insignia on his chest and had looked up at him provocatively with sea-blue eyes. "Jacob, is there anywhere we can be alone together?"

He had forgotten his question in the course of their subsequent embrace.

During the night in their small, cold hotel room Jacob had begged her to leave Paris, to go to Portugal where his parents had been trapped by the advent of war. Old Dr. Jardine was ailing. He would love to have her and Leo by his side. The family would take care of them. And Portugal would be safe. It was not at war. Jacob urged, persuaded, outlined details. Sylvie simply said, "And you? Then we would be without you." Finally, she had acquiesced. "I'll see."

She had kept from him until the very last the fact that Erich and Anita had been interned as enemy aliens. She was living alone with Caroline and Leo.

"*Jardine, schnell, kommen Sie hier.*" The nurse's brusque tones stirred Jacob from his reverie. Quickly he fastened the last buttons of his prisoner's garb and stepped out into the noise of the crowded infirmary. He looked up and down the length of the room, the men huddled in their beds, the bandages, the moans, the blank staring eyes. There was pain here, but more than that, fear. For a brief moment his own anxiety shaped itself into the figures of Sylvie and Leo, supine on the narrow camp bed.

The next instant the vision was dispelled by Fräulein Kalb's repeated "*Schnell.*" Jacob focused on a French soldier struggling, shrieking. "*Ma main! Ma main! Qu'est-ce qu'ils ont fait de ma main?*" He worked to calm the man whose left arm ended where his hand should have been. But at the back of his mind, his own questions took on the insistence of a refrain. Where were Sylvie and Leo now? Where had the war taken them?

Sylvie was on the road. A road leading from Paris toward Orléans, a crammed road reeking of human fear, carnage, desolation. All of France seemed to have taken to this road. Whole families trudged. Old men, women and children. Vehicles of all descriptions loaded with the possessions of countless houses. Perched atop them, struggling along beside them, their owners or any strays who had been picked up on the way. A human trail moving slowly, silently. Breath was too precious to lose on words.

Sylvie was among them. Yet her shining eyes, the curve of her lips, gave the impression that she was on some other road; that she was engaged on some boundless adventure on a highway heady with the scent of speed and freedom. Sylvie was coming into her own. For once, life around her, outside her, teemed with a drama greater than that of her inner imaginings. It had happened gradually. First there had been the exhilaration of crossing frontiers and taking Leo to his grandparents in Portugal. Then, before she had had a chance to miss Leo, Erich Breuer, the Austrian composer, had returned from the camp where he had been interned. Without his wife. A silent, thin, ghostly shadow, he had immured himself in the coach-house at the back of the garden refusing Sylvie and Caroline's company. Two days later they had found him swinging from a rafter, his face a grotesque mask.

They had stared at him for a long time, Caroline sobbing; Sylvie in fascination. So this was death, she had thought. So simple, so easy. A matter of choice and a bit of rope. Something that could be managed at any time.

The thought freed her. It gave her energy. She embraced Caroline, unseeingly comforted her. From that moment, a change took place in the two women's relations. Solid, sensible Caroline—the steadfast woman who protected Sylvie, who had effectively been her mainstay since her parents' death, who had lived with her, ministered to her during the terrible months of her pregnancy—vanished. It was Sylvie now who made all the decisions, who leapt mercurially into action and tended to a Caroline grown fragile, ineffective.

Something else had come along to change Sylvie. And that something bore the name of Andrzej Potacki. It had been early in the war, a cold, gray, wintry day. For lack of anything to do, Sylvie had taken Leo to the Musée Grevin, the wax museum on the grand boulevard, and then to the café opposite. She had been remonstrating with her son, calling him, as she did, Leo and Tadzio by turn. She had felt more than seen the young man next to her staring. Then he had approached. She saw a shock of overlong blond hair, a narrow, reckless face with a wave of a nose which tilted slightly at its tip.

"*Jestés Polka?*" he asked abruptly.

She nodded.

"*Ja też.*" They were both Poles. He had come home with her, stayed for a few days in the house. It had happened naturally enough. He seemed to have no fixed address and his words, the rise and fall of Polish on his lips, held her rapt. It was almost as if her earlier wish to return to Poland, a wish ruptured by the war, had taken on reality in his presence. The more she looked at him, the more she thought she could see her father in him, or perhaps, a grown version of her brother. That shock of blond hair, the slim, quick, graceful movements. And the language, the soft rhythms evoking memories. Even the content of Andrzej's talk brought back something of those distant years, the unfathomable intricacies of Polish politics, the wish, passionately felt, for a free untrammeled nation, a wish now hampered by the Germans, who through Andrzej took on for Sylvie the vivid reality of personal, not abstract, enemies. She listened to him for hours, played the piano for him, medleys of romantic longing, the pieces he told her he loved best, the pieces her father had loved best. Leo adored his pranks. Sylvie felt completely at home with him.

After a few days, he disappeared. No excuses, no apologies. Just an easy going. Then he came back again. Always, there was a present for Leo, for herself, for Caroline. Some delicacy which was difficult to find. He was mysterious in his movements, unpredictable, but she trusted him instinctively. Let him come and go as he pleased. They had become friends. More than that. There was a kinship between them.

With Andrzej, she was transported back to that reckless, adventurous, untroubled Sylvie of her Polish childhood. It was as if she had never left that confident place in herself, never been sent away to France. She was still romping through fields and forest with her brother, Tadzio, in a space which was full of naughtiness, but was untainted by anxiety, unhampered by any split between wish and action. There was never any question of going to bed with Andrzej, for all his playful gallantry. And the lack of that dimension gave

Sylvie a different strength. Caroline, once Leo had been safely taken to Portugal, almost became the worried child Sylvie and Andrzej had to protect.

Andrzej had not been there on the afternoon of June 9 when Jacques Brenner, still in soldier's uniform, appeared at the house in Vincennes and told them in no uncertain terms that it was time now to pack up and go. Go south.

"And Jacob?" Sylvie and Caroline had asked in unison.

Jacques had shrugged, a new terse authority in his voice. "He's clever enough to find you wherever you are," he had said.

Sylvie had recognized his imperative. They had left the following morning, taking the minimum of luggage and whatever food the house contained. Sylvie was not attached to her possessions. Only her clothes, the stuff of her appearances spoke to her.

By the time they were nearing the village of Dourdan, their car numbered six passengers. They had picked up a woman and two small children, an old priest, and a man in ill-fitting farmer's blue whose legs seemed to be giving way beneath him. His broken French soon betrayed him as a fleeing British soldier. It was through Robbie, for that was the name he gave them, that Sylvie learned of the devastation she was later to understand had been the Battle of Dunkerque, when some 300,000 French and British soldiers fell victim to the lightning attack of Hitler's bombers. The British who survived and had not made their way back across the Channel in fishing or rowboats or anything that floated joined the great exodus to the South. A vast migration of peoples fleeing the Führer's troops.

It was Robbie who, as the sky just outside the village of Dourdan darkened with the thunder of aircraft, pushed them out of the car and forcibly heaved them into a ditch by the side of the road. Bombs hit the ground with an explosive thud. The heavens rained with gunfire. Sylvie, like a small excited boy on his first trip to the cinema, was transfixed by the movement of light, the barrage of sound. She could not keep her head down.

Caroline's nails dug into her arm. Her sobs mingled with the shrieks and screams around them. "We're going to die," she stammered. "Sylvie, we're going to die." The dust which clawed at her nostrils smelled of blood.

Sylvie slapped her angrily. "Of course not, you goose! We're going to live." The words held a triumphal bellow.

❖   ❖   ❖

Late that night, in the eerie hush that follows battle, their car, now windshieldless, shuddered to a halt just outside Orléans. "Damn," Sylvie swore softly. "We're out of petrol."

"That's it, then. We've had it." Caroline trembled.

"Ninny," Sylvie rebuked her. "Everything will be fine. Trust me." She put her arm round her shivering friend. They huddled together and slept. At dawn, Sylvie announced to Caroline that she was setting off in search of gasoline and food. Caroline was to stay with the others and guard the car.

"Robbie should go with you," Caroline protested.

"And help me with his formidable French?" Sylvie looked at her in amazement for a moment and then determinedly set off.

The lines for gasoline were a mile long, a rambling snake gorged with ramshackle vehicles and weary bodies. Sylvie's patience, never notable, snapped. She marched to the front of the line. "I'm with an ambulance of wounded, just outside town. Quick." She said the first thing that came to her mind and did so in an authoritative voice. She placed her two cans firmly on the ground and swinging her hair back, put a hand assertively on the hip of her trousers. "Quick," she repeated.

The attendant looked at her suspiciously and then shrugging, filled her cans.

Sylvie nodded an abrupt *"Merci"* and set off. She suddenly felt gleeful, like an actress at the climax of a successful performance. Survival, she reflected, was a question of instinct. Her instincts would serve her.

When they finally arrived after a maze of stops and starts and detours at the Jardine house atop the hills behind Marseilles, they learned that the Germans had occupied Paris.

Sylvie had two simultaneous thoughts. She must somehow find out if Andrzej had managed to escape south; she must discover Jacob's whereabouts. She gazed out at the deep summer blue of the Mediterranean and played with the ring Jacob had first given her. With a superstitious certainty she knew that while that ring was on her finger, Jacob could not die.

A few weeks after Marshal Pétain, hero of the First World War and now spokesman of defeat, had signed an armistice with the Germans, Jacob was sitting with his friend Jacques in the latter's Paris apartment. They were musing over the events of the past weeks, plotting future possibilities. By a mixture of what he himself termed one-quarter guile and three-quarters luck, Jacob had escaped from his POW camp. Lieutenant Schrader had all too happily—and, Jacob suspected, in full knowledge—sipped the late-night bromide Jacob prepared for him and had slept peacefully while Jacob donned his perfect fit of a uniform. The keys to the jeep were in its pocket and with only momentary trepidation as he shouted a brusque *"Sieg Heil"* to the guard at the camp gate, Jacob had sped into the countryside. In the darkness of a forest, he had abandoned the jeep, begged a change of clothes from a nearby farmhouse, walked, cycled, somehow stumbled his way to a still functioning French field hospital. In the chaos of retreat, no one questioned the origin of an able pair of medical hands.

What went on in those subsequent weeks, he preferred not to remember, certainly not to talk about.

When it was clear to Jacob that the French army was now poised to become an army of collaboration, he deftly disappeared again, and made his way back to Paris, a Paris which had the strange emptiness of a ghost town, where Nazi boots thudded through desolate streets and swastikas flew from the Arc de Triomphe and the Eiffel Tower.

He had been grateful to find their house at Vincennes empty, bearing only the marks of a relatively orderly departure.

Jacques, however, was at home. He had ostentatiously popped a cork as soon as Jacob entered.

"I was saving this last bottle for your arrival." He lifted his long-stemmed glass into the light and looked lovingly at its mellow tones. "From now on all the champagne will go to the Germans," he said ruefully.

Jacob sipped, hugged his friend, smiled. "Seeing you I might almost be lulled into thinking nothing had changed." His eyes clouded over. "But, of course, everything has changed."

"Yes, everything." Jacques laughed wryly. "At last, at long long last, I have a sense of purpose."

Jacob looked quizzically at his friend.

"Come with me this afternoon. A small group of us are meeting at the Musée de l'Homme."

Jacques, a lover of mystery, refused to say any more.

In a dusty back room of the Musée de l'Homme, a handful of men sat talking quietly. Their pallor, their graying temples and erect carriage immediately spoke to Jacob of the senior orders of the civil service. Suspicious glances were followed by a few hushed words from Jacques. They then welcomed him with polite nods.

The oldest of the men rose. In subdued tones, which nonetheless commanded their full attention, he spoke. "There are only a few of us here today. That is how it must be. But I know that across the country other men, other women are meeting, will meet, in mind if not in body. What we have to defend is more precious than our lives, our homes and the soul of France: it is a spiritual freedom, our very image of the world, of life. Our tasks now are not yet clearly defined: but if we are vigilant, we will see them as they present themselves to us. Whatever our daily jobs, our first goal must be to make things difficult for the occupying power, to create networks of subversion, of resistance and in due course to defeat them."

He sat down. The hush in the room was broken by discreet voices, suggestions. Jacob found himself contributing. He indicated the need for blank identity cards, official stamps, papers. So many were fleeing, would have to flee. British soldiers. Refugees from the east.

They nodded. Names were mentioned. Possible contacts. Empty flats. The need for caution.

The group dispersed, singly, inconspicuously.

Jacob, catching Jacques' nod, left the Musée before him. He walked through streets depleted of cars, deviated into a courtyard when he saw a group of Gestapo approaching, made his way by a roundabout route to the café in front of Jacques' apartment. It was one of the few to have reopened since the Occupation. As he sat staring into the street, he noticed a large car pull up in front of the apartment. A woman emerged. He blinked, looked again. With a sense of unreality, he leapt from his chair and dashed from the café.

"Mathilde." He spoke her name softly only when he stood directly behind her. Something in her carriage, in the severe cut of her Red Cross uniform made him refrain from throwing his arms around her.

"Jacob, I hoped I might find you here," she said in the low formal tones of someone addressing a distant acquaintance. But her dark eyes danced.

Only when they had reached the safety of Jacques' flat did they embrace. And Jacob released her only when he found that the embrace, despite himself, was becoming something more than the expression of a reunion between long-parted friends.

The Princesse's mobile features took on a roguish expression. "So, mon ami, I find you alive in all ways."

"In all ways." Jacob, echoing her, smiled a little wistfully.

"And Sylvie, too, I have learned is safe and well and little Leo is in the arms of his grandmother."

Jacob's astonishment was written on his face.

She laughed. "Don't look so surprised, my friend. Yes, I know things. I have friends in many places. Sometimes one's position is an advantage. That is why I have come."

The Princesse paused, foresaw his next question, told him Violette was safely ensconced in Switzerland. She too hoped to be returning there soon. Then she assessed him. He was leaner, his face etched with new lines, a new grimness in his eyes. She knew what they hid. She had seen it herself: the harrowing explosions, the maimed bodies, the fear, the deaths. And now the helplessness of defeat; the realization of what for years they had most dreaded: a Nazi victory and all that it implied.

She knew she could trust him implicitly, that he would carefully consider what she proposed. Yet she didn't know how to begin: it was a matter they had never broached together.

"Jacob." She plunged. "I imagine that you are now thinking of going south, rejoining Sylvie."

Jacob nodded.

She cleared her throat. "I think it might be better if you didn't. Safer. There will be laws soon. Like there are in Germany. Laws against . . ." She stumbled and Jacob finished her thought for her.

"Laws against the Jews. Foreskin laws."

The Princesse flushed a little. Nodded. "They will come, I know. It could endanger you, Sylvie . . . ."

Suddenly Jacob laughed. The corners of his eyes crinkled with a mirth that had become uncustomary. He took the Princesse's hand, pulled her along with him. "You see," he said, taking something from a drawer which seemed to contain nothing other than socks. "I have considered the possibility."

She gazed at what he handed her, read the identity card, "Jules Lemaître." The Princesse smiled. "He is not unlike you." Then, with an air of mystery, she dug into her shoulder bag. "Here is another possibility. *Voilà*, M. Marcel Derain."

Jacob met her eyes. Then, with a sudden sense of the conspiratorial playfulness which had characterized their meetings in an epoch which now seemed an eternity ago, Jacob lifted her in his arms and twirled her round the room. "Which shall it be, Madame la Princesse?"

"Well," she said with a pertness which sat oddly with the severity of her uniform, "you were once both my master and my Jules, so Jules Lemaître let it be."

Jacob nodded, serious again. "And I knew him, worked with him, saw him die. There is no family to speak of."

They were silent for a moment, each remembering their dead. Then they talked, quickly, intently, with the knowledge that time was short. The Princesse told him of a doctor in Montpellier who had set up a clandestine organization which placed Jewish refugee children in remote villages; Jacob might want to work with him. He had only to name her. She had a plan for a link to Switzerland. Money would help. It was available. He listened carefully, told her of Jacques' group, gave her the keys to his house, the consultancy: they might come in useful.

She rose. "Tomorrow morning a friend of mine, the secretary to the American ambassador, leaves for Bordeaux, in an official car. It could be arranged that you accompany him south." The efficiency of her tones masked her fear for him.

"Mathilde." Jacob took both her hands in his, kissed them. "You are formidable."

She shrugged. "We all need to be formidable these days, eh *mon ami?*" They embraced, each realizing but hiding from themselves the knowledge that it might be for the last time.

While Jacob was making his way across the demarcation line into unoccupied France, Sylvie was trailing her way through the narrow winding streets of the old Marseilles harbor area. Sylvie liked the Vieux Port with its congested, cobbled lanes, its dealers in dope and vice and petty crookery of all descriptions. She liked the grubby, sun-tanned children, the lithe youths and dark-eyed secretive girls. She liked the louche, overdressed men, the skimpily clad prostitutes and sailors. The sense of a dense human mass in ceaseless activity, the knowledge of a black market which now burgeoned and thrived suited her. What suited her less was the constant presence of police, who had all too quickly shown themselves to be servants of their German masters.

But what Sylvie liked least of all was the funereal atmosphere of the house on the hill. With Dr. and Madame Jardine gone, the gathered refugees spoke in muted voices, exuded fear and an aura of impending catastrophe. It had all grown worse in the last week, ever since those ridiculous anti-Semitic demonstrations here and in Toulouse. She worried about Jacob, wished he would return and somehow sort them out. Caroline was proving useless. The mood of the house seemed to suit her, as if she too had become a hapless Jewish refugee waiting for doom. For the moment, only Joseph Rittner demonstrated any spunk. He organized the day's activities, made sure the vegetable gardens were tended, reassured the group that their papers would soon be arriving, that they could soon leave, somehow. At least Caroline listened to him, followed him with loyal doggy eyes wherever he went.

Sylvie shivered, despite the blazing sun, as if with premonition.

Money was running out. Old Dr. Jardine's clinic for workers had been closed and between them that group of doctors and psychiatrists seemed to be incapable of earning a penny. And they didn't have ration cards. Which made the garden all the more important. And her own activities. She smiled a little proudly at herself. She was becoming quite adept at negotiating on the black market. Her job at the Hôtel du Midi helped. Soon she might just take a permanent room there. She was sure Madame Castelnau would allow it.

Two days ago she had fired old Dr. Jardine's housekeeper.

The ostensible reason had been money. But Sylvie had another purpose. She had a feeling that in the long term it would be better if no outsider knew what went on in the house. It was too risky. In any event, Caroline could manage things. It would give her something to do, keep her busy.

She herself was more than busy enough. She had found her job just a few days after they arrived, as soon as she realized that she couldn't bear sitting around in the bleakness of the house. She had brushed her hair into an elegant knot, donned uncustomary silk stockings and her celadon suit with its square shoulders. For once, despite the gasoline rations, she had driven rather than cycled into Marseilles and done the rounds of the big restaurants and hotels. She had told them she could play the piano, sing, entertain, act as hostess, had done so in Paris. She named clubs.

At the Hôtel du Midi, the largest of the hotels in the Vieux Port, she had struck it lucky. Madame Castelnau had lost her husband a year back; her son, who managed the dusty, rambling hotel with her, had still not returned from the front. She needed help, help with clients so she could be freed for other tasks.

Small shrewd eyes had assessed Sylvie from the midst of a plump tranquil face.

"Let me hear you," Madame Castelnau had said and led Sylvie into the bar where an old highly polished piano stood unused. Sylvie had played, a little Mozart, a playful Satie; and sung, some light boulevard songs, a mellow ballad, a risqué wartime number filled with innuendo which had been making the rounds. She stopped short at jazz.

The old woman's eyes had lit up. *"C'est bien.* When can you start?"

"Now, tomorrow," Sylvie had answered. "When you please."

"And clothes? Have you got clothes?" The woman made a suggestive gesture which looked comical on her portly form.

"Some." Sylvie smiled, jubilant.

Sylvie began to play. At lunch in the restaurant, some light classical music in the best of taste. The customers complimented Madame Castelnau, gave Sylvie tips. In the evening, in the bar, a melody of pieces which grew more risqué as the night progressed. By the second week, word of mouth had got round. The Hôtel du Midi buzzed with new clients. *"C'est bien. C'est très bien, ma petite,"* Madame de Castelnau congratulated Sylvie as she watched her daughter-in-law, Nadine, calculating the till receipts. Only the daughter-in-law with her thin, sallow face did not look on Sylvie with benevolent eyes.

Sylvie didn't care. In her third week at the hotel, she saw Andrzej in the bar. It was what she had hoped for. One of her prime reasons for making herself public.

He was waiting for her when she had finished. "I had counted on your finding me," Sylvie said, letting him take her hand and kiss it with that effortless gallantry which he made particularly his own.

"Had you any doubt that I would?" he grinned, his long lips curling mischievously. "I promised you that if you came to Marseilles, I would find you. And I always keep my word."

Sylvie looked happily into eyes of a blue density that matched her own and which stood only an inch or two above hers.

"C'est votre petit frère?" Madame Castelnau interrupted their greeting.

"Oui presque. Almost my brother," Sylvie laughed. Andrzej, a year or two younger than her, looked absurdly boyish.

Andrzej had bowed, then taken her arm and guided her out through the mile of darkened lanes toward a small secluded café.

"You're obviously well, a little tigress in performance." He poured water into her pastis, gave her his familiar crooked smile.

"As you can see." Sylvie's laugh tinkled more merrily than it had done for weeks. "And you, have you found what you came for?"

He nodded mysteriously, offering no explanations. Instead he deflected her with a rebuke. "You're using your name. You shouldn't be. Or Jardine's. At least not publicly, on stage. Tell Madame it's too difficult. Get yourself a professional name, something simple. He gazed at the wine racked behind the bar and grinned with a flash of white teeth. "Latour, that will do. A fine Château. You can't get any more French than that. No one wants Poles, and your husband's family is too well known." He suddenly looked serious. "Has he come back yet?"

Sylvie shook her head, apprehension marking her features.

"Never mind." Andrzej's low staccato raced on. "I'll watch out for you, while I'm here." He stopped her querying interruption. "No questions. But will you do something for me?"

"Of course."

"Good. You can keep secrets, I know." He looked round casually and then presented her with a pretty packet which bore the hallmark of a leading pâtisserie. "It's not for you"—he threw her a dazzling smile—"though I wish it were. Take it to the Seamen's Mission in the harbor tomorrow. Give it to the pastor there, not anyone else. Only him. Ask him if there's anything you can do for him. Tell him André sent you. Got that, André, not Andrzej." He rose. "I have to go now. I'll walk you back to the hotel."

"When can I see you again?" Sylvie asked before he left her. "Where can I reach you?"

"*I'll* reach you." He waved her a cheery goodbye.

Sylvie, looking after him, had thought he resembled nothing so much as a carefree angular youth off on some devilish prank. But she knew, from their previous talks, that beneath the casual manner, there lurked a precise, methodical brain and a single-minded dedication: a dedication to a free Poland.

She thought of all this again now as she approached the white-washed façade of the Seamen's Mission and she clutched her large bag to her side. She smiled graciously at a passing *gendarme*: she had taken to this game of smiling, making a virtue of being something of a local celebrity. It was better than shuffling past the brutes and exuding suspicion.

Then she saw a familiar form coming toward her. She was about to call out "Robbie" when she stopped herself and looked again. The clean-shaven man in the neat blue suit looked and didn't look like Robbie, the British soldier who had driven south with them.

He made no gesture of recognition as she came abreast of him, but when she walked into the mission, he followed her.

"You had me frightened for a moment there, Sylvie. I thought you were going to shout at me in English right in front of the copper. You know they've got orders to round us up."

"I almost did," Sylvie said ruefully. "Stopped myself just in time."

"What brings you here?" Robbie asked.

"I've come to see the pastor." Sylvie looked round. The room was filled with a bevy of men, all of whom seemed to have grown mute with her arrival.

"It's right through here." Robbie sped her up some stairs and then gave her a curious glance.

"No, Robbie, I'm not taking up religion, if that's what you're thinking."

"I'm sorry to hear that, young lady."

A voice with a softly distinct accent interrupted her. Sylvie looked up into a kindly, smiling face.

Robbie coughed. "This lady asked to see you. She's the one I told you about, the one who gave me a lift here."

The pastor ushered her into his office. "And what can I do for you, young lady?"

Sylvie gave him the prettily wrapped parcel, mentioned André's name. She peered inside the box as the pastor opened it, thought she saw a stack of ration tickets, before he casually put the box on his desk.

The pastor assessed her: from behind thick glasses gray eyes twinkled, saw a young woman of no little attraction, and what was it, something else, yes, a childlike impulsiveness. There it was, now. She gripped his hand.

"André said I might be able to help. I should like to help."

The pastor took his time, patted her hand. What had André told her? That young man too was a little reckless. But clever. He had already provided him with some useful tips, not to mention other things. The pastor knew that he was involved in decoding work. There was a group of them in an old château on the outskirts of Marseilles. Caution was necessary, on all fronts. Yet more and more fleeing British soldiers arrived at the mission every night. And money, materials and contacts were necessary if the task of getting them safely back to England were to continue effectively.

"I could, for example, bring you . . . clothes." Sylvie said the first thing that came into her mind. They must need clothes, she told herself. Robbie had new clothes.

The pastor smiled. "That would be useful." He decided he would trust the young woman. Her instincts were good. He had learned to make snap assessments himself in the last few months. "But you mustn't come here." He coughed, twinkled. "People would begin to wonder what a delightful young woman like yourself was doing in a mission which caters to vagrants and down-and-outs."

"Oh, I'm very charitable," Sylvie countered impishly and then grew serious. "But, you know, you can always send people to me. I see a lot of people in my work, a lot of men in particular chat to me." She said it matter-of-factly, with no trace of vanity.

"I can well imagine," the pastor murmured. He coughed. "That, too, could have its uses. Though you must be careful, young lady. Many people now are quite happy with the situation, think France is safe, at peace. They may not look kindly on the help you're giving us."

Sylvie nodded sagely, as if she fully understood his meaning. She didn't until after she had spoken to Robbie, who was waiting for her by the door of the mission. He explained to her that he would be leaving France in a few days' time, that he wanted to thank her. As she left the mission, it suddenly came to her what the pastor was up to. Clandestinely returning soldiers to Britain. The thought made her skin tingle. It made her want to help him all the more.

The weeks passed. Sometimes to Sylvie the war seemed simply to be an elaborate game of hide-and-seek. A game she enjoyed above all others. She had learned not only how to barter for ration tickets but where to get counterfeit supplies. She made forays into houses she could only imagine were criminal, as well as visits to wealthy mansions. She became increasingly adept at dressing down or dressing up, one moment a streetwalker, the next a lady of rank. She passed packages, papers, books, newspapers, all containing illicit materials, and sometimes information, without batting an eyelid, only with a little pleasurable increase in her pulse rate. She still smiled at the police.

It occurred to her that the art of counterfeiting must be the only thriving one in this period. It was an art which exhilarated her. An art not so different, though more valuable, than stealing apples in the marketplace.

Andrzej was behind some of her activity. He had come only once more to the Hôtel du Midi to hear her sing. More often she would find a note, couched as if it were a message from an ardent admirer, left for her at the hotel. "Mademoiselle, your singing is a delight. I would so like to express my regard personally. Might you consider meeting me at the Café des Quatre Sous on Wednesday at 4:00."

The first time, the note was signed "André Philippe." After that the names changed, but she always knew it was him. Andrzej gave her tasks. She proved efficient at them. They grew in riskiness. The greater the risk, the happier Sylvie was. Only once had she almost been caught out. She was picking up a newspaper left on one of the hotel bar tables, which she knew had been left for her.

"I wanted to see that." Nadine, Madame Castelnau's daughter-in-law, had all but torn it out of her hands.

Sylvie had stilled her initial anger and smiled. "Oh please, Nadine, I only have half an hour before my next act. I'll give it to you then." She had raced up to her room, heart in mouth, taken out the offending envelope, and in less than the promised time returned the paper politely to Nadine. She didn't like that woman.

One night in the bar of the Hôtel du Midi, Sylvie was idly sipping her between-sets drink and chatting to the bartender when the drift of a conversation at a nearby table made her prick up her ears. Two men talking, one stroking his moustache over moist reddened lips. "Tomorrow, tomorrow morning will see the end of all that. The *Rosbifs* and their charming pastor have been getting away with things for too long." He banged his fist on the table and then catching Sylvie's glance winked at her lasciviously.

She gave him one of her cool professional smiles, but her mind was aflame. The pastor, the mission. A raid might be imminent. She must warn him. There was no one else the man could be referring to. She glanced at her watch. Five minutes before her next set, ten at most. And it would be courting trouble to try to get to the mission so late. What could she do?

Sylvie sauntered slowly but deliberately through the crowd toward the door.

"Where do you think you're going?" An irritated voice stopped her. "You're on in just a minute." Nadine tapped her pencil sharply against the till.

Sylvie swallowed an expletive. "I'm just going up to my room to check on the lyrics for a new song I want to try out," she said sweetly.

She tripped lightly up the stairs and raced to her room. Hastily, she scrawled a note, folded it into the first book her hands fell on,

André Gide's *Les Faux Monnayeurs*. Then, down the stairs and out
the door. "A breath of fresh air. That's what I need," she said to no
one in particular.

At the hotel door, she paused. Whom to trust amidst this gaggle
of urchins and night strollers? She called to a young boy with a
peaked hat and fixed him with stern eyes. "Take this to the mission
for me. Half your money now"—she pulled out a hundred-franc
note—"half when you get back."

The boy grinned, his face a mixture of cunning and greed. *"Bien
sûr, mademoiselle. Tout d'suite, mademoiselle."* He sauntered off.
Sylvie allowed herself only a moment in which to look after him,
before taking a deep breath and letting the hotel doors enclose her
once more.

She couldn't sleep that night. At the first light of dawn, she pulled
on the trousers she had taken to wearing in the daytime in order to
conserve her existing clothes, and made for the mission. The youth
hadn't come back for the second part of his payment, and she had
no idea whether her note had reached its destination.

The sky was a milky gray, the harbor only beginning to struggle
into morning life. Only the pavements still teemed with yesterday's
litter and seagulls aggressively asserted their rights over the remains
of the night. A slow-moving sailor desultorily kicked an empty box
of Gitanes aside and looked out on a placid sea. Sylvie carried her
shopping basket. She had an excuse ready, if she were stopped. She
wanted to be first in line at the butcher's. According to the rationing
calendar, it was a meat day. She had missed the last.

And then, as she was nearing the mission, she saw them. A group
of eight gendarmes making their way determinedly toward their joint
destination. Sylvie gazed into the murky water which lapped at the
odd array of skiffs and yachts and feluccas moored closest to shore.
With a sudden frenzied energy, she screamed. A resonant heart-
stopping shriek. And then another and another. She looked round
her wildly. She could see windows opening, heads bending to the
scene. She hoped against hope that from the midst of the slumbering
mission, too, someone would hear her cries.

Still screaming, Sylvie raced toward the policemen. "Come, you
must come." She pulled the first one along with her. "Quickly.
There's a soldier in the water. A dead soldier," she howled. "All
bloated. Horrible. Quick." They followed her suspiciously.

"Look, there." Sylvie pointed to the edge of a boat where something bobbed rhythmically. She shrieked again. "The poor man. You

must do something. You must get him out." She tugged frantically on the sergeant's arm.

The men stared into the water. "There's nothing there," one of them murmured. "She's imagining it."

"I'm not imagining it," Sylvie bellowed. "I saw him, I tell you I saw him. Maybe he's floated under the boat." She started to cry, great deep sobs which shook her frame.

"Can I help, gentlemen? Can I be of any use? The lady seems troubled." The pastor was at her side, concern wreathing his gentle features.

Sylvie continued to sob, but from the corner of her eye, she saw the looks of consternation passing amidst the policemen.

"She's mad," one of them muttered. "She says there's a dead man in there."

The pastor shook his head sadly. "A poor old derelict, no doubt. They do throw themselves in from time to time. Come, my dear"— he took Sylvie's arm—"let these gentlemen see to all this and let me find someone to take you home. A nice hot drink and you'll feel better." He led Sylvie away. When they were at a little distance from the police, he winked at her, "All safe, my dear. We're ready for them."

From the midst of what were now genuine tears, Sylvie returned his wink.

Exhilarated and triumphant, she made her way back to the hotel by a circuitous route. There was a note waiting for her. She tore it open rapidly. "Even the execrable *café national* is not too bad at Le Petit Poucet. Meet me there today at noon? Antoine."

Andrzej. Sylvie smiled to herself, changed quickly and rushed to the Boulevard Dugommier. Andrzej wasn't at the bar yet. She sat down at a small back table which she knew he would prefer and waited.

Two cups of liquid—which bore no relation to coffee but which tasted only mildly of acorns—later, there was still no sign of Andrzej. Sylvie began to fidget. Andrzej was normally punctual. She sipped some water and tried to still a nagging worry. There was nothing wrong. He had only been delayed. But the mixture of waiting and worry collided in her with another, a deeper anxiety. Jacob. She had still had no word from Jacob. Sylvie pushed her chair violently back from the table and signaled to the waiter. As she counted out some change, she asked, "There hasn't by any chance been a message for me from Monsieur Antoine?"

"Are you Mademoiselle Sylvie?"

Sylvie nodded.

The old man laughed. "You should have said so sooner. He's been delayed. He wants to know if you can manage a picnic. On Sunday. Meet him at the turn-off to Bertin's farm at nine. And he says to bring as much food as you can in your bicycle basket. It's a party."

Sylvie suddenly giggled. "You men, you never seem to have time to do any shopping."

"*Et c'est comme ça.*" The waiter shook his head sagely and watched her saunter gaily off.

Sunday dawned with a crisp autumnal clarity. Sylvie, her bicycle laden with two baskets, wound her way slowly over the hills toward Bertin's farm. She had woken with a flash of ill temper. She knew what lay at its root. They had been expecting her today at the house on the hill and Caroline's displeasure on the telephone when she had announced she wasn't coming had irked her. Irked her doubly, because even if she had made the visit, she would not have been able to bring any more than extra ration tickets and the continuing promise of suitable papers for any of the inhabitants. Despite her growing range of contacts, this was still something which eluded her.

She would tackle Andrzej on the question today. He *must* be able to help. And help with locating Jacob. Despite herself, worry about him encroached on her consciousness with increasing frequency. If only she knew where he was. If only she could send him one of the photographs she had received of Leo. Other women she knew had had letters from husbands who had been taken prisoner. But for Sylvie there was still no sign. Today. Today there would be a whole day to talk it over with Andrzej and see what could be done.

Sylvie slowed down to let a truck pass and then, the wind in her hair, sped down the final incline before the turn-off to Bertin's farm. She scanned the countryside for Andrzej, but there was no sign of him. All she could see were two figures busy with the vines in a nearby field. She turned off the road and waited, hoping he wouldn't be too long. And then suddenly, she heard a rustle and he was there, leaping out of a roadside gully, embracing her, kissing her on the lips with a ferocity which confused her. She drew back.

"Quiet, Sylweczka." He held her to him, whispered in her ear. "Today we're lovers. You know how to treat a lover. Especially one who might be being watched." His eyes laughed as he stroked her chin playfully. "The name by the way is Guillaume Pacquette. Got that?" He kissed her again, with a great show of passion, but his lips were oddly impersonal.

Sylvie grinned and only then noticed that his left arm was in a cast. Her concern formed itself into a question which he stopped. He nuzzled her hair. "Don't worry. Just a little veteran's paraphernalia. Guillaume has been in the wars. And if you look over his shoulder, you'll see how those two over there are distinctly interested in his lovemaking. The Gestapo are sometimes found to be wearing strange uniforms these days. So another embrace, please. Make it look good, Sylweczka."

Sylvie giggled. "And here I thought we were going on a picnic."

"We are. Of sorts. A picnic with a purpose." Andrzej gave her a mischievous glance, pulled his bicycle out of the gully and tried to strap one of her baskets onto it. Sylvie helped him solicitously, letting her hand linger on his shoulder.

"I know the most wonderful picnic spot. Stream, woods, fields. It's only about twenty kilometers away."

Sylvie's face dropped.

"All for a good cause," Andrzej nuzzled her ear again and whispered.

They set off at a leisurely pace, pedaling over hills, coasting down steep cypress-clad inclines, stopping occasionally for a drink, always ostentatiously playing the lovers Andrzej had designated them as. The roads, as the morning progressed, held their usual Sunday complement of cyclists and walkers and Sylvie began to feel she was playing to an ever-growing audience.

At last, when the sun stood high in the sky they turned off on to a small dirt road which led only to a field and beyond that into a dense wood. Where the grass met the trees, they spread the blanket Andrzej had brought and rested.

"Are you going to tell me what all this is about?" Sylvie asked as she handed him a glass of wine.

"About?" Andrzej looked at her impishly. "Why, it's about a little innocent lovers' outing, perhaps a little foray into the woods for mushroom picking. And for picking up other wondrous produce of the forest."

"Is that all?" Sylvie's tone was skeptical.

"That's all you need to know, my pretty one. Aren't you enjoying yourself?"

Sylvie gave him a little girl's grimace.

He raised his glass to her and then reached to caress her hair.

From the corner of her eye, Sylvie saw two men walking their bicycles toward the top end of the field. She smiled, brushed Andrzej's cheek with her lips.

When the men had disappeared over the crest of the hill, Andrzej rose. "Now put your arm around me and we start on our mushroom picking. Lots of mushrooms and even more cuddles." He embraced her again, his free arm moving up and down her back. But his eyes were scanning the middle distance and the new tension in his body had nothing to do with the proximity of hers.

After the clear sunshine of the field, the dense woods felt somber. They stooped every so often to pile mushrooms into one of the baskets. Andrzej was silent, sniffing the air around him as if he were following a mental map. The springy carpet of earth and moss gradually brought them to a little rivulet. Andrzej's face lit up. He quickened his pace. They followed the winding of the stream to a small clearing dominated by an ancient cypress.

"Here, Sylvie. What do you say? It's a fine spot for a picnic." Without waiting for her to reply, he spread the blanket beneath the old tree. While Sylvie laid out the food she had brought, she saw Andrzej scatter an obscure heap of dried leaves and branches and glancing furtively around him, bring out from the loosely piled earth a rectangular case. He opened it quickly. Sylvie's breath caught. A wireless transmitter. And then another. Small. No more than thirty centimeters wide. For a moment he met her eyes. His own were gleaming. Then with deft movements, he took a tiny screwdriver from his pocket and dismantled one of the radios. Valves and wires disappeared amidst the copious harvest of mushrooms in the basket. Andrzej gave her one of his reckless smiles, swallowed a few mouthfuls of food and then urged her off the blanket which, neatly folded, now served to cover the second radio and the remains of their food.

"So this is what you call a romantic picnic, my poor little wounded hero?" Sylvie teased him in a whisper.

"A romantic *Polish* picnic." He squeezed her hand. "Brilliant, aren't they? Have you ever seen anything so small? Perfect. Made by Polish hands." His tone changed. "When we get back to our bicycles, the baskets go on mine. If by any chance we're stopped and anything happens to me, tell the *patron* at Le Petit Poucet."

Sylvie looked at him seriously. "Nothing will happen. But we take one basket each, otherwise it looks odd. And if we're stopped, let me do the talking, Guillaume Pacquette. Your French still leaves something to be desired."

"Oui, Mademoiselle Latour," Andrzej bowed, chuckling. "And don't forget, we're still lovebirds."

Their bicycles lay innocently where they had left them. No one was to be seen in the surrounding fields. Gaily, they strapped their baskets onto their bikes, adding the bathing suit Sylvie had brought, some tools, an empty bottle, into the general jumble. They set off whistling.

Three kilometers along the road in the dip of a hill they suddenly saw a straggling line of vehicles and people. And police.

"Damn," Andrzej swore beneath his breath. "A security check." He glanced quickly at the lie of the land on either side of the road. "Shall we try and get round?"

"Too late," Sylvie murmured. Two more cyclists were gaining on them from behind. They looked eerily like the two men she had seen in the vineyard earlier. "Just remember to act the wounded soldier," she said to Andrzej sternly as they neared the roadblock.

No sooner had they joined the line than Sylvie put her arm round Andrzej and started to grumble in a voice loud enough for all in the vicinity to hear. "It's terrible. You fight for your country. Get wounded. And they still harass you at every turn. It's not fair." She turned to the man nearest to her, an old farmer. "He's just out of bed, you know, his first outing. Poor thing. Here, Guillaume, drink this." She passed Andrzej a flask of water. "He looks awfully pale, doesn't he?" She looked for confirmation to the others.

Andrzej did indeed have the grace to look pale. "I'm all right," he murmured. "Ça va, Sylvie."

"Poor darling." She kissed him lightly. "Does your arm hurt? Here, let me hold your bike. Why don't you go and sit down by the side of the road, over there."

Andrzej was about to comply when a voice from the front of the line rang out, "Come here, you two, you can have my place. I'm not in a hurry. Here, let these two go first," the man who had an austere wrinkled face addressed the motorist and two other cyclists in front of him with an air of authority. "The boy's not well. He needs to get home to rest." He dropped his own bicycle by the side of the road and came to take one of the two Sylvie was holding. Then he urged them both to the front of the line.

"Oh, vous êtes trop gentil, monsieur. Too kind," Sylvie thanked him. She kept one hand on her bicycle and one protectively on Andrzej's shoulder. When they reached the police, she carelessly all but dropped her bicycle on the gendarme who asked her for her papers. He looked at her *carte d'identité,* cursorily, glanced at her face and waved her through.

Sylvie took hold of her own bike and Andrzej's. "He's not feeling well," she said to the gendarme. "His arm, you know." She gave him a sweet smile which bore a trace of pride and waited impatiently while the police examined Andrzej's papers. This time the check was more thorough. Andrzej's identity card was passed from one gendarme to the next and finally to a third. Sylvie's pulse raced. She felt her knees growing weak. They couldn't be stopped now, not after she had got through with the radios. *"Quand même,"* she heard herself addressing the gendarmes, *"vous n'allez pas lui faire des problèmes quand il est faible comme ça."* She looked into the tallest policeman's eyes and tapped her foot impatiently.

The man, looking a little shamefaced, motioned Andrzej through.

Sylvie patted him maternally on the back. *"Ça va, cheri?"*

Andrzej nodded.

They did not speak until they had pedaled for some ten minutes; then Sylvie pulled off the road. "I have to stop for a moment. I'm exhausted."

Andrzej grinned. "Hardly surprising, Sylweczka. After that grand performance.

"Did they suspect you were you?"

He shrugged. "They probably put up the block because they found out there was a drop the night before last."

"A drop?"

"Some goodies from the Brits. Our basket contents amongst them."

"I see," Sylvie breathed. "So that's who you work for."

"I work only for Poland." He flashed her a dark look and then burst into laughter. "And *you* are a distinct asset, my Sylweczka. But we have to get on. Otherwise those two thugs who were behind us will catch up."

"Thugs?"

"SS. They daren't make themselves public since this is supposed to be Pétain's Free and Independent-of-the-Germans France." He chuckled grimly. "But they're here and a good half of the French police are in cahoots with them. And if we don't carry on, we may find them on top of us. Which wouldn't be pleasant. Don't worry, Sylvie." He intercepted her frightened look. "They haven't got much on me yet, particularly since our baskets are still with us. And they'll want more before they pounce. You, my dear, have been more than a perfect foil, a lover beyond any suspicion." For good measure, he gave her a kiss.

She left him at the gateway of a large house outside Marseilles.

It was only as she was making her way back to the Hôtel du Midi and reviewing the day's events that she considered how odd it was that Andrzej's kisses had never moved her beyond the excitement of creating their shared spectacle. Comrades in purpose, Sylvie thought. Her brother in subterfuge. How different it all was from her last meeting with Jacob.

And then she remembered. The day's adventure had obliterated her intention of speaking to Andrzej about locating Jacob. Anxiety suddenly replaced exhilaration. All the nervousness she had kept at bay during the day pounced on her in her solitude. She imagined Jacob in the hands of the SS. Imagined him lying in some dank prison. Almost, she reversed her direction and turned back to find Andrzej. No, she couldn't do that. But tomorrow. Tomorrow, she would leave a message for him. At the café. Jacob had to be located.

And then, miraculously, that very night, as her eyes perused the clientele of the hotel, Sylvie saw him.

The lights were low in the large ballroom of the Hôtel du Midi. On starched white tablecloths, candles flickered, reflected a thousand times in ornate mirrors. She was standing just to one side of the pianist who now accompanied her several evenings a week. As was her way, she let her gaze rest on different men in turn, following the rhythmic dictates of a love song, half spoken, half crooned. One of the men her eyes fell on in this way was sitting alone at a table in the corner of the room. There was something in the set of his shoulders, in the aloof yet intent cast of his head which drew her gaze again. Sylvie missed a beat. She felt rather than saw the slight mocking inclination of his lips. She raced through another number, then cut short her set. Only the sheer habit of professionalism made her slow her steps, exchange a few bantering words with regulars as she moved implacably toward the corner table. Jacob, at last.

He spoke before she did, stopping her exclamation.

"*Mademoiselle, vous chantez fort bien. Je vous félicite.*" With a polite formality, he congratulated her on her performance.

Sylvie was taken aback, at a loss for words.

Then he smiled, the smile she remembered which began in his eyes and gradually worked its way to his lips. Imperceptibly—she was not sure she had seen it—he winked. And again, before she had a chance to say anything, he began to list the numbers he preferred, warming her with his enthusiasm, yet keeping her distant. "And do you know," he continued his litany, "*A l'hôtel d'Algers, je vous ai rencontré?*" He hummed an unrecognizable bar of music and then filled in some words, "*A l'hôtel d'Algers, je vous ai rencontré, c'était minuit, plus ou moins samedi.*"

Suddenly the glaze lifted from Sylvie's eyes. He was making a date with her, tonight, at that vast ramshackle Hôtel d'Algers on the other side of the harbor. It was her turn to smile and she made it a dazzling one.

Of course, she thought as she meandered back to the small stage. Andrzej had more or less warned her early on. It was better if she weren't known as Madame Jardine. Jacob, too, must be aware of that. Or perhaps he had his own reasons. She asked the pianist to play a familiar tune. Then she leaned sensuously against the high-backed piano and improvised, her lips curling lazily over the words which seemed to shape themselves of their own accord:

> "*A l'hôtel d'Algers*
> *dans un autre pays,*
> *je l'ai rencontré*
> *c'était le samedi*
> *l'homme de mes rêves*
> *mais seulement le samedi.*
> *Dimanche il était parti.*"

Jacob, watching her, felt the moisture in his palms. She had understood. But trust Sylvie to take his own coded words, and fling them back at him with a twist in the tail. He loosened his collar a little. Indeed, he would be gone tomorrow. But they had the space of a night. It had been too long, far too long. He had forced himself to wait, stay away from her until everything was in place, until work brought him here. In Marseilles, there was always the danger that he might be recognized and there was no point running unnecessary risks. It had taken a while to establish his new identity in Montpellier, to become Dr. Jules Lemaître with a post at the hospital and some part-time work with a local GP who needed the help. The first gave him access to the dying and with the dying came official papers which could with a little cooperation from colleagues be tampered with. The second gave him access to people's homes, a sense of who was on whose side. Both were useful in terms of the real work—moving Jewish refugees to safety.

He had begun on the Princesse's suggestion by helping Dr. Weill with his children's line to the hinterlands. Then had come the establishment of a line to Switzerland which had, only a few weeks back, taken him as far as Grenoble. He preferred to check out the contacts himself. He found the work exhilarating. Saw that people trusted him, listened without questioning. Were infused with his seeming calm. And now, the establishment of a line through the Pyrenees. It was necessary: anti-Jewish measures were now flowing fast and furious both from the Occupied Zone and in Vichy France.

It was this last line which had brought him here, with papers for three of the inhabitants of his father's house. Perhaps he shouldn't have come himself, but he could no longer stay away from Sylvie. In the last weeks, he had dreamt of her repeatedly.

There had been news of her, of course, through that underground network which now worked with greater efficiency than the telegraph system itself. He had known where she worked, what she was engaged in both at the hotel and in lesser measure in her clandestine activities. That knowledge when it arrived had fueled his hunger for her and had both fed and assuaged his anxiety for her safety.

And now, here she was. More striking than even his dreams had allowed for. Jacob breathed deeply, as if the air had grown thick. He could smell her, smell that sweet musky scent which lingered around her when she was performing. He tore himself away from it. He must leave before her. At the Algers, they would be safe. He knew the *patron,* knew the night attendant.

Sylvie, gazing in Jacob's direction in the midst of a number, saw an empty chair. Longing swept through her. She had been singing for him and now he was gone. She curtailed the encores she was usually pleased to give and left the hotel just after midnight had chimed. She felt the gaze of Nadine of the hundred eyes, as she had begun to call her, trailing her.

Jacob was waiting for her in the small untidy bar of the Algers. Wiser now, she did not even attempt to greet him. She simply met his eyes, held them. They were so dark. Sylvie shivered. There was something new in them, something intransigent. She took the hand he held out, felt its strength, unfamiliar now. She walked with him past the hotel attendant, who nodded without looking up.

Two endless flights of stairs. An unfamiliar corridor, dimly lit, in which his shadow seemed huge. Who was this man she was following? A whiff of danger, of the illicit, filled her nostrils. It excited and frightened her at once.

Jacob opened a door into a darkened room, lit two candles. They gazed at each other in the flickering light for a long moment.

"Sylvie." It was the only word which passed between them and it was less word than sob. He traced the line of her face, her long graceful neck and then with an abandon she didn't associate with her husband, found her lips. The hunger in him woke her to his passion, centered her own. It was a hunger she didn't recognize in him, a deep ache which she didn't know if she could fill. Yet it reminded her of something, of that unquenchable thirst she had felt in the first days of their affair when she came, a slip of a girl with an inexhaustible excitement, to his flat on the Île Saint-Louis. Past memory flamed present desire. When he pulled her down on top of him in the middle of the soft sloping bed, her mind receded. All she could feel was the unutterable pleasure of this thrusting object which yoked them.

That pleasure for Jacob was haunted by images which pursued him, though awake he was able to keep them at bay. Bodies staring into dusty space on desolate fields; bodies like his now, on their backs, limbs askew; faces distorted by the surprise of sudden death. He turned Sylvie over, buried his face in her breast, thrust, thrust at the pain, urging it to life, purging it in her pleasure. When his cries came, he muffled them in her skin, letting the tears flow instead.

"I've missed you, Sylvie," he said, when breath would allow him. "Missed you too much. I would have come to you sooner, had it been possible."

His eyes when she looked into them were haunted. "Talk to me," she said. "Tell me about you."

He told her what he could, hid more, turned the questions back at her, listened intently, stroked her, her hair, her glistening skin, until she wanted him again and again. In her, he nonetheless evaded her. Jacob has become elusive, she thought, said it to him. He smiled, but his eyes were still. He held her tightly, so tightly. They slept.

When she awoke to the bright Mediterranean light, he was already gone. Only the bed bore the traces of his presence. Sylvie fingered the sheets.

On the single chest lay an envelope. She opened it. A thick roll of money tumbled out and a hasty note. "I will come back as soon as I can. Be well. Be safe. My love."

She still didn't know the name the man she had slept with bore. I am a whore, Sylvie thought. She smiled.

CHAPTER
TEN

*O*n a grimly cold morning, late in the harsh winter of 1941, Dr. Marcel Derain reported to the prison camp of Chambarran outside Grenoble.

The guards were expecting him. *"Ah oui,* Dr. Derain. You're replacing Dr. Bertrand this week."

"Yes, poor old Bertrand is suffering from influenza." Derain wiped the mist off his spectacles with a large handkerchief. "But he'll mend. Another week or so."

The guard glanced at Derain's identification. The man didn't look too well himself. His coat seemed too heavy for his sloping shoulders and he had a vague, preoccupied air, as if the last thing he wanted to do was take over Bertrand's duties. He dragged his feet as they marched toward the camp infirmary.

Derain made his rounds slowly, talking to the patients, dragging his stethoscope or thermometer from his black bag with a bumbling ineptness, bumping mistakenly into a German guard. So it was with some surprise that the Canadian officer in the corner bed found, once his abdomen had been examined, that his blanket was neatly folded over what his fingers quickly ascertained was a sharp-edged file, a set of papers, a length of rope. He listened more carefully to the doctor's rambling words, his tone of innocuous comfort. He was being given sleeping powders, which would also kill the pain, and if he and his fellows wanted to send a word of thanks to the good, but ailing, Dr. Bertrand who had tended to them so well thus far, he could be reached at 17 rue Sebastopol.

The Canadian understood instantly. These were his escape orders. He had a week to make use of the tools. Help would be waiting at the given address. He wondered if Bridges in the next bed, his companion in self-inflicted illness, had received the same instructions. He would find out later. For the moment, he watched the doctor continue his slow, lumbering rounds. Clever, this Frenchman. No one would suspect anything of that clumsy, ineffectual man, whose eyes seemed almost blind behind the thick spectacles.

From the camp, Dr. Derain made his way to the University of Grenoble. In its environs, he began to move more quickly. He had a lecture to give, a stand-in lecture for Dr. Bertrand's anatomy class, and he was already late. With a steady thoroughness, he took the assembled students through the rudiments of the nervous system. When the hour drew to its end, he asked in a mumbling voice that three of the students stay behind. Dr. Bertrand had left some notes for them.

One by one, he addressed the students. The nature of his communication, however, was hardly medical. It contained precise details of time, place and date for the pickup and delivery of a child. As well as a warning. The previous week, the line had been betrayed. Caution was necessary. The passwords must be carefully adhered to. To each student, he clearly enunciated the new sets of questions and replies. To each, he also gave an envelope containing the large sums necessary for the guides.

Then with his slow, awkward tread, Dr. Derain walked the short distance to the Hôtel des Montagnes. It was only as he neared room 418 that his pace changed and he took the thick spectacles from his eyes. He knocked on the door, three quick taps, followed by a pause, then four louder ones.

Princesse Mathilde opened the door and gazed at her visitor with a momentary consternation.

"Jacob!" She closed the door quickly behind him. "Jacob, I wasn't expecting you. What's happened?"

"A little problem on the line." He shrugged. "An informer. I should have suspected. They rounded up one of the guides and two Canadian officers we were moving as a favor to Jean Beaulieu." He anticipated Mathilde's question. "The children are safe."

"And you're here as Derain?"

Jacob nodded. "Old Bertrand has been as compliant as ever. More so. I have his prison round this week." He grinned.

Worry creased Mathilde's features. "You shouldn't, Jacob." She frowned. "It's too risky."

He put his arm round her and smiled his old teasing smile. "Whereas you, Madame la Princesse, do nothing which involves any risk at all." They gazed into each other's eyes and for a brief moment enjoyed the sense of shared action and shared secrets.

For over a year now the clandestine escape route Jacob and the Princesse had established had functioned with only a minimum of hitches. The line moved Jewish children from Paris or one of the notorious internment camps to Switzerland, often passing through Grenoble, a center of Gaullist sentiment and resistance activity, which thus offered a variety of "safe" houses. In Grenoble and its vicinity Jacob worked in the persona of Dr. Marcel Derain. What brought him here officially was the occasional series of guest lectures on neurology he gave at the university at the behest of his old colleague Dr. Bertrand. In Montpellier and the southwest, Jacob went under the identity of Jules Lemaître. Jacob Jardine had now formally been ascertained to have died in action.

The line which ended with the Princesse in Switzerland had thus far transported over one hundred children. Occasionally Mathilde would cross the frontier with her false-bottomed suitcase which contained the large sums necessary for financing the operation and bring one or two children back with her on the train herself. She felt little fear when doing this. Her imposing stature, her title, her unblinking gaze quelled even the most officious guard's queries. And her alibis were always impeccable. There were old sick relatives with grand names to visit in France and the children she sometimes personally brought back with her were pupils for the school she had opened in the Château Valois. She was, after all, not unknown as an educator if anyone cared to check. Nonetheless, she didn't make the journey to France too often. It was safer not to arouse suspicion unnecessarily and jeopardize the entire operation.

Jacob and she had last met outside Grenoble some four months ago. It had not begun as an auspicious occasion. Jacob had just made his way back from Paris across the demarcation line and his distress, however veiled, was evident to her in his every gesture. It took her several hours to extract the full painful story from him.

In Paris he had been to see one of their contacts, Sophie Stein. It was a household which sported the yellow star the Nazis had imposed on the Jews. Like so many others, Sophie had begun by wearing the star because she was a law-abiding citizen and she couldn't believe that the French, her friends, her compatriots, would allow anything terrible to happen to the Jews. When her husband, a foreign Jew, was taken away in October of 1940, she started to realize her mistake. But she didn't want to leave her home. She had two small children and she still hoped her husband would return. Nonetheless, contacted by the underground, she began to work with them, occasionally feeding children into Jacob's network.

Jacob had come to see her while in Paris, because he wanted to convince her it was time to flee south. He had heard rumors which made it clear to him that her time was running out. He arrived too late. When he rang the bell of her flat in the Marais, the Gestapo opened the door. He took in the situation at a glance. Sophie was pressed against the wall, her small daughter in her arms, her son whimpering by her skirts. Blood was running down her face. In front of her there stood a second officer, thin faced, his eyes a cool, callous gray.

"I'm a doctor," Jacob said evenly. "I had a message that a child was sick here."

While he was pulled into the room and then shoved unceremoniously into a corner, he heard the second Gestapo officer mutter, "There will be more than one sick child here unless Mrs. Stein names some names."

"I don't know what you want from me," Sophie mumbled.

With a savage gesture, the German ripped the little girl from her arms and threw her forcibly against the floor. The child howled, struck her head against a table leg, was silent. Jacob lunged forward. "We don't treat people like this in this country," he shouted, landing a punch on the man's chest with all his strength. He felt him fold and then from behind, something struck him at the base of his neck. The last thing he remembered seeing were the small boy's dark eyes weeping silent tears.

He woke in a prison cell. No sooner awake than the interrogation began. Yes, he was Dr. Jules Lemaître. No, he had never before visited the house in question. No, he had no more than the usual animosity toward the Germans, but the Gestapo's behavior toward that woman and her children had been inexcusable. They locked him into a cell again, took away his clothes, his black bag. In the distance, he heard screams, unceasing, intolerable.

Some time later his interrogation was renewed. No, he wasn't

Jewish. The officer must know that only two percent of Jewish doctors were now allowed to practice. So how could he be? A French officer had walked into the room at that point, but his interrogator pressed on. But Dr. Lemaître was circumcised, wasn't he? The men who had stripped him down had noted that. Yes, but the circumcision was hardly religious. Jacob had his story ready. It had had to be performed when he was eighteen, due to an infection. They could check the hospital records. They were on file. He named place and date and then, staring at the French officer, demanded to see a lawyer, demanded to be allowed to ring his colleagues to alert them to his whereabouts. He had done nothing wrong except lose his temper. After his continued insistence, they finally allowed him to phone. He rang Jacques. Within two hours, his release had been arranged. Two hours after that, he ascertained that Sophie Stein and both her children had disappeared.

He left Paris the next day. He knew he had been lucky. The same strings could not be pulled a second time. He chastised himself mercilessly. If only he had come to Sophie's house sooner. If only he hadn't overreacted and punched the officer, then Sophie and her children might still be safe. But in himself he knew that his action had probably only hastened things a little. What he had witnessed was a daily occurrence, an instance of widespread suffering and pitiless atrocity. The only hope for change was to loosen the Nazis' stranglehold on Europe.

By the time he reached the Princesse's address outside Grenoble, he was consumed by a cold, implacable rage. Even after she had extricated the story from him, it maintained its icy grip. *"Eh oui, mon ami,"* she had said to him. "That's what all our efforts are about now. We shall overthrow that barbaric regime. Somehow. Meanwhile you and I play mother and father to an endless stream of frightened children. Hitler's orphans. We do what we can." She shook her head sadly and took his hand, trying to stroke some warmth into him.

He had fallen into her arms as if life lay there. A life which had nothing to do with heinous and random suffering and plots and schemes and the vertigo of changing identities; a life always and ever constrained by the sense that whatever one did wasn't enough; a life lived with death as a familiar. They had spent the night together, made love slowly like old friends who had time on their side. And they had slept, a deep untroubled sleep, a parenthesis in that straining sentence which was war.

As they surveyed each other in the Grenoble hotel room now,

they both remembered that last meeting. A stolen moment which could not be replicated on this occasion. Jacob's time was pressing. He had two more meetings in the hills outside the city that evening. They exchanged the necessary information. Money for the increasingly expensive guides who led the refugees over the precarious mountain passes was unearthed from Mathilde's case. They embraced mutely. And then Jacob walked out into the frosty night.

Two days later, he returned to the camp at Chambarran for the second of the week's routine visits. But something had happened to disturb the routine. Guards at the gate were numerous. He was instantly marched into the Commandant's office, his bag, his coat, his clothes ruthlessly searched. Jacob knew how to read the signs. Beneath the placid, bumbling exterior of Dr. Derain, a little thrill went through him. There must have been an escape. Successful, he hoped. Security had been trebled.

The Commandant looked at him with increasing displeasure as his bag revealed nothing more surprising than the usual doctor's implements. The man scowled. "Dr. Derain, two prisoners have escaped from the infirmary since your last visit. What do you know about it?" The voice which came from the plump face was threatening. He plied at the bottom and sides of Jacob's bag with stubby fingers and then threw it impatiently across the room.

Jacob allowed the surprise to settle slowly on his face and then looked with a fearful man's caution at the Commandant.

"I? I know nothing. How dreadful for you. I am sorry, Monsieur le Commandant." He stooped a little more into his capacious suit. And then he looked directly into the man's eyes, his own sheltered behind the thick spectacles. "Monsieur le Commandant, would a man like me dare to come back into your camp if I had helped an escapee?" A tiny self-derisory smile tugged at his mouth.

The Commandant looked at him closely and then blurted out, "Let him do his rounds."

The officers tailed him. Jacob walked with Derain's blundering countryman's gait toward the infirmary and slowly carried out his duties under watchful eyes. The Canadians were gone. His part of the return favor to Beaulieu was accomplished.

When he left the prison, he made his way by a circuitous route back to the University. From the locker room, he picked up a case and went to the station. The train to Toulouse was on time. Jacob found a seat in the third carriage. As they neared the first stop, he walked slowly to the lavatory. There, he changed quickly into a well-fitting suit; ruffled the pomade out of his hair, so that its tousled curl returned; exchanged thick spectacles for a pair of heavy horn-rimmed glasses; put Derain's papers into a compartment in his case and took out Lemaître's; and donned a soft gray hat. When the train started to move again, he joined the line of newcomers and with a busy, efficient man's brisk pace strode into a different compartment.

As he sat down and pulled out of his pocket an old medical journal, he wondered wryly to himself at the skills war had taught him. Not only him, but countless others. A welter of resources untapped in peacetime. He was continually amazed at people's endurance, their fierce loyalties, the instant, unspoken camaraderie which grew up between strangers engaged in common tasks. He marveled at the ability the war had spawned in all of them for living in the present, from moment to discrete moment, as if the future, a time after the war, was akin to a heavenly afterlife and not part of the continuum of existence.

He was also struck by the reserves of cunning individuals had—a defensive cunning which prior to the war he had seen openly at work only in his patients, who could fabricate endless ploys to keep the integrity of their madness intact. Now he saw instances of that cunning blossoming everywhere—in the rich spontaneous fictions people concocted to get themselves out of a tight spot, in the ingenious games of hide-and-seek they devised, in the subtle ruses and masterly feats of timing. The paranoias of occupation had given birth to countless novelists.

They had also, he reminded himself grimly, given birth to a slew of informers. He must take greater care in the future to guard the network against them.

Nadine of the hundred eyes, sallow-faced Nadine behind her till at the Hôtel du Midi did not like Sylvie. She did not like Sylvie under whatever name she bore, Latour, Kowalska, Jardine. For, oh yes, she knew that Sylvie had several names, and what reason for several names if there was nothing to hide?

Nadine did not like the way Sylvie looked. The way she swung the blonde mane of her hair over her shoulders. The cut of those vampish dresses which clung too closely to her body. She did not like the way Sylvie flounced round the hotel like some *grande dame,* acting as if she owned it, when the fact was the hotel belonged to her mother-in-law and would by rights soon pass down to Nadine and her husband. She particularly did not like the way the attention of each and every man at the hotel, including her husband, focused on Sylvie as soon as she walked into the room.

That was how it began; it was only the start of it.

Her loathing for Sylvie became an obsession. It entered into the realm of madness. She rocked herself to sleep with it at night, detailed its parts in her dreams, woke to the confused throb of it, fueled it with new matter in the course of the long days.

All the lacks in Nadine's own life found their cause, their reason in Sylvie.

And, as is the way of things, what had begun as a pungent private envy took on with the passing months the gloss of a public virtue. Envy rationalized, transformed Sylvie into a public enemy. She became, for Nadine, the focal point of everything which stood in opposition to the reigning moral order of France: the sanctity of family, *patrie*, church. A visible threat, an outsider from the capital with its loose ways, its squalid morality, its lack of patriotic fervor.

From early on in Sylvie's employ at the hotel, Nadine would purse her thin lips in distaste and comment to her mother-in-law, "Maman, don't you think you should tell that new performer to dress with a little more propriety?"

"Mmmnnn," Madame Castelnau would usually mumble obliquely and pay little heed to her.

Or Nadine might say, "Maman, we run a respectable establishment. Just watch that performer sidling up to the men. Why, she's no better than a slut. It isn't proper." She never spoke Sylvie's name, as if her lips might be sullied by the sound.

When, after a time, Nadine's comments had taken on an irritating frequency, Madame Castelnau one night turned on her daughter-in-law. "I want to hear no more about this, Nadine, do you understand? I am in business. Since 'the performer,' as you keep calling her, has been with us, business has been better than ever. We run the most successful bar in Marseilles." She looked shrewdly at her daughter-in-law's narrow, sullen face, her thin, rigid shoulders, and was filled with a sudden repugnance. Why, the girl was now almost thirty and still she had given her no grandchildren. "The customers don't come here to watch you sitting behind the till, you know," she added with a touch of malevolence. "If I were you I would forget about Sylvie and pay a little more attention to your husband."

With as much majesty as her plump frame would permit, Madame Castelnau shuffled away.

Nadine was silent for a few weeks. Then she tried a new tack. "Albert," she said to her husband one night. "You know, I think that singer we employ is Jewish."

"Jewish," Albert said amiably. He was a slow-moving man with soft undefined features. "Why, she's as blonde and blue-eyed as a Bosch goddess." He hesitated for a moment. "And even if she were, what does it matter to us? Maman knows what she's doing." He switched off their bedside lamp. "Now go to sleep and don't worry your head about it."

"Albert, I was in her room the other day, and I found a store of ration coupons." Nadine hadn't meant to confess her prowling, but now that it was done, she rushed on. "She could get us into trouble with the police. We should get rid of her."

"Mmmm," Albert mumbled. A deep snore escaped him.

My husband has the instincts of a coward and a traitor, Nadine thought.

With all the stealth of vengeful envy and the cunning of pettiness, Nadine watched Sylvie, made inquiries, pursued her. She knew Sylvie dealt in the black market, knew she sometimes spent nights elsewhere, knew about the house on the hill, knew Sylvie made regular visits there. What she didn't know was quite what to do with her knowledge. Her loathing of Sylvie was tempered only by a fear of her mother-in-law. She bided her time.

Her time came early in the autumn of 1942. It was then that the step-by-step amassing of anti-Jewish laws, aimed first at refugees, then at restricting the activities of French Jews and turning them into second-class citizens, crystallized into deportation orders which extended to all Jews in France.

Sylvie knew that Nadine of the hundred eyes had all of her eyes on Sylvie. She had even once caught her unmistakably trailing her toward the house on the hill. But with the easy contempt of a woman at once beautiful and fearless, Sylvie could not imagine what Nadine could do to her. Madame Castelnau, she knew, was on her side. In the two years since she had had Sylvie on her stage, her hotel had become one of the most successful establishments in the Vieux Port and one which drew an increasingly select clientele. Various other hoteliers had tried to tempt Sylvie away. Each time, Madame Castelnau had raised her salary, offered her a share of the proceeds. Except on weekends, Sylvie now performed only in the evenings, had her own supporting band, an extensive wardrobe, two of the rambling hotel's best rooms designated for her use. The Hôtel du Midi suited her: she was effectively her own mistress there.

And so Sylvie became only a trifle more vigilant. She had in any case more important things on her mind than Nadine.

Andrzej had disappeared. She had heard nothing from him since the spring. Nor could she make contact with him through any of the usual sources. The secret decoding center where he had worked had been raided. She didn't know whether he had escaped or been arrested. With Andrzej gone, so too was her source of orders. She felt rudderless. And also stricken with worry for the man who more and more had taken the place of her lost brother.

Sylvie wished she could take advice from Jacob, wished he would involve her in the work he was doing. He came to see her, always unexpectedly, every three or six or eight weeks. Every time, just after he came, a few of the changing flow of inhabitants in the house would disappear, a few more arrive. She knew he was involved in the organization of an escape route, but he would never tell her the name he used or where he was based. She had only the number of a *poste restante,* in case of emergencies. Nor, no matter how much she pleaded, would he engage her in any of his work. "It's too dangerous, Sylvie," he would say stroking her skin, so that she curled closer into him, "too dangerous. Who knows what either one of us might say, if we were rounded up, tortured . . ." The phrase, left hanging, always stopped her questions.

Increasingly, their nights were spent in a coupling which left little space for words. It was as if language carried with it the threat of betrayal, while the continuing menace of the war left solace only in the flesh.

With Andrzej gone and Jacob away, Sylvie, outside her working hours at the hotel, now spent more time with Caroline at the house on the hill. There was a good reason for this. In April, Caroline had had a baby. Sylvie sometimes joked to her friend that the baby was partly hers. In any event, its arrival had been impelled by her intercession.

From the very beginning of their stay in Marseilles, Sylvie had noticed that Caroline was nurturing a secret passion for Joseph Rittner, a gaunt Austrian Jew, whose gentle ways and soft speech calmed and ordered the floating and often frightened population of the house on the hill. He was a tall, erect man whose face would have been ugly but for the luminous brown eyes which transformed it and settled it into a precarious beauty. He had large capable hands whose movements reassured, steadied.

Caroline clung on his every gesture, ran to his unbidden command. When after some six months Rittner was still politely addressing Caroline as Mademoiselle, Sylvie decided to do something about it. Life, particularly in these times, was too short for unrequited passions. Then, too, Sylvie felt, Caroline needed some happiness. Over the long years of their friendship, she had grown progressively quieter, as if she were old before her time, as if Sylvie's tumultuous existence displaced her own, made it recede.

Sylvie, when she was not preoccupied with her own needs, was capable of great generosity.

One day, she asked Caroline to come and have a walk with her through the cypress-clad parkland which bordered the elegant old house. She took Caroline's arm and when they had gone a little distance, said, "Caroline, you've been working too hard. Why don't you borrow that blue dress of mine you've always fancied, do your hair and take Joseph to the opera and dinner at Castelmuro's. It'll do you both good to get away from here."

Caroline flinched. "You're mad, Sylvie. It would be too dangerous for him. We might be stopped. In any case," she added softly, "I couldn't ask him."

A note of exasperation crept into Sylvie's voice. "You're in love with him. I know you're in love with him. And you've got to do something about it. You can't just go on and on and on like this. This endless politeness."

Caroline flushed crimson, extricated her arm from Sylvie's.

"Well, say something. Do something. If you can't take him out, invite him to your room. You know he won't take the initiative. He feels he's a guest here, on sufferance, a Jew. Most of the people here think this is your house, you run it, you're the *grande dame.*

"Caroline," Sylvie shouted at her friend who had begun to walk away from her. "Caroline, if you don't do something, I'll talk to him myself."

"You wouldn't dare." Caroline veered round, looked at her friend threateningly.

"I would," Sylvie taunted. "You know I would. I give you a week."

The two women stared at each other, unconsciously assuming the expressions, the very posture which had characterized them as schoolgirls. Sylvie, daring, provocative; Caroline, angry, a little hurt, a little bullish—but suddenly, because of it, because of the taunt, spurred into her former self again. The girl who would take up Sylvie's dares.

A week later, when Sylvie returned to the house, she knew without having to ask that everything had changed. Little secret glances sped between Caroline and Joseph. There was a softness about her friend's lips, a new ease in her movements.

"Well?" Sylvie stole a moment with her friend away from a meager lunch table which that day catered for eight.

"Well." Caroline squeezed Sylvie's hand, flushed crimson and then hugged her. "Oh Sylvie, he's wonderful, it's wonderful."

"Good," Sylvie grinned. "You deserve a little happiness."

The little happiness had blossomed. It had lightened the atmosphere of the house. Caroline now bustled, spreading hope amidst the fleeing transients, trying to rid them of the past nightmares which traveled with them, trying to lessen their fears of an apocalyptic future. Her energy grew at the pace of the baby within her, fueled by Joseph's steady smile. She had never, Sylvie reflected, been so beautiful.

Even on that Sunday when they learned that Walter, one of the refugees who had been longest in the house, was dead, Sylvie reflected, Caroline had only trembled a little, and then rushed to assuage the fears of the others. Walter, having at last built up his precarious strength enough to make the arduous and treacherous journey through the Pyrenees, had taken his own life, just as he had almost reached the last hurdle in his trajectory toward America, the new world.

Joseph, that afternoon, had told them one of the many stories he slowly unfurled through the long days of the house's enclosed existence. His arm lightly on Caroline's shoulder, he had recounted the story of a little German boy with a great love of books. A gentle little boy, who as he grew into youth and manhood had gradually collected a vast treasure trove of books. A library of precious tomes which charted the history of Europe—arcane editions, picture-laden folios, recondite philosophy texts, fictions, cabbalistic scripts in German and French and Greek and Hebrew and Italian, the languages he had learned. A library which in time began to include slim volumes of essays, gemlike epigrammatic narratives which bristled with insight and gnomic utterances. His own.

On the day when Hitler and his henchmen decided that books, with the exclusion of *Mein Kampf* and its ilk, were to be burned as repositories of Semitic decadence, the precious library found its place amidst the flames. Its owner, physically and morally beaten, unable any longer to earn his living by publishing, accepted the invitation of friends to France. He mourned his library, a little world which encapsulated a vastness. He tried to do battle against its destroyers in the only way he knew: by writing. But sadness engulfed him, deflecting his efforts. His friends told him stories of a new world, a world where he could rebuild his collection, but his loss trailed him, made him heavy so that he dragged his steps ever more slowly. And it seemed to him to be not only his loss, but the world's. The loss of centuries of civilization. His friends counseled hope, drew pictures of a civilization built afresh, a better world. But he could only look at them blindly, through the mists of his own pain. On the precipice of the new, he decided he could not bury his bitterness at the loss of the old. So in generosity, he flung himself backward over the precipice, to be buried with the past and the culture he mourned. So as not to contaminate the spirit of the future for others. For us.

The nine pairs of eyes focused on Joseph were wet.

"That was Walter's story, wasn't it, Joseph," Sylvie murmured. "I never knew . . ."

He smiled at her gently from his gnarled face, then lovingly stroked Caroline's stomach. "The angel of the future. It is our task to prepare for it," he said softly.

Caroline glowed.

In April the baby had come, a tiny red-faced girl with vast brown eyes. They named her Katherine. Joseph had delivered her himself and Sylvie, watching the proud father and attentive mother, had thought of Leo, of Jacob. Though she was hardly prone to self-reflection, Sylvie knew that she had robbed Jacob of something in those early days of Leo's life. She would make it up to him, she thought with a sudden pang. When the war was over. When the *sales boches* were defeated and Poland and France were free. She missed her little boy, missed Jacob, missed Andrzej.

Meanwhile, there was more work to be done than ever. Caroline could no longer run the large house, make the countless necessary visits to Marseilles, get in supplies, deal with petty officials, barter. Everything grew scarcer and scarcer as the French economy was bled dry to support the occupiers and their war machine. Everything more and more difficult. And paying for help could prove treacherous in this clandestine household. No matter how much Joseph and the guests helped, the burden now fell on Sylvie. She didn't mind.

Caroline was happy. And the two of them had grown closer than ever. At every turn, Caroline looked to Sylvie—for advice on how to deal with the baby and in order to share her pleasure in that small life. A small life which had come amongst them through Sylvie's intercession.

Sylvie reflected on all this as she sped toward the house on the hill early one September morning. She was pleased with herself. She had managed to get, amongst other things, a whole side of lamb and the soap so essential to little Katherine's diapers. She was looking forward to her visit. Every three days seemed to bring vast changes in the tiny creature.

The drive leading to the house had its usual peaceful grandeur. Tall poplars huddled against blue sky and then the house appeared, etched on a precipice, behind it the vast stillness of the sea. As always there was a hush about the place and Sylvie, thinking nothing, leapt out of the car. Suddenly she heard a rustle behind her. She turned and saw a small shy boy emerging from the bushes.

"Gabriel, tu joues cache-cache?" she smiled at the boy. He had arrived only two weeks before, a timid creature with those haunted eyes, too old for his years, which she now knew as the mark of the refugee. She didn't want to know what those eyes held, but she liked this little curly-headed boy from Berlin with his broken French. She held out her hand to him.

As he approached, she saw that he was crying. "What's wrong, Gabriel? Have you hurt yourself?"

He shook his head. Sylvie gazed at him and then suddenly her skin prickled. "The others. Where are the others?" she asked, her voice thin.

"Partis. They're all gone. The police came. There's only me." Tears rolled silently down his thin cheeks. "I was playing in the park. Two days ago. When I came back they were piling them into a big van. I hid."

Sylvie held him tightly. Her mind raced. "Come with me." She pulled Gabriel after her toward the house. It was locked. "You've been sleeping out?" He shook his head and pointed to an open window. "Good, clever boy." Sylvie patted him as she unlocked the door.

The elegant ordered rooms looked as if they had been struck by a tornado. Books, papers, chairs were strewn everywhere. Madame Jardine's antique porcelain which had graced the airy sitting room lay in smithereens. Sylvie looked round with a shudder, refusing to allow her mind to dwell on the scene which had led to this devastation. Briskly she locked the door behind her, all the while making soothing noises to Gabriel. But her mind sped, tumbled, balked. Where had they all been taken? Where was Caroline? Little Katherine?

First things first. Gabriel had to be taken care of. Sylvie raced the Citroën down the winding roads to Marseilles and parked behind the Hôtel d'Algers, her and Jacob's meeting place. She knew that the owner must be one of the links in Jacob's operation. Gabriel would be safer here in the short term than with her. Old Vassier would know, would understand what needed to be done. She asked to see him alone and was shown into a dusty office which smelled of stale tobacco and musty socks. Vassier rose with the agility of a younger man from his deep leather chair. His wrinkled tortoise face was as ever contemplatively benign and betrayed nothing of his thoughts.

"Ah, Mademoiselle Latour. Always such a pleasure for these old eyes to see you."

Sylvie smiled briefly and then took on a businesslike tone. "Monsieur Vassier, a young cousin of mine has been landed with me for a short time. I think he would be happier here with you than at the Midi, with all its noise." She lowered her eyes demurely. "You understand. In my position . . . Could you look after him for a few days?"

"Why, of course, my dear." Vassier patted her hand paternally.

"He'll be sent for very soon," Sylvie added, letting the sentence hang.

Vassier passed a plump hand over his shining scalp, as if it still held a head of hair. "Don't worry, my dear. Just bring him to Madame."

Sylvie went to fetch Gabriel and when she returned Madame Vassier, a tiny birdlike woman, was waiting for them in her husband's office. "How lovely. A cousin of Mademoiselle Latour's to stay with us. You will help me with my work, won't you . . ."

"Gabriel," Sylvie supplied.

"Gabriel," the woman finished, drawing the small boy to her. He looked after Sylvie with fearful eyes.

She smiled at him reassuringly. "I shall be back to see you later, Gabriel. Be good."

Sylvie turned away. The weight of that apprehensive yet resigned glance slowed her step. Children shouldn't look like that. Why,

Gabriel was only a few years older than Leo, whose features she remembered as bold, unshadowed. Sylvie shivered. Thank God she had listened to reason and taken Leo to the safety of his grandparents in Portugal.

But there was no time now for musing. Sylvie walked rapidly through the bustling narrow streets to a post office and hastily scribbled a message to Jacob. It was the first time she had dared to use his poste restante number. "Everyone has gone. Please come." She signed it "S," not knowing whether what she had written was clear enough or vague enough, but trusting to Jacob. Then she went back to the Hôtel du Midi and plotted.

Sylvie knew through Marseilles' impeccable word of mouth network that most of the Jewish refugees who were rounded up in the area found their way to the notorious camp in Gurs in the Basses-Pyrénées. It was rumored that in the cold winter months thousands of them died there of starvation, of typhoid, of dysentery. But Caroline wasn't Jewish and Caroline was her first point of concern. Could she have ended up there or in some prison? Or was she simply roaming the streets searching for Joseph? Sylvie disqualified the last possibility. Wherever she had been taken, her name would certainly exist on some official list. If there was one thing the German occupation had established in France, it was the rigidity with which lists were kept and adhered to. Lists and files and forms and documents for everything. It was what had made counterfeiting such an honorable and lucrative profession.

What she needed now was quick and certain access to files, Sylvie decided. And she thought she knew how that might be possible without recourse to that potentially dangerous personal trip to a police station.

Quickly she donned her smartest wool suit, tied her hair into a smooth knot and perched low on her brow a little rounded hat with a pert peacock feather. Then she made her way out of the hotel. Just outside the door she met Nadine of the hundred eyes and rather than the usual curt nod with which the woman addressed her, thin lips formed into an uncustomary greeting: *"Ça va, Mademoiselle Latour?"*

There was something about the lilt of the voice, the slight sneer around the lips, the hint of a triumphal color in the eyes which made Sylvie stop in her tracks. A light glimmered and then exploded for her with the clarity of a revelation. Nadine, of course. Nadine-of-the-hundred-eyes. Nadine the informer. Nadine who had followed her to the house on the hill. Nadine who seethed with visible malice. Sylvie's hand rose, poised for a resounding slap. And then she stopped herself, drew her shoulders back, looked at the smaller woman as if she were a pernicious slug and just about as bothersome. *"Ça va très bien, madame. Merci.* But you, you look as if you might be sickening."

It all happened so quickly that Nadine wasn't sure she had heard Sylvie properly, had seen the raised hand. Wasn't sure that Sylvie knew. Nadine wanted her to know, wanted her to realize that Nadine was the stronger. Wanted to gloat. Watching Sylvie's receding form, sensuous even in its briskness, apparently carefree as she made her way down the street, Nadine felt her hard-earned triumph trickling through her fingers. She sped after Sylvie. She couldn't contain herself any longer.

"Now you see, Mademoiselle Latour—Kowalska—" beady eyes gleamed at Sylvie from a pinched equine face—"you may be able to put things over on a lot of people, but not on me." Vindictiveness settled over her dark features. "Those dirty Jews of yours have had it now. And your own days may be numbered." Nadine sneered.

"You had better start counting your own, you informing vermin, you and all your repulsive kin," Sylvie lashed out and then, with an icy withering glance, strode away.

Nadine looked after her in smug satisfaction. Now that contemptuous bitch would mind her manners, would know who held the reins of power.

But Nadine's satisfaction didn't last long. That very evening, half an hour before she was due to perform, Sylvie left the Hôtel du Midi. None of Madame Castelnau's entreaties could make her stay. When the poor woman remonstrated with her, demanded reasons, Sylvie simply said, "Ask your daughter-in-law. Ask her."

Madame Castelnau didn't need to ask. She understood everything in a flash without digging for details. She finished Sylvie's slap for her. It was a resounding one. It left Nadine at least temporarily cowed.

Meanwhile, Sylvie, with the help of a tousled street urchin, carried her bags to the Hôtel d'Algers. She needed to be out of the public gaze for a while to put her rescue of Caroline and Katherine into effect. That afternoon she had gone to the Villa Pastré to see her new friend the Comtesse. She had been to this remarkable residence with its grand vaulted veranda and its acres of parkland in Montredon just outside Marseilles several times before. The Comtesse Pastré held open house for stray artists and writers who had fled the occupation to find refuge in the free city of Marseilles. And she did so with panache and liberality.

Sylvie had first been brought there by an artist friend. The atmosphere, despite the scent of the sea, had reminded her of Paris days which now seemed long past. And the Comtesse, who was part Russian by origin, had been drawn to the gifted and beautiful young performer she considered her fellow Slav. She had asked Sylvie to return whenever it pleased her to do so.

Sylvie had done so today because she sensed that the Comtesse, with her innumerable contacts in high places, would know exactly which senior official could help her discover Caroline's whereabouts. She had not been wrong. The Comtesse had offered to intervene personally. Now all Sylvie had to do was wait. It was the task which was most difficult for her.

She refused to sing at the Hôtel d'Algers, despite Vassier's entreaties. She filled the waiting hours by trying to bring a light into Gabriel's eyes. It became something of a mission. If she could do that, she thought superstitiously, Caroline would be saved. She fed the little boy the precious chocolates admirers had given her. She took him for walks by the sea, named boats for him, telling him one would carry him to a new and distant world where there was chocolate every day. She stroked his hair and cuddled him, thinking he needed human warmth. He was always gracious, polite, grateful, but his eyes never gave up their haunted look as if they were eternally fixed on a scene he couldn't divulge. She took to reading him to sleep at nights from a tattered copy of *The Count of Monte Cristo* she had found in the hotel. She acted out whole scenes for him to make up for his scanty French. It was during one of these scenes, on their seventh night together, that Gabriel laughed. A pure childish carefree laugh. She hugged him. That night she slept with him cradled in her arms.

The next day a note arrived for Sylvie with a single word written on it. Gurs. So now she knew the worst. She waited three more days in the hope that some word might come from Jacob. During those days, she found out everything she could about Gurs. Vassier was a great help, as were other friends.

A plan began to take shape. In order to execute it, she needed a high-ranking military letter on Caroline's behalf. Sylvie made use of the underground network she had become familiar with over the last years, this time pulling the strings herself. The letter on its stolen stationery and with its forged signature was obtained. But still no word from Jacob.

Her patience exhausted, Sylvie decided to set out on her own.

Armed with her store of gasoline coupons, she drove the large Citroën as quickly as she dared through a rain-drenched landscape, under skies which turned a colder steely gray the closer she drew to the foothills of the Pyrenees. She spent the night in a small village. Beside the old empty hotel, a swollen brook rushed angrily over worn stones. In the morning everything was swathed in chill cloud. Sylvie drew her coat round her and inched her way toward the village of Gurs. The roads were narrow and winding and she could see no more than a few feet ahead of her. She had hoped to get to Gurs early. She stumbled on the camp, rather than found it, closer to noon, by which time a pale wintry sun emerged to give her a sense of her whereabouts.

At a threatening signal from an armed guard Sylvie drew up at the camp gates. She took a deep calming breath and stepped out of the car. With her flowing golden hair, her fine loosely cut black cashmere coat, and the silk stockings she did nothing to hide, she looked like nothing so much as a starlet who had strayed on her way to a glamorous party. She approached the guard. "I have come to see Monsieur le Commandant," she said in a voice which left no doubt that the meeting had been prearranged.

The man looked at her curiously, altered his menacing stance, and said, "Monsieur le Commandant is not here."

"But that can't be," Sylvie trilled. "I have come especially to see him. I have a message"—she lowered her voice to a whisper—"a personal message from Vichy."

The guard stared at her in consternation. Sylvie could see his mixture of disbelief and apprehension: she might just be telling the truth. She talked on, capitalizing on the apprehension, confusing him with her insistence. "It is imperative that I speak to him. The matter is urgent. Fetch his deputy." She put all the force of her personality into her voice, tapped her high-heeled foot impatiently on the ground. The guard eyed her, then gestured to his double at the other side of the gate, simultaneously asking Sylvie for her papers. She whisked them in front of him authoritatively, then stepped back as he turned to murmur to his mate.

As she waited, Sylvie identified the smell that had besieged her nostrils despite the cold. The reek of human excrement. And something else. The stale foul odor of human bodies closely cramped together. It turned her stomach. As she breathed it in for fifteen, then twenty, then thirty pacing minutes, that smell became for Sylvie irrevocably the smell of death. By the time a young soldier at last came to fetch her, her fear, her nausea had been transformed into a luminous anger. It sharpened her performance, gave it the edge of truth.

The slight gray man who confronted her on the other side of a cheap functional desk in the small bare room was immediately at a disadvantage. In the grim atmosphere of the camp, Sylvie with her perfect skin, her animal grace, radiated health, evoked a world of natural power. Her air of command, her directness, erased any possibility of ambivalence or suspicion.

"There has been a mistake," she said as soon as the barest formalities of introduction had been made. "My cousin, Caroline Berger, has been brought here by mistake. I have come to fetch her."

"That is not possible, Mademoiselle. We have our information, our orders."

Sylvie pinned him with a contemptuous glance, drew herself up to her full height. "Ah, but you see, it is altogether possible. As your Commandant would know, if he were here." She paused for a moment, and then, as if she had suddenly decided that she could honor this man with her confidence, she sat down and looked beseechingly into his eyes with the conspiratorial seductiveness of a young girl.

"You see, it's a delicate matter. My cousin had a liaison"—she lowered her voice to a whisper so that the soldier in attendance wouldn't hear and she stumbled over the offending word—"a liaison with . . . with a high-ranking officer. She came south to have the baby. I don't know how she stumbled into the arms of the police, found herself amongst Jews, but I know, I can understand that she wouldn't defend herself. Divulge her secret. Break her trust with General . . ." Sylvie stopped. She fumbled in her bag. "You see he wants her back, and the baby." She flashed her letter before him.

The man examined her letter slowly and then looked again at Sylvie. Her air of calm expectation seemed to convince him. But still he hesitated. He was not a brave man. This whole thing was not in the rules. And rules governed his existence. He cleared his throat, avoided Sylvie's direct gaze. "Monsieur le Commandant will be back at five. It would be better to wait for him." He rose, averted his face. "You can sit in the next room."

Alone in the bleak cubicle, Sylvie suddenly grew frightened. The wait seemed interminable. From the window she could see row upon row of identical barracks. Somewhere in one of those squalid structures were Caroline, Katherine. She had to move, had to go to them before her nerves gave way. Her high heels clacking, she strode past a soldier, murmured, "I need some air." At a glance from his superior, the soldier followed her.

Sylvie walked. Walked past grim barracks, peered in to see gray, huddled forms, empty apprehensive eyes. She saw a group of men, straggling prisoners, being marched, their shoulders hunched, their limbs too weak for their bodies. She saw a man fall, felt the thud of a soldier's rifle as it hit those gangling legs. She stilled her cry, forced herself to walk on. It was cold. A wet wind enveloped her, bringing with it that high rancid smell. She shivered. There were women now. Women and small children forming a haggard line. In their shaky bluish hands, they held tin bowls. As Sylvie neared the front of the line, she saw a thin gruel poured into those bowls from a large pot. The woman at the front of the line dropped her bowl with a clatter. Liquid disappeared into stony ground.

"Clumsy fool, you'll go without now," a raucous voice shouted. The woman walked blindly on, unhearing, undeflected by the sound. Someone shoved the dropped vessel into her hands. She held it to her, unseeingly cradled it to her breast.

Sylvie gazed at that stooped, slow-moving form: wispy hair flecked with a gray which was also the color of the lined face, blank dark eyes. She stopped short, swallowed hard. And then with a determined gesture, she walked toward the woman, took her arm. When the guard tried to stop her, she hissed at him, "Don't touch me. Take me to the Commandant straight away. Look, just look at what you have done to my cousin." She put her arm more firmly round Caroline, forcing those automaton gestures into swifter movement. Caroline did not seem to recognize her, looked blindly through her.

"Katherine. Where's Katherine?" Sylvie murmured. There was no answer from her friend. And with a sudden swift realization, Sylvie knew. Knew with a terrifying certainty that there was a hole in Caroline's arms where Katherine should have been. In that moment, the full horror of that pervasive smell twisted her bowels and her heart. She dragged Caroline forward, past those grim barracks, those desolate faces.

As they neared the HQ, a man came toward them deliberately. "And where might you be going, Mademoiselle?"

Sylvie looked at him, looked at the stripes on his jacket coldly. "I am coming to see you. And then I am taking my cousin home immediately," she said in blunt indignant tones. "You can see the state that she's in. And all because of you, because of your stupid mistake." She turned on him a face of citizenly outrage. The emotion was genuine. "I shall complain. Complain in the highest quarters, Monsieur. Madame la Comtesse d'Espinailles will complain as well."

He was about to interrupt her, but she pressed on. "And when we find out why my cousin's baby, why the General's baby has disappeared . . ." She let the sentence hang, its threat unspoken.

The Commandant stared at her. Angry, adamant eyes outfaced him. "Mademoiselle," he murmured in what were now placatory tones, "I do not round people up. I simply run this camp."

"In that case"—Sylvie gave him a contemptuous glance—"you will kindly see us out of this camp instantly."

Only when they were a good five miles away from the camp did Sylvie pull up at the side of the road. Not a single word had yet passed Caroline's lips. She took her friend in her arms. Caroline's body was rigid. Sylvie realized there was nothing she could say to erase the weight of that dead baby which lay like a canyon between them.

"I'm taking you home, Caroline." Sylvie stroked the dirty, wispy hair. "Home."

"You should have left me there." A cracked unrecognizable voice emerged from her friend's dry lips.

Sylvie pressed her closer.

"Left me there to die," Caroline muttered.

Silence covered them.

Sylvie drove on. And in the silence of that bleak late October afternoon she was suddenly filled with a pure, intense loathing. It floated over everything she had seen at Gurs and with a venomous insistence settled itself on the figure of Nadine. Nadine of the hundred eyes became all enemies to Sylvie. All enemies incorporated into a single vicious entity. She had saved Caroline and now she would wreak vengeance on the despicable creature who was responsible for all her friend's misery.

After the war, when Sylvie tried to tell people of how she had stolen Caroline from the arms of the camp, they looked at her in disbelief, as if she were concocting a tall tale. They couldn't imagine that it had been quite that easy; but then neither could they imagine the horror of even those camps.

This war, with its daily heroisms and daily atrocities, strained the bounds of peacetime belief.

Jacob arrived in Marseilles at the turn of the year, just after the Germans had taken over the whole of France. He had been prevented from coming sooner. Sylvie's message had reached him late. His first instinct was to go to her. But he had weighed up his desire to see her, to comfort her against other commitments. The latter had won. As had his sure sense that to see her at that moment would endanger them both and implicate others.

As the Allies began to make dents in the German war machine, retaliatory measures in the occupied zones grew ever fiercer. Police vigilance increased and acts against the Jewish population and resisters multiplied. For some time now, Jacob had been worried about the safety of the house on the hill and Sylvie's too frequent visits there. He had already decided, before receiving Sylvie's note, that the house had outlived its use. The present group of inhabitants would be the last. But he had been too late.

Jacob quickly ascertained that the group had been removed to Gurs. He had spent several weeks there working as a doctor during the winter when the typhoid epidemic was at its height. Over a thousand of its sixteen thousand inmates had died of disease or starvation. He knew that it was possible to get people out: he had done it before. But it would be too risky for him to go back there again. He set about making contacts with other medical personnel and the Red Cross. Three days after Sylvie had left Gurs with Caroline, two men were smuggled out of the camp in a Red Cross ambulance. One of them was Joseph Rittner. Jacob did not learn until later that he had been recaptured crossing the Pyrenees. He did learn that there was no one in the camp by the name of Caroline Berger.

Now he had come to Marseilles to say goodbye to Sylvie. The German occupation of the Southern Zone dictated new strategies. It was imperative for him to go underground: the moment for armed resistance had come. Any future contact with Sylvie could only endanger her and the success of any operations he was involved in. He knew that his very love for her made her his Achilles heel. Yet he wanted desperately to see her, to hold her if only for one more time.

Jacob, however, had not sufficiently prepared himself for Sylvie's state, for the difficulty of a meeting which was in reality a parting.

Never compliant, Sylvie was now vehement. When he slipped into her room in the Hôtel d'Algers late on that chill January night, she flew at him in a storm of irascibility.

"You, where have you been? I haven't seen you for months. I wrote to you."

A torrent of abuse covered him. From within it, he watched her, marveled at the savagery of her eyes, at her beauty. He tried to take hold of her, cover her words with a kiss. But she pummeled his chest, drew away.

"No," she said fiercely. "I need to talk to you. Do you know what they've done to Caroline? She's a ruin. She can hardly speak. They killed her baby. She, she, that woman," Sylvie spluttered, "that Nadine of the hundred eyes. She killed her. It's all her fault. I want you to help me get her. Stamp out those putrid little informers."

"Calm yourself, Sylvie." Jacob's voice was soft. "We're not fighting a war against individuals. It's the force of the Nazis we have to break."

Sylvie looked at him coldly. "The Nazis have been very polite to me. Very correct. Nadine, on the other hand . . ." She made a murderous gesture. "She deserves to be wiped out. And if you don't help, I shall do it myself."

"Sylvie." He shook her, gripped her shoulders. "Sylvie, listen to me. I've come to say goodbye. I may not see you for some time."

"You haven't seen me for some time as it is," she countered him caustically.

Jacob shrugged, his eyes sad. "I'd hoped . . ."

She cut him off. "*Where* are you going?"

"I can't tell you that."

"You're going to fight, aren't you? And you're leaving me here. What am I supposed to do? Do with little Gabriel, with Caroline? And what's become of Joseph?"

"He's out now." Jacob tried to take her hand, but she drew away again.

"I want to come with you," she said suddenly, her expression adamant. "I'll have a gun. I'll be able to kill."

"You know that's not possible, Sylvie."

"Why not? Other women do."

He ignored her words. "I'll see that the little boy is taken care of. If you need help, Vassier is reliable."

"You'll see to this. You'll see to that," she taunted him. "Well, you can see to taking me with you. See to exterminating that verminous Nadine."

His dark eyes burned into her. Yes, it was true, other women fought. But if Sylvie were with him, if anything should happen to her, or him, then he knew the secrecy of any operation was at risk. He stiffened his shoulders, his face grim.

"Here." He reached into the pocket of the coat he hadn't yet taken off and drew out a large wad of money. "You might need this."

She threw the money at him. "I'm not your whore," she said tersely.

He shrugged, turned to go.

Sylvie watched him open the door. It was like an event in slow motion, the movement of his back, his arm, his fingers, detailed, time-stopped.

"Jacob," she called after him softly. "Jacob."

He turned back to her.

She ran to him, planted a hot girlish kiss on his lips. "Take care," she said.

"You too." He stroked her hair once. They looked into each other's eyes intently.

She was too proud to ask him to stay.

The next day Sylvie accepted an offer she had long put off from the Provençal, an elegant hotel which seemed to grow out of the steep rock wall on the other side of the harbor. Caroline and Gabriel would stay under the watchful eye of old Vassier. If Sylvie couldn't join Jacob, she would fight her own war.

Caroline was still in a mute daze. Nothing Sylvie could do could shake her from it, no stroking or cajoling or talk of happier days when the war would be at an end. She had formed a strange silent bond with the boy, however, and in quiet ways they took care of each other. Two victims, Sylvie thought, her heart going out to them.

When she had made her arrangements at the Provençal, Sylvie confronted Caroline. "You're in charge of Gabriel now. I'm going back to work."

Caroline didn't answer.

Suddenly her silence infuriated Sylvie, made her feel paralyzed, insubstantial. "None of us have our own children these days," she raged at her. "None of us."

Caroline shuddered but made no reply.

Sylvie's anger instantly subsided. She walked across the dingy hotel room and tried to put her arm around her friend. "Soon, soon the war will be over and Joseph will come back and you can have another baby," she said, repeating what she had said innumerable times before.

This time Caroline murmured, "You should have let me die. Let me die where Katherine died." She sank back into a threadbare armchair and stared into the middle distance. She hated herself, hated that ugly guilty face that confronted her in the mirror when she washed, a face that was not Katherine's. Katherine's pinched little face in death had not been her own either. She had not complained. Simply shriveled like a leaf and faded away. Caroline had held on to her tiny weightless form for two days until one of the guards grabbed it away.

It made no sense. None of it made any sense. This life, the camp, the others she had heard of, Katherine's death. Why? Why was she still alive? How could she still be alive? She had no right. Without Katherine. Without Joseph. She tried to focus on Sylvie. She was no use to her either. No use to anyone. "You don't understand, Sylvie," she said faintly, as if she were talking to herself. "I don't want to live, don't want to survive. Not in this kind of world."

"Yes, you do," Sylvie replied stubbornly. "Joseph will come back. Jacob said he was out. He'll come back and you'll have another child and everything will be fine."

Caroline trembled. Joseph would never forgive her for letting Katherine die. She remembered those vile guards and how they had torn them apart, separated them, flung Katherine into her arms, pushed Joseph brutally away so that he stumbled. She remembered the sadistic gleam in their eyes as she had shouted and cried. Suddenly a hatred equal to that she felt for herself found its way onto the features of those men.

She looked at Sylvie, tuned into that voice, still talking—cajoling and angry by turn.

"This is no time for philosophy," Sylvie was saying curtly. "It's time for action. We're going to take our revenge. We're going to make her pay, that informing bitch who was responsible for having you rounded up, for little Katherine's death. Make her pay slowly." Her features burned with a vengeful wrath Caroline dimly recognized. It was like the anger that had smoldered there when, as girls, they had planned in intricate detail the pain they would inflict on the nun who had persecuted them. Caroline sat up a little straighter.

She didn't remember Sylvie mentioning a woman before. But perhaps she had. It was often hard to tune in to Sylvie's voice.

"Yes, you'll see." Sylvie, now aware that she had her friend's attention, took her hand and clasped it firmly. "We'll take our revenge. Very soon now. I promise you."

The sudden return pressure of Caroline's fingers gave her renewed energy. Yes, she thought, there was nothing like vengeance to give one a taste for life.

Sylvie proceeded carefully. This time she was taking no chances. No longer could she afford to underestimate Nadine of the hundred eyes and her ilk.

After the Nazi occupation, Marseilles was a changed city. The teeming life of the streets thinned out. People avoided each other's eyes. They might confront those of a gray-uniformed German or a black-shirted Gestapo officer or, as the months went by, the even more dreaded gaze of the hated Milice, whose brutality became legendary. It was better to be unseen and unseeing.

Sylvie followed this rule of invisibility. Except when she was on stage, where her light burned more strongly than ever. The clientele of the Provençal was different from that of the Hôtel du Midi. It was an upper-class establishment and as the year rolled on it increasingly became the haunt of German officers and their French collaborators. Sylvie changed her style and her repertoire.

Before the war she had seduced her audiences into a kind of warm complicity. Now, sheathed in her own glittering beauty, she radiated an electric contempt. She had learned some old German cabaret songs and a cold sexuality emanated from her as she barked and crooned the words of a foreign language. An impassive hetaera, a white goddess for whom her audience of lovers were mere playthings, she generated a brilliant white heat. The Germans adored her. They besieged her with requests, with presents, with invitations. She accepted nothing. One young Gestapo officer was particularly insistent. There was something about his flat high-cheekboned face, his lash of blond hair, his steel blue eyes, smoldering and icy by turn, which excited her. She took to sitting at his crowded table between sets. Oberstleutnant Wilhelm Berring talked to her of poetry, of music, of distant mountains, but behind the words, there was an intractable force, willing her, seducing, coercing. Sylvie, aware of that will, was drawn to it. And drawn to challenging it. For the moment she gave nothing but the dramatic allure of her presence. And its cachet in that club where she was the supreme object of desire.

With his cunning tortoise eyes Vassier warned her. "Some of our people do not like women who befriend the occupiers."

"Befriend?" Sylvie laughed shrilly and then grew serious. "I have my reasons. Tell your people. My record hasn't been so bad. I should be trusted."

"You're playing with fire, Sylvie." Vassier shook his head. "What would your man think?"

"He has nothing to do with it." Sylvie was adamant. "In any case, I can be of use to you. I can overhear things, use my ears."

"In a nightclub?" Vassier was skeptical.

"You'll see. Men talk, they boast . . ."

He shrugged. "Be careful, Sylvie, you're in the lion's den."

Sylvie was as good as her word. She had a little German. She started to listen, mingle more with the clientele, sit at a variety of tables. Often she had no knowledge of what use what she heard might be, but she had a sure instinct for significance. She reported to Vassier. Once or twice Vassier beamed. He patted her. "I was wrong about you, *ma petite.*"

They were not major matters Sylvie reported, no intelligence about troop movements or deportations. But in a world where newspapers and radios lied and all useful information was secret, Sylvie could be instrumental. Sometimes it was a word dropped about a raid the Milice were about to perform. Another time, it was a drunken self-aggrandizing narrative about some *maquis* who had been picked up and what had been done to them. Little scraps of matter which were pieced together by those who had access to larger pictures.

It was not what Sylvie saw as her main task.

She had begun her plan of vengeance on Nadine of the hundred eyes. It had to be a long intricate process which filled the woman's days with misery, so that she suffered acutely, woke each day bathed in sweat. With avid detail, she concocted her scheme, excited Caroline into participation and then reported back on each step. Caroline lived for these reports. Gabriel, her only other link with the present, was gone. The boy had been spirited away one night on a journey which would take him to Switzerland. Not even the chocolates Sylvie stuffed in his pockets could lift the gloom which covered all of them. Now Caroline did nothing but repetitiously clean and tidy her room and gaze out of her window on to the past. Only Sylvie's vengeful fire warmed her.

Sylvie had started by writing little anonymous notes to Nadine. Insidious schoolgirl notes of the kind which read, "Your moment is coming, you scum." "There is not much longer now." Notes calculated to torment and instill fear. Soon the notes grew longer and more elaborate, detailing the tortures which would be inflicted on Nadine. They would compose these notes together, spend long afternoons cutting and pasting words from newspapers into intricate messages.

Sylvie also paid young boys to harass Nadine, make catcalls and then when Nadine turned, to shout out, "Oooo—a hag." Sylvie was pleased with herself. She had seen Nadine on a number of occasions in the street and she looked dreadful. An ugly frightened woman who could not walk without looking over her shoulder.

Then Sylvie decided the time had come for the climactic act in her little drama. She anticipated it with a cruel relish.

To bring it to fruition she needed the connivance of one of her Germans. She chose Oberstleutnant Wilhelm Berring. She suspected he would rise to the task, if the stakes were high enough.

He had often invited her to have dinner with him on her night off and now at last she accepted. They went to Marseilles' most exclusive restaurant and she was amazed again at the plenty available in German quarters when in the markets, for the French, there were shortages of everything. When their meal was at an end and they were sipping a Courvoisier, she let him take her hand and stroke it. He was at once romantically reverent before the supreme pedestal of his exalted goddess, and insistent. Mademoiselle Latour must give up her other admirers. He would make it worth her while. There was this lovely apartment. It could be hers. He looked at her meaningfully, let his eyes skim her neck, her bosom.

Sylvie's laugh tinkled. "You are so generous, Herr Berring. But you know it is out of the question. I am not free. Not free to be with you." She played lingeringly over the words, drew a single nail slowly over the back of his hand. "Even this. Even tonight is dangerous to me." She met his gaze and then suddenly pulled back, looking with deliberate casualness over her shoulder.

"Why? How can it be dangerous? Is there a man?" Fingers gripped her arm.

Sylvie shook them off lightly. "No," she crooned softly. "Not a man. That would be easier, perhaps." She laughed, a cold, low, electric laugh, challenging him. "No. Not a man. A woman." She shivered, as if a chill wind had suddenly crept over her. "A woman who watches me. A woman who hates Germans. Who hates me. Who thinks I am sinning against humanity by even speaking to you." Sylvie watched his face, saw the rush of anger, the tension of control. "And so I have to be careful," she continued in what was almost a whisper. "Have to make sure I don't overstep the mark of simply earning my keep by singing. Or else I may wake up one morning to find myself in a pool of blood." She passed her tongue over her lips as if tasting that blood, as if tasting him. She laughed again. "So you see, *mein lieber Herr*, something keeps me back from that apartment you so charmingly describe. And what may happen within it."

"Who is this woman? If she is all that stands between us, then . . ." He took a walnut from the table and crushed it with one deliberate gesture in his fist. He smiled, a little whimsically. "Tell me, Mademoiselle Latour, who is she?"

"Ah no, it is not so simple." Sylvie looked with poignant melancholy into the distance. "She may be a single woman, but there is an organization behind her, a powerful organization." She dropped her second bit of bait, letting the word *maquis* hang unspoken. "You could not possibly contend with that."

The negative enraged him. "Could not," he repeated. "There is nothing that *we* could not, *I* could not do"—his eyes rested on her— "for you."

Sylvie lowered her eyelids, thoughtfully traced the lines of the tablecloth with a delicate finger.

"Who is she?" Berring closed his hand over hers. His voice grew low. "Speak her name and you will be free. Free for me."

Sylvie hesitated, as if the act of naming, its implicit betrayal came to her with difficulty. She played with the ruby on her throat, brought it to her lips, let it fall back heavily between her breasts. The grip on her hand hardened. "Tell me." There was an urgency in Berring's tone. "I will make sure that any harm she has done you is amply repaid."

Sylvie lifted her gaze to his. Her eyes sparkled with a hard brilliance. "I would like to see her suffer. Suffer slowly for each malicious act she has performed. And know it was because of me." She drew in her breath, saw her excitement reflected in his features. A shared exhilaration in cruelty. "But, it cannot be. There would be reprisals. There . . ."

"Trust me," Berring cut her off. "I will arrange everything." His lips curled into a thin line. "Everything. And then . . ." Below the cover of the tablecloth, he touched the silk of her knee. Sylvie's face was impassive, judging. Slowly she took a cigarette from her evening bag, allowed him to light it, puffed once. And then, her gaze challenging him, holding him, she wrote a name on a slip of paper. Nadine Castelnau. Hôtel du Midi.

A week later, amidst the bustle of the Provençal, he motioned her to his table. "It's done," he said. His eyes glimmered with a new intimacy as he raised her hand to his lips.

Sylvie perched on the edge of a chair, crossed one long silken leg over the other. "Good," she drawled, taking a deep breath, savoring her revenge. "I only hope she knew through whom."

"Your 'message' was conveyed." He chuckled over the word. "My men tell me she begged your forgiveness."

"Very good." Sylvie's eyes sparkled to the bright silvery tune of the rhinestones on her dress. She felt for a moment as triumphant as if she had won the war. She wanted to rush back to Caroline and tell her, tell her instantly.

"And now, my cruel beautiful one, shall we meet after the show?" Berring's hand curled insidiously round her arm and kept her by his side.

Sylvie turned a laughing face on him. "I'm afraid, Herr Oberstleutnant, another night's delay is in order. Tomorrow night, perhaps, or the next. To kindle your ardor a little."

He bowed, his eyes steely. A little nerve played in his jaw. "Tomorrow night, then. My car will be waiting."

Sylvie blew him a careless red-lipped kiss.

As soon as she could the next day, Sylvie went to see Caroline. She was buoyant with her triumph, the success of her simple Old Testament understanding of justice. An eye for an eye. "It's done," she said as soon as the door of Caroline's room was closed behind her. "It's done." She took her friend in her arms and danced her round. "Nadine won't spy or inform anymore. Tortured by the very people she's so loyal to." She giggled girlishly. "Katherine is revenged. We're revenged."

For a brief moment, Caroline smiled, tasting vengeance, keeping pace with her friend. Then she stopped, slumped into a chair, looked dismally at the wall.

Sylvie shook her. "What's the matter? It's done, I tell you. Everything we planned for."

Caroline's voice when it came was hoarse. "It doesn't bring Kath-

erine back, Sylvie. Nothing can bring Katherine back. The Germans
are still our masters, still committing unspeakable acts. And Joseph,
Joseph." She hid her face in her hands, sobbing silently.

Sylvie felt suddenly drained. She looked unhappily at that bowed
head, stroked it listlessly. "But we've had our revenge on Nadine."
Her voice was pleading.

Caroline's tear-stained face stared up at her. "If only there had
never been a Nadine. If only . . ." She stopped herself. Her hands
flew up to her face, hiding it, hiding her thought.

The unfinished sentence coiled between them. Sylvie finished it
in her own mind. If only she had never gone to the Hôtel du Midi.
Of course, why had it never occurred to her, she thought grimly. In
some way, Caroline held her responsible for Katherine's death.

Sylvie fled. She walked aimlessly through the wet gray streets of
the old city. She felt depleted. All the drive had gone out of her
personal war, shaped as it had been by her loyalties to friends. All
her acts of spontaneous courage had been for them, in their defense,
not performed out of some deep and intractable sense of abstract
justice. And now she had lived out her passions to no end. She was
alone. Caroline was removed from her. She had not seen Jacob since
that fateful night when they had argued instead of lying in each
other's arms. The news Vassier occasionally gave her of him was
merely a testimony to his continuing and, as the old man implied,
heroic existence. Andrzej seemed to have vanished from the face of
the earth. She had been unable to trace him. She was alone.

Sylvie watched the waves, saw the world close in on its horizon.
She felt abandoned, impotent, aimless.

Even her performance gave her no satisfaction that night. Men's
eyes devouring her, but leaving her untouched. She made her round
of the tables. The conversations she half heard made no sense. Men's
voices droning, boasting, endlessly considering the movement of
troops, the advance of the Americans here, the retreat of the British
there, Mussolini, Stalin, Hitler, Hitler, Hitler. She suddenly hated
them, hated them all, but with no passion.

When after her last set a message came to tell her a car was
waiting for her, she was momentarily bemused. She had forgotten
all about Herr Oberstleutnant Berring. She had certainly never had
any intention of taking up his invitation. Indeed, she had never
thought at all beyond the completion of her personal mission. And
now as she tasted the notion of going off into the night in a sleek
car and compared it to the thought of a lonely, defeated bed, there

was hardly any question of choice. A German. Why not? She could test her power a little further on the hated Germans.

The chauffeur brought her to the very door of the apartment and then, bowing briskly, left her. Sylvie smoothed the lamé of her long dress and knocked. Berring came to the door himself, took her hand to guide her into a richly appointed salon. His tone was angry. "You are late. I cannot stay long tonight."

Sylvie shrugged. "I work late, as you know."

He took it, then said more softly. "I thought you might not come." He was gazing at her intently.

"Did you?" Sylvie arched her brows, laughed, slipped her stole off her shoulders and filled his hands with it. She strolled away from him, taking in the room, caressing the heavy velvet of a sofa, the dark sheen of a grand piano. He poured her a glass of champagne. She took it nonchalantly, continued her stroll, her cool assessment of her surroundings. She paid no attention to Berring.

Suddenly he gripped her shoulders from behind, veered her round to him and kissed her violently on the lips.

Sylvie stroked the lapel of his uniform. "Not so fast, my lieutenant. We are not children. We have time. Time to get to know each other." She smiled into that hard face, slipped from his arms. "A little more to drink. Perhaps a dance."

He moved deliberately to the gramophone, a slow crooning number, poured more champagne into her glass. His eyes, dark, steely, never left her.

Sylvie sipped her drink, held his eyes. She moved back toward him, put her arm lingeringly on his shoulder, started to dance, her body skimming his, drawing him on. Her fingers slipped beneath his jacket, nails found skin. A rush of breath. Sylvie's laugh tinkled. "I adore dancing," she breathed. "Don't you?"

He tried to kiss her again, but she evaded him, put a finger to his lips. She could feel the tautness in his limbs. "Would you like to see me dance?" Her lips brushed the place where her finger had been.

"It depends on the nature of the dance." His mouth curled, a thin tense line.

"Oh, I was thinking of a very special dance. A performance. Just for you." Sylvie put a throb into her voice. She eased his tie from his neck, led him to the sofa. "There," she crooned, "comfortable?" She floated sinuously away from him, began her own gyrating, rhythmic movement. Then, with a hoarse little laugh, she unzipped her dress, let it fall slowly from her shoulders, lifted it with a high-heeled foot into his lap. "Just for you," she mouthed.

He brought the garment to his face, breathed in Sylvie's fragrance. His eyes flickered over her, saw the long silky expanse of her swaying body, the pallor of skin where dark stockings ended. His features grew strained, his lips dry. He reached for his drink, a cigarette, sat further back in the sofa.

Sylvie, impassive, read his desire as if from a great distance. It was no different from the hotel, she thought dimly. This was what they all saw, all those ogling men, who worshipped her from within their private little peep-show fantasies. Sylvie stripping. Performing. Like this. She cupped her hands over her breasts, circled her nipples, released the lace of her bra, swung her hips closer and closer to him with a riveting motion, so that he couldn't prevent himself from reaching out for her.

"No, no, not yet." She evaded his grasp, moistened her lips. She caressed smooth hips, released a stocking and drew it lingeringly down her leg. She heard the uncontrollable rush of breath and met his eyes for a moment. Then slowly, deliberately, she brought her foot to his crotch, rubbed. And again. "Oh yes, we must release the prisoner, give him air." With sure, unhurried fingers, she unbuttoned his trousers, let her cool hand trail over his stiff penis. A groan escaped him. She drew away again, continued her own rite, stroking herself, swaying, touching herself there, humming a little tune. His eyes were wild. His hand moved involuntarily to grasp his penis. Rub. Then with a savage gesture, he released it, reached for her, pulled her down to him. "Ssshhh," Sylvie whispered. Still smiling, holding his gaze, she pressed his penis between her breasts.

It was all over in a moment.

His eyes focused on the sperm which moistened her. And then suddenly, he slapped her hard across the face. She arched backward, her face downcast, oddly penitent beneath the strands of golden hair. A tear glistened in the chastened gaze she turned up at him. "I thought it was what you wanted," she said in a demure little girl's voice, "what you all wanted, what you dreamt of. A private, an intimate performance."

He scowled.

Sylvie shivered. "I'm cold." She reached for his Gestapo jacket and wrapped it round her naked body. Then with long, even strides she went to pour herself another glass of champagne. In an instant he was next to her, nuzzling her breasts between the rough folds of the jacket. "Perhaps you are right," he whispered. There was an air of confusion on his features. He glanced at his watch. "I must go. We have just broken a particularly tiresome *maquis* group. I have work to do. Tomorrow, no, the next night, I shall come back. You will be here?"

Sylvie nodded. "I will try."

"Make sure." His voice was a stern command, but his eyes as he lifted the jacket gently, almost apologetically, from her shoulders, held a plea. It accompanied the formal bow, the respectful clicking of heels.

When the door closed behind him, Sylvie burst into gleeful laughter. It rippled from her throat as she washed and dressed. Then quietly, stealthily, she slipped from the flat.

Later that night, Sylvie dreamt. Dreamt uneasily. Dreamt of Jacob. He was was calling to her. He needed her. He was in a dark place. A pit smelling of earth. She woke in a sweat. She had the indubitable sense that the call was real. Jacob needed her and last night she had been toying with a German officer. She shuddered.

It was not that she felt guilty. Guilt was not in the repertoire of Sylvie's everyday emotions. Nor was the concept of marital fidelity. If she hadn't slept with another man since Leo had been conceived— despite what appearances may have suggested—it was simply that she hadn't wanted to. And she was loyal to Jacob, if not faithful. What she had done last night had nothing to do with him, except in so far as she still irrationally resented his unwillingness to have her with him.

What she felt now was more akin to panic. Something she had heard last night in the hotel in her listless state came back to her. A gleeful voice in German, above the clatter of the rest: *"Ja, wir haben eine ganze Gruppe gehaftet. Und der Capo ist einer Wichtiger."* This, coupled with Berring's parting comment, gave her a sudden uncanny sense of certainty that Jacob was in danger. Jacob, the important leader. Jacob captured.

She dressed hurriedly. As the first light of dawn shivered in the crack of the heavy curtains, Sylvie stole from her room and stealthily made her way to Vassier. She raged at him, told him he had to find out quickly, now, instantly. Jacob was in danger. She would go to him herself, she would save him.

Sylvie raced to Caroline's room, shook her. "Wake up, Caroline."

She shook her hard. "You have to wake up. You have to help me. Jacob's been captured. Jacob. We have to go to him."

Caroline sat up sleepily.

"You have to help," Sylvie was shouting. A chaos of words poured out of her. "I'll make it all up to you. You'll have another baby with Joseph. I'll have another. I'll give her to you." She was pummeling her. "Caroline, you're my only friend."

Caroline rose. She embraced her friend.

Jacob turned over slowly on the plank in his dank cell. There was no part of his body which didn't ache. When he coughed, blood and mucus tore out of him. Urinating was an agony. Two of the nails on his left hand had been pulled out. He didn't know how much longer he could go on.

He had coached himself for this. Prepared a list of false names, false addresses he could give to his torturers, should the occasion arise. He had held out even before releasing these. They wouldn't trust them if they came too quickly. But even now, now that he had reached the point of confessing these, the torture continued, more brutal than before, at shorter intervals. Perhaps they already knew the names were false. He had no notion how much time had passed. Day blended into night with no mark of difference. He was underground. The scrawls he had made on the walls might bear no relation to real time.

Perhaps they simply enjoyed the torture. He wished he had one of those capsules the Americans carried in their teeth. To end it all. Before it was too late. He thought dimly of his comrades. How many had been taken after that last fatal meeting in the empty barn? Everything had been going so well; the group had been working so well together. The power station explosion had run with the precision of clockwork. And in the last weeks alone, they had managed to dynamite a much-used section of track; had engineered the escape of over fifty of their men from the hill-town prison. They were just awaiting a new cache of arms, when the Germans had sprung. How many of his friends had been taken? How many were still alive? Their faces leapt out at him clearly now from the darkness. He chased them away. Better not to see them. Not to have their faces in his mind. Sylvie and Leo suddenly lodged there instead. No, no, not them. Not them again. He censored their images. It was dangerous. He might breathe their names. Might mumble something as they prodded and poked and stamped on his defeated body. He prayed that they would shoot him soon.

There they were again, the heavy door creaked. Perhaps now, perhaps they would do it now.

Jacob felt rough arms heave him up. Two men marching him, dragging him to the interrogation chamber. He began in his mind's eye to draw the map of the human body, first the skeletal frame with each bone and joint named, then the intricate route of the nervous system, the tracery of veins, arteries, blood vessels; the lobes of the brain. The effort of concentration lifted him into another space: it was his survival tactic for interrogations.

But they were taking him further today. Jacob looked down the dim vaulted corridor with its exposed beams. Perhaps today really was the day. His heart raced. He imagined the firing squad lined up in the bleak morning light. He allowed himself the pleasure of holding Sylvie, her cool body close against his. He saw Leo, no longer a baby now, but a boy carrying a school satchel. He sent a silent message to Mathilde, to Violette, an *envoi* willing them to well-being.

He was outside. The night was dark. Painfully he breathed crisp air into his lungs. Voices barked. German. No. He didn't want to hear.

He was being lifted, pushed into a black van. It lurched into action.

So it wasn't his day. Jacob held himself with difficulty on the wooden seat. Hope, stupid, irrepressible hope, sprang up in him. He focused his mind on the intricacies of the nervous system again.

He didn't know how long they had driven when the van pulled up short. The guard who had sat with him dragged him out, pushed him into the back seat of a waiting vehicle.

"*Au revoir, monsieur. Bonne chance,*" the man said in French. He doffed his Nazi cap with a smile.

Jacob stared at him in confusion. But before he could say anything, before he could get his bearings, the car he was in sped away.

Through the blackness, he distinguished two women in the front seat, both hooded in nuns' cloaks. From the driver's hood, a wisp of unmistakable blonde hair escaped. A laugh rose in Jacob's throat, hesitated there, and then exploded in a single rush of sound.

"Sylvie," Jacob whooped. "Sylvie."

CHAPTER
ELEVEN

I n the latter part of August of
1945—the momentous year when formal treaties, at least, declared
that the world was at peace—a curious scene unfolded on one of
the *quais* of the Paris Gare de l'Est.

Three women, one man, two children. The man, bearing two mid-
dle-sized cases, walked determinedly in front of the group. His face
beneath the soft brown hat was set in grim lines. Trailing him, running to keep up with him, occasionally settling a hand on his arm,
a laughing woman, blonde hair loosened over a coat which hung
from her shoulders. Behind them the two children, a dark curly-
haired girl of about ten, hand in hand with a slender blond boy, a
little smaller than her, evidently frailer. And then the two other
women, one erect, stately, walking with measured steps which left
no doubt of her certainty of her destination; the second, head bowed,
her gait sluggish, awkward, as if at any moment she might pause and
question her whereabouts.

The odd thing about the party was that it was impossible to tell
who was doing the leaving, who staying behind. First the man
boarded the train. The blonde woman, after a moment, followed.
Then the whole party disappeared into the coach. One by one they
each came out, until only the man was left on the train, while on
the platform, the blonde woman held on tightly to the boy kissing
him over and over again. And then, just as the train shuddered into

life, the man and the blonde woman changed places. The man clung to the woman's wrist, prevented her from mounting the second step. "Please, Sylvie, I beg you. Don't go," he mouthed over the mounting clamor of the engine.

A moment later, it was too late. The train heaved into action, the woman encased in its iron depths folded her fur-lined coat over her arm and looked with satisfaction into the distance. The small group waited, a little forlornly, for the wave that never came.

Sylvie Kowalska Jardine, almost six years to the day after she had initially planned a return to Poland, was now at last on her way. She knew that the others were adamantly set against her going. Jacob, Leo, Caroline, even the Princesse and Violette who were on a passing visit. She didn't care. Only Leo gave her a fleeting pang: he was such a quiet, dutiful child, physically almost the replica of her brother, Tadzio, but without Tadzio's mischievous sparkle. A child, she thought, brought up in the claustrophobic proximity of old people whose anxieties shadowed his movements. A child who had, with the close of the war, come back into their midst like a shy stranger. Now, four months later, he was still timid, hesitant.

Like a woman struggling out of a smoke-filled room where the fumes threatened to engulf her, Sylvie took a short choking breath.

She needed, she had to get away. Life after the initial euphoria of liberation had taken on a dreariness which bordered on desperation. Some days she could see no reason for getting out of bed. Jacob seemed to have lost all interest in her, seemed more intent on his mother, who was still mourning the death of her husband. He trailed guilty depression wherever he went. All he could think about were the dead, whose numbers seemed to grow daily. Or of the survivors of those horrendous extermination camps which she wanted to hear no more about. He spent all his time now working with those survivors. It was as if he had disappeared inside them.

Caroline, if anything, was worse. Her days were composed of visits to the missing persons' office, interminable waits by the telephone, scrambles for the post. She was looking for Joseph, her hope straining against her fear in an uneven contest.

If only the baby that was growing in her had housed itself in Caroline, Sylvie thought. That would have made things better all round. Caroline would have a purpose in life, outside her obsessive search. And she would have a friend again, rather than a funereal vestige of the Caroline of old.

No one knew about the baby. Not even Jacob. She hadn't told him and he was too preoccupied, rarely came close enough to her, to notice. He had stopped making love to her altogether now. Sometimes she felt he had embraced death, averted his eyes from her body because it reminded him too painfully of life.

She knew when the baby had been conceived. Sylvie laid a hand surreptitiously on her stomach and felt the slight taut bulge, still too small for anyone to notice unless they were looking particularly. It had been on the eighth of April, exactly a month before the war in Europe had finally ended. Jacques had arrived in the house, bearing a bunch of celebratory flowers. Kissed her, whistled a birthday tribute. Jacob had looked aghast. He had forgotten. He had tried to redeem himself by pretending he had planned a surprise birthday dinner at the Ritz. They had gone to the hotel, eaten what these days passed for an excellent dinner. As long as she had concentrated only on Jacques' witticisms, and not focused on Caroline's ashen face or Jacob's abstracted eyes, she could almost imagine that the last six years had never been.

Later, at home, Jacques had asked her to sing. She had sat down at the piano and picked out a few tunes, and then almost as if she had been inspired, she sang. Sang the coded lyrics Jacob had improvised for her in that first wartime meeting in Marseilles:

> *"A l'Hôtel d'Algers*
> *dans un autre pays,*
> *je l'ai rencontré*
> *c'était le samedi*
> *l'homme de mes rêves*
> *mais seulement le samedi.*
> *Dimanche il était parti."*

And then, she had added a new stanza:

> *I saw him again*
> *I don't quite know when*
> *A world had gone awry*
> *Perhaps it was April 45*
> *That man of my dreams*
> *Things had changed it seems.*
> *We had lost our dreams.*

Jacob had stared at her as if he were seeing her for the first time after a long absence. Then, when the others had gone, he had made love to her. Made love with a kind of desperation which their coupling could only momentarily assuage, a search for oblivion.

In an odd way she remembered that day as the last significant day of her life. Since then everything had been gloom and pettiness. Sometimes Sylvie felt her hold on things was loosening. There was no one to talk to except Leo, no one to reflect her being, to notice whether she looked well or poorly, to shape the borders of herself. Increasingly she found herself daydreaming about the past, lost in the sheer exhilaration of the last few years.

How different it had all been then. How well she remembered the look of wonder on Jacob's face as he learned how she and Caroline had planned his escape from prison, then sprung him. A look of wonder which extended to each touch, each excited glance during his period of convalescence in that remote farmhouse. And then had come the exhilaration of sabotage. Three times they had worked together, before Jacob had again insisted on going his separate way. Three times she had had the opportunity to marvel at Jacob's cool implacability. It was as if there was another, a different man housed in him as he calmly uttered unquestionable orders; infused them with his own determined purpose. With him, danger, the swift secrecy of laying explosives, was merely an incident in a longer narrative which bore a triumphant end. Even Caroline had blossomed in his atmosphere of quiet resolution and incontestable hope, laying aside her depression to work beside them. Yes, those had been the best times. Sylvie could still feel the tingle in her fingers, the catch in her throat when she pushed down the lever on the detonator.

And all in order to return to the banality of a Paris flat, to hunt in bare shops for everyday needs.

Andrzej's letter had come as a godsend. It had taken weeks to reach her, had chased her through a variety of addresses. In its enigmatic terseness, its bravura, it was pure Andrzej.

"Silweczka!" he addressed her in the caressing diminutive, "Poland is free and again in chains. I trust you and yours are well. I salute you. Andrzej."

That was the extent of it. There was no address. Only a postmark. Krakow. Sylvie had hugged the letter to her for two days, breathed in Andrzej's unshackled air. Then without telling anyone she had gone about purchasing a train ticket, getting the necessary visas.

Only a week before her planned departure had she announced her intention to Jacob.

A look of utter astonishment had come over his face. "Sylvie, this is madness," he had said. "Poland is in ruins. A wasteland. There are still pockets of fighting. It's no place for a woman on her own. And the journey. You'll never get there."

She had looked at him scornfully.

He had tried quiet persuasion. "If it's your Babushka you want to see, you know very well that there is almost no chance that she's still alive. Why, even before the war, it was hardly likely. Sylvie, be reasonable."

"I too am allowed to pay homage to my dead" is all she had said to him.

Eventually she had told him of the letter from Andrzej. An edge of anger had entered his voice. "You don't know where he is, Sylvie. There's no address. And it's irresponsible. What about Leo? He needs you."

Sylvie had been deaf to his protests. She had spent her last days taking Leo to the movies, to a concert. And she had packed her bags. One full of whatever durable food she could find. Another with clothes. One evening Jacob had walked in and thrown in her face the information he had gleaned about Andrzej: it was more than Sylvie knew for certain.

"Andrzej Potacki. Mathematician. Twenty-eight years old. A lieutenant in Anders' army. Probably parachuted into Poland last year. I guess that makes him a hero in your books." He had sneered the last at her.

It had dawned on Sylvie that he was jealous. And his words had confirmed her suspicion. "I trust you intend to come back," he had said coldly.

"I imagine so," she had answered, her tone equally cool. But a little note of triumph played in her ear.

That night she had slept in Leo's bed.

Sylvie looked out of the murky train window. Gray drizzle. Flat barren land. Here and there, the remnants of an abandoned tank. The train moved, slowly, heavily, in fits and starts. Destination seemed a distant idea unrelated to its fitful progress. Goods trains rattled past them as they made interminable stops at innumerable small stations or on desolate stretches of track. Reims, Chalons, Chaumont. The changing flow of passengers who shared her compartment was silent, wary. They avoided each other's eyes. It was hardly any different from the wartime trains, Sylvie reflected, except that the passport and ticket checks were carried out with a semblance of politeness. Nonetheless, as they crossed the border into Switzerland, she was grateful for the diplomatic pass the Princesse had, at the last moment, procured for her.

At Basel, she stayed overnight in a small hotel. Her dreams were in Polish. She was a small girl, running, running. When she woke she had difficulty remembering where she was. But at least the train left the sleepy station on time. In Zürich it was another matter. The platforms teemed with people and languages. The train to Vienna was delayed and then delayed again and again.

Sylvie, sitting in the crowded waiting room, had the sense that she was hovering somewhere outside her body. She clung to her suitcases as if they were her sole grip on reality. When at last she boarded the train, she sat back in her seat and instantly closed her eyes. She prayed that she might not wake until they reached Vienna.

She had forgotten about borders.

At the small market town of Feldkirch, they were all suddenly and ominously ordered off the train. Passports were barked for. A thorough search was in place. The smallest minutiae of cases were turned over, sniffed. Fear tugged at Sylvie, fastened on her throat, a fear she had never felt during the war, not even when at the last, her small cases were filled with rifles. It caught her unawares, perhaps precisely because she was unprepared. She managed to hold herself up only by leaning heavily on the wall of the station. A man, seeing her ashen face, took her arm. "Yes," he murmured, "just like the Nazis. Habits don't change quickly."

Not until the first dawn light glimmered were they allowed back on the train.

At Innsbruck, Sylvie was told there would be no trains to Vienna until the following day, if then. Tears started to stream down her face. The teller took pity on her, told her there was a train in an hour to Salzburg. Perhaps she might like to visit Mozart's birthplace.

Sylvie wanted to kiss him. The sprightly line of a Mozart concerto formed in her ear. She hummed inwardly. In her mind's eye, her fingers flitted over keys. Sound poured out, drowning the bustle of the station. Playing, Sylvie waited, still playing, boarded the Salzburg train. In Salzburg, the station hotel had a room for her. She forgot about food, wanting only the comfort of a bed. Sylvie slept. In her dreams, she was in the pink house. Her parents' house. She was sitting at the grand piano. Mozart flew from her fingertips. "Pa-pa-

PA," her father, standing beside her, sounded out the rhythm. She looked up for his approval. *"Dobrze, dobrze, bardzo dobrze."* His smile gleamed white. He patted her head, let his hand rest on her shoulder. Sylvie took it, brought it to her lips.

She woke again to a feeling of displacement, in time as much as in space. There would be no trains, she was told, until later. No, no one was quite sure when. With a sigh she left her cases at the station and sat in a small café to sip something that went under the name of coffee. Then she wandered through the town, stumbled upon Mozart's birthplace, paid homage. The cobbled streets, the colors and proportions of the houses, reminded her of something, what was it, long ago. She couldn't quite place it.

When she finally reached the station again, she was told a train was about to leave. Sylvie rushed, scrambled with her cases. She suddenly realized that she had lost her sense of destination. The journey itself had taken over, a journey which seemed to be as much about taking her back in time as across space.

They arrived in Vienna late that night. But the station still swarmed with frenetic activity and a maze of foreign tongues. Sylvie's head reeled. Every second person seemed to be in uniform. A welter of uniforms: Russian, British, American, French. She walked over to a Frenchman. Hardly trusting her disused voice, she asked about hotels. He looked at her as if she were a madwoman, then pointed her toward a kiosk. There a man told her in no uncertain terms that there were no rooms to be had in Vienna. Sylvie felt the tears leap again to her eyes. She shook herself. What was the matter with her? She tried to see whether there were any benches where she could sit. If worse came to worst, she told herself, she could stay the night in the station.

Sylvie trailed her cases listlessly round the station. She saw people bedded down on the floor, a woman with a child, an old man. When she thought she could walk no more, she spotted a station café and breathed a sigh of relief. She walked in, queued for a place, and at last found herself at a small dismal table. The man behind her was shown to the same place. Sylvie looked at him briefly, a small man with lanky hair, the traces of a moustache. She concentrated on placing her order.

When she had finished, he addressed her. *"Sie suchen ein Zimmer?* A room?"

Sylvie watched his shifty eyes, but despite herself, found herself nodding.

He smiled craftily, rubbed his thumb against two rather grubby fingers. "You have money? Real money? Dollars?" He spoke now in broken English.

Again, despite herself, Sylvie nodded. She clamored against her own fear. Why, this man was no different from the black marketeers she had spent so much of the war with, she told herself firmly. Murder was hardly his business. But she held tightly to her bag.

He drank his coffee, watched her crumble her tasteless cake, let her pay for him. Then he took her bags and gestured for her to follow him. For that at least, Sylvie thought, she should be grateful.

They walked silently through narrow, cobbled streets, keeping away from the main thoroughfares. At last, in a tiny dark lane, huddled against the gothic bulk of St. Stephansdom, he stopped in front of a house and pressed a buzzer. There was an answering ring. Sylvie followed him up three narrowly curving flights of stairs to where a door opened on a small, neat, middle-aged man with a trim Hitler moustache.

"*Kommen Sie hinein, kommen Sie hinein,*" the man welcomed her smilingly. Then with a gesture of distaste, he passed Sylvie's guide some bills and closed the door on him.

Sylvie looked round her: a small spare flat, but tidy. Her host chatted to her in his rapid sing-song Viennese. She followed only half of it, had the sense that he was telling her his life story, a whirlpool of words and events which culminated in a dying wife and a door being opened on a room with a vast double bed, a dark ornate wardrobe. She looked longingly at the clean, ironed sheets.

"*Ja, ja, Sie sind müde.*" He smiled and smiled, a clown's smile which didn't sit naturally on his face. "*Ja, aber nur Ihren Pass bitte.*" He launched into a story about a man who had snuck out on him in the middle of the night, asked apologetically for her passport. Sylvie showed it to him, then with an instinctive cunning withdrew it. "*Ich bezahle Ihnen jetzt,*" she said, reaching for her purse.

He looked a little hurt, but whipped the money away from her.

She didn't know quite what it was, but she decided to sleep with her clothes on, tuck her bag under her pillow. She didn't like Vienna, Sylvie thought, as she sank into the soft bed. She would do her best to be out of here tomorrow.

As it was, Sylvie spent five nights in Herr Karl's flat. During that time she was treated at length to his theory of a watery apocalypse which would sink this mired world in the way it deserved. She was also made privy to his habit of polishing his five pairs of boots, his visible wealth, daily, as she sipped her ersatz coffee in his tiny kitchen. The rest of her time was largely spent arguing with stubborn Russian officials and waiting for the pass and the ticket which would take her first to Ostrava and then to Krakow.

Paris seemed a million miles away from St. Stephansdom, a city in another universe.

On her last night at Herr Karl's, Sylvie decided she would allow herself the luxury of getting fully undressed, of washing herself slowly from top to toe at the tiny sink in preparation for her departure. She paused for a moment in the process to gaze at the mound of her stomach. For a flickering second, it occurred to her that this whole journey was a kind of madness. Then she slipped naked between the bedsheets and wandered quickly into that world of dreams which was becoming as real to her as her peregrinations.

She was startled from sleep by a sound she couldn't quite place, the catch of a breath, the creak of a floorboard. She felt cold, pulled the blankets over her from where they had strayed. It was then that she felt a weight on the bed. She sat up, opened her eyes. In the glimmer of a single candle, she saw Herr Karl perched at the very edge of the bed.

"*Ja, ja, das bin ich,*" his voice crooned strangely. "It's only me."

She took in the baggy pajama top, the hand wrapped round an erection, the scraggy testicles, the glazed eyes. She wanted to hit him, but she stayed her hand, wrapped the blanket more tightly round her. He moved to pull it from her, to caress her bare shoulders. Sylvie drew away.

"Herr Karl," she said in an icy voice. "I am a married woman, a pregnant woman."

She saw him blink, saw the rubbing hand falter, and then the croon came again, "*Ja, ja, das macht nichts.* It doesn't matter. You're so beautiful." He pulled her toward him, tried to move her hand to his crotch. She kicked him, leapt out of bed. She didn't know what fed his excitement more, the sight of her nudity or the kick. But his eyes shone brighter than ever; the erection strained. He came toward her.

"Herr Karl, I shall go straight to the police," Sylvie screamed, hearing the absurdity of her own voice. She drew herself to her full height. She was a good head taller than him. "The police, you hear."

"The police," he said in a strangled voice and the word brought the sperm teeming out of him onto the bed's whiteness. "I am your police." He looked at her triumphantly with a hint of menace, a trace of revulsion. "And there's no reason, Frau Sylvie, to be so high and mighty," he cackled. "You're just a Pole, aren't you? You know what Herr Hitler thought of the Poles. Racial vermin. Slaves. A nation that deserves to be swept off the face of the earth." He laughed his gleeful mad clown's laugh and pointed to a tiny peephole in the wall opposite the bed. "I have seen you before. I know what you women get up to."

With a cocky gesture he left her shivering in the cold room.

Sylvie packed her bags and stole silently from the flat. An acrid taste of disgust left with her. She felt numb, disoriented. It was as if, for the first time, the foul residue of war had penetrated her, enveloped her very person. She sat huddled in the station, waited for the train and finally embarked on the last lap of her journey. It took her through Ostrava and then after another change, another delay, at last to Krakow.

When she finally disembarked in the once royal city, her disorientation seemed to have grown. She no longer had a precise sense of why she had come, the imperative that had forced her to this journey. It had taken her almost two weeks to complete an itinerary which should have taken at most two days. To her those two weeks stretched back into a time whose starting point had lost its distinctness.

She walked through ancient, dimly familiar streets which reeked of sewage and poverty. Thin children played in the shadows of houses. People scurried. Everywhere Russian blended into Polish making her feel that she had lost her grip on her native tongue. A room, she thought dimly, I must find a room. Rest. She saw notices pinned up on buildings, inspected them. They didn't lead her to rooms. They were pleas, endless exhortations: "If anyone has seen a boy of eight with brown hair who answers to the name of Thomasz Przemyk, please inform Rosa Przemyk at . . ." "Disappeared in Warsaw on 5 August 1944, Tadeus Komorowski, 50. Any news welcome . . ." Sylvie read, started visibly to shake. Then she remembered, Andrzej, she must find Andrzej, put notices up, on the walls, in the papers.

"Pani szuka kogós?" A woman approached her, an old woman with a crinkled face and a thin smile, a woman wearing a flowered headscarf. Sylvie saw Babushka, knew it was and wasn't her.

"Tak. Yes—no," Sylvie replied, "I'm looking for someone, but I'm also looking for a room." A woman, she thought, I can trust a woman.

"I was told the Russians have filled the hotels, but I need somewhere to stay."

The woman inspected her, took in the rich fur-lined coat, the slightly worn cases.

Sylvie tried to counter her suspicion. "I've come from Paris, but I'm Polish. I've come to look for someone. Can you help me?"

The woman hesitated, then nodded. She looked hungrily at Sylvie's bags, took one from her. "Come with me."

She led her to a nearby building, up a dark, narrow staircase. "Here we are," she said.

Sylvie's heart sank. A bare, tiny flat. Three small rooms, of which the biggest was the kitchen. The only decoration was a small wooden crucifix, the portrait of a saint.

The woman ushered her into a bedroom, removed children's things from the bed, exhorted Sylvie to unpack, showed her a rickety wardrobe in the hall. "This is fine, isn't it? Clean." She patted the narrow bed. She chatted, told Sylvie her name, Pani Baran, went to boil some water so Sylvie could wash, watched her open her cases. Sylvie saw the hunger in her eyes, handed her a large sausage.

"Dziękuję, dziękuję," she bowed, bobbed, rushed away to hide her treasure.

Sylvie sat down on the bed and wept.

The next day Sylvie extricated herself from Pani Baran's two children, who followed her every move, and made her way to the French consulate. Princesse Mathilde had insisted in no uncertain terms that she must go to the consulate, must present the letter Sylvie was holding to the consul. Sylvie now saw her wisdom. She had no idea where to begin her search for Andrzej, apart from the hit-and-miss strategy of the countless random announcements. But when she arrived at the consular building, she was emphatically told by a woman whom she thought could be either a housekeeper or a secretary that there was no one in. The consul was away. For at least two weeks. Her stress on the importance of her mission, her plea that she was looking for a friend, held no sway. The woman simply shrugged. "Put an ad in the paper," she said.

Sylvie kept back her tears, bought herself an execrable meal in a dowdy restaurant, found a newspaper office, returned desultorily to Pani Baran's. Her hostess, when she told her, was more sympathetic to her problems. She patted Sylvie's shoulder. "Come with me," she said, then hesitating, added, "Put on a hat."

She led her to Krakow's central square and through the doors of the ancient cathedral. In its damp awesome depths, she stopped in front of a painted statue of the Virgin Mary. She urged Sylvie to pray, to pray for the return of Andrzej. She lit a candle, bowed her head. Shivering, Sylvie imitated her gestures. She was transported back to the last time she had prayed in front of the Virgin, to the time when Tadzio and her parents had died. Her mind reeled. But then as now, prayer would not come to her.

Pani Baran, however, smiled with a calm certainty. She led her to one of the cafés on the square. Despite the cold, despite the lack of anything Sylvie considered distinctly edible, it was crowded with voices and people. Pani Baran took her to a back table where an old gnarled man sat smoking an acrid cigarette. She spoke for Sylvie, named Andrzej Potacki. The old man gestured them into chairs, puffed at his cigarette, reflected, murmured Andrzej's name over and over. Then he shook his head. *"Nie wiem."* He smiled toothlessly. "But come back in a day or two. I'll keep my ears to the ground, make some inquiries." In the next breath he addressed Sylvie. "Do you have cigarettes?"

It was her turn to shake her head, but she reached in her purse and gave him some change. He nodded rhythmically, *"Dobrze, dobrze."*

Sylvie lived out the passage of the days, counting them until the consul's return. Each day she explored another sector of the city, scanned people's faces, read the walls, the newspapers. Each day as Polish gradually invaded her consciousness, she felt she was being thrown back further into her past. Certain streets at certain angles in particular lights spoke to her. Certain smells leapt into her nostrils, threatening her with their unnamed familiarity. She found it increasingly difficult to imagine Jacob. But at each corner, she thought she saw a face from her childhood.

Exactly two weeks and one day after she had first gone to the consulate, she returned. This time he was there. Sylvie presented her letter, waited. She was, respectfully now, ushered into a sitting room by the woman who had originally turned her away. It was the first time in weeks that she had been in an atmosphere which spoke of comfort. She sank back into brocade cushions, breathed deeply.

The sound of a French voice startled her. *"Madame Jardine, je suis enchanté."* There followed a neat little speech which paid compliments to Sylvie, to the Princesse. "If I can be of any assistance . . ."

Sylvie looked at the trim older man, the elegant cut of his suit.

She talked, explained, shed a tear. At the end of the interview, she found herself a guest of the consul's, if only for two weeks. He was so sorry; another staff member was arriving then. Space would be tight, but for now, he welcomed her.

Sylvie emerged with the sense of a minor triumph. She knew that there were no real grounds for it. She was no closer to finding Andrzej. But the consular building gave her the impression of being on firm terrain rather than in a dangerous swamp in which the earth might give way at any time and swallow her up.

Pani Baran was not equally pleased to see her go. Nonetheless, she insisted on helping Sylvie pack, insisted that she have a bath before leaving. She brought out the old tin tub Sylvie had seen her use for the children. She watched Sylvie undress and began to chortle. "I knew you couldn't be growing fat on our food, Pani Sylvie. So the man you are looking for is the child's father." She shook her graying head, began a litany of names, of men who had disappeared, died.

Sylvie, feeling her head whirl, cut her off sharply. "My husband is very much alive and in Paris," she said definitively. The statement suddenly brought back Jacob. For the first time since she had left Paris, she began to wonder why she had come here.

She left Pani Baran all her remaining food. It meant more in that world of lacks than paper money.

A week in the consulate brought no news of Andrzej. Sylvie let out two of her dresses, had another made, wrote a letter home. Out of pride, the writing of it made her reaffirm her certainty that soon she would locate Andrzej. She also said that she was searching out any living relatives. And, the letter added, she had decided that she would visit the family home. It was a thought that had hovered at the back of her mind and at that moment became a determination.

But first the consul suggested that she visit Warsaw. There was a man he knew there who had been with Anders' army. He had many contacts, might be able to help.

Sylvie packed a single case and traveled to Warsaw, a continually interrupted journey which lasted a day and most of a night.

She arrived in a desolate, wintry wasteland which beggared description. Ruins had been spoken of, but in her mind's eye, these had borne a picturesque tinge. The reality was the horror of utter devastation. Narrow lanes carved through torrents of fire-blackened rubble, eerie windowless shells of houses, looming staircases attached to scorched, fragile façades. Here and there a wooden cross, shriveled flowers, announcing a grave. And everywhere the scribbled messages, like incantations, evoking the missing. A city of the dead. The disappeared.

Sylvie made her way through debris. At every turn, small groups of men, women and children worked with bare hands, the occasional spade, to clear the waste. Amidst it Sylvie shivered to see bones, skeletal remains. She averted her eyes, tried to be as brave as these children. At last, at the corner of a small square which boasted the fragment of a pedestal and an armless cherub, she found herself in front of the address she had been searching for.

The consul's friend. He was sitting in front of a small stove which gave off a mere whisper of heat. A cavernous man with an empty sleeve pinned neatly to his jacket, in a room where the wall looked as if it might precariously tumble at any moment.

"Come in, come in," he welcomed Sylvie.

She stated her business. He looked at her oddly as she gave him Andrzej's name.

"Yes, I know him," he said, then paused.

Elation flooded through her.

"But I don't know where he is."

Something in the way he said it gave Sylvie a start. She recognized that tone. What was it? She gazed into the man's eyes. And then she located it. It was the whiff of the clandestine, the guarded.

"Can you find him? Get him a message from me?"

Her excitement made him smile.

"I'll try, but I can't promise."

Sylvie told him where she would be staying.

"Don't hope too much," he cautioned her as she left. "And try other means, any means you have."

Sylvie nodded, thanked him. She couldn't help the happiness that murmured inside her.

Two weeks later, in that dismal city it subsided. A cold wind gusted in from the plains. A remorseless slate sky quashed all possibility of hope. She had tried to trace some relatives with a prewar address she still had. She had walked from street to indistinguishable street, picking her way carefully, to no end. No one seemed to know anything. The Russian officials she tried to talk to made short shrift of her inquiries. They treated her as an enemy. She began to see that even the desolation around her was not going to guarantee a true peace.

One day amidst the ruins, in a narrow street-level room, she found a hat shop. The absurdity made her laugh and then cry. The tears became a regular occurrence, catching her alone, in public, unawares.

Beneath the tears, the only reality seemed to be the reality of waiting. She was filled with her waiting. Every day she went to see the consul's friend. Every day, he shook his head lugubriously. She tried other sources, pinned messages to walls. To no avail. She began to understand Caroline's madness. The sheer inert weight of increasingly hopeless anticipation. Its tentacles filled the air one breathed, bowed one's shoulders. She had a desire to hold her friend, weep with her.

After another period of waiting, she felt herself suffocating, cracking under the burden. Time seemed to have lost its significance. She had forgotten how long she had been here. Only the sight of her growing belly in a cracked mirror one day made her aware of its passage. She decided to go to Lodz. She had another address there. Another set of relatives in the giant industrial city. But here, too, the search proved fruitless.

She returned to Krakow, to the safety of the consulate. She no longer had a distinct sense of who Andrzej was. Why she was looking for him. She walked up to blond men in the street, peered into their faces, apologized. His image had grown hazy. Sometimes, despite the persistence of her search, she forgot who was its object. Andrzej's name took on the shape and substance of her father, the flickering form of her mother. One morning she woke up whimpering, "Papush, Mama."

In the shadow of a forgotten dream, Sylvie decided it was time to visit their graves.

The next day there was a letter from Andrzej. She couldn't believe it. She wanted to dance for joy. He said he would come to see her. He couldn't give a precise date. But he would come. Sylvie had a sudden image of her father embracing her. Saw herself and her brother running joyfully through the woods, playing mischievous pranks. Saw Andrzej. She lay down on the bed and smiled.

The quality of her waiting changed, became increasingly tangled up with memory. Days merged into weeks. Still Andrzej didn't come.

She sat in her small back room and sewed. None of her clothes fitted her. She was making two skirts into one in a crazy patchwork. Her fingers moved clumsily, actions blinded by tears. When would he come? She felt heavy, inert.

The consul came to her room. His eyes moved from her thin,

strained face to the now sizable bulge of her belly. He cleared his throat politely. "I have been thinking, Madame Jardine, perhaps it would be better if you returned to France this week. I have a friend leaving. He could accompany you."

Sylvie looked at him as if through a haze. Her hands flew protectively to her baby. "Yes, yes," she murmured, acknowledging his concern. "But I need another week, perhaps two," she mumbled vaguely, unable to imagine a leaving. "My friend is coming. And I need to go to my parents' grave."

He didn't scold her, didn't think her mad. He had seen her condition before. Hundreds shared it. He simply shook his head, a little sadly, and then tried to make things easier for her. He said he would arrange for her ticket to Lublin.

So that the consul wouldn't confront her too often, she forced herself to spend time in public places, sitting in the few central cafés. One day she overheard two journalists speaking English. They were talking in low voices about battles in the east, partisans, resistance against the Russians. That's where Andrzej would be, she thought dismally. That's what his first card had been about. "Poland is free and again in chains." That's what he had meant. He was fighting, fighting still. She went up to the journalists, told them she had heard them, asked what places they had been talking about. Blurted out that she wanted to go there. Had to find somebody. Somebody named Andrzej Potacki.

They looked at her as if she were mad. "That's no place for a woman," one of them murmured. And the other added, "In one of the villages I went to, half the women had been raped. Cossacks, they told me. Raped. Even the pregnant ones." He looked significantly at her stomach. They advised her to go back to France.

Sylvie walked slowly back to the consulate. It had become almost impossible to talk to anyone. No one understood. More and more, the only reality seemed to lie in the shadows which moved within her.

And then Andrzej was there. A knock came on her door and the little maid bade her go to the rear sitting room. She walked heavily, opened the door to see a man in a greatcoat restlessly pacing the width of the room.

"Andrzej." Sylvie spoke with difficulty. She felt her legs giving way. The maid held her, directed her to the sofa. Sylvie sank heavily into its depths. "Andrzej, is it really you?" Her voice was a hoarse whisper.

He was at her side, clutching her hand. "Silweczka, you mad-woman, what are you doing in this godforsaken country?"

The maid closed the door on them discreetly.

Sylvie stared at him. He was thin, his face gray, but his eyes still danced beneath the incorrigible fall of his hair. "Andrzej." She repeated his name, again and again. She held him. "I've come to find you. I've found you." A teasing smile curled her lips. "And now I'm going to take you away."

"Madwoman." He shook his head, gazed at her tenderly. Then, like a mischievous younger brother he patted her stomach. "And this, is this my Christmas present?"

Sylvie lowered her lids shyly, avoided his question. "You *will* come to France with me, won't you?" She held his hand tightly.

He groaned comically, but his face was serious. "Silweczka, you're a brave girl. And it's wonderful to see you, to see you alive, well. But you have no idea what's going on." Suddenly he looked round him suspiciously, lowered his voice, spoke with urgency. "It's not France here. This country is still at war. Nothing is over for us." His eyes grew fiery, intent. "We didn't live like rats in cellars for years, didn't lose millions of our people, our cities, in order to be slaves of the Russians. You understand?"

Andrzej speaking with the reckless intensity of her father. "In Warsaw the Russians, our supposed saviors, let the Germans massacre us, let us die like flies." He made a savage gesture in the air and Sylvie could almost see the crushed creatures fluttering groundward. "Like flies. And they held their fire. They want us as their slaves, want our wealth. Why, at this very moment, they're transporting thousands of people . . ." He paused, looked round him again a little wildly.

"But that doesn't concern you. All you need to know is that some of us are still fighting. Partisans." He gripped her fingers so tightly, she thought they would break.

"So I can't go anywhere with you, Sylweczka." He looked at her sadly. "But I am pleased to see you. Pleased to see you so well. A little mamuśka. And now you must go back to where it is safe."

Sylvie's face fell. What color it had had drained out of it. "You mean straight away?"

He nodded slowly. "We have one night. Tonight, I shall take you out and show you the lights of Krakow"—he laughed bitterly—"feed you up on pheasant and wine. After all, we have both traveled a long way to see each other. But tomorrow"—he patted her hand gently now—"tomorrow, we shall put you on a train for Paris."

"No." The tears streaming down Sylvie's face did not prevent her voice from being adamant. He couldn't leave so soon. She argued, pleaded, convinced him that he should at least accompany her to her parents' house.

The train to Lublin should have taken a matter of hours. With the chaos of communications, it took them the best part of a day. Sylvie didn't mind. She sat in the cold carriage holding Andrzej's hand. She felt she was floating, floating somewhere between past and present. Scenes from her childhood flitted into her mind, like fragments of dreams. Girlishly she evoked them for Andrzej in the language of that childhood.

Night had fallen by the time they reached the town. Andrzej said they must find a room there. Miraculously he located one with a large clean double bed. They slept side by side in their clothes, a vast eiderdown sheltering them. Like two innocent children who still had hope. Sylvie dreamt, dreamt of home, of her father caressing her, of the smell of cherry jam, of trees.

A paradise before the fall.

But in the morning, Andrzej's restlessness was palpable.

"Sylweczka." He took her hand, looked at her earnestly. "I must get back to my men. They need me."

Tears leapt into her eyes.

He put his arm round her shoulders. "There are journeys it is important to make alone, Sylweczka," he said softly. "Believe me, it will be better." He leapt into action. "I will find you a driver."

Minutes later he was back. He pulled her toward a horse and cart, helped her onto the wooden plank next to a grizzled man whose face was half hidden by his cap, covered her legs with a blanket which smelled of hay and stables. "Pan Stach will make certain you get there safely. He knows the house well." Andrzej embraced her. She could feel the nervousness of his energy, his desire to see her off.

"Be brave, Sylweczka. We will meet again when Poland is free."

He stood waving as the cart clattered into motion over uneven cobblestones, a slender young man with bold blue eyes in a vast greatcoat. The wave brought back the memory of another, the sight of a small receding form, Tadzio waving her into a distance from which she would never return to meet him.

❖   ❖   ❖

They had hardly left the recurring rose and cream and stucco of the town when the first snowflakes began to fall from a leaden sky. Thick white flakes which blew and danced and settled in brown earth. The swirl of whiteness, the horse's slow rhythm, induced trance. The driver's gruff voice came with a jolt.

"I knew your father. An upstanding man," he said, addressing the wind. He receded into silence, shook his head, grumbled. "Now, now the Russians are in the house. Before that it was the Germans. Turned it into a hospital. Carried out experiments. *Wariaci*. Madmen," he mumbled into the scarf he had drawn round his neck.

Sylvie didn't know whether he was referring to the Germans or their victims. She shivered. Felt the baby thump. She asked him about Babushka, Pani Kasia. He grumbled, said nothing, then after a while, nodded vigorously, "*Tak, tak, Pani Kasia. Umarla.* She died, before the war."

She had no distinct sense of how long they had been on the road. The snow had stopped. Increasingly, subliminally, she began to recognize things: a farmhouse, a hamlet, the curve of a hill, a dark expanse of forest. Then, a drive, the tracery of chestnut branches glimmering with snow, a small fluted church spire. Her pulse raced. There it was, the house, the low huddle of the stables. Warmed pink against the slate of the sky.

"Shall I come back for you?" Pan Stach asked her.

Sylvie nodded, then shook her head.

He watched her confusion, shrugged. "If you want me, tell Mietek to fetch me," he gestured in the direction of the stables. Sylvie saw two jeeps oddly stationed in front of them.

She let the large brass knocker resound. She waited. What would she say? She felt insubstantial, a little like a ghost. The knocker was too low on the door. Paint crumbled against her coat as she brushed its surface.

A woman in a shabby nurse's uniform was looking at her. Sylvie opened her mouth, but no words came out. The nurse gazed at her, then smiled suddenly. "Has your time come?" She took her arm, took her small case, led her in.

"No, no," Sylvie protested. "This was my home, before the war. I've come to see it. Visit my parents' graves. My brother's." For some reason, she started to weep.

"Yes, of course," the nurse crooned disbelieving. She stared again at her stomach, pulled her along.

Sylvie trailed after her, unresisting now. She was alive to the strange hush of the house, the occasional scream, murmurs, whimpers. She peered through the door of what had been the main sitting room, saw rows of beds, reclining bodies.

"Come." The nurse urged her up the broad staircase, past her parents' room. "No, not here." She pulled her along, opened a door. The music room, Sylvie thought. But there was no piano, no polished cello erect by its little stand. Instead four beds, three of them occupied by women.

She was taken to the bed by the window. Sylvie looked out: in the dimming light, she saw the small chapel, a stretch of meadow, trees, trees. Her coat was pulled off her while she stared.

"It will be all right," the nurse crooned. "Nothing to it. Now take your clothes off. That's a good girl. Tell me your name. Have you got papers?"

Sylvie offered no resistance. She stared out of the window. Heard the cascade of a Liszt étude, her father's voice, "Faster, faster," Tadzio laughing. She lay back on a plump pillow. Closed her eyes. Moved her lips silently. She heard the women whispering in the distance, "She doesn't look well, poor thing."

Sylvie dozed.

She was startled awake by a male voice. Russian mixed with Polish. In the yellow glow of a bedside lamp, she made out a tall man in officer's uniform. A handsome face, eyes of a liquid darkness. He sat down by the bed of the woman next to her, stroked her hand. "You'll see, Hanka, it will all be over quickly. You'll be fine. We'll have a strapping boy. Soon we can all go back to Leningrad. It's a beautiful city. The boy will love it." He talked on, softly, coaxingly.

Sylvie sat up a little. She liked the sound of his voice. But in Hanka's vast gray eyes there was only mute terror. He coaxed her out of bed, wrapped her in a robe. "The nurse thinks a little stroll down the corridor will help your circulation. Come." They went slowly from the room.

"What a man, that Ivan Makarov." The old woman from the bed opposite Sylvie's spoke. "So gentle, so handsome. But that Hanka"—she shook her head—"I don't know. She's so frail. He brought her in early. Useless, really, there's hardly any staff about. Frightened, I guess he was. I don't think they're married," she added maliciously.

"And he only talks about sons," the woman from the corner bed piped up. "Thinks she'll give birth tomorrow maybe, to a Messiah." She laughed gleefully and then started to cough.

"Maybe she will," one of the nurses muttered. "Did you see the size of that gold crucifix around her neck? That must have cost a pretty penny. They were rich, her people. Don't know what the war's left them though. She's lucky to have that Makarov."

Later that evening, a priest came to their room. It was Christmas Eve. The women crossed themselves, prayed. Sylvie saw Hanka's lips moving frenetically. "Please, please give me a boy, a strong boy."

Sylvie turned away. For the first time, she paused to consider her child. Her thoughts flitted to Caroline, her endless mourning. Caroline would be happy with the baby. She would let her bring her up. It would bring Caroline back to life. A little Katherine.

She woke to cold blue light inching through the shutters. Her gaze fixed on wallpaper. A broad gold stripe, then a narrow gold stripe, then a band of cream and again and again. The music room. Sylvie felt hot, her mouth was parched. She was home. She repeated it to herself, "I am home." She edged out of bed. She had to see her parents: the thought hammered in her. Had to see Tadzio.

They had put her clothes somewhere. Yes, the wardrobe, a hideous ramshackle thing. Where had it come from? Sylvie moved heavily into her clothes, her coat. She walked quietly down the corridor. She peered into the library. A cluster of odd desks, but her father's was still there. She looked at it longingly, but a sound made her close the door quickly. She crept down the stairs. No one. No one by the door. She opened it. The rush of cold air grabbed at her cheeks, cooled her hot forehead. She walked down the little side path, round patches of frosty snow, to the chapel. She searched in the tiny graveyard. There it was, one stone, already speckled with green. Three names simply carved. A cross. Two crests. Sylvie stared. Turned away.

There was no one there, the thought came to her. No one at home.

She walked. Walked across the meadow to the woods. Morning brightness through a tangle of branches glistening with frost. A man approached her, nodded suspiciously. Sylvie pushed on. Babushka's cottage, a steep-roofed square of wood. The terrace. A sliver of smoke from the chimney. She almost stopped to knock. Changed her mind. Ferns peered brown through the crackle of light snow. Sylvie walked. A clearing. The gamekeeper's house. She shivered, hurried on, her steps stumbling, her hands clammy despite the cold.

Memory pressed on her. Her mother was walking beside her. Long strides, hands in jacket pockets. "Here, it was around here I think they found you." She paused, swung back blonde hair. "Silweczka, do you remember anything? Do you remember who it was? Who did it?"

Sylvie flushed. Shame tugged at her, groped with his black-rimmed fingers at her entrails. She pushed him away. Panicked. "No, Mama." She shook her head vehemently. "No. I told you I don't remember anything."

Her mother took her arm. "Never mind, Sylweczka. It's probably better that way. Soon, you'll be in Paris. It's beautiful there." Her mother's calm voice.

"I don't want to go, Mama. I don't want to go. Please, please don't send me," Sylvie pleaded. Her mother paid no heed, talked on, described the marvels of the city, the Ezards, their kindness.

Sylvie turned on her. "You want me to go away. You hate me. You hate me," she shrieked, pounded her arm. Tears, hot humiliating tears, poured out of her.

"No, Sylweczka." Her mother tried to still her. "You don't understand. Your father . . . your father has found all this very difficult. He's upset. It's difficult for him to think of you growing up, grown up." She shrugged. "And then, you may have noticed. I'm going to have a baby."

"No." Sylvie stared at her. She couldn't, wouldn't believe it. "No," she howled. "No. Not a baby. You can't. You'll go away. You'll take Papush away. Like last time." She grew hot, confused. "He'll never forgive me. He thinks I'm dirty. I hate you," she shouted. "I hate you."

Sylvie ran. She wanted to kill her mother. Kill the baby. She ran deeper into the world of the forest. She hated her. She could hear her ragged breath trailing her, her voice, "Sylweczka, wait," and then a thud, a cry. Silence. For the flash of a second, Sylvie was jubilant. She had killed her. Killed her. Now Papush would have to keep her here.

Then she turned. Her mother lay sprawled on the ground where she had stumbled. She gripped her stomach. There was a trickle of blood from her forehead against the pallor of her face. And then, lower down, lower, a dark spreading patch. "Sylvie, run to Papa, run quickly," she groaned. "Quickly."

Sylvie ran with the speed of panic.

Hot panic flashed through her now too as she found herself rushing clumsily over the frozen earth. Running, running. She tripped, fell heavily onto cold ground. "Mama, Mamuśka," she called to the trees, "I'm sorry. I'm sorry. Don't die, Mama. Mamuśka." Her hands gripped her stomach. The baby lurched. She thought she could feel warm blood trickling, oozing down her legs.

Sylvie dreamt. She was hot. So hot. So cold. She was being carried. Her mother was being carried. Her throat ached with dryness. "Drink," a voice said to her. "I'm sorry, Mama," Sylvie pleaded, sipped. "Sorry. It's Papush I hate, not you. Don't die, please don't die. It's Papush. I hate men," she sobbed. "Don't die. Please stop bleeding. Please."

A scream sounded through hush. Sylvie didn't know whether it was hers or her mother's.

Hands prodded her. Voices murmured. Indistinct.

"It's not too bad. Not too much blood."

"Keep her warm."

"It's the other one I'm worried about. If anything happens to his boy, Makarov will make us pay the devil."

"What a day. One, too frail by half, praying nonstop. The other half-dead of exposure."

"It's the screams I can't stand."

"Lucky we moved the old ladies out."

"She keeps calling for her mother. Told me she lived here."

"She's delirious. It's the fever."

"Doesn't hear me when I speak to her."

"Give her some of those powders. It won't hurt her."

"And some broth for the other one. She's so weak."

"I wish she'd stop calling for her mother."

"Thank God Christmas is over and the doctor is back tomorrow."

"Not as bad as last Christmas, though. Is it?"

"I don't know."

"Here, Pani Hanka. Drink this."

Hot, so hot. And the pain. The pain in her back.

Sylvie slept, dreamt. Dreamt bodies and babies. And voices and cries, all jumbled and tumbled together. She didn't know for how long. Then louder screams, again and again.

"It's Hanka. Where's that doctor?"

Screams again and then that tiny murmuring frightened voice, "Please God, give me a boy, please, please."

Sylvie opened her eyes. She saw Hanka's translucent face. The terror there. Pain wrenched across her. Her own cry merged with the other woman's. Hot confusion pounded in her head. She caught her breath across the crest of another contraction and then again and again.

"Not both of them together." The nurses bustled. "There, there, darlings, not so loud. You'll disturb the other patients. Here, breathe some of this."

A mask clamped to her face. Nausea. Sweat poured down her. Her head swam. She couldn't tell her cries from Hanka's. The pain.

"Breathe, little mother, breathe. Go on."

A cloth, cooling her forehead.

"Oh God, she's bleeding."

"Where's that doctor? He should be here."

"Here, this will help."

"Push, dearie, push. Now, now."

"Yes, yes, you're there, once more."

A hot, searing pain tore through her. She screamed, screamed again. Over the din she heard them.

"A boy. A boy."

"Hers is a girl."

"A big healthy boy."

Sylvie heard Hanka murmur, "Yes, a boy. A boy. A boy, Ivan."

The fragile cry of babies, a whisper, a hiccup.

Sylvie fell back on the sheets, looked over at Hanka. No more screams now. Her eyes were shut. Silence. Only the nurses' uniforms whispered.

"*Boże mój, Boże mój*. Poor child. Poor thing. Poor Makarov."

Sylvie woke at the crack of dawn. She glanced at Hanka. White, so white, like her mother had been, there on the ground in the woods. With the spot of red spreading through the sheets. Poor thing, poor thing. Gray eyes fluttered open. A faint serene smile. And then the eyes closed.

Sylvie stared and stared.

Then slowly stiffly, she crept out of bed, tried her feet. They held her. But her thoughts were askew. Sore. Like the soreness inside her. She was cold. So cold. Mama was dead. Mama, Mama hold me. Help, she must get help. Caroline, help me. Where are you, Caroline? Poor child, poor child. Katherine. Poor Katherine.

Sylvie fumbled clothes, dressed, put on her coat. Her hands shook. Two babies lay sleeping peacefully in cots at the end of the room. She studied them closely. Breathing. They were both breathing. Two fistlike faces beneath dark, downy heads. Four tiny wrists and clenched fingers. Sylvie stared. Then determinedly she lifted one tiny form, wrapped it in a blanket. Stealthily, she made her way down the stairs. Mama, Mamushka, I've brought you your baby. See, Caroline, your baby. Look, look, aren't you happy. Pleased. Pleased with me.

Cold air lashed her face. Where were they? Where were they?

The stables, she remembered. The stables. She knocked loudly. "Take me to Pan Stach. Please, please, take me to Pan Stach."

Ten days later Jacob Jardine arrived at the French Consulate in Krakow. He was worried. Deeply worried, as he had increasingly been over the months of Sylvie's absence. The telegram summoning him had been something of a relief. He had come as quickly as was feasible, hoping that the word "unwell" the telegram used was not a euphemism for "critical."

He stood there now in the rococo sitting room and twisted the lighter in his pocket.

"Dr. Jardine, I'm so glad you were able to get here so quickly. I hope our telegram didn't frighten you unduly. It's just that Sylvie, Madame Jardine, was ill when she came back to us. Feverish. A little delirious. A postnatal infection, I imagine."

Jacob's mouth fell open.

"No, no," the consul rushed on. "Nothing serious. She's much better now. And the baby, the baby is just fine. We hired a nanny to look after her. But you can imagine, this is hardly the place for a mother and child."

The man smiled, waiting for Jacob to speak.

An embarrassing silence while conflicting emotions played over Jacob's face.

"Of course," the consul filled it, "it would have been better for the birth to have taken place in Paris. But your wife insisted on staying, insisted on visiting her parental home. Never mind. It's all for the best. And the baby has been no trouble. A sweet little girl. Hardly ever cries."

Jacob tried a smile, murmured thanks. He was desperately trying to digest what the consul was saying. He found himself ludicrously counting months as he followed the man up the stairs.

"I shall leave you now," the consul said politely, as he knocked on a door. "Of course, you are welcome to stay here for a night or two."

Jacob took in the room, saw a gray-haired woman rocking an

ornate cradle and humming; saw a frail Sylvie reclining on a sofa, her eyes fixed on empty space. He didn't like that unseeing stare, didn't like the memories it aroused in him of another room, many years ago, in the south, in Roussillon. He composed himself.

"Sylvie." He took her cool, limp hand. "Sylvie, I'm here. I've come to take you home."

She turned her head, looked at him as from a great distance. But her eyes focused on him. She gave him a watery smile. Nodded.

Jacob relaxed, kissed her forehead.

She gazed up at him. "I didn't tell you. Thought you wouldn't let me leave. But there's a baby. It . . ." She paused, a little confused. "She . . . she came just a little early." Sylvie stood up, walked slowly toward the cradle and picked up the tiny bundle. "Here." She turned to Jacob. "She's yours. For you and Caroline." She stretched the bundle toward Jacob.

Jacob took the baby, looked into the tiny face. Calm gray eyes stared at him as if they could see him. He smiled, held the bundle close.

"Yes," Sylvie murmured. "I thought you would be pleased. Caroline will be pleased. I've named her Katherine."

Jacob averted his face. He couldn't tell her, it wasn't the moment to tell her, that Caroline had taken her own life the preceding month.

PART III

CHAPTER
TWELVE

biting November wind whipped through the canyon of the street and caught at Katherine's coat, depositing an array of candy wrappers and bus transfers at her feet. She clutched her school satchel more closely to her, holding it like a shield against the elements. One more block and she could hop onto the bus which would take her to Grand Central Station. No one had seen her. No one would, she promised herself. Only her friend Antonia knew where she was headed and she could be trusted to keep a secret.

The bus appeared just as Katherine turned the corner and she leapt onto it confidently. Everything was working according to plan. She would be at the station just in time to catch the train. Her teacher wouldn't worry, since she had alerted her that she was going to be away and promised to bring a note on her return. That meant she had a good eight hours' start before anyone need even think about her absence. And by that time she would be safely in Boston. Katherine sat back in the warmth of her seat and watched Central Park give way to the shops and office towers of midtown Manhattan.

At the age of thirteen Katherine Jardine was an adept New Yorker. She could maneuver her way round streets and crowds and subway lines with the ease of a native. There was no trace of the foreign in her speech, except perhaps in the greater clarity with which she enunciated her sentences. She was also an adept liar. It was not something she liked to do or resorted to very often. But when she did, it was always performed with complete aplomb and without the slightest trace of hesitation or reddening of cheeks. She lied out of expediency. As she had done to her teacher yesterday. As she would do tomorrow, if she needed to, to realize her plans. And her plans now were very clearly set in her mind. She was running away from home. And she was determined not to return.

Katherine lined up at the ticket counter and proclaimed her destination in a clear voice. The clerk looked at her oddly as she took her purse out of her school satchel and carefully counted out the exact money.

"Isn't Boston a long way for a kid like you to be going?" he asked.

She looked at him directly with her cool gray eyes. "I'm going to meet my family," she said quietly. "They're waiting for me at the station."

The attendant was suspicious, but cowed. There was already something about Katherine's face that made questions an imposition. Tall for her age, she held her shoulders straight, her head, with its abundant sheen of hair, high. She had a composure well beyond her years. And her beauty was already more than a promise. Of all this Katherine was only dimly aware. For beneath her apparent self-possession, there was a driving urgency. Over the last months, she had realized that she had to leave home or something terrible would happen. She couldn't quite locate the nature of that terror, she didn't know exactly what evil it was that would occur, but she felt it tangibly. It was there as soon as she passed through the doors of their East Side brownstone. It circled round her as she moved through the house and sometimes it settled in the look of pure hatred that emanated from her mother's eyes when they rested on her.

Katherine sat back in the train's cushioned seats and as it pulled away from the platform, she breathed a sigh of relief. The first part of her plan had been safely accomplished.

She had tried to talk to her father about her fears. But Pappy, who was always so willing to engage with her for hours and talk about school work or play chess, only patted her on the shoulder and fobbed her off with platitudes when the question of her mother came up. "Your mother is a little depressed at the moment. It will pass." Or, "Don't worry, Kat, it will all get better soon." Well, now that she was no longer there, he would have to pay attention; would know that she had been serious. Or would he? Katherine stirred nervously in her seat. He had been so absentminded of late, so preoccupied with his work, his writing, the morality of being an expert witness. She still didn't understand what he meant by all that, no matter how much he explained. All that she knew was that he was increasingly away from home, at meetings, conferences. And that left her solely in her mother's power.

Katherine shivered and drew her coat more tightly round her. She tried to think of something more pleasant. The hills now, through which the train was winding its way, were pretty. Katherine rummaged in her satchel. She had brought almost nothing with her— two pairs of underwear, stockings, a toothbrush, two books. More would have made her flight obvious. She drew out a book. The photograph she always used as a bookmark fluttered out of it. She looked at the picture. Yes, that had been the happiest time of her life. The crossing. Pappy and a dark little girl who was herself leaning against a lifeboat.

She was almost six then. Mother and Leo had been seasick for the duration of the crossing and had lain inert on deck-chairs. Pappy and she, on the other hand, had had a whale of a time. She could still remember it all intensely: the swimming pool in which she had learned to do a dog-paddle; the ring game; the endless stretch of blue ocean; the vast liner as big as a city through which she and Pappy had wandered endlessly. Then the excitement of the New York skyline seen from a distance, its jutting towers like a giant's cardboard cut-outs poking into a blue sky. After that, it had all changed. She couldn't remember the details, only the sense of confusion that everything was different—the language, the schools she had been sent to one after another. And Pappy was always busy. Still, there was Leo. They had grown very close. He had helped her. And then Leo had left for college. That was when the evil had grown.

Katherine glanced at her small watch. Only a few hours and she would be with him again. Pappy had given her that watch. He had given her so many things, beautiful things, little surprising things when he came back from trips. Some of the most treasured had disappeared or been broken. That was when she had begun to recognize the evil.

She remembered the moment distinctly. She was ten. She had come home from school with Antonia. Thankfully, her mother wasn't in and Doreen, the maid, had plied them with milk and cookies. Then they had gone to Katherine's room. Instantly Katherine had realized something was wrong. The doll, Angelina, her favorite Venetian doll, with the masked porcelain face and carnival gown, the one

Pappy had brought her. She was gone. Katherine looked round the room. No, she was nowhere. She dashed out to Doreen and asked her where the doll was.

"Ah, I'm sorry, honey. Angelina got broken. Your mother said she fell off the shelf and smashed. I picked up the pieces myself. I'm sorry, honey." Doreen turned her broad kindly face away and busied herself with dinner preparations.

"Where is she, Doreen?" Katherine asked in a low voice. "I'm sure I can fix her."

Doreen shook her head. "No, you can't, honey. Your mom's gone and thrown her down the incinerator. I told her you might want the pieces and the beautiful dress, but she just said you were too big for dolls anyway."

Katherine's eyes filled with tears and she rushed to her room. "She hates me, Antonia. She hates me," she said in a steely voice.

"Who? Doreen?" Antonia asked incredulously.

"No, my mother," Katherine said bluntly. She hid her face.

Not that she could explain it in so many words, but Katherine had long since stopped trying to win her mother's love. There had been too many occasions on which she had tried to please, hoped for hugs or even smiles, times when she had practiced the piano and cleaned her room assiduously, only to be met by jibes, or slaps, or worse still, beatings. She went through phases when she felt intensely guilty, as if there were something that she couldn't quite locate that she had done to provoke her mother's wrath. At other times, she sensed that whatever she did, it made no difference. It was her very presence that was at fault. If her mother was intent on finding something wrong, she would. Then, the lashings would follow; the strap on her bottom; the ruler over her palms; the stinging slaps. Katherine bore it. She was trapped. If she told her father, then as soon as he was away there would be a worse incident. Now she hoped only for her mother's indifference. When she was home with her, Katherine walked softly, spoke almost not at all, kept to her room. Anything to prevent an incidence of temper. At dinner on the night when her doll had been broken, however, Katherine was too upset to pretend to be invisible.

They were sitting as they always did when her father was home, in the large airy dining room which looked out on the stone patio where in the summer clematis bloomed white and purple. Katherine knew each of those stones, each of those flowers intimately—so often had she concentrated on them so as not to cry or react to her mother's jibes. Tonight, as soon as they had sat down, Katherine said to her father, "Angelina is broken. She's gone."

"Oh, I'm sorry, Kat. How did it happen?"

Katherine shrugged and looked directly at her mother. "She knows."

"So, you're wailing to your father again. You never stop, do you?" Sylvie spoke in French, as she normally continued to do in the house, and glared at her daughter.

"Hush, Sylvie," her father interjected. "I'll get you another doll, Kat, next time I'm in Venice."

"She's too old for dolls. And she's got plenty left. You always spoil her. If it's not one thing, it's another." Sylvie was venomous.

"You broke her, didn't you? You did it on purpose. Because I loved her." Katherine leapt out of her chair and dashed from the room. Behind her, she heard her mother saying adamantly to her father, *Elle ment.* She's lying, as usual."

Then they rowed. She hated that. Her mother's endless stream of accusations. "I should never have had that brat. You should never have brought me here. I hate this stinking, boring country. Hate it. Do you hear?"

And then her father, his voice cold, steely. "That's enough, Sylvie. You're working yourself into a state. Calm yourself. Leave the child be."

"You've always preferred her to me. You . . ."

Katherine shut her door quietly, blocking out the sounds.

After such rows, her mother would sometimes stay in her room for days on end or trail round the house like a blind stranger, oblivious to Katherine's existence. Sometimes, and Katherine didn't know which was worse, she would stamp round and rail, flailing out at Katherine at the slightest excuse. And so Katherine learned that it was better not to provide an opportunity for a row. She tried hard not to complain to her father.

After the incident of the doll, at irregular intervals other objects precious to her had disappeared from her room or been broken in her absence. She pretended not to notice. But the sense of a malicious presence at work grew in her. Then, this autumn it had all become much worse. Katherine thought she knew the occasion that had sparked it. It was after her mother had come home from a solitary trip to Rome. The time without her in the house had been blissfully peaceful. Nothing, Katherine noted only to herself, had vanished from her room. And what with Leo home for a part of the holidays, life had been wonderful. The feeling of joy even persisted until two weeks after Sylvie's return. Then Leo went back to Harvard.

Katherine was into her third week of the semester. She had gone to school in the morning with a slight cough and a sniffle. By lunchtime she was distinctly unwell and the school nurse told her she had a temperature and sent her home. She had walked into the house and shouted her usual, "I'm back." An uncharacteristic silence answered her and Katherine assumed everyone, including Doreen, was out. She poured herself a glass of orange juice and carried it up the stairs to her room. When she got to the first landing, her mother's bedroom door suddenly flew open and her mother burst out. "What are you doing here?" she shouted.

Katherine was so surprised she dropped her juice. Sylvie looked disheveled. Behind her through the open door, Katherine saw a man she thought she recognized as the porter. But she didn't have a chance to look, for her mother's hand struck like lightning across her face. "That's for your spying. And now you'll run and tell your father, won't you?" Sylvie struck her again with greater force so that Katherine knocked her shoulder hard against the edge of the bannister. "And that's for carrying tales."

Her mother reeked of alcohol. Katherine held back the tears with difficulty. She had stopped crying when her mother hit her, partly out of pride, but partly out of spite because she always felt her tears gave her mother pleasure. "Nurse sent me home early because I'm ill," she said in a small voice and walked slowly up the stairs.

That Sunday, Antonia was having a birthday party. The girls had been plotting it for a month in great excitement. Antonia had invited some boys. Katherine had even bought herself a new dress for the occasion out of her own pocket money topped up with a little from the bank account into which her own presents went. She hated the dresses her mother made her wear, somber unattractive things in rough heavy wool or dull summer cotton; and she had asked Leo to go shopping with her and help her choose. They had selected a full-skirted velvet frock in a deep royal blue which set off her auburn hair. She had worn it twice, once when she had gone out for dinner with her father and Leo and on the night of Sylvie's return from Italy. But when Katherine came to dress for the party, her dress was nowhere to be found in her wardrobe. Katherine's heart skipped a beat. She charged off in search of her mother.

Both her parents were sitting in the living room reading.

"Maman, have you seen my blue dress?" Katherine asked in a quiet voice.

"Mmmm?" Her mother pretended not to hear her.

"My blue dress. I can't find it."

Her father looked up. "She means that pretty velvet dress, Sylvie. The one she wore for your homecoming."

"Ah, yes, that one. I gave it away when I was clearing up. It's quite unsuitable for a young girl," her mother answered casually.

Katherine's face grew contorted. Jacob looked on helplessly. "I'll buy you another. Tomorrow," he said softly.

"But it's Antonia's party today." This time the tears trickled down Katherine's cheeks.

"You've plenty of other clothes." Her mother's tone was firm.

Two days later, at the bottom of her wardrobe Katherine found a crumpled heap of blue. She lifted up her dress. Down the front of it there was a long slash. She imagined that slash through herself. That was when the terror had taken a grip on her. Her father was away. She trod carefully in the house, trying to keep out of her mother's way. When he returned, bearing a brand new dress in a rich burgundy shade, she had shown him the blue one. She said nothing. Her eyes spoke for her.

Jacob hugged her. "I'll sort it out," he said in a tired tone.

That evening she could hear raised voices emanating from her parents' room. Loud, angry, hideous voices. She wanted to go and stop them. Instead, she buried her head under her pillow and cried.

Then, the following week, the essay on *Jane Eyre* she had been working on for her English class disappeared from her desk. She had discussed it with her father just a few days back. She couldn't understand why Rochester kept his wife in the attic. What kind of madness did she have? They had talked about it at length over dinner. Now the essay was gone. Katherine hugged herself in fear. That was when the plan of running away had begun to formulate itself in her mind.

She told Antonia about it in a hushed voice the night her friend came to sleep over at her house. Normally, she preferred to stay over at Antonia's when the occasion arose. But this time, Antonia's mother had rung to ask whether Antonia might stay at the Jardines'. They were going to be out late and their help was away. The girls talked in whispers.

"She hides my work. Breaks my things. She's after me, out to get me. I know she is."

"But why?"

"I don't know why. I just know I have to get away. I have to."

"But where will you go?"

Her mother burst in on them. "That's enough from you two. I know what you're up to. Antonia, you go and sleep in Leo's room. I'm not having any nastiness in my house." Sylvie's tone would brook no questions. The girls had looked at each other curiously and Antonia had trailed obediently after the older woman. The next day, after Antonia had left, Katherine was told that her punishment was that she would have to stay in her room over the entirety of the weekend. Bread and water would be brought to her. "And you're lucky to get that, given what you've been up to," Sylvie said coldly. Angry at the injustice of it all, Katherine was yet relieved to have an excuse to stay out of her mother's way. She was growing increasingly scared. She had noticed, over the last weeks, that her mother had not been wearing her favorite ring. That incident so many years ago when she had been punished for the supposed loss of the ring was etched indelibly in her mind. She was terrified of a recurrence of the scene. Confinement in her room was preferable to a great deal else.

On the day when Katherine came home to find the easel her father had given her collapsed on the floor and the careful copy she had been making of Vermeer's "Girl with a Mandolin" splattered with red paint, she made her decision. But first, she would give her father a final chance. She had talked to him twice already about wanting to be sent away to school and he had looked at her sadly, saying, "But you're too young, Katherine. And I should miss you." She would miss him terribly too, and she hadn't pursued it. Late that evening she knocked at his study door and tried again.

"Pappy, I want to go away to school. I *need* to go away. It will make things better. For you as well."

"Yes, Kat." Jacob removed the glasses he had taken to wearing. He looked tired. "I think you're right. I shall start looking into places for next year when you begin high school. We should talk about the kind of school which would be best for you."

"I need to go *now*," Katherine cut him off.

"But that's not realistic."

Katherine took her father's hand and pulled him toward her room. "Look," she said. She hadn't cleaned up. The pots of paint lay splattered all over the carpet. In the midst of them her own besmirched picture, the broken easel.

"Come with me." There was anger in Jacob's voice and stance as he led her toward Sylvie's bedroom. Sylvie was stretched out on her bed, a diaphanous negligée fanned out around her.

"Sylvie. There is a terrible mess in Katherine's room. What has got into you? It's the child's work."

Sylvie sat up startled. "And you think I did that?" she asked, incredulous. "It's her mess. She always leaves a mess."

"She doesn't, Sylvie. You know she didn't do it," Jacob enunciated slowly.

"And you believe her." Sylvie's voice flew off into an upper register. "The little tale-carrier. You always believe her." Katherine stole away. She didn't want to hear any more. In bed, in the dark, she formulated her plans. She would go to the bank tomorrow at lunchtime and withdraw all her money. No, perhaps only enough to get her to Boston and a little on top. Otherwise it might arouse suspicions. Then, once in Cambridge, she would convince Leo that she had to stay with him: he would listen to her. She was certain of that. Then she could go to school in Boston or something. Her mind beyond the escape itself went blank.

Katherine looked at her watch again. It was lunchtime and she was suddenly very hungry. She had been too nervous to eat the evening before and she had skipped breakfast this morning. She walked toward the restaurant car—a long-legged girl with burnished hair and haunted gray eyes who gripped her school satchel as if it contained her life.

When she got there, all the tables were occupied. She hesitated and then sat down at the far end of one where a lone man was wholly immersed in a newspaper. The waiter handed her a menu and she studied it intently, doing her sums all the while. Everything was far more expensive than she had anticipated.

"I recommend the sole meunière. It's the only edible thing on this train," a voice instructed her emphatically from across the table. Without looking up, Katherine gave her order hurriedly to the waiter.

"I promise you, I'm right," the voice intoned again. "I travel this route at least once a week. I hate airplanes."

At last Katherine glanced at the owner of the voice. He was an old man, older than her father, with a shock of white hair and long drooping moustaches which sat incongruously with his very correct pin-striped suit. Under his shaggy brows, there were eyes of a decidedly twinkling blue.

"So, now you can take that coat off and come and sit opposite me here and put that satchel you're gripping so decisively there. I'll watch it, don't worry. No one will steal it." He was laughing at her. Mutely Katherine obeyed his instructions.

"Yes, now that I can see you better, I can say that you are a decidedly pretty girl, even if the cat has eaten your tongue." He grinned gleefully. "In Berlin, where I come from, oh yes many years ago, before those foul Nazis besmirched the country, they would have said of you that you would make a great beauty, a *grande dame sans merci*. But that doesn't mean anything to you, does it?" Katherine heard a distinct cackle. "No one in this godforsaken country speaks any languages."

"A great lady without mercy," Katherine was goaded into responding.

"Well, well, well. Not only beautiful, but also clever. Let me offer you some of my wine, young lady."

Katherine shook her head emphatically.

"A little bread then?"

She accepted greedily and bit into a slightly stale roll. The man watched her. "So, now that we are becoming friends, you can tell me your name."

Katherine was about to reply and then remembered herself. She bit off her words. Just then the waiter brought their order and she was saved from having to say anything. As soon as her plate was on the table, she dug in ravenously.

The old man opposite laughed. "It does me good to see a young appetite." He nibbled at his food and studied her reflectively. "So you are off on an escapade. No, no, you don't have to tell me. It's a secret, I know. And your name is a secret too." He lowered his tone in merry complicity. "I shall call you Schatzie. That means sweetheart, my little treasure. My name is Thomas Sachs. It's a real name. See?" His eyes twinkled and he brought a card out of his wallet and handed it to her. Katherine read, "Thomas Sachs, Sachs Enterprises." She handed it back to him.

"No, no, keep it. You never know when it might come in useful. And now that you've finished bolting your food, tell me something about yourself. Tell me a story. I'll order you a large ice cream as a reward."

Katherine hardly had a repertoire of small talk. She scanned her mind, but it was blank of everything except the worry of her escape.

"Well, tell me about what young girls read then," he persisted.

"I've just read *Jane Eyre*." At last Katherine had found a subject. She spoke about the book fluently and with passion, almost forgetting to eat her ice cream.

Thomas Sachs listened intently and only occasionally interrupted. "Yes, it's as I thought," he said when she had finished. "You are decidedly an intelligent young lady. Now, if you will excuse an old man his habits, I shall go off and smoke a cigar. I do not like to pollute the atmosphere for other diners." He put out his hand and Katherine shook it. It was cool and dry. "And do not worry about your bill. It is already taken care of. Thank you for keeping me company."

Katherine just managed to say thank you in return before he walked away. He was small, wiry, Katherine noticed, and had the light, quick step of a far younger man. She suddenly realized, as she went back to her seat, that she felt more cheerful. Thomas Sachs had turned flight into adventure.

When the train reached its destination and Katherine stepped out of the old station, it was already dark and bitterly cold. Light feathery snowflakes were falling. She hesitated. She had intended to take a bus, but in the dark everything looked unfamiliar and slightly forbidding. She had been here only once before. The details of getting to the house her brother shared with three other students in Cambridge now seemed more intractable than she had foreseen. She decided to join the long taxi line. It moved slowly and she cursed herself for having forgotten her gloves and scarf. She thrust her hands into her pockets and stamped her feet on the ground, willing warmth to come into them.

It was then that she heard the word. "Schatzie." She looked up and saw the high, gleaming shape of a Rolls-Royce double parked beside a taxi. Thomas Sachs was looking out of the back window. "Can I give you a lift anywhere?"

Katherine nodded gratefully. Decidedly this man was her good angel.

The chauffeur held the door open for her.

"Just tell Hans your destination."

Katherine blurted out the memorized address and sat back in the comfortable warmth of the car. It was vast. A small bar was open in front of them bearing bottles of whisky and brandy. Darkened windows separated them from the chauffeur.

"I take it someone has forgotten to come out and meet you." Thomas Sachs tsked under his breath. "I take it too that you are not a habitué of Boston." He didn't wait for her reply. He flicked a switch and spoke: "Hans, the scenic route, please."

In the light of passing streetlamps, Katherine could feel Thomas Sachs looking at her curiously. "Tell me, Schatzie, how old are you?"

"Sixteen," Katherine lied. She had prepared her new age, if not her name.

"Mmmn," he said reflectively. "It's not an insubstantial age, though everyone looks so young to me now." He shook his head sadly. "Come, come and sit close to me and keep an old man warm."

Katherine hesitated.

"Come, I won't harm you." He took her hand and drew her closer. She leaned lightly against the soft wool of his dark cashmere coat. He smelled of a lemony cologne. "You see, that over there is the celebrated Boston Common. There are forty-eight acres of it. And that granite obelisk is the Bunker Hill Monument which you will have learned about in school. The people of Boston still take their revolutionary glory seriously. In the daytime you can come back and look at the Old State House we're coming up to and see the cobblestones which mark the place where blood was shed in the great Boston Massacre. And that is the glorious Charles River . . ." He interrupted himself. "You know, Schatzie, the more I look at you, the more you remind me of a certain Titian. Very fetching, distinctly fetching." Dry lips brushed against her cheek. She didn't pull away. It felt comforting, like when her father kissed her. Except for the tickle of the moustache. Thomas stroked her hair, guided her hand to his lap. Silence enfolded them. Then his breath in her ear seemed to grow hot, irregular, a little hoarse. Katherine abruptly withdrew her hand, edged away.

Thomas laughed. "Well, Schatzie, it's a good thing we have arrived. I'm sure you will agree." His eyes crinkled humorously. Katherine, meeting them, found herself smiling in return.

"Yes." He patted her shoulder, grinned ruefully. "I shall make sure that you are properly welcomed, and then, well, if you should need anything or wish to see me, you have my card. Now, before you go"—he took her hand again and held it—"you must tell me your name. As a special thank you. I shan't tell it to anyone else."

Katherine believed him. She smiled the special smile which was so rare and which lit up her gray eyes. "Katherine Jardine," she said. "And thank you."

She had, though she didn't realize it, made a friend for life.

The one thing Katherine hadn't bargained for when she executed her well-laid plans was that her brother Leo might not be home when she arrived. As it was, she was greeted at the door of the ramshackle house by a complete stranger, a young man who looked at her oddly. He had certainly not been here on the day that she and her parents had briefly visited Leo's quarters.

"Hello," Katherine mumbled clumsily. "Is Leo here, Leo Jardine?"

"I'm afraid he's out. Was he expecting you?"

Katherine shook her head. She stretched a hand out to the gangling youth. "I'm Katherine, his sister. May I come in and wait?" she blurted out.

The young man stood aside. Katherine walked in and as she did so heard the smooth engine of the Rolls pulling away.

Nick Stanton examined the young girl, who clasped her school satchel nervously. "Leo may be quite late," he said. "Past your bedtime."

"That's all right. I'll . . . I'll just wait, right here." Katherine perched on the edge of an overstuffed sofa. "I've come all the way from New York."

Nick Stanton gazed at her with an uncustomary scowl. He was expecting a visit from the young woman he had been wooing assiduously and he had carefully orchestrated the evening so that all his housemates were out and he had the house to himself. Now he had Leo's baby sister to contend with. Well, not quite a baby. He would have to get her to cooperate. He couldn't very well throw her out.

"Like a drink of some kind?" Nick asked, trying to think how to begin.

"Yes, please, if it's not too much trouble." Katherine looked round her in some confusion. She was suddenly close to tears. All the turmoil of the past weeks pressed down on her now that she had arrived at her destination: this slightly tawdry student house with its worn second-hand furniture where she was so obviously unwelcome. She gulped down the proffered glass of Coca-Cola quickly.

Nick cleared his throat. "I'd kinda hoped to be alone here tonight. Do you think you could come back later?" He saw her face fall and the tears fill her eyes. "Or, could you go up to Leo's room and—

well, wait there?" he said in a rush. "I'm expecting a friend . . ." His voice trailed off.

"Yes, yes, of course." Katherine stood up abruptly. "I won't be any trouble." She rushed up the stairs to the top of the house where she knew her brother's room was before Nick had a chance to show her the way. She closed the door softly behind her, took off her coat and folded it neatly on the small divan bed and snuggled down in the flowery corner armchair. Leo's room. She recognized his intricate paperweight on the desk, his books, the old chess set, the orderly arrangement of things. She was safe at last. The tears now streamed down her cheeks. She was safe. She dozed.

In her sleep, she saw a body slashed from breast to navel. It was hers. Blood slowly coagulated round the edges of the gash. A youth came in. Who was it? She couldn't identify him. He was naked. From between his thighs a vast penis jutted. It moved imperceptibly toward the wound. No, a voice shouted. It came from the slashed body. Hers. No, she could see its face now. It was her mother. There was a malicious smile on her face.

"Kat, Kat, wake up. You're dreaming."

Katherine's eyes fluttered open. "Leo," she said in disbelief. "Leo." She hugged him, held on to him tightly.

Leo returned her embrace a little stiffly. "Kat, what on earth are you doing here?" His consternation was clear. Leo at the age of twenty-one was a tall, broad-shouldered youth with a shock of golden-blond hair, sea-blue eyes and a slow, steady manner. And he provided many a Radcliffe girl with ready material for reverie. He loved his sister, but this love was always overlaid with a trace of anxiety. Now, he was more than slightly taken aback to find her in his room.

"I've run away," Katherine said simply. "I had to. There was nowhere else to go."

"But Kat, you can't simply run away. Mom and Dad will be beside themselves with worry."

"I had to," Katherine repeated. She studied her brother. He wasn't taking her seriously. "She's going to harm me in some way, Leo. I know it. She wants me dead," she said slowly. There was no trace of excitement in her voice, just a statement of cold fact. Katherine wondered at the words herself as they left her mouth. Yes, they were true, though she hadn't thought them that way before.

Leo moved away from her and paced the narrow length of the room. "You're exaggerating, Kat," he murmured. "I know Mom gets excited sometimes, slaps you, but not that . . ." Even as he spoke, his words sounded hollow to him. There was a conviction to Katherine, a tremulous sadness about her. Leo couldn't bear to think what she meant, what she might have been through. It was always that way. Even when he saw his mother behaving unpardonably with her, he couldn't quite believe what he witnessed. It always seemed like a momentary aberration. Sylvie was so different with him, like another being. And so he gave Katherine all his protective tenderness, but he couldn't bring himself to blame his mother, to judge her. He watched his sister.

"I want to live here with you," Katherine said at last. "I won't be any trouble. I'll help you keep the place clean. I'll go to school. There must be one nearby." She poured out the details of her fantasy.

"But Kat, that's not possible. You must know that. Look at this place. Four men. Four students. We can't take care of a little girl. The others wouldn't stand for it," Leo added lamely. "Now you go to sleep. I'll use the sofa downstairs. And in the morning"—he glanced at his watch—"we'll ring Dad and sort something out."

"No," Katherine said emphatically. "No, I'm not going back to that house." She looked at her brother, disappointment and fear mingled in her face. "If you don't want me here, I'll go somewhere else. I'm not a child."

"But you are, Kat, you are." He gave her a tender, persuasive smile. "We'll speak to Dad in the morning. It'll be all right."

He was placating her, like her father did. A pat on the back and everything would be fine. "He's not there, Leo," Katherine said. She paused for a moment. "I'm afraid of her. Can't you understand?" She met his eyes and held them.

Leo felt a chill go through him.

"At least, let me stay here for a few days. Don't ring her. I'll arrange something," she said wildly.

"Let's sleep on it." Leo kissed her on the forehead. "It's late now. You've been dreaming. Everything will be clearer in the morning. All right?" He gave her the slowest, steadiest smile he could manage.

A cold gray light made its way round the corners of the curtains and trickled into the room. Katherine woke from restless sleep and groggily studied her whereabouts. Then, in a rush, she remembered. She leapt from the narrow bed. There was a funny ache at the base of her spine. The knickers she had gone to sleep in felt wet. She looked down, saw a streak of red on her legs. It was on the bed, too. She groaned. Not that. Not that too. Not now. Angrily she pulled the sheet from the bed and thrust it in the corner of the room in a tight heap. She was dismayed and embarrassed. Her period. "The curse," Antonia called it, for she already had hers. She talked about it gaily, almost with pride. "Woman's curse. For our sins. Every month, regular as the moon. A reminder." Almost, Katherine sat down on the bed and cried. She would have to wash the sheet later. Was there a machine in the house? She hadn't noticed.

Her mother had sent the curse to her now, to punish her. With a violent gesture, Katherine pulled her dress over her head, not bothering about the hideous bra her mother had bought her and forced her to wear to bind her small, pointed breasts. She rushed to the bathroom, washed and stuffed paper into her fresh underpants. Now to face her brother and his housemates. She felt depressed. Nothing was working according to her plan. Perhaps she ought simply to go home and lock herself in her room forever, like Rochester's mad wife. No. Then her mother would have won. Katherine threw her shoulders back and walked slowly down the stairs.

When she reached the bottom, she could hear her brother's voice from the living room. She took a deep breath, was about to go in when she heard her name. "Yes, yes, don't worry, Katherine's here with me. Yes, I'll bring her back." She didn't wait to hear the rest. In a trice, she had flown up the stairs, grabbed her coat and satchel, and quietly made her way out the door.

Her brother had betrayed her. Katherine was distraught. She couldn't quite believe it. Why hadn't he waited, at least until her father was home? She wandered aimlessly through the cold morning streets, not sure which way she was going or what direction to take. She found herself amidst a cluster of shops and saw one announcing "Drug Store." Remembering her new needs, she embarrassedly asked the man behind the counter for a box of napkins. He wrapped it in a brown paper bag, an object to be hidden. Katherine found a small restaurant with a soda fountain. She ordered a glass of milk, gulped it down and then rushed off to the ladies. She stuffed the remaining napkins into her satchel. Something at least had been accomplished. But what was she to do next? A hotel? She counted her money. There were almost fifty dollars left. It would last her for a few days. Yet would she manage to register in a hotel without arousing suspicion? She examined her face in the small mirror. It looked strange and far too young. With a sinking feeling, Katherine rearranged the items in her satchel. A card fluttered out. Thomas Sachs.

The house, from the road, looked monumental, a colossus of a residence, with gothic spires, hewn out of dark stone. An ornate iron gate presided over its entrance. Large dark pines stood like sentinels guarding the sweep of wintry garden. To Katherine, a New Yorker, used to apartment blocks and intimate brownstones, it was trebly impressive. Had she felt less desperate, she would have turned back. But Thomas Sachs was now her only hope. She pushed the bell at the side of the gate. It let out a long clang. No one came. She waited and then tried the gate. It was open. She hurried along the path, past matching stone lions, up a few stairs to the imposing door. Here, she rang again quickly, before she lost her nerve.

A tall, suited man answered.

"I have come to see Mr. Thomas Sachs," Katherine mumbled. "He's not expecting me, but I would like to see him."

"Whom should I say is calling?" the man said in an accent she had only ever heard in the movies.

"Katherine Jardine." She hoped Thomas Sachs remembered her name. She waited in a hall rich in oak paneling. There was a series of engravings on the wall which caught Katherine's eye: dark, somber images where clusters of fraught figures seemed to howl.

"Mr. Sachs will see you in the morning room. Come this way." The man's face was expressionless as he took her coat and satchel. He led her into a large room where a floor-to-ceiling window gave out on a garden dominated by a fountain and a single curving oak, its tracery of branches lavish against the steel-gray sky. The *bergère* he motioned her to sit on was plumply comfortable. Katherine waited. It was a good room, she decided, severe, yet opulent. She already had an eye for such things. The furniture was a trifle heavy for her taste, but its wood gleamed brightly and the deep blue hues of the rugs were softly reassuring. On the curve of one wall stood a beautiful old grandfather clock, its pendulum swinging rhythmically.

"So, you approve of my Biedermeier." A voice startled her. Thomas Sachs stood to one side of her, his blue eyes bright beneath the shock of white, swept-back hair. He was wearing a gray suit with a light polo-neck sweater which made him look younger and at the same time more intimidating than he had the day before.

Katherine nodded. "You see, I've come." She tried a smile which sat oddly on her worried features.

"And I'm very pleased that you have," he said when she didn't continue. "What can I do for you?" he asked.

Katherine stalled. She didn't know where to begin. "I hope I'm not disturbing you." It had suddenly occurred to her that he probably had a family, a wife.

"Only a little. The telephone calls can wait and my first meeting is not until lunchtime." He examined her shrewdly. "But perhaps you might like a little something to eat now, a little hot chocolate and some cinnamon toast." Without waiting for her response, he pulled a long cord, gave instructions to the butler and came to sit opposite her. "Now, Schätzchen, tell me what is the matter. Truthfully, please. I am sure you have not come here to satisfy an old man's whims." He gave her a kindly smile and waited.

"My brother didn't want me to stay with him," Katherine blurted out. "I've—I've run away from home you see and ..." Katherine poured out her story with not much sequence but with a great deal of feeling. She had never spoken to anyone so openly before, not even her father, and when she had finished she trembled a little with the emotion of it.

"Poor Katherine," Thomas Sachs said softly. "Come, let us have a little warming drink and then we will think." He motioned her to the small round table she hadn't seen being laid out and urged her to drink and eat. "Now, Schatzie, how do you think I can help you?"

"I don't know." Katherine shook her head so that the long auburn sheath covered her eyes. "Perhaps I can stay here," she whispered an entreaty.

"Tell me truthfully, now. How old are you?" Thomas Sachs asked.

Katherine lowered her eyes. "Thirteen. I'm sorry I lied to you yesterday."

He smiled. "Women rarely manage the whole truth about their age, at one end of the spectrum or the other," he said. "But let us think clearly. If you were to stay with me, it could only be with your parents' permission. No, no, don't interrupt me and look at me with those wild eyes. You know that is true. You wouldn't want to have me arrested for abduction or worse crimes." He laughed, his face crinkling. "Would you?"

Katherine shook her head. "But I won't go home," she added emphatically.

"No, not today. Perhaps not tomorrow. But in a few days' time it might look a little different."

Katherine rose from the little table. "Thank you for listening to me." She made to leave.

He caught her arm and held it hard. "Don't be a stupid girl, Katherine. Sit down. Have you got money? Clothes, stuffed into that little bag of yours? What shall you do? Sleep in bus stations? Be picked up by the police? Sell that young body of yours?"

Katherine looked shocked.

He laughed. "You see. You have not thought things through properly. I know that you are serious in your wish to leave home. It is a wise decision on your part. You should not be in the same place as your mother. I shall talk to your father for you. I have been a good advocate in my time. We shall find you a school somewhere." He patted her hand. "For the time being, you shall stay here. Roberts will fix up a room for you. Later on today, we shall get you some clothes. That dress you are wearing is an offense to my eyes." He bowed slightly and left her.

Thomas Sachs was as good and as generous as his word. He was also a shrewd judge of character. In his nigh on sixty years, he had lost two fortunes and built up a third. A prosperous publisher in Berlin, he had left that city in 1935, with his paintings, some furniture, and what money he could easily bring with him. He refused to live under a regime which sanctioned the burning of books; nor, since many of his friends and the writers he published were Jewish— as, indeed, he sometimes felt himself to be—would he tolerate the government's anti-Semitism. His wife and two sons, despite his admonishments, had said he was exaggerating the danger of the Nazis. They said they would follow later, perhaps, once he was set up in America. Meanwhile they would keep the family firm going in Berlin. He could do nothing to persuade them to join him and they had left it too late. Now they were all dead.

In the United States, he had begun by setting up a small press which published German writers in translation, books which kept the Germany he knew alive. The company had grown, diversified, prospered, taken over other companies. He was now a rich man. A rich man who had three loves—women, books, and the satisfaction of having made an unexpectedly canny deal, in that order. He had never married again, preferring the easy sensuality of mistresses and high, but fleeting, passion. Too much had been vested in his first family. Too much lost.

This little Katherine intrigued him. She had the makings of a passionate woman. He had liked the way she laughed at him in his old man's vice. He also liked her spirit. He would see what he could do for her.

A few days later two men sized each other up none too discreetly in a Park Avenue office. One paced with long-legged strides behind an impressive desk and every now and then ran a hand through his tangle of salt and pepper hair. The room, despite its ample proportions, seemed too small for him. His brow, above piercing dark eyes, was furrowed in concern.

The other sat back in leisurely fashion in a comfortable armchair and elegantly crossed one loose-trousered leg over another. His blue eyes beneath the shock of white hair bore a trace of irony. But his face was set in sympathetic lines.

"Let me get this quite clear. You say you met my daughter on the train to Boston, that she was running away from home, that she ended up on your doorstep when her brother refused to house her?" Jacob Jardine eyed the smaller man suspiciously. He felt like hitting out at him, this kidnapper of his daughter. As if the movements of violence would eradicate a reality he preferred not to acknowledge and bring the girl back. But he controlled himself. He had sufficient cause to suppose that Thomas was only a messenger, merely the bearer of bad news.

He had come home late the previous evening from a tedious conference to find Sylvie in a strangely seductive mood, a champagne bottle at the ready, her favorite music pulsing through the house. Only when he had asked her about Katherine had he realized that something was seriously amiss. Sylvie had told him with a dreamy insouciance that Katherine was away in Boston, staying with a charming man called Thomas Sachs. And who, Jacob had asked in disbelief, is Thomas Sachs? Sylvie had shrugged and gestured carelessly toward the telephone. "There's a number somewhere over there." Jacob had rung instantly and spoken to the man who now sat opposite him.

"That is correct. And, as you heard from her own mouth on the telephone this morning, she is fine, though she refuses to come home to you and your wife." Thomas Sachs stressed the final word a little. "She wouldn't even speak to her when I first rang your home."

Jacob looked away, out of the window at the stretch of blue winter sky above the uniform roofs of the Park Avenue apartment blocks. He had been half-afraid something like this might happen. He hadn't acted quickly enough. Anger at himself coiled within him. He turned it momentarily toward the man in front of him. "I shall come and fetch her straight away," he said brusquely.

"Come by all means," Thomas Sachs said patiently. "I can well understand that thinking of your daughter in a stranger's house is not easy. But"—and here he turned the whole force of his energetic presence on Jacob—"I would suggest that you do not attempt to bring her home. She is too frightened, too tense, like a coiled creature ready to do harm. To herself or to others. We have talked a little about it. And, though I believe she is at heart a sensible girl, she might be driven to do something silly. At the moment she is quite well, having a little, let's call it, holiday." Sachs smiled his irresistible smile. "And it makes me quite happy to have a young person with me."

"What has Katherine told you?" Jacob asked, trying to keep his voice calm. It wasn't that he feared betrayal. It was simply that the Katherine he saw through Thomas seemed a stranger.

"Oh." Thomas threw off the question lightly. "That she doesn't get on with her mother. That she fears her, when your wife has had a little too much to drink." He paused. Thomas, obedient to codes of privacy, didn't want to overstep the line. But Jacob's eyes encouraged him. "That she can't communicate with her, particularly when your wife is depressed."

Thomas was polite, matter-of-fact, as if he were speaking of everyday matters. But Jacob read what was unspoken. It grieved him. He turned away, stared out of the window. The move to America had never achieved its aims. It had not helped Sylvie get over Caroline's death. She had never found a life here, a raison d'être. She had remained a stranger and her bouts of listless depression had grown along with her drinking. And she would take no counsel from him. When he had realized that she was closed to him, he had suggested that she consult an analyst. To no avail. However, on the advice of an acquaintance, she had gone to a clinic in Pennsylvania: she retired there periodically now. They pumped her full of drugs.

Jacob paced the room for a moment. When he was honest with himself, he had to confess that he had tried to draw brackets around that part of his existence that was Sylvie. In the normal course of things he was benevolent, but absent: he did not allow himself to be drawn either in anger or in passion. And when he was drawn, it was usually in rage. Attempting to keep the semblance of peace, of ordinariness, he had, he now realized, sacrificed Katherine.

He turned back to Sachs, warming to the man because of his

evident concern for Katherine. "You see all this, Mr. Sachs." Jacob gestured at the wall of books, at the divan where his patients normally lay. "I have read and thought and practiced and observed and written for over a quarter of a century, survived a world war, and still I have not been able to provide a home in which my children may be happy."

Thomas Sachs chuckled. He had taken in the shelf full of Jacob's own writings, he had paused at the artful photograph of a striking blonde woman who he had no doubt was Jardine's wife. He knew that he was in the presence of one of the few men he might recognize as an equal, a kindred spirit. "That, Dr. Jardine, is not a challenge many of us can say we have met. Though at least," he added with a hint of grimness, "you still have the wherewithal to keep trying."

Katherine spun round the room and watched the bottle green fabric of her new dress lift and swirl with her. She caught the effect in the floor-length mirror and smiled. It was a new kind of smile. Slightly tentative, it warmed her eyes and elicited response. The few days she had spent in Thomas Sachs's company had already begun to have an effect on her. Under his generous tutelage, she was developing a narcissistic interest in herself.

It was a healthy narcissism. Up until now Katherine's posture of confidence had been an act of will, a daring of elements which might prove as hostile as her mother. The show of bravura hid a guilty timidity. Inside her, there lived a small frightened creature she felt was unlovable. Thomas's eyes forced her to take account of something different in herself and to begin to value it. He nurtured the young woman in her. And Katherine began to like this young woman who swirled gracefully in front of the mirror.

He had taken her to Boston's leading department store. There, with an expert hand, he had picked out an assortment of dresses, skirts and blouses for her to try.

"But I don't need all this," Katherine had protested.

He looked at her sternly. "Beauty is not a question of need. If you are to sit opposite me at table and walk through my house, then I prefer you to look your best, which I know will be very good indeed." He lifted out a white silk blouse trimmed with fine lace, felt the fabric and handed it to the sales assistant who stood behind them. "We will try this one as well."

Katherine shook her head mournfully. "I won't be able to repay you for years."

"Katherine." He gave her a fond smile. "You have still not realized that I am a very rich man. I have very few desires left—a fine picture, a good bottle of wine, a visit to the opera. My payment will be to see you in these clothes. That will give me far, far more pleasure than my money. And now run along and try these garments. And remember, I want each one paraded before me."

She had dutifully done so and together they had selected an array of clothes in the deep greens and blues, the rich wine shades that Thomas said best set off her porcelain skin and burnished hair. "Black will come later. You are still too young and I shall save myself that delight," he had added. Then he had sent her off to the lingerie department with the assistant, admonishing her to choose the prettiest undergarments. "Even if they aren't for my eyes," he had added with a twinkle. "It is important for a woman to feel beautiful everywhere." Finally there had been shoes and a fine pair of leather boots. Katherine had been as excited as a child on Christmas morning. She only wished Antonia were there with her to help her think over all the things Thomas said. As it was she stored his words to mull over in her room.

It was a spacious room on the second floor of the house overlooking the garden. The furniture was of glowing mahogany, the bedspread a thick white cotton cover of intricate design. There were always freshly cut flowers in a blue vase on the table. But what Katherine liked best were the corner shelves which housed three miniature cities, carved out of wood and painted by an expert hand so that they evoked future urban landscapes. Dream cities, she thought of them as and wondered at them.

On her first evening at Thomas's house, after the shopping spree, she had shyly come down to dinner in one of her new dresses. She was self-consciously aware of the silk slip, the new bra next to her skin and she had walked stiffly into the room the butler ushered her into. Thomas, sitting in a deep armchair in front of an open fire, was browsing through the newspaper and he took off his reading glasses to look her over. "Very nice, Schatzie," he said, his eyes twinkling. "Very nice. But now you must forget you are wearing new clothes and relax into what I know is your natural grace." He motioned her toward the sofa and abruptly began to talk about politics.

"Have you heard about this new senator everyone is proclaiming as the next President, John F. Kennedy?"

Katherine nodded vaguely.

"I am going to put my money on him. He seems to have a slightly democratic, even a socialist cast to his conscience. In this country it is only the older, the inherited rich or a few intellectuals who are relaxed enough to think about the unprivileged. The rest are too busy worrying about holding on to what they have or getting more."

Katherine looked at him quizzically. "But Thomas, would you give away everything you had?" She gestured at the richly appointed room.

"And what makes you ask that?" He looked at her shrewdly.

"I thought you suggested you were a socialist," Katherine said hesitantly.

A booming laugh came from his wiry frame. "Even if I had said I was, which I am not, though I admit to certain sympathies, I can see that you are prey to the usual set of misconceptions. Socialism does not mean the equal distribution of misery; but simply the desire for a little more wealth, a little more justice all around." He laughed again.

Katherine flushed. Thomas noticed her discomfort. "I am not laughing *at* you, Schatzie. You are right to speak your thoughts. I like it when you question me. You are also right to suggest that I would not like to part with all of this. Come." He took her arm and led her to the dining room, where the gleaming long rectangular table had been impeccably set for two. The food was exquisitely cooked and discreetly served. The wine would have delighted a connoisseur.

Thomas Sachs was indubitably a hedonist. But he was as much a voluptuary of the intellect as of the senses. He bored easily and though he loved beautiful women of all dimensions and aspects, he had rarely bothered to see them twice if there was not some fire of the spirit or intelligence to intrigue him. He said as much to Katherine on their second evening together. She had been asking him about the little wooden cities which adorned the shelves in her room.

He looked pleased. "Ah, you have noticed them. They are by a fine German artist called Feininger. I have some of his paintings as well." He led her into his study where she had never yet been.

Katherine was moved by the delicacy of the paintings, the playful motion of shapes which suggested rather than depicted. "But this one, this one is splendid." She stopped in front of a small canvas. "It's not by the same artist, is it?"

"Yes, you definitely have an eye, Schätzchen," Thomas beamed. "That is one of my great favorites. A Paul Klee. And to think I almost sold it just before the war to pay for a meal and a tawdry hotel room."

Katherine looked at him in disbelief.

"Oh yes, Katherine. The world changes. In London, just before the war, almost no one had heard of Paul Klee, although in Germany he had been famous for some years. I had taken two of his canvases out of the country with me. I was in transit in London. By some mix-up, my papers didn't seem to be in order and I had to hold on there until the proper American visa came through. I hadn't planned that and what funds I had were coming here to the States. So I was desperate. I went to the National Gallery and offered to sell the two Paul Klees I had carried with me, to tide me over. Only one person at that great institution had heard of Klee, a poet and art critic by the name of Herbert Read. His committee told him he could offer me two guineas for each picture. I was hungry. I considered it carefully. Finally I decided to decline politely and throw myself on the mercy of an acquaintance instead." He chuckled. "And now these pictures are worth a small fortune and I would part with them even less. I am glad you appreciate them."

"They're exquisite," Katherine breathed. "So wistful and sad, yet playful. I like them very much." She found herself telling him about the Vermeer she had been painstakingly copying, and then with a shudder of its destruction.

Thomas took her hand in both his and stroked it gently. "Schatzie, I am going to pay you what for a man of my years is a great compliment. The more I see of you, the more I esteem you. Too often with young women here it is not the case. You are not only lovely, you also have fire and intelligence. Do not let anyone stamp either of those out."

On Friday Thomas left the house before breakfast. He had warned her that she would be on her own, with only the butler for company, until Saturday when he returned. He had given her a book to read, Thomas Mann's *Buddenbrooks,* which he recommended highly. It would serve as a substitute for school. She also had the run of the library and she could of course go out, as long, he warned her with a sardonic look, as she didn't wander off with strange men. Katherine remembered this with a smile in the midst of her reading. The house felt lonely without him, but she realized that the strange feeling she had was one of happiness. She thought she could stay here forever in this big solid house where Thomas translated the world for her. It would all end very soon though now. Her father would be back in New York on Sunday and Thomas had already carefully explained what he intended to do. She had stopped being so afraid once she had heard him talking to her mother. Thomas, she sensed, could convince anyone of anything.

On the Saturday evening she dressed carefully in her favorite of the outfits Thomas had bought her: the white silk shirt with its lace collar and cuffs and a full blue skirt. Beneath the shirt, the mirror showed her that the small fine flowers of her delicate bra could be seen. Katherine was pleased. Before the fire in the sitting room, she waited impatiently for Thomas and his approval. He gave it as soon as he appeared.

"It does me good to come home to you, Schätzchen. You are looking more lovely than ever tonight." He bowed to her a little formally and then with only a hint of self-mockery kissed her hand. After the butler had served him a whisky and her a lemonade, Thomas came to sit beside her. "And how have you been in my absence, Katherine?"

"Very well, thank you," she replied politely and then with a trace of irony in her voice, added, "I finished *Buddenbrooks* and walked only in the garden. There wasn't a single strange man in sight."

He cocked a shaggy eyebrow. "Really? You astound me."

She giggled and suddenly in the softly lit room felt brave. "Thomas, that night in the car, when you drove me to my brother's, you ..." She paused, changed her mind.

Thomas looked down at his drink. "I thought you might ask me about that some time," he murmured. "I believed you were older than you are, perhaps a little bit more experienced, because of your bravery in accepting a lift. No, let us be quite honest. I hoped both those things. I desired you and—how shall we put it—I am as they used to say a little bit priapic."

Katherine looked at him uncomprehendingly.

He shrugged. "How can I explain it to one so young? I like women, Katherine. I like to give them pleasure and to take it. I am no puritan. Women excite me and I am not frightened of them. I respect them. Sex need not be a big loaded word, burdened with anxieties and fears and emotions. Sometimes, of course, it is; but sometimes, too, it can be simply pleasure, equally shared. No"—he looked into her eyes—"when you are older we shall talk about it some more."

"But now," Katherine pressed him, "now you don't desire me anymore?"

There was a hoarseness to his laugh. "Now, Katherine, it is different, though you shouldn't, in your innocence, provoke me too much." His eyes played over her blouse and she noticed that his hand around the whisky glass trembled a little. He stood up. "I am not a monster. And you are a girl, let us even say a young woman, who is a guest in my house. Very soon, I shall meet your father, who is certainly younger than me. What shall I say to him? That I have been seducing his daughter? No, no, that would not do."

"But if I were older . . ." Something in Katherine drove her to make him more explicit.

"When you are older, we shall see. Perhaps we shall talk again. Now stop behaving like an arch temptress and let us go to table."

With the dessert, Thomas brought up the topic again of his own accord. There was a peculiar sparkle in his eyes. "Katherine, I am glad we had that little talk before dinner, even if it made me a trifle nervous. It was intelligent of you to bring it up. It is better to speak of such things than keep them hidden." He raised his glass to her. "Now I shall tell you something which I wish you to remember, even if we do not meet again soon after this week."

Katherine's spoon tumbled from her hand. It seemed an impossible thought. "Even if I go away to school, I shall want to see you. Please," she added.

He smiled reassuringly. "Yes, yes, but listen to what I say. I have noticed in this puritan America of ours that beautiful women are rarely permitted to be clever. There is a division of labor. Silliness is for the beautiful, intelligence for the homely. It is because the men here are too often afraid of women and seek to control them. Intelligence would make them more difficult to control. And to please them, the women dampen their intelligence. Where I come from, we were taught to prefer the best of everything. I want you to promise me that you will keep your intelligence as alive and as visible as your beauty."

His eyes bore more seriousness than she had ever read in them. "I promise," Katherine said in a small voice, not quite sure what it was she was pledging, though in later years she would have ample occasion to reflect on what he said.

"And now, for once, we shall both drink to that." Thomas Sachs poured her a glass of wine.

"Kat, *ma Petite* Kat." Jacob Jardine paused at the door of Thomas Sachs's gracious living room and looked at his daughter. She rose and walked toward him shyly. There was something different about her. Her walk, perhaps. Her manner. Her expression. She looked, yes, the thought troubled him, like a woman. Then he smiled and opened his arms to her. She ran into them and pressed her face against his chest.

"I had to do it," she murmured, "had to make you believe me."

He patted her reassuringly. "You were right. I was obtuse." Jacob released her and greeted his host and his son, whom he had asked Thomas to invite to this reunion. As the evening proceeded and conversation unfolded, Jacob was haunted by a sense of strangeness which he couldn't quite pinpoint. It was not only that his daughter in this prepossessing dining room seemed an unfamiliar creature, that his son was slightly uncomfortable, and that Thomas with his mercurial wit and ironic eyes felt like a friend recovered from a distant past. It had more to do with the easy communion between Katherine and Thomas Sachs, the way his eyes sometimes fell on her when she wasn't looking.

That was it, Jacob suddenly thought. They were like a couple of newlyweds, fondly excited by each other's company, by the experience of their first dinner party. The notion shocked him. The matter of Katherine's school had to be sorted out quickly. He cleared his throat.

"Katherine, I spent yesterday calling a variety of schools in the New England region."

Katherine looked at him expectantly.

"None of them was prepared to take you on in the middle of the semester. Nor even, without a great deal of fuss, before next September."

Katherine's face dropped and Thomas was about to intervene when Jacob hushed him.

"Then I had an idea which I would like to try out on you. I spoke to Princesse Mathilde and asked her about the school Violette went to in Switzerland. It is a proper school, not just a training ground for debutantes. Princesse Mat says she is certain that they will have you. She will ring me back about it tomorrow."

Katherine's features registered her surprise. She met her father's eyes, then Thomas's. "I don't know," she said hesitantly. "It's very far away."

Again Jacob prevented the other man from speaking. "Yes, but it is a good school. I could fly over with you at Christmas, or even before. You could get to know Princesse Mat and Violette again. They would be like a second family to you. Their home is not far from the school. My only worry is that the majority of your classes would be in French. Do you think you could manage?" Jacob spoke it as a challenge.

Katherine was torn. She could see that a simple yes would please her father. But Switzerland—it was so remote from everyone. Yet the alternatives seemed dismally uncertain. After a moment she looked up from her plate and directly at her father, "Yes, Pappy. I think I can. Let's give it a try." She was rewarded by the pleasure which suffused Jacob's face.

CHAPTER
THIRTEEN

n the eve of her departure for
Switzerland, Thomas Sachs had given Katherine Jardine a little parcel and a brief, admonitory speech. "In here, my dear, you will find
the standard guide for innocents abroad." His eyes had twinkled.
"Never forget you are leaving the continent of dreams for the land
of memory. And things there are rarely quite what they seem."

"Are they here?" Katherine had asked.

"No, no, perhaps not." He had grinned devilishly. "But then the
world has grown smaller since Mr. James cruised on his ocean liner."

When Katherine had opened the parcel, she had found a copy of
Henry James's *Daisy Miller*, but she had been too excited to read.
She had been even more excited as the blue flames whipped from
the bulky Boeing's engines and New York's familiar skyline was metamorphosed into a dark sea of twinkling lights.

And now as they descended on Geneva, she pressed her forehead
against the pane of the oval window and breathed deeply. Beneath
her, hills grew into majestic mountains and a lake glistened in early
morning light.

"It's wonderful." Katherine clutched Jacob's hand. "Beautiful. I'm
glad you talked me into it."

In the month since the decision had been taken that she would
come to school here, her feelings had turned from foreboding to
anticipation. One of those weeks had been spent at Thomas's house

and then her father had come to fetch her home. "Your mother has gone off on a little holiday," he had announced vaguely and Katherine had returned to New York and to school. She was happy to see Antonia again. The girls had so much to discuss. And Antonia's enthusiasm about a Swiss school "like all those glamorous women in the magazines" had infected a more cautious Katherine. "I shall convince the parents to let me come and stay with you in the holidays," Antonia had promised.

Katherine's mother had come home only the day before they were due to leave. She had been pale, listless, disaffected and Katherine was stricken by remorse. Was it her fault? Had she imagined the violence of the previous months? No, the pain surfaced in her mind all too readily. She wiped it away. Nonetheless, guilt pricked at her. And Sylvie's pallid face and lusterless eyes as she said goodbye to her daughter stayed imprinted on her memory.

The bustle of passport control and customs clearance over, father and daughter emerged into the pristine arrivals lounge. A slender gray-suited man instantly walked over to Jacob. *"Docteur Jardine? Soyez bienvenu. La Princesse vous attend chez elle."*

"Is that the prince?" Katherine whispered to her father.

Jacob smiled. "No, that's Pierre, the chauffeur. There hasn't been a prince for some years. Mathilde doesn't like getting up too early these days. We should be at the château just in time for breakfast."

As they drove through the frosty morning light along the winding borders of the lake and up, up, into the mountains, Jacob chatted to the chauffeur about his wife, Thérèse, about the forecast for skiing conditions, about Pilkou and Martine, the Princesse's dogs. Katherine was suddenly acutely aware that he sounded boyish, happy. Though she knew that her father traveled to Switzerland, she had had no idea that he was so well acquainted with the Princesse's household. Somehow that was a comforting thought. It made the meeting with the woman, whom she had often heard referred to but whom she remembered meeting only once briefly in New York, less daunting.

Soon, as the large Mercedes climbed narrow roads, the magic of the landscape erased all else from Katherine's mind. Hillside pastures dotted with cows and steep-roofed chalets gave way to dramatic slopes. Mont Blanc, sixty miles distant, loomed massively present. And when the château the Princesse had now occupied for over twenty years emerged from amidst snow-clad trees halfway up an escarpment, she felt dizzy with the beauty of it all. For Katherine the landscape bore none of the familiarity of a picture postcard. Everything from the vertiginous slopes to the twin spires of the château which gracefully echoed the greater majesty of the peaks was breathtaking, awesome.

Princesse Mathilde, when she and Frederick had originally taken over the château, had been similarly inspired by its location. In 1937, she had felt she had had enough of the pernicious course of human history. And though she had been sensitive to the château's own architectural beauty, she had stripped one entire back portion of the interior in response to the natural environment. What resulted was a vast room whose span of glass and white walls welcomed the mountains in. The furnishings were raw in their modernity, leather sofas, thick white rugs over glistening natural wood, pictures whose vibrant abstract shapes echoed the landscape without representing it.

It was in this room that Princesse Mathilde, a dramatic figure in a long black hostess gown, welcomed them. Her eyes, despite her years, still held their fire and, though her figure had thickened somewhat, to Katherine's young eyes she seemed the very embodiment of the word *regal*. Mathilde and Jacob embraced in the manner of old friends and then the older woman held Katherine at arm's length and scrutinized her.

"Your father didn't warn me quite what a striking young woman you had grown into," the Princesse said in English with a wry glint in her eye. She hugged Katherine. "I hope we shall become the best of friends. You must treat this place as your second home."

Katherine smiled politely. Then, as she felt a large paw on her thigh, she unbent a little.

"Ah yes, Pilkou and Martine don't want to be forgotten. You must shake hands with them, Katherine. They have been so well brought up, they put the rest of us to shame." The Princesse laughed delightedly. "I'm afraid these two, despite their growing girth, are my constant companions. They're one of the reasons I now make everyone come to me, rather than traipsing round the world." She shook her head in self-mockery.

"Now Mat, you know your notion of a retreat would put most people's social diaries to shame. Don't give Katherine the wrong idea," Jacob intervened playfully.

"The first lesson on entering this house, Katherine, is that you must take only half of what your father says to me seriously," the Princesse responded in kind. "But it's time to sit down to breakfast. I think Cook has outdone herself. I asked her to prepare everything as it might be in America, so that you would feel at home. I suspect she imagines you are built like a giant."

They followed the Princesse into the dining room, where a sideboard heaved with food—cereals, fruit, muffins of all description, hot rolls, a jug of freshly squeezed orange juice. No sooner had Katherine helped herself than a maid appeared with a silver platter heaped with pancakes. "You see." The Princesse smiled as Katherine gasped. "And we must eat as much as possible or she will be deeply insulted."

While they ate, the Princesse and Jacob began to chat in French. As Katherine watched them and listened, she was suddenly aware that her father seemed different than he did in New York. There was a lightness to his gestures, a ready smile on his lips. He was utterly relaxed, at home. For the first time it occurred to Katherine as a conscious thought that he might find life with her mother a trial in ways which didn't only concern her. The notion, now that it was clear, depressed her. She had been selfish in coming here. She was abandoning him.

Princesse Mat read her thoughts.

"Katherine, I haven't yet told you how pleased we all are that you shall be going to school here and be with us at Valois frequently. I hope it will provide your *parents*"—she stressed the word—"with an excuse to come and visit me more often." She stood up and extended a hand to Katherine. "But now you probably want to rest. We have fixed up a room which you can call your own." She put all her expressive charm into her smile. "Violette has even advised me as to what you might like. You'll find a pile of novels, a record player, an assortment of Elvis Presley and Dave Brubeck records . . ." She pronounced the names as if they were utterly outlandish.

Jacob chuckled. "Princesse Mathilde has always had the aspirations of a fairy godmother."

Mathilde gazed at Katherine benignly. The girl looked as if she could do with a fairy godmother, or perhaps just a mother. Jacob should never have allowed it to go this far. But then men were never very good at seeing what was in front of their noses. For all her beauty, Katherine had a wary look about her, as if she couldn't afford to laugh or cry or show any sign of emotion. She was contained, far too contained for a girl of her age. She had none of that innocence or boundless enthusiasm that the Princesse always saw as the stamp of the American girl.

This Katherine instead reminded her a little of those refugee children she had housed during the war, ever polite, ever ready to comply, but as old as the world and never altogether of it. As if at some point in their lives they had decided that the only way to survive was to retreat to a still center in themselves. A magically barred inner space, removed from everyday life. They guarded it superstitiously, for while it remained impenetrable, they felt they could stay alive, whatever the horror of the world outside.

She would have liked to take the girl in her arms and hold her for a long time.

Not privy to the Princesse's thoughts, Katherine smiled. She had the sense she was inhabiting a dream from which she had no desire to wake. Everyone was so kind, so good to her. Everything was so beautiful.

The dream persisted throughout her stay at Valois. They drove to a point higher up the mountains where the snow was already thick, and Katherine had her first skiing lessons. The sense of whizzing through the snow with only hills and trees around her made her jubilant. She loved the speed, the recklessness. She felt triumphantly free for the first time in her life. She was grateful that Sylvie had not taken up the Princesse's invitation to join them for the holidays and, a little guiltily, that Leo hadn't either. Instead of Leo, there was Violette.

Violette, dark-haired, vivacious, instantly installed herself as Katherine's loquacious elder sister. She fussed, gave advice which she laughingly contradicted the next minute, and talked enthusiastically about the business she had just initiated. Violette had set up as a paper restorer, an arcane occupation which took precise scientific skill but involved her in outlandish escapades with police and businessmen or lawyers. Having worked as a freelance for a while, she had recently opened an office in Geneva.

Over a lavish Christmas dinner which Katherine thought must have taken Cook weeks to prepare, Violette regaled them with tales of bizarre exploits. She talked as if she had taken on the mantle of Philip Marlowe, a female arch sleuth for whom the teeming underworld held no secrets.

"So after the fire, Himmelbrau and Strick called me in to see whether I could do something to re-establish their client files—thirty years of legal practice up in smoke. I set to work with my little bag of magic potions and do you know what I discovered?" Violette paused to make sure everyone's interest had reached an appropriate pitch. "I found as the charred remains came to light that one of

their employees, who had left the firm last year, had been embez-
zling them for years and had set fire to the premises so that no trace
could be found of his dirty work. Now the police never stop ringing
me," Violette laughed triumphantly.

"My daughter has a highly developed sense of adventure," the
Princesse said wryly. "I don't know where it comes from."

"Yes, you do, Mat," Violette countered her. "Apart from the tiny
genetic component, it has everything to do with Madame Chardin's
establishinent. Oh yes, Katherine, the school you are about to go to
is a very special sort of place." She paused dramatically.

Katherine saw her father exchange a worried look with the
Princesse.

"Don't let Violette provoke you," the Princesse laughed. "Madame
Chardin is a model of academic rectitude."

"So she must be. She has helped to mold our wonderful Violette."
Jacob looked happily on Violette, gaining reassurance from her presence if not her words. In any event, he consoled himself, nothing
could be worse for Katherine than the situation that had developed
at home. With the exception, perhaps, of a continued stay with the
dangerously attractive Thomas Sachs. And Madame Chardin would
take Katherine away from both.

"A model of rectitude Madame Chardin may be, and a dab hand
at Latin declensions and trigonometry, but what the girls get up to
is something else," Violette countered mysteriously.

What the girls got up to was something Katherine was to learn
only gradually. Her first impression of her new school filled her with
trepidation. It was not the premises themselves. The school was
perched on a hillside at the edge of a little village halfway between
Geneva and the Princesse's château. A pastoral atmosphere prevailed, despite the looming brick of the three-story structure with its
adjoining chapel and outlying houses.

What Katherine found daunting was the ambience within: the
large unsmiling woman who sat at a table in the entrance hall and
stiffly handed her two sheets of paper, one with a map of the school
which showed her own room clearly marked, the other with a long
list of instructions printed in four languages, French, German, Italian
and English; a smell which mingled disinfectant and scouring soap;
the difference in temperature between the stifling main body of the
school and the chill of the outlying wing where she found her room.

Pierre, the Princesse's chauffeur, deposited Katherine's bags in
the middle of the room, smiled reassuringly and said goodbye. He

would be back in three weeks, he reminded her, to take her home for the weekend. Every third week, the girls were permitted to have visitors or to leave the premises for the weekend. In between the school was a world wholly unto itself.

Madame Chardin was an educator with very strict ideas. She believed that girls needed a fair dose of daily and vigorous exercise. This was partially accomplished at seven in the morning when the girls ran three times round the school grounds, unless a particularly heavy snowfall made running utterly impossible; and again in a physical education period in the afternoons. Food was also strictly controlled and no sweets or biscuits were allowed in rooms.

That apart, moral education was high on the agenda, followed with varying degrees of import by botany, languages and academic subjects. Madame Chardin was a Protestant with distinct Rousseauist leanings, but she had read her Rousseau with an eye to institutions. "Natural" leanings might come first, but these were regulated with the severity of a drill master.

Some of this Katherine gleaned dimly from the set of house rules she read through three times in a room distinguished only by orderly barrenness. There were three beds, three cupboards, one desk and no external signs that anyone inhabited the space. For a girl who before her recent adventure had never been away from home alone for more than a weekend, the prospect which this room and Madame Chardin's rules evoked was a daunting one. Had Katherine been able to forget the fear her mother instilled in her, she would have wept out of homesickness. As it was, she thought with longing of Antonia and the informality of her school in New York where teachers could even on occasion be construed as friends.

"So you're the new girl." A voice stirred her from her reverie and Katherine turned to see a tall slim sandy-haired girl enter the room followed by a smaller rounder figure. The tall girl stretched out her hand. "I'm Portia Gaitskell and this is Marie-Hélène Beaumont," she said in a French which bore the traces of English. "And don't pay too much attention to all that gumph. She only gives it to us to scare us when we arrive."

The two girls laughed and Katherine smiled a little warily in response.

"This is your bed and your cupboard." Portia pointed to the bed furthest from the window. "You can unpack now or we can show you round the premises first. 'It is your duty, girls, to make your new colleagues feel at home here,'" Portia suddenly said in stentorian tones which made Marie-Hélène burst out in giggles.

"Portia does an impeccable rendition of Madame Chardin," Marie-Hélène said in a softly mellifluous voice. "As you'll see. Here, have some of these. They'll make you feel right at home." Marie-Hélène opened her wardrobe and reached into the pocket of an ample winter coat to bring out a box of truffles.

By the end of that evening, after she had sat through a dinner in the large school refectory, listened to Madame Chardin's opening speech of the term, and lain in the dark listening to her new roommates, Katherine did indeed begin to feel if not at home, then at least marginally more comfortable.

As the weeks progressed, the only thing which troubled her was that her new friends had seen so much more of the world than she had. Granted, Marie-Hélène was a year and Portia two years older than her. But it wasn't a question of age. They had both already seen and lived through so much and they were fearless in the way they connived to break the school rules at every opportunity. Their intricate scheming spoke of defiance, but also of a love of conspiracy for its own sake, conspiracy prompted by group living within a regimented and closed institution.

As an initial reaction the girls' parents might have been shocked by what they got up to. On second thoughts, however, they might have reflected that these little conspiratorial activities prepared them quite as adequately for life as the main curriculum. Portia's father was an ambassador and the family had lived in Nigeria, China and Washington—places where scheming was hardly a novelty. Marie-Hélène's family were wealthy French industrialists and her summers were spent in a variety of exotic locales, which spurred the girl's fantasies.

Between them the schoolgirls represented a United Nations of wealth and prestige. Katherine felt young and inexperienced in conversations which spanned the pros and cons of marriage, the intricacies of divorce, the complexities of couture and, most frequently, the vagaries and mysteries of men. And she was initially awed by the plots which the girls concocted as they sought to shame a particular teacher or fellow pupil, or simply to escape at impermissible hours from the school grounds. Sometimes she remembered Thomas's parting words to her and thought that perhaps she was indeed something of an innocent.

At first she tended to listen and take in what was said in order to mull over it in the quiet of her own bed. She wrote long letters home to Antonia in which she translated the other girls' lives in terms that made sense to her. She also wrote to her brother, whom she had mostly but not altogether forgiven for his betrayal of her to her mother. And she wrote to her parents, keeping her tone light and giving away little of her present life.

Thomas Sachs received her longest letters and wrote the longest in return. Their correspondence provided an alternative education for Katherine. He suggested books she might read and when she had, she wrote to him about them. The ensuing exchange over the months turned the whole cast of Balzac's *Comédie Humaine* into Katherine's familiars and gave her an awareness of greed and ambition, love and betrayal far beyond her years. Thomas's witty and sometimes acerbic voice became the other side of her inner dialogue. When it sometimes emerged from her own lips, her teachers or friends would look at her oddly, wondering whether they had heard her correctly.

By June, when the little mountain flowers covered the lush meadows with their brightness, Katherine had adjusted to her new life. Rarely did dreams of home and her mother come to haunt her. She lived in the present tense of the school with its totally absorbing pattern of routine and minor rebellion. Only when the other girls exchanged confidences about their parents and sometimes lambasted them with the particular competitive cruelty adolescents are prone to, did Katherine retreat into silence. She was still unable to speak about the circumstances which had brought her to Madame Chardin's. She preferred not to think about it.

With the Princesse, she was still timid. The woman inspired her with an admiration which made closeness difficult. Yet Katherine trusted her, as she had never trusted an older woman before. Sometimes she found certain phrases, certain inflections creeping into her French which she recognized as belonging to the Princesse. She was pleased to find them.

One day, she had shyly asked the Princesse whether Portia might come and spend a week with her at the beginning of the summer break. "Of course," the Princesse had answered. "There is nothing I like more than having the house filled with young people."

Pierre came to pick them up in the long Mercedes and they piled in with all their bags and appurtenances. Their end-of-term hilarity matched the bright sky and light frolicking tufts of cloud. Château Valois, when they reached it, looked more beautiful than ever amidst the fresh green of early summer leaves and dappled sunshine. Even the much-traveled Portia paused in the ripple of her chatter to exclaim her appreciation. Katherine found herself smiling happily as if the compliment were directed at her own home.

The Princesse came to greet them as soon as they were over the threshold. She hugged Katherine and stretched out a welcoming hand to Portia. Then she said, "There's a surprise visitor here for you, Katherine." Her voice sounded a little strained, but only Portia caught the odd pitying look she gave Katherine as the girl rushed toward the salon.

Katherine fully expected to fall into her father's arms. But as she made out the figure who stood darkly outlined against the blaze of the picture window's light, she stopped abruptly short. The Princesse and Portia looked on as mother and daughter, now almost of an equal height, one blonde, the other dark, took each other in. A hush descended on the room. Then Sylvie walked toward Katherine and pecked her lightly on the cheek. Katherine flinched perceptibly.

"Hello, Katherine, you're looking very well," Sylvie said with a falsetto of enthusiasm which grated on Katherine's ears. "It must be Europe. I've never believed that New York was good for anyone."

Katherine could find no words. She stared at her mother as if she were a ghost, a ghost with streaming blonde hair who wore a tightly unmaternal black dress and puffed incessantly at her cigarette. She glanced anxiously at Portia. How would she judge this peculiar entity which was her mother? Katherine shivered with ugly premonition.

The Princesse stepped in, held the precarious social balance of the group together. She engaged the girls in a description of their schooldays, made them chat.

Sylvie puffed at her cigarettes, and then in the middle of one of Katherine's sentences abruptly stood up. "I've never been very good at school," she said in a bored voice. She sauntered from the room, paused at the door, and turned.

"Katherine, you'll be pleased to know that I'm only here for a few days. Then it's off to Rome." She gave her daughter a look which combined challenge and malice and then left them.

Katherine sat rigidly in her chair. Princesse Mathilde chatted on, pretending nothing was amiss. She was angry at Sylvie. She had urged her to be kind to Katherine and the woman had promised. But then Sylvie had never been controllable. The Princesse sighed and then with a smile urged the girls to go off and unpack before having a swim. The pool had just been cleaned and called out for swimmers.

Katherine, as they made their way up the stairs, made no attempt to answer Portia's unspoken question and engage in confidences about her mother. Beneath her external calm, she raged and felt frightened by turns. Sylvie was no longer the withdrawn, slightly pitiable figure she had last seen in New York. She was fueled by a frenetic energy which spoke to Katherine of danger.

Over the next days, the girls swam, took long walks, talked, and ate Cook's meals which seemed more wonderful than ever after the school's frugal fare. Katherine tried to enjoy it, tried to forget her mother's stalking presence. But at every turn it caught up with her, here to laugh belittlingly, there to make a venomous comment, about Katherine's hair, her clothes, her French accent. Katherine unconsciously reverted to her childhood tactics, withdrew, tried to make herself small, invisible.

The Princesse stepped in to defend her at every turn. One day Sylvie turned on her. "Stop behaving like her mother," she said bitingly. "You and Jacob have done quite enough together." Sylvie paused and then burst out in a shrill laugh, before leaving the room.

It was the Princesse's evident flush which made Katherine begin to speculate. What was Sylvie implying? What was the "quite enough" that Mathilde and Jacob had done? Thomas had warned her that things were never quite what they seemed in this old world. Could it be that Mathilde and her father had . . . She stopped her thoughts. But they kept returning. She embroidered on them. How she would have liked to have Princesse Mat as a mother, Violette as a sister. Yes, perhaps that was why they were so kind to her.

The thoughts provided her with a refuge from Sylvie.

Toward the end of the week Katherine was called to the telephone. The voice at the end of the line made her break into smiles.

"Hello, Schätzchen. I'm in Geneva. Shall I take you out?"

"Thomas!" Katherine pealed in delight. "Yes please. But wait, I must check with Princesse Mat." After a moment, Katherine returned to the phone.

"Mat says you're to come to dinner tonight and stay over. Then, if it's all right, my friend Portia and I can drive into Geneva with you tomorrow."

The familiar chuckle warmed her ear. "Anything your heart desires, Schätzchen. It will be a pleasure."

"It will be quite a party, then." The Princesse's dark eyes shone when Katherine reported back to her. "Like the old days. My two grandchildren arrive this afternoon with their nanny. Violette is driving up from Geneva with from what I can make out is her latest beau and two friends. Then there's Dr. Mohr and his wife. And Sylvie. I must go and warn Cook about the growing numbers." The Princesse moved into action with the energy of a much younger woman. But before she left the room, she turned back.

"Katherine." She looked into the girl's unreadable gray eyes, appreciating the fineness of her face. "Katherine, my dear, you must try not to mind too much about your mother." She paused for a moment, seemed to be about to say something else, then changed her mind. "I, we all, love you very much. You know that." She held Katherine's gaze, smiled seriously, then with a swirl of skirts hurried away.

For the rest of the day, Katherine felt oddly blessed. As she clambered over the steep Alpine meadows with Portia, she told her friend for the first time about Thomas and how he had helped her when she had nowhere to go. She didn't go into the reasons for her running away from home, but she extolled Thomas's role.

"A veritable knight in shining armor," Portia laughed. "Come on, let's go back and make ourselves beautiful for him, for the evening. I'm dying to try out my hairdressing skills and I've got these two absolutely sumptuous dresses which haven't been worn for ages. You can try them and see which you like."

The girls hurried back excitedly, then, bathed and scented, they tried on combinations of clothes and hair for effect.

"The trouble with you, Katherine Jardine, is that you look too good in anything and everything," Portia said wistfully as Katherine slipped into the borrowed blue silk dress with ruched sleeves. "If I ever have a man, remind me not to introduce him to you."

"The trouble with you, Portia Gaitskell," Katherine countered, "is that you're too good for any man. And don't forget it. But just in case you're intent on finding an admirer tonight, I've decided which way your hair looks best." With a few deft strokes of the brush, Katherine gathered up Portia's fine sandy hair into a loop at the back of her head and let its length trail her shoulders. From a small vase, she took two of the daisies they had picked that afternoon and wound them strategically in Portia's hair. Portia was delighted with the effect. She had already had occasion to notice Katherine's skills, skills with arrangement, with colors and shape. Their room at school, within a few weeks of Katherine's arrival, had by a few deft touches and additions acquired a new look.

"And now you should really wear the white dress. A proper English rose," Katherine suggested in her usual hesitant tones.

"While you provide the contrast as a proper femme fatale." Portia laughed and looked at Katherine's shapely figure swathed in blue silk, the glow of her bare shoulders darkened by the sun.

"No." Katherine met her friend's eyes in the mirror. "I look ridiculous decked out like this." As ridiculous as my mother, she thought to herself, but said aloud. "Not at all how I feel." With rapid movements, she slipped out of the revealing dress and pulled a girlish white frock out of the wardrobe. "This is much more my style."

Portia smiled and twisted some daisies through Katherine's thick auburn hair. They examined themselves in the mirror. "Snap," Portia said. "Two of Madame Chardin's prize ingénues."

The windows of the Princesse's salon had been thrown open to make it one with the vast slab of a marble terrace. Here some of the assembled company sat watching the sun set in rosy Technicolor behind a jagged peak. Katherine and Portia were amongst Violette and her friends, Simone, Yves and Carlo Negri. While Violette entertained them with stories of increasing complexity, Katherine from beneath lowered lids stole occasional glances at Carlo. She had never seen anyone quite like him before. There was a slow sensuous laziness to his movements contradicted by the dangerously hard angles of his face, the flashing darkness of his eyes, which no matter how covertly she looked at him seemed to be gazing at her. He was like a large, beautiful cat, poised and motionless, but prepared to leap. Katherine was rapt by his magnetism. It made her feel uncomfortable and strangely vulnerable. She forced herself to concentrate on Violette's lurid tale, another installment in her life with the police.

"Violette is in love with death," Carlo suddenly interrupted in a soft but resonant voice.

Violette looked at him defiantly. "There speaks the man who drove us here at such breakneck speed that I began to take pity on his poor Ferrari's engine. We left Simone and Yves behind in a trail of dust just outside Geneva." She shook her dark curls woefully.

"Ah yes, when it comes to that, Violette and I are two of a kind," he said with mock mournfulness. "These old, old families, you know. The genes want a rest."

"Genes, yes, how they mark one." Sylvie sat down next to Carlo, a little too close. She smoothed her elegantly cut celadon dress.

"Though I sometimes think Violette is more like me than my own daughter." She laughed loudly. "You have a sense of adventure, my dear."

Katherine saw Violette look at Sylvie with frank admiration. "But I can't sing like you. Otherwise I might trade in my detective work for a life on the boards."

"Song, yes. My gift from the gods. The Dionysian gods." She threw Carlo a sultry glance.

"Why don't you sing for us now?" Carlo said lazily.

"Oh, I couldn't. My voice isn't what it used to be."

"Go on, Sylvie. We'd enjoy it," Princesse Mathilde encouraged her.

"Well, if you like." She looked at Carlo again, moved to the piano, ran long fingers over the keys, and then in a low, sultry voice began on a medley of wartime numbers.

Katherine averted her eyes. She couldn't bear the sight of her mother preening, her squirming body. She watched Portia to see the effect Sylvie was having, watched Carlo and Violette. And then suddenly, Sylvie called out to her.

"Katherine, come here. Come and accompany me. You must still remember some of the numbers you were taught. A simple one. Let's start with 'La vie en rose.'"

Katherine wanted to run. She hated playing. She could sense the scene coming, foresee the inevitable criticism, the malicious put-downs. Her fingers stiffened under the memory of the innumerable raps on the knuckles Sylvie had given her in the past.

"I didn't know you played," Mathilde's warm voice intervened.

"She doesn't play very well." Sylvie's laugh tinkled. "But I've tried. Lord knows, I've tried to teach her. Come along, Katherine. Just a little accompaniment. You can manage that, surely."

Katherine felt the hush in the room grow ominous in its waiting for her. Suddenly in that tremulous silence the French voices had left, a fragment of the buried past rose in her like a wave of nausea. "You can manage that, Katherine," Sylvie said to the gathered guests. "Surely at your age you can manage that. Girls of four don't wet their beds night after night. Like some untamed beast. It's disgusting. The sheets stink. The mattress. Disgusting."

Shame, cloying, dirty, engulfed her. Katherine's legs trembled, refused to take her weight.

"I can do 'La vie en rose.'" Portia leapt up. "Katherine's not in the mood, are you, Kat?"

Katherine shook her head bleakly.

Portia tried a chord, then another. Sylvie's voice burst upon the room. Jarring, electric. Katherine sat tautly at the edge of her chair. It had been averted. The scene had been averted. She closed her eyes for a moment and took a deep breath.

Then from behind her she heard the butler announce, "Thomas Sachs." Thomas. Escape. She could escape. Katherine leapt up and moved with alacrity toward the hall. The Princesse was already shaking hands with him and Katherine held back a little. He cut a striking figure in his dark dinner jacket, his shock of white hair swept back from his wide forehead, his clear blue eyes alive with irony. Thomas, how glad she was to have him here. Glad of his glow of appreciation as his gaze rested on her. She rushed girlishly into his arms.

"It is very very good to see you, Schätzchen," Thomas said in a low voice. He held her by the shoulders and kissed her in continental fashion on the cheeks.

They walked toward the salon together, arm in arm. As they approached, Sylvie's song beckoned to them, enfolded them. Suddenly, from the threshold of the room, Katherine saw her mother through Thomas's eyes. A mother whose eyes and gestures were seductively alive. A mother in an elegantly cut celadon dress which moved with her body. A mother whose blonde hair was wound back in a demure knot, but whose lips were pursed in the semblance of a kiss. The mother she had portrayed to Thomas as a monster of iniquity.

Applause covered that mother as her song ended.

Katherine tensed.

"You must be Mr. Sachs. What a pleasure it is to meet you at last." Sylvie moved toward them at once. "You've been so kind to poor Katherine and I'm so grateful to you. She's such a difficult child, you know, always imagining things." Sylvie wrapped her hand round Thomas's arm and led him toward a far corner. Katherine followed in growing horror. Sylvie's voice was warm with complicity. It wooed Thomas, complained lightly of a problematic child, while her gestures told him how attractive she found him. Katherine looked on in confusion. Thomas seemed to be succumbing to Sylvie's charms as much as to her narrative. She wanted to intervene, to warn him, but her limbs, her tongue, were frozen.

The dining-room table was sumptuously set with the Princesse's family silver and vast candelabra. The Princesse presided at one end, while Thomas had been placed as guest of honor at the other. To his left was Sylvie. To his right, a nervous, embarrassed Katherine. Next to Katherine sat Carlo.

The gourmet dinner Cook had prepared tasted like sawdust in Katherine's mouth. She felt trapped in the web of narrative her mother was spinning about her. Each time Thomas or Carlo tried to draw her into conversation, the words died on her lips. She knew she was behaving like a silly child, the little girl she no longer was. But she could do nothing, while Sylvie's presence drew everyone like a charm. The fact that Carlo was sitting next to her, overhearing the conversation, indolently gazing round the table or raising his glass to sip the delights of the Princesse's cellar, only made things worse.

As a half-eaten plate of delicious *boeuf en croûte* was lifted away from her, Katherine heard her mother say, "And do you know, one day when Katherine was tiny, she stole the engagement ring my husband had given me." Sylvie looked with limpid eyes into Thomas's face. "I told Dali about it and he simply chuckled. 'Quite, quite right,' he said, 'little girls have to be jealous of their mothers and of their daddy's affections.' " Sylvie laughed with a silken tone. "And it never changes, never."

Katherine's face had grown contorted. Thomas's hand, patting her knee reassuringly, did nothing to still her emotions.

"Sometimes"—he smiled at Sylvie urbanely—"I think we inflict the oedipal story on our children and attribute emotions and intentions to them which are more properly our own. Perhaps we have got things the wrong way round. Perhaps it is fathers who are jealous of the sons who will soon replace them. Or mothers who are jealous of their daughters. While the children are merely innocent mirrors who reflect what we wish to see."

"Perhaps," Sylvie replied sweetly. "But in my case, I can tell you it was quite different. The ring was merely one instance."

"Bitch," Katherine mumbled under her breath, not knowing how the word had made its way to her lips. She rose abruptly from the table. "Excuse me, I'm not feeling very well."

She rushed away before anyone could stop her, rushed too quickly to hear Carlo say, "I don't know, I think if I were the beautiful Katherine's mother, I might suffer the occasional twinge of jealousy."

he arched hall of the Palazzo
was cool with the marble and stone of centuries. A coolness unimag-
inable in the pulsing outdoor heat of that Milan afternoon. It enveloped Sylvie, chilled the dampness of her forehead, calmed the fever
which had brought her here.

For two days she had surreptitiously watched the gateway of the
magnificent house from the cover of a plane tree on the other side
of the road. She had observed the Palazzo's comings and goings,
trying to sniff from them a sense of the life within. The clandestine
nature of her task, the whiff of danger, filled her with excitement.
It reminded her of another time. Another Sylvie. The Sylvie of the
underground, the war, its risks. The charge of being incognito. She
felt as if, at last, after all those American years of stifling tedium and
vagueness and oppressive normality, she were again herself. There,
in the secret shade of the plane tree.

Sylvie followed the dark-suited man who had opened the vast
polished door to her, trailed past antique busts of senatorial gaze.
In the loggia there was a hushed stillness, broken only by the rampant color of geraniums pouring through columns from the courtyard
beyond. She was shown into a library of gracious proportions, ushered toward a chair. From nowhere another dark man appeared,
bearing a tray, a jug of Campari and soda, a tall iced glass. He
hovered, moved invisibly into the background.

Sylvie waited. Let the tranquillity of the Palazzo lull her.

Four years. It had taken her over four years, but here she was at last.

She remembered the point of origin of her journey distinctly.

She had been in the clinic in Pennsylvania. It was her third visit there, perhaps her fourth. It was 1956. She was forty. In tangible decline. The weight of that age sat heavily on her shoulders, marked her body, tore at her mind. No one she had loved, no one she considered her own—neither her father, nor her mother, nor her brother, nor her friend Caroline—had reached such a ridiculous age. An age which, it struck her, had no future.

Jacob hated her going to the clinic, but she went whenever things at home got too difficult. She liked it there. Liked it in part because Jacob disapproved. Liked the plump nurses who wore ordinary clothes and smiled inanely and constantly. Liked the other patients with their erratic ways. Liked the doctors who let her say and do anything she pleased. As long as she didn't drink. She didn't mind that. They gave her pills which kept the world at a distance, muted things, let her dream. Jacob hated the pills.

She liked the grounds too, the little woods, far from the ugly clamor and harsh odors of the city.

That time, a little boy had been there. A little boy of about eight, small for his age, curly-haired, dark. He sat in a corner, sat very still. His only movement was in the tears which crept down his pale cheeks. For some reason, Sylvie took solace in him. He reminded her of something, of some repressed part of herself.

She sat near him, not too close, not too far. She saw how he refused everything. Food. Talk. Attention. But she knew he was aware of her. Not too near. Not too far. One day he looked up at her, met her eyes.

She waited until he did it again. Then she went up to him.

"I'm going for a walk," she said. "If you'd like to come . . ." She let her invitation hang. He gazed at her hesitantly. She didn't move. She waited. Waited for perhaps five minutes. Then he nodded.

They walked slowly, silently, in the grounds. Sylvie took an apple from her pocket. Bit into it. Offered it to him. He looked at it and then, after a moment, bit into it ravenously. They didn't speak, but the next day and the day after that, the walk was repeated. On that day, Sylvie asked him his name. He didn't answer for a while and then, as they made their way round the little lake, he answered, "Ivanov." Then, changing the intonation, "Ivan."

"Ivanov," Sylvie repeated. "Ivan," she said again, sniffing the sound. Something in her leapt and then faded. "A nice name," she said.

The next day Ivan started to speak to her, haltingly at first, in an English which wasn't quite English, and in disconnected bursts of speech. He had been in the States for only a few months. A stray little Hungarian boy, sent away from his strife-torn country by his mother, to a new life in America with adoptive parents who didn't understand him. Who were doing their best, but *couldn't* understand him, not only because of the gap of language. And who, at their wits' end, had sent him here. Sylvie understood. Understood the dreams and images that tormented him, the listless refusal of his shrouded days. He reminded her of little Gabriel, of so many others during the war. She hugged him to her, stayed by his side, let him speak when he wanted to speak, held him when he cried.

One day while they walked, he asked, "Do you already have a little boy like me?" He pressed her hand, all but beseeched her.

His words set up a buzz in Sylvie's mind. They whizzed and flew and darted into murky corners. She gazed at little Ivan, bent down to kiss him. "No, not a little one." She shook her head. "But I wish I did."

His words brought back another scene. Her parents' house but not her parents' house. After the war. Two women lying in beds, their mouths round with cries. She floated above them, then leapt into one of the bodies. Her own. Sylvie in labor. The nurses barking like hyenas, braying like donkeys. Noise. Too much noise. In the bed next to her, a frail girl. What was her name? Hanka. Hanka pale, screaming. And a man. Ivan, of course. Ivan Makarov.

After that, the memory faded but lay there, in the back of her mind, refusing to leave her alone.

For three more weeks at the clinic, Sylvie kept Ivan company. She stopped taking the pills. And while she walked or sat with him, she thought, pondered her life, dredged up scenes, remembered. When Ivan went home clutching Sylvie's address in his hand, Sylvie left too. She was suddenly burning with the fire of a new task.

She had forgotten about the obstacle of her immediate family. When she returned to New York, she bumped against them with a vengeance. She would have told Jacob about her new purpose, but she knew he would see it as another sign of her raving, a sign of some new imbalance, and would try to search for causes, try to talk her out of it. In any case, she hated him, hated him for never making love to her anymore.

And she hated Katherine. Loathed the look of innocent reproach lodged in those cool gray eyes. Loathed her fearfulness. Hated that slim body with its perfect skin which always nestled into Jacob's embrace. Sometimes her loathing was so great that she even forgot her new determination.

At first she thought she might take Leo into her confidence. The detective agency she had approached had given her no results. All she had to go on was a name, a place of birth, the suggestion of an address. They thought she was mad. Leo, she finally decided, might think the same. In any case, he was just a boy, engrossed in his new university life. He might even turn against her and she cared for him.

So Sylvie decided she would enlist the Princesse. Princesse Mat always knew how to go about things. She had friends in high places everywhere, contacts in embassies. Sylvie flew to Switzerland.

She didn't tell Princesse Mat the whole story. In any event, she had begun to like the idea of a secret. A secret always buoyed her up, gave her a sense of adventure. She told Princesse Mathilde that she wanted to find the son of her old friend Andrzej Potacki, yes, yes, the Andrzej who had died with the partisans after the war. The child, she told the Princesse, had been left in the care of a friend of Andrzej's, a Russian. Yes, it was strange that he was Russian, but history too was strange. Ivan Makarov was his name. A certain Ivan Makarov. Perhaps he was an officer. Sylvie wanted to find him. Things were so awful in Poland, in the Soviet Union. But now it was all opening up a little. Maybe the child could be located. Sylvie wanted to see him, to give him things, to help.

The Princesse had looked at her curiously. But Sylvie had convinced her, vowed her to secrecy. She knew that the Princesse suspected her of having taken Andrzej as a lover, but that only made it all the more plausible. What did she care what the Princesse thought, as long as she helped her.

And the Princesse had helped. She knew of agencies. She knew the Polish ambassador, the Soviet ambassador.

It took a long time, so long that Sylvie had almost given up, had gone back to the clinic several times.

And then last summer, there had been word. They had traced a son of Ivan Makarov to Milan of all places. He had apparently been adopted by a wealthy industrialist. In a fever of excitement, Sylvie had flown to Milan. She had no idea what she would do, but she needed to see the boy.

She had found the Palazzo easily. But its size, its ostentatious wealth had daunted her. Sylvie bided her time. She haunted the gateway of the house, waited for the boy to emerge. And then, one morning, she saw him. A slender youth with dark tousled hair and eyes of a stormy blue. The eyes, she thought, were unmistakable. She wanted to rush up to him. But something held her back. For three days running she returned to the house at the same time. Behind her dark glasses, she constructed for herself the illusion of security.

One day, she called out, and he turned. She fled. She had no idea what to say to him.

She returned to New York. Here everything was worse. Katherine's very presence seemed to provoke her at every turn. She was the incarnation of everything that had gone amiss in Sylvie's own life. And the girl now flirted outrageously with Jacob, with Leo. Sylvie's rancor against her became the measure of her universe. She started to drink again. She took another lover. Nothing helped.

And then Katherine was gone. The relief of it. Sylvie began to think more clearly. What did she want? Things twisted this way and that in her mind. And then she hit upon a scheme.

Again she enlisted the Princesse's help.

She wanted to write a series of articles, perhaps a book. It would give her something to do. A book about the children of the war, displaced children, children who had not been brought up by their natural parents or in their home countries. Hitler's orphans. Stalin's orphans. The Princesse had to help her. Give her introductions. She knew all about those refugees. From the war. Last summer when she had gone in search of Andrzej's son, she hadn't been able to bring herself to speak to him. The articles would provide a way. Please.

Sylvie had come the closest she had ever been to begging.

The Princesse's eyes were sad. She had looked at Sylvie for a long time before speaking. Then she had nodded slowly, and said, "Sylvie, you know that you've found yourself an elaborate means of coming to terms with your own childhood. Just remember that, my dear. All this is about you. And there may not be any magical answers out there."

But the Princesse had written letters, smoothed the way, given her a literary pseudonym.

And here Sylvie was, waiting in the cool hush of the Palazzo. She sipped her drink. Sat up straighter. Remembered herself. She was a journalist. She had coached herself in the role, prepared her questions. She pulled out a notepad from her briefcase, opened the tape recorder she had brought. She prided herself on the last. It was the sign of her new trade. She wound tapes, set up her microphone.

She was only sorry that the brief formal note which had arrived from the Palazzo granting her an interview of no more than ninety minutes' duration had stipulated that photographs would not be permitted.

Sylvie, the actress, rearranged her broad-brimmed hat, crossed one tapering leg over another and smoothed a stocking. She wanted him to think her attractive, to like her. And there he was at last, a tall youth in a light summer shirt which showed her how his shoulders were already visibly broadening. Her breath caught. She stood.

He came toward her with outstretched hand. "How do you do? I am Alexei Gismondi."

"Laura Stirling," Sylvie remembered herself.

There was another man with him, a minder, Sylvie thought, perhaps an English tutor. They made small talk, about Italy, the weather, New York. Alexei's English was stilted, but adequate. Sylvie, warming to her role, conjured up fantastical pictures of New York days and dangerous nights, brought a laugh to his lips. Then she explained her purpose. She wanted a profile of Alexei, his present life, something of his past.

The boy smiled at her, a smile half whimsical, half serious. Her heart bumped. He was so like his father.

Alexei Gismondi gazed calmly at this woman. So this was a New Yorker, he thought. She must have been very pretty once, so blonde. He had met very few Americans in his life and his image of New York was a product of films and *gialli,* the thrillers he loved to read. It was a world which howled with car chases and teetered between excitement and extinction. He imagined this woman draped on Humphrey Bogart's arm and walking into a seedy bar. The picture worked. He panned toward a piano, saw her saunter over to it.

Sylvie called him back, smiled with wide curling lips, asked him to describe his days.

"They are exceedingly boring," Alexei answered honestly. Everything was boring compared to his books and the films he swallowed voraciously. "I go to school, come home, do my work, have English lessons. I would be far more interested in hearing you talk some more about New York." He looked at her earnestly.

At the age of fourteen, Alexei Gismondi was hardly adept at self-revelation. Since his move to Italy, he had led a cloistered life in the luxurious Palazzo. Up until two years ago, he had been tutored at home. It was his English tutor who had convinced his uncle that films were an excellent way to learn the language. And so his education in Hitchcock and Huston and Wilder had run parallel to his study of English.

Then his uncle had decided that it was time to send him to school. He needed the company of other children. But he had not yet formed any firm friendships. His uncle's wealth, the chauffeur-driven limousine which brought him to and from school, cut him off as securely as did his own past. Despite the fact that he had drawn a cord between his previous life and the present one, he was not exactly lonely. He lived a great deal in his fantasies and he enjoyed these. He had something of the solitary about him, something of the dreamer, although he had none of the dreamer's physical clumsiness.

All this Sylvie began to learn as she watched his graceful gestures and questioned him. She provoked him first to talk about his interests, the books he read, the films he watched. Then gradually, imperceptibly, she led him into the trickier terrain of the past.

"So the Gismondis are not your parents?" she asked casually.

"Oh no, I thought you knew that. They are my uncle and aunt, on my mother's side."

Sylvie flinched despite herself.

"They have adopted me now, of course, so I bear their name, though Lara, my aunt, sadly died two years ago."

"And your own mother?" Sylvie prodded.

Alexei's eyes grew cloudy. "She died when I was born," he said softly. "She was Polish."

"I was born in Poland, too," Sylvie offered.

"Oh yes?" Alexei didn't pursue it. "I don't speak Polish. My father took me to the Soviet Union when I was very small. We lived in Leningrad, then in Moscow," he said proudly. "Then . . ." His voice trailed off.

Sylvie recognized the look that came momentarily over Alexei's face. Fear. The traces of fear. It was gone as soon as it had come and he re-established his public gaze. "But that is all over. My uncle and aunt had no children. They adopted me. They have been very good to me."

What Alexei didn't tell Sylvie about, what he spoke of to no one, was that last year he had spent with his father.

His memory had grown into a series of fading snapshots. He could flick the pages of the album at will. But around the frames of the pictures everything was dark. Except for that last year, when the blurred skelter of images wouldn't stay in their frames and played about with a kaleidoscopic frenzy. The emotions of that period still lived within him.

Each section of the album began with a key image. There was Leningrad, his father in his uniform kneeling by his side and explaining to him how quickly the waters of the Neva flowed, flowed into the Gulf of Finland. There was Moscow, the great military parade, the pride of the Soviet Union trooping in front of them and his father pointing to a man, not so far from them, a man with a big moustache and dark eyes. Stalin, his father whispered in pride.

Then came Budapest, the Embassy where people talked in hushed voices. His father was different then. Something was worrying him. He could smell it on him. He would rarely stoop down to explain things to Alexei.

And then, in that last year, came the great journey north. An endless journey in a train toward a landscape which was all snowy vastness. This was where the pictures refused to stay still. The blizzards stirred them, made them leap and flurry, like his father's anger.

He saw his father only rarely. Basha looked after him in the small village. But each time his father appeared, he looked grimmer. One day he took Alexei along with him. It was cold, so cold in the jeep that it was with difficulty that Alexei kept his eyes open. When he did, he saw rows upon rows of dismal huts; and then a little further, gangs of men walking, walking and falling and still walking. He saw one man hitting another. It frightened him. He wanted to cry, but the tears froze on his face.

His father drove on. There was the forest. And there were men chopping at the trees. Alexei could see their faces. They were terrible. Empty. Like skulls. He closed his eyes. His father shouted at him over the noise of the engine, "I want you to see, Alexei. I want you to see."

When they got back to Basha and the small house, his father embraced him. "I want you to remember today, Alexei. You may not understand now, but I want you to remember. It is why I am sending you away."

It was then that Alexei began to cry. They stood huddled beside the small stove and his father waited for his tears to subside. "This is a great country, Alexei. Never forget that." His father lowered his voice. "But the revolution has strayed. Soon, perhaps, it will come right. Justice is on its side. But for the moment, it is better that you are further away. Your permit has come. You shall visit your aunt and uncle. It is what your mother would have wished."

Alexei knew that when his mother's name was invoked, there was no arguing. He nuzzled against his father. "And when shall I see you, Papa?" His father held him closer, but didn't reply.

Two days later, a Comrade Tulayeva came to fetch him. From above her vast chest, she looked at him disapprovingly. He knew instinctively that tears would not be in order, might even prove treacherous.

He never saw his father again.

At the Finnish border, a sturdy man with a dark face and a broad smile waited for him. He had a thick coat with a fur collar, bright white teeth. "I am your uncle Giangiacomo," he said to him. They were the only words Alexei understood until he reached Milan.

"How old were you when you arrived in Italy?" The American journalist broke into his thoughts.

"I had just turned seven," Alexei responded calmly. "You can see why I remember so little." He smiled, glanced at his watch.

What he remembered clearly was his arrival in this house, his sense of confusion, his awe at its size and grandeur. Why was he being taken to a government building? Then, his aunt, her long cool fingers tracing his features, stroking his hair. She smelled strange, like no one he had ever met. But she could speak a little Russian. She told him this was home. She was kind.

Later he recognized that smell. It was the odor of churches, the sharp lingering sweetness of incense. Lara took him to the cathedral. He had never been to a church before. It was cold, cavernous, darkly littered with pillars. She knelt before a statue of a woman with a pure face, not unlike her own. She crossed herself, looked upward with pleading eyes, then shut them fast. He had no idea what she was doing.

He learned soon enough. Lara went to church every day. She introduced him to priests, told him stories of saints which frightened him. Had him confirmed. She also told him that it was prayer that had brought him to her. After she died, the renegade thought came into his mind that perhaps it was a surfeit of prayer in those chill damp churches that had killed her. With her gone, he never went back to church.

He didn't know why these thoughts had come back into his mind now. Perhaps it was the contrast between this leggy blonde journalist who claimed she was Polish and his aunt, so pale, so retiring.

Alexei rose.

"Oh, is my time up already?" Sylvie looked at him in dismay. "Why, we hardly seem to have begun. Perhaps, perhaps you could take a few moments to show me the house, your room, where you work?" She looked at Alexei with a plea.

The youth nodded graciously. "I don't see why not," he said despite his minder's disapproving glance.

The man took her aside for a moment. "You understand, Miss Stirling, anything you see in this house, anything Alexei may wish to show you, cannot find its way into your article," he said in a low voice which carried a note of threat.

Sylvie looked at him in some perplexity.

"I know, I know you come on the highest recommendation. Otherwise Signor Gismondi would not have granted you this rare opportunity. But we do not allow journalists into this house normally. Signor Gismondi insists on the strictest privacy."

From behind her she heard Alexei laugh. "He has good reason. Once my uncle allowed a magazine team to do a feature on the interior. The next week we were burgled." The story seemed to delight him.

"Oh, I wouldn't mention anything specific," Sylvie said. "It's not my style," she added with bravura. "It is only Alexei I am interested in."

The youth grinned, a trifle embarrassed now. More like a child of his own age. Sylvie suddenly remembered how uncomfortable in his own skin Leo had been at fourteen. But Alexei had a poise, a calm. She wondered where it came from, how deep it went. She had a moment of pure desire in which she wanted to shout to him that he must come away with her. Now. But she only gripped her bag more firmly.

He turned away from her, discomfited at her glance. Yet polite, so polite. He gestured for her to precede him through the door. They walked round the loggia to the other side of the house where Alexei threw open a door on a spacious reception room.

"We entertain in here. Though it's been rather quiet since my aunt died."

Sylvie saw a room of classical proportions, a ceiling painted with the voluptuous splendor of the Baroque, prepossessing marble fireplaces, mirrors, an array of sofas, lamps of the finest porcelain, polished wood. Splendor. But she wasn't interested. Instead, she asked Alexei, "Your aunt. What was she like?" She gestured around the room, encouraged him. "She must have been a woman of great taste."

Alexei looked a little wistful. "Yes," he answered hesitantly. Then as if he had on the spur of the moment decided to take her into his confidence, he added, "But she was always a tiny bit sad. She felt guilty, she once told me. Guilty that she had been the lucky one. The one of the three sisters to be sent to Italy, before the war. She was the eldest, my mother the youngest. My aunt was the one who went to all the trouble of trying to get me out of the Soviet Union." He looked sad, a little boy now.

"You loved her," Sylvie murmured.

Alexei nodded. "She was very kind to me."

"Have you any photos of her, of yourself?"

Alexei wavered. His photographs were private.

"It is getting late, Alexei," the minder intervened. "Signor Gismondi will soon be home. You know he likes you at the table punctually."

"Oh, but your room, I should so like to see your room." Sylvie tried to delay the moment of her departure. She felt restless, at odds with herself. The boy showed no more than a formal interest in her.

They walked up a grand staircase, first the minder, then Sylvie, then Alexei. She thought she could feel his eyes on her legs. Men's glances were so much more direct here. Even this boy's. She swallowed. Moved more provocatively.

His room gave her a subject. It was a large room with windows that looked out on grounds. Inside it was all clutter. Yellow-backed books everywhere, a shelf full of Russian tomes, then a desk, neater this, with school materials ranged. At one end, a screen with a home projector, a camera, reels of film, a splicer.

"You make movies?" Sylvie asked.

Alexei grinned. "Hardly movies. Just little bits of this and that. My uncle bought me a camera for my birthday."

She could see the enthusiasm in his eyes. "Would you show me a little bit of this and a little bit of that? I'd love to see what you've done."

He held back, but she convinced him. She realized as he started to load the projector that he probably didn't have many people to talk to. Sylvie started to chat about films she'd seen recently. He raved about Hitchcock, about Bogart and Raymond Chandler. The atmosphere grew easy between them. While they talked she glanced at three photographs framed on a shelf. A blur of fair hair, a delicate face, young. Hanka, she remembered. Behind her, standing, a man in a Russian uniform. Makarov, she thought, though she didn't recognize him. Then two portraits, distinct, calmly posed. A burly man. A slender, frail woman, her eyes filled with longing. Alexei's family.

Sylvie was confronted by the utter pointlessness of her presence. Tears rose haphazardly to her eyes as she watched the sequence of silent film Alexei showed her in the now darkened room. A street, the details of a door, a handle, the grain of the wood. Then a woman coming through the door. Her face in close-up, anxious, shadowy, the brow furrowed. The camera followed the woman along a gravel path. Feet on pebbles. Walking quickly. She could almost hear the crunch they made. Then grass. The camera moved up the woman's body to her eyes, searching, searching. Peering downward. And then a smile, full lips curling, eyes sparkling. She bent. Something glistening through grass. The woman picked it up. The camera zoomed in on her hand. A ring. Then nothing. The rattle of the projector.

"That's as far as I've got with this bit."

"Who is the woman?" Sylvie asked, needing to know.

"Oh, that's Anna. She works here. She let me film her. She also teaches me French. She gave me the idea for this footage. I think it's from some French writer. A woman loses some jewelry she thinks is real. But it's not. It's fake. It's a complicated story and I've only used elements of it. There's only so much you can do with a Super Eight," he shrugged.

"Oh, but you've done it beautifully. The atmosphere is wonderful. I want to know what happens next," Sylvie enthused.

"Do you?" Alexei looked at her skeptically. "It's only an exercise. Not the real thing. I'd like to do the real thing."

And there she had it, Sylvie thought. Her answer. Alexei was more interested in film than in anything else. She looked at him. So distinctly his own person that there was no space for her. If he had been in a sorry state, if he had needed anything, then she could have helped him, perhaps eventually told him. As it was, Alexei was a closed case.

Yet she desperately wanted him to acknowledge her, to have some impact on his contained life. "If you ever want to meet anyone in movies—" she began. But a knock at the door interrupted them. A woman's voice, murmuring in Italian.

"Signor Gismondi is home, Alexei. He is waiting for you." There was a hurried exchange between the boy and the woman Sylvie recognized as Anna.

Then Alexei turned back to her. "Perhaps you would like to meet my uncle?" he said politely. "He has asked to see you, since you are still here."

Sylvie nodded, willing to do anything to prolong her visit.

They went down the stairs again, this time to another room, a smaller reception room. A barrel-chested man in a well-cut suit stood to greet them, gripped her hand firmly. He assessed her with shrewd eyes, but his lips smiled. "Good evening, Signora Stirling," he said in strongly accented tones. "I may call you by your pen name, yes?" he added.

Sylvie had a sense that he was threatening her. She panicked for a moment, and then seeing the beam on his face, smiled as calmly as she could in response. Had she really expected that one of Italy's leading industrialists would not check her out before letting her into his house? What did it matter, she thought. She had achieved her purpose, at least in part.

"Of course, the Princesse has told you," she murmured.

"Yes, yes." He waved the matter away with a gracious gesture. Sylvie noticed that despite his short legs, his girth, he had a grace about him and a power.

A tray with crystal glasses was brought. Cool champagne. Sylvie drank it with relief.

"I also know that you speak French, which would suit my poor tongue much better. But then my son would be left out. My son has not yet had adequate lessons in French."

Sylvie looked at him curiously, glanced at Alexei.

Signor Gismondi missed nothing. "So Alexei has been referring to me as his uncle?" He tousled the boy's hair with a friendly gesture. "He is stubborn, my Alexei. Not a bad thing. He would like to think that his father is still alive. Though, of course, there is almost no hope. The poor man disappeared into Stalin's camps, you know." He shook his head in disgust. "*Povero popolo.*

"Still, eh, we have to concentrate on the future. Fathers, uncles, what does it matter?" He focused his gaze on Alexei. "You are happy here, eh, Alexei?"

The boy nodded, his embarrassment visible only in the slight stiffness of his limbs.

Signor Gismondi glanced at his watch. Sylvie knew it was her cue. She rose. "A great pleasure to meet you, Signor Gismondi. And your son. He is a very fine boy. Talented," she said in even tones which didn't reveal the effort it cost her.

She shook Alexei's hand, held on to it a little, savoring the cool texture. "Thank you, Alexei."

He looked into her eyes dreamily. He was seeing Lauren Bacall sauntering across a room, shoulders high, slim hips moving. Imagining Marilyn Monroe, the wide mouth, the perfect teeth.

"You will, of course, send me a copy of your manuscript before it goes to press." Signor Gismondi followed her to the door. The words were less a request than an order.

Sylvie gazed at him in momentary confusion. She had forgotten her alibi.

"Of course, of course." She recovered herself, spoke effusively. "Though it will take some time. I have quite a few more interviews to do." She smiled, her old dazzling smile, the smile of Sylvie the performer who spoke to men's hearts as well as their groins.

Signor Gismondi was not unsusceptible. "I shall look forward to it, whenever it arrives." He bowed.

Over the bulwark of his body, Sylvie waved to Alexei. His eyes were already elsewhere. She was invisible to him, already forgotten. Sylvie took her leave. At the front door of the Palazzo Gismondi, she was handed her tape recorder, her briefcase. Her hands trembled.

In the moist warmth of the evening, she leaned against the wall which encircled the Palazzo. She was tired out. She thought of Alexei, his life, its wealth, its comforts, his family, so substantially lodged in him that nothing could remove them. And she thought of her tiny incursion into that life.

The life of her son.

She felt as if she had given her last performance.

And now depression tugged at her. Four years. It had taken her four years to meet him and within an hour it was all over. She remembered again the scene she had recalled at the clinic. The scene that had sent her on her journey. But this time she knew its ending.

She saw the two women lying in their beds. She saw the nurses, heard the noise. In the bed next to her, Hanka, pale, screaming. Then murmuring, "A boy, a boy for Ivan." Her child. No, Sylvie's child. No, no, Sylvie had a girl, Katherine. She wanted a girl. Yes, yes, a girl for Caroline. A girl for Jacob. Sylvie floating, choosing between two cots, two babies. Boy and girl. A girl for Caroline.

Katherine for Caroline. A boy for Hanka. Her son, Sylvie's son for Hanka.

Everything had become clear to her because of that scene. Her hatred for Katherine, the dismal turn of her life. Her resentment of Jacob for not recognizing that the daughter he adored was not his. He should have been able to see it sooner, see it instantly. Understand why Sylvie couldn't stand the sight of the girl. He was cleverer than her. But no, he idolized the girl from the start. She made him blind. She could do no wrong in his eyes. She, it was she, Katherine, who had stolen Jacob away from her. From the very first, as soon as he had held her, he had had eyes only for her.

Sylvie had brought a cuckoo into her own nest.

And her son? She had found him, seen him, shivered at the resemblance to Jacob, but he was as distant as he had ever been. Not some peasant boy she could steal away with the promise of a better life, but a youth sheltered by his wealth, closed to her.

All the excitement that had buoyed her up over these last years drained out of her. What was there for her now? Only a return to the barrenness of her life. A life without Alexei. A son no sooner found than lost. A fleeting moment. Never to return. Almost like death. Like Caroline's child. No sooner had than lost.

Sylvie walked. The streets were crowded with evening strollers. Young couples, arm in arm. Not much older than her son. Her Alexei. Laughing. They didn't see her. Saw only each other. Their present. The future in each other's eyes. She wasn't part of it. She was invisible to them. Invisible. An invisible vessel for voices. Random sound teeming inside her. A bleak flat voice surfacing. "You understand nothing, Sylvie. Nothing. Katherine, my child, my future, died before me." Caroline's voice. Dead. Burbling empty sound. "Get her away from here. Take her away. I can't stand the sight of her." Papush. Look, Papush. Look. I have a son for you. Dead. Dead like you. Dead babies.

Sylvie walked. Unfamiliar streets. Shadowy crowds. A shadow herself.

She found herself back in her hotel. The bar. Yes. A drink. She needed a drink. Everywhere around her, couples, murmuring, gazing into each other's eyes. And she, alone. Invisible. Sylvie drank. And then a voice, a real voice, a stranger's voice, addressing her in English. "May I join you, signora?" Sylvie focused. A young man, looking into her eyes. Seeing her. A warm smile, a flash of bright teeth, directed at her. "Another drink?"

Sylvie nodded, sat back. A live voice, chatting. "You are a stranger here, *si?* Alone? Milan is a beautiful city. I could show you, show you some attractions." The smile again, seeing her. Admiring. A young face. Unlined. Alive. A young man's face. Like Alexei. She saw Alexei in him. Sylvie sipped her drink. Smiled serenely into eyes which saw her.

"What is your name?"

"Umberto."

"How old are you, Umberto?"

"Eighteen."

"Eighteen," Sylvie echoed. She was still at the convent. At the convent with Caroline. The games they played. With the nuns. At her parents' house. The makeup. The forays into café. Strangers' eyes staring. That one. She would have that one. Sylvie sidling, smiling with red lips. Their hands, touching her, desiring. Caroline over her shoulder. Watching mutely, angrily.

Umberto was stroking her hand. "I will take you dancing, *si?* And then . . ." His eyes trailed over her slowly. "And then . . ." He flicked his tongue over full lips.

Sylvie let him take her arm, floated. Floated on a young man's arm through the lobby, smiled proudly, a little vainly at the graying assistant manager behind the desk.

"Che cosa fai in questa casa?" A hiss came from the manager. The arm on Sylvie's stiffened, dropped. "I told you not to come in here again."

The graying man turned to her, his face battling between pity and contempt. "You should know, signora," he said softly, "this young man will charge you for your pleasures."

Sylvie looked at him uncomprehendingly for a moment. Then, with a sudden savage gesture, she struck Umberto hard across the face. He scurried from the hotel.

Sylvie shook.

The manager grinned. *"E meglio cosi.* Much better."

A loud self-lacerating laugh broke from Sylvie. Fool. She was a fool. She looked wildly round the lobby. People staring. A humiliated fool. There was nothing, nothing here for her.

She caught the first plane back to New York.

Jacob was kind, solicitous. But his kiss was not a kiss. Merely a hollow formality. He didn't see her either. Saw only her state. Was she drinking? Taking pills? Was her mind wandering? That was what his eyes asked, while his mouth spoke hollow questions. Had it been a good flight? Had she enjoyed her holiday? Being patient with a patient. That's all it was.

Almost, in the midst of the new apartment that she hated as much as he did, though it had been decorated to her own specifications, she said, "I have been to see my son." That would have made him stop, look at her, see. But no, he was asking her about Mathilde, about Katherine. Katherine again. That's all he cared about. He had bided his time, not asked her straight away, waited. Oh, she knew him so well. His little supposed sensitivities. But the question had been there all the time. All he could think about.

All he saw in her was the absence of his daughter.

Almost, she brought it out. "She is not your daughter." But she didn't. She could predict his empty stare, the calm voice, soothing her. "Sylvie, stop fantasizing. I know you wish it were so. But a wish is only a wish." She could have pushed it, prodded an old wound. "No, not your daughter, someone else's." And then? Then he would shrug, a little stiffly, look away. "All so long ago. So many years. What does it matter? Our daughter, nonetheless."

No, she was more cunning than that. She had a better way of rupturing that patient impassivity, of making him look at her. Listen.

Sylvie poured herself another drink, smoothed her dress. "That nice man Thomas Sachs was there. Such a nice man." She sat back in her chair, crossed her legs slowly. Oh yes, he was listening now, four ears in place of two, all his eyes on her. "A gentleman. I think your Katherine is in love with him." She laughed.

Jacob leapt up. "Why do you say that?"

"Oh, we women know these things." She taunted him, waited for the press of questions. Teased him with hints, then elaborated details of look and stance and voice as they passed between Katherine and Thomas, conjured up a possible affair, a marriage.

Sylvie laughing, enjoying herself, enjoying his discomfort.

He made love to her that night. Love in the dark. Her and not her. Was it what they used to call love, that cursory groping devoid of excitement?

The next day listlessness overcame her. She wandered round the empty apartment aimlessly. The tape recorder sat there. She pushed the switch. Alexei's voice. Sylvie listened. Over and over, she listened. She started to doodle with the tape as accompaniment. Random scratchings of her pen. Trapped animals with human bodies. Birds with frightened eyes. Mutilated fantastical creatures. For days she doodled.

One evening Jacob found the pad. "You're drawing again, Sylvie. These are wonderful." He bought her paper, inks, pens, charcoal. Encouraged her, his eyes warm.

Sylvie drew to the accompaniment of voices. Alexei's voice, one of many. She no longer had any need to switch the tape on. Each word, each intonation, lived inside her. But sometimes, she still did. And while she drew, one of the many voices inside her set up a repeated chant, "What should I do? What should I do?"

Jacob was excited about the drawings, named them her Bestiary. She started to tear them up, slowly, deliberately. Whichever drawing he particularly commented on in the evening was certain to have disappeared by the next day. He stopped commenting.

One afternoon he came home when she had the tape on. "What's that you're listening to, Sylvie?" he asked.

She looked at him dimly, hardly aware of the voices on the machine. Then, with a careless gesture, she switched it off.

"That was you, wasn't it?" Jacob was curious.

Sylvie sat up straighter. He was concentrating on her. The full force of that old gaze. She smiled. "Didn't I tell you? I'm researching a book. That was one of the interviews." The words came to her lips with no forethought.

She saw his initial skepticism. "No, you didn't tell me."

"I like my little secrets, you know." She laughed, her low, throaty laugh.

"What is it about?"

Sylvie babbled, saw the skepticism settle into belief. He'll believe anything if he wants to, one of her voices said. Anything but the truth. Perhaps she could try the truth on him now. "Jacob," she started, but he was already hugging her, congratulating her.

"A brilliant idea. A grand idea. How far have you got with it?"

"I'm just starting."

"Well, you must tell me all about it. If you want to, that is." He was a little wary now. "On the way. We can talk more on the way. I must shower now."

She looked at him quizzically.

"You haven't forgotten, Sylvie? It's the party tonight. For my new book. Leo will be there."

She had forgotten.

The room in the Fifth Avenue complex was crowded with half-familiar faces. Analysts, writers, doctors, journalists. She couldn't remember their names. She felt dizzy. It was so long since she had been to a party like this. She clung to Jacob's arm, saw him spirited away on a tide of compliments. Loud flattering voices. Leo. Thank God, there was Leo. Her tall, blond son. She had hardly seen him over the last months. She hugged him, held on to him.

"Everything okay, Mom?"

She nodded. "And you?"

"Just fine. Must find Dad to add my congratulations. Have you read the new book?"

Sylvie shook her head. "Have you?"

"Most of it. It's interesting, even if it is by the old man." He gave her his lopsided grin. "Let's go and find him." They wound their way through the crowd. "What have you been doing with yourself?"

"Oh, this and that. Drawing a little again. Thinking about doing a book myself."

"That's great, Mom." He squeezed her hand. "Don't let the old man get all the plaudits."

And that, Sylvie thought, was that. Everything fine and dandy as long as she was gainfully occupied. And what if she told Leo now that she wasn't writing a book, wasn't doing anything? Told him she was thinking about his brother? A brother he had never known? A brother whose voice was now lodged firmly inside her? He would look away, refuse to meet her eyes. Try to change the subject.

They found themselves trapped in a little group. A bulky round-faced woman in a huge hat was holding forth in stentorian tones. "And that's the trouble with men." Her dark eyes bore down on Leo. "All of them. They tell you you'll never have to iron their shirts. You do it once, twice, as a special gesture, to please them, and then before you know it, they expect it, week in, week out and grump if it doesn't happen. Surprise transformed into the habit of expectation. Never give men anything. Isn't that right, Mrs. Jardine?"

Sylvie looked at her blankly. Saw expectant faces. Who was this woman? "I wouldn't know," Sylvie mumbled. "I've never ironed a shirt." Open mouths. Laughter. Sylvie turned away.

"Good one, Mom," Leo beamed at her. "There's Dad. Wait till I tell him how you put down that old harridan."

Put down? Sylvie gazed at him queerly, thought about what the woman had said. In essence she agreed with her. She might never have ironed shirts, but she too had once upon a time brought Jacob little surprises, little presents. Stories, they had been mostly. Stories about herself. He liked stories best of all. Stories intrigued him, excited him. She couldn't remember whether the stories were true or not, but she thought dimly that they had both hoped they were. Jacob certainly had cared about their truth.

And then, after a time he hadn't. It wasn't only that he wasn't interested in her any longer. What had he told her once? In the world of psychoanalysis there was no distinction between truth and fiction. Only what was uttered mattered. And now she was trapped by that. A glass bowl, enclosing her, with Jacob staring in—smiling, benevolent, disinterested. Anything she said was only a symptom of her condition. No truth. No world outside the bowl. How could she puncture that glass? How could she make him see? Make him feel? She had to do it. Make him see the truth about Alexei. Feel the truth about what she had done. To him. For him. For Caroline. To them all.

She was tired. So tired. So many voices. In her. Around her. She needed to escape.

The following week Sylvie went to the clinic in Pennsylvania. She breathed easier here. Nobody bothered her. Asked anything of her. And she dreaded the winter holidays. All that semblance of seasonal good cheer. That pretense of family life. It was better here. She could think her own thoughts. She stayed. And stayed. Took up residence. Going home only occasionally. To see Leo. To see Jacob. They looked strange to her. Unreal. They kept trying to speak to her and yet they didn't see her. They didn't let her think.

One day when the sticky buds on the trees were at their plumpest and the sun gleamed a promise of summer, Sylvie took her sketch pad down to the little lake in the clinic grounds. She perched at its edge and let her pen, as was her wont, run automatically over the creamy paper. Line took on shape and form. A mermaid with dark, tangled hair. She spoke in Caroline's voice. "It's cool here. So cool. So nice. So quiet. Only the water ripples." Sylvie looked at the lake, the water rippling in the breeze. Its depths murky, secret. There was a mermaid there, too. Just like in her drawing. She looked again. A tangle of dark hair. A woman's body. A grimace. Sylvie screamed. Screamed and screamed again. An attendant came running. She pointed, stared.

There was commotion at the clinic. Everyone was transfixed. Transfixed by the death. From the lowliest attendant to the senior doctor through all the patients. They could talk of nothing but that. And even in their silences it was there.

The senior doctor addressed them all in a memorial service. Sylvie could barely remember the woman who had drowned herself, but through his words she took on the grand status of a tormented romantic. That was when the idea lodged itself in her. It brought a smile to her lips. Made her feel light, buoyant, as airy as those soft spring clouds. Death had them, had them all by the short and curlies. Just like after the war. What had they done, all of them, Jacob, Caroline, all of them, but stare wide-eyed into the face of death? Medusa's unremitting gaze. Sylvie laughed.

She sat by the lake and drew and laughed. A scorpion's body flowed out of her pen, the crushing claws, the segmented middle with its spider's legs, the tail, large with its sting; and between claws and body, a Medusa's head, with cold, unlidded eyes. She looked at her drawing and was pleased. Where had she heard that scorpions when threatened by fire stung themselves? Yes, but the tail kept its sting. She laughed. She would fracture that glass bowl which kept her imprisoned once and for all. Jacob would see her as she was. They would all see her. But what was the sting? Sylvie drew.

A week later, she left the clinic and went home. Jacob, looking at her, thought she seemed happier than he had seen her in years.

"It's good to have you back," he said.

Sylvie smiled secretly.

"Is the book going well?"

"Mmmnn. In fact, I need to go to Europe to do a little more research."

"If you think you're well enough?"

"Oh, I'm quite well."

She couldn't stop smiling. She would see Alexei again. One last time. She flew directly to Milan, checked into a hotel, telephoned. Ah no, the young Signor Gismondi was not in. He was on holiday. Would be away for some weeks. Where? Where was he? Sylvie wailed. Could the lady please identify herself? He was not at liberty to give Signor Gismondi's whereabouts. Sylvie hung up. She started to shake. She hadn't counted on this. She couldn't wait. She wasn't strong enough. She paced her room, back and forth, back and forth. And then it came to her. Of course, Mathilde. Princesse Mathilde. She would spend some time with Mathilde. Wait at Mathilde's.

But Valois wasn't auspicious. She had forgotten Katherine's aura there. The Princesse was enchanted with Sylvie's daughter. Could speak of little else. Nothing Sylvie said seemed to penetrate her loyalty to that daughter who wasn't hers. Sylvie drank and babbled. But Mathilde wasn't seeing her. Wasn't listening. Wouldn't hear what she had to say. She couldn't stay here. Couldn't. And Katherine would be coming soon. No, not that. Sylvie fled.

It was on the return journey to New York in a plane which seemed motionless, caught in an eternity of blue, that the plan came to her. It came, as so much did for her now, in the cadences of a disembodied voice. A voice which ordered the clocks back, which made a nonsense of time. Time moving back while her body, her life, moved forward. Just like that, Sylvie twisted the dial on her watch, saw the woman beside her do the same. They were all doing it, everyone, moving time back, at the simple behest of a voice. Sylvie stared at her watch, twisted again and again. And now it was yesterday and the day before that and the day before that. So simple. An order from a disembodied voice. Yes, yes, now she had it. Her own disembodied voice, speaking. Speaking the truth. Moving the clocks back. Now, she knew what the sting in the tail would be. They would remember her. Remember her in years to come.

Sylvie gazed out at the eternity of blue and took a long, deep breath. She felt strong again. Calm. Only the details remained to be arranged. Yes. And then she had merely to wait. To wait for the appropriate moment. A moment to commemorate Caroline. Just before Christmas.

Yes. She smiled serenely.

CHAPTER
FIFTEEN

Beyond the sheltered glaze of
Princesse Mathilde's drawing room, the snow fell lazily. Thick, heavy
flakes silently covered the sleeping earth. The Princesse, looking out,
felt old. As old as the peaks she could see from her window. She
fingered the envelope in her pocket, drew it out, read the brief lines
again without seeing.

It wasn't right. Dying shouldn't be a matter of choice. Not for the
young, the healthy. The privileged. Not after all the unnatural deaths
these last years had already witnessed. It disturbed the order of
things. Ruptured lives. The girl, how would she feel? And her
brother? And Jacob?

Irritation, unleashed, now flooded through her. Sylvie had always
been selfish. Selfish in her impulsiveness, in her unthinkingness, in
her assumption that the world moved only around her. And now,
selfish in her dying. Forcing them all to retune their lives to the
pitch she set.

The Princesse crumpled the telegram into a tight ball. Then, with
a visible change of heart, she carefully smoothed it out again. No,
she wasn't being fair. An ironical smile played over her features.
Here she was, sounding, even to her own ears, like a puritanical
Swiss burgher, imposing a moral code on Sylvie that had never been
hers; forcing her into a mold which was alien to everything that

made her Sylvie. It was Sylvie's unconventionality that had always fascinated them all. And she had chosen to die as she had lived.

Princesse Mathilde jabbed at a log in the stone fireplace and watched the sparks leap angrily upward. She wondered how Jacob was taking it. He must be distraught, agonized. She should rush to comfort him.

A little thought pounced on her, took her unawares. He would be free now. Perhaps . . . She stopped the fantasy in its flow and chastised herself. Here she was in her sixties and still dreaming like a schoolgirl about a man. A man she had had an affair with some thirty years ago.

She corrected the picture. Not any man. The only man she had ever wanted. The only man who had ever wholly captured her imagination in a lifetime of meetings and travel and ceaseless activity. She glanced at the outlines of her image in the vast window. People told her she still looked wonderful. Flatterers. Time trapped one in a masquerade with costumes of its own choice. Sometimes when she caught a glimpse of that woman with the drooping lids, the pronounced cheekbones, the crêpey neck in a strange mirror, she didn't recognize her as herself at all. An old woman who looked, as the flatterers said, remarkable. But an old woman, nonetheless. An old woman ridiculous in the presence of desire.

An old woman dreaming. Musing. If only all those years ago she had not been so strapped by convention. But no, she had no regrets. It could not have been otherwise. It was not a matter of "if only . . .", but rather a nostalgia for a different, a parallel plane of existence, a nostalgia for a future she could never have lived.

An old woman made older by the suicide of one whom she still considered a girl. She wondered if during that last frenetic occasion when she had seen Sylvie there had already been a premonition of the end. A hint she had been blind to because the very notion of suicide was so antithetical to her own nature. Sylvie had raved, raved with that undertow of intensity which always made her seem to be speaking the truth. The Princesse shivered. Could she have done anything to save her?

Jacob must be asking himself the same questions now. She imagined him at his desk, his head in his hands. Jacob filled to the brim with sorrow for the woman whom, despite everything, he had loved. She could almost write his hurt for him, his wonder at another of Sylvie's acts, trace the workings of his mind as it ferreted out reasons, laid blame at his own doorstep. And she could hear the tittle-tattle round the world's psychoanalytic tables, the shaking of a hundred eminent heads. "Oh, but did you hear? Yes, suicide. His own wife. I always suspected he was improperly analyzed. That old guard. They never took proper time over it." And on it would go, the dissections, the speculations, the dismantling of Jacob's work.

And Katherine. With sudden decision, the Princesse pulled the bell cord. All this musing was simply a way of deflecting the inevitable moment when she had to face her. The girl wouldn't, couldn't take it well.

Mathilde had planned a party for her, a party to celebrate her sixteenth birthday in a week's time. Katherine had looked so achingly beautiful when Mathilde had talked about it. The shyness, the hesitancy, the gratitude, all spoke in that face which drew the eye and held it. And now?

Princesse Mathilde was a brave woman. But her present task daunted her. She remembered the last occasion on which mother and daughter had met. Well over a year ago now. She hadn't been privy to the goings on at the opposite end of the table, but she had a distinct, almost tactile memory of the girl fleeing, the usual calm repose of her features fractured. And then the tremulous silence round the table, ruptured by Sylvie's insouciant laugh.

"A cup of hot chocolate, my dear?" The Princesse glanced at Katherine's cheeks, pink from her walk, and gestured her toward a chair.

Katherine smiled, nodded.

The Princesse collected herself. It was all so difficult. The girl had settled into her new life now, had begun to relax. Madame Chardin was pleased with her. It had taken time but her written French as well as her spoken was now first class.

"Was it lovely out in the fresh snow?" Mathilde delayed.

"Beautiful." Katherine breathed happily. "I've been sketching. Would you like to see?" She presented her pad to the Princesse. Mathilde looked, recognized the cluster of tall pines, the little bridge, the stream rushing beneath it. Katherine had drawn it all with snail-like whorls of her pen, a multitude of curving strokes, so that the landscape had a hectic life of its own, at once like and unlike itself.

"You're getting very good, Katherine. I think we should perhaps provide you with some extra lessons."

The girl shrugged. "It's not quite right. You see there, the light"— she pointed to a corner of the drawing—"I couldn't capture it. It's all too dismal, too heavy."

Princesse Mathilde paused, waited for hot chocolate to be deposited, sipped. The girl was always so hard on herself.

"Katherine, I have to tell you something I would rather not have to say," Mathilde plunged in and then hesitated. The girl looked at her expectantly, wariness gathering in her gaze with each passing second.

"A telegram arrived this morning. I'm afraid . . . I'm afraid your mother has committed suicide." It sounded so blunt, but there was no way to say it delicately. And the girl had to know.

Katherine sat silently for a long moment, her eyes growing perceptibly wider, the color draining from her cheeks. Then abruptly she got up and turned away from the Princesse.

"Good. I'm glad." A cracked voice broke from her. A moment later she turned back. Horror was written on her features. "I didn't mean that," she mumbled and raced from the room.

Katherine lay on the bed which had become hers and gazed blankly at the ceiling. The sentence curled round in her head over and over like the whorls of her picture. "Your mother has committed suicide." Two antithetical emotions pulled at her. One side of her screamed with delight. Good, good. She's dead. She won't be able to kill me. The other throbbed guiltily. I killed her. I wanted her dead. Pappy said she was frail. Unwell. It's my fault. Between the two emotions, Katherine was paralyzed. She lay dry-eyed and motionless on the bed and was still lying there when the maid came to ask her if she was packed.

Jacob sat in the plush chair and stared directly ahead. On the raised dais in front of him lay Sylvie's coffin. Next to him, on one side, Katherine, her hand resting in his. On his other, Leo, his face pale. All around them the solemnity of other faces in mourning.

Mourning. What did the word mean? Most of the people here had hardly known Sylvie. Yet they had come. Come without immediate invitation. A great many of them, out of respect for her, for him, for the grief which was meant to inhabit him, but which for the moment, he knew, he only represented. A community of grief.

It was a strange place, this. Not a chapel, yet built to resemble one. Like a theater set in which they were all spectators of the drama of death. God was absent, yet the trappings of his churches were in place. The mock-Gothic arch. The purples and burgundies. The pulpit from which he had spoken his set text in memory of Sylvie; and Jacques, his friend Jacques, had evoked in mellifluent

French a Sylvie of old. The hush was there, despite the music he had chosen. Music to evoke her, music she might have favored. Raucous, black. And Gershwin's *Rhapsody*, the one that had started them off on this road together.

Sylvie had no taste for the funerary. If anything, the Sylvie of old would have preferred a noisy wake, frenetic dancing, a bacchic rite. But that was impossible here.

He had spent his grief in the day and night he had sat at her bedside. Gazing at her. In her death, she was very young. Young in her frailty, her pallor, her flowing blonde hair. A mere girl draped in her favorite nightgown of black silk sprawled luxuriantly on white sheets. A girl play-acting.

She had created her own mise-en-scène. A dusky rose in the bed-side vase. A copy of Baudelaire's *Fleurs du mal* on the pillow by her side. A bookmark showed the page: *"J'ai plus de souvenirs que si j'avais mille ans"*—"I have more memories than if I were a thousand years old." And the note. To him. Perched on the table beneath a bright green apple and a bottle of pills. A single word. *"Assez."* Enough. Beneath it, one of her fantastic beasts, a scorpion with a Medusa's head. He had pondered the drawing, its cold angry gaze, the intricacy of the creature's skeletal limbs. Her parting gesture, almost a battle cry.

And he had read the poem over and over again, though he knew it well. Yes, it was pure Sylvie. It captured her state: the limping weariness of her days, her sense of abandonment. She was that cemetery abhorred by the moon, that old sphinx, ignored, forgotten by a careless world. Yet still an enigma. Her countless memories, her secrets, her store of billets-doux and romances, gone with her.

There had always been men and once he had cared a great deal about that. He remembered their last jealous scene, all those years ago, in Paris, some time after her return from Poland, a journey she had always refused to talk about. He had confronted her. "It won't make any difference, Sylvie, but I just want to know whether this child is mine or someone else's. Andrzej's, perhaps?"

She had looked at him for a long time, at first solemnly and then with mounting anger. "What does it matter what I say? You won't believe me. Yes. No. What does it matter? You love your suspicion." Then raging, she had added, "Men, men can never know who their children are. A B C D or E, any one could be my children's father."

And, of course, she had been right. On both counts.

What he had loved about Sylvie had always in part been his inability to pin her down, to capture her. To know her. She was the very embodiment of his desire for the unknown, the unknowable, the other. In death, she had returned to that and returned his desire.

Jacob had sat by her bedside and cried. He remembered the many faces of Sylvie, the child-woman with the mischievous glance who had stolen apples in the Paris market, the girl he had obsessively trailed, the passionate creature who had boldly come to his flat and pleasured him to the point of pain, the frightened child who pushed him away and clung to him simultaneously. He remembered the proud, fearless Sylvie of the war years, the seductive Sylvie on her many stages, feeding off her music and the eyes directed at her, and giving back amply in return.

He grieved for what was lost and what had never come to be. In himself as well as in her. The maimed Sylvie of the postwar years, receding ever further into a life he couldn't penetrate. The Sylvie he had failed to help or to come to terms with. A Sylvie for whom the promise of America with him had not borne fruit. For whom its freedoms had proved stifling. A Sylvie who abhorred her aging image in the mirror. The cruel Sylvie, the Sylvie of the drinking and drug bouts. The Sylvie who couldn't contend with motherhood, with the loss of her youth.

He knew that he had failed her. He had ceased wanting her. And then ceased trying to erase the distance between them. He had stopped caring and replaced feeling with form, the patterned semblance of a twosome, a family life.

Grief gave way to a guilt which gnawed at him.

Her suicide was a reproach.

It was also something else. He must try to communicate that to the children, who were filled with evident self-recrimination, Katherine particularly.

He must try to explain to them that Sylvie's suicide was above all an appropriate finale to her life. A brave transgressive choice for a woman who felt she had reached her end. "Enough." She had struggled to shape the messiness of life into a whole, like an artist. And like an artist, she had chosen the moment, the scene of the full stop.

Sylvie's coffin slid away, swallowed up by flames they couldn't see. He couldn't link that final event with Sylvie. It was no longer a part of life. She lived on in them, in their memories, not in the ashes he knew he would soon be given.

Jacob squeezed Katherine's hand, urged her up. How tall she had grown, and beautiful. Almost a woman in her simple black dress beneath the auburn sheen of her hair. And his son, his golden son, so like his mother. Sylvie had left him these two. He had a great deal to be grateful for. He ushered them to the door. It was time for leave-takings. They formed a little row. The three of them. The survivors. Murmured condolences were offered, accepted.

Katherine was trembling. He caught Princesse Mathilde's eye. She was already at Katherine's side, embracing her, leading her to a corner. Mat had a genius for sensitivity. His debts to her were never-ending and yet she had never once made him feel that he owed her anything. Her tact always and ever gave him back his freedom. He would willingly, he suddenly thought, die for her.

The crowd was thinning. Only a small cluster remained. Jacob embraced Mat, his daughter, his son, Violette, Jacques. What remained of his family.

"Shall we go?" he said softly.

The long black limousine drove them through the wintry city. The Princesse had insisted that they gather at the Waldorf for a light lunch. Insisted that Katherine's friend Antonia join them.

They sat round a quiet corner table. Food arrived. Katherine, unable to swallow, listened and watched. Everyone was talking, reminiscing, laughing. The laughter shocked her. Antonia was asking Leo about medical school, hanging on his words. Katherine half overheard. She realized that she didn't know this young man who was her brother. She had rarely seen him outside the context of the family. Despite the letters, he was a stranger. They had barely spoken for what seemed like years.

Katherine sat shrouded in silence. Her mouth wouldn't form syllables, wouldn't open. It quivered.

She remembered the note she had penned to her mother after their last meeting. "You're a vile, stupid woman. I wish you were dead." She had felt wonderful after she had written it, as if at long last, rather than simply running away, she had struck a blow for herself.

She had left the note in an addressed envelope on her desk and it had vanished. Had the maid picked it up, had it posted? She was too afraid to ask. And then, back at Madame Chardin's, she had forgotten about it.

"Don't you want your pâté, Kat?" Leo asked her for the second time.

Katherine shook her head.

"I'm ravenous. They don't feed us at med school." He took her plate.

Why wasn't he more upset? He loved Sylvie, was her favorite.

Leo read her mind. "Cheer up, Kat. Sylvie hated long faces. She wouldn't have wanted you to be miserable." He bit his lip as he said it, for of course in the past Sylvie had often wanted Katherine to be miserable. He put his arm round her for a moment. "Am I being callous? The way I put it to myself is that Sylvie made a choice. The people I deal with in the hospital every day aren't usually in a position to make choices." He squeezed her shoulder, shrugged.

"Yes, and forty-six is quite old enough to die," Violette murmured. "After that, what's a woman good for?"

Katherine's eyes flew to the Princesse. She hadn't heard. But her father had. There was an odd expression on his face. He was looking wistfully at the Princesse. He pecked her lightly on the cheek. Jacques did the same now, but with exaggerated fervor. The Princesse, her face glowing, caught Katherine's gaze. She smiled a benevolent smile.

That night her father sat on the edge of her bed and stroked her hair, as if she were still a little girl. She asked him, "Will you marry Princesse Mathilde now?"

Jacob looked at her in surprise. "Why no, it hadn't occurred to me to propose." He hesitated, wondered if he should tell her. But no. The moment wasn't right. "Not that she would have me in any event." He laughed the matter away.

Katherine's wide gray eyes quizzed him.

"Would you like to have the Princesse as a mother?" he asked her softly.

"I don't know," Katherine mused. Her glance played over a room which was no longer her own. "I've sometimes thought she *was* perhaps my mother," she suddenly said in a rush and then paused, turning the statement into a question.

Jacob forced her eyes to his. "No, Katherine," he said evenly but with an undertow of insistence. "Sylvie was your mother." He stroked her hair again, lightened his voice. "Though I know the Princesse loves you as if you were her own child. You are happy in Switzerland with her, aren't you?" he murmured, hesitated. "I wish you had known your mother in her youth, before we moved to New York. She was quite different. She . . ."

Katherine cut him off. "I want to come back here. Come back to live with you in New York."

The note of determination in her voice was not one Jacob wished to dispute.

And so Katherine moved into the spacious apartment on New York's Upper East Side, overlooking Central Park and a stone's throw from the Metropolitan Museum. It was the place that Sylvie had insisted on buying once both Katherine and Leo were no longer at home. For Katherine, the place held no memories, yet she disliked it intensely. It was so obviously Sylvie's lair. It reeked of her. Smelled of her depressions, her movie queen tastes, from the satin-clad bed refracted in a multitude of mirrors to the living-room chaise-longue where she had lain curled for hours.

She returned to her old school. Academically, there were no problems. American history aside, Madame Chardin's had more than adequately prepared her and Katherine set her sights on college, on Barnard, or Radcliffe or Sarah Lawrence. She worked hard and enjoyed it. She also began to read her father's books, Freud, Jung, Melanie Klein, the psychoanalytic canon, which became the subject of endless conversations between them across a dinner table which most often they shared alone. She loved these evenings with her father, was constantly aware that Sylvie's absence had the benefit of bringing the two of them closer. And she treasured that closeness above all else. She invented a hundred little things to make him happy, to bring a smile to his face. To obliterate the memory of Sylvie.

In other ways, Katherine's life was less pleasurable. Her friendship with Antonia apart, she had always been something of a loner and her peers now looked at her slightly askance. She could read the gossip in their eyes, see the speculations about her absence in Switzerland, her mother's suicide. They considered her strange, standoffish. Katherine was indeed aloof, but out of reticence rather than intent. She was also a little out of step with her schoolmates. She did not share Antonia's interest in dissecting last week's date and plotting the next. She had hated the one double date Antonia had talked her into, hated the squirming disaster of the back seat of the car, the searching hands, the prescribed wet goodnight kiss. Nor did she manage to swoon at the sound of Elvis's voice or at the mention of Big Bopper. She sometimes thought that Madame Chardin's school had succeeded in turning her, despite herself, into what that portentous lady called a "European."

Increasingly she felt, without putting it into so many words, that all she wanted was to read, to paint, and to make her father into that person she had seen with the Princesse: a light, carefree, witty, happy Jacob.

As the weeks grew into months, a plan took hold of her. She would redesign the apartment, transform it so that it became a proper home, a space where friends could come, a place for gatherings, a home like the Princesse's, which always hummed. Katherine took to her plan with her customary thoroughness. She read interior design magazines, browsed for hours in department stores comparing the textures and colors of fabrics. She wanted to do sketches, prepare everything, and then surprise Jacob with her scheme.

It was to Thomas that Katherine turned for help. Thomas, whom she met once every week or two, for dinner, or a trip to the theater, or, if it was the weekend, a forage round the Upper East Side galleries or a visit to the Whitney or the newly opened Guggenheim Museum. It was Thomas who had on their many rambles first made her see the city in all its architectural wonder, distinguishing between façades, pointing out detail.

So she told Thomas about her plans, one Saturday in the Russian Tea Room. Told him with great enthusiasm.

"Already a homemaker," he chuckled. "A young Jacqueline Kennedy."

She was aware of his implied criticism. It confused her. "What's wrong with that?" she asked, bristling a little.

"Now, now, Schätzchen, you mustn't be so quick to take offense." He patted her hand.

If he had chosen to, Thomas might have told her in no uncertain terms what was wrong. He might have said to her that sometime in the middle of the nineteenth century a cult had grown up around the idea of the home. A safe private oasis far from the madding crowd, a sphere where calm and all the virtues flourished. A beautiful place over which a feminine angel presided, soothing the weary brows of males tossed in the storms of the big bad world.

He might have told her that in the United States for over a decade now, the journals and magazines and guide-to-life books, aided and abetted by manufacturers, traders, and advertisers, had sung the song of the perfect home and the perfect homemaker. And that now at last, they had found their perfect heroine, Jacqueline Kennedy. That most glamorous of all the angels of the hearth, who had come in her little pillbox hat to preside over the purest and most gracious of all houses, the White House.

He might have told her that she, Katherine, had fallen under the spell of all this, but with a difference. The difference being that Katherine was doing it all in the name of another who was not her husband, but her father.

As it was, Thomas merely patted her hand and said, "This is a very good idea of yours, Schätzchen, and of course I shall help you in any way I can." He had no desire to put an old man's damper on her youthful excitement.

He began to take her to antique shops, sought out trade exhibitions of fabrics and contemporary furniture, bought her books on design—on Bauhaus, which brought him back to his own youth, on the Viennese Secession with its decorative flights and insistence on utility.

Katherine was an able and eager pupil.

He loved her eagerness, her hunger for knowledge. He loved the way her eyes, fixed in an intensity of concentration, widened as he spoke.

Sometimes her beauty so took him by surprise, that he lost the thread of speech. There was a quiet wistfulness about her, a reticence, a grace which reminded him of one of Leonardo's Madonnas. She held him completely.

He also worried about her. Worried about her attachment to her project, which he read correctly as not only her desire to make Jacob happy, but to replace and improve upon her mother. He worried about her lack of friends of her own age, yes, even male friends.

Often, after he had left her at the door of her apartment, he would ridicule himself. An old man with a Pygmalion fantasy. An old man, who had lived too much, striving to create the perfect woman. It would lead to no good. Yet she compelled him. One of the few women who had done so over time without the complement of sexual gratification. He made no approaches to her of that kind. He laughed at himself. He was like an enamored father, an old fool. Too often after he had seen her, he felt restless, driven to correct this unhappy image of himself in the arms of another. He would ring up one of the women in his little black book and pay for his excesses. Thomas had the vitality of a far younger man.

Katherine knew none of this. All she knew was that she counted on Thomas. He was one of the still points in her sparsely peopled universe. She didn't think about it, but in her mental geography, the vivid world consisted of herself and her father at the center; Thomas and Leo, a short distance away; then a little further, the Princesse and Violette and Portia whom she still corresponded with regularly. Antonia, as the year pressed on, was gradually dropping off the map.

It was the end of May when Katherine put her plan to Jacob. Three sketchbooks full of it.

They were sitting opposite each other in their usual places at the rectangular dinner table Katherine always set with tablecloth and candles and fresh flowers.

"Pappy," Katherine began, "Pappy, I think we should have the apartment done over. Look, I've planned it all." Her excitement shone in her eyes as she showed him her sketches.

"These are wonderful, Kat." He turned the pages slowly as she evoked her dreamscapes for him. He saw that through them she was imagining a new life. A new life filled with friends and dinners and parties. A new life with him, before the old had been properly buried. Displacing Sylvie before she had come to terms with her. He didn't want to destroy her pleasure, but its implications worried him. She needed to understand what she was doing.

"Wonderful," Jacob murmured. "You've worked very hard." He looked at her. "We'll do it. We'll get the decorators in and do it."

Katherine beamed, leapt up and kissed him.

"Yes." He waited until she had sat down again. "Yes, we'll expunge Sylvie. Exorcise her." He said it lightly, then added: "Because this is what all this is about, isn't it, Katherine?"

Katherine looked away, all her excitement vanishing. The very mention of Sylvie's name filled her with a rage which was instantly followed by guilt. It tied her up in knots. Why had her father brought Sylvie up now? Why couldn't he just get over her?

"No, that's not what it's about," she murmured. "I just thought it would be nice to have a change. This place is hideous." She looked up at him boldly.

Jacob smiled. "I might agree with that. I'm not particularly thrilled by Sylvie's last exercise in interior decoration." He sipped a little wine. "But I want us to be clear about what we're doing. Don't get me wrong. I don't think there's anything terrible about expunging Sylvie. We don't live in memorials."

"But?"

"But I want you to understand what you're getting rid of. I want you to know a little more about your mother, come to terms with her."

Katherine pushed her chair back brusquely. "I think I know quite enough."

"Do you, Kat?" Jacob moved to sit on Sylvie's darkly velvet sofa, urged Katherine to sit next to him. "You know, before the war, before you were born, before illness took a grip on her, Sylvie used to love parties, just like the ones you've been describing to me. She would sit at the piano and sing. Electrify us all."

Katherine played with her hair nervously. "I don't want to know, Pappy. I don't want to think about her."

Jacob put his arm around her, this daughter of his who was almost a woman. He smiled. "Oscar Wilde once said that children begin by loving their parents; after a time they judge them; rarely, if ever, do they forgive them. I don't want you to forgive Sylvie. I just want you to judge her with a fuller picture at your disposal. For your own sake."

Katherine's tension erupted. She pulled away from him. "I never loved Sylvie. You know that. And I'm fed up with hearing about her. From you. From Leo. Don't I count for anything around here? You've never loved me, none of you."

"That's utter nonsense, Kat, and you know it." Jacob's eyes suddenly blazed. "What *you* don't understand is your mother and my loyalty to her. What you don't know is that she saved my life during the war."

Katherine hesitated for a moment, stared at her father. He always took Sylvie's side. Even now. Even now that she was dead. A strange raw voice burst from her. "And what you don't understand, have never understood, is that Sylvie tried to kill *me.*"

She raced sobbing from the room.

Jacob didn't follow her. She had to come to terms with his loyalties, whatever the pain it caused her. Feeding her fantasies was no use. It would only make for more difficulties later on. Somehow Katherine had to learn to make a space in herself for Sylvie. And Sylvie *had* saved his life. Saved it in her own inimitable way. By methods which didn't sit well in peacetime America.

A grim expression furrowed his brow. Lying, acting, counterfeiting, cheating. Sylvie's heroisms of war were to Katherine the signs of a bad mother. How to make her understand?

He would take her to Paris. Perhaps there he would make her see a little better.

And while they were away, he would allow her little dream to come to fruition. They would have the decorators in.

The holiday was not a total success.

It wasn't that Katherine wasn't enamored of Paris. No city she had ever walked in was half so beautiful. The winding river, the curve of the bridges, the elegant uniform façades, the glistening and various roofs, the limpid skies, the bright markets with their wares tantalizingly displayed, all spoke to her. As did the museums which she visited assiduously, as if Thomas, her mentor, was ever at her side offering another pair of eyes.

But she was impatient of their return to the home she had created in endless sketches; impatient too of Jacob's incessant meetings with colleagues, with acolytes who sat transfixed, listening to him as if they were on their knees. She was slightly wary of him in this city which for him was replete with memories. She never knew when a walk might lead them past a location which was imprinted with Sylvie's presence. After an initial resistance, she let him talk on when this happened, but she turned her mind away, only half listening. She didn't want to know.

Jacob, aware of this, persisted nonetheless. Not that he could have stopped himself from remembering. Paris was his city. Sylvie's city. The cobbled streets and the boulevards spoke to him, told him tales he thought he had forgotten.

Princesse Mathilde came to see them for a weekend. It was the weekend on which Katherine had arranged to fly to London to visit Portia. Seeing her father with Mathilde briefly, she was again impressed by how happy they always were together. It made no sense to her, the couplings people chose. She was tempted somehow to ask the Princesse why her father had not married her instead of Sylvie, but it was not a question which could easily be put.

London was a revelation. Portia's family house was in one of the Nash terraces overlooking Regent's Park. The girls walked in the Rose Gardens and caught up on the past months, discussed the future. Portia had a place at Newnham College in Cambridge. She tried to persuade Katherine to apply there too.

Katherine demurred. "I couldn't be that far away from my father. He's all alone now."

Portia giggled. "That's the difference between us. I can't wait to get away from the Aged Ps again. A full month with them is already too much."

"I used to feel that way when my mother was alive," Katherine offered. "But now, things are different."

"Mmmn, mothers," Portia grunted. "At least yours wasn't a bore. She had a sense of the dramatic."

Katherine gave her a strange sideways look.

She returned to Paris, impatient now for the holiday to be over. They were to spend their last days there with her aunt Nicolette's family in Neuilly where they had just moved. She hardly knew them, had met them only once, Jacob had reminded her, at her grandmother's funeral in Portugal, before they had left Europe for America. All but one of her cousins was now grown up, her uncle dead, and her aunt had decided to come back to France.

Fearful at first of the reunion, Katherine found herself charmed by her aunt, who reminisced comically about Jacob's youthful exploits. Charmed too by her four cousins, their husbands and wives, all of whom treated her with instant familiarity, and their children who caroused through the house with unstoppable stamina, much to her aunt's hilarity. She promised herself that she would keep in touch with them.

She was surprised by the notion which came into her mind: this was the first *real* family she had ever experienced. She found herself envying the easy banter between her cousins and aunt, the argumentative informality of mealtimes, the laughter and bustle and hugs.

When they got back to New York, to the new apartment, she would make sure that their home was like that. A thought dawned in her. Leo would be coming back to New York now to work in a hospital where he could specialize in tropical medicine. Perhaps he would move into the apartment. Yes, she turned the idea over in her mind. Yes, a home for the three of them.

But Leo, when she put the idea to him, was aghast.

He had grown into a slim blond young man, slightly ashen from his long hospital hours, a little frenzied and erratic in his gestures which spoke of bouts of sleeplessness and an adrenaline-fueled energy.

"What, you want me to move in here? Are you mad?"

They were sitting in Jacob's study and he looked from his sister to his father in amazement. "I'd go crazy here. Why, the two of you are like recluses out of some dated European movie." He gestured wildly around the room. "Books, books, pictures and books. That's all I ever get around here. No, Kat, it's not for me."

Katherine grew pale. Jacob smiled.

"And you know what, Kat?" Now that he had started, he threw his sister a challenging look and rushed on. "You're square, Kat. Pretty, yes. But altogether square. You're turning into an old frump before your time. Look at you, that little skirt, that little blouse. Why, I bet you don't even have a pair of jeans. Why should you?

You're living in the Middle Ages. This is America, kid. You hear me? America. Not Europe."

"I do have a pair of jeans," Katherine said bleakly.

Leo stopped in his tracks. His tone softened. "Well, get them on, kid. Get them on and I'll take you out with me tonight." He posed a mute question to Jacob, who nodded. "Come on, hurry up."

Katherine rushed off nervously. Jacob grinned. His son at least had swallowed America whole. He didn't disapprove. He was in fact increasingly proud of him, of his dedication to his work, his plans for working in trouble spots abroad. And a little fraternal criticism would do Katherine no harm.

Leo took Katherine to the Village. It was as if in that short distance from the Upper East Side she had crossed a magic dividing line into another country. The narrow streets swarmed with young people. The girls' long hair flowing over tight turtleneck sweaters, eyes darkened against pale skin. The men, jacketless, their sweaters like the girls'. Every second door opened onto a café or club. Sound thrust out of them on the milling pavement. The moan of a sax, earnest voices, the rumble of laughter.

Leo led her into a club. Small crowded tables, lights so dim the faces were hardly perceptible. Everywhere the curl of smoke. On a tiny stage, a black man at a piano, his face impassive beneath an odd hat, his fingers thick yet darting, running lightly, effortlessly over keys. Rich syncopated sound, cool, playful. She sat back intrigued. She had never been to a jazz club before. Never heard of Thelonius Monk. She watched her brother. He was engrossed in the music, his eyes half shut, his body swaying lightly. Like the others, all of them, in a musical trance.

In the break, a large sandy-haired young man in a black leather jacket came over to their table. He slapped Leo on the shoulder.

"Hiya man, what's up?" His eyes slid over Katherine with a mixture of disdain and interest. "Who's the chick?"

Katherine was surprised by the voice. Low, rumbling, sleepy. With Portia's accent, but trying to sound like something else.

"My kid sister," she heard Leo say.

"Ya? No kidding. Groovy sister." He smiled a flash of white teeth at Katherine and from nowhere pulled up a chair, which he turned back forward to the table. He leaned his chin on it and looked intently into Katherine's eyes. "Hiya, kid sister, the name's Ted. Ted Mercer."

"You're English, aren't you?" Katherine asked.

"How'd you guess?" The man laughed. "And here I thought I'd perfected my American. I've been trying to get your brother to give me lessons." He looked at Leo, but Leo was paying no attention to them. He was scanning the smoky room, fidgeting a little nervously. Then he leapt up, waved. A slender young woman made her way toward their table. Tight black slacks, black skinny-ribbed top, a length of ash-blonde hair cut with a fringe which met her arched brows. She kissed Leo lightly on the lips. "Didn't think you were coming tonight," Katherine heard her murmur.

"I tried to ring you, Claudia. Didn't get you."

"Can't stay. I'm meeting Pete."

Leo held on to her hand. "Tomorrow then?"

"Maybe, ring me." She pulled away, smiled at Ted, waved.

Leo sat down, his expression glum.

"A ball-breaker, that one," Ted offered.

"What do you know about it?" Leo prickled.

Then, as if he had suddenly remembered Katherine's presence, he turned to her, a little embarrassed. "Want to go somewhere else, Kat?"

"I don't mind," Katherine said softly. "Whatever you prefer."

"Can't blow now, folks." Ted decided for them. "The man's about to start." He turned a comical face on Katherine. "Think my American's coming on?"

"She wouldn't know," Leo muttered.

Later, on their way home, Katherine suddenly realized what it was that had been troubling her throughout the evening. The girl, the girl Leo had kissed, Claudia, she was like Sylvie. Like Sylvie in the photographs. The thought depressed her.

Over the coming months, Leo opened her eyes to the other Manhattan, to another America. He took her, sometimes with Claudia, sometimes with Ted or other friends, to a variety of jazz clubs, to The Five Spot, The Village Vanguard, to cabarets like The Premise where satire thrived, and to poetry performances. She was disconcerted and then enthralled by Lenny Bruce's spitfire monologues, his explosive mix of four-letter words and Yiddishisms which hit at the gut of hypocrisies. She warmed to Ginsberg's chanting lines, to a whole panoply of poets and satirists who launched a full-scale assault on upright and uptight America. She learned a look and a posture and a set of adjectives which passed for being hip in the Village. It wasn't difficult.

And sometimes she thought that whatever Leo said, she nonetheless preferred her quiet evenings with her father or her outings with Thomas.

By the beginning of December, the finishing touches had been put to the apartment. Katherine, as she walked through the enlarged sweep of the living room with its creamy raw silk textures, its mix of low-slung sofas and older more ornately curved chairs, was radiant with satisfaction. She saw a new life unfolding. She saw feet sinking into the thick pile of the new rugs whose abstract patterns evoked the work of contemporary artists. She saw tantalizing gatherings round the bold rectangle of the dining table. She envisioned the admiring glances of guests as they noted the sculptural perfection of the two McKintosh chairs poised in the foyer. She saw the foundations of home.

Jacob, sharing in her delight, thought that he had perhaps been wrong to worry.

They planned a New Year's Eve dinner party, a double celebration of their transformed home and the dawn of the new year, 1963. A new year without Sylvie, Katherine thought with a mixture of guilt and jubilation.

And so, on the evening of December 31, 1962, Jacob, Katherine and Leo waited in a living room decked in flowers and soft lights for the first guests to arrive. Katherine in a dress of milky white shantung, simple in its A-line but rich in its texture, a dress which she felt matched the calm of the room they were sitting in. A dress which enveloped her in an aura of purity. Jacob, trim in his dinner-jacket, his dark eyes sparkling darker against the graying of his thick hair; Leo, blond, relaxed, despite the effort it had cost him to put on a suit for the occasion.

Guests began to arrive. The psychoanalytic contingent first. Dr. and Mrs. Gross, Dr. and Mrs. Ellenberg, an old stooped bearded man, Dr. Evans, with a deep voice, who chucked Katherine a little lasciviously under the chin and cackled to himself eccentrically. Then, a woman Katherine didn't recognize, blonde, statuesque in a sculpted magnetic blue dress which revealed an expanse of creamy throat on which a single jewel radiated. Jacob held her hand a little lingeringly before he gravely presented her to Katherine and Leo as Dr. Camille Briand. Something in his demeanor made a tremulous question form in Katherine's mind, but it fluttered away at the distinctive sound of Violette's infectious laugh.

Violette, briefly in New York, galvanizing the room with her presence. Violette, her hair cut short in raffish pixie fashion, so that her eyes looked luminously large. Violette in a mannish black silk trouser-suit, decorated only with an intricate artist's clasp.

"And yet another Violette, this time," Jacob teased, lifting her off her feet, a note of warm approval in his voice.

"I'm masquerading, playing fashion games," she whispered so they could all hear, "unlike *ma belle Katherine,* who will never feel the need to. *Ça va, petite?*" She hugged Katherine, then corrected herself, "*Ma grande,* I should say, since you now tower over me."

"And Leo, my favorite man."

He kissed her on the cheek, cutting short the second as he spied a new arrival.

"Claudia, Claudia." He called his girlfriend over and held her hand tightly.

"I can see I've been displaced in Leo's affections." Violette pouted wryly. Both she and Katherine gazed at the girl's openly sensuous movements, the clinging magenta frock, the dramatically outlined eyes against the pale skin, the fall of blonde hair.

"Well, well, well," Violette murmured, "a man's taste revealed." She caught Katherine's glance and smiled conspiratorially. Then, with a dramatic gesture, she put a hand to her brow and turned to Jacob. "I'd almost forgotten. I took the liberty of inviting my friend Carlo along. Carlo Negri—you remember, Katherine. The madman has just flown in from Rome on a whim, to spend a few days with me here. It's all right, isn't it, Jacob? He'll be around in a little while. He wanted to rest and freshen up before foisting himself on you."

"Of course, of course, Violette." Jacob smiled.

Katherine read a slight strain in Violette's voice.

She echoed her father's assurance, ensured another place at table. The room was now alive with people. Corks popped, glasses tinkled, delicate canapés were served, laughter sounded. Thomas appeared, dapper in a dinner jacket. Blue eyes twinkling. He surveyed the apartment, surveyed Katherine. "Wonderful, Schätzchen, wonderful. You have done well. And you look like a blushing bride. Is the dress a hint? Do I see a groom?"

He caught her embarrassed flush, the flash of anger in those cool eyes. "Now, now, don't tell me that you put on that dress tonight in all naïveté?" he asked humorously. "Let me go and congratulate Jacob. On the success of the refurbishment, I mean," he chuckled, his expression roguish. "And then I shall come back. I have a little present for you."

He left her just as Carlo Negri was shown in. It had been over a year since Katherine had seen him and again she was struck by the magnetism of those coal dark eyes, the indolence of his gestures as he took her hand and playfully brought it to his lips. *"La bellissima Katerina,"* he murmured. "The one woman for whom I might almost leave my roulette table." He held her gaze.

Katherine felt pinioned by that look, unable to break through the invisible circle it created around them. It was at once agreeable and troubling.

"Ah, Monsieur Negri, a pleasure to see you again." Thomas came to her rescue. "I was just going to ask Katherine whether she might like to have her slightly belated birthday present before we go to table."

"Oh yes, please."

Thomas went out, came back a moment later with an object draped in blue velvet which he positioned carefully on a low table. He gestured to Katherine and she slowly lifted the velvet. A hush fell over the room as the gathered guests looked on. It was broken by a chorus of "Ahs" as every eye focused on a perfect piece of sculpted oval marble.

"A Brancusi head." Jacob was the first to speak. "Thomas, you really shouldn't have." Anger tinged the polite comment. Again Jacob thought he must bring himself to do something about the increasing hold this man had on Katherine's life. Yet it was so difficult. He could find nothing to say against Thomas. Nothing, except warnings about precisely those things he didn't want Katherine to think about.

"No, you shouldn't have," Katherine echoed, but her hand was drawn to the cool translucent stone, a stark primordial form with its blind but all-seeing eyes intense in their repose. "You shouldn't have."

"I know I shouldn't have," Thomas laughed, "but I wanted to."

"It's beautiful, achingly beautiful." She squeezed his hand. "Thank you."

"To make you happy, Schätzchen, I would give more than a Brancusi," Thomas said softly.

"I guess there are some benefits to being little Miss Purity nineteen sixty-three," a sultry voice intoned behind them. They turned. "We haven't been introduced." Claudia, her face bland, her body speaking, stretched out a hand to Thomas.

"Indeed not." Thomas bowed.

Leo flushed, gripped Claudia's arm. "Dinner, I think."

"*Ne t'en fais pas.*" Carlo was at Katherine's side. "Some of us value a little purity." Dusky eyes enveloped her. He lifted his glass, curled long lips, "To Katerina, *la madonna del Nuovo York.*"

"Oh these Italians with their madonnas." Violette overtook them, groaned. "I sometimes think Carlo would be happiest if we could all be reduced to the purity of a primitive ovum, like your Brancusi." A dark look passed between them, excluding Katherine.

Food was served. A warm turbot salad and garlic croutons, pheasant tenderly arranged on wild rice, an array of cheese, crème caramel, each course with its own choice wines. Glasses were filled, and emptied and filled again. A laughing toast from Jacob to Katherine for having transformed this little corner of Manhattan. Conversation hummed. Katherine smiled. She wondered if that warm glow inside her was what people called happiness.

Later there was music. Carlo took her hand. "*Puis-je?*" He guided her, pressed her close. His body swayed sinuously against her, sure, strong, lulling her into rhythmic obedience. Katherine danced. Felt the dance's pleasure. He lifted her chin to look down into her eyes, a dangerous look. Katherine arched away. The hand on the small of her spine moved firmly, imprisoned her. "*Bellissima,*" a caress in her ear.

Then he was gone. Other arms around her, Leo's friends, Ted Mercer, old Dr. Evans, leering, Thomas, elegant, light on his feet, Jacob, warm, witty, relaxed, whispering, "Thank you, Kat." A champagne glass in her hand. Dr. Gross booming the countdown. "Five, four, three, two, one."

"Happy New Year." A chorus of voices and corks popping. Katherine was being kissed. Carlo, a warm flicker over her lips, the receding harsh planes of a dark face. Violette's eyes on her, on him. Sardonic, challenging. "Surely big sisters should go first." There was something in the way she said it, something in the rapid toss of her head. But there was no time to ask. Other lips came, other arms. "Happy New Year." A new year without Sylvie. Katherine smiled and smiled.

Soon after midnight, people began to leave. Violette asked Katherine if she could use her room to freshen up a little.

"Of course."

Katherine followed her. There was something, something she needed to ask. It was difficult. She was still slightly in awe of Violette, her worldliness, her sharp tongue. She watched her at the mirror. Outlining lips, vivacious eyes.

"How's Mathilde?" Katherine began. "I miss her."

"As energetic as ever. She's been asked to sit on a human rights commission and now she's full of stories of gruesome tortures in Turkish prisons, of Russian poets locked up in psychiatric wards." Violette grinned. "It suits Mat to a T."

"I think she's wonderful." Katherine paused, took a deep breath, looked at Violette's face in the mirror, her own next to it. "Violette, is Mat my mother? I've always thought that maybe . . ." She let the sentence hang.

Violette's expressive face in the mirror passed through a variety of emotions. She turned to Katherine, put her hands on her shoulders. "Hasn't Jacob told you? He said he would tell you. Tell you now that Sylvie's dead." She shook her trim head with a gesture of impatience. "Kat, it's not that Mathilde is your mother." She hesitated. "It's simply that you and I share a father."

"Share a father?" Katherine echoed, astonishment distorting her features.

Violette nodded. "Yes, you're my little sister," she looked at Katherine anxiously. "I've known since Frederick, Mat's husband, died. I was pleased to find out, I must say. Frederick was always such an old stick. And Jacob, well . . ." She laughed, threw Katherine an inquiring glance. "It's wonderful, isn't it? The idea of Jacob and Mat as lovers. Oh, a long time ago. Before Sylvie." She turned back to the mirror, made a great show of powdering her nose. "A wonderful illicit romance which resulted in me." She grimaced comically. "It still thrills me to know my queenly mother did something improper at least once."

Violette stopped herself as she caught the expression on Katherine's face. "It isn't so bad, is it, Kat? Leo wasn't unduly upset. He guessed ages ago." She squeezed Katherine's hand. "You were the last, the baby," she said softly. "I thought Jacob had told you."

"He didn't tell me." Katherine thought she might cry. She felt dizzy, confused. All the still places in her life seemed suddenly to have shifted dramatically. She had a sense of having been betrayed, cheated, deceived.

"Don't take it like that, Kat. It hardly matters anymore. It's ancient history." Violette looked at her. "Aren't you pleased to have an older sister?"

"It's not that. It's not you. It's just . . ."

Violette kissed her. "Look, we'll talk about it some more. I'm here for a while, working. But now I really have to go. Carlo's waiting." She hugged her. "Happy New Year, little sister."

Katherine lay back on her bed, the party forgotten. Thoughts buzzed through her like swarming bees. Circles within circles of deceit. Betrayal. Jacob had two daughters. He hadn't told her. She had always thought of herself as singular, as Jacob's only daughter. It had sustained her. But she had only been one of two. She recalled Jacob's constant praise for Violette, the birthday presents they had bought for her together, his frequent trips to Switzerland. She felt a tug of jealousy. And beneath it, that refrain of betrayal. No one was to be trusted. No one was reliable. Not even Jacob.

Was it one of the reasons Sylvie had hated her? And was it guilt that had made Jacob so patient of Sylvie's attacks on her?

Confusion pressed on her, mingled with humiliation, consolidated into anger. Jacob should have told her. She *wasn't* a baby. Katherine rose. She had to speak to him. She wanted to shout, "Why? Why didn't you tell me? How could you not tell me?"

She looked for Jacob. He wasn't in the living room. She stole away before anyone could talk to her. He wasn't in his bedroom either. She breathed in the cool Japanese atmosphere she had worked to create for him, looked at the slatted chairs, the pale grays, the yellows. Why? Why hadn't he told her? She wanted to sob.

She paused at the door of the study. There were voices. Jacob's. And smooth French-accented tones. Camille Briand's. That woman he had danced with. Katherine shivered, listened. They were talking about a problem child. A girl whose mother had died. A girl who thought she had killed her mother. Fantasy and reality colliding.

They were talking about her.

Katherine swallowed hard. How could he? To that woman. She pushed open the door without knocking. There they were sitting next to each other on the sofa. Something reeked of intimacies exchanged.

"Kat, come in." Jacob's gracious smile. "We were just talking about a case of Camille's."

"I bet." An uncustomary surliness spoke through her. She closed the door again without saying another word.

Suddenly a memory engulfed her. Another room. A stairwell. Sylvie, in one of her negligees, smacking her hard. Behind her, in the depths of the bedroom, a man. Katherine rubbed her cheek where the pain had been.

Parents. She'd had enough of parents.

She strode back to the living room. Thomas was still there.

"Thomas, can I come to Boston with you?" she asked him abruptly.

"You mean for a little holiday?" Lively eyes quizzed her.

She nodded, then shook her head. "I mean now."

He looked at her queerly. "I hadn't planned on going back tonight."

"Tomorrow then?" Katherine's tone was insistent.

He met her on it. "I'll send Hans round to fetch you. At one o'clock."

Katherine gazed out of the window on to the snowy expanse of Thomas's garden, the trees graceful in their white covering, the dim outlines of the vast central sculpture. She turned and surveyed the room that was always hers when she visited Thomas, its architectural simplicity, the reassuring certainty of the heavy polished wood, the playful cubes and rectangles of the little Feininger villages which she had spent so much time dreaming over in the past. The crackle of the smooth white sheets, already turned down in readiness on the immaculate bed.

Yes, she realized suddenly, that was it. She always felt at home here. More at home than in Manhattan.

She lay down on the bed and tried to think things over. When she woke with a start, it was already late. But she felt refreshed. Full of a dawning sense of purpose. She showered, quickly slipped on her black wool frock, a string of pearls. Thomas always preferred formal attire for dinner. It was an old-world custom he adhered to.

He was nursing a drink in the living room and listening to the strains of a Bach cantata when she came down.

"Better, Schätzchen?" His eyes surveyed her. "Yes, I can see you are better." He gestured her toward the velvet armchair opposite him.

They sat quietly, following the contrapuntal intricacies of the music. When the piece had run its course, Thomas addressed her. "And so, Schätzchen, are you finally going to tell me what this visit is all about?"

Katherine looked at him, looked at the intelligence in that strong face, the vivacity of the eyes. She gave him a slow smile. "I will. But first," she laughed, "I think I heard you say something about dinner. I'm starved."

Thomas groaned. "I had forgotten about these young appetites.

Come, Schätzchen, I am sure it is all ready." He led her to the dining room, where the table shone with the gleam of heavy silver, the intricate curves of candelabra.

No sooner had they sat down than they heard the distant ring of the telephone. Roberts came to the door. "It is Miss Victoria. She insists that she must speak to you." Katherine heard him, despite his soft tones.

"Yes, yes." Thomas folded his napkin neatly again. "Excuse me for a moment, Schätzchen."

When he reappeared and the wine had been served, she asked him, "Who is Miss Victoria, Thomas?"

She felt him considering.

"A friend," he said casually. "Now, Schätzchen, pay attention to the plate of hors d'oeuvres Roberts is offering you. I recommend the artichoke hearts."

"What kind of friend?" Katherine pressed him.

"A ladyfriend. Does that satisfy you?" Blue eyes teased her.

Katherine grew suddenly morose, knew it was irrational. But she persisted. "Do you go to bed with her, Thomas, make love to her?"

He put his fork down, looked at her sternly. "Katherine, I could say to you, that is none of your business. But I will be honest with you." He held her eyes. "Yes, I do go to bed with Victoria on occasion. I was supposed to see her tonight. That is why I had to take the call. Does that satisfy you?" He watched the emotions play over her young face; the stir of anger, the hint of disappointment and then a smile settled, hesitant, ravishing in its innocence.

"Thomas." She looked down at her hands for a moment and then confronted him. "Thomas, will you marry me?"

He gazed at her and after a second burst out laughing.

"Is it so funny?" she asked quietly, her hurt in her eyes.

"No, no, Schätzchen." He stilled himself. "It is only that I have never been proposed to so abruptly, so boldly before."

"But will you, Thomas, now, soon?" Gray eyes questioned him with the full seriousness of her young being.

He met her seriousness. "I will consider your proposal," he said slowly.

It was not the answer Katherine had hoped for. Tears rose in her eyes. She hid them while Roberts served creamy chicken from a steaming casserole.

Thomas, his voice light, asked for his compliments to be sent to Cook, asked for a little more wine. He was biding his time. Surveying

Katherine. She was hurt by his answer. But what had made the girl propose to him in this way? It was wholly unexpected. He would have liked to take her in his arms, to stroke the vivacity of that auburn hair, yes, those full young breasts. He stopped his imagination. But there was something more at stake here.

"Schätzchen." He forced her to meet his eyes. "You must not be upset. You cannot simply propose to me with no more reason than the discovery that I happen to sleep with a woman and expect an instant answer. It must have crossed your imagination before that I make love to women. I am not dead yet." He saw the shadows flutter over her face.

"No, perhaps it has not crossed your young imagination. Never mind, that is not what is at issue. But marriage"—he paused—"marriage is a serious proposition. For you, perhaps even more than for me."

Katherine pushed her chair clumsily away from the table, stood up. "I don't feel very well, Thomas. Excuse me."

He didn't care for her, Katherine thought. Not really. Not when it came to that. To what he did with women. Like her father. She was just a child. Unimportant. A plaything. An occasional recreation.

He moved quickly after her, took her arm. "Come, we shall sit by the fire and talk quietly." Despite her resistance, he maneuvered her into the living room. Made her sit on the sofa, poured a glass of brandy. "If you are old enough to propose to me, then you are old enough for this." He tried to lighten the atmosphere.

He took her hand, stroked it softly. "Now, Schätzchen, tell me. What has occasioned all this? Are you pregnant? One of those young men you see?"

She pulled away from him, aghast. "No, of course not," she said adamantly.

"Well, that, at least, is a relief." Thomas smiled. "So tell me."

Katherine gazed into the fire, the leaping flames, let her eyes play over the fine marble hearth, the painting by George Grosz above it, with its hectic planes, its lurid faces, a satirist's black view of life in the metropolis. She spoke slowly. "It's just that I like it here with you. I like to be with you. I would like to live with you."

She turned to him, lips slightly parted, eyes wide, entreating him.

He kissed her. She gave him soft, warm, innocent lips, unmoving beneath his. He could have, he knew, urged her into response. She was passive in his arms, willing, willing him. But he let her go, only cradling her in the circle of his arm.

"Tell me, Katherine, tell me. There is something troubling you. Something perhaps since I have last seen you. That man Carlo?"

Katherine shook her head and relaxed into the fold of his arm. She looked again into the flames. "I've learned that Violette is my sister. My half sister," she murmured.

"I see," he said softly. "But that should be no reason for grieving. You have always liked the Princesse. And Violette."

"I know," Katherine mused, perturbed. "But I feel betrayed. Cheated somehow. Jacob should have told me. He treats me like a child." She didn't tell him the rest about her father and Camille, or the thoughts that had tormented her that long night.

"I understand." Thomas got up, paced. "So you have come to me to make a double betrayal of it. Tit for tat. Your father with the Princesse. You with me." He paused, knowing eyes tinged with irritation looked down on her, challenged her.

"No." Katherine leapt up, away from him. Her face was flushed. "It's not like that."

"Isn't it, Schätzchen? Think about it. You ask me to marry you, perhaps first to seduce you. No? Not because you're drawn to me particularly." He grasped her arm, made her turn to him. "But in order to pay your father back, to teach him a lesson."

"That's not true." Katherine struggled to free herself from those fingers which gripped her too fiercely, from that intelligence which probed into her.

He pulled her closer to him. His face was on a level with hers, his pupils were strange, bright. "So you want to be a woman, Schätzchen?" he murmured.

Katherine, fraught, stood rigidly against him.

Suddenly he laughed, a little harshly, let her go. "No, Schätzchen. This is not the spirit in which one becomes a woman." He turned away from her, poured himself a drink.

She stood where he had left her, gazing into the flames. She felt humiliated. The eyes on her back were laughing at her, judging her.

Thomas sipped his brandy. He could smell her fear. It was no good. The moment was all wrong. He could take her upstairs now, try slowly to elicit some response from that virginal body. Show her what she thought she wanted. She wouldn't protest. But she didn't want him. Not now. Not ever, perhaps. It was all some impulsive reaction to her father. And he, he who was used to the subtle caresses of experienced women, did he want the responsibility of that fearful flesh? His eyes strayed over her, that long elegant body, the beautiful head, waiflike now, somehow lost.

"Katherine, it's no good. Not yet. You're still a child," he said softly, as evenly as he could. "Tomorrow, you will go home. To Jacob. Try to understand him a little. Youth is so unforgiving. So impatient of human frailty."

She said nothing, wouldn't face him.

"And perhaps you shouldn't play with these things, Schätzchen. Not just yet. Not until you're older."

She wanted to hit him for saying that to her. A child, always a child, powerless, humiliated. Her eyes blazed at him as she fled to her room.

The next *day* she insisted on leaving.

Saying goodbye to her at the station, Thomas looked at her sternly. "You mustn't take all this too much to heart, Schätzchen. You're troubled now. And sex is always a little problematic at first. In a little while, we shall sit and laugh over it." He squeezed her hand. "And reconsider your proposal." He smiled.

As she turned away from the limousine, the last thing Katherine felt like doing was laughing. Resentment burrowed inside her. She was irritated, indignant. They all treated her like a child. A child to be cajoled, lied to, patted. But she was seventeen. In other cultures women of seventeen had families, worked. She had had enough of these old people who looked down at her from their height of years, who always knew what was best for her. Well they didn't know what was best for her. Didn't know what was best for themselves half the time. Look at her father. No sooner one woman in the grave whom he had cheated on, a woman who had been miserable enough to kill herself, than he was in bed with another. Another cold blonde bitch. Katherine tried the word and liked it. The bitch and he were probably in bed making another child together.

Jacob was in fact at the Plaza Hotel dining with Violette.

"You should have told her." Violette fingered the heavy pendant round her neck and raised eyes at him that both accused and laughed. "It should have been you. Not me."

"I know," Jacob sighed. "She hasn't spoken to me since. Simply left a note to say she'd gone off with Thomas. Wasn't sure when she would be back. God knows what the two of them are up to together." He shook his head slowly, poured Violette a glass of wine. "It's so difficult with Kat. She's so sensitive. Runs back to her lair, if I so much as breathe about the past. Not like you." He smiled a slow admiring smile at Violette. "How are you, my vagrant daughter?"

"Your thick-skinned vagrant daughter is not at her very best." Violette rolled her eyes.

"And are you going to confess your sins to your analyst daddy?" Jacob matched her tone, but he was aware that Violette was troubled, had been aware since her arrival.

"What would you say if I told you I was pregnant?"

He looked at her attentively. "I don't know. I might ask you if you were pleased. I might ask you who the father was. I might ask you if you were contemplating marriage. I might jump up and clap my hands. I might hope to be a better grandfather than I'd been a father." He stopped and met her eyes. "Tell me, Violette. What do you want me to say?"

"I want you to tell me I'm a silly ass for letting it happen."

"*Et voilà*. You're a silly ass for letting it happen." He paused. "You don't want the man?"

"Want is hardly the problem. He's an addiction. I've thought of replacing him with heroin. Breaking the habit would be easier." She smiled her roguish smile. "The problem is we're no good for each other. It's like a race. Who can do the worst, the most exciting things to whom. And first. It takes a lot of imagination." Her eyes grew stormy. She took out a cigarette, lit it slowly, brooded. "You see, we're totally alike and totally unsuited. If we got married, we'd kill each other." She hesitated. "And I don't want a child. And he doesn't know."

There was a gravity in her face he had never seen there before. "*Ma pauvre Violette*." He knew, without having to ask, who the man in question was. Instead he asked, "And why do you have this particular addiction? Why this craving for stimulus? Perhaps if you had a child . . ." He let the sentence hang.

She finished it for him. "I'd die of boredom instead. Life is short, Jacob. I like to pack my minutes."

"And so you try to make it shorter."

She looked at him for a moment and burst out laughing. "Are you offering that as an interpretation?"

Jacob shook his head sadly. "You know I've never been able to combine being a father with analysis. Just look at the three of you."

She kissed him. "You're the best father I've ever had. And the three of us are fine. Just remember that."

"I'll try." Jacob grinned, grew serious again. "And you . . . No, I won't moralize. You know I'll back you up in whatever you do."

"I know, Jacob." She looked at her watch, rose. "But I'm convinced the stimulus is better than the boredom. My very own tender trap."

Jacob helped her with her coat. He had a sudden sense that Violette had more of Sylvie in her than Sylvie's own daughter. Sylvie, tempered with Mathilde's quick wit and humor. He sighed. That mysterious female continent. Still a mystery after all these years.

Katherine, as she wandered restlessly round the Manhattan apartment, felt as trapped as Violette. For the first time since she had moved back into the house, she knew she couldn't face an evening with Jacob. She was angry, seething. She poured herself an uncustomary drink, and grimacing, swallowed it down in two gulps.

Then, with relief, she remembered. There was a gathering at Ted's tonight. He had mentioned it to her at the party.

She liked Ted. He was a big burly man who made her feel comfortable. Though he drank too much and when he did, his American accent slipped and the BBC tones came through. He told scathing stories about his life at Oxford, about his home in Yorkshire, stories in which the humor dipped into anger the more he drank. Sometimes the rancor in these stories frightened her. She wondered what his lectures were like, but she had never taken up his invitation to come to CCNY and listen.

Yes, she would go to Ted's, Katherine determined. She slipped into her Village gear, a black ribbed dress, fishnet tights, pale lipstick, boots. Her reflection dissatisfied her. She still looked like a child. Kid sister Katherine. Indignantly, she forced the dress down over one shoulder, leaving it bare; piled her hair up loosely on top of her head. Looked at herself again. Jewelry, that's what she needed. With sudden grim resolve, she pulled a large box out of the bottom of her cupboard. Sylvie's jewelry. She had never used it before. She fingered glittering necklaces, gold and silver chains, bracelets, beads, brooches, earrings. Tentatively she tried a few and then, with something like exasperation, chose heavy bangles, a choker with ruby-red stones and matching pendant earrings. A different Katherine looked out at her from the mirror. That Katherine smiled with her lips open.

Ted's apartment was in the East Village, an assortment of dank rooms almost devoid of furniture but with a variety of rugs and cushions and mattresses scattered around the floor. In most of them now music throbbed, thick white candles flickered and couples danced or sat in little intent circles and chatted above the din. Katherine could smell the high sweet scent of marijuana.

In the last room, there was a pocket of quiet. Ted was declaiming to a small hushed group. Long sonorous lines of verse. She had known that he wrote poetry, but she had never read or heard any of it before. She listened attentively. An incantatory rage came from him. Images of men, crushed together. Underground. In a mine. A wail. A rush of rich metaphor. The mine became one of the circles of Dante's *Inferno,* a London tube, a heaving labyrinth. He was good, Katherine thought. Very good.

When he reached the end, she went up to him, shyly told him how much she liked what she had heard. He embraced her, thick heavy arms crushing her, the smell of alcohol. "Thanks, kid. And where's your big brother?"

Katherine shrugged. "I've come on my own."

"Really?" A shaggy eyebrow rose.

"Really."

"And your glass? Where's your glass?" He placed one in her hand, poured thick red wine. "To poetry and all that rubbish." He clicked her glass with his, smirked, and drank to the bottom. "And now I'll show you how poets dance." He took her into the next room, performed a little pantomime of swiveling hips and stormy eyes, then wrapped his arm around her. "I'm not very good at this," he murmured in her ear. "Now, Brian, Brian here is a whiz of a dancer." He motioned her toward another man, made the briefest of introductions and set them off.

Brian smiled. "Gotta do what the big man says."

Katherine danced. There were any number of nameless partners, telling her she was a cute chick, trying to fondle her. On occasion, she would meet Ted's eyes, and he would wink, and nod his head encouragingly. Still the kid sister to him, she thought dismally. She looked round for Leo, but he was nowhere to be seen. She hadn't spoken to him since New Year's Eve, since Violette had told her. And suddenly she wanted to see him, to tell him she knew.

Katherine meandered through smoky rooms. Couples, everywhere now, their arms around each other. The last of the bedrooms was dark, empty. She was about to turn around, when she heard a low moan. And then, she saw him in the corner of the dim room. He was kissing Claudia, his body straining against hers, his hands cleaving her bottom. Katherine stifled her cry, turned guiltily away, but Claudia's laugh stopped her.

"And here comes kid sister, right on time. Daddy's little girl, seventeen going on forty-five." She examined Katherine brashly from luminous blue eyes, laughed again. Then she ran her fingers through Leo's hair, challenging him with her look. "Next time you want to get your cock into me, Leo, why don't you leave kid sister at home?" She flounced away from him, past Katherine and out of the room.

Leo looked at Katherine mutely, but his eyes accused her.

"Sorry," she murmured. And before she could stop herself she blurted out, "She's just like Sylvie, isn't she?" She looked at Claudia's receding form, the blonde hair, the narrow swinging hips, with distaste.

"And what's wrong with that?" Leo turned on her. "If only you were a little more like her, you'd be a lot less of a drag."

Katherine's mouth dropped.

"Yes, Daddy's girl." Irritation covered his face. "Claudia's right. But you know something, that darling father of ours was mad about Sylvie. Have you looked at those photographs of her from the Paris days? She was breathtaking. I don't blame him. They weren't even married when I was conceived. He couldn't keep his hands off her."

Katherine had a sudden desire to vomit. This too, on top of everything else. She felt the ground giving way beneath her feet. She scanned Leo's angry face helplessly.

But her silence seemed only to goad him. "You should go and get laid," he muttered and left her.

Right, Katherine thought, that does it. She marched furiously back toward the front room, poured herself a glass of wine and downed it quickly. She scanned the dancers, saw Claudia moving vampishly against another man, Ted. As if an unknown force were compelling her, Katherine strode toward the woman, pulled her away from her partner. "Ball-breaker," she said loudly, so loudly that everyone around them turned. Then, with a resounding smack, she slapped Claudia's face.

Leo, watching from the corner of the room, dropped his glass in amazement at Katherine's unexpected wildness. Then he froze, saw as if in slow motion Claudia raising her arm, hitting out. At empty air. Ted had pulled Katherine away, was navigating her toward the other end of the room. "Do something about that little twerp," Claudia was hissing at him.

He put his arm around her absently. "It's okay. Ted's lecturing her." He led Claudia away, looked back to wave to Ted and saw in astonishment that Katherine was planting a kiss very firmly on his lips.

"Leo told me to get laid," Katherine was saying to Ted. She looked seriously into his eyes as they danced.

"By me?"

She pressed closer to him, let her hips move as she had seen Claudia's do.

"Me, huh? The man definitely has taste," Ted quipped. He eyed her curiously. "Are you sure, kid sister? Have you ever done this before?"

Katherine recoiled. "I am not a kid. And I've had enough of being a sister. Anyone's sister. Or daughter."

Ted stroked her hair, slowly pulled out the combs which she had used to keep it up. "Hard growing up, isn't it?" he murmured.

She put her head in his shoulder. They danced, After a while, he asked her, "And *have* you done this before, Katherine?" Deep-set eyes quizzed her in the candlelight.

Katherine shook her head, hid her face again in his shoulder. "But I want to," she mumbled.

He led her to the far room where she had found Leo. "You stay here and think it over quietly"—he put another glass of wine in her hand—"and I'll go and see if I can get rid of the remaining folks." He ruffled her hair and grinned.

Katherine looked around her. This was Ted's bedroom, she realized. There was a small desk, strewn with books and papers. She glanced at them, saw some lines of poetry. She picked up a leather-bound volume. Shakespeare. The Sonnets. She rifled through pages. Drank. Then, remembering herself, she slipped off her dress and went to lie on the bed. She closed her eyes. The room reeled and she opened them again, tried to focus on the book, waited. The apartment grew quiet. And then Ted came in. He looked huge as he gazed down on her.

"Not much on, I see."

Katherine put her hand out to him. Tried to make her eyes look sultry, the way she had seen women do in films.

As he bent to her, she thought she heard him murmur, "Well, well, well. My present from Leo."

He kissed her. A tongue probing, dry. Hands on her back, firm, strong, rubbing. It wasn't unpleasant. She closed her eyes. She saw Leo with Claudia, his arms round her, straining. She arched against

Ted. A man's body, she told herself. She wouldn't be a child any-more, wouldn't. A laugh came to her lips now. Ted was putting a condom on, milky plastic stretching. She stifled the laugh, kissed him.

He lay beside her, hands caressing her, one leg astride her, rub-bing, stroking. Her eyes seemed to be on the ceiling, watching them. And then his voice, taut, low, drowning them out, intoning, "Listen Katherine, listen:

> "Th' expense of spirit in a waste of shame
> Is lust in action; and, till action, lust
> Is perjured, murd'rous, bloody, full of blame,
> Savage, extreme, rude, cruel, not to trust; . . ."

She had never heard the sonnet. She listened, listened to the rise and fall of his voice in her ear, a rumbling incantation which made her almost oblivious to the movement of his body. The words cov-ered the hot ache inside her, the sense of an object that didn't belong, ripping, invading.

> "Enjoyed no sooner but despisèd straight;
> Past reason hunted, and no sooner had,
> Past reason hated . . ."

His voice grew louder as he reached the crescendo, words laboring against breath.

> "All this the world well knows; yet none knows well
> To shun the heaven that leads men to this hell."

The last word was a caustic rasp.

And then nothing for a few moments, until his voice came again and he lifted himself from her.

"And there you are, young lady. The bloody deed is done."

She followed the direction of his eyes and saw the bloodied sheet.

"I hope Leo is pleased," he murmured.

"And me."

"Oh yes. And you." He looked at her strangely. "But what you don't understand is that it's Leo I'm doing it for." He laughed oddly, then stroked her hair. "You're a sweet girl, Katherine."

In the taxi, on the way home, Katherine didn't know whether she should be jubilant or in tears. She consoled herself. If that was all that separated her from childhood, it wasn't much. A few lunges. A little blood. Not much. What was all the fuss about? Would Leo be able to tell the difference? Her father? Would anyone know? It didn't matter. She knew. Knew that she was no longer a child.

Katherine gazed out at the empty Manhattan streets.

She had liked the sonnet.

y the time Alexei Gismondi
was seventeen, he was rather further along the road to sexual knowledge than Katherine Jardine. Milan may have been a bustling modern metropolis, capital of Italy's postwar economic miracle, but in
matters of sexuality, the habits of the city's bourgeoisie harked back
to a previous age.

When Alexei was fifteen, his uncle brought him to a woman. A
woman who would initiate him into the ways of the sexual world.
Alexei went back to her and other women like her many times. It
was soon evident to him, engrained in him, that there were certain
women one could make love to. And there were other women.
Women like his aunt. Women one met socially. Women one might
talk to, perhaps in the distant future marry. Women one could
secretly desire, but who were pure, untouchable. Women who were
mothers. One could always tell the two kinds of women apart.

The problem was whether one could ever bring them together in
one person.

This disjuncture was the one which most preoccupied Alexei in
his young life. But another came close second. It had to do with his
two fathers, or rather his uncle and his father. On the one hand
there was his uncle, shrewd, practical, energetic and yes, kind. His
uncle and everything he stood for. Wealth wrought out of industrial
riches. A vast entrepreneurial empire run with paternalist generosity,

but with power and profits solidly centered on the Gismondi family. An empire which ran hand in glove with the regime of the Christian Democrats and their many-tentacled system of patronage. An empire to which Alexei, sheltered and pampered, would one day be heir in partnership with his cousin, Sergio.

It was this, as he well knew, that he was being groomed for.

On the other hand there was the person Alexei thought of as his real father. A father who paradoxically grew stronger, more substantial in him, the further he receded into the wintry mists of time. A father who was vast, who loomed larger than he had when Alexei was knee-high and whose last words to him about the justice of the revolution took on increasing weight when an adolescent Alexei was able to fathom their meaning.

By the time he had reached his final year at the *Liceo,* Alexei had read a great deal about the history of Russia and the makings of the Revolution. He had also read Karl Marx and Trotsky and imbibed a critique of a nefarious capitalism which seemed to him altogether apt. Words like *exploitation, alienation* and the *struggle of the workers* were part and parcel of his everyday vocabulary. As he drove in the car his uncle had bought him through the tawdry high-rise suburbs of Milan where the workers, many of them migrants from the peasant South, lived, he felt hotly guilty at his unearned privilege, distraught by the injustices and inequalities of everyday life.

He was hardly alone.

Throughout the sixties public debate in Italy raged around these very issues. There was a deep sense in many that the resisters, the left, the very people who had freed Italy from the grip of Fascism were those who had been cheated out of the economic miracle of peace. In 1963 the Christian Democrats, who had ruled Italy since the war with their advocacy of church and hearth and capital, were forced to form a coalition with the Socialists. Everywhere there was talk of an opening to the left and what it meant.

If Katherine Jardine had chanced upon Alexei and his friends arguing in a Milan café she would have felt like an alien creature—separated from these youths, who were in many ways her peers, by something far more than the Italian language. The very weight given to certain common words—*Communist, Socialist, American*—the values attributed to them, would have divided them as irrevocably as devils and angels. Yet if the subject under discussion were movies, their idiom would instantly have shifted to a shared one. Marilyn

Monroe, Marlon Brando and, of course, the entire Disney cavalcade were common currency. America's legacy to the world.

Alexei's interest in film had not abated. If anything it had grown into a consuming passion. His studies at the *Liceo* at an end, he wanted nothing more than to be able to plunge into the world of Cinecittà. But it was clear to him that this was a near impossibility. Giangiacomo Gismondi had insisted on university and Alexei, whatever his feelings, knew that in this he must follow his uncle's will. He was, though the fact was never spoken, acutely aware of the debt of gratitude he owed his uncle. More than that. Whatever the nature of his nascent political ideas, he liked the man, respected him. He knew, too, how much he meant to this man whom he still thought of as "uncle," but whom he called "father."

They made an odd couple when they went out together. Giangiacomo, with his bald head, his girth, his florid gestures and genial manner. Alexei, towering over him. Slender, somewhat withdrawn, with his tumble of dark curls and reflective air. Invitations from Milanese hostesses, particularly those with daughters a little younger than Alexei, or indeed widowed sisters appropriate to Giangiacomo, were hardly scarce.

Those who had not met them before and heard them introduced as father and son were always slightly perplexed. Whispered questions followed and then, "Ah, of course, the Russian . . ." Nor were people quick to forget them. Giangiacomo's ready wit. The intelligent blaze of Alexei's eyes, that look which seemed to see more than one wanted to reveal. Once they had positioned Alexei in their minds, people would often comment, "Yes, yes, I suspected he wasn't Italian." It had something to do with the quality of his silence, his restraint.

Within himself, at these gatherings, Alexei hardly felt restrained. He was filled with excitement, the excitement of looking, of finding the telling detail—the movement of a napkin over red lips, the clench of a hand at the turn of a conversation, the swing of a trousered leg. The excitement of framing shots, of observing as if through the eye of a camera, of imagining the frame through Hitchcock's eyes, or Rossellini's, or Huston's.

The faculty of seeing was the one through which Alexei breathed. It was not a passion which was immediately visible to others. And it tended to position him outside any group.

Giangiacomo Gismondi was always surprised, when they sometimes talked over these gatherings, by how much his son had taken in just when he had thought him most absent. A useful quality for an executive, he would reflect to himself proudly.

Toward the end of his last term at the *Liceo,* Alexei determined that he would continue his studies in Rome. He had two reasons of equal weight. He wanted to be out from under his uncle's all-embracing shelter. And he wanted to be in the proximity of the Italian film industry. He convinced his uncle of the validity of his decision and Giangiacomo conceded. But he insisted that Alexei live in the family flat in Rome.

"Your mother always preferred it there," he told Alexei. "It would please her. And your being there will give me an extra excuse to visit my favorite city." He laughed and shrewdly assessed his son. He was not blind to Alexei's reasons for wanting to leave Milan.

Alexei merely observed that whenever his fathers wanted to affirm the validity of their choices, they called on the weight of the absent mother. That much, at least, they had in common. He remarked on this to his closest friend, Enrico Mazzocchi, as they flew together to Sicily at the outset of the summer break.

"You can't argue with the dead," Enrico commented wryly, as he sipped another in his endless intake of Coca-Colas, "so they're a perfect source of authority. The Sicilians, you'll see, are stigmatized by the weight of their dead. That's why they manage to carry on their vendettas over generations. The virtue of the dead is unquestionable."

He was elated by this visit to Sicily. He had seen Rosi's film *Salvatore Giuliano* six times over the last years and was fascinated both by its brilliant semi-documentary technique and by the story of this contemporary Sicilian Robin Hood who had been sold out by the politicians. When Enrico had asked Alexei whether he wanted to spend a few weeks with his family in their villa there, he had accepted with alacrity. The *Mezzogiorno,* the South, the problem this underdeveloped agrarian area posed, was something much discussed in the magazines and newspapers he read.

But nothing, certainly not Rosi's harsh camera, had prepared him for the sheer sensuous splendor of the island. As the car drove them along sinuous roads which wound below the dark ancient cone of Etna, he felt he had stepped into another time. A time which did not set its clock by the pulse of Milan. Before him stretched a coastline of jagged cliffs and great rock towers, a sea of purple and iridescent green. In this lush corner of the island, pockets of wildflowers still thrust their myriad colors through golden grasses. Citrus trees were heavy with the weight of orange and lemon.

Enrico's family villa sprawled starkly white and Moorish above the cluster of houses and church and ancient temple which formed the small town of Cefalù. When they stepped out of the car, lizards flickered eletric green across the ground. The air was heavy with the buzz of bees and the sweetness of thyme and mint.

"*Ti piace?*" Signora Mazzocchi turned her handsome sharp-nosed face to him.

Alexei nodded.

"Yes, I can see you're already under the spell of the place."

"Don't get too spellbound," Enrico cautioned him with a lopsided grin. "Or we'll never budge from this place. There's a lot more to see. And I'm going to show it all to you."

Enrico was as good as his word. The very next day at dawn they set off into the interior, up steep bumpy roads where they met only the occasional Vespa or mule. Lushness turned to rocky escarpments and then to sunbleached plain where the corn danced lazily in the wind. In one field, the harvest was already in progress. They stopped to watch. Young men stripped to the waist bending to clasp an armful of stems and slicing through them with a sickle. Old men in red headcloths, handkerchiefs at their throats, tying sheafs together with grass twine.

"It's as if the machine age had never come."

"It hasn't in most of the South," Enrico said flatly.

"I know." Alexei paused. "I have to fight the lure of the picturesque. It all looks so beautiful, so right."

Enrico snorted. "From the outside. For us tourists. From the inside it's grueling labor. And for what? For a few loaves of bread. They're all probably relatives. In a couple of days, they'll go to a cousin's patch and repeat the process. Listen, they're singing."

Alexei listened. "I can't make out a word. It's dialect."

"What did you expect? Tuscan? A little aria from Verdi?"

Alexei glanced at his friend, startled at the edge in his voice. "No, no I didn't," he said softly. "You really care about this place, don't you?"

Enrico shrugged. "We've had the villa for five years now. They still treat us as if we were creatures from Mars. From that other planet called the North of Italy. They hate us. And with reason. We've got everything. They've got their patch of land, a few grapes.

And toil. Year after year. Over and over. That's what they're singing about."

Alexei listened, tried to make out the words. Then the rhythm changed. Incantation turned into a series of sprightly ripostes, one man after another.

Enrico's mood lightened with the melody. "They're growing bawdy, now. There's plenty of that. Singing about the King and Queen doing it. The weight of balls." He chuckled. "All that and yet they see the grain, bread itself, as holy. Reverence side by side with bawdiness. It's altogether pagan."

They drove on, arguing. About the stranglehold of the Mafia and the priests. About the trap or comfort of superstition. In a nearby village, they stopped to stretch their legs. Women and girls, a length of lace or embroidery in their hands, sat in small groups in front of the huddled stone houses. Their presence hushed their voices. Only old weathered faces wrapped in black allowed themselves to glance at these aliens.

By midday they had reached the antique splendor of Agrigento. Vast pagan temples caught between the blue stillness of sea and sky. Zeus and Juno and Hercules, Castor and Pollux, Demeter and Persephone roaming like ghosts in an acropolis of roseate columns, only to find themselves in a Norman church. The pagan bumping into the Christian and co-existing.

Alexei was entranced by the beauty of it all and fascinated by the collision of cultures. Pagan deities become patron saints, one for every crop and every stone, and each one in need of propitiation. A world of blazing sunlight and dark fears. A world centuries away from the machines and assembly lines and televisions of the North.

The next day he astonished himself by agreeing to go to church with Enrico and his mother. He had not entered a church since his aunt's funeral, though it was only in the last year or so that he had found reasons in the books he read to substantiate what had been a choice based in part on loyalty to his Russian father.

The sleepy central square of the small town was abuzz with people, more of them, Alexei thought, than its precincts could hold. Women and children in their Sunday finery; bow-legged old men in soft hats resting on benches in front of the mellow baroque façade replete with finely carved statuary. Alexei could feel rather than see the eyes on him. At first he thought it was because he seemed so much taller than those around him. Then he realized that it might also be because of the paucity of young men. Of course, so many had left for the North, for other countries.

Inside the church was cool despite the heat of the day.

While the priest in his ornate robes intoned the mass, Alexei's gaze wandered. The expression on those faces, those murmuring lips reminded him of his aunt, her delicate features, her beseeching eyes raised upward toward a heavenly dome. Suddenly the burly form of his uncle Giangiacomo interposed itself in his vision. He was struck as never before by the difference between the two of them. How had they ever come together, that man with his unstoppable energy, his peculiarly animal gait? And that woman, as fragile as a china cup, all refinement and lassitude and intense devotion? A sudden image of them coupling leapt into his mind. He banished it. It was unthinkable. A desecration. Perhaps that was why they had had no children. The direction of his thoughts upset him. He forced himself back to the present.

His gaze rested on three young women in white muslin who stood out at the end of his row amidst darkly clothed elders. The one closest to him had a purity of profile which arrested his gaze. Raven hair beneath lace haloed in the light of stained glass. A high rounded forehead, hooded eyes, a straight classical nose, and then the contradiction of full reddened lips. He watched her kneel, belatedly remembered that he was part of the congregation and also knelt to pray. But his eyes stayed on her, on the grace of that head bent in utter submission.

Suddenly she shot a glance at him, dark, doubly secret in that atmosphere of hushed reverence. The hot nakedness of that glance, its potent intimacy, troubled him. It was as if for a moment there had been only the two of them in a private space, a bedroom.

He watched her, waited for the repetition of that look. It didn't come. There was only now, as the congregation rose and trooped into the blazing sunlight, a demure young woman with lowered lids shepherded by a gnarled old man through the fray of shouting children.

"Stop staring." Enrico followed the line of Alexei's gaze and roused him from his reverie.

Alexei jumped. "Was I?" he mumbled.

Enrico nodded, laughed. "Very obviously. You'll get yourself into trouble."

"Who is she?" he asked quietly.

"Who are they, you mean." Enrico's eyes rested on the backs of the three girls in white and the old man.

Enrico's mother overheard them. *"They* are our nearest neighbors. The villa is on land we bought from them. Old Bagheri used to be quite a wealthy peasant, but I think they've fallen on hard times. It would have to be hard times for a Sicilian to sell an outsider land. His wife is dead; the eldest son has gone north and the eldest daughter is already settled. That leaves three daughters who will cost a pretty penny to marry off. Dowries, you know."

They stopped in the small café at the end of the square and ordered coffee. Alexei noticed that Enrico's mother was the only woman in the darkened room.

"I warned Alexei of the dangers of staring," Enrico chuckled.

Alexei could feel himself flushing, could feel the imprint of the girl's secret glance on his face.

Signora Mazzocchi sipped the strong sweet coffee and looked reflectively at Alexei. "Enrico's right. Eyes in Sicily speak loudly. And with them marriages are made, honor defiled, vendettas begun."

"And it always starts in church," Enrico said with a touch of malice.

"The only regular meeting place. Otherwise the young are kept strictly apart," his mother concurred.

"There's an old proverb here," Enrico added. " 'Everyone can go to church' "—he paused dramatically—" 'and prison.' " He laughed. "Chances are you won't see the lovely Miss Bagheri more than three times in the three weeks that we're here."

"A ghastly state of things," Alexei said lightly. But in his mind, Enrico's words took on the form of a challenge.

On the way back to their villa, Signora Mazzocchi pointed out the Bagheri home. It was the last house in the town, a crumbling but not unimposing residence which bordered on a grove of gnarled olive trees. From behind the curtained upper floor balcony, Alexei thought he heard the sound of voices. He looked up and sensed rather than saw those eyes gazing down at him. Incomprehensibly, he shivered in the noonday heat.

Later that afternoon, while they were lounging round the pool, Signora Mazzocchi announced that she would be going to the Bagheri home that evening to pay her seasonal respects.

Alexei, who had been unable to settle into his book and had instead resigned himself to a daydream in which three girls in white featured largely, felt an unaccustomed nervousness coil in his stomach.

"Would you both like to accompany me?" Her words seemed to come from a great distance. Not trusting his answer, Alexei jumped noisily into the pool.

"Yes, why not," he heard Enrico say. "You want to come to the Bagheris', don't you, Alexei?" he shouted after him.

Alexei nodded vaguely and then plunged again into the cool water.

The room into which old Bagheri sternly ushered them looked as if it had never been penetrated by a shaft of light. A large worn refectory table in the midst of which stood a ceramic bowl of dried flowers ate most of the space. An old woman who didn't look at them deposited a tray on it and shuffled away. Signor Bagheri poured silently and gave them each a glass of pungent wine, a golden biscuit.

They made desultory conversation about the weather, the poor crops, the poorer fishing, the latest series of Mafia "accidents" in Palermo. All the time Alexei waited impatiently for the appearance of the three girls. Signora Mazzocchi seemed to read his mind.

"And your daughters?" she asked.

"They are well, good children, the holy mother be praised," the old man answered. Alexei sensed the suspicion in the look he cast over himself and Enrico. "Giulia has had an offer from Signor Novellone. Father Paolo arranged it," Bagheri said with a touch of pride. "And he tells me my youngest, Francesca, has the makings of a vocation." A smile with a touch of guile lit his lined face.

Alexei flinched. Was Francesca the girl whose eyes had left an indelible trace on him?

"How splendid." Signora Mazzocchi kept the conversation flowing and then rose. It was time for them to go. Signor Bagheri must come and repay their visit. The peaches were doing very well this year. He must help himself. They couldn't possibly eat all of them. She chatted their way out through the darkened hall.

Behind a closed door, Alexei thought he heard the murmur of girlish voices. He paused. And then, just as he had lost all hope of seeing her, the door opened a fraction and from shadowy depths he felt those eyes blazing at him once more.

When Enrico didn't engage him in forays around the island, Alexei took to strolling slowly in front of the Bagheri house or along that stretch of orchard where the two families' properties adjoined. He didn't know quite what drove him to it, but whatever it was, it was strong enough to withstand Enrico's teasing.

One sultry afternoon after siesta, he was rewarded by the sight of the three girls sitting at a short distance in the cool of the olive grove. They were embroidering, their hands and voices lively over the chatter of the cicadas. One of them turned at the rustle of his footsteps. Alexei, lost as to a form of greeting after his long wait, simply nodded and walked on. There was silence from the girls and then a rush of giggling. He perched himself a little higher up the slope where he could see them quite clearly, if not in detail, and listened. Their talk wafted over to him with the fluttering of the sea breeze. From what he could hear he was certain they couldn't see him. He felt like a spy. But he kept his ground.

They were talking about Giulia's forthcoming wedding. How many pillows and sheets there still were to embroider, the guests who would come to the party. And then one of them asked, he wasn't sure which, "And do you think old Novellone can still do it? He's almost as ancient as Papa." A spatter of giggling. Alexei flushed. He heard the tones of a reprimand, from Giulia, he imagined, and then another giggle. "He's probably all shriveled, a prune. You'll have to dance for him, like Susannah before the elders."

He was certain, though he had never heard it, that the voice was Francesca's. The words startled him. So girls, too, proper girls, thought about these things. A kaleidoscope of possibilities invaded him. He lay back, closed his eyes, saw Francesca's sleek head bent demurely in prayer, the hot flash of her look. He felt himself stirring.

"Ale-e-e-xei." Enrico's call brought him back. He stumbled up, sensed with a tinge of shame the girls' startled looks, rushed toward his friend.

"We're off to Palermo for the evening. Have you forgotten?"

"No, no, just dozing," Alexei mumbled. "It's the heat."

Enrico looked at him a little skeptically.

The next day the girls were there again. This time, it was Francesca who sat facing the Mazzocchi property. He recognized the classical modeling of her face instantly, the secret heat of those hooded eyes as they rested on him for a moment, before again returning to their work. Today he made his way unobtrusively, silently, to a slightly different spot above the girls. He didn't know what it was that imposed his stealth, but he knew he didn't want to be noticed by the others. He sat resting on the twisted gray bark of an olive tree and watched the picture the girls made in the distance.

The breeze today had changed direction and he could hear only the indistinct murmur of their voices. To his right, a little further up the hill on Bagheri's land, a tethered goat rhythmically munched at strands of straw, wisps of herb.

Suddenly, he saw Francesca rise and saunter up the hill. Nervously, he watched the slow movement of her hips in the full skirt. She seemed to be coming directly toward him. He sat transfixed, not daring to move. Could she see him? When she was almost abreast of him, she reached into her pocket and with a casual gesture threw something over the tumbling rock terrace which divided the two properties. Then, without raising her eyes, she carried on up the hill, her pace unbroken, toward the goat. From her pocket, she now brought a clothful of potato peel and apple cores and laid them on the ground.

Alexei didn't dare to breathe. He still didn't know whether she had seen him. It was only when she had completed her meandering trajectory and rejoined her sisters that his eyes chanced on the object which she had thrown over the terrace. A stone, odd in its whiteness. Alexei picked it up. Paper. Paper wrapped around the stone. His heart leapt. He uncurled it carefully. A message in minuscule writing. "Tonight at midnight, in the goat shed."

He wanted to jump up and shout his glee. It was so unexpected. So unbelievable. He would be able to talk to her, to see her, perhaps, his throat caught, even to touch her.

Well before the appointed hour, Alexei slipped out of the villa and trod as softly as he could over uneven ground to the meeting place. An ocean of stars lit his way and illumined the small shack which stood just a short distance over the terrace on Bagheri's land. He perched on the dry earth and waited, imagining Francesca's stealth. She must, nervously now, be making certain that her sisters were asleep, slowly creeping down creaking stairs, carefully, silently, unbolting a door, then racing, racing toward him. He imagined her light-footed tread, the nimble motion of her body, the warm flush of her skin, her full reddened lips. Excitement suffused him. He waited.

He waited well past the appointed hour. As the air grew chill, he began to worry. Worry that she had been found out. That old Bagheri had caught her, punished her. That her elder sister had stopped her, talked her out of coming. Then his worry took on a tinge of suspicion, of anger. Perhaps it had all been a hoax. Perhaps she had never intended to come. Perhaps her sisters had put her up to it, to make fun of the alien. A gnawing disappointment succeeded the anger. She wasn't interested in him. He had misinterpreted her look, misread the meaning in those eyes. The message might even have been for someone else. She had a secret beau. He had stumbled on the place where they left each other messages. His imagination ran riot. He envisaged her delicate body in another's arms, her secret eyes warm in adoration on another's face. He grew hot despite the chill of the night.

In that eternity of waiting, Alexei ran through a whole gamut of emotions he had never before experienced. They made up the primary repertoire of the man in love.

By the time the first chirrups of the dawn chorus had begun, his longing for Francesca had taken up the whole of his being. He wondered about her, wondered whether a girl like that, a girl who prayed in church, a girl whose family Signora Mazzocchi visited, might let him kiss her. He wondered what her father had meant by a vocation. Wondered about the note which nestled secretly in his pocket.

It was the first time that a woman had invaded the entirety of his imagination. He was no longer himself. He cursed the day's plans which would take him with Enrico to Gela. He wanted only to see Francesca, to force her gaze to rest on him if only for a moment, to clasp her in his arms.

All that day's sights and journeyings passed him by in a haze. The only palpable event was his waiting. He had already determined that he would return to the appointed spot that evening. Like a pendulum, his mood rhythmically moved from hopeful anticipation to despair.

That night a sliver of a moon dulled the stars, but lit the hump of the hills and cast a shadowy glow over the olive grove. Alexei took up his vigil at the side of the shed. He had promised himself he would stay here only an hour. More would be demeaning.

He didn't have long to wait. A few moments past midnight she was there, a slight figure in a white shift weaving swiftly through the trees. Trapped in the weight of his imaginings, Alexei didn't have words with which to greet her. He stared, trembling slightly, at the proximity of that profile which had haunted him, at the shadows her thick lashes cast on the purity of her cheeks.

Suddenly she looked straight up at him. "I'm glad you've come. I couldn't make it last night," she said shyly, softly.

Joy rushed through him. He took her hand, so small in his, and led her behind the shed, where it seemed to him they were sheltered from the houses.

"My name is Alexei," he said at last, unable to think of anything else.

"I know." She smiled, showing tiny white teeth against the redness of her mouth. "I'm Francesca."

"I know. Francesca." He tried the name for the first time on his lips, felt its weight. "Francesca," he repeated. He felt the pressure of her fingers and there seemed nothing else for him to do but to kiss those slightly parted lips. She smelled of orange blossom and wild thyme and as she pressed close to him, he was ashamed of the sudden surge of his body. Her lips were so innocent, so tentative, not like the women he had kissed before, been with. He wanted to protect her from himself. He let her go.

But she stayed close to him. Her fingers fluttered through his hair. "I saw you in church. You know, don't you. I thought you looked like the picture of our Lord in the Cappella Palatina. I told my sister, Theresa," she said softly. Her words, coupled with the reverence in her eyes and the sensation of her touch, confused him. He gazed at her, still not quite believing she was there.

"I have to go now. They might find me out." She drew away from him.

"No, please, not yet." He caught her hand, pulled her to him, kissed her passionately now in anticipation of her absence. When he let her go, she flitted down the path.

"Will you come tomorrow?" he whispered after her breathlessly.

"Perhaps. I'll try." She threw him a dark look from brooding eyes.

Alexei leaned heavily against the shed and watched her fleeting form. He didn't move for a long time.

The next night took a decade to arrive. Alexei went through the gestures of conversation, the forms of enthusiasm for what he saw in Messina, but at every turn Francesca invaded his thoughts. Enrico cast strange glances at him, but Alexei pretended not to notice.

It was Saturday. There were guests at the villa and they took an eternity to depart. It was gone midnight before he was able to slip away. He rushed, a little recklessly, to the appointed spot. She was already there.

"I thought you might not be coming." She pouted at him, her eyes downcast.

"I couldn't get away sooner. I've thought of nothing but you all day." He looked at her wonderingly, not quite sure of her reality, that raven head which glowed in the moonlight, the pallor of her upturned face. He touched the shoulder which the shift left bare. So slight, so delicate.

She shivered, moved into the circle of his arms, gave him her lips. He was suddenly aware of the surprising fullness of the breasts pressed against him. Hesitantly he touched their curve. She took his hands and cupped them round that firm heaviness.

"A perfect fit." Her laugh trilled softly. Shining eyes darted at him. "Much better than my own."

A train of imaginings rushed through him, making his loins bound. Her small fluttering hands on her own body, secret, alone, in the dark of night. Exploring. The pleasure of it. And then that face raised in innocent adoration. He drowned the images in the moisture of her mouth. She moaned, drew away, laughed.

"Let me see it," she challenged him. "Let me. I've never seen one. A big one. A real one. Is it like a snake?"

Her words with their mixture of childish curiosity and longing startled him. He felt shy, but her fingers encouraged him.

"Oh." She looked at his erect penis doubtfully. "No, that would never fit." She touched it tentatively.

Alexei drew in his breath, turned away from her.

"Have I hurt you?" Her voice was all remorse. She wrapped her arms around him, buried her face in his back, snuggling against him. "I'll let you touch me. I have a little snake too. He dances."

He kissed her fiercely to cover words which made him dizzy. Her eyes wide, serious on his face, she brought his hand to her mound. It was hot, so hot between her thighs. He rubbed that prickly softness, groaned. With a little cry she leapt away.

"It's Sunday. It's not right." She shook her head so that her hair tumbled heavily over her face. From its midst, she frowned. "I must go," she said, but she lingered for a moment and he stepped toward her. "No." She avoided his arms, scrambled down the hill. Then, coltishly, she looked back at him, giggled. "But I won't tell Father Paolo. No, that I won't."

The next day he set out for church, before Signora Mazzocchi and the new house guests, and with an alacrity which mystified Enrico.

"Is this a case of a Sicilian conversion?" his friend asked him wryly, as he matched his pace to Alexei's rapid one.

Alexei shrugged, not trusting the reasons he might find.

The row they had sat in the previous week was already full and

there was no sign of Francesca or her sisters. In his desperation to
find her, Alexei moved against the flow of people, accidentally jostled
against old Bagheri. The sisters were behind him.

"*Scusi, scusi, signor,*" Alexei mumbled, hoping that his face didn't
show his embarrassment.

The man grunted.

Alexei scuttled into the first place he could find. Enrico, amusement tugging at his dimple, was right behind him. "So now I know
what brings you to church. Remember, I warned you. Watch your
eyes," he murmured to Alexei.

Alexei paid no heed. He waited for a repetition of that look from
Francesca. It never came. Her devotions as she knelt and prayed
and intoned the mass seemed absolute. Not even when it was over
and Alexei lingered in the line of her gaze, did her eyes rest on him
with a glimmer of recognition. He was distraught. He began to think
that he had imagined those heated kisses of the previous night. He
even went out of his way in the crowded square to pay his respects
to Signor Bagheri, exchange a few words with him. But the girls,
immersed in their own conversations, paid no attention to him.

Nor did Francesca appear at their midnight rendezvous or in the
olive grove at all over the next few days. Alexei was beside himself.
He almost turned to Enrico for advice, but he couldn't find the
words with which to do it.

On Wednesday evening, while he was changing for dinner, the
maid came to Alexei and said Signora Mazzocchi would like to see
him in her own sitting room for a few moments. He was taken aback
by the unusual request, but he made haste and within minutes he
was knocking at her door.

She was arranging flowers in a bright ceramic bowl and she gestured him casually toward a cane chair.

"Are you enjoying your stay here, Alexei?" she asked as she
clipped an inch of stem from a perfect crimson rose.

"Very much, thank you," Alexei murmured.

Hazel eyes met his and studied him. "I had a visit from the priest
today, Father Paolo."

Alexei grew warm at the mention of the name he had recently
heard on other lips. "Oh yes," he mumbled, played with the button
of his shirt. "I haven't met him yet."

Signora Mazzocchi left her flowers and perched on the table closer
to him. "He told me you had been seeing the youngest Bagheri
girl?" It was a question which asked for confirmation.

Alexei shrugged uncomfortably, nodded.

Signora Mazzocchi tried a half smile and gazed at the youth. He was beautiful, she decided then, though it was not a word she usually applied to men. It was something to do with the serious set of those lips, the expression of those deep eyes. He would be capable of great passion some day. But not yet. She continued with her task, a delicate one.

"You know in Sicily girls do not see young men unchaperoned. And even then . . . Francesca's family is an honorable one."

Alexei squirmed, said nothing.

"I do not think your father would approve of your marrying or even being engaged so young," she plunged on.

Alexei leapt up. Those words, so formal, so definitive, belonged to another world. They had nothing to do with Francesca. With him. With what they felt.

"I know. I know what you're thinking." Signora Mazzocchi looked on him kindly. "In any event, Father Paolo confirmed old Bagheri's hint that Francesca has a vocation. He doesn't want her deflected from it by the chance appearance of a young man from the decadent North."

"What's it to do with him? With them?" Alexei's growing anger crept into his voice.

"Everything." Signora Mazzocchi laughed lightly. "Young girls are hardly free to make their own choices here. Or in Milan for that matter. Francesca is only sixteen."

Alexei turned away from her, but her voice stopped him on his way to the door. "Alexei, I suggest you do not try to see Francesca again." It was said casually, but Alexei heard the sternness of the warning. Signora Mazzocchi put a hand on his arm, made him turn to her. "This weekend there is the Festa, that will take your mind off things. And then, soon after that, we go. You understand what I am saying?"

Alexei nodded. Not trusting his voice, he moved swiftly from the room. It wasn't fair, he raged inwardly. Wasn't right. He was being treated like a criminal. He had visions of Francesca being forcibly constrained. Kept from him. He rushed out of the house. Without thinking where he was going, he strode toward the olive grove.

They had done nothing wrong. Nothing that called for this form of adult intervention. He justified himself. Exonerated the two of them.

And yet Francesca must have spoken to the priest. Confessed to him. He remembered her promise not to tell Father Paolo. And yet she had. He must have wrung it out of her. She hadn't met his eyes at church that Sunday. Hadn't come to their rendezvous. He recalled for the hundredth time the details of their last meeting. She had been as eager as he was. He hadn't forced her to do anything. He didn't understand. He must speak to her, see her.

Alexei found himself by the little hut which marked the site of their love. The goat was still tethered there tonight, its jaws engaged in endless motion. If only Francesca would come. Alexei threw himself down on the earth, breathed in its fragrance. Wild thyme, like Francesca. How could he reach her? Get past her father? Each scheme that presented itself to him, as he lay there, took on a note of added desperation.

His eyes fell again on the goat. It was nuzzling something white on the ground. A cloth. His mind raced. The cloth Francesca had brought the goat tidbits in. Could it be hers? Would she come to fetch it again? Could he leave her a note in it? If someone else found it, it would compromise her. But he had to take the chance. He located a smooth round stone, thought of a message which could be construed in a variety of ways, inscribed it on a small leaf he tore from his notebook, wrapped it round the stone, and placed that on the cloth.

All he had written was a list of pleases and buried amidst them the word "come."

But he felt a little better. The single action, no matter how small, had at least ruptured the monotony of his passive waiting.

Later that night, after a dinner during which he managed to conduct himself with a modicum of normality, he returned to the spot. He did not expect to see Francesca, but he needed to be there. The goat was gone and to his delight so was the cloth, bearing, as far as he could make out, his secret message. He leaned against the stone wall of the hut and gazed at the moon. In the distance he could make out the mellifluous sounds of a shepherd's pipe. He was surprised to find himself uttering a prayer. A prayer that must, he imagined, be addressed to some pagan deity of place who could waft Francesca to him, unveil her from the bark of an olive tree, hew her out of the rocky escarpment.

And the next evening, almost as if his prayer had taken flesh, she was there, magically released from the shadowy folds of the hill. He rushed toward her breathing her name, but she eluded his embrace.

"I've come, but only to tell you that I can't anymore. I've promised."

There was no luster in the eyes she focused on him. Her face looked small, sad.

"What is it, Francesca?" He reached for her again. The way she evaded his touch angered him. Despite her protestations, he took hold of her hand, held it fiercely and pulled her up the slope toward the shelter of the hut. "What's happened?" In the somber light he examined the curves of her face.

She shrugged listlessly. "Father Paolo has forbidden it. He is right."

He stroked the heavy fall of her hair. "But we haven't done anything bad," he murmured.

Her eyes flashed suddenly with their old fire. "I wish I were a man," she said bluntly. "Then nothing is ever bad. Wrong."

Her words, their bitter edge, took him aback. In that instant, he was blindingly aware of the gulf between them. "No—yes." His words stumbled. "I'm sorry. I . . ."

"It's not your fault." Her hand fluttered to his cheek and then darted away again, checking itself. He caught it in mid-air, drew her down, so that they sat together, leaning against the stone wall. Gently he wound his arm around her, thrilling to the smooth skin of those soft rounded shoulders. They gazed at the shapes the moonlit incline thrust at them, each buried in private thoughts. He could hear the rush of her breathing. The ache it set up in him seemed unappeasable. She seemed to share it for she turned to face him, her lips parted.

"One last time can't matter," she murmured. "I shall have all of eternity to repent." Dark eyes challenged him and in a rush of passion, he pressed her to him, kissing her eyes, her cheeks, her neck, her lips. She clung to him fiercely, her whole fiery body intent against him. And then in a rush she disentangled herself.

"Goodbye, Alexei." Her lips formed the words soundlessly.

And then with a sad little submissive wave, she was off.

He stood watching her for a moment, his limbs growing cold. And then anger uncoiled from his stomach and surged through him. He ran, ran like a man possessed, down, down the incline toward the thud of the sea. Ran past the moored fishing boats of the bay toward a neighboring cove. There he almost tripped over a couple, their bodies intertwined. They sat up, disturbed by his footfall. The woman's skin shone bare around the brief darkness of her bikini. "Northerners." The word rose to Alexei's lips with the emphasis of a curse.

He was surprised by its appearance there. Surprised by the strength of his identification with Francesca. A mere question of geography separated her from this bikini-clad woman on the beach. A woman who could fearlessly wrap her arms around her lover, bare her body to the breath of the sea.

Alexei clambered over boulders, leapt into the next cove, and dropping shirt and trousers in a heap, plunged into the sea. With all the savagery of his youth, he pounded out his anger, his sense of injustice on the waves.

He saw Francesca only one more time. It was on the last night of the Festa as the brightly decorated floats moved through the heaving lantern-lit streets of the town. Amidst the shouts of the hawkers and the crowds, she wafted past, a waxen figure in a holy scene with the Christ child at its center. Head lowered in rapturous adoration, she looked in her crimson and purple gown like a saint in a medieval icon. For a moment, he thought her angelic smile was directed at him, but he realized his face must be indistinguishable in the crowd.

"Francesca, Mother tells me, is destined for the convent at Agrigento," Enrico informed him as he followed the direction of Alexei's gaze.

A blaze of fireworks saved Alexei from the task of replying. Not, in any event, that he could have found words to suit the confusion of his emotions.

It was only in later years that this became possible. And then, his means of expression was the medium of film—a film which subtly explored the condition of women in the South, the fetters which trapped them, fetters which bred a peculiar sexual heat, fetters of family and tradition and poverty.

And then Rosa had come to hone his sense of justice with a razor-sharp tongue and force him to read the dictionary of desire through another set of eyes.

CHAPTER
SEVENTEEN

*E*ven after she had accepted his proposal, Katherine Jardine was unable to say for certain when her wanting of Carlo Negri had begun.

Perhaps it had already been there all those years ago when she had first met him in Switzerland at the Princesse's with Violette?

No, it wasn't at that first meeting. Although she had already been aware of him in that distant past. And again in New York. The magnetism of his eyes, those indolent gestures.

But even if desire had been there, she wouldn't have recognized it then. She would certainly not have been able to acknowledge its existence. That was possible only now.

Katherine sighed and spread her books out on her preferred table in the stacks of London's Courtauld Institute. Thick volumes whose contents by turn excited her and induced a daydreaming stupor— Panofsky's *Meaning in the Visual Arts*, Momigliano's work on the Renaissance. Richly colored plates on heavily embossed paper, Leonardo, Titian, Rembrandt.

Another few months and her three-year course at the Institute would be at an end. Three years of reading and discussion and intent looking. Three years of living in London and exploring the entrails of the sprawling city. And now there was the terrifying hurdle of her Finals.

But she couldn't concentrate today. It was no use.

She pulled out the letter she had only glanced at before setting off from her flat on Highbury Fields that morning. Four pages in Jacob's dense hand. She skimmed to focus on the relevant passages.

"I have had a letter from Carlo Negri asking for your hand in marriage."

"Her hand." The expression was so antiquated, so absurd, Katherine thought. It leapt out at her from Jacob's fluent prose like a piece of mistaken phraseology. But she could imagine that Carlo, too, in writing to her father had used dusty formalities. He had told her he was going to write, murmured something about families, appropriate forms.

Katherine read on.

"I must say, I was rather surprised. I had no idea things had gone so far. Marriage, my dear Kat, is a serious thing, and without wishing to fall into the trap of clichés, you should at least *believe* it will last forever."

Irritation suffused her. How could Jacob take that tone with her? Had he thought seriously about marriage when he had wed Sylvie, believed it would last forever? And even if he had, what good had it done?

"Carlo is a good twelve years older than you, a man of a certain experience. He may want different things of marriage than you do. You're still very young. I had thought, when we last spoke of these things, that you wanted to work, to pursue a career, and not to settle into childbearing straight away.

"Still, if marriage is your wish, I shall, of course, not stand in your way."

There was a PS. "Have you spoken with Violette about all this? I believe she knows Carlo rather well."

Katherine winced with a mixture of guilt and triumph as she thought of her half sister. Imagine Jacob suggesting that she talk to Violette about Carlo now, as if all that hadn't happened, hadn't been over eons ago.

With an irritated gesture she crunched her father's letter into a tiny tight ball and took a piece of paper from her folder. "Dear Pappy," she began with hard sure strokes, then changed her mind: "Dear Jacob, I want Carlo. We shall let you know details of the wedding. Love, Kat."

As she sealed the letter, she wondered again at the certainty she felt about that wanting if about nothing else. When had it really begun, this wanting of Carlo?

That first summer in Rome? Yes, that must have been it. That first glorious month on her own in the world's most beautiful, most surprising city, a city which seemed to contain all of recorded time within the precincts of its seven hills.

For her course at the Courtauld, she needed another language and she chose Italian over German. Jacob, once he had been convinced of her determination to study in London, had agreed that a month in Italy learning Italian would not be a bad thing for a budding art historian. Princesse Mathilde had seen to the rest, had arranged for her to stay with an old friend of hers, Maria Novona, who lived in a vast flat a stone's throw from the Villa Borghese.

Maria Novona had arranged a little afternoon party for her, so that she could meet some young Italians, since her course catered only to foreigners. Whether by the Princesse's intervention or by pure chance, Carlo Negri had come to that party.

He had arrived a little late and Katherine had been aware of his eyes even before she had consciously acknowledged his presence. He had given her one of his lazy smiles by way of greeting. *"La bella Katerina,* now a student in Rome," he had said lightly, his gaze resting on her just a moment too long before taking in the crowd of young men and women around her. "When this is over, will you come with me for a drive? I'll show you some sights." She had nodded her agreement and he had then withdrawn to talk to Maria Novona, not engaging with the group again, though she had the impression that his attention never left her.

A drive with Carlo was like nothing else she had ever experienced. She had been terrified at first as that gleaming low-slung Ferrari had raced demonically over narrow roads past Frascati and up into the Alban Hills. But then, just as she thought she must cry out, ask him to slow down, the sheer exhilaration of speed had taken her over. Her mind, all her anxieties had seemed to dissolve so that she was aware only of the wind rushing through her hair, the flickering movement of light in trees, the sheer physicality of hurtling recklessly through space. There was no past, no future, no responsibility, only that headlong movement. And the shape of that man at her side controlling it.

When they had pulled up above the lake and the Castel Gandolfo, her knees, her hands were trembling. She didn't know whence the strength had come to resist Carlo's kiss. But somehow, perhaps from sheer force of habit, she had turned her face away and extricated herself from the car. After two repeated nights with Ted some months back, nights where there had been no Shakespeare to lull her senses, awkward nights which gave her little pleasure and less satisfaction, she had decided that all that was not for her. She even went so far as to think that the pleasures of sex might well be an invention of her father's generation, a great con perpetrated by the disciples of Freud. It was a time when she felt most bitterly about Jacob.

Carlo, unlike some of the young men she knew in New York, had not persisted. She had heard a low, sardonic chuckle behind her, *"E bene, è così,"* and then he was beside her, looking down at her, his eyes at once dangerous and approving. It was from that look, without quite knowing why, that she dated the start of their relationship.

The next day a card had arrived inviting her and Maria Novona to take tea with Signora la Contessa Buonaterra, Carlo's mother.

"You are honored, Katherine. La Contessa is very selective with her guests," Maria Novona had said with an inflection Katherine didn't quite understand.

The Buonaterra family palazzo was some ninety kilometers outside Rome. As its gloomy gray stone façade emerged through the cypress-lined drive the following Sunday, Katherine shifted uncomfortably in her seat. The heavy baroque weight of the building with its formidably muscled reclining figures oppressed her, blotted out the sun's rays. She preferred to let her eyes rest on the symmetry of gardens sculpted out of hilltop, and beyond, the blue haze of the sea dotted with tiny islands.

A servant in full livery opened vast doors to them, led them through an expanse of echoing hall to a vaulted room which at first glance seemed to Katherine to be peopled by marble and painted figures. But some of them moved—like ghosts amidst the somber grandeur, statuesque women in extravagant gowns, silent men tottering under the weight of years. Katherine dragged her steps, looked up at the ceiling with its bold images, so much more vibrant than what was in front of her.

The Palazzo Buonaterra was grander than any house she had ever visited. She had had no idea that Carlo lived this way. And when he emerged smiling, white-suited, alive, from the depths of the room, she had to look twice to make sure it was him. He seemed to read her astonishment, for his lips twisted into a leisurely irony. "Welcome. Welcome to the familial pile," he murmured just for her ears, and then ushered her and Maria Novona to a far corner of the room. "Mama will want to meet you. We must pay respects to her first."

The familiarity of the word *mama* seemed to bear no relation to the figure who sat regally in a chair which to Katherine had all the appearance of a throne. She felt somehow that she should curtsey but she had no idea how to go about that gesture.

"Ah Signora Novona and Signorina Jardine, the young protégée of Principessa Mathilde. And how is the dear Principessa?" Pale gray eyes examined her from above a haughty, jutting nose. Katherine felt as if each detail of her features, her clothes, her movements was being surveyed, judged, all while the thin mouth moved, smiling a little, eliciting response from her. The Countess seemed principally interested in details of her parentage. There was an additional smile when Katherine named her mother, a murmur, "Ah yes. Kowalska, Polish, Catholics, I know of the family." And then, "Sit by me, child. Take some tea," and a host of other introductions, cousins, uncles, aunts, politicians, judges. At one point, she had intercepted a glance between mother and son, a glance of, what had it been, complicity?

When Maria Novona had stood to leave, Katherine had breathed a silent sigh of relief. Carlo had accompanied them to the door of the room. "I think, Katherine, you have passed the Roman mother test," he had whispered to her, his long lower lip curling.

She had seen him only once more during that first stay in Rome.

"Have time for a coffee, Katherine, before the lecture?"

A familiar voice startled Katherine from her reverie.

"Oh yes, sure." She looked dazedly at her fellow student and housemate, Chris, and tumbled her books into her bag.

"You've been working too hard. You've got the pallor of one of those swooning pre-Raphaelite maidens," Chris joked, flicking through the pages of a book and pointing to a fiery-haired Rossetti. "See?"

"I'm fine, Chris. Fit as a Rubens," Katherine insisted. She liked Chris. They were mates. Together, over the years, they had done the galleries and museums, arguing over the Rembrandts in the National Gallery, gazing at the impressionists at the Tate, venturing into the Institute of Contemporary Arts in Dover Street.

But today, she was devoid of conversation. The mood of reminiscence wouldn't leave her. It obliterated Chris's words, followed her into her four o'clock lecture, where she succumbed to it.

Throughout that first year in London, she had heard from Carlo only once. A cryptic postcard had arrived from New York. King Kong atop the Empire State Building. The message in Italian read *"Saltare o non saltare."* To leap or not to leap. *"Auguri"* and his name, signed in a bold hand. She had spent some time pondering the words and then set the card aside.

Life in London was too busy for a great deal of reflection, what with her courses, trips to museums, and weekend visits to Portia in Cambridge, where they cycled through tiny streets or punted along the magical Cam and chatted endlessly. Increasingly, too, there was a small circle of friends with whom she went to Beatles' concerts, for strolls along Carnaby Street or the King's Road, or to a mass of theaters from the Royal Court to the Aldwych to a series of thriving fringe venues. The men she had singled out as friends at the Courtauld seemed content not to make passes at her. If one of them did, she froze him with her cool gray eyes and said she was distinctly not interested. She might also repeat the line about sex being the great Freudian con. In her closer circle none of them minded. And London had so much else to offer. It had been a wonderful first year.

And then, the next summer she had returned to Rome. She had passed her Italian exam, but nonetheless she knew that her Italian was poor. On top of that she had chosen the Italian Renaissance as her special subject and Rome was a treasure trove to her.

She had no immediate intention of contacting Carlo in Rome. But during her first week there, she went to a club with a group of acquaintances from her previous visit. She was dancing with one of them. A slow number so different from what she had grown used to in London, and she had the uncomfortable feeling that her flimsy King's Road skirt showed far too much leg for conservative Rome. In order to cover her embarrassment, she flung back her hair which she now wore, London fashion, in a long loose mane.

It was in the midst of that gesture that she met his eyes. There was a hint of anger in his features before they settled into their characteristic insouciance. He nodded, smiled a little mockingly. For some reason, she could feel an uncustomary flush rising to her face. He was dancing with a tall slim blonde who looked as if she had stepped off a catwalk. Katherine watched him covertly. She liked the way he danced, those sure, effortless movements.

A few moments later, he came over to their table. "You should have told me you were in town," he said in a proprietary tone. "I'll take you out for lunch tomorrow."

"No. No, I can't at lunchtime," Katherine demurred.

"For dinner, then. At eight. You're at Maria Novona's?"

Before she had a chance to answer, he nodded briskly and was gone.

The next morning as she was leaving for class, a vast bouquet of gardenias met her at the door. They were for her. She searched for the card. Carlo.

Sometimes she thought it was that fragrant array of flowers he sent her daily throughout that period in Rome which fed her love. No one had ever sent her flowers before.

At other times she knew that they were only the backdrop to something deeper, darker.

That evening he drove her at his usual daredevil pace to the outskirts of the city and parked amidst trees in front of the glow of a restaurant. He turned to her, his eyes bright with the excitement of the speed, and lightly skimmed her thigh where her skirt left it bare.

She had lurched away from him, as if his touch scalded her.

He had shaken his dark head mockingly. "So much womanly leg and still a child. Come, Katerina." He forced her face to him and kissed her, slowly, deeply. She had never felt anything like that before. It was like the wildness of the car hurtling through space. It made her forget everything but his lips. And it frightened her. She struggled away from him. Fled from the car.

He was next to her in a moment, his hand resting lightly on her shoulder. "There is time, *mia Katerina,* plenty of time. But soon, soon, I, we, shall make you a woman."

He began, throughout those weeks in Rome, to woo her assiduously. One night it was dinner and dancing on the Via Veneto amidst the blazing flashes of the paparazzi. The next, the race-course. On the weekend, he took her to the family estate and patiently taught her to ride. And when her horse began to gallop aping his and she cried out, he stopped only after some moments, relishing, she sensed, her fear, which made her a little more pliant in his arms. His kisses grew bruising, more ardent, as did hers, despite herself, in response. But still, she didn't quite know why, she resisted him. Turned away.

One day he had insisted on taking her on a round of designer boutiques so that she would be appropriately dressed for the morrow's occasion. She didn't quite recognize the elegant figure that paraded before his connoisseur's eyes and acknowledged his choices.

The special occasion turned out again to be the racetrack, but this time he was driving and her heart bounded to the speed of his car as it looped and vanished before her eyes. She remembered something Violette had said, years ago, about old families, about being in love with death.

He came second and dejection haunted their evening.

"What do you do when you're not doing this?" she asked him, trying to draw him out later in the lamplit cavern of the restaurant.

He laughed, the planes of his face suddenly mischievous. "I look at my land. I gamble," he said. "And make love to beautiful women."

She flushed.

"Some of them like it." He gave her his dimpled smile.

"I . . . I might like it," she countered him, irked.

"Yes, yes, I think you might. Soon, yes, Katerina. Very soon." He paused for a moment, reflected, and said with a note of seriousness, "I like you, Katerina. I'm gambling on you." Then he chuckled. "And there are other kinds of gambling, of course, the stock exchange amongst them."

That night he had let her go without trying to kiss her. She had missed his lips, the scent of his hair, those arms tight around her. Like she did now.

"Miss Jardine, are you with us today? I asked whether you had brought the Donatello slides with you."

"Yes, yes." Katherine fumbled in her bag, embarrassed. She was no use to anyone this afternoon. Jacob's letter with its admonishments had provoked a flood of reminiscence.

The lecturer's words flowed in the dimmed light and Katherine tried to concentrate on the screen in front of her. But all she could see was Carlo in that khaki flying suit he had worn on the last weekend they had had together in Rome.

But she had woken that day bathed in sweat. A dream, a nightmare haunted her eyelids. She couldn't quite make it out. It had something to do with her mother. She hadn't dreamt of Sylvie in a long time. But she had been there in that dream. Very tall. Forbidding. In a black dress. And Katherine, it must have been a very little Katherine, had brushed against her legs, wanting to be lifted, needing to feel arms around her, holding her.

And then she had woken, remembering nothing more, except the sense of that need, the hunger. And with it fear.

The roar of the plane's engine had been deafening. But the excitement on Carlo's face had infected her. And the sheer pleasure of being suspended in space over the hills of Rome. Seeing the frame of the Colosseum, the white mass of the Capitol, the winding Tiber, the tiny streets and then the dome of the St. Peter's from this new perspective, she had felt light-headed, exhilarated. And as they had looped toward the sea and he had told her it was her turn to take the controls, her initial terror had slid into a joyous intoxication.

When they had landed, her heart was pounding and her knees were like jelly. She was grateful for his arm around her, the solid strength of his body.

"You're beautiful." He had kissed her lightly on the forehead. "Have I told you often enough?"

They had driven to the coast and walked arm in arm along an empty beach. She felt airy, light, as if the plane had moved her into another sphere, swallowed all the fears she might have. And when his arms folded around her and he kissed her, she returned his passion with an uncustomary freedom. He pulled her down on the sand and covered her with his body so that she could feel every inch of him indented against her. Desire, coursing, unfamiliar, bounded through her, drowning her.

"Yes, Katerina, yes, at last," his breath moaned in her ear. And suddenly in that moment, she didn't know quite what brought it on, perhaps the fact that she was lying down, perhaps the fact of his voice, her dream came back to her and with a panic, she wrenched away from him and ran, ran as fast as she could along the expanse of the beach.

If she drowned in the need that he wakened, then he could be the only one to save her. The thought formulated itself foggily in her mind as she ran, repeated itself over and over until it turned to nonsense. But she was running as if to save her life.

They didn't speak on the way back to Rome. And when she uttered a hesitant thank you, he didn't respond. The car sped away almost before she had had a chance to close the door. She could see the surly set of his shoulders. She felt desolate, felt she would never see him again. At the same time, she had a sense of relief. As if she had been given back herself.

But a day later, he had turned up in order to drive her to the airport. There was a different light in his eye, the mockery tinged with pain, as if somehow he had at once won and lost a bet. She had chattered unstoppably in order to cover her confusion. And when it was time to say goodbye, he had looked at her with what she could only read as frank admiration. "I shall see you in London, perhaps," he said. And then playfully, so that she wasn't sure of his intent, he had whispered, "You'll save yourself for me."

He had begun to come to London, a day here, a weekend there, usually without warning. He had shown her a London she didn't know, the London of breakfast at the Connaught and Mayfair gambling clubs and polo weekends in country houses. He had friends here, acquaintances, an international set which mingled rock stars and photographers, gentry, politicians and debutantes. They were hardly the circle in which she normally moved. She felt shy at first, ill at ease. And when the men made passes at her or the photographers asked her if she would sit for them, she looked to Carlo dubiously. Usually, all she could read in his face was his habitual indolence with a glint of irony. Sometimes, there was something else, which she thought looked like approval.

In those months, he no longer tried to kiss her, though occasionally he would stroke her hair, trace the lines of her face. It puzzled her, distressed her. She had asked him one night hesitantly. "Don't you want me anymore?"

He had turned smoldering eyes on her. "*Mia carissima Katerina*, I am not a little boy. When you are ready, you will let me know. And then, perhaps . . ."

"Now, will you kiss me now." Her voice broke as she said it. They were sitting in front of her flat in the Porsche he had hired for the weekend.

"Now?" He had taken her hand and caressed it slowly, finger by finger, so that she could feel each inch of her skin. "Just a kiss?" he had teased her.

She had nodded abruptly.

And almost in mimicry of her, he had shaken his head. "No. I'm not ready."

"I hate you," she had raged at him before she could control her words. "I hate you and your snooty useless friends with their Rolls-Royces and their horses and their empty heads and . . ."

He had caught her arm just as she was about to bound from the car and pulled her to him, kissing her so that desire leapt at her entrails, kindled her cheeks.

"And I, little Miss Jardine from Madame Chardin's school, I think I am rather beginning to love you. Though you are growing into an intolerable intellectual snob with your Vietnam demonstrations here and your Donatellos there and your professors this and that. Don't forget there would never have been an Italian renaissance if there hadn't been those contemptible families like mine to finance it."

Her lips still tingling, her ears ringing at his use of the word *love*, she had been unable to summon a response. All she wanted to do was to ask him to repeat the first part of what he had said, to kiss her again. Instead she sat quietly, unable to move or to speak.

"Perhaps," he had said after a moment, "you should invite me to meet some of your friends, since you despise mine so much."

"All right. Tomorrow. For lunch. Or a drink. I don't know if there's any food in the house." And with that she had raced breathlessly from the car.

She remembered every detail of his arrival at the house in Highbury Fields which she shared with a group of friends. Carlo, in uncustomary jeans, a dark blue sweater, a leather jacket thrown casually over his shoulders. He had stood quietly by the door of her room and looked with something like amazement at the narrow bed, the desk with its load of books, the wall above it with its collection of postcards.

"Yes," he had said softly, "just as I imagined it. All you would need to do is replace the postcards with a crucifix and we have the perfect novice's cell."

"What do you mean?" she had blurted out.

"I'm just teasing you." He had smiled and reflectively traced the line of her cheek. "And these friends, are you going to dare show me to them?"

"Since you've dressed appropriately for the occasion, I just might." It had been her turn to tease.

"I didn't want to put you to shame," he laughed.

The ring of the doorbell saved her from having to reply. "That must be Portia. You remember Portia, my friend at Madame Chardin's?" She raced to the door, hugged Portia, who was grumbling that she could stay only a little while since she had to be at a meeting; called her housemates together, all five of them, Chris and Tim and Jude and Penelope and Sally, made introductions, poured a not very wonderful wine and watched.

Carlo had sat quietly in the big sagging chair, but despite his jeans, his quiet, he had exuded a style, a magnetism, a sun-warmed glow which marked him as ineradicably foreign. Chris and Tim with their shaggy beards and student pallor faded into insignificance. Her girlfriends, Portia apart, tittered a little too much. Still, she had been anxious for him, worried that her friends might draw him out on politics or books he hadn't read, or simply ask him what he did. But the hour before he stood to go passed smoothly enough.

At the door, the sardonic smile now firmly back on his face, he asked her, "Well, did I pass the friends test?"

Katherine squirmed in embarrassment. "I'll tell you next time we meet," she managed to say.

Only when she closed the door did she remember that his words echoed those he had used to her in his mother's house. It perplexed her, but she didn't have time to think about it, since Portia now followed her inexorably back to her room for what she called a private chat.

"Kat, you're not in love with that man, are you?"

Katherine had never considered that particular formulation and its expression had brought the color to her face.

"If you are you're even madder than I think. Why, he must exude that charm on at least ten women a week and pop them into bed quicker than you can say Jack Robinson. You—who won't even come close to a decent man's bedroom."

They had had the argument about Katherine's recalcitrance every time she had gone up to Cambridge to see her friend the previous year.

"He's very kind to me," Katherine said softly, but she was bristling.

"Kind!" Portia flopped on to Katherine's bed and made as if to throw a pillow at her. "Kind? Katherine, how many times do I have to tell you that you're an exceedingly beautiful woman. Men like that are not noted for their kindness to beautiful women. You're going to get your little tootsies burnt, not to mention more delicate parts. Why, he's just a playboy. A playboy with a lot of filthy lucre. We agreed on that years ago, if you'll remember, when we were at Princesse Mat's."

"You don't know him, Portia," Katherine murmured.

"No, that's true. I don't know him." She looked at her friend curiously. "Next thing you'll tell me is that he makes your pulse race and your heart go pitter-patter and that he's going to carry you off to his castle on his white charger. What kind of books have you been reading, Kat? Fairy tales, I bet. These are the nineteen sixties."

Katherine turned away. It was useless trying to explain to Portia.

"All I know, Miss Jardine, is that if I was going to hop into bed, I'd do it with Chris or Tim and build up my repertoire, sharpen my nails a little before digging them into the likes of Signor Negri. And

I imagine they'll be a lot *kinder* than his Italian highness." Portia stood up to go. "Want to come to this meeting with me?"

Katherine had demurred.

The next time she had seen Carlo was over the Christmas holidays in Switzerland. She had not known he would be there, but she had told him that she was planning to stay with Princesse Mathilde. And when Mat announced one night that Carlo had rung and would be coming by the next day, Katherine was overjoyed.

Princesse Mathilde, who seemed to see everything despite her years, noticed that too. "You saw a little of Carlo in Italy, I believe," she said casually, lifting a poker to prod the fire.

"Yes." Katherine leapt up. "Here, let me do that. And in London," she added.

She had long since rid herself of any momentary animosity she had felt for Princesse Mathilde over the revelation that Violette was her half sister. In fact, the first time she had seen Mathilde after that, the Princesse had taken her aside and talked to her at length about her relationship with Jacob. She had done so with such feeling and humor and honesty that Katherine had thrilled to her story and wished again that Mathilde were her mother. As it was, she felt closer to the Princesse, trusted her more intimately, than anyone else.

And so she had not been afraid to intimate, in the face she presented to the Princesse, something of her feelings about Carlo.

Princesse Mat had merely murmured a noncommittal "I see," and patted her hand. Katherine had been grateful for her tact, her lack of an instant judgment.

The next day Carlo had arrived early and having paid his respects to the Princesse had whisked her off to a village high up in the Alps where he was staying and where the snow was already thick on the ground. The coil of his presence had wound instantly round her, though there had been something different about him, a seriousness round the eyes, a certain concentration about his features which closed him to her. They had spoken little, a desultory query about her studies, another about her friends. Then the business of skiing had taken over. She had known that he would ski beautifully, but nonetheless, she was rapt by the swift grace with which he maneuvered the steep slopes. And she had stopped looking at him only when the mountain demanded her entire concentration.

Later, she was as always breathless with the exhilaration of it, and it was only after they had shed their gear and she had a drink in her hand that she realized she was alone in the chalet with him. Realized too that it was perhaps the first time that they had been alone in a house together. Perhaps he had the same realization then too for he came up to her and in a single fluid gesture relieved her of her glass and took her in his arms. His kiss shook her with its intensity, reminded her of Roman nights, and she clung to him unwilling, unable to let go. It was then that he had murmured in her ear. "Perhaps, *mia Katerina,* it would be a good idea if we were to be married." She had arched away from him, searched for his eyes, uncertain that she had heard him correctly.

He must have taken her surprise for indecision for he stepped away from her. "You will think about it. Yes. It is a big step, I know, for a young woman." With that, he had looked at her intently, taken her hand again, stroked it, as if it were a precious, a fragile object.

Confusion had invaded her. He wanted to marry her. Somehow the notion had never occurred to her. Marriage. To be wed to Carlo. Yes. She wanted to shout. Yes. He wanted her. Not the way Portia had said. But *really*. For good. She had found her tongue again only when they were back at the Princesse's house. She had made him roll down the window of the car. "Yes," she had said to him shyly. "Yes, Carlo, I will."

He had sped after her and lifted her into the air. Kissed her a little clumsily, like a joyous youth. Then they had walked into the wintry night together. "It remains only to get the permission of the families."

She had balked a little at this, but she had seen the flash of his old indolent smile. "*Mia Katerina,* you will learn that in my family very little is serious except birth, marriage, and death. They are the three occasions on which we go together to church. I imagine, too, that your father would wish to have his permission asked."

For the rest of that holiday period, he had showered her with presents, treated her like an idolized figure on a pedestal. She felt cosseted, cared for, caressed. Now that his desire was spoken, legitimated by the promise of a future, her own flowed forth untrammeled. She wanted always to be near him, to touch him, to hold him. Kisses weren't enough. Sitting at dinner, or driving through the shadow of the towering slopes, she would imagine him naked beside her, his body glowing, the movement of his limbs.

One night, she had said as much to him. He had cast vibrant eyes on her, stroked her face. "No, Katerina, now we must be like good children and wait for the sanction of the priest." His cheek dimpled playfully. "And dream about the pleasures of our wedding night."

On the weekend, Violette had driven up from Geneva. Soon after her arrival, she had asked Katherine to go for a walk with her. It was one of those crisp clear days when the snowy peaks seemed within arm's reach and the branches of the trees traced a network of dark filigree against the sky. They trudged companionably along a woody path, caught up on work and studies. Then Violette stopped and looked at Katherine.

"Carlo tells me he has proposed to you. That you have accepted."

Katherine was startled. She hadn't known that Carlo had seen Violette. And there was something of an accusatory note in Violette's tone. "Yes," she said tersely, began to walk again.

Violette read her expression. "Ah, you didn't know Carlo had already told me. You thought he'd wait for the grandmama's approval before mentioning it." She laughed brusquely. "Carlo tells me most things. We go back a long way, you know."

Katherine didn't like the implication of that. She looked away, her face stiff.

"Don't worry, Signora la Contessa Negri will approve. Mat's name will be mentioned frequently. And the old crow is getting desperate for *bambini*. Carlo hasn't been very accommodating until now. But I guess Mama has finally got through."

The cynicism in Violette's voice grated on her, opened up a chasm of suspicions. "You sound jealous," she said brutally, in self-defense.

Violette was silent for a moment. "Yes, yes perhaps I am," she responded softly. She picked up a stone from the path and threw it forcefully against the stump of a tree. "Are you sure you're doing the right thing, Katherine?" Her voice was quiet now, reflective.

Katherine nodded vigorously, started to walk again with brisk steps. She was tempted to run away.

Violette matched her pace. "Carlo is not an easy man, you know. He's restless, moody. He . . ."

"Is that why you didn't marry him?" Katherine cut her off vengefully. For the first time the thought that Violette and Carlo had been lovers, real lovers, bedtime lovers, had crystallized itself in her mind. She didn't know why it had taken so long for the notion to rear itself consciously. She was a stupid innocent. But now that it was there, it took on the substantiality of a vast secret edifice that couldn't be overlooked, that had to be negotiated cautiously.

"No, no, that's not why." Violette's face had that look of painful honesty which made her so like the Princesse. "No. He simply never asked me."

The sentence hung there between them in silence. Katherine didn't break it. She felt jubilant. Carlo loved her. It was her he had asked.

Violette continued after a moment. "The timing was never right, I guess. And we're too alike. Power games."

Her voice had a reedy quality. Katherine didn't know what it hid.

"And then, I don't think I want children. I'm not sure I can have any anymore." She paused.

Katherine's steps faltered. She stopped to look at her sister. "I'm sorry," she said, meaning it. "Why? Why can't you?"

Violette surveyed her intently and then shrugged. "It's too complicated to explain. And it's not the end of the world." She put her arm around her. "What I was trying to say is that Carlo is . . . well, he's fine. But you mustn't have too many illusions." She hesitated as if she were about to say something else. Changed her mind, smiled. "I'm sure you'll be a wonderful mother, if only to make up for Sylvie."

Katherine flinched at the mention of Sylvie. "Let's go back," she said tautly.

"Oh come on, Katherine." Violette, ever perceptive, was aware of her recoil. "I know Sylvie was beastly to you, but you'll have to come to terms with her some time. Mat once said to me that Sylvie was simply a woman ahead of her time. If she had been born in my generation, everything would have been different for her. She might have been like—well, like me." Violette laughed wryly.

Katherine hadn't joined in with her.

She had dressed carefully for dinner that night, a dress for Carlo's taste, soft velvet, elegantly cut, hugging her body, at once revealing and concealing. There were to be only the four of them, the three women and Carlo. She had not seen him since her conversation with Violette and suspicions like fleas bit at her body giving her no peace.

But the glow of Carlo's eyes on her as she came down the stairs had assuaged her.

"*Carissima Katerina,*" he murmured, kissing her lightly on the forehead and reaching for her hand. It was the first time he had ever touched her openly in public and she was surprised. His soft words explained everything. "I have told Princesse Mat about us and she has given her approval. That means my mother will not resist. I imagine your father . . ."

She squeezed his hand, held on to it as they approached the others.

"Katherine, I'm so pleased." The Princesse embraced her. She looked at Carlo speculatively. "And Carlo, Carlo is already like a member of the family."

Katherine had smiled and smiled.

Later, toward the end of dinner, Violette had dropped her bombshell.

"Well, since it's a week of announcements, I might as well make mine. I'm getting married too. Christian Tardieu is the lucky man. We thought we would do it quietly, over Easter, if Leo and Jacob can make it then."

While Violette talked, Katherine read the startled expression in Carlo's face and then something else, what was it, something darker, a challenge. But he was all congratulations and good wishes. Then he said, half jokingly, "Perhaps we can make it a double wedding."

"Ah, no." The Princesse was emphatic. "Your mother will never stand for that suddenness. And in any event, Katherine will want to complete her degree. In June, perhaps. June would be an appropriate month for you."

Katherine had watched Carlo carefully when Christian Tardieu, a shy burly man who was all affection for Violette, made his appearance. But she could detect nothing unusual in his behavior.

And when he had held her tightly that night under the twinkling blanket of wintry stars and seared her lips with his heat, all her suspicions had been obliterated by the weight of their double and acknowledged passion.

On her return to London, she had instantly told Portia of her plans. They were sitting in a pub opposite the British Museum near the publishing firm where Portia now worked.

"You're having me on. I don't believe it." Portia looked at her aghast.

"Well, it's true. We're getting married, probably in June. I'm sorry it doesn't please you."

"It's not that. It's just, well it's just as if you'd swallowed all the romances in the world, hook, line and sinker. What about all those things we talked about? The career you were going to engage in. Museum work. You're, we're still so young. Marriage is for old people."

"There are galleries in Rome. Carlo has nothing against my working. We've talked about it."

Portia sat mute.

"Portia. First you tell me you're worried because he's going to
love me and leave me. Now you're against it all because he won't
leave me. Well?"

Portia looked at her skeptically. "You're in love, right?"

Katherine nodded.

"Well, there's no talking to women in love."

"But you'll come to the wedding. Be my bridesmaid?"

Portia groaned. "Who else?"

Portia had been right. There was no talking to a woman in love.
And very little ability to concentrate. Katherine sighed. She would
have to get today's lecture notes from somebody else. And she must
stop daydreaming, settle down to work. Study. Study hard.

Carlo would be coming to London in two weeks' time. And then
they would set the date.

The date was a Saturday at the end of June.

The Contessa had insisted that the wedding take place in the
chapel on the Palazzo grounds and the party be held there afterward.
Generations of Buonaterras had been married here. In any case,
what else had she to do but organize parties? And this was one she
had been looking forward to for many a year. She gave one wing of
the Palazzo over to Katherine and her family and friends. Another
to Princesse Mathilde and her family. No, no, she wouldn't hear
anything to the contrary. They must all come, stay here with her,
for as long as they wished.

Only Carlo was banished from the house for two days prior to the
event.

"We can allow ourselves to play with certain forms, Katerina. But
for the groom to see the bride before the appropriate moment is
bad luck. And I am superstitious."

Katherine, without Carlo there to shore her up, felt more than a
little lost in the midst of this cavernous splendor. But the Princesse
was there and Leo, so bronzed and handsome after his year in Tanzania, and Jacob, a little melancholy but so careful of her now that
she was going to be given over to another. And Portia, with that
slightly puritanical glint in her eye, reminding her that she didn't
altogether approve, but filled with curiosity about the world of the

Palazzo. Only Thomas was missing. She had rung him to persuade him to come, but he had demurred, insisting it was not his place. She would have liked him to be there.

The day of the wedding dawned with that crystal Mediterranean clarity the poets celebrated. From her window, Katherine could see across the miles to the meandering line where shore met sea. And already, despite the earliness of the hour, the Palazzo was humming. In the gardens, under the cover of ancient trees, the tables were going up. Crystal and silver and china tinkled. Flowers appeared in wild profusion. Instruments. A band. And all, Katherine thought, for her and Carlo. Wonder enveloped her.

Princesse Mathilde and Portia helped her dress, along with a maid. The dress was one Mat had traveled specially to London to help her choose. She had insisted, proclaiming that one needed an older woman at such times and she understood such things, knew a designer. They would do the Contessa and Carlo proud. She felt responsible.

The dress had arrived at the Palazzo two days before in a vast box. A satin fairy-tale gown, Katherine thought, looking meaningfully at Portia as she slipped into it. A tiny lace collar, a hundred minuscule buttons along closely fitting lines which gave way below her hips to volumes of material and a long lace train.

"Yes." The Princesse looked at her approvingly. "Simplicity with a touch of splendor. It suits you to perfection. Carlo is a very lucky man." She mused a little, rearranged a stray lock of Katherine's heavy burnished hair, took from a box a tiara with a fine lace veil attached to it. "This was mine. I thought you might like it instead of what we chose in London."

Katherine gazed at a crown of silver, a multitude of sparkling stones. "No, no, I couldn't," she protested.

"You can and you must. I have no use for it and as you know, our dear Violette, with her modern ideas, insisted on the outrageous simplicity of a suit for her civil wedding." Princesse Mat laughed. "So this needs an airing. You can pass it on to one of my grandchildren or yours at the appropriate moment."

"Go on, Kat," Portia urged her. "You've gone this far, so you might as well go all the way."

Katherine let the Princesse place the tiara on her head and arrange the veil.

"There, my dear. A bride to perfection. How does your English rhyme go? 'Something old, something new . . .' "

"I've brought the 'something borrowed and something blue.' " Portia smiled. "There." She handed Katherine a pale blue handkerchief with a picture of Alice in Wonderland embroidered on its edge.

The girls burst into giggles.

The bells chimed. From the chapel doors the strains of the organ poured onto the grounds. Katherine clung to her father's arm. Rising panic overtook her. A sea of unknown faces. The heavy smell of flowers mixed with incense. She straightened her shoulders, looked through the haze of the veil straight ahead at the gold and Venetian blue of the altar. That was beautiful. She had examined it yesterday with her art historian's eyes and marveled at the purity of color and figure.

And then he was there. Carlo. Like a stranger. So dark, so fine. That little devilish smile tugging at the corner of his lips. She didn't listen to the words of the ceremony. Wasn't sure that she understood them. She was aware only of the proximity of that man, her husband. He took her hand, slipped a fine golden band on her finger. He had already given her a ring to mark their engagement, a diamond in an antique setting. It was beautiful, but she had an age-old dislike of rings. She could hardly bring herself to wear it. Now this. But it felt all right. So light.

And then he kissed her. Softly. For the first time she met his eyes. They were darkly serious, intent. It was then that she suddenly realized how very meaningful the ritual was for him.

The Princesse looked on. Mused. The girl was in love. She radiated it. And Carlo? Perhaps he was, too. She hoped they would be happy. But what did it mean, in any event, to be in love? Love could be as blind as parental will. It was no guarantee of anything.

She looked at her own daughter, her husband. No. Violette wasn't in love with Christian. But he suited her, was in love with her. He would be good for her, would settle her a little. Violette had been floundering. Too many years of living on the edge. And he had a little boy, a son from a previous marriage. That, too, would calm her a little, give her a center, she hoped. She had stopped trying to interfere in her daughter's life years ago. It never had the desired effect.

She smiled. Looked at Jacob. Still so straight, so handsome. She had been in love with him once. And then they had been friends.

Were friends. Rare friends. The kind who knew each other's secret lives, could read the flicker of an eyebrow, the curl of a lip. She knew now which she valued most. She had only a residue of patience left for that world of excess, of heights and depths and blind gropings. But then she was old. Time, so much time, pulling at one with the force of gravity, weighing down one's shoulders. She straightened hers.

Jacob walked past her to the march of the organ. He met her eyes, smiled. It made her feel younger. But she could read his worry. He was worried about Katherine. Always worried. Ever since she had been tiny. He didn't know what to make of Carlo, wouldn't perhaps have known what to make of any man who so fully stole his daughter's desire. She returned his smile. Hoped, and since she was still in a church uttered a tiny prayer, that she would never have to mention Sylvie's last visit to her.

Katherine, in a dream, danced. Head high, graceful, in Carlo's arms. Eyes locked. Brimming with promise. Around them, other couples. A melody of pastel gowns and light suits. Her father with the Princesse. They changed partners. Now, at the peak of her love, she could be generous to him. "Perhaps you'll be next," she radiated, "with the Princesse." He laughed, kissed her, collided with Portia and Leo. "And you two after that. That would be too wonderful. Please." They blushed in unison.

Katherine danced on. A welter of arms. Men she didn't know. Smiling faces. And then the car. Gleaming white. Carlo beside her. Portia at the window, throwing rice, kissing her, whispering, "Remember, Katherine, they live happily ever after."

s the bells tolled over
Katherine Jardine's wedding, Alexei Gismondi's dreams were not
dressed in bridal white. They wore the riot of colors of his rebellious
generation and the magical hues of celluloid.

He was in the second year of his studies at the Philosophy Faculty
in Rome. After three months at the University, it had become plain
to him that his actual course was a total charade. Dull professors
reading inaudibly from the even duller books they had written on
Plato or Aquinas or Augustine. Dusty overcrowded halls filled with
bored students. Soporific lectures without a smattering of intellectual
excitement or an iota of relevance to the world in which they lived.
No questions, no exchange, no argument—just a stream of words
from a lazy figurehead empowered by tradition. One could just as
easily and far more fruitfully stay home and read the given texts in
order to regurgitate them in ridiculously inept oral exams.

This was the first lesson Alexei learned at the University of Rome.
He was hardly alone in mastering it. Throughout Italy, France and
Germany, students universally agreed on one thing: university structures, the contents of courses, were abysmally antiquated and ripe
for change.

The second lesson Alexei learned, and it followed with total logic
from the first, was that any education that was to be had was available only outside the lecture halls. In student refectories and cafés,

in a variety of gathering places from piazza to crowded flat, friends met to laugh at the ineptitude of the "official" curriculum. And to discuss what really mattered to them.

This unofficial curriculum was broad. It ranged from the living conditions of students and workers to the writings of Marx and Freud. It confronted the fact that Italy's economic bubble had burst and jobs for graduates were no longer easily to be had. It took up Lorenzo Milani's book, *Letta a una professoressa*, a vibrant challenge to an educational system which discriminated against the poor. It focused on the war in Vietnam and liberation struggles in the third world. It questioned moribund conventions, censorship and bureaucratic corruption. It monitored and confronted the rise in violent activity by groups of fascist thugs.

And it debated what was to be done.

It was the unofficial curriculum which led students into the streets of Rome and Milan, Turin and Trento and Naples.

These were students who wore suits, had short hair and scrubbed faces. They were the sons, and occasionally the daughters, of lawyers and judges and doctors, teachers and businessmen, civil servants and industrialists.

In the spring of 1966 one of these students, Paolo Rossi, was killed in a clash with fascists at the University of Rome. Alexei had known him vaguely. It was after that death that he, too, took to the streets in protest, participated in occupations.

Paradoxically, it was also that death, which led him finally to his dream site, Cinecittà, Italy's very own Hollywood.

It happened in this way.

Giangiacomo Gismondi had come to Rome the week after Paolo Rossi's death. In the richly appointed apartment above the Spanish Steps in which Alexei now lived with his friend Enrico, he waited for the boy's return from the University. Alexei was late. Never a patient man, Giangiacomo paced the room between phone calls and barked orders with increasing menace.

When a disheveled and dusty Alexei finally appeared sporting a black eye, Giangiacomo was already in a temper.

"Look at you. Where have you been?" Giangiacomo snapped at him.

"At a demo." Alexei's tone in response was more curt than usual.

"A demo? A demonstration?" Giangiacomo snorted. "Is that what you go to university for?"

"A friend of mine has been killed by fascist thugs and you sneer?" Alexei challenged him, ready to continue the battle of the streets.

"When a friend dies, one arranges a funeral, not a demonstration," Giangiacomo retorted.

"And allows the fascists and their friends in power to go quietly home to bed. Your friends, I imagine." Alexei was angry now, insolent.

"What do you know about fascists?" Giangiacomo growled. "You weren't even in nappies when we put an end to Mussolini."

"Oh, so there are no fascists left now that Mussolini is dead?" Alexei exuded sarcasm. "No fascists in Italy? No crypto-fascists in America fueling the military-industrial complex, exterminating the Vietnamese? Making a mockery of democracy? No fascists in Rhodesia? In South Africa?"

"Empty rhetoric. Stupid, empty, student rhetoric." Giangiacomo spat. "Not even as intelligent as the Communist union leaders. If I hear that you've been to one more of these demonstrations, I'm cutting off your allowance."

"Fine. You can do that as of today." Alexei stormed from the room.

A moment later, he put his head round the door again. "And if you'd like me to move out of the apartment, just say so and I'll pack my bags."

Giangiacomo simply stared furiously at him.

The next day Alexei took up the contact he had through a friend of a friend of a friend to Cinecittà.

He had visited the vast studio complex before and been both enthralled and a little bewildered by that maze of activities which go into the making of a feature film. But now he wanted to be more than an observer. He wanted a job.

He struck it lucky. A third assistant director was needed on a comedy about to go into production the following week. The script was a hundred pages long, a hundred pages tracing the complicated love life of a provincial Don Juan. It was Alexei's job to keep track of the various takes and their details.

Every morning now, Alexei woke at the crack of dawn to drive the thirty kilometers out of Rome to Cinecittà. His first day on the job, he improvised a complex numbering system to record what was going on.

Films are rarely shot in narrative sequence. Locations and sets prescribe the order of scenes. The production schedule had it that the first week's shoot would cover all the scenes which took place in the hero's country house and grounds—created out of nothing in one of Cinecittà's studios. Alexei noted the position of actors, the duration of takes, angles, retake upon retake. The whole thing was grossly complicated by the fact that the director had not yet made a decision on his leading man and three actors were vying for the part. By the third day, Alexei threw out both script and numbering system and simply started to write down everything that happened in minute detail.

The production was scheduled to run for ten weeks. It stretched to thirty. As the other assistant directors left to take on prior commitments, Alexei rose to first assistant. He had stopped going to lectures altogether. On weekends, he borrowed notes from friends and erratically caught up on reading. He felt it didn't matter. He would somehow manage exams. And what he was learning now was far more interesting to him.

He was fascinated by the chaos of filmmaking. A chaos which at its end would have to be transformed into order. As if life with all its accidents, its differing points of view, its illusions and deceits could somehow be reassembled to breathe meaning.

Sometimes, during lax moments, he would sneak away from his own production to watch Fellini at work in another part of Cinecittà. Fellini, the master of chance, who rarely worked to a script, but allowed a story to unfold through the play of atmosphere and accident and the infallible direction of his own distinct eye. Watching Fellini, a comment he had never understood crystallized in Alexei's mind. It was from the French filmmaker Jean Renoir. Film, he had said, was a huge machine in which everything is prearranged, but where reality enters suddenly through a door you have purposely left open in order to violate what was prearranged.

What Alexei loved almost as much as the actual making of the film was the camaraderie which developed amongst the team. For those weeks, they were a little world unto themselves, with their loves and their squabbles, but all united, all with their defined roles, in the disparate activities which would somehow become a movie.

During his third week on the production, the wardrobe mistress responsible for the lead actor came up to him during a coffee break.

"It's you I'd like to dress." She looked up at him from dark laughing eyes. "I'd make you into a Russian count, complete with fur hat."

"How did you know?" He smiled.

"Know what?"

"That I was Russian."

She chortled, "I didn't have a clue. Sheer genius, I guess. Whoops, there's my call. See you." She waved, dashed off.

He watched her receding form: a trim woman with electric shoulder-length hair, blue jeans, white shirt. He searched his mind for her name. Laura, it came to him. He would have to remember.

Two days later, she invited him into her dressing room. Mirrors, racks of clothes. "I can tell you, Gianni is no joke." She did a little mimic dance and imitated the lead. "What do you think, Laura? Just a little extra tuck here. No, no, that's not right." She pranced and strutted in front of the mirror, held her breath, stuck out her chin. And then, played herself. "Oh no, Signor Gianni, you look *delizioso*. Your fans will be breathless."

Alexei laughed.

She leaned against the dressing-room door, shutting it firmly behind her. "Now, you, on the other hand . . ." She lifted her face to him.

He suddenly realized she was waiting to be kissed.

"Mmm." She urged him on, her eyes laughing.

Work permitting, they made love almost every day. During lunch breaks. Amidst the clutter of the wardrobe room. He would bring sandwiches, wine. She would add fruit, a slice of cake. They would make love, eat and laugh. After the day's shoot everyone was too tired for anything but sleep. He found out only after two weeks that she had a husband. She laughed about that too. "Don't pull a face, Alexei. This is cinema. That is life, eh, *mio caro?*"

He knew what she meant. The two worlds rarely coincided. When he left the precincts of Cinecittà, he hardly thought about Laura. He imagined it was the same for her.

Alexei was happy. When the end of the university term came, he had been meant to go and work in one of Giangiacomo's factories, "to learn the business" as his uncle put it. Alexei explained to him that he already had a job in as important an industry. Giangiacomo, a little rueful over the outburst that had caused all this, took it in his stride.

"How much are you earning, Alexei?" he asked.

Alexei told him.

"And if I doubled it?"

Alexei shook his head. "I'm doing what I want. It's important to me."

Giangiacomo nodded. He was, he realized, proud of him. Proud of his determination. "Good boy," he mumbled.

By the time the shoot was over, Alexei had over four thousand pages of notes. "Bravo." The director shook his steel-gray head plaintively. "Bravo, Alexei. We have 125,000 meters of celluloid and your weighty document is probably the only thing that will enable us to reconstruct it in the edit." They looked at each other and chuckled.

The special screening for the crew of the film took place in November. On a whim, Alexei invited Giangiacomo to accompany him.

In the preview room, Giangiacomo laughed until the tears ran from his eyes. He was, as the director later whispered to Alexei, the very best member of the audience. Alexei himself could barely manage a smile, so intrigued was he by the film's transformation. He could see how each cut had been made, each take selected and how, miraculously, it all finally hung together.

When the credits rolled and Alexei's name appeared on the screen, Giangiacomo let out an audible breath. He patted Alexei's knee. "Congratulations, Alexei, congratulations."

Two days later a bulky package addressed to Alexei arrived at the apartment above the Piazza di Spagna. Enrico looked on as Alexei opened it.

"It's too big for a bomb," his friend teased wryly.

"More like a small cannon," Alexei agreed.

It was, in fact, a sixteen-millimeter camera. Alexei whistled beneath his breath.

"You know, Giangiacomo is quite mad," he said to Enrico. "On the one hand he prevents me from going into film, insists on university. On the other he gives me this."

Enrico shrugged, teased him. "He simply thinks you're the best son who ever walked the face of the earth."

"And that," said Alexei, "is probably because I'm not altogether a son." He stroked the camera, played with the lens, set up the tripod.

"But if you don't put that object away for a while and do just a little work, you'll never leave this godforsaken university," Enrico counseled him.

Alexei pretended not to hear. He was already dreaming about the uses he would put the camera to. He did work, but intermittently. His energies went mostly into a little documentary he had planned, a documentary about his friends and their political views. Faces spoke squarely to camera, criticizing the university hierarchy, the realm of privilege, the condition of workers and students, the corrupt sell-out which was Italian politics. Interspersed with the faces were shots of Roman workers' quarters, the blank faces of students in lecture halls, strutting professors. The film had little aggression. It was cold. A document.

He thought, when he saw the rushes, that he would throw it away.

But he learned something from the experiment. He learned that the world's reality was not the camera's. He learned that fabrication might be the only way to find truth through the camera's lens. He went assiduously to the movies to see how other directors did it.

That spring there was no work to be had at Cinecittà. The vogue for Italian westerns had come in and productions had moved to Spain and Yugoslavia. Alexei, feeling a little guilty about Giangiacomo, finally agreed to spend a part of the summer working in his Milan complex of factories.

Giangiacomo's idea was that Alexei should spend a month apprenticed to a production manager in each of the two factories, one making refrigerators, the other cookers. The last month would be spent with senior management, familiarizing himself with sales and accounts.

"I think you'll find it is almost as much of an adventure as Cinecittà," Giangiacomo said to him slyly.

Alexei shrugged. "I hope you don't expect four thousand pages of notes."

"No, not that. Perhaps just a little conversation at the end of it."

Despite himself, Alexei was excited when he arrived at the factory complex some fifteen kilometers outside Milan. He had insisted on checking in without Giangiacomo and as he walked through the corridors to Signor Bassani's office, his natural curiosity took over. The buildings were new and on this floor, an atmosphere of chrome and leather and airy functionalism prevailed.

Signor Bassani was a man of about thirty-five with an easy manner. His deference to Alexei, marked at the start of the week, almost disappeared by its end. He showed Alexei round the shop floor, explained the workings of the various parts of the assembly line, the depot, the warehousing systems, introduced him to the shop stewards, to the rest of the senior personnel.

Alexei was fascinated by the beehive of activity. He avidly watched what seemed to be a seamless stream of operations. He was particularly intrigued by the assembly line. From his vantage point on the ramp above the shop floor, the movement of men and machines had the rhythmic quality of an intricate dance.

It was only in his second week, when he got down on to the shop floor, that his impressions began to change. He noticed the glazed look in the men's eyes as they performed their repetitive functions, chained to the rhythms of the machine, eight hours a day, six days a week. He imagined himself in their place, constantly in the blare of that noise, in the midst of those acid smells.

In the bright new canteen, he took to chatting with them.

Many of them were from the South. They were shy with him, withdrawn. But he persisted. One of the men, he discovered, was from Cefalù. He talked to him about the beauties of Sicily. The man, whose name was Augusto, looked at him with suspicious eyes. "Beauty, yes," he said to him, "but no jobs."

His eyes reminded Alexei of Francesca, dark, hooded, secret. He wanted to ask him if he knew her, if he knew what had become of her, but Augusto gave him no opportunity.

One evening, he asked if he could drive him home. Augusto shrugged. "If you like."

He made no conversation, except to say, once, abruptly, that he missed the sea. Then he merely sat and directed Alexei toward a high-rise block on the outskirts of Milan.

Alexei had hoped he might be invited in, but there was only a mute thank you to be had from Augusto.

He befriended one of the shop stewards, Emilio, a thick-set older man who had no reservations about joining him for a beer. Alexei asked him about the Sicilian.

The shop steward shrugged. "They have a rough time, these Southerners. No life really. Country boys. A little lost. They live four to a room and sometimes do bed shifts with the night workers. One goes to work and the other goes to bed. It saves money."

"I see," Alexei murmured.

At the end of his second month at the factory complex, Alexei found himself in a rage. He confronted Giangiacomo.

"It's appalling. Inhuman."

"What's appalling?"

"The way you treat your workers."

"The way I treat my workers?" Giangiacomo was all surprise. "What's wrong with the way I treat my workers?"

"One of them fell asleep on the line today and his salary was docked."

"It'll teach him to sleep at home." Giangiacomo was restrained.

"Home? Do you know how these people live? Four to a room. It's inhuman. What they do is inhuman. The same motion, day in day out. No talk. No choice. No satisfaction. Just domination from above for a pitiful wage."

"Student claptrap," Giangiacomo rumbled. "My workers are well paid. Safety standards are good. The canteen is new. People queue up for jobs in any Gismondi company." He paused. "Alexei, if a man falls asleep on a line, he jeopardizes the rest of the men. You should understand that. His salary is docked as a warning," Giangiacomo explained with unusual patience.

Alexei stared at him angrily. "Look at the way we live. There are twenty rooms here. We never use half of them. And look at the way they live. There's something very wrong."

"Oh, so it's revolution now, is it? Spread the profits. Distribute the wealth. Like in the Soviet Union, eh? An equal distribution of misery. That's what you want. I'll tell you something, Alexei." He glared at him now. "They would die in the Soviet Union to have factories as well run as mine."

"We're not talking about the Soviet Union." Alexei glared back. Mention of the Soviet Union was always a sensitive point between them. "We're talking about Italy. Exploitation in Italy."

"Bah," Giangiacomo grunted.

That autumn when he went back to Rome, Alexei threw himself into student activity. He felt he had a new fund of knowledge now, a new fund of experience to contribute to the discussions which raged. It seemed to many of his friends that students and workers could be put in the same equation. Both suffered from conditions imposed on them from above. Neither had any voice, any degree of autonomy. Students, like workers, were the legitimate bearers of revolutionary aspirations. Together they would change things. Overthrow the old regime, build a new world where justice reigned. And the place to begin was here, now, with the very matter of their everyday lives.

There was a thrill to disrupting those tired droning lectures, to invading those musty oral examinations and disputing the marks students were awarded, to taking over university halls and running courses, to investigating the problems of Roman workers, to marching, to skirmishing with fascists and police. A thrill and a certainty of purpose.

Excitement was in the air. The excitement of shared aspirations. Aspirations shared over continents. A giant festival of shared hopes. In America, in Germany, in France, in Britain, the students were marching. Against Vietnam. For civil rights. In the autumn of '67 Milanese students occupied the universities. In Turin they set up a free university where the things they wanted to know were taught. Everywhere they protested, put on street plays, staged happenings, sang, danced.

Then in Rome in March of '68 things took a sudden ugly turn. Students had been violently evicted from the Faculty of Letters, locked out of the Valle Giulia. The call came to reoccupy it. Alexei, along with some two thousand students, heeded it. With his Leica round his neck, which he carried everywhere in order to document activity, he made his way with the crowd to the park in which the building stood. He was armed, like his fellows, with the usual supply of eggs and tomatoes.

Before they even reached the park, something happened which no one had expected. The police charged. Drove jeeps straight into the crowd, threw tear gas.

Sirens wailed. Pandemonium. Alexei ran, aiming his token missiles, angry at their ineptitude. Through the clouds of smoke, he saw a woman fall, saw her hit, dragged. Blood. Her face in the crowd was a replica of Francesca's, high rounded forehead, reddened lips, raven hair. A purity. He rushed toward her, but was shoved back. He picked up a stone. Hurled it at the nearest policeman.

Everywhere around him objects were flying. Students were fighting back, tearing up benches, using planks as clubs. A great wave of communal anger.

Resistance.

A few hours later he found himself, bruised and beaten, in a crowded police cell. There was a mixed mood of triumph and despondency amongst the inmates. Triumph because they had fought back, had not simply fled the onslaught. Despondency because they were in a cell, unequal to the opposition.

Alexei's mood was somber. The violence, the blood, had shaken him. He couldn't get rid of the image of that woman lying helpless on the ground, trampled. Francesca. The thought wouldn't leave him. But it couldn't have been her. She was in a convent. In Agrigento. Another kind of cell. He shivered, stood quietly at the back of the cell, didn't speak.

Giangiacomo came to bail him out the following day. As they left the police station, the cameras clicked and popped in rude cacophony, microphones were thrust in Giangiacomo's face, in Alexei's.

His uncle all but dragged him into the waiting car. He didn't speak. From the set of his jaw, Alexei knew that rage was being forcibly contained.

They didn't stop at the flat. After a struggle through traffic and round cordoned-off streets, he realized that they were headed for Milan.

They drove in silence. Alexei's head ached. He felt a bump on his forehead he hadn't noticed before. His body was stiff, sore. He lapsed into sleep. When he woke it was dark. They were home in Milan. He hadn't been there since the previous summer and he sank with something akin to gratitude into his own bed. A doctor came to see him. Giangiacomo stood by as he checked limbs and ribs, bumps and bruises. Still he didn't speak.

The next morning Alexei showered and made an attempt to shave round the bruises and scratches on his face, before going down to breakfast. He wasn't a pretty sight but he was ravenous.

Giangiacomo was already at the table. "Here." He thrust a stack of newspapers at him. "Now you can feel pleased with yourself." He glared at Alexei and strode out of the room.

Alexei looked at the papers. On a series of front pages, amidst images of the streets of Rome, he saw his own swollen face staring out at him, sometimes next to Giangiacomo's, sometimes alone. The headlines blared: "Student riot in Rome." "Industrialist's son arrested." "Gismondi's revolutionary heir." "Gismondi heir attacks police." "Gismondi millions take to the streets."

Alexei's heart sank.

The evening papers were even worse. They carried details of Alexei's activities, traced him back to the summer he had spent in one of the Gismondi factories, implied that he had created trouble there, interviewed workers to see whether they backed father or son. There were also lists of the Gismondi holdings. Profiles of Giangiacomo. Profiles of Alexei. One of them mentioned Alexei's Soviet parentage, implied shady dealings with the KGB.

Alexei was astounded.

"Well?" Giangiacomo confronted him over dinner. "What have you got to say for yourself?"

Alexei shrugged, toyed with his food. "I'm sorry. Sorry you've been implicated. As for the rest . . ." He straightened his shoulders.

"As for the rest, you're prepared to attack the police, assault the forces of order? Is that what you're saying to me?"

"Attack the police?" Alexei was incredulous. "It was your forces of order who attacked us, attacked us with their jeeps and their tear gas and their truncheons. Fascist pigs." Alexei's voice rose. "I was there. All you do is read your right-wing papers and think it's the truth." He pushed his chair back abruptly, "There's no point talking to you about this."

The next morning the letters began to arrive. Heaps of them, over the next weeks. Letters addressed to him. Addressed to Giangiacomo. Threatening letters. Menacing letters. Letters saying he should be deported, hung, excommunicated. Packages containing dead mice, amulets. Congratulatory letters, addressing him as Comrade. Letters proposing marriage, affairs. Letters with photographs, locks of hair. Letters offering better, more deserving children for adoption than Alexei. Letters asking for money for a variety of worthy causes. Begging letters.

The letters repelled him and fascinated him. He had become the subject of other people's imaginations.

A public property. But the fabric of those imaginations compelled him. How extraordinary human beings were!

He had had no further confrontations with Giangiacomo. They were polite to each other, civil, meeting mostly over breakfast. The letters formed a kind of bond, a silent conversation. They passed them between each other with a shake of the head, occasionally a chuckle.

Then on the fourth day, a different kind of letter arrived. Giangiacomo's face grew grim. He passed it to Alexei. "This is what I have been afraid of."

The letter was composed of bits of magazine cut up to form a message. Its gist was that unless Giangiacomo left a million lire at a certain place at a certain time, his son would be kidnapped.

"Utter nonsense," Alexei laughed. "A schoolboy prank."

Giangiacomo looked at him contemptuously. "If you don't value your life, I do. It wouldn't be the first case of this kind in Italy. I shall alert the police."

"But you won't pay."

Giangiacomo shook his head. "No. But you shall have a bodyguard. And for the next week or so I don't want you out of the house."

Giangiacomo was firm, stilling all of Alexei's protests.

The next day, amidst the plentiful post, there was another letter of a similar kind. This time the implication was that Alexei was complicit in the demand for money, which was to go to a revolutionary grouping, and that he would aid and abet his own kidnapping.

"Your friends?" Giangiacomo asked him sternly.

"Don't be ridiculous." But he began to share his uncle's worries. He spent his days lying around in his room, pacing the house, sprawling in the inner courtyard where the sun was already hot. There were two orange trees there, planted in large tubs. He gazed at them. Remembered the woman lying in the Roman street, remembered Francesca. Her scent came back to him, the heat of her stolen caresses. She was imprisoned now, trapped in the cell of her nun's order. Trapped by her family into the cell of church and tradition.

He too was trapped now. Imprisoned in the world of his uncle's millions. Unable to go out, to move freely.

The irony of it didn't escape him. But it didn't lessen the sense of feeling trapped.

He raced round the courtyard, his prison's very own plush exercise ground. He ran until he was exhausted and then sprawled again. It was while he was lying there thinking about Francesca that the notion of the film came to him. A film which distilled the essence of Sicily. A film about a woman trapped in the sensuous splendor of that island and her own body, fettered by the conditions of her sex and society. He dreamt the film piecemeal. Began to make notes.

The following week the post had dwindled a little. There were the now usual requests for charitable contributions, another kidnapping threat which made Giangiacomo seethe. And also a different letter. A letter with a neatly typed envelope, somewhat official in character. Inside it another envelope bearing a sheet of handwritten paper, a faded photograph and a small velvet pouch. The letter was in English in a large sprawling hand. Alexei read it with some difficulty.

Dearest Alexei,

By the time you receive this, your twenty-first birthday may have come and gone. But I send you my very best wishes and a small token of the love which should have been yours.

Before it is no longer possible, I wish to tell you that I am your mother. This telling is the last pleasure I offer myself.

Do not ask how this can be so, for I will no longer be here

to tell you. It is all already so long ago and lost in the shadows of history.

But know that I have loved you, however briefly, and wished that it could be more.

I have seen that you are well and that is my consolation.

My dearest son.

Yours ever,

Sylvie Kowalska.

Alexei read the letter three times. There was no date. No return address. He was mystified. He passed it to Giangiacomo, then gazed at the faded face in the photograph and opened the small pouch. A ring, a pretty ring, inscribed with the same initials. S.K.

He looked queryingly at Giangiacomo.

His uncle shook his head. "Another madwoman. Here, look at this one."

Alexei read the letter his uncle handed him.

"Dear Signor Gismondi, I am a widow of youthful age. I have one son of my own who has turned out to be every mother's dream. I am certain I can accomplish the same miracle for you. Your son needs a woman's hand to steer him on the right course. I would be willing to meet you . . . etc., etc."

Alexei laughed. "The mothers are queueing up. But the tone here is not quite the same as Signora Sylvie Kowalska. I wonder . . ." He looked at the small black and white photograph again, showed it to his uncle. "And she has a Polish name, like my mother."

"Your mother was called Hanka Burova, as you know, and she died in a nursing home just outside Lublin a long time ago. Your father buried her there with his own hands." Giangiacomo stared at the photograph. Alexei saw a tinge of consternation pass over his features.

"Do you know her?"

Giangiacomo shook his head abruptly. "People are very bizarre."

"And she sends me this ring. A pretty ring. Strange. I wonder who she is."

"I'll see if I can find out anything."

That night Giangiacomo came home late, after Alexei had already had dinner. He called Alexei into his study.

"I have been talking to the police." He paced, his burly form too energetic for the width of the room. "No, don't interrupt me." He motioned Alexei into a chair and laughed. "Yes, those fascist pigs, but it's funny how when they're protecting one they acquire a different name. They tell me that all things considered, it would be better for you not to be here, at home, in Milan."

"That's fine, I'll go back to Rome." Alexei was eager.

"No, you will most definitely not go back to Rome." Giangiacomo scowled. "That address is equally well known. And I do not want you out in the streets again."

"I will do what I must do," Alexei flared at the order.

"You will do what I tell you as long as you are my son," Giangiacomo glowered. He didn't give Alexei an opportunity to speak. "You will go on a holiday until all this is over, the publicity, the troubles . . ." He waved vaguely. "And when you come back, you will come to work with me, and we will let it be known that that is your choice."

"That's preposterous," Alexei fumed. "I have to get my degree. I . . ."

Giangiacomo cut him off. "You have just spent months telling the world that there is no degree worth getting at an Italian university. It is a strange moment to plead academic duty."

"That's not the point. I have to go back to my life, to Rome." Alexei leapt up, looked threateningly at Giangiacomo. "I have no intention of coming to work with you. Of being a stooge to capital. Of cavorting with the fascists."

"You will do what I say as long as you are my son," Giangiacomo shouted now.

"Give your millions to someone else then," Alexei blazed back. "Get married, make yourself another son. Your own son."

Silence filled the room. In that moment, Alexei realized that he had overstepped the limit. When it came, Giangiacomo's voice was very low.

"Fascists, Alexei? You talk of fascists so easily." He laughed strangely, a sound more like a moan. "Do you know what the fascists did to me? Real fascists? Mussolini's Blackshirts? Do you know that I am only half a man? Incapable of having children?" He sat down heavily. "You are the only son I will ever have."

Alexei stared out into blackness. Murmured, "I'm sorry. I didn't know. Forgive me." After a long moment, he added, "I will do what you ask."

He went to Sicily for his enforced holiday. He wrote the script that was burning inside him.

$\mathcal{I}$n the hush of night the boat
moored at the island. Rugged limestone crags etched in moonlight.
The fragrance of sun-warmed greenery. The sharper tang of the sea.
A score of stone steps leading up, up. Katherine and Carlo, hand in
hand, walking. Walking through the doors of a Castello perched on
a hilltop. A Buonaterra Castello on a Buonaterra hilltop on a Buonaterra island. Everything in order. Everything arranged. Just for them.

A honeymoon imagined just for them.

Katherine thought she should pinch herself. But she didn't want
to.

Cool tiled floors. Pale ochre walls. A table set with majolica.
Oysters, crusty bread, champagne. Carlo's eyes. Dark, teasing. Skimming her face, her shoulders, her breasts. Pausing. A kiss, slow,
playful, drawing her on, promising, promising.

The bedroom. White. A low wide bed in its center. Waiting. Her
silk nightie already waiting. Waiting for the shape of her body.

"Mia Katerina. Mia sposa." His voice low, enveloping her. Like
his arms. Strong. Gentle around her and then bolder urging her
body, her lips, so that she was aware only of the texture of him, the
shape of head, shoulders, back, the scent of hair and cheek.

"I want to see you. I have never seen you." Fingers, delicate on
buttons, the lace of her bra, unfastening, tracing curves and nipples,
smoothing skin. A mingled rush of breath. And then lower, stroking,

kissing, urging her underpants off. Looking. The palpable sensation of his eyes on her nakedness. They distanced her, from him, from herself. But she read his desire in them.

And then he was kneeling to her, his arms molding her hips, that dark head buried in her thighs. The flicker of a tongue. A different pleasure. She felt shy, pulled his head away.

"I want to see you too," she said hesitantly, fingering his shirt.

He smiled, undressed quickly, unselfconsciously, his back to her as she perched on the bed. A muscled athlete's body, smooth bronzed skin.

"Do I pass?" he asked as he turned to her. Her eyes fell on that arching penis. He laughed at the focus of her gaze. "Does he scare you? He is usually quite friendly." He wrapped his fingers round his penis as if he were shaking a hand. His eyes caressing her, grew darker, more somber. He covered her body.

No, she wasn't scared of it, of that, the thought flashed through her mind as she curved her limbs to his weight. No, she wanted only to please him. Wanted, too, to obliterate those eyes, her eyes which watched them again from the ceiling. Not frightened, no. Simply distant, curious, watching the kisses which covered her breasts, her belly. Watching her own response, the arch of her body, her hands digging into his back, her lips shaping into a moan.

"Carissima." His breath in her ear, harsher now. And then, slowly, carefully, that jutting penis probing between her thighs. She was ready for it. Not frightened, no. Its entry was sanctioned by the security of "forever." Forever desired. Desire forever assuaged.

She opened to him, her knees high. She could see them from the ceiling, see the thrust of his body, and then another thrust, and another mingled with a cry of—what was it? Astonishment.

And suddenly, there was the force of his hand across her face. Hitting her, jabbing at her, again and again. His voice raucous. "Puta. You've cheated me. Putana," over and over. She cried out with the surprise and the pain of it, no longer a pair of eyes, but a body, a hot, hurting self.

And in the midst of that pain, the thrust at her face, the lunge at her entrails, her body shuddered, surged against him, heaved, loosened, wave after wave, cry after cry of hurt. And pleasure.

His face as he stood looking down on her was somber, filled with a dark contempt. "Whore." The word curled with malevolence around her. He spat emphatically on the floor and strode away, leaving her cowering, alone, in the white room.

Katherine wept. Wept silently. She didn't understand. Didn't know what had happened to her. It was all so sudden, the dreaminess of his caress, and then all at once, incomprehensibly, the cruelty, the pain, the contempt. And her body, racked into response. The humiliation of it. She huddled beneath the sheets, like a small child, and curled into a ball of weeping misery.

After a while, she got up and walked on trembling legs to the bathroom. Where had Carlo gone? She wanted to talk to him, question him. Her face in the mirror looked wild, bruised. She washed, wiped herself there where she teemed with their joint wetness. She shuddered. Why had he called her a whore? What had she done? He would have to come back. He couldn't leave her alone. She wanted him to look at her again with those eyes full of playful adoration. She pulled on the new nightie, straightened the bed, waited. Her face ached. There was a hole where her heart should have been.

Eventually, she didn't know how much later, he returned. He stood over the bed. Tall, menacing, in a robe of midnight blue. It was as if he didn't see her. As if she weren't there. With a savage gesture, he thrust something at the bed.

"For the servants. *Someone* needs to be satisfied." A harsh voice, filled with repugnance.

Katherine saw red liquid oozing across the bed.

Before she could say anything, he was gone.

But it was then that she understood. A hysterical laugh rose to her throat. A virgin. She wasn't a virgin. It was too ridiculous. They were in the second half of the twentieth century and the man she had married was distressed because she wasn't a virgin. What difference could it make? He had never spoken to her about it. Never mentioned it. Never breathed a word. She reflected on the course of their relationship, saw for a moment how he might have thought she was a complete innocent. But it was too silly. Absurd. Tomorrow she would explain to him. Tell him how it had no meaning. There was no other man in her life. No men. They would laugh about it.

But from the recesses of her mind stories tumbled forth, feudal stories which ravaged her dreams. About the rights of Italian noblemen, the droit du seigneur, the land rights to virgins. About unclean women, booted, eschewed, burnt. About the magical chastity of the Madonna, the universal mother, redemptive, sacred.

She woke, frightened, not realizing she had slept, to the noise of a knock. Sun slashed through the shutters making a cell of the bed.

"Signora." She leapt up at the sound of the maid's voice, told her to come in, but rushed to hide in the bathroom. Her face in the mirror was bruised, uncanny. The woman called to her through the door. She had brought breakfast and a message from Signor Negri. He had had to go to the mainland. He would be back this evening.

Katherine ran the bath. Waited until she was sure she had gone.

So Carlo had fled. She shivered.

The shutters had been thrown open to the glistening blue of sky and sea. A table perfectly set for breakfast with white linen, a silver coffee jug. The bed, too, had been changed, sparkled white. That hysterical laugh rose to her throat again and choked her. Perhaps the telltale sheet would be hung outside the Castello, proof of the master's virility. She had heard of that custom.

Proof too of his wife's purity.

With a shaky hand, Katherine downed cup after cup of coffee. She had to pull herself together. She would swim, sunbathe, walk around the island. It would calm her, prepare her for Carlo.

She tried to cover her bruises with makeup, donned vast sunglasses, a bikini, shorts. The island was tiny, no more than three miles in diameter. From the Castello the sea was visible all around her. A scattering of small houses clustered around the pier. She walked away from them, clambered over rocks, came across a stretch of vineyard and then on a promontory at the furthest tip of the island lay down to purge herself in the sun's rays.

When she woke, the sun was low on the horizon. In the distance she could see Carlo's yacht already moored. She had a sudden wish to run in the opposite direction. But there was only the sea. She scrambled down the precipice and dived off a rock into the crystalline water. So cool. She swam until she had no breath left and then struggled up rocks to where she had left her things. A rustle woke her to another presence. She looked up to the promontory. Carlo, his eyes on her. She waved, called his name. He turned his back on her, walked away.

The maid came to tell her dinner was ready. At last, she would be able to talk to him. She gave a final brush to her hair, adjusted the strap of her muslin dress, looked at her face. There was nothing more she could do about the bruises.

He was standing, white-suited, severe, on the vine-covered terrace. "Ah, Katerina. There you are. I trust you have had a good day." His voice was even, formal. His eyes didn't meet hers. She saw the old retainer who had welcomed them yesterday, placing some dishes on the table.

"Thank you, yes," she said matching his tone.

"You swam?" His gaze flickered.

She nodded. "I thought you had seen me."

He didn't answer, stared out at the sea. "Would you like a drink?" he asked politely.

She wanted to put her arm on his shoulder. Force him to acknowledge her fully. He looked so brooding, so handsome. Despite herself, a tremor of remembered passion coursed through her.

"Carlo." Her voice cracked.

"Some wine, perhaps a gin?"

"Wine," she murmured.

"*Un po' di vino bianco,* Rodolfo."

When the servant had left them, he turned away from her completely. Didn't speak.

"Carlo," she tried again. "We must talk. Please."

"Talk, Katerina? Words have such fluid meanings. They don't change facts."

"Facts. What facts?" Her voice rose. "You don't understand anything."

"Katerina, this is hardly the moment," he said sternly. A second later, Rodolfo was upon them, bearing a tray, large globes of chilled wine.

The servants, Katherine thought. Never in front of the servants. She sat through a dinner which seemed to go on interminably. Carlo ceased to speak to her as soon as they were alone.

She tried once more to engage him when the zabaglione had been served. "Please, Carlo, listen to me."

He looked at her reflectively, his gaze straying over her bruised face, her bare shoulders, her bosom.

"Later, Katerina."

But there was no later. He didn't come to her that night. Or the next. Or the next. Though that morning, he walked into her room early, waking her. He looked at her coldly. Then without speaking, he rumpled the sheets on his side of the bed, tossed a pillow. The laugh rose to her throat again. "Don't tell me, the servants will be suspicious," she mumbled.

He left without saying a word.

During the days, he vanished. And each dinner was a repetition of the first, but with an added tenseness, an increase in forced politeness so that Katherine began to feel that tone might totally usurp the possibility of any other. They were meant to stay here three weeks, three weeks of glorious honeymoon isolation before the boat was intended to cruise them to a variety of coastal spots. She couldn't bear it any longer.

On Sunday she took her courage in her hands and after the lights in the house were out went in search of his room. She walked in without knocking and he leapt up from the chair where he had been sitting. Newspapers were sprawled on the table. A bottle of whisky, half drunk.

"What are you doing here?" He looked at her threateningly.

"I . . . I couldn't sleep." Katherine shivered, put her arms around her chest. She hadn't prepared her lines and confronted by him, she didn't know where to begin.

"Couldn't sleep?" Sarcasm whipped at her. "Couldn't sleep. Perhaps you need a little injection of male for a sleeping tablet. Is that it? And there's only me here to provide it." The ferocity of his eyes scared her.

"It's not like that, Carlo. You don't understand."

"Don't understand?" He took her by the arms and shook her so that her hair tumbled over her face. She could smell the whisky on his breath. "Don't understand that I married a liar? A slip of a girl who tricked me into believing she was pure?" His fingers dug into her painfully. "Who kept me at bay for a year, two, while she was having it off with others. And then cheated me into marriage. Marriage which is a sacrament." He slapped her, hard across the face.

Tears leapt into her eyes. "No, Carlo, no. It's not like that." But the depth of his rage made her mute, helpless, like a child. Words wouldn't come. She turned away from him, made for the door. He dragged her back. Lifted her chin so that she had to confront the fury in his eyes.

"Why did you do it? Was it for money?" He spat the word to her. "The Buonaterra fortune. Eh? Like a whore. For money."

"I loved you, Carlo," she said softly, the tears streaming down her face.

"Love?" The word seemed to fuel his wrath. "There is no love with whores. Only this." He flung her down on the bed and with one swift gesture loosed his trousers. "And this is what you have come for." With a scowl, he tore off her panties and lunged into her, his hands kneading her breasts, his breath at her ear, a savage chant to the cadence of his thrusts, "Liar, liar, cheat, liar, liar, cheat."

Despite herself, despite the tears, she came to his rhythm in great bounding waves. Afterward, he looked at her as if she were a piece of refuse the sea had washed up. He left the room abruptly.

Katherine sobbed. She felt dirty, defiled, degraded—all those words whose meaning she had never fathomed. And lost. So lost. He hadn't even kissed her. There had been no tenderness, no caress. And yet she had responded. Responded tumultuously.

The next day, she didn't leave her room. Told the maid she was feeling ill. Which was, somehow, the truth. She gazed out of the window, wishing there were someone she could talk to, go to. She was a prisoner. A prisoner in a fairy tale partly of her own making. And a grim tale it had become. The pun startled her, made her think of Portia with her "happily ever after." But she couldn't have told Portia about any of this. It was too demeaning. She wouldn't have understood.

The maid brought her lunch, dinner, was kind. Katherine decided to stay in her room for another day. She couldn't face Carlo. She saw his boat leaving, returning. If only she could go, on one of those little fishing boats. And never come back.

He came to her room after dinner, just as she was scheming means of escape.

"I'm told you're ill," he said. He looked tired, his eyes bleak. "Shall I call a doctor?"

She shook her head. Tried to find her tongue, her courage. "Carlo, I should like to go. Leave here."

He gazed at her as if she were deranged. He paced the room, back and forth, back and forth as if he too were a prisoner in a cell. "Ah no, my little Katerina," he said at last. "It is enough that I know my shame. We will not tell the world. A man and his wife have their honeymoon. The time has already been prescribed. We will not change it."

"I will go mad," she said softly.

"Madness doesn't come so easily," he refuted her. The sardonic expression she had not seen for what seemed like years settled on his face. It reminded her of better days, of London. She took her chance.

"Carlo, it's not how you think. What you say about me. There was only ever one other man. A long time ago. It wasn't important." She blurted it out.

"Not important. A long time ago." He laughed harshly. "You see, you talk like a whore."

He had trapped her again. They were talking two different languages, two different value systems.

"And why should I believe you? I don't believe you." He took her hand, ran his fingers up her bare arm, touched her lips. She trembled. "You see, you like it too much. You couldn't have waited a long time. Not like a good little girl, not like a wife." He spat out the word. "But like a whore."

"Only with you, Carlo. I like it only with you."

"That's what all the whores are taught to say."

Again that trap. She was not a person, with her own history. But a category. One of two categories. A wife or a whore. A virgin or a slut.

"Shall I prove to you again what a whore you are?" His hand on her arm caught her by surprise. Roughly, he stripped her robe from her so that she stood naked before him. Ruthless fingers played over her body, circled her nipples, while all the time cold eyes watched. She caught her breath, steeling herself, but his mouth came down on hers fiercely, punishing her. She gasped.

"You see?" A pitiless laugh. He switched off the light, tumbled her onto the bed.

That night he made love to her—though in retrospect she knew that would not have been the name the romances gave it—in a variety of postures which wrenched her body. Each time, as the climax neared, that voice rasped triumphantly in her ear, *"Puta, puta, puta,"* and then the waves burst upon her.

He left her at dawn.

She didn't sleep. She bathed, looked at her whore's limbs, waited for the sounds of the house. As soon as she heard them, she dressed. A bikini, a sun frock, a broad-brimmed straw hat. She went down to the terrace, had some coffee, waited for him to leave the house.

Sure enough, around nine, he made his way down the steps to the little pier. She raced after him. "I'm coming with you today," she said.

Astonishment spread over his features. And then he mumbled, "Suit yourself."

She perched on the deck of the yacht, the sea spray fresh on her face. Watched the island recede with a sense of jubilation. He didn't speak to her, but he whistled tunelessly as he steered. She recognized that concentration in him. Like when he was driving.

A little glimmer of hope pulled at her. The old Carlo was still there. Perhaps, perhaps, he would see her again as she had been before, as she was.

They moored at Baia on the pretty little Bay of Pozzuoli. He suggested a drink at a beachside terrace. She felt like whooping at the normality of it, as if she had just awoken to find that the past days had been a dream. She dared to touch his arm. But he pulled away, frowned. At the café, he was polite, formally solicitous, aware of the eyes on them. Then he left her, saying he would meet her back at the beach around four.

She watched him, that tall, handsome man with the indolent stride whom she now had to call her husband. She wondered whether she should try to find a bus, flee. She imagined herself returning to London, to her friends. To New York and Jacob. They seemed further away than another planet.

She strolled, visited the Temple of Mercury, the ancient Roman baths, nibbled a roll. Then she went down to the beach, swam, stretched out. Men pursued her like wasps. It was as if they could smell the sex on her. One, particularly persistent, settled himself next to her, talked at the wind. She sat up once, twice and again to tell him to leave her alone. It was then that Carlo chose to reappear.

"Put on your dress," he said brusquely, thrusting it at her. He took her arm and half pushed, half pulled her toward the yacht. His eyes blazed, but he said nothing more, not on the boat, not at dinner.

But later, much later, he came to her room. "So now we know why you wanted to come with me. One isn't quite enough for women like you, is it? You need two, three." She smelled the whiff of his excitement, knew, with a sudden deadly realization, that there was no point arguing. "Why pay for a whore, when I have one right here?" He gripped her shoulders, pushed her down, down to her knees. "Here," he thrust his burgeoning penis in her face. She took him, gently in her hands, wondered at the rush of breath which escaped him. He wound his hand round hers, rubbed, again and again. His eyes were wild. Then, he pushed himself into her mouth, gasped. She thought she would choke. But he forced her movements. In, out, in, out until he heaved into her with a great groan.

She cried.

He kissed her then, almost tenderly. Almost conciliatory, as if the humiliation had gone too far. "Only half a whore," he murmured. He lifted her on to the bed, trailed his fingers over her body so that she shuddered, tucked her in. "Sleep well," he said. And then bent to her ear. "We shall have to teach you to use your tongue."

❖ ❖ ❖

Their life took on a rhythm. When she saw him by day, he was formally punctilious, opening doors for her, pushing in her chair, offering her drinks. But there was never any real exchange, only stilted conversation. At night he came to her, usually in the dark and they performed their rites, rites punctuated by the cry of *whore* at the apogee of their pleasure. She felt humiliation, pain and ecstasy all at once, so that the two became indistinguishable.

She also felt trapped. But it was the trap of an addiction, so though she thought desultorily of leaving, she knew she couldn't, wouldn't. Sometimes, she sensed, it was the same for him.

By day she grew increasingly depressed. They didn't leave the island after three weeks. He suggested casually that it would be better if they spent the rest of the summer here. She knew there would be no point in arguing. She didn't even know any longer whether she wanted to go.

She began to have dreams, by day when she lay in the sun, as well as by night. In them she was always a child. A child who couldn't speak. Mute. Trapped without words. No one understood her. No one listened. They punished her. Punished her for sins she hadn't committed. Slapped her. Called her names. Liar, liar, cheat, whore.

The dreams frightened her.

At last the time came to go back to Rome. They moved into an old palazzo, not far from the Capitol. It had been divided into two gigantic apartments. Ornate wainscotting and parading nymphs curved round a vast staircase. But their floor had been scrubbed bare, whitewashed. There was only the minimum of furniture.

"I thought, all those months ago, that you might want to have a hand in the decor," Carlo murmured to her as a maid fluttered over their arrival.

But Katherine had little energy for it. There was an endless round of visits to make, family, people to be met, and regular trips to the Buonaterra estate so that la Contessa could see her only and favorite son and her new daughter-in-law. Katherine felt she was drowning.

She went to see Maria Novona.

"How beautiful you look, Katherine. Carlo must be making you very happy."

Katherine gazed into the gilded mirror over the fireplace and saw herself through another's eyes. It was true, she thought, with a sinking heart. She looked beautiful, bronzed face, shining hair, eyes tinged with a new meaning, an expression she couldn't recognize. Her body betraying her, once again.

She left, more distressed than when she had arrived.

Carlo, their formal social life apart, was rarely around. He never told her where he was going. There were no nights out in clubs, none of those wondrous drives and expeditions which had marked their courtship. He even began to stay away some nights. When he did, she missed him terribly. An addict without her drug. And she felt even more deeply humiliated. The drug didn't have the same potency for him.

But her mind cleared a little.

One day, she went into his room as he was dressing. Carlo with his indolent grace knotting a tie before his reflected image.

She perched on a chair. "I want to go back to America," she said bluntly.

He looked at her strangely. "You miss your father. You would like to visit him?"

"No—yes," she stumbled. "I want to get out of this, all of it." She gestured wildly around her.

"Out? Of this?" He stared at her blindly, then understood. He laughed maliciously. "*Mia Katerina,*" he said with a threatening patience. "We do not have divorce here." His eyes pinioned her, surveyed her slowly. "Here, we live with our mistakes."

The ready tears sprang to her eyes. "So you agree it is a mistake," she said softly.

He touched her face as if he had suddenly woken to it. "Come, put on a pretty dress. I shall take you out this evening."

He took her to the Via Veneto where the paparazzi's bulbs flashed at their passage. They sat and sipped a daiquiri, made their way to a jazz club, danced. But it wasn't the same, Katherine thought. Carlo's eyes flickered round the room, landed on the swing of another buttock, the lift of another skirt. Afterward, he made love to her, but only perfunctorily.

She realized that they had never slept together for the length of a night in the same bed.

Her dreams grew worse, took on an obsessive intensity. Sylvie appeared in them with growing frequency, her figure blending with Carlo's. Punishing, hitting. It terrified her. She spent whole days in bed. She thought she might call her father, ask him to come to Rome. Help. But a remnant of pride prevented her. "Here, we live with our mistakes." Carlo's voice, haunting her.

She thought of getting a job. After all, she had got a First. But the effort involved seemed insurmountable. She didn't know where to begin, how to raise the matter with Carlo.

Then she started to vomit. Regularly, every morning, after she got up. She went to a doctor. He confirmed what she already knew. She didn't tell Carlo for a week.

When she did, finally, he looked at her with boyish joy, swung her around the room. Her heart lifted. Then he stopped, looked at her sternly. "It is mine, yes?"

That hysterical laugh rose in her. "No. It is Rodolfo's." She named the old retainer at the Castello. "Or perhaps Tom, Dick, Harry's, any man's in the world, except yours."

He gazed at her curiously for a moment and then joined in her laughter.

He kissed her with the first tenderness she had known in months. He grew solicitous, kind. He took her to shops, to antique marts, filled the apartment with flowers. It began to feel like a home, with the nursery as its point of pride. He bought her clothes to shape her pregnancy, soft little dresses with appliqué collars. He would look at her adoringly, each day checking the progress of her belly, stroking it softly. She wanted him, wanted him inside her. The continuing intensity of that desire confounded her. But from the day that she had announced her pregnancy, there was no longer any question of that.

She had the blinding realization that motherhood had redeemed her from whoredom. But he slept only with whores.

She began to take an interest in her pregnancy. When the baby started to kick, she was filled with a sudden joy. She thought about how she would be good to her, hold her, cuddle her, talk to her. Always, in her own mind, the baby was a she. Carlo used the masculine. Amidst all the smiles he gave her, it didn't trouble her.

But she was a little bored. When the rainy, winter days didn't permit walks, she began to read again. There were not many books in the house and she thought nostalgically of her father's copious library. But she read what there was. One day she came across a book in French buried behind some others in the bookshelf. *Justine*, by the Marquis de Sade. It rang a vague bell. She read. The book revolted her and compelled her. Sexual terrors perpetrated on an innocent.

Carlo found the book on her bedside table. He scowled. "Hardly suitable reading for a mother-to-be," he mumbled, took the book away.

She found it again. Scanned the introduction. It was full of termi-nology—*sadism, masochism, perversion*. Terms she remembered from those months she had spent browsing through Jacob's shelves, words that had flown through their conversations. Terms half understood.

Hands folded protectively round her belly, she began to muse. To think about herself. To think about Carlo. According to those terms, she was a masochist. She took pleasure in pain, in humiliation. The notion distressed her, haunted her. Her dreams came back. Sylvie's huge, overblown form predominant in them. Not Sylvie in the flesh, but an atmosphere, a voice, accusing, oppressive, cruel in gesture and language. Liar, cheat. Or simply absent, there but not there, unreachable, untouchable, unhearing.

A child, a toddler, herself, Katherine, reaching out to someone not there. Arms waving in the void. Aching, longing. And then that slap, a hit. She was there. Maman was there. Oh, the pleasure. A touch, a slap. Maman saw her. Touched her. But the touch was hard. Hurt. The words, cruel, nasty. She was a liar. Katherine was a liar, a cheat, dirty. Dirty pants. But still Maman saw her, acknowl-edged her, touched her. Katherine cried. Sobbed. Alone in bed. Dirty. But alive. Seen. Touched. Touch. The relief. The pleasure.

Katherine, hands on her growing belly, her daughter, mused. Thought. Lost in trickles of memory. Probed. Her father's daughter. Her mother's daughter. Pain, pain better than nothing, the void of nonrecognition. Pain become pleasure. Escape from pain, from humiliation by making it into pleasure. Pain become eroticized. Little Kat struggling to be.

Violette came to visit. Bustling, energetic. Katherine threw her arms around her, surprised at how genuinely pleased she was to see her. Violette was full of new plans. She was giving up her work, was going to train as a lawyer. Like her husband.

"Mat, needless to say, is thrilled. I think she's always harbored a secret fantasy of herself as a lawyer. And here I'm going to fulfill it for her at last." Violette laughed, comfortably, deliciously.

Violette was changed, Katherine thought, somehow less frenetic, less shrill.

She read her mind. "Yes, I'm happy, for what it's worth," she grinned at Katherine. They were sitting in a restaurant off the Piazza

Navona. "And you? You look well. The pregnancy suits you." She glanced meaningfully at Katherine's protruding stomach.

"Yes, I'm well," she smiled.

"To tell you the truth, the whole idea has always terrified me." Violette passed her hand through hair that had again grown curly.

"And me," Katherine admitted. But she relished the secret tumble of the baby within her.

"And Carlo?" Violette gazed at her inquiringly. "No, you don't have to say it. I know. He's the proudest father-to-be in the whole world," she chortled, then looked serious. "But the two of you. Are you well together?"

Almost, Katherine wanted to confide in her, try to air something of her feelings to another being. But she couldn't bring herself to. Didn't know where to begin. It was all so hidden, so dark. It didn't belong here in the light of day. So she simply nodded.

"Well, that's a relief," Violette gazed at her speculatively. "Yes," Violette murmured.

The next evening Violette came to have dinner with them at the apartment. She was full of oohs and aahs about the arrangement of things, about the spectacular nursery with its hand-painted mural, a zoo replete with elephants and tigers. They chatted companionably over dinner, Violette as always full of recondite tales which made them giggle over their plates. Katherine was not unaware of Carlo's pleasure in seeing Violette, the glances he cast in her direction.

But he was so affectionate to her, so careful that she ate and drank and sat appropriately, that she didn't mind. She had got used to the idea that she was the precious vessel, the sacred container of the future. It was a better role than some others.

She retired early. It was late in her pregnancy and she was sleepy, preferred lying to sitting. As she was undressing, she remembered that she wanted to give Violette something to take to Mat. It was an article on special schools she had cut out of the *Corriere della Sera* and it mentioned Princesse Mathilde and Jacob and a school they had founded in Paris years ago. Katherine had never known anything about it.

She went back to the sitting room with her package. They were standing there by one of the luxuriant palms, bodies tensed, gazing at each other. Carlo's hand gripping Violette's shoulder. Katherine paused, eavesdropped, despite herself.

"You *will* come. Later. I want you to." Carlo, urgent.

Violette shaking her head. "No."

"I'm sorry," Katherine said quietly, "I just wanted to give Violette this to take to Mat."

Violette had the grace to flush. Carlo simply looked surly.

Katherine lay in her bed and gazed up at the ceiling, her heart pounding. It was not, she rationalized, as if she hadn't known. Violette predated her. But now . . . She had no illusions about Carlo's fidelity to her. She knew, without having tangible proof, that he went to women. It was the way of things. Sanctioned by the society. Men, real men, couldn't be expected to contain themselves for all those months. In the abstract, she hadn't minded terribly, had turned her thoughts away from it. But faced with the reality, with the real presence of Violette, that look, that hand on her shoulder . . . it made her feel sick.

She stroked her stomach. After her daughter was born, all that would change. She would see to it.

Natalie Marina Negri della Buonaterra was born on the first of July 1968. Katherine thought she was the most beautiful creature in all the world. She lay gazing at her for hours, watching those tiny hands grasping that absurdly dark tuft of hair, the luminous eyes, that puckered rosebud mouth folding itself around her nipple, sucking, sucking. She stroked and cradled and held her, crooning softly, unwilling to let her go even for a moment.

Carlo, after an initial flicker of regret that his baby wasn't a boy, looked on adoringly. He, too, held the baby, rocked her, sang, little snatches of opera, nonsense tunes, patted, pampered. They were, for those first months, the happiest family in the world. The hundreds of pictures recorded it—the three of them in the clinic just outside Rome, at home in the nursery, at the Palazzo with the Contessa; Natalie in a dozen different poses, at Katherine's breast, in Carlo's arms, alone waving her legs in the air.

Jacob came to visit, to ogle his granddaughter, to hurl her in the air. He was pleased. He had been wrong. His daughter was contented. All his anxieties, silly paternal ravings. Carlo was good to her, mad about the child.

Katherine looked at him, looked at all her visitors, her well-wishers, lovingly. From a little distance. Her bond was with Natalie. She slept when the baby slept, woke when she woke, in a continuum which enclosed only them. When those little lips closed themselves around her nipples, when that cry ceased, she felt for the first time that she was needed. A being who wasn't superfluous in the world.

When Natalie was six months old, Leo stopped in Rome on his

way to New York. He brought with him a beautiful black woman, tall, stately, a fellow doctor from the hospital in Tanzania. Carlo's eyes, mesmerized, followed her round the sitting room. Katherine felt ashamed. She tried to make intelligent conversation with her brother, with his colleague, but her mind, unused, refused to formulate thoughts. And she could smell their disapproval, their contempt for the luxurious apartment, for Carlo, for her, with her idle life, her nannies, her maids. She clutched Natalie to her and she thought about the world her brother inhabited, the scarcity, the illnesses containable by wealth, the children, orphaned, dying. She held Natalie more closely.

Later she said to Carlo, "My brother thinks we're decadent."

He shrugged. "In Rome we think decadence is good. We have a saying. 'Only with decadence can you have culture.' Bread, bread is not enough. We need beauty to live. And Rome is beautiful. We are not barbarians."

A moment later, he added, "And don't tell me that puritanical brother of yours doesn't screw that black beauty he brought with him."

She felt like slapping him.

But after that, gradually, she began to take an interest in things. She read the papers every day from cover to cover, amazed that so many things had passed her by, student uprisings, changes in government. She began to have the need to do something, like an itch, slight at first and then as she scratched it, stronger and stronger. She wrote to Portia asking her if any of the magazines in the group she worked for might be interested in having the occasional article. A round-up of Roman galleries, say. It wouldn't—she thought about this carefully—take her away from Natalie.

Portia said they would give her a try.

The letter brought relief and anxiety. She had no confidence. She looked at herself carefully in the mirror. Her figure was almost back, but she needed new clothes, a new hairdo. She had her hair cut stylishly shoulder-length, bought an array of clothes, smart suits with short skirts and Edwardian jackets, loose black trousers which accentuated her height, ruffled silk shirts, Indian print dresses with swirling skirts.

With Natalie sometimes in tow she made the rounds of the galleries, meeting owners, going to vernissages. An article was accepted, then another. She was jubilant. She hugged Natalie. And she felt her mind working.

Carlo was quick to notice the change. She wasn't altogether sure he liked it, but he didn't comment. Now and then, however, his eyes flickered over her. It stirred something in her, something which since Natalie's birth she had almost forgotten. Once stirred, it bubbled and boiled. She wasn't sure she liked it. She lay in bed at night thinking.

Carlo hadn't come to her in almost two years. And suddenly she wanted him, wanted his hands, his weight on her body, him inside her. But she was also afraid. She didn't want the drug, the addiction, the humiliation, the pain. Yet she sensed somehow that she was different, that Natalie had changed her, that she had changed. And the desire, day by day as she watched Carlo lazily folding a napkin or rocking Natalie on his knee, night by night alone in her bed, grew in her.

One night, in the early hours, she couldn't stand it anymore. She went to his room. She knocked, went in. He wasn't there. It shocked her. She knew that when they spent weeks in the Palazzo during the hot months, or on holidays, he sometimes spent nights away, in Rome. But here at home, she had always assumed that he came back, slept here. He was always there in the morning for Natalie. She was astounded at her own ignorance of his life. And angry.

By rights now, he should be with her.

And she wanted him.

She crawled into his bed, sniffed his scent, curled up, waited.

The dial on the bedside clock showed five when she heard his footsteps. He switched the light on, saw her.

"What, may I ask, are you doing here?" A low voice, containing irritation.

"I . . . I wanted to see you."

"Well, now you have seen me, you can go straight back to your room."

"Where have you been, Carlo?" Katherine didn't move.

"That is hardly any of your business."

"Being here is your business."

"Since when?" He looked startled.

She hesitated. "Since now, since always." She stretched out her hand to him. "I want you," she said softly.

"Katherine. It is late. I am tired. Please go to your room now."

She shook her head, restraining tears. "I'm not going."

"Very well, then." He looked at her grimly. She suddenly noticed new lines on his face, a kind of desperation.

He took off his jacket, his trousers, and leaving his shirt on he lay down beside her on top of the blanket. She tried to take his hand.

"Go to sleep," he said, turning his back on her. He slept within seconds.

When she woke, he was already up, playing with Natalie. He avoided her eyes.

"Carlo," she said to him over breakfast. "Carlo, let's have a weekend together, just you and I."

He looked at her strangely, almost in fear. "Without Natalie?"

She nodded. "She'll be all right with Lina for a few days."

"Where would you like to go?" he asked stiffly. "Venice, Monte Carlo?"

She shrugged. "Anywhere. So that we can be alone together a little."

He didn't say anything but a few nights later he came to her room. She was reading.

"*E bene.*" His lips curled in a smile which was also distaste. He switched off the light, perched on the bed, played with her breasts perfunctorily and then heaved into her. She arched to him, sought his lips. But they were far away. She could feel his coldness, his distance, yet despite herself, her body moved with him. It was over too soon. He stood up.

"Carlo," she called after him.

He didn't give her a chance to speak. "You are happy, yes? We will have another baby soon."

The next day she went to the doctor and had a diaphragm fitted. She didn't want another child. Not yet. Not like that. Out of coldness.

He came to her regularly now, once a week, dutifully. The child-making machine. Shielding herself from the full horror of the past, she thought that in a way this was worse than before. Before, in spite of the cruelty, the slaps, there had been passion. His and hers. A kind of love. Now, there was nothing. Only her memory of passion, which she fantasized for herself out of the shape of his body, the trace of a kiss, the rumor of a touch. Yet she waited for him, wanted even that. A new kind of humiliation smoldered. The humiliation of rejection, the lack of desire.

In his own time, he took her to Venice. They drove and she was aghast at the new recklessness of his driving. Before she had sensed his excitement, been aware of her own. Now she felt there was only a need for obliteration, an obliteration harder and harder to obtain. It frightened her, but the fear bore no attendant exhilaration. She thought that perhaps she had changed. That perhaps he had too. But they had moved in opposite directions. She thought of Natalie, wanted to hold her. As soon as they arrived at the Danieli she phoned home, desperate for the peal of that little voice.

The weekend was not a success. They saw friends, trailed through museums, on the surface a perfect couple. But at night, in the vast bed, he read the newspapers. She tried to touch him, lifted the silk of his robe. He moved her hand away, carelessly.

"You don't want me," she said, a dismal statement.

He turned a page of his paper. "You are my wife. The mother of my children. That is enough."

"It's not enough for me," she said softly.

He didn't rise to it, read on.

Suddenly, she shouted at him. "You have a mistress. That's where you take your passion. Tell me. Admit it."

He looked at her grimly. "Katerina, don't be a child. Go to sleep."

"I'll find out. I'll go home. Take Natalie with me. Get a divorce there. Find a lover," she shrieked at him.

He slapped her. The sound rang between them. Cold. Dispassionate. There was nothing on his face except irritation. She returned it with contempt.

She went to the bathroom. Locked the door. Cried. Violette had warned her, she suddenly thought. What was it she had said about Carlo? His moods, power games. He must have been with Violette for years. On and off. What was it about her which fueled his desire? Violette, so vital, always different, while she, Katherine, was boring, always the same. She looked at her tear-stained face in the mirror. People, others, found her attractive. She knew that. But not him. And yet he had, once, all those years ago. Had desired her then. She remembered his eyes warm on her, his kisses. She loved him when she remembered. It flooded over her.

She would reawaken that love in him. She would follow him, find his mistress, emulate her. Yes. She would try.

She washed her face. Went back into the darkened room. Later that night, he came in to her. In her hope, she clothed him in the robes of desire and clung to him.

But after that weekend, he stopped coming to her almost altogether.

They spent the summer months again at the Palazzo. Despite the beauty of the place, despite the grounds across which Natalie, beaming, exploring, joyously hurtled, Katherine hated it there. The formality of those endless dinners, the vapid faces of the extended family, the Contessa herself, with her advice on child-rearing, her endless conversation about Princess so-and-so and Archbishop whatever— Katherine felt it would all stifle her. And Carlo, so polite, and so utterly removed, his eyes never meeting hers. It was unbearable.

When he announced that he had to be in Rome for a few days, she begged him, "Take us with you. Please."

He demurred, "It's too hot. It will be unhealthy for Natalie. You're better off here."

The next day, pleading work, an article, she asked the Contessa's chauffeur to take her to Rome. She arrived at midday, browsed through galleries amidst countless tourists. Carlo was right. It was too hot. She went back to the apartment. He wasn't there. She showered. Without quite knowing why, she changed. A black trouser suit of loose silk over a little camisole. She made herself up carefully, tucked her hair into a large black straw hat. Then she went to sit in a café opposite the apartment, watched its door, waited.

He arrived. Almost, she went up to meet him. But something kept her back. An hour later he came out again, changed, his face freshly shaven. He was whistling. She rose, trailed that graceful, sauntering stride. He got into his car. She hailed a cab and feeling like a criminal, asked the driver to follow Carlo. She thought in the traffic that they had lost him, but in the narrow streets beyond the Spanish Steps, they found him again.

He pulled into a tiny gap between two cars. Katherine waited and then as he moved down the road, she paid off her cabbie and followed him once more. It was dark, the streets filled with strollers enjoying the breath of evening, but through their midst she saw him turn into a lane and walk into a porticoed house. She stopped nervously in front of it, paced. What was she to do now? A laughing group of people, women in long gowns, men in light summer suits, walked through the doors. Perhaps it was a club. She rang the bell.

A man opened it, looked at her curiously, asked if she were a member. She gazed at him blankly. "I'm afraid this is a members only club," he said to her sternly. She almost told him she was Signora Negri, but something held her back. She waited. When another group of people arrived at the door, she took her hat off, put on a large smile and sauntered in with them.

She followed them up a marble staircase. A large domed room, chandeliers, gaming tables. So it was that kind of club. Covertly she looked around for Carlo. She spied him toward the back of the room, his face intent on the roulette wheel. There was a glazed set to his features, a grimness in his eyes. But there was no woman on his arm. She wanted to laugh, go up to him, kiss him. But she didn't. He wouldn't have been pleased. Instead, she made herself small at the room's distance from him. A man came up to her, grazed her with his eyes. Would she like to come downstairs for a drink with him, perhaps something more? His gestures insinuated.

She shook her head, walked away, found another position. A while later, she saw Carlo making his way out of the room. She followed him from a distance, down the long staircase. But he didn't leave. Instead he continued through another door, down more steps.

It was darker here, arches, columns. Catacombs. From somewhere, the rhythmic din of music. Couples dancing slowly, desultorily. Smoke, smoke floating everywhere in bluish light. The high sweet reek of marijuana. She lost Carlo, almost tripped over a couple on the floor, embracing, kissing passionately. Another space, cushions on the floor, bodies writhing, a tumble of limbs, clad, bare. An arm around her, embracing her, holding her, forcing her lips. She pulled away. The man followed her with bemused eyes, lurched on. On to another woman.

Carlo, where was he? Panic rose in her. A man waved his erect penis at her, leered, satyr-like, crushed her breast with his hand. She stumbled, cowered against a column. It was then that she saw him, standing, not far from her. A woman in front of him, on her knees, her hands caressing his hips, her hair tumbling over his loins, her tongue, licking, sucking. Another pair of arms around his chest. Another woman behind. No. No. Katherine stared. Transfixed. Not a woman, a man. A cock probing into taut buttocks. Carlo's face contorted, straining, gasping. His eyes, bright, dilated. Pleasure. Such pleasure. He was coming. Coming into her mouth. She could feel it, hear his shout.

She cried out over it, "Carlo."

He looked blindly in her direction. Focused. Grim eyes, the curl of a lip. He pulled her up, over to him. "A new little whore." He turned to his friends. "Quite pretty, really. Look." He ripped off her jacket, tore open her camisole. Held her under the chin. "Quite beautiful in fact. A little Madonna of the Rocks. No? Look, Giovanni, for you, perhaps?" He thrust her at Giovanni. "I think she'll like you. She's dying for it. See. She's wet already. No, no"—he pulled her back—"let me prepare her for you." He kissed her, cruelly, painfully, his face a mask of derision, loathing. "There now, she's ready. Take her." He pushed her away.

Katherine ran, stumbling, crying. Somehow, she could never remember how, she made her way back to the apartment, put on fresh clothes, found a taxi to take her the kilometers to the Palazzo. The next day she packed some bags. For herself, for Natalie, for the nanny, Lina. She made excuses, said a friend in London needed her. She left.

Two nights later, the telephone in her Hyde Park hotel room woke her. When she picked it up, there was no preliminary greeting, only a trail of abuse.

"*Puta.* Who have you got in your bed? Eh? Tell me. Tell me, you whore?"

Carlo. Surly. Drunk. She could almost smell the whisky on his breath.

"In London to play at Messalina? Rome isn't good enough for you, eh? Tell me, whore."

Katherine hung up without saying a word. Her hands were shaking. She reached for a glass of water, then dropped it, as the phone rang again. And again. She didn't answer it. Forced herself to lie completely still in that room whose silence was intermittently punctured by the telephone's insistent ringing. Finally, she took her courage in hand and, as coolly as she could, told the switchboard that she would not be taking any more calls that night, whatever their source, no, not even from her husband. She was grateful only for the fact that Natalie and Lina in the room next door were undisturbed.

Somehow she managed to get through the next day, take Natalie to the zoo, eat ice cream in the park, smile attentively.

And then late that night, it started again. She picked up the receiver and heard that harsh slurring voice, thick with insults. How dare he? Anger suddenly filled her, pulled her off the bed. How dare he talk to her like this after all that had happened? She started to scream into the receiver, "Leave me alone, Carlo. Don't ring again. Let me be."

An odd hush met her eruption and then his voice again, cold now. "Let you be? Let you be with whom?"

"With whom? There has to be someone, does there? Well, I'll tell you what there will be. There will be a divorce. In America if not in Rome. I'm going home. Now leave me alone."

"You are going nowhere." Carlo's tone was menacing. "I am coming. Coming right now to take you back here. To bring my daughter home. *My daughter."* The force with which he hung up resonated in Katherine's ear.

She lay back on the pillow, exhausted. She could picture him so clearly, that sullen handsome face, the eyes desperate in their anger, the hand almost crushing the glass it held. She could see his tensed shoulders as he paced the room like some imprisoned animal. And then the leap into action. Yes, she could see him bounding into the car and driving. Driving wildly. Driving here.

The image almost paralyzed her. And she sat up again. She didn't want to go back. Couldn't go back. Not to that. And he would come here and force her. Compel her with his presence. Force her through Natalie. "My daughter." His emphasis echoed threateningly in her ears. No, no, not that. She had to get away. Now. Instantly.

Katherine threw her clothes into her bag. At the first light of dawn, she woke Natalie and Lina. With a bright smile, she announced, "I thought we'd go to the country today."

It was because of that journey into Sussex that Katherine did not hear until two days after the event that Carlo was dead. Killed in a car crash as his car careered over the Alps.

She cried.

CHAPTER
TWENTY

*T*he headquarters of Gismondi
Enterprises occupied a large dignified block in the heart of Milan.
From his airy office at the summit of the building, Alexei could
glimpse the tracery on the roof of the Duomo just a few streets
away.

He glanced at it now, then turned his attention to the briefing
sheet which lay on the ebony rectangle of his desk. He read intently
for a few minutes.

A smile tugged at his lips and finally settled. Giangiacomo was at
it again, casting him as the firm's troubleshooter.

Alexei leaned back in his chair and gazed at the single silver-
framed poster on the wall opposite him. His film. *La Donna del
Sud.* He had learned, just yesterday, that it had been awarded
another prize at a festival. Pleasing.

But now Giangiacomo wanted him to contend with the women
from Milan. A different proposition, that. Alexei chuckled.

After those years of turmoil in his early twenties, they had arrived
at an easy relationship, he and Giangiacomo. During the summer
months Alexei had spent in Sicily, tempers had cooled. And since
there was nothing to do there but read and plot his film, he had
somehow managed to pass his exams, get his degree.

Then there had been his period of military service. Strangely, he
had enjoyed that, enjoyed being thrust together with men from such

different backgrounds. But Giangiacomo had contrived to have his period of military service cut short.

Contacts. The web of contacts. He wondered whether the article he had read recently in an American paper was true: seven phone calls would bring you in touch with anyone from any walk of life in the whole world.

And influence. Giangiacomo certainly seemed to have a great deal of that.

He had come back to Milan to work with Giangiacomo at the headquarters of Gismondi Enterprises. Giangiacomo set him tasks. One week it was to research the viability of a small company making window blinds and write a report. The next to sit with the chief accountant and go through cash flow projections for the electrical appliances sector. The third to observe union negotiations at the refrigerator plant. The fourth to do a survey of what customers in a major department store looked for when they went in search of lighting fixtures. The fifth to work with an advertising accounts executive on a new campaign.

And so it went on. Alexei didn't like to admit it, but he enjoyed the experience, found it intriguing.

Sometimes, when he brought Giangiacomo back a report which pleased him, his uncle would say, "You see. It isn't so tedious here. Not for a young man of your natural curiosity."

Giangiacomo also took him along to meetings in New York, in Paris, in Milan, with various company managers, bankers, other executives, union officials. At the end of such meetings, Giangiacomo would often turn to him and ask for his impressions, his comments, his views.

One day, after Alexei had worked with him for some six months, Giangiacomo said to him, "Alexei, I am very pleased with you. You are valuable to me, particularly in meetings, very particularly in those interminable negotiation meetings. You are observant, you listen, you are attentive to detail, you never seem impatient or irritated, and you sum up dispassionately, fairly, as subtly as a lawyer." He beamed. "I think I am going to give you a raise in salary."

Alexei colored a little. "Thank you," he murmured. He was flattered by his uncle's pleasure. He, too, had grown to respect him more, not for the qualities his uncle had named, but for his energy, his drive, his humor. Watching Giangiacomo at work was like observing a well-tuned dynamo.

But Alexei was intent on something other than being an employee of Gismondi Enterprises. He cleared his throat, braced himself for a row.

"It may or may not be the moment to tell you, but I'm determined now to take up film-making."

Giangiacomo's features registered utter surprise. Alexei didn't let him interrupt. "I have found backers, a production company prepared to invest in my script."

"You have found backers?" Giangiacomo's features below the bald pate settled into skepticism.

Alexei nodded. "We have a production schedule. We intend to start casting in a month's time. Then film on location in Sicily."

Giangiacomo met his eyes sternly. Then suddenly he let out a loud guffaw. "My secretive son." He embraced him. "We must drink to this. Bring out the best champagne." He clapped Alexei on the back.

They drank. Alexei was both surprised and delighted at his uncle's equanimity.

"And tell me, Alexei." Giangiacomo looked at him shrewdly. "Why didn't you come to me for finance?"

Alexei shrugged. "You don't have a production company."

"I see"—Giangiacomo gazed at him reflectively—"I see." He paused. "And how long will it take to make this film?"

"About six months."

"You know, Alexei." Giangiacomo took a sip from his glass, looked at him ruefully. "I have to make a confession to you. Our argument all those years back about fascists? Well, you were right." He scratched his head. "I was mistaken. They are the same nasty thugs today, with their bombs, and their violence, and their protectors in high places. To think that in nineteen seventy-two almost nine percent of Italians can vote for neofascists. I can hardly believe it." He shook his large round head sadly. "I was wrong."

"Thank you," Alexei murmured. "Thank you for saying this."

The film, once the editing had been done, took seven months to complete. Seven intense glorious months, a number of them in a small seaside town in western Sicily. He didn't know in retrospect what had meant more to him. The months on location, living and working with a group of people who created their own world in order to invent a parallel universe on the screen. Or the months spent in the dark intent isolation of the editing room, where the strips of celluloid were slowly reassembled to breathe an imaginary life. But he knew he had never before been so happy, felt so totally at ease, so sure.

Giulietta Capistano, a young actress, had played the lead, the woman he had still at the beginning of the shoot thought of in his mind as Francesca. He hadn't realized at the outset what an intimate business directing actors was, how keen the knowledge of each movement of the brow or lips, each gesture, became. So that one dreamt their bodies. And dream flowed seamlessly into that counter-reality which was the time of the production.

By the end of the first week, he had fallen in love with Giulietta. Or was she simply the consummation of Francesca? He didn't know. They made love, secretly, shyly at first and then with a heat which was an echo of the island's. He was not unaware of the irony of that fulfillment. What had been impossible in reality, what remained impossible in his film's narrative, was shadowily realized in the world which existed between the two of these. Gradually Giulietta's image usurped Francesca's, so that in later life, he could not separate the two.

Wanting to continue that love, he had seen Giulietta again several times in the wet autumn of Milan, but always with a sense of shock. They both acknowledged, a little sadly, that the affair was over. Giulietta had a new part. For Alexei, she continued to exist, time-stopped, in the flickering images of his movie.

The film finished, a project that had obsessed him for years, he was at a loose end. He started to dream new ventures.

Giangiacomo wanted him back at Gismondi Enterprises. Was persuasive, insistent. A wave of strikes had been sweeping Italy. His uncle claimed that they were in part the work of radical infiltrators, Alexei's old friends, he scowled at him.

"If that is your analysis of the situation, then what you are saying to me is that you want me to work against my friends?" Alexei looked at him incredulously. "Not a very sound move, I would have thought."

"I want you to come and work with me. Full stop. And sometimes, only when it's necessary, to be the final point of call in these disputes. You understand them, understand these people's language."

"And you think I can be co-opted for the company's needs that easily. That's insulting. How do you know I won't move to the other side?"

Giangiacomo had looked at him for a long time. "I think you'll be fair. You have, it's become clear to me, a sense of justice. I think you know that I am not a mad dictator. I believe that what is good for the workforce is, on the whole, good for the company."

"And what if I think the power structure should be turned topsy-turvy? That profits should be shared?" Alexei teased him, egged him on.

"Bah! Student claptrap. Anarchist fantasies. You don't believe a word of it. Just think of your film. Did you work on the principle of a naïve collective? Did you allow the sound man to make decisions about cuts? Did the person who made up your actress determine her lines? Would you have got a lead actor if you paid him the same as an extra? Codswallop, all of it."

"No, of course not. Now *you're* being deliberately naïve. But I listened to the sound man if he had a point to make or said his accommodation was terrible. And we all ate together," Alexei added, a little lamely. "Anyhow, it's not a useful analogy. We weren't a vast enterprise."

Giangiacomo chuckled. "And will you all share in the proceeds?"

"Hardly. It's not my decision. A production company invested in the film, not me."

"And if it were you, dare I suggest to you that you wouldn't? Because if you did, there would be no money to invest in the next film. It follows for Gismondi Enterprises. No profits, no company, no jobs."

Alexei smiled. He had rehearsed the arguments to himself many times. He knew that on this level at least, on the level of the total transformation of capitalism, he had for the past years had few illusions. But that still left a vast area for improvement. "I'll think about what you propose," he said to his uncle. "But I have my own proposition to make as well."

He brought out a sheaf of papers, neatly bound, presented them to his uncle. "I've been thinking of forming a film production company within Gismondi Enterprises. A high-risk business. But with some advantages. This is the business plan. Since you won't let me go, we might as well try and combine our interests. Will you have a look?"

Giangiacomo's laugh boomed across the room. "I always knew you were a shrewd negotiator, Alexei. I always suspected it. Tit for tat, eh my son?" He laughed again. "I will study your proposal carefully."

And so Alexei had moved into the office at the top of the Gismondi building. Occasionally troubleshooting for Giangiacomo, gradually putting the machinery and projects in place for the production company.

His secretary buzzed. "The women have arrived, Signor Gismondi. Shall I send them through?"

"Give me another minute, Daniella." He glanced quickly at the list of demands again. A curious case, this one, a new development.

Alexei rose as three women filed into his office. One a middle-aged matron with a round pleasant face; the second a neatly dressed young woman, her hair pinned demurely into a bun; the third . . . Alexei looked again. A blaze of red hair overtook the muted colors of his office. A vibrant, electric blaze floating above a delicate, lightly freckled face, a slight, supple, blue-suited form. She looked all of eighteen.

The redhead spoke first. "Maria Buora, Bianca Morelli"—she pointed to the other two women—"and I am Rosa Venturi." The voice that came from her was bigger than she was, sure, bold.

"Please, *signore*." Alexei gestured them toward chairs.

He noticed that Rosa Venturi perched at the very edge of hers.

"You know why we are here," she said evenly. Green-flecked hazel eyes pinioned him. The voice didn't give him time to respond. "We, the women at Conti's, want equal pay with the men, the description of our jobs upgraded so that there is no question of our right to that equal pay. We want access to more highly skilled jobs. We want a women's representative on the Factory Council. We want a negotiable maternity leave with a minimum of three months with full pay and jobs held until we return." All this she barked out in a staccato voice.

"Is that *all* you want, Miss Venturi?" Alexei cocked an eyebrow.

"No, that is not all we want, Signor Gismondi." She met his eyes, immune to their irony. "That is merely a beginning. And if we do not get it, we will withdraw our labor. There will be no canteen. The factory will not be cleaned. The entire small-parts division will walk out. And so will a portion of the design team."

Alexei looked at her. All that fire emanating from the small frame. "May I ask why you haven't gone through the proper channels, worked through your union representatives? None of this, as I understand it, came up in the last round of negotiations."

Rosa Venturi flashed him a contemptuous glance. "Signor Gismondi, if we have come to you directly, it is because our unions have no interest in our just demands. Ask my colleagues here."

Alexei glanced at the other two women, whose eyes were cast down. They looked fearful. Finally one of them nodded.

"Our *male* union representatives"—Rosa Venturi's tone dripped acid—"see women as an unpaid service industry. Women wash their dirty underwear, take care of their screaming children, dish up the pasta. And are there to be screwed."

The word fell into the still air of the elegant office with a clatter. Rosa's colleagues flushed. Alexei wasn't sure of the color of his own face. But her eyes were on him.

He chuckled. "I dare say, Miss Venturi . . ."

"This is not a laughing matter." She pulled him up short. "And since our union representatives are male to a man, they cannot begin to see us as fellow workers with a set of grievances as important as their own."

"Indeed." He looked at her seriously. "But you are asking for rather a lot, all in one go. It will take us time to consider this." He paused. "I shall send someone down from head office to have a look into affairs at Conti's."

"Send a woman," Rosa Venturi said abruptly. "Oh, but no, of course, you probably don't have a woman on your senior staff. How silly of me to suggest it." She looked at him benignly, masquerading innocence.

"I'll come myself," Alexei said.

"And you, as the maker of *La Donna del Sud*, imagine that you think like a woman?" She laughed, her small nose turning up in derision.

Alexei looked at her in open surprise.

Her face suddenly fixed itself in politeness, as if she had gone too far. "We can hope for no better," she said tersely, stood.

He held the door open for them, only to be taken up short. "We can open our own doors, Signor Gismondi. We hardly need the veneer of polite tributes to remind us of our supposed helplessness."

Alexei stood back. "I can hardly imagine you as ever being helpless, Miss Venturi," he murmured under his breath.

As soon as they had gone, Alexei buzzed his secretary. "Find out about this Rosa Venturi for me, will you. A detailed CV."

He was irritated. And intrigued. He had realized as soon as Rosa Venturi had opened her mouth that she was not the usual member of the workforce. Her choice of words, her accent, betrayed other origins. But he had never met her like before. In the circles in which he moved, discussion of feminism, of women's rights, of male machismo, had in the last year hardly been rare. But in his office, across a negotiating table, and with the forceful ardor which Rosa Venturi had brought to it . . . never.

As soon as he could in the following week, Alexei drove down to the Conti plant. He had been there only once before and he didn't know it well. But he did now know something more about Rosa Venturi. She was twenty-four, the daughter of a schoolteacher from Bergamo. She had studied law for three years and then dropped out. The legal studies explained something of her ability to argue. It didn't explain the fierceness, the fire she brought to the task.

Alexei, at the age of twenty-seven, was still in something of a quandary about women. His youthful encounter with Francesca had left a deep residue, the texture of an identification, an understanding. But with that exception, he tended to float in and out of relationships, never quite sure how they had begun, never desperate for them to go on once they seemed over. His affairs had the aura of a dream, deeply present, and yet not quite substantial. Women liked him, liked his hesitancy, presented themselves to him. He was sensitive to their desires, tended to idealize them, was always a little breathlessly aware of what he thought of as their fragility.

He had never lived in close proximity with a woman, not even, effectively, a mother.

If he had been asked to put into words what it was about Rosa that intrigued him after that first meeting, he might have said it was the sense he had of her being substantial. A fierce compact mass of resistance. He could reconstruct everything she had said, every flicker of her eyes, every electric shake of that ruddy head.

When he went to the Conti factory that rainy morning, he had the sense that he was embarking on a new kind of adventure. He talked first with the manager.

The man threw his hands up in the air. "It's that woman. Everything was fine until she came here. We should never have hired her. And I've thought of sacking her, but she does her job adequately, fulfills regulations to a T. And now the women see her as a leader. She started having these informal meetings with them, before I realized what was going on. Twice a week, like gossip sessions, we thought. In the canteen, where she works. And now!" He struck his head with his fist.

Alexei went to see one of the union representatives. Here the reaction was rather more aggressive. "That one. That Venturi. All the problems started with her. We thought everyone would be happy when the Factory Council was set up last year. But no, she started to petition. Make demands. Barged in once and harangued us with a long speech. Joan of Arc. And she's turned the women against us. They all seethe with suspicion now."

"You know what she needs." The man made an obscene gesture with his arm. "Eh, a few *bambini*. That would sort her out."

"And did you try?" Alexei asked with pretended naïveté.

"That one," the man grumbled. "She's an icebox."

Alexei spent some time in the various workplaces, watched, listened. During the lunchbreak he went to the canteen. Rosa was behind the counter, her uniform bristling blue and white, her hair bright. He helped himself to a glass of wine, asked for a plate of pasta. Her eyes challenged him. "Spying?" she mumbled. "We need some action soon, next week." She turned to the next person in the line.

At the end of the afternoon, he waited for her to emerge from the building. She was with a group of women, talking volubly. He signaled to her. "Can I give you a lift home?"

"I'm not going home," she said blandly.

He shrugged. "A lift elsewhere then. It might be useful if we talked."

She followed him to the car park. "Cavorting with the enemy won't do you any good," she said, defying him with every inch of her presence.

He looked at her for a moment and then unlocked the door of the car. He didn't speak again until they had left the factory grounds. Then he said, his tone a little grim. "We are trying to run a company here, Miss Venturi, not a sex war. This used to be a relatively happy firm. Now——"

She cut him off. "Happy? What do you know about it? The women weren't happy. They were just cowed, docile. Used to being exploited."

Alexei's eyes flickered. He braked too hard at a red light. It was raining, the ground sodden. The car squealed. He switched the position of the windshield wipers. "What are your interests here, Miss Venturi? You're hardly our usual canteen worker."

Her voice too was even. "You know my interests. I imagine they were put quite succinctly in that fat brief you had on your desk. And if that was too difficult for you to read, we stated them when we came to your office."

"We?" Alexei murmured. "Would the other women in the company be quite so adamant if you weren't there?"

"Are you threatening me with the sack?"

"Hardly." Alexei laughed. "That wouldn't be my job."

"Good. Because we'd all be out tomorrow on a case of unjust dismissal. I do my job well."

"I'm sure," Alexei muttered. "But it seems to me you do have an unusual interest in calling strikes. Strikes without the unions' sanction. Have you thought what would happen to your friends if they were all dismissed? I imagine they need their jobs."

He could feel her compact body growing taut. Stiff with emotion. "You can drop me here," she said abruptly.

"Here?" Alexei queried. They were in a tawdry area of high-rise workers' flats.

"Here," she ordered. She turned to him as he pulled up short, her face fierce. "Mr. Gismondi, it won't come to that." Her voice was low, carrying a hint of menace. "I have friends, journalists. It wouldn't look good for the supposedly benevolent head of Gismondi Enterprises, *your* father, to be seen sacking a bunch of helpless women. It might tarnish his image." Suddenly, she laughed with girlish glee.

He had an overwhelming desire to shake her. "And you think a little publicity would trouble Giangiacomo? Shake Gismondi Enterprises?" he derided her.

Their eyes locked.

"Oh no," she said softly after a moment. "I have no illusions. Only a bomb or two would shake Gismondi." She realized she had gone too far, opened the door, got out quickly, then turned back to him. "Next week. We want our answer by next week."

"You shall have it when everything has been duly considered," Alexei murmured.

He watched her walk toward the door of one of the apartment blocks. Blue jeans, booted feet, a short jacket. And that blaze of hair. He stopped the direction of his thoughts. But he waited, not quite sure why he was waiting.

She didn't reappear.

Alexei asked management at Conti's to do figures on salary differentials, complete with job descriptions; on the numbers of women who had left the firm because of pregnancy; on the impact of possible changes on running costs and profits. The figures troubled him. Rosa Venturi had a point.

He went to see Giangiacomo.

His uncle groaned. "If we give in, it will spread."

"It will probably spread in any event," Alexei said. "It's in the air."

"Will they walk out?"

Alexei shrugged. "Probably. It's their leader. She wants the publicity." He felt a surprising little shudder of betrayal as he said it.

"The publicity will make it spread quicker," Giangiacomo muttered. "Hammer out a compromise. The factory's solid enough."

Alexei composed a letter, a cogent open letter, explaining what was possible, what not. In his mind, he had a firm picture of Rosa as she read it. Her anger, a little glimmer of self-satisfaction in those flecked eyes.

The answer came within a few days. It accepted everything Alexei had proposed gratefully. It didn't bear Rosa's signature. He found out she had left the firm the day after his letter had arrived. A low whistle escaped him.

A week later he was still thinking about her. At odd moments, her voice came into his ear, a voice filled with passionate outrage. He found her telephone number in a file, rang her. He was told that she no longer lived at that number. The level of his disappointment surprised him.

Alexei buried himself in work. The production company was in operation. He sifted ideas, treatments, dreamt a new film of his own.

Then one evening as he was walking through the Galleria off the Piazza del Duomo, he saw her. Trim legs in high heels, a belted black trench coat, a cloud of bright hair. He caught up to her.

"You disappeared."

She took in his presence, laughed. "My job was done. It's up to the others now."

He matched his step to hers. "What job?" he asked.

She gave him a sardonic glance. "The job of waking them up. Women of the world unite, you know." Her tone was friendly, complicit.

"Can I buy you a drink?"

She glanced at her watch. "Why not?"

They sat down at one of the café tables in the Galleria. "What are you doing now?" he asked.

"Oh, this and that." She smiled vaguely. He watched the avidity with which she drank her Campari, small quick gestures, the long curve of her throat.

She met his gaze. "You want to fuck me, don't you?"

Alexei's mouth dropped. "I hadn't quite considered it yet." His eyes lingered on her face, the reddened lips. "But now that you put it so forcefully . . ."

Her laugh was deep, spicy. "Don't look so surprised. Women aren't asleep. They know about these things." She stood. "Thanks for the drink."

He put out his hand to stop her. Cool skin. She flushed. Pulled her fingers away.

"Where can I reach you?" Alexei asked.

"I'll reach you. When I'm ready."

Bag swinging over her shoulder, she strode away.

Some weeks later, he was working on his new script in the apartment he had moved into near La Scala, when he was surprised by a ring at the door.

He opened it to find Rosa standing there.

"No, I'm not an apparition," she responded to the look on his face. "Are you going to invite me in?"

She sauntered past him. Tight blue jeans, a leather jacket, her hair half bound in a loose scarf. He could smell the night on her.

"Nice place." She glanced round. "It's nice to see how the rich live." Her voice dripped sarcasm. "You could put a few families in here."

"Do I sit back while you give me a political lecture," he said irritated, "or do I play delighted host and offer you a drink?"

She laughed. "You offer me a drink."

"Good, because I'm tired of platitudes and I might find myself arguing that the rich used to live a lot better. *And* there were fewer of them." He didn't know quite why he was so angry. Perhaps it was that he had been working well and hadn't particularly wanted to be disturbed. Perhaps it was simply her rudeness. He glanced at his watch. It was past eleven.

"I know, I know, it's late." She saw his gesture. "But I thought you of all people might have a bed for me for a few nights. I'm between flats."

He looked at her covertly while he uncorked a bottle of wine. She was examining his pictures, fingering the books on the coffee table. He handed her a glass. Stood over her. "Is that an invitation? Or are all the hotels in Milan fully booked?"

She shrugged. "It's what I said. I need a bed." Hazel eyes provoked him.

He kissed her. Cool firm lips, opening to his.

She pulled away. "You didn't ask my permission."

Alexei laughed. "You didn't resist."

"No, perhaps not." She met him on it, surveyed him critically. "You're not unattractive. A little too male for my taste." Her nose crinkled.

Alexei felt uncomfortable, stripped bare, naked before the scrutiny of that gaze. Suddenly he chortled. "Where did you learn to do that?"

"What?" She pretended not to understand.

"Stare like that." He mimicked her, slowly trailed his eyes over her body.

She chuckled, took her jacket off, threw it on the sofa. A blue sweater, tight around small unbound breasts. "By observing men," she confronted him. "So, do I get a bed?"

"I haven't decided yet. I have a lot of work to get through tonight."

She looked at him queerly. "You're an odd fish, you know?" She sat back in the sofa, curled her legs under her. "Have you got any food? I'm ravenous."

"Help yourself." He pointed toward the kitchen.

She moved with alacrity. After a moment, she called out. "Who does your cooking? Who washes your socks?"

He followed her, leaned against the kitchen door and watched her cram cold meat into her mouth.

"An exploited servant whom I pay nothing and force into my bed every night."

Her face dropped. "I didn't know. They . . . no one told me. When is your wife coming back?"

Alexei smiled, put his arms round her. "Idiot," he murmured, "you can't see the truth for your ideas."

She flushed, squirmed away from him. "Don't patronize me, rich boy."

He looked at her coldly, moved to go back to his desk.

"Do I get a bed?" Her voice followed him.

Alexei didn't turn. "Third door on the left. For one night."

"Thanks."

He tried to concentrate on his script. With little success. He was tautly aware of her presence, the sound of the shower, her movement through the flat.

And then suddenly, she was standing in front of him, wearing his robe, her hair darkened by water. She met his eyes, walked toward him, a little smile tugging at her lips. Soft fingers ran down his shirt. "Now. I'm ready now," she murmured.

"I'm not sure that I am," Alexei resisted her, *"now."* She shrugged. "That's the way it is with men. They always have to choose. Always have to decide. When. Where. How." She moved away.

"It must be pleasant always to have your views so easily confirmed," he muttered. "A palpable delight."

She threw him a scathing glance.

He caught up with her at the door. "All right. Now. My room? Your room? On top? Underneath? Standing up? On the floor? Choose." He was gripping her arm tightly. She turned to face him, features posed in contempt. With a ragged breath, he found her lips, her throat, the curve of her bosom. He felt angry. He had never felt angry like this with a woman before. And he was keenly aware of the excitement with which she met his anger. Teeth nipping his lips. Nails raking his back, digging, probing. She pulled him down onto the floor of his study. "Here, here," she whispered, covering his mouth, tugging at his trousers. He heaved into her with a moan, thrust heavily, deeply, wildly, coming into her urgently as if he had waited too long.

She was smiling when he looked at her, small white teeth bared. "Nice," she said reflectively. "A little too violent, a little too much like a man, but nice." She had the air of a cat licking her whiskers.

He gazed at the expanse of her body amidst the tumble of the robe. Satin skin. Miniature perfection. He turned away, stood. "You're perverse," he muttered. "You provoke me into behaving like an animal, so that you can tell me off for being one."

"Provoke?" She looked at him innocently. "You don't have to be provoked. You can walk away. Read a book. You don't have to prove your manhood." She tied the robe tightly round her. "That's the difference," she murmured scathingly. "Men can walk away."

Alexei did. He went to the kitchen. Made a cup of coffee.

She followed him a few moments later. "Are you going to offer me one?"

He looked at her a little grimly, shook his head. "No. I don't think so. That's women's work. You can make your own."

Her nose crinkled.

"Perhaps"—he stared at her—"perhaps when you have the grace to treat me as something other than a generic male, as something other than a random representative of your hated species, then I might just consider offering you a cup."

Rosa laughed, a low rumble. "You sound a little like me. Those are my lines." She mimicked him, "I'm a person, not the incarnation of Woman."

"It's gracious of you to notice." Alexei stirred his coffee, looked at her reflectively. Standing there, leaning against the counter in his white robe, she did indeed look like the incarnation of fragile, innocent femininity. And yet within that small frame there was all that fierceness, that polemical ardor. He noticed the direction of his thoughts, had enough self-critical awareness to see that his surprise at Rosa's contradictions was precisely what she was attacking. It didn't make him relent. Instead, he said, "I don't like politics in the bedroom."

"Politics are everywhere," she replied, her face serious. "Everywhere that power is." She gazed at him for a moment, eyes wide, direct. "But I'm not unfair. You can choose next time."

"That's generous of you," Alexei muttered. "But there may not be a 'next time.'"

There was. Later that night and again and again and again for the course of the weeks that she stayed at the apartment. So that he came to know every fragment of her body, every inch of that smooth skin from the curve of her foot to the hollow at the base of her neck, to the smattering of freckles around her nose. And yet every time he saw her or held her afresh, she continued to surprise him, her face and body like quicksilver.

Over the weeks, he began to think that, despite her polemics, it was the sudden sexual encounter which most excited her. Whatever she proclaimed, however she verbally resisted, it was the surprise embrace, in the shower, in the midst of breakfast, in the stealth of night, that roused her to greatest passion. He felt a little triumphant in this knowledge since it belied what he called her superficial politics.

Then he realized that he was mistaken. It was not the accosting male that excited her, but the heightened pleasure of the transgressive. Anything that broke the rules, implied danger, was illicit, exhilarated her. One evening while they were sitting in the darkened back rows of the cinema, he felt her hand at his groin. She was stroking him, rubbing. In consternation, he felt his penis bulge. He took her hand away. She kissed him on the neck, "Don't be so bourgeois," she whispered, drawing his hand to her mound, shifting herself, so that she sat on him, wriggled. He could feel her heat, her moisture. He kissed her full on the lips and again that hand, teasing him until he thought he would burst, there, amidst the other spectators, like a rampant teenage boy.

When the lights came on, her eyes were bright, a green haze. She pulled him along, ran past people, past a policeman, into the darkness of a lane. She flung her arms around him, leaned back against the brick of a wall. "Here," she murmured. He came into her with a groaning fury. A few minutes later, when they bumped into the same policeman at the corner of the lane, she smiled a polite "Good evening," and then looked at Alexei with mischievous joy. That night they made love again and again with an increasingly reckless abandon.

Her scent began to trail him through the streets of Milan.

He was astounded by the force she exerted over him. He felt taken and taken over. Yet at the same time, he felt protective of her, wanted to shelter her. Somewhere in the long nights of their lovemaking he had discovered a vulnerability, a hidden fragility which he suspected was at the root of her fire. A vulnerability that had been converted, overlaid with the fierceness of her outrage, and transformed into an indignation with the way things were. She talked in her sleep. Small smatterings of sound. Her blind face clenched. Fear. He had mentioned it to her one morning, and she had refused to share his bed after that. He rued the fact that he had spoken.

In the hours they spent talking and arguing, he realized that part of her fascination lay in her certainty. She was pitiless in her judgments. Intemperate. Sure. He had never had that kind of absolute conviction except when he was filming. An absolute sense of what was right. It both riled him and intrigued him.

Gradually, she ceased to treat him as a mere example of the enemy, the patronizing male sex. She talked to him intelligently, cogently, about his film, which she admitted to liking, about other projects. But she refused to understand how he could work for Gismondi Enterprises.

About herself, she was secretive. All he knew was that she was looking for a new job, that she had done a few days' work here and there. And that she wouldn't accept his help in finding one. Nor would she meet his friends. He learned nothing except the blandest facts about her past.

And then suddenly without warning she was gone.

Buoyant with the expectation of seeing her, he had raced home from the office. It was a Friday and he had thought they might drive out for the weekend toward Padua. He wanted to explore some locations for his film.

But the apartment was empty, bereft of any trace of her. Her toothbrush was gone, the small overnight bag. Only a note remained on his desk. "Thanks for the room. See you some time."

A hole formed inside him. A hole the size and shape of Rosa. He thought he might fall into it. She had left no forwarding address. He had no idea where she might have gone. He knew none of her friends, her family.

Despair overtook him. Into that despair, the thought tumbled that she had gone off to another man. Rosa in bed with another. Red hair fanned over another's pillow. Limbs askew, clasped round another man. Her shudders, her cries, her nose crinkling in disdain. Rosa.

Jealousy began to fill the hole where Rosa had been. It sat heavily with him on the sofa as he gazed into nothingness. It followed him round the length and breadth of the apartment as he retraced the sites of their love. It angered him and mortified him.

He loathed his passivity. The next day, to break it, he chased through the office files and found her family's address. He rang, asked for her. A man answered, told him in no uncertain terms that Rosa Venturi did not live there and would never live there again.

Alexei walked blindly through the streets of Milan. He haunted the Galleria where he had once bumped into her.

He remembered the block of flats where he had once driven her. He went there, studied an anonymous list of names, then sat in his car and watched the block for hours.

When he finally returned home, he realized there was nothing for it. She had disappeared.

He could concentrate on nothing. After midnight, he went out again, prowling the streets, hoping to catch a glimpse of her. He was in a rage. How dare she simply vanish like that? Without warning. Without a word of endearment. He was faced with the agonizing notion that he meant nothing to her. Was simply a temporary address.

When a prostitute propositioned him on a tree-lined avenue, he followed her to a dusty hotel room, lost himself in a body which his imagination shaped into another form and punished with the passion of his anger.

Afterward he felt ashamed. He couldn't meet the woman's eyes, left her a large sum. "Any time you want me," her voice rang after him.

As he walked home, he could hear Rosa's voice, lecturing him contemptuously on bourgeois habits, his abuse of women.

After a week of evoking Rosa's figure at every turn, Alexei threw himself into work with a grim energy which battled against the black melancholy in him. Rosa, he told himself, would not come back and if she did, he didn't want her. He finished his script, traveled to Rome, to Paris and Los Angeles to investigate co-production finances for his new company, saw two treatments move from page to production. He accepted invitations to the kinds of parties he had eschewed, wild parties where drugs flowed as liberally as food and drink, staider parties where he found himself the eligible darling of the society matrons.

And then, as suddenly as she had vanished, Rosa walked back into his life. It was a Friday evening in April. He had just come home. And there she was a few minutes later, framed in his doorway. Her hair was a little longer, wilder, but the jacket, the jeans, the wide eyes, the freckles were all the same.

"Hi. Want to come for a ride? I've borrowed the most wonderful motorbike." She smiled at him engagingly.

Alexei wanted to shout, to berate her. Wanted also to embrace her, to beg her never to leave again. All he said was, "Isn't it a little late?" His voice was grim.

Her face fell. She shrugged. "It's a great bike. I only have it for a few days. We could go into the country."

He scoured her expression. Nothing. No guilt. No remorse. She looked a little pale. That was all.

"Are you going to invite me in at least?" She touched his hand and as he flinched and pulled back, she walked in. "It's nice here. I'd forgotten how nice," she mused.

"Are you planning to stay?" Alexei asked with heavy sarcasm.

She looked a little hurt as he said it. "If you'll allow me. Just for a few nights. I'm . . . I'm between flats." She walked up to him as she said it and traced the line of his cheek gently with her fingers. "You're nice too. I'd forgotten."

He met her eyes and was bewildered by what he saw there.

"Oh Rosa." He crushed her in his arms, kissed her savagely and then more gently as if that kiss could bear all the weight of months of anger and yearning and loss. When he released her, she looked at him wistfully for a moment. Then she smiled. "Does that mean you'll come for a ride?"

When he nodded, she looked as gleeful as a child.

They sped through the city, and then faster, ever faster through the countryside. Rosa in front, her hair flying beneath the grip of her goggles. Alexei behind, holding her, loosely at first, and then tightly, ever more tightly as the bike picked up speed. He could feel the mounting tension in her body, its excitement echoing in his own. Darkened fields, wind, night, and the two of them in the vastness, racing.

She turned a little dangerously off the highway into an uneven side road and then into another, even narrower. She pulled up short, clambered off. "Here. Shall we stop here?" There was a rich depth in her voice.

In the moonlight her face looked ghostly, pale. But her eyes were wide, clear, asking him, urging him. He took her hand, kissed it. She laughed, a strange clear sound in the open night and then she whisked away from him, running, running on to a stretch of field, throwing herself on the bristly earth. He came after her, more slowly, a little reflectively, almost as if his desire didn't match hers, as if at the last moment, he might turn and go. He stretched out beside her, didn't look at her, focused on the stars.

"Rosa, I don't want it now. Not if you're going to disappear again."

She kissed him, soft lips, fingers caressing his hair, his chest, his groin, rubbing, rubbing. Each of her gestures clamored with its double in his memory, intensifying sensation until he could bear it no longer. He moaned and in that sound, he sensed that he was lost. He covered her with his body, thrust into her, thrust to erase time and its passage, thrust to erase the pain of her going, until the waves of her coming encircled his, obliterating everything but the present.

"You see, Alexei," she said afterward as if she had read the movement of his thought, "if everything were as simple as now, the sky, the earth, our bodies, nothing else, no power, no corruption, no injustice, no fascist cops, no poverty, then I would stay with you. Stay for as long as it lasted." She looked at him a little sadly.

He took her hand, kissed it. She had changed in the time of their separation, he realized. She was less strident. She was talking to him, not to an example of the male species. And there was something else, too, something he couldn't quite fathom. A kind of desperation. It had been there in her lovemaking, a desire for release, for forgetfulness, beyond the excitement.

He touched her again. Made love to her gently, achingly. When it was over, she cried. Soft, silent tears.

"Paradise is a story we tell ourselves," Alexei murmured.

He lifted her in his arms. "Come. I'll take you somewhere. Somewhere you'll like."

Alexei drove this time, remembering the surge of the machine, its power, from his time in the army. For an hour, they sped over quiet roads, through a sprinkling of villages and then up, up into hills. They stopped in front of a large house of gracious proportions, nestling amidst cypresses in old grounds. Stone unicorns guarded the front steps. A lone dog barked in the distance.

Alexei dug in his pockets for a ring of keys.

"Is this yours?" Rosa asked speculatively. She looked around. A wide hall, tapestries, a single sculpted figure, mottled white; a living room with deep rounded chairs, a flowered sofa, polished wood, a fireplace, the logs piled in readiness. Quiet luxury. Peace.

"Is it yours?" she repeated.

"In a manner of speaking." Alexei shrugged. "Ours for now. Please don't lecture me."

She chuckled. "Not tonight. Not now."

They stayed in the villa for two days. Two long days and longer nights in which they walked along the borders of Lago Maggiore, sat in the grounds, talked, made love, and talked some more, about life and justice, politics and revolution. He was again startled by the force of her convictions, the vehemence of her beliefs. The force gave her a fire which sparked him, warmed, even when he disagreed.

When Sunday evening caught them by surprise, Alexei knew that now more than ever he could not bear to let her go. Panic gripped him with the thought of her disappearance.

He concluded for the first time that he was in love. The logic of that thought led only one way.

He asked her while they were taking a last stroll through the grounds. Took her hand and formed his lips round the words. "Rosa, will you marry me?"

He heard the startled breath which escaped her.

"I love you," Alexei said simply.

She didn't reply for a moment, but she didn't drop his hand. Then, she said in a low voice, "I could say I will never be another in the list of your possessions, a piece of Gismondi chattel. But I won't say that." She paused. "I think we understand that now, between us."

When she didn't speak again, Alexei turned her toward him, gripped her shoulders, sought out her lips. She lowered her head away from him, shook it. "No, Alexei. Sex, yes. Marriage, a machine to keep society stable, no." She shook her head again. The sweep of her hair tickled his face.

"And love"—she shrugged—"I don't know what it means. It doesn't enter into my plans." Her voice took on a husky passion. "Life is about more important things than a little cozy twosome." She looked at him, a little sorrowfully, her face earnest.

But he was angry. "There's nothing to say, then," he murmured. "Let's go."

He insisted on doing the driving and he raced, too fast, dangerously winding through the traffic in the hours that it took to get back to Milan.

By the time they reached the apartment, his anger was spent.

"I don't want you to go." He turned to her as she sat on the bike, his eyes holding a plea.

"It's better if I go. I'll only be trouble."

"Where will you go?" His voice was harsher than he had intended. "Do you have anywhere to go?"

"I'll find somewhere," she said softly. "Don't concern yourself about it."

He grasped her shoulders. So frail. So strong. He met her eyes. "I can manage a little trouble. Please. Stay."

A smile spread over her lips. "But not forever."

"No," he met her on it. "Not forever."

CHAPTER
TWENTY-ONE

*P*ortia Gaitskell addressing a large crowd in a dusty hall in midtown Manthattan. Portia, her hair cut functionally short, her face devoid of make-up, her eyes glowing, her voice sure, authoritative as she led her audience through a hidden history, the *real* history of women. Portia, invoking man as the enemy. Men as the perpetrators of systems which oppressed women. Systems of knowledge which legitimated male power and mutilated women. Made women into objects—objects of hatred or desire—but always and ever passive objects, robbed of their subjectivity. Robbed of the ability to act, to take control of their lives, to construct their destinies.

Katherine, watching, listening from the audience, was proud of her. Proud of Portia's mastery of the crowd. Proud of the confidence with which she mustered her arguments. Proud to know her. Portia, her friend.

She was also a little in awe. It had been almost three years since she had seen Portia. There had been letters, of course, the occasional phone call. But somewhere in those three years, Portia had learned how to weave her tongue round words which had never passed Katherine's lips. Words like *patriarchal, phallocentric, sexist*. Words which carried keys to the workings of the world, which explained the relations between the sexes. Words which resonated with purpose, direction, certitude.

Katherine in contrast had no certitudes, no explanations. Except where the specificity of her work was concerned.

It made her feel strangely out of step.

Portia, invoking Ibsen, *A Doll's House,* written almost a hundred years ago. Nora, refusing the "sacred duty to husband and children" and proclaiming another duty, just as sacred—"My duty to myself."

It was odd, Katherine thought. She didn't consider Natalie in terms of duty. She loved her. She didn't want to be made to feel guilty for that love. It came first. Natalie came first. And then her work, a different order of things, which she adored, which was necessary.

Later, there were drinks. Women, milling, congratulating Portia. Women in baggy overalls, in loose dresses, faces animated, breasts unbound. There were a few men, too, feet shuffling. A little uncomfortable, but their faces poised in smiles. Good men, gentle men. Men trying hard not to be part of a hated category. Men nervously prepared to be part of a future which wasn't only theirs.

Katherine stood on the sidelines. She didn't look right. Her dress was too good, her lipstick too much in evidence, her stockings too smooth. Her manner too reserved. There was a little circle of quiet around her.

Portia broke through it. "Katherine, you made it. I'm so glad."

"You were wonderful, remarkable."

They smiled at each other, still two girls from Madame Chardin's School. Embraced. Portia introduced her to others, many others. "Katherine Jardine, the new true force in the Museum of Modern Art."

Katherine flushed, demurred. She had been at the museum for only a year, a stripling of an assistant curator. But Portia's approval felt good. She basked in it.

It wasn't, as she found out later that night, after they had had a crowded, noisy and jovial dinner in Chinatown, by any means a wholesale approval.

Portia accepted Katherine's invitation to come home and stay with her rather than in her hotel. Katherine proudly showed her round the brownstone she had moved into just a few months ago and which was still in the process of being done up. They tiptoed into Natalie's room and looked at the warm sprawl of the small body amidst cuddly toys. Katherine kissed the sleeping form, hugged her.

And then, a bottle of wine between them, they sat and talked and caught up.

After a while, Portia went on the attack. "All you can tell me is Natalie this and Natalie that. What about you? I want to know about you."

Katherine balked. "She's my daughter. I love her. I'm not one of your Noras, you know, abandoning my child so that I can set off on a long and arduous struggle for self-fulfillment." Acid came into her voice.

"*Your* daughter? Surely you mean your and Carlo's daughter? His little treasure. You're just perpetuating his memory, living in his shadow, by investing all your emotions in your daughter. You haven't mentioned a single other human being except Natalie since I arrived."

"That's utter tripe, Portia. I've never heard such tripe." Katherine was angry. "I never think of Carlo. You know nothing about it." Katherine knew too well how she had made an active task of forgetting Carlo after his funeral. She didn't want to remember. Only forgetting made life possible.

But then Portia knew nothing of her relations with Carlo. She had never told her, not on the occasion when she had fled Rome, nor afterward.

Still, her friend's certainty was deeply irritating.

"You're just obsessed by men," she said in a slightly calmer, but still terse, voice. "Yes, yes, you talk about women, but the source of everything, the motive cause of everything, the measure of everything, is Man."

Portia's face grew contorted. But Katherine for once wouldn't let her interrupt.

"Well, I don't know Man. I know a few very specific men. My father, Thomas, my brother, I don't hate them. But there are no men in this house, not in fact or memory. Just Natalie, and Doreen, who helps take care of her, and me."

Suddenly Portia burst out laughing. "Katherine Jardine, that's the longest speech I have ever heard you make. And who knows, there may even be a little truth in it." She took a long, reflective sip of her wine. "Still, it's not quite right. I mean you, *you* don't seem quite right. It's all too disciplined, too closed off. I know, I know, there's work. And then there's Natalie. Where are your friends? Why aren't you part of things? There's a huge women's network in this city."

Katherine sat back in her chair, fingered thick, pale brocade. She shrugged. "I've never been a good joiner. You remember that. I'm hopeless at the general. Remember in London, you were always trying to get me to join this group and that?" She paused, looked at her friend with a trace of irony. "But at that time, if my memory serves me, the cause was Vietnam. I still remember the refrain at the demo, 'Where has Harold Wilson gone? Crawling to the Pentagon.' Then it was revolution, liberation for everybody. Now it seems it's liberation for only half of everybody. Just us women."

Portia grinned. "I got tired of stuffing envelopes and being tea lady and having men only half as intelligent as me giving me orders. So I've graduated into the women's movement. Men can take care of themselves. In any case, they need us more than we need them. Otherwise, no more Natalies."

It was Katherine's turn to laugh. "You'll meet her tomorrow and then you'll see why she takes up so much of me."

Because she had promised Portia she would, Katherine went a few weeks later to a consciousness-raising group she had recommended. It took place in an airy but slightly ramshackle apartment on West End Avenue. The women were mostly her age or slightly younger, a mixture of postgrads and students from Columbia and NYU, some teachers, a social worker, a painter. She exchanged a few words with one, then another, sipped her instant coffee and sat, a little nervously, at the edge of her chair. Others positioned themselves on the floor, squeezed into sofas, a desultory gathering, so that Katherine was not quite certain that the session had begun, when in fact it had. She was surprised by its content. Somehow she had expected that they would talk issues. Talk about inequalities, about women's role in the workplace, about the need for independence, about rights. She had done her homework, gobbled up since Portia's departure Simone de Beauvoir's *The Second Sex*, Kate Millett's *Sexual Politics*.

But this was more like a group confessional, a sharing of experiences, most of them to do with sex and with their own bodies. A woman began by saying how her boyfriend had left her life when she had suggested that they try something other than the missionary position, do it with her on top.

Men were threatened by women's desire, another commented, it robbed them of their power, their potency.

They talked of the experiences they had had of men hating women's bodies, telling them their "twats" were smelly or large, doctors refusing to examine them, assuming complaints were psychological, hysterical; their own sense of abasement.

"But remember, sisters, we're beautiful," another said, "blood, secretions, smells and all. We're not plastic dolls, men's masturbatory fantasies."

And so it went on, through men, menstruation and masturbation.

Katherine was terrified lest someone ask her to speak. She had never been adept at confession and she felt that to do so in front of a group of strangers would be a breach of everything she was. She found it distasteful, an invasion of privacy. Then, too, she felt that she had so little experience compared to these women. She had thought about so little. There had really only ever been Carlo. And that was in a different time and a different place. Another world. She didn't want to think about him, about that. She had buried his memory with his body.

Yet the women's words forced those years back on her. She too had felt abased. And how. She had been not only a prisoner of an old-fashioned marriage but a prisoner—and she had realized it at the time—of sex. Of her own desires. She remembered how, when the telegram had come announcing Carlo's death, there had been, amidst the tears, a jolt of relief. She would never now have to confront the implications of that last terrifying scene with him. Never have to see him again. Never have to think about it.

She had gone back to Rome, been a dutiful widow, stayed for two months with the Contessa. Visibly, she had mourned. Inwardly, she had cut herself off, detached herself. And then, when she could face the world of the Palazzo no more, she had fled with a bad taste in her mouth, a taste to which she gave the word *decadence*.

She had made no decisions at the time, but simply led her new life. The life of a widow. Everyone kind to her, everyone sorrowful. But inside herself, she was happy. She was free. She had given herself over first to the care of Natalie and then gradually to work. She had never consciously determined not to involve herself in other relationships, but that will had grown within her. There was no need for that whole murky world, that tangled undergrowth of sexual relations. She was fine as she was.

And, Katherine thought, as she fled from the group, though it was comforting to know that other women might share her feelings, she really didn't want to explore those feelings anymore.

Waiting at the bus stop she recognized one of the other women, a woman who, like her, hadn't spoken.

"Hi." The woman smiled. "Pretty heavy stuff."

Katherine nodded.

"I was petrified," the woman admitted. "It was my first time."

"Mine too."

They sat together on the bus. "I'd hoped we might talk about children, but I don't suppose anyone but me has any." The woman grinned.

"I do, a little girl," Katherine beamed.

They both suddenly laughed.

"Have you got time to come back for a drink?" Katherine asked.

The woman nodded. "By the way, I'm Betty Alexander."

Katherine had made a friend.

The months rolled into years. Katherine was promoted. She was good at her work. She had a highly attuned sense of the visual. If in the mounting of exhibitions, she said one picture should be hung next to another, or an object placed in a particular position, her decision inevitably turned out to be the right one. She was meticulous, without being pedantic. Her catalogues could never be faulted. And she had a composure which seemed to be unbreachable. No matter what the pressure of work, she was never ruffled, never raised her voice. Then, too, she was good with artists and collectors, a beautiful woman who listened to them attentively and intelligently so that they felt cared for, looked after.

Increasingly, she was asked to travel, to Paris, London, Cologne. She stayed away from Rome. As often as she could, when these trips were to last more than a week, she took Natalie and Doreen with her. She liked being in Europe. Sometimes she thought she preferred it. But New York was home.

Her work blended into her social life. There were countless openings, dinners to meet someone or other, business lunches. It wasn't that she refused to go out with men. She did go, when she found them agreeable. But when it came to anything more than conversation, she simply said politely, "Oh no, I'm not interested in that." The way she said it, her gray eyes intelligently directed at them, her composure intact, her voice quietly dignified, meant that they didn't dare confuse her "no" for a partial "yes."

Increasingly, though, she found she preferred to go out with her gay or women friends.

In her relations with men, as in so much else, she knew that she was buoyed up by the women's movement, without ever having directly been a part of it. It made the flow of her life seem to have been the result of conscious choices. By all appearances, she seemed to be a woman who had determined on a career, a woman who had decided to bring up her child single-handedly; who had chosen to live alone.

Katherine knew it wasn't quite like that, though gradually she began to believe in the Katherine of appearances as being all of herself. Even her move into the field of modern art and away from her academic specialization in the Renaissance, which had been propelled by her wish to have nothing to do with Carlo's world, with Rome, now took on the gloss of being a deliberate aesthetic choice. She relished the clean bright lines of the contemporary, the hard intellectual edge of conceptual art, the ironies of pop. Preferred it to the textured world of the Renaissance, with its sense of the sacred and of sin.

Only her father sometimes jarred her into remembering that she wasn't everything that she now seemed. And Natalie.

When Natalie was six, she asked her mother over the Sunday lunch, which was as often as possible a family event, "Mummy, how come I'm the only girl in my class who doesn't have a daddy?"

Katherine caught the conspiratorial glance which flew between Jacob and Leo, felt the interrogator's beam of those liquid dark eyes which her daughter had inherited from Carlo.

"I've told you, sweetie, your daddy died when you were very little." She kept her voice even and didn't flinch before Natalie's gaze.

The girl frowned, pushed her food round her plate.

"But when people die, they don't come back," she said reflectively.

"That's right, darling. They don't come back." Katherine watched that little face with its perfect skin, watched it straining, wanting to hold her, to embrace her. But she knew she had to let her finish her thought.

"Does that mean I'll never have a daddy?" she asked, the tears clouding her eyes.

"Never is a long time, Natalie," Jacob interjected. "You might acquire a daddy before then." He winked at her.

She leapt into his lap. "I wish you could be my daddy, Gramps. But you can't 'cause you're my grandpa. And Uncle Leo can't be, can he, 'cause he's my uncle?" She looked at Leo seriously.

"That's right, Natalie," Leo murmured.

"That's too bad. 'Cause I'd like a daddy of my own, like the other girls." She threw her arms around Jacob's neck.

"And I'm sure you shall have one, one day."

Katherine pushed her chair too noisily away from the table and stiffly went to fetch the pudding she had spent half the morning making.

That evening, after Natalie was tucked up in bed, Katherine turned on her father. "You shouldn't encourage her like that, tell her stories about daddies she's going to have."

"And why not?" Jacob let the full force of his gaze fall on his daughter. "You don't intend to mourn forever, do you?"

"I've told you before, I'm not mourning."

"Well then, what is it?" He poured her a drink, handed it to her, watched her groping for an answer. "What is it, Kat?" he murmured again.

"Nothing." She lowered her eyes.

"You haven't become a man-hater, as the papers would put it?" He smiled at her gently.

"Of course not." She was adamant.

"Well then?" Jacob prodded.

"I just haven't met anyone I like."

"I see," Jacob said, not believing her.

"Don't use that tone on me," Katherine overreacted. "I haven't seen you exactly rushing to get remarried."

Jacob mused, fondled his glass. "I'm an old man. It's not the same. Even so, I haven't cut myself off altogether. As I suspect you have." He shook his white leonine head. "Eh my little Kat"—he stroked her hair fondly—"sometimes one has to let go. Otherwise the future . . ." His voice trailed off.

On the whole, these days they got along extremely well. Katherine felt none of the rancor she had once had for him. He was her mainstay and a bantering camaraderie prevailed between them. But after that night, every few weeks or so, he would ask if he could bring a friend along to Sunday lunch. It was invariably a far younger male friend, nice enough, intelligent enough. Katherine froze. Froze doubly in the presence of Natalie and under the strength of her father's obvious intent. It spoiled those occasions for her, made her relations with him tense.

Leo, too, when he was in New York, began to come round with one friend or another. Irritated, she chided him, "I'm not in the marriage market, you know."

"Well, you should be," he responded sedately.

"I don't see a ring on your finger."

He shrugged. "It doesn't suit my line of work. But you, with Natalie, there's no excuse."

To evade their purposes, Katherine started to invite Betty Alexander to join their family Sundays. They had become, since that inauspicious meeting of the women's group, fast friends. Betty's little boy, Tim—the product of a teenage fling whom Betty had insisted on keeping—was two years older than Natalie and the children played happily together while the women chatted. Shared their frustrations about work, about the conflicting demands of children and jobs, about the satisfaction they took in their children, which it seemed unfashionable to voice, almost as if that were the most guiltily secret of pleasures in this heyday of liberation.

When they had first met, Betty, who was a legal secretary, had been in severe financial straits. Katherine, always generous to a fault with her closest friends, had lent her the key money which enabled her to get a decent apartment in a co-op. She had done the same for Doreen and her family. Carlo's legacy had been substantial and though she had at first considered refusing it so that all ties with him were severed, Thomas had convinced her that this would be a wholly idiotic move. "Why should your daughter suffer because of your puritan conscience?" he had told her emphatically, and Katherine had seen the sense of it. Still, she was careful to keep what she thought of as Natalie's legacy intact: the brownstone was in her daughter's name.

During the winter of 1975, Katherine was particularly busy at work. She hadn't seen Betty for some weeks, when they finally determined to meet one evening for coffee. Katherine thought her friend looked a little nervous.

"What's wrong, Bet?" she asked. "Having trouble with one of your beaux?" Betty, unlike Katherine, had a string of boyfriends, most of them altogether unsuitable and the women often spent hours laughing over the foibles of her love life.

"It's not quite that," Betty demurred. She was quiet for a moment and then she looked directly up at Katherine from amidst the tumble of her blonde curls. "I've decided to get hitched up," she blurted out.

"Oh." Katherine gazed at her, before turning abruptly away and fumbling with some dishes. "Who's the lucky man?" she asked in as bright a voice as she could manage.

"Dave. David Thompson. I think I've mentioned him before. He's a junior partner in the office. He gets on brilliantly with Tim." Betty's words raced, almost as if she were offering apologies.

"I'm very happy for you." Katherine's tone sounded false even to her own ears. She felt like crying, felt absurdly betrayed.

Betty put her arm around her. "I think I know how you feel, hon. But soon it'll be your turn."

"No, Betty." She shook her head bitterly. "It's not what I want."

A few weeks after the turn of the New Year, Katherine packed Natalie into the car and set off to Boston for a weekend with Thomas. They had become fast friends again after her return to New York. Katherine had relegated her distant proposal to Thomas to the sphere of a childish aberration which they could occasionally joke about. He, ever tactful, simply assumed that her marriage with its unfortunate end was private business. A year after Carlo's funeral, he quoted Wittgenstein at her. "Death is not part of life." It was time for her to move on to other preoccupations.

Katherine, driving, with Natalie safely belted into the back seat, remembered his perfunctory tone on that occasion and smiled. Thomas was her mentor, the one close friend with whom she shared her work, her ideas about art. And he was as besotted with Natalie as Jacob, spoiled her with presents, talked to her as an equal, read her Grimm and Kästner, allowed her to play with the magic little Feininger villages that she herself had once been so in love with.

Sometimes Katherine reflected that she could solve all her problems, put Jacob and Leo and Natalie's anxieties to rest, in one fell swoop by marrying Thomas. The husband and father everyone but she seemed to want. But the moment for that, if there had ever been one, had passed.

Two years earlier Thomas, in order to replace his English butler, had acquired a housekeeper who Katherine suspected also served other purposes. She was a rounded blonde of about forty, with the features of a doll-like Fragonard shepherdess. She spoke with a Southern drawl, but beneath the sweetness, Katherine sensed a bullying will.

Susannah Holmes. She put Katherine's nerves on edge. Susannah always managed to appear in a room when Katherine and Thomas were deepest in conversation. The way she tidied Natalie's toys away at the merest opportunity and followed her around with a falsetto "darling" drove Katherine mad. She didn't know how Thomas could put up with the woman, though it was true that the house seemed impeccably run.

As a result of Susannah, Katherine had stopped going to Boston with any regularity. She saw Thomas in New York, for dinner, for a vernissage, for an occasional expedition with Natalie. This weekend she had made an exception. There had been too few opportunities to see him of late. He made the trek to New York less regularly. She had to remind herself that Thomas was getting on. He would be seventy this year, though to her he seemed to have changed remarkably little over the years.

"Schätzchen. And my little Natalie. Welcome." Thomas answered the door himself and Natalie bounded into his arms.

Katherine smiled. Natalie was all warm enthusiasm and lack of inhibition. A happy, lively girl in the normal course of things. Not at all like herself at that age. For that she was constantly grateful. She had done one thing right in her life, at least. The slightly plaintive tone of her reflection surprised her.

"Come, come, my two beauties. First some lunch, and then, before the sun goes down, we must build a snowman. I have tested the snow in the garden and it is perfect." Thomas romped round them as if he were as young as Natalie.

Lunch was brought by a young man.

"Mmm." Natalie gorged herself on soup and crispy rolls, pausing only to answer Thomas's questions about school, about her dancing lessons.

Katherine, curious about the young man, inquired casually at one point, "Has Susannah gone?"

Thomas chuckled. "Only until tomorrow. To visit her sister. I know you don't like her, Schätzchen." His look teased her. "You are not quite as unreadable as you choose to believe."

"Mommy is perfect." Natalie, thinking she sensed criticism, rushed to Katherine's defense. "Well almost." She burst out laughing at the face Thomas pulled.

They played away the afternoon in Thomas's garden, pleased at the vast snowman they created and, at Natalie's behest, a snowlady to keep him company.

"There." Natalie patted her mittens together. "Now tomorrow we can make them some snowchildren."

Thomas sought out Katherine's eyes.

Later, after a game of Monopoly, and dinner, and countless stories—which Natalie still wanted Thomas to read to her, though usually now she read for herself—the two of them lounged in front of the fire. They chatted idly about this and that, about the vagaries of the art world, about Thomas's decision at last to sell his publishing firm.

At one point, he said to her. "I don't know, Schätzchen. You seem to me a little bit strained." He examined her face.

Katherine shrugged. "I'm working hard. Perhaps it's my age." She laughed, the sound too shrill. "I'm thirty now, as you know."

"Yes, a ripe old age," he teased her, seemed to let it pass. But then he said, "Perhaps you need a man, a regular man. You have thought about it, I'm sure."

Katherine prickled. "You're as bad as Jacob. As bad as Leo. Always trying to marry me off. I thought we had now agreed that the nuclear family doesn't work." Her voice was contemptuous.

"I wasn't necessarily suggesting marriage," Thomas murmured. He stood to fill her glass, gazed down at her reflectively. "Perhaps just, what do you call it these days, 'a relationship.'"

She snorted. "What is it with you men? If a woman's a little off color, all you can think of is that she isn't getting it regularly." She scoffed at him, "Is that it, Thomas? The infallible cure for all female maladies, a regular dose of cock? I didn't know you were a closet Freudian."

"Now, now, Schätzchen," Thomas said softly. "There's no need for such a reaction." He sipped his brandy. "It's strange. You remember when we first became friends, I said to you a beautiful woman has to be careful not to play down her intelligence in this country? And, of course, I meant play it down in the interest of possible sexual partners."

Katherine nodded.

"I almost wish now that I had said something a little different. Now, I *would* say something different. I would say to you that an intelligent woman shouldn't perhaps defend herself too much against the beauty of her sexuality."

Katherine swallowed her brandy, made as if she were about to retire for the evening.

"Don't go, Schätzchen," Thomas held her back. "I am not attacking you."

"But you wouldn't talk like this to a man." She confronted his eyes, challenged him. "You wouldn't say to him, 'Max, all your problems will be solved by the regular exercise of your penis.'"

Thomas chuckled. "I might. You forget that I have always been in favor of a little sexual liberation. You children inherited it from my generation, my compatriots, Marcuse and the others."

"I'm tired, Thomas, I'm going to bed."

"Sit, Katherine. Forgive an interfering old man. I don't like to see such beauty as yours wasted. Come, I will tell you a funny story which will amuse your women friends. Perhaps it will prove to you that I am not just an unreconstructed sexist. I was gossiping with a woman friend of mine in the publishing house the other day about a colleague of ours who is having problems with his marriage. He is a man of about sixty and some twenty years ago, he married a woman much younger than himself. A very pretty woman. He would bring her to office parties and parade her around, show her off, hungry for other men's eyes to fall on her. 'Yes, show her off. Like a penis,' my woman friend said to me. 'And now, now that she's older, there are problems. After all, what can you do with an aging wrinkled penis?' " Thomas laughed loudly. "That is good, no? 'What can you do with an aging penis?' "

Katherine smiled. "As I said, you're just a closet Freudian. Jacob would be pleased with you. Both sexes enamored of, obsessed by the mythical, magical phallus." She stretched. "Well, here's one lady who's opting out." Katherine rose and kissed him goodnight lightly.

He held her back, his face unusually grave. "Tomorrow, Katherine, I am going to make you a proposition I have been thinking about."

"Oh?" she queried him, lingered.

It was at this moment that Susannah Holmes flounced into the room. Two red spots burned in her cheeks.

"What proposition?" She looked at Katherine with unrestrained hostility and then turned suspicious eyes on Thomas.

Katherine stiffened. The odious woman was an eavesdropper on top of everything else.

But Thomas smiled calmly. "I didn't expect you back this evening, Susannah."

"Well, I'm here," she drawled.

"So I see."

"Goodnight, Thomas." Katherine moved away, pointedly avoiding Susannah. But then, at the door of the room, she turned back. "If you think, Ms. Holmes, that Mr. Sachs is proposing that I take your place as his housekeeper"—she emphasized the word—"then you are sadly mistaken." With that she nodded curtly and left.

How she disliked that woman.

Thomas's proposition, as Katherine found out the next afternoon, was not of the kind she had half imagined. With a seriousness which spoke of considered reflection, he proposed to her that she leave the museum and set up her own gallery. "Enough of the old art bureaucrats," he said to her. "They are tiring you out. You want something different. More stimulating. I can see it now, the Katherine Jardine Gallery. I will help you with the business side. You'll learn quickly enough, I'm sure. I can be a silent partner. What do you say, Schätzchen?"

She demurred at first. It would be too risky. Too risky for him. She couldn't accept that. But the more they talked, the more the idea appealed to her. Her own space. An adventure with Thomas. And she could see that he was excited by the notion. Something to replace his publishing interests.

"Why are you so good to me, Thomas?" she asked him as they sipped the fragrant tea Thomas preferred. "I've done nothing to deserve it."

He patted her shoulder. "You have been like a daughter to me, an interesting daughter, and you have given me a wonderful granddaughter." He looked at Natalie, who was peacefully working on a large drawing. "That is more than enough."

"Well, well, well. Playing happy families again." Susannah Holmes walked noisily in on them and surveyed the scene. With rapid irritation, she picked Natalie's paints and water and brushes off the floor and urged her into the kitchen. "We don't want a mess, do we, child?" The southern tones sat oddly with her quick gestures.

"I was finished anyhow," Natalie proclaimed, bouncing into Thomas's lap and giving him a hug.

Susannah's eyes showed distaste, but Thomas grinned.

The next day at home Katherine wrapped up two Robert Natkins she had purchased and had them sent to Thomas. "We love you," she wrote on a card. "Thank you."

She was excited about Thomas's idea of the gallery. It wouldn't leave her. Over the years since her return to New York, she had slowly acquired a small collection of her own, buying the work of young artists here, there and everywhere, whenever she fell in love with a canvas. Having her own gallery would mean that she could spend more time exercising her own tastes, rather than fulfilling the needs of an institution.

She mused about the gallery during her next solitary trip to Europe, thought through details. It should be possible. It wouldn't even necessarily be that much of a gamble if she were cautious. She knew people, knew artists, knew the business.

The thought of the gallery kept her buoyant. But within her there was also a kernel of something else, something she didn't want to face. Thomas's words about her state of being had hit home, despite her spirited defense. And they came on top of her father's, on top of Betty's announcement of her marriage. She felt something akin to desperation. She transmuted it into activity. In Paris she filled every inch of space in her diary with appointments, visits to galleries, even a trip to Neuilly to see her aunt.

Then one night over dinner with a group from the Musée d'Art Moderne, something happened to her. She didn't know quite what it was. Perhaps she had drunk too much, was too tired, but she found herself returning the glances of the man opposite her. When he asked if he could see her back to the hotel, she nodded. Nor did she deny him her room. Or her body. A wildness gripped her. Another Katherine took her over. One she didn't know and didn't particularly want to make the acquaintance of. Passionate, frenzied. A woman who took as much as she gave. And then forgot about it. Love with a stranger. Uninvolved. Inconsequential. Secret. Even from herself.

She stopped in London to have a quick look in at the Tate, the Whitechapel and the ICA. She went to see Portia, who was sharing a house in Islington with another woman.

"Still no man?" she said brazenly to her friend.

"They're not good enough yet." Portia grinned. "Soon perhaps. There's one on the cards. He claims he loves cooking and washing up. And you?"

Katherine shook her head. "Still just mothering and working."

"And waiting for your father to grow up." Portia laughed at the surprise on her friend's face. "I've started to think Freud might have had something."

Katherine groaned.

"Well, whatever you're doing it suits you." Portia grew more serious, examined her friend closely. "You look terrific. I'll end up thinking you've done it the right way round, if you're not careful. First marriage and a child. And then the rest. My lot are all going to be geriatric mums."

"Nothing is quite what it seems," Katherine murmured. And then, more brightly, told Portia about the notion of her own gallery.

When she returned to New York, she started somewhat erratically to look around. Walking through the Village, or SoHo, Madison Avenue or the Upper East Side, she would find herself examining spaces, thinking, perhaps here. Or here. She did research on the subject, talked to other gallery owners about their turnover, their expenses. She also mentioned it to Jacob. He was enthusiastic about the idea. "Since I can't seem to get you married off"—he chuckled as she froze momentarily—"a new project may not be such a bad thing."

On her next trip to Cologne, she talked at length with some dealers. Also without thinking about it, she repeated the French episode. A man, a hotel room, a single night. No ties. No commitments. No questions asked. No memories. It became something of a pattern. But never on home ground. Never at home. Never near Natalie. A secret. Containable. Controllable.

Natalie and Doreen came to join her in Geneva. They traveled to Princesse Mathilde's. She was as always delighted to see them. Natalie played with the dogs, gamboled over the grounds. She said to the Princesse, "You must come and stay with us in New York. I would like that."

"Perhaps, one day," the Princesse demurred without refusing. "I'm feeling my years now." She turned to Katherine and laughed. "I prefer lying around here and simply looking out of the window."

"Nonsense," Katherine refused the Princesse's age. "You look as beautiful and fit as ever."

She smiled at Katherine reflectively. "I would, however, like to make one little trip, if you'll allow it. I'd like to take Natalie to visit the Contessa. She hasn't been well and I know you won't take her. But Natalie should meet her grandmother before the old thing, silly as she is, dies."

Katherine turned away. The proposition startled her and troubled her. She had never known the Princesse had views on all this.

"Katherine, look at me. It is only right that Natalie should meet her. And I know, though I don't know why, that you won't go." The Princesse scrutinized her with all the intelligence of her years. "Natalie is not you. She may, when she's older, hold it against you. That you kept all that back from her. And I feel responsible."

"I'll think about it," Katherine said softly.

"I count on you." The Princesse was sterner than usual. "And I shall tell the Contessa that it won't be long now."

Katherine did think about it, thought about it through the entirety of the long flight home. The prospect filled her with unbearable anxiety. She had wild fears of her child being stolen away from her

or seduced into the enchantments of a Roman labyrinth. She held
on to Natalie's hand tightly. Held on to it as if it were her own life.

On May 10, 1977, the Katherine Jardine Gallery was ready to open
its doors to an expectant public.

Katherine, after much thought and consultation with Thomas, had
chosen a prime site just off Madison Avenue, a mere stone's throw
from the venerable Metropolitan Museum and amidst galleries
whose reputation was securely established worldwide. She had
selected this location for two reasons. The first was that it was close
to home and Natalie. She knew that she would be increasingly busy.
The second was that her gallery, where she had determined to show
brazenly contemporary work, would provide a contrast to the staider
establishments in the vicinity, something it might not have done in
the increasingly trendy streets of SoHo.

And then, too, she had fallen in love with the space, its gracious
proportions, the long generous sweep of the two main rooms, the
rounded arches which led into more intimate alcoves, the cheerful
blue and white awning at the front, from which banners could be
hung announcing shows.

On the night, Katherine was a bundle of exhilaration and nerves.
None of this was visible on the surface. As always, her gestures were
calm, unruffled, and her features bore no trace of her emotion. In
a tailored linen dress, set off only by a rakish clasp of bold design,
she was the very image of elegant composure. The papers and the
magazines had already commented on this.

Thomas had insisted that she hire a publicist who would spread
word of the gallery's opening and, as a result, profiles of Katherine
had appeared in a variety of places. Seeing herself refracted through
a public lens in this way had thrown her into commotion. She didn't
recognize herself in anything she read.

Male journalists had waxed lyrical over what they called her
arresting beauty—a beauty, as one said, which forced you to search
your mind for the forgotten original of which it seemed to be a type.
The women journalists preferred to focus on her status as a working
mother and on her ideas for the gallery, which were, they said,
unique—a gallery which linked an exploration of tradition with an
exhibition of the new.

There were barbs as well: a little scurrying into her professional
past brought out the armies of envy alongside the well-wishers. People said she was cold, implacably ambitious, a medusa who van-

quished her opponents by turning them to stone. Others called her judicious, intelligent, compelling. She was labeled everything from Ms. Iron Pants Jardine to The Show's Best Exhibition.

Over the last weeks as the articles came out, Thomas had simply patted her hand and consoled her with the statement that all news was good news prior to the launch of an enterprise.

He had been with her a great deal during these last months while the gallery was being refurbished and ideas took on material form. As soon as the space had been found, she had determined that she would open with a sequence of shows which introduced current art from Germany, work which boldly combined paint and other materials to reflect with a tortured melancholy on that country's bitter twentieth-century history.

It was Thomas who had hit on the idea of juxtaposing images from the twenties and thirties with the contemporary. His eyes had sparkled when he had suggested that Katherine select apposite pieces from his own collection to exhibit alongside the work that was for sale.

Once he had convinced her that he had no reservations about loaning his canvases, was indeed enthused by the notion of sharing them with other eyes, she had thrilled to the idea. It was a brainstorm which sparkled with possibilities. The past and the present side by side, one illuminating, reflecting upon the other. Continuity and rupture.

Katherine had selected the work for sale and then over slides they had endlessly discussed juxtapositions, placings, materials for the catalogue. More than once, his eyes had glowed over her and he had said, "You do know, you really do know exactly what you're doing."

"And since I know," she had smiled, "I also know that you must write an article for the catalogue." She had swayed him and he had done so in the witty, terse style which was his. Katherine was more than pleased.

And now there it all was—the pictures hung, the objects and sculptures and lights carefully positioned, the floors polished to a high sheen, the champagne glasses and catalogues at the ready.

Katherine checked once more that everything was in order and then raced up the stairs to the second level.

Thomas, with Natalie at his side, was chatting with the twins, Joe and Amelia, whom she had hired as her assistants. Their shy serious grace had won her over from the first and they had proved as deftly efficient as she could wish.

"Come, Schätzchen, let us have our own private celebratory drink before the crowds arrive." Thomas winked at her and popped a cork. Then with an air of great formality poured champagne. For her, for an excited Natalie, for the twins, for himself.

Katherine watched the man whose life was now so inextricably bound with her own and whose presence seemed to extend back as far as she could remember into her past. Thomas, her good angel. Thomas, whose movements were a little slower now, but whose eyes, as he turned them on her, were still those of a young man, replete with humor and energy. She raised her glass to him.

He twinkled as he raised his. "To the Katherine Jardine Gallery. It will be a great success, I know."

"Thanks to you," Katherine glowed at him.

He shook his white head. "No, Schätzchen. Thanks to you." He squeezed her hand, teased her. "In these feminist days, you must at least learn to accept the responsibility of your own achievements."

"Oh Thomas," she giggled. "Still trying, always and ever trying to teach me how to be a good woman." She kissed him.

"Who knows, one day I may succeed. What do you think, Natalie?"

Dark eyes gazed at them both with mock solemnity. "Maybe," Natalie said tentatively. "Just maybe," she grinned.

"You little horror." Katherine embraced her and then announced, a little breathlessly, "It's time to open the doors."

She held on to Thomas's hand as they made their way down the stairs.

"It will be a great success," he whispered emphatically in her ear, giving her courage. "I know about these things."

And as the crowd coming through the doors separated them and Katherine recognized in its midst a welter of critics, collectors and cognoscenti, she knew that Thomas was more than probably right.

*J*acob Jardine put his arm firmly around his daughter's shoulders, took Natalie's hand and forced them both to walk. Walk down the long leafy avenue of the cemetery. Away from Thomas Sachs's grave.

Katherine was weeping. Blindly, silently. Weeping the way he had only ever seen her weep as a small child. There had never been any visible tears for Sylvie. Nor had she shed any at Carlo's funeral. But now, all the tears she had stored over the years seemed to have burst forth. Decades of tears released in the ten days since Thomas's death.

He had meant even more to her than Jacob had ever realized.

But then, for all their closeness, there was always a great deal about his daughter that he never altogether knew. She had locked herself away in her little box of secrecy many years ago. Already as a small child. And he hadn't wanted to probe too much, to interfere, to control with that terrible controlling knowledge of his profession.

And a professional distortion had resulted nonetheless, he now increasingly thought. Oh yes, he had managed to avoid some of the traps he had seen his colleagues fall into. He had eschewed the little controlling experiments on the domestic terrain, the veiled extended analyses by the all-seeing father, the spilling over of analytic ploys on the home front. And their often tragic results. But he had failed in the opposite direction, cut himself off, not intervened quite enough. With Sylvie and with Katherine.

He kept his arm firmly around her and guided her and Natalie toward gates, already closed. They were the last mourners in a darkening cemetery. There had, to start with, been a great many of them. Thomas was known, liked, and men of all generations in trim pin-stripe suits had come, together with hatted women, their faces sad, respectful, a little uncomfortable as the living always were in the presence of the dead. But now, there were only the three of them: his daughter, her shoulders too straight, her face all but obliterated under the vast black hat; Natalie, gripping his hand for reassurance.

Jacob found the guard. The well-oiled gates were opened. He led his little family toward a waiting limousine.

Yes, he thought again, as he settled into the seat and patted Natalie's hand, where the most important things were concerned, Katherine couldn't, wouldn't turn to him. Perhaps that was the way it had to be. But he worried. A father's prerogative. Worried about her solitary state. Worried about the emotions, the anger he could feel simmering beneath that mask of cool composure, that self-control.

Worried, too, about that secret little box she had stored within her. Her box of memories, locked, forgotten, even it seemed by herself. Sylvie, Carlo, whatever they had meant, whatever she had felt for them, locked and stored into oblivion. Denied existence. And with them, a part of herself. So much energy put into the act of denial, into the process of forgetting. It fueled distortions. Made her resist intimacy. It was dangerous.

What if something should trigger the lock on that secret box? Would Katherine cope? Had Thomas's death done so? Was she coping now? That tear-streaked face was turned away from him.

Jacob held Natalie's hand more closely. How often he had pondered those twin pivots of memory and forgetting. His life was spent in the work of memory, the work of unearthing the buried past, bringing unconscious memories to the light of day, making them visible and hence robbing them of their dark force. Making memories forgettable. Without forgetting, life was impossible. Memory trapped one in the vicious grip of repetition, a rat's treadmill, a constant return to the poisonous point of departure.

The twin pivots of memory and forgetting. The line stretched between them was the tightrope of life.

Natalie was shivering, despite the warmth of the evening. He was worried about his grandchild, too. Katherine was almost too close to her. Despite all the demands of work, she guarded the girl too nearly. Tried to play mother, father, sister, friend, all at once. She was making up for Sylvie's lacks. But Natalie might end up resenting her. Resenting her, too, for Katherine's obliteration of her father.

He looked at the two of them, saw Natalie plant a kiss on Katherine's face. No, she didn't resent her yet. Perhaps she never would. Perhaps he was simply an old fool with outmoded ideas. After all, all those years ago he had been wrong to worry about Katherine and Thomas, about his interest in her. A silly jealous father was what he had been, like a character out of a Molière comedy. And now, Katherine was doing so well. He was proud of her. And these weeks of tears might help. Help unblock her somehow. The self was not a fixed entity hewn in stone. It was a fiction, a story we told ourselves to live by. And those stories could change, shift. Until the end came. And then others took up the narrative, determining its course, in part by its end.

"Thomas would have been pleased with the manner of his death," Jacob suddenly surprised himself by saying. The words hung there unanswered over the hum of the engine. But he had to go on now he had started. It was necessary to speak about it, if only for Natalie's sake. "So quick, so clean, in his sleep. Without illness. His mind still as sharp as ever. A Thomas sort of end."

Katherine didn't respond. She gazed out of the window.

"But he won't come back," Natalie said softly after a moment. "The dead don't come back."

"No," Jacob murmured, remembering another conversation. "They don't come back. Except in our thoughts. And that is something."

"I miss him already," Natalie said. "I'll miss him forever. He always gave me such good advice."

Jacob squeezed her hand. "I'll try to give you good advice in his guise now." He allowed himself a little laugh. " 'Old men love to give advice. To console themselves for not being able to set a bad example.' A very intelligent Frenchman called La Rochefoucauld said that once, Natalie."

She smiled at him kindly, as if to console him for his efforts.

Katherine lay in her hotel-room bed, a whisky glass in her hand. Jacob had taken Natalie down to dinner. It was a relief to be alone. She wasn't good for anything, for anyone. She seemed to be able only to weep. Thomas's death, so sudden, coming so soon after the opening of the gallery when she had last seen him brilliantly alive, had shocked her out of any semblance of composure.

She replayed the sequence of events again in her mind. They hadn't seen each other for a week after the opening, but they had spoken every day. And then, one day, when he hadn't rung, she had simply assumed that he was busy, had other things to get on with. The next morning, she had rung him, but there had been no answer at the house. She had tried again, later. Still no answer. Perhaps he had omitted to tell her that he would be away for a few days.

So the next day, she tried again. Susannah picked up the telephone. Katherine, as always, irritated by Susannah, asked for Thomas in cool, professional tones.

"He's dead," the voice had replied, point-blank, almost blithe.

"What?" Katherine had shrieked into the telephone.

"Yes, Miss Fancy Pants. Died this morning at the Charles Hospital."

Katherine had caught the first plane for Boston. She didn't believe that voice. Didn't recognize it. The drawl was gone. Susannah was lying.

But Katherine had gone to the hospital. Nurses had confirmed Thomas's death. She had asked to see him, and then when they realized she wasn't a relative, she had had to beg, exhort, scream to be granted that permission. A nurse, in order to keep her quiet, had finally led her to a cold, gloomy room. And there, when the sheet had been drawn back, she had seen Thomas. A pale, slightly puffy Thomas, but his face his own. A trace of surprise hovered over it.

She had kissed him.

Two hours later, the weeping had begun. It still wouldn't stop.

Thomas was dead. Thomas who had been a true friend to her. Her closest friend ever since she could remember. Thomas who had stepped into her life and saved her from it. Saved her from her mother. Thomas who had chided and advised and loved. Thomas, who had watched and sheltered and cared. Thomas, whom she had never repaid. Who had only given. Dead. Dead in the flesh. She had seen him. The physical finality of him.

Not like Sylvie or Carlo. She thought of them now. She had fled from them. Wanted them obliterated. And everything in herself they stood for. But Thomas, who was good. Who had done good. Whom she loved. Who was her better self.

She felt small. Alone. Utterly abandoned. No matter how many times she told herself she must pull herself together for Natalie's sake. No matter how many times she told herself Jacob was still there. She still wept.

Over the coming weeks and months, the weeping gradually ceased. But at odd times, never predictably, it would still come upon her, take her by surprise, contorting her face in the midst of a meeting or at table with Natalie, so that she had to run to a lonely place and hide until it ceased. Out of the weeping came the sense that she must behave as Thomas would have wished her to. She worked harder than ever to make a success of the gallery. She lavished care and affection on Natalie and Jacob, on those closest to her.

Three months after Thomas's death, his will was read. No impersonal executor's letters for Thomas. He had asked for the community of his legatees to gather, to inspect each other, to recognize the presence of his mind and estate at work after the passage of his body.

Katherine and Natalie were summoned to a midtown office which smelled of old leather and pipe tobacco. Amidst the small group already gathered, most of whom she didn't know, Katherine spied Susannah Holmes, wrapped in a lavish mink.

Katherine managed a nod, before averting her eyes and taking Natalie to a window seat in the far corner of the room. As they waited for Thomas's lawyer, who was also his executor, to read the will, she told Natalie the story of the towering spires they could see in magnificent detail from the window.

But her thoughts were on Susannah. She had forgotten about Susannah. Forgotten how much she despised the woman. Despised the way she had taken charge of the funeral proceedings as if she were Thomas's wife. Despised the curt way she had rung the gallery on the day the opening exhibition was over to order the return of Thomas's pictures. Susannah constituted the only part of Thomas's life that Katherine found it difficult to allow.

The executor called them to order. He read, his voice a decisive monotone, gathering phrases in its stride, neutralizing, equalizing. Buried somewhere in his bland delivery, there was Thomas's own playful tone, his tastes, his wishes, the forms in which he wanted to be remembered. Katherine held Natalie's hand tightly, wondering what she made of it all. There was a substantial legacy, greater than she had somehow ever imagined. There were bequests to a score of charities, to Harvard for the establishment of a Chair, to PEN, to the Academy of Letters for the institution of a prize for translators of German fiction.

She started as her own name rolled off the executor's thin lips.

"To Katherine Jardine, who has for many years been like a daughter to me, I leave my house with all its contents and my collection of works of art (bar three) for which she shared my love."

Katherine started to cry. With half an ear she heard that Susannah and a variety of other individuals had received substantial legacies. And then Natalie was named. Natalie Jardine Negri della Buonaterra, "to my youngest friend whose life is all to be made, I leave the three villages by Lyonel Feininger and the remainder of my estate to be kept in trust for her until her twenty-first birthday."

"What does it mean, Mommy? What estate? Where is it?" Natalie whispered when the voice had stopped. "Isn't Thomas kind? My favorite villages. Can I put them in my room?"

At Natalie's voice, the man in front of them turned and smiled at her. "What it means, young lady, is that you are a very lucky girl."

Katherine, trying to control her tears, whisked Natalie away. She could feel all the eyes in the room turned on her daughter, the murmurs, the hum of voices, already speculating, wondering whether Natalie might be Thomas's child. She must take her out of here before Natalie was poisoned by the tongues.

Near the door she all but collided with Susannah Holmes. "Bitch. Scheming bitch." The woman's words slapped her. "Think you got what you wanted? Well, don't be too sure."

Katherine looked at her as if she were mad. She all but dragged Natalie to the elevator.

"Don't let her upset you, Mommy," Natalie said in the maternal tones she had increasingly taken on of late. "She's just silly, that Susannah."

"You're right, hon." Katherine smiled at her daughter's seriousness. "I'll tell you what. Let's go to the Russian Tea Room, where we always went with Thomas, and eat as many of his favorite cakes as we can."

Ensconced at a table in the Tea Room, Katherine explained to Natalie what Thomas's will meant.

"But that's amazing, Mommy." Natalie played with a *mille feuille*, her face unusually solemn.

"Yes, it is," Katherine murmured.

"I'm really happy about the villages." She suddenly looked as if she were about to burst into tears.

"Me too, I love them too." She forced a smile. "Thomas has been very good to us. Too good. And do you know what we're going to do?" Suddenly Katherine's smile became real. "We're going to turn his house into a public museum." The idea had just come to her and as she spoke it, she knew that it was right. Something for Thomas. A visible memorial to his life and taste. She grew excited, communicated her excitement to Natalie. "The Thomas Sachs Collection, like the Frick. My favorite kind of museum. A home that has been lived in, loved. A home with all its pictures for everyone to share. Won't that be grand?"

Natalie was infected by Katherine's delight. She began to smile. "You mean nothing will be taken away? It'll be just as it was?"

"Well, almost." Katherine dreamed, schemed layouts in her mind's eye. "We'll have to move some of the furniture, arrange the pictures and sculpture a little differently. But all the work will be kept together, everything that he loved in one place, his place. Undispersed. Okay, Nat?"

"Okay." Natalie jabbed a piece of cake and began to chew. "Sounds good to me."

Three days later, all Katherine's dreams evaporated into a foul heap. A special delivery letter in a long legal envelope arrived for her at the gallery. As she read its contents, her eyes grew wide in disbelief, her face ashen.

"What's up, Kat?" Joe, one of her gallery assistants, was at her side. He brought her a glass of water.

She drank. Didn't answer. Read the letter again. She couldn't believe its contents. Susannah Holmes was contesting Thomas's will, suing the estate, claiming that Thomas had promised to marry her, claiming the house, the pictures, the largest portion of Natalie's legacy.

Susannah. Thomas's wife. His concubine. The word fell into Katherine's mind and stretched its wings covering everything. She started to shiver. She felt dirty, sullied. Susannah swathed in her furs. Without her southern drawl. Without her mask. A squalid woman, sullying Thomas's memory. Casting her vulgar shadow backward through time, dirtying Thomas, cheapening everything. Wanting money. Everything for gain.

Thomas's woman. His wife. He had chosen her. Lived with her. Thomas profaned. Her friend. Natalie's friend.

She sat still for a very long time.

"Shall I cancel your next appointment?" Joe's voice seemed to come from a great distance.

Katherine nodded. "Cancel all of them for the rest of the day," she murmured.

She looked at the letter again. She had always suspected, of course. Known about Susannah. Known she was more than a housekeeper. She forced herself to think about it. To focus on the Thomas she hadn't been privy to, had preferred latterly not to know. It was not the kind of relationship they had had at the end. Yet he had never been secretive about his sexual needs. Had never hidden their existence. He had merely been tactful about specificities, about the women themselves. Which was as it should be. As she had been for different reasons.

It was she who was prudish. Who didn't like to acknowledge the existence of that other Thomas. He disturbed her, this Thomas of sexual games. This Thomas who was Susannah's. Why had he chosen her? That horrible woman. Why not Katherine?

No, that was not the way to think. She stilled herself. Recalled Thomas's voice. He would chide her for thinking that way. She could almost hear him answering the question she had put. "There are many different ways of loving people, Schätzchen. And sometimes, with some of us, time does us a disservice. It keeps us out of step. We never meet in the sexual dance. But there are other dances. Other forms of music, equally resonant. Sometimes more resonant."

Hearing his voice calmed her. Thomas was not serious about sex. He did not cloak it in the robes of religion. He was not a Lawrentian romantic. Far from it.

Suddenly she remembered other names in the will. Other women had been left substantial sums too. She hadn't been paying careful enough attention, but she thought Susannah had been given the largest amount. Thomas was a fair man. A generous man.

Katherine rescued his image from the murky colors she had over-laid it with. Susannah's colors.

He had, she reflected, written his will with all his faculties intact. He had known what he wanted. It was his "will." She mustn't allow herself to sink passively to Susannah's volition, simply because of the force of the woman's greed. That's all it was. Nothing more. Not a feeling for Thomas. Not a plea for justice where wrong had been done. She and Natalie had dreamed a museum for Thomas together. She wouldn't let her daughter down. And Thomas would have liked the idea.

Katherine picked up the telephone and dialed the executor's number. She would help the estate fight Susannah's claim. Fight it to the bitter end.

The legal battle took her over with an intensity she would not have found imaginable. It colored her days and nights, her working hours as well as her dreams. She woke with a bitter taste in her mouth, her mind full of arguments which she rehearsed over and over in the course of the day. Arguments against Susannah, arguments which increasingly became a vindication of Thomas's honor, his good sense. Her Thomas.

The executor put the case in the hands of one of his junior partners, a woman of about Katherine's own age who he claimed had a great deal of experience in this field.

On the occasion of her second meeting with Julia Katz, the woman looked at her forthrightly and said, "I have to tell you, Ms. Jardine, that I'm usually on the other side in these cases. I believe, I believe very strongly, that women who live with men should have the same rights as those legally bound to them in marriage. Men cannot be allowed to use women as mere playthings, as sexual objects, and consider themselves unattached. Have no responsibility for their continuing welfare."

Katherine stared at her for a moment, saw a dark woman with fiery eyes and quick gestures, a woman of purpose, a woman she had thought she might like. She closed her notebook firmly and rose. "Well then, Ms. Katz, there is really no reason for you to be burdened with this case." Katherine's voice was cold. "I'm surprised the estate has chosen you to defend the integrity of Mr. Sachs's will. It, and my daughter and I as its principal beneficiaries, should be seeking advice elsewhere."

"On the contrary." Julia Katz grinned engagingly. "The executor feels that if the estate's defense convinces me, then the hearing will be a pushover." She looked a little rueful. "I was simply making myself plain to you. Sit down, Ms. Jardine."

Katherine hesitated, then slowly, warily, she sat down again. She hadn't paused to consider the larger implications of the case at all. She suddenly heard Portia's voice in her ear. "It's the principle of the thing, Kat. A woman standing up for her rights, the rights of women, against men, against exploitation. Anyhow. It's not as if you or Natalie need the money." Portia's voice clarified things for her.

"Ms. Katz." She met the young lawyer's eyes. "We are not dealing with a divorce case here or even a case of a man chucking a woman he has grown tired of out of a home which is rightfully hers. We are dealing with a dead man's will, his wishes for his legacy. Susannah Holmes was amply, more than amply I imagine knowing Thomas, paid for her services as a housekeeper for three years. If she performed other services"—Katherine's face twisted in distaste— "then I can only suggest the sum left to her, the substantial sum of a quarter of a million dollars, should be more than sufficient recompense." Katherine paused, then murmured with repugnance, "She's just a scheming fortune-hunter."

Julia Katz chuckled. "That's what she says about you, of course."

"About me?" Katherine's confusion was evident in her face.

"Why yes." Julia was amused. "Haven't you thought about it? She sees herself as the rightful wife. You're the other woman, seducing Mr. Sachs away from her, scheming for your own ends."

Katherine spluttered, "Ridiculous. That's ridiculous. That's how that greedy woman would think. The . . ." She controlled herself. "Ms. Katz, Thomas Sachs was my dearest friend since I was thirteen. I knew him for far longer than that . . . that woman."

Julia Katz's eyes glimmered with irony. "Well, we've now established that you don't like her. And I imagine she doesn't exactly love you. Fortunately, the law doesn't function according to individuals' tastes. So let's see what kind of case we've got here. Ms. Holmes is claiming that Mr. Sachs intended to marry her, that she only stayed with him because of that promise, an oral agreement which he would have kept if his death had not intervened. She is arguing that she therefore has a right to the house and its contents and to a larger proportion of the estate, that he would have changed his will but death took him by surprise."

"When were the last changes made to the will?" Katherine interrupted her.

"A year before his death."

"But he would have known what he wanted by then. Susannah had already been with him for some time. It was then that we began to talk about the gallery." Katherine was emphatic. She told Julia Katz about Thomas's involvement in the gallery, their joint plans, his silent partnership, though in the end she had refused any financial investment from him. "I'm not interested in Thomas's money," she finished with a plea in her voice. "I do want the collection and the house to be kept intact. To make a museum of it. I'm prepared to use my own funds for that, raise more from other sources."

"Okay." Julia looked at her curiously. "I think we've got the makings of a case. But it won't be straightforward. There may be nastiness."

Katherine shrugged. "It's worth Thomas's memory to me." She shook Julia's hand. "He was a good man, you know. He deserves better than the likes of Susannah Holmes squandering his beloved pictures on furs and diamonds."

But Katherine didn't like the nastiness. She didn't like the prying steps the lawyers were taking to amass their evidence; their questions to all of Thomas's colleagues and former mistresses about his relations with Susannah, with her, about his intentions.

She liked even less Susannah's sudden appearance one rainy spring day in the gallery.

Katherine, on the stairs, heard the woman's voice, hard, callous, brooking no response, telling Joe that she wanted to see Katherine Jardine now.

She met Joe halfway up the stairs.

"There's a woman who . . ."

"I know, Joe," Katherine comforted him. "Give me a moment and then send her up."

Katherine positioned herself behind the glass slab which was her desk and pretended to write.

"So this is The Katherine Jardine Gallery." Susannah flounced in, drawled, did nothing to hide her venom.

Katherine saw a Susannah with gilded hair, a bright red couture suit. She didn't speak, waited.

"Must have cost old Tom a good few grand, this dump."

"I beg your pardon?" Katherine was astounded by the implication.

"I beg your pardon," Susannah mimicked her. "Beg away, Miss Hoity-toity. You must be good at begging to have gotten all you did from old Tom. Oh, don't pretend you don't know what I'm talking about. Seducing the old codger with your hoity-toity words and your hoity-toity manner, beguiling him with that little brat. Too good for me, he thought. This dump was too good for me. Couldn't take me here. How much did the place cost him then?"

"This is *my* gallery, Ms. Holmes." Katherine's tone was icy. "I paid for it. Please leave. Now."

"I'm not going anywhere." Susannah sat down on the chair in front of the desk to give emphasis to her words. "Not until you agree to my claim. I've had it with waiting for these lawyers. Agree now, or . . ."

"Don't be ridiculous," Katherine hissed, looked at her as she might look at a bevy of vermin. "It has nothing to do with me."

"Don't be ridiculous," Susannah aped her. "So high and mighty, aren't we? But he couldn't get it up with you, eh? Your royal highness was too good for sex. Too good to spread your legs. Had to have it with me. With the servants, eh? Bet your royal highness wouldn't dress up in little ruffled maid's skirts. Without panties, of course. No panties for old Tom, just seamed silk stockings. That made him hard as a ram." She laughed, her mouth a red slash.

"Don't be vulgar." Katherine's hands were trembling. She clenched them in her lap.

"Vulgar, am I? Not good enough. You're the one who made him think I wasn't good enough for marrying. Hoity-toity bitch. He would have married me if it hadn't been for you. He liked my ass. Liked my tits. He'd put his cock just there"—she flaunted her ample breasts—"and get me to suck away."

"Get out," Katherine hissed.

She laughed again. "Upsets you, does it? Well, it's going to upset you a whole lot more if you don't give me what I want. 'Cause I'm going to tell the world, tell the court, tell your little brat, every little bit of what old Tom did to me."

Katherine rose. "If you don't go now, I'm going to phone the police." She picked up the telephone receiver.

Susannah stood, taking her time. "And one more thing, I might just put it about that your little brat is his. That wouldn't make you happy, would it? It would distress the darling." Her voice reeked malice. "So you know where to send your agreement."

Katherine watched her, as if in slow motion. It seemed to take an eternity for her to turn, for the stiletto heels to reach the door. And then suddenly Katherine's mind snapped back into gear. She called after her, her voice controlled, "If my brat, as you choose to call her, is indeed Thomas's daughter, then I think you'll see that you have no case at all, Ms. Holmes."

The woman swung round and gave her a poisonous stare before proceeding down the stairs.

Alone, Katherine found herself shaking. She paced, looked out the window at passing cars, at two strollers in flowered dresses. She tried to collect herself. Perhaps she ought to ring Julia Katz right now and give up the whole thing. Let that disgusting woman have what she wanted. Let the whole thing be over and done with.

She felt exhausted, limp. She fell into the soft gray sofa which spanned a corner of her office and let her eyes fall on the single painting the room held. Two figures gazed with incurable melancholy into a windswept sky, a darkening sea. It was an Edward Hopper she had bought a little while back for too much money, but she was transfixed by the mood of the image. The painting had spoken to her, wouldn't leave her alone.

She took solace in it now. A thing of beauty, fixed against the transience which its very subjects suffered from. No, the thought suddenly crystallized in her. She wouldn't let that woman take over Thomas completely, whatever her sexual claims. Thomas had given his collection to her. For a reason. She would fight to keep it. Keep Natalie's inheritance. Keep his wishes, his memory intact. Susannah's threats were empty. Her descriptions wouldn't sway any court. That's why she had come here to bully her today.

Yet Susannah's words continued to torment her. They conjured up a different Thomas, opened up a window on an intimacy she would rather not have seen. The scenes she glimpsed through that window obsessed her. Sometimes Susannah's figure, like a vulgar laughing vamp from a Fellini movie, metamorphosed into herself. Her buried escapades with strangers in foreign cities began to flit before her eyes. They laughed at her with Susannah's red gash of a mouth. Threatened to swallow her. Obliterate her.

Katherine rang her father, asked if she could stop round and see him on her way home. She needed, she realized, to talk to someone. And there was only Jacob.

She didn't often come to the apartment now. Jacob tended to visit her and Natalie at their home. And it felt a little odd to be sitting opposite him in the room she had sought so fervently to create all those years ago. It hadn't altered much, though Jacob had got rid of the modern carpets and replaced them with the Persian rugs he favored.

"All this legal business must be getting on top of you," he said, reading her mind after they had exchanged a little desultory small talk.

"It is." She tried to smile, but her lips felt stiff.

"There's nothing like an encounter with the law to drive you into the arms of an analyst." Jacob laughed softly. "The legal system is society's sanctioned dream of paranoia. Tell me the latest."

She told him. Told him about Susannah's visit, not everything, but in essence.

"And you're distressed because of her vile manner, because you've been forced to invade someone else's secrets. But most of all because you can't make a retrospective saint of Thomas?" Dark eyes surveyed her shrewdly. "Is that it?"

Katherine began by nodding and then shook her head vehemently. Denied his words. "No, it's Natalie. Natalie would be so upset if all this came out in court, all the detail. And the estate might lose."

Jacob studied her, waited for her to go on. When she didn't he said, "Are you sure it's Natalie you're worried about and not you? After all, she needn't be at the hearing."

Katherine didn't answer directly. "She's a horrible woman." Her voice shook. She stood up, paced the room. "Nasty, horrible. I don't know why Thomas . . ." She left her sentence unfinished.

"Kat, look at me. Thomas was a man, not an angel. This woman was his mistress, a consenting mistress. Whatever they did together was their business. She hasn't suffered from it. He obviously didn't, since he chose for it to go on. You're upset because she wouldn't have been your choice. But then, other people's sexual preferences are usually a mystery to the outsider. And sexuality is always disruptive, seen in daylight, publicly. That's why we like to tame it by dressing it up in the language of love."

Jacob chuckled. "What Susannah Holmes has done is akin to parading naked down Fifth Avenue. The secret, the clothed, rampantly displayed. Though I thought your generation had done away with all that. Everything open. Everything permissible. Isn't that what the sexual revolution is all about?" He smiled at her kindly as she scowled. Teased her.

"Thomas has done nothing wrong, Kat. Sex isn't a moral issue, though people construct moralities around it." He paused. "It is, though, a way of eluding death." He let the phrase hang for a moment, so that she was forced to confront it.

"Come and sit by me, Kat. You're overwrought."

She sat by him, let him put his arm around her, soothe her. She wanted to contradict him, to say that for her sex was a kind of dying, a blotting out of herself. Yes, that was what she felt. And Thomas, the Thomas she knew and loved was being blotted out by Susannah's crass evocations. But she couldn't bring the words out.

Jacob chatted, his voice playful. "I heard this wonderful Woody Allen line, 'Is sex dirty? Only if it's done right.'" He chuckled. "You remember your Yeats, 'Love has pitched his mansion / In the place of excrement.' And sometimes, according to our wishes, we transform that place into a temple. But it hasn't altogether moved.

"I worry about you, Kat," he said gently. "You split yourself apart. You want things to be either all good or all bad. I guess it's to do with Sylvie."

Katherine stiffened. He hadn't mentioned her mother for a long time. "Why do you say that?" she asked. Her voice felt rusty.

"You've made her into the 'bad mother,' which I know she was.

In part. To you. Cold, cruel, rejecting. And sexy." He stopped abruptly and then hurried on, as if he had exposed too much. "And I imagine you've made Princesse Mat into the 'good mother.'" He studied her for a moment.

"And now, I think you're struggling to maintain Thomas as the 'good father,' the perfect man. I imagine, if he was anything like the man I think he was, he would have been the first to reject the idealization. No man with that ironical twinkle in his eye, no good Berliner of Thomas's generation, would deny his portion of wickedness." Jacob laughed.

"Remember, Kat, the end of that poem, 'For nothing can be sole or whole / That has not been rent.'" He paused, let her consider it, then laughed again ruefully. "And that's enough of my babble for this evening. Otherwise you'll have to start charging *me* for a fifty-minute hour."

Katherine tried to smile. "And my fees are high."

"Shall I take you and Natalie out for dinner?"

She nodded, kissed him. "Thanks, Pappy."

"*Ça ira, petite.*" Jacob switched to French in response to her childhood appellation. "Thomas's testament will sort itself out. That Holmes woman wouldn't have come to you directly, if she didn't already sense her case was going badly."

In herself, Katherine knew that Jacob was right. Right about many things. She needed to ruminate over them. It had helped to talk to him.

But it didn't eradicate the foul taste in her mouth which that scene with Susannah had left behind. Nor its implications. They festered in her as she waited for the case to be heard, waited for any subsequent moves on Susannah's part.

Something else happened during those endless months of waiting. Obsessing about Susannah, she began to see her as a type. A type who proliferated in the streets of the city. A type who was the very personification of greed. An all-consuming greed. And that greed was everywhere. It seeped out of the grates of the subway and poisoned the city.

In her corner of New York the greed was cloaked in its most unobtrusive, most modest garb. It wore the muted coat of good manners and good society. Camouflaged greed, with its brothers envy and desire. A trio of endless insatiable craving. She could smell their heated, slightly rancid odor tainting the crisp spring air as she walked to work.

Oh, the greed was well hidden here. Not like in Susannah's red mouth and her hungry eyes. Here, in this Upper East Side of Manhattan, it was kept under control. There were venerable museums and established galleries to disinfect the atmosphere. Stylish boutiques mingled with old world curio shops and ramshackle booksellers. A veneer of European culture to obscure the subterranean greed that propelled the American dream.

But it was still palpably there. She could see it in the women's faces: that leap of hunger as they gazed at the parade of fashions coolly displayed in the shops. The snatched furtive glance at the orgy of freshly baked bread and cakes which diets wouldn't permit. She could read it in the covert looks of brisk executives, subliminally comparing the attributes of wives and mistresses to those of sleekly groomed passersby—and all the while tallying up the relative values of stocks and shares.

The greed paid no attention to the weather. It infected the sky, which this spring was of a perfect untrammeled blue. It hovered over the pale trees, poised to unfurl their plump sticky buds.

It even invaded her gallery.

It bore the figure of a fat little man with thinning black sleeked-back hair and a vast signet ring displaying four equally fat diamonds. A client. A client with all the proper introductions and credentials. A client with a vast bank account. A client who trailed on his arm a towering lacquered blonde whose fingers and wrists and neck glistened with the trappings of wealth. A blonde who was another incarnation of Susannah.

The two sat and looked unseeingly at the canvases the twins displayed for them from the storeroom. Katherine looked on and wondered. What had these images to do with this fat beaming figure with his self-satisfied smile, his endless talk of market values and good investments? Nothing, Katherine thought. Nothing. But they were united by the intractable logic of greed. The client's desire to possess the canvas.

It was not only a desire for money, for financial value. She knew that. She could see it in the wistful expression which sometimes scurried across her clients' faces. It was also a hunger for something else. The prestige, the status the canvases conferred with their incontrovertible tag of luxury culture. They were attempting to buy the inaccessible, the unnameable, the spiritual value the square feet of the canvas locked into itself and radiated indiscriminately.

Perhaps that was what Susannah wanted as well. That was why she was set on Thomas's collection.

Perhaps it was what she, herself, was in search of. Something to take her away from the squalor of greed and sex and ceaseless want.

Katherine sighed, halfheartedly made a sale. Then she went home. Increasingly all she wanted to do was to spend time with Natalie and her schoolfriends. She felt free with them. Greed was kept at bay.

At last, the case was heard, Katherine, her body numb, dimly heard the court rule in the estate's favor. Thomas's will was to stay as he had intended. Katherine unclasped her hands and slowly rose.

"Bitch," Susannah Holmes hissed at her as she crossed her path. "Tight-assed rich bitch."

"Tight-assed Rich Bitch vs. Greedy Scheming Whore," Katherine confronted her at last. It gave her pleasure to roll the crude words off her tongue. She threw Susannah a withering look. The woman's lipstick was askew. She saw her mouth drop. That too gave her pleasure.

"The court has ruled. Goodbye, Ms. Holmes." Katherine strode away.

She walked home. The streets had suddenly lost their ominous smell of greed. They were simply the streets of New York, shabby, seedy, bewitching, exhilarating by turn. She felt light.

She hugged Natalie and hugged her again. "This weekend we're going to Thomas's house," she announced triumphantly. "And we start work. There's a lot to do."

"Oh Mommy." Natalie bounced.

When they got there, Jacob in tow, the house was ghostly in its covering of white sheets. Katherine paused for a moment, shivering at the signs of Thomas's absence. Then with a vigorous gesture, she pulled the sheets off the breakfast-room sofas, one after another. "Come on," she urged the others.

That done, she guided them up to Thomas's bedroom. On the wall, opposite the bed, there was a drawing by George Grosz. She knew it well. A plump prostitute with greedy lips, her private parts bared to the furtive streets of the city. "We'll give this to Susannah," Katherine said reflectively. "She deserves a little bit of Thomas."

She looked at Jacob, signaling that the words were intended for him, but she addressed Natalie. "What do you say, hon?"

Natalie looked at her mother curiously and then met her smile. She nodded sagely.

"That's my Kat," Jacob beamed. "That's my daughter."

CHAPTER
TWENTY-THREE

flash of red hair. The briskness of heels on stone, a light, animal quickness. Rosa.

Alexei ran, turned a corner, placed a hand on a slender shoulder. "Sorry. So sorry," he mumbled.

"Non fa niente." A stranger smiled, recognized confusion.

Alexei loped away, nursing a mixture of disappointment and embarrassment.

A year, one long year had passed since he had last seen Rosa and still her form appeared to him around every corner. In this last week, somehow, it had been even worse. Perhaps because he had finally finished editing his film, a film he would have liked to have shared with her. But it was madness thinking he would suddenly bump into her, here in Rome.

Alexei sat down at one of the tables in the Piazza di Spagna and watched the passersby.

The shape of a brow here, the redness of lips there, the swing of an arm, the flick of a hip. The pieces of Rosa. But not her.

It was strange the way he now felt he knew her. Knew her better than when she was with him. At those times the mercury in her temperament, the electricity between them had taken over.

A phrase tumbled into his mind. Ready made. Perhaps he had read it somewhere. "Knowing people is what we do to them when they are not there."

If that was the case, he had had ample occasion to know Rosa. He could still taste the despair he had felt when she had gone that second time. A sense of loss so total that he could find no words for it. As if he were a child for whom language had not yet formed.

A distress equal to the wonder of those previous weeks.

The weeks after she had refused his proposal of marriage.

She had been tender then, only playfully argumentative, as if the sex war were over at last between them.

The evening the results of the May 1974 referendum on divorce were declared, they had celebrated with a bottle of champagne.

"I don't know why I'm celebrating," Alexei had joked. "All I want to do is marry you."

"You know very well why we're celebrating." She had taken on her sometime look of a stern schoolteacher. "It's a breach in the power of the church. We're fractionally more free now. Though there's a long way to go." Then she had laughed, her voice rich, dark, unlike her. "Anyhow, wanting marriage is a happier desire than wanting divorce."

That night, as if suddenly she trusted him, she had not risen from his bed after their lovemaking, but slept with him peacefully, her bright hair fanned over his chest. In the morning, she had brought him coffee in bed.

"You see, you would make an excellent wife," he teased her.

"Don't joke, Alexei." Her face was serious. "Don't make bad jokes." She had looked so desolate that he had pulled her to him and covered her with his love.

It was then that he had started to woo her, inventing a coupled future, buying her presents, insisting that she go out with him, go shopping with him. "I want to see those glorious legs of yours sometimes," he had laughed.

"You see them in bed. Isn't that enough?"

"I want to see them and you in front of my friends, in restaurants, dancing, at parties. I want you to meet Giangiacomo."

"You know that's not possible." She had cut off his fanciful flurry.

"Why? Why not? You think I care if anyone recognizes you as a notorious industrial troublemaker? Because that's what you are, isn't it?" He had put words to it at last. "That's what you get up to when you're not with me?"

She had turned away from him, but he carried on. "What do I care if that's your work? And if I don't care, they won't care. I'll say, 'Meet my wife. She goes into factories and makes people think about their conditions. She's brilliant at it.' " He had laughed, enraptured of his dream.

"You don't understand anything, Alexei," she had murmured, still not facing him.

He had wrapped his arms around her, nuzzled her hair, her neck, breathed in her perfume. "I understand that I love you."

She turned in the circle of his embrace. Looked confused, as if she might cry. But then, her eyes had suddenly taken on a mischievous sparkle, the irises ringed, dark. "All right, take me shopping. Keep the system turning. Fulfill your consumerist desires. Just remember that I'm not your possession."

They had made the rounds of the boutiques. Rosa in dusky blue silk. In emerald green. In a saucy black catsuit. They had gone dancing, gone again to the house by the lake, made breathless love amongst the chattering cicadas. The chemistry between them was so potent that Alexei was lulled into feeling it would never end.

And then, suddenly, one night, she had refused him, refused his touch.

"Why?" He had looked at her in bafflement.

"I don't feel like it," Rosa had shrugged.

"Don't feel like it?" He had run his fingers along the bodice of her dress to where it met the tawny glow of her skin. He could see her instant response. "Don't feel like it?" He had gazed at her in amazement.

She had run to her room, slammed the door. He had forced his way in.

"You're going away. That's it, isn't it?" he had said grimly.

She had shrugged.

"Why? Why are you going?" he railed. "If you can't find a job, I'll find you one. I'll give you money."

"I have to go," she said quietly, her eyes on the wall.

"Who says you have to go? What for? Where are you going?" He was shouting.

"You promised not to ask any of those things." She met his glare, her face expressionless.

Desolation settled over him. "When will you be back?"

She shrugged again. "A week, a month, two. I'm not sure."

"But you'll be back? I have to know." Pain gripped his throat.

She had not responded, simply kissed him lightly, fraternally on the lips.

For the first two weeks of her absence, he had managed well

enough. She had left all the clothes he had bought her. He consoled himself with the fact. And he was busy. Had to go to Rome, to Bari, do location work on his film, which had been bubbling into readiness. And then, in the course of the third week, depression had hit him. She wasn't back. She wouldn't come back. He grew listless. Energy, of which he usually had a large store, left him. He was interested in nothing, could concentrate on nothing.

Except on Rosa, who was gone. He thought of hiring a detective to trace her, but put aside the thought when he imagined her anger at being found. He tried to understand what had made her the way she was. He knew so little about her, still. The family seemed ordinary enough. A father who had been part of the Communist Resistance. A mother who kept house, a much younger brother. It explained nothing of her fire, her stringent idealism. She had told him little of friends, of former lovers, though he realized these had not been lacking. In a way, he hadn't wanted to know, and they had been so caught up in each other that the past meant nothing.

But now, now he needed to know.

Alexei spent days and nights brooding on Rosa, replaying their conversations, their lovemaking, and as the weeks passed, despairing of her return.

And then, one chill December night, he had opened the door of the apartment to find a lamp alight in the sitting room. Over the edge of a high wingback chair, he saw a single strand of red.

"Rosa," he uttered hoarsely, "Rosa."

She leapt up with a cat's grace. Alexei gazed at her. She was radiant. Beautiful. More beautiful than he had remembered her. Her hair lavish, her eyes deeply lustrous. For a moment he had the impression she had just been to bed with another man. There was that feline look of both excitement and satiation about her.

And then she had flung her arms around him, kissed him ardently. "I'm back," she mouthed, making him forget everything, tugging at his coat, his shirt, kindling his passion until they fell together, there on the floor and made urgent, endless love.

Afterward she laughed. "I guess I've missed you."

"There was no one else?" He eyed her skeptically, smoothed her shirt over her bared breast.

She shook her head, still smiling.

"Where have you been?" he queried.

"Ask me no questions and I'll tell you no lies." She made a small moue, teased him.

He grimaced, got up. "Can I get you a drink?" he said politely. But he was angry. Her insistence on silence made a nothing of his despair over the last weeks. He poured some wine, handed her a glass. It was then that his eyes fell on the stack of newspapers by the chair she had been sitting on.

"Catching up on your reading?"

"Mmmn. We live in exciting times." She came to sit on his lap, stroked his hair. "You grow more handsome with the months." She scrutinized him. "My absence must be good for you."

"I dare say," he muttered, looked at her intently. "I could say the same for you. Where have you been, Rosa?" He had to know, the need gnawed at him.

"What does it matter? I'm here now." She laughed, her tone excited, her face alight. She snuggled closer to him.

But he stiffened against her, moved away as if in retribution. He picked up one of the scattered papers. A photograph showing a union leader sprawled on a sidewalk in Turin. One of a number maimed by the Red Brigade. Another photograph of a fascist bomb attack in Brescia. A headline about the release of a magistrate kidnapped by the Red Brigade. Alexei threw the newspaper back on the floor.

"Bah. You call these exciting times? They're disgusting times. Terrorism on the right. Terrorism on the left. Lives destroyed. People murdered."

"I'm happy to be back, Alexei," she said softly, deflecting him.

But he didn't want to be deflected. He was angry at her, couldn't bring himself to rage at her directly, so he baited her. "And the terrorists on the left? It's incomprehensible what they're up to. They'll ruin the hopes of any kind of democratic socialism in this country. They'll run us right into a police state as everyone shouts for protection against bloodbaths, against anarchy," he railed at her, as if the responsibility were all hers.

Now she met him on it, her face aflame. "Ha. You used to call yourself a child of Marx and Coca-Cola. Now the Coca-Cola has taken over altogether. Long live the multinationals and their culture of placebos. You've turned into a real Gismondi." She pinioned him with contempt, hurried on. "When was there ever a revolution without blood? And what system has ever been toppled without a revolution?"

They had argued about this before. But as he looked at her now, he thought he heard a new vehemence in her tone, a cold, hard rage, mingled with the ideological purity. If he had cast her in one of his films now, it would have been as a Diana, burning with the ice of high principles.

Alexei responded softly, his own questions pitted against hers. "And where has revolution ever got the people? Those very people you pretend to care so much about?"

As he murmured the words, he had a sudden, swift and certain realization. He glanced at the newspapers again and then looked at her sharply. "That's where you've been," he breathed. "You've been with them. The brigades. How stupid of me. Tell me, Rosa. Tell me." He gripped her arm.

The color drained from her face. "Don't be ridiculous." She struggled away from him, raced for her room, slammed the door. He heard the turn of a key in a lock.

Alexei paced. Of course. He had been blind. He hadn't listened to her, hadn't heard. Her sudden inexplicable appearances and disappearances. Her refusal to tell him how she spent her days. He remembered seeing her in the street one day, wandering aimlessly, looking into shop windows, her consternation when he had approached her, the abrupt way she had looked over his shoulder. She must have been following someone. Of course. That was one of the things she did with her days. He remembered too her adamant refusal to meet his friends or have him meet hers. He had thought in part it was a desire to be only with him, in part a refusal to be talking with the supposed enemy. But her secrecy had another motive.

He had a sudden devastating sense of unreality. Everything he had felt, had experienced in the last months was thrust into cataclysmic doubt.

He poured himself a whisky, gulped it down. The heat in his gullet was real. Nothing else. He had told himself a story about Rosa and the story had no grounding, no truth. He, he who prided himself on his powers of observation.

What was he to her but a cover? A mere cover. An address where she could rest. Where she wouldn't be suspected. A comfortable address that provided the occasional fuck.

Alexei marched to her door. Banged on it. "If you don't open this, I'll break it down," he shouted, not recognizing his voice.

She opened it.

"That's the truth, isn't it? That's where you go? And I, I'm just a cover? A convenience?"

She turned from him, went to sit in an armchair by the window. "Believe what you like," she said coldly.

Alexei stared at her, saw a fragile figure with a pale face beneath a blaze of red. His rage was strangled in his throat.

"Who drove you to this, Rosa? Who? Who's forcing you to it? I'll beat him up. You can't carry on like this. It's dangerous." He was babbling.

Her eyes grew icy, green. "Why do you say who? Why don't you ask what? Why do you assume it's a man? I'm quite capable of thinking without a man. All I have to do is look around me. Oh no, not here, not in this beautiful Gismondi apartment. But out there. Where you never see."

Sorrow filled him. She had admitted it now, inadvertently. "You know that's not true, Rosa. I see, just as well as you. I just draw different conclusions," he murmured.

The admission sat between them like an insurmountable boulder. They looked at it in silence, examined it.

She took the first step. "What are you going to do now? Turn me over to the police?" she asked with a small laugh.

"Don't be ridiculous. You know me better than that," he barked.

She scrutinized his features, her own serious. "I'll go in the morning. First thing." She sighed, a fleeting sadness. Then she was brisk, efficient. "We'd better get some sleep now."

He nodded, unable to rise.

She turned back the coverlet on the bed, paused, looked at him again.

He rose slowly.

"Alexei," she called after him. "I didn't just use you. I loved you. Loved you in my own way. But as I told you once, there are things more important than love. Love, revolution, they're not in the same order of things."

She loved him. She had never said it before. "Oh Rosa." He gathered her up in his arms. "It's madness. Give it up. Stay with me."

Her eyes resisted him, stern. "I can't now." She kissed him lightly, moved away. "I've made my choices."

"You can do more useful things. Not this terrorist lunacy."

"We're not lunatics." She turned on him. "Half the things the press attribute to us aren't true. We're very specific in our targets."

He gazed at her, wanting her, despite everything. That tone of utter conviction in her.

"And if my turn were to come up? Or Giangiacomo's?" he suddenly said.

She wouldn't let him finish his thought. "Who knows. I might even be able to protect you." She laughed, suddenly bright, as if the question had already been considered, answered. "Goodnight, Alexei."

He didn't move. He didn't want to be left alone with his thoughts.

"Still here?" She searched his face. "You're not by any chance wanting to share a bed with a terrorist?" She was impish.

"I was prepared to share my life," Alexei murmured, embracing her.

She had left him in the morning, despite his protests that it was safe to stay here, to stay with him, that he would never breathe a word.

Two days later he had come home to find the apartment in a shambles. The door had been broken into. Everything was topsyturvy. He had looked round in dismay. Called the police. And then strangely, when he had checked each room more carefully, he hadn't been able to find anything missing. Yet drawers and cupboards had been turned out, mattresses lifted from beds. A shambles. The break-in worried him, gave him an uncanny feeling. He had told Giangiacomo about it the next day.

His uncle had looked at him queerly. "Sounds as if whoever it was was searching for something. Have you got any company files at home? Documents?"

Alexei shook his head. "It's just what I thought. But I can't imagine what anyone could have been looking for."

Giangiacomo shrugged. "Let's be grateful it wasn't worse. But keep a watch on things. A watch on yourself. These are not easy times." He looked at his son skeptically. "Be wary of some of the company you keep as well."

Alexei had seen Rosa only one more time.

It was early on a rainy morning at the beginning of March, just before he was due to leave Milan. He was dressing when the bell surprised him. Giuseppa had her own key and it wouldn't be her yet. He looked through the spyhole the police had recommended he have put in, saw a hatted figure he had to look twice at to recognize.

"Rosa." He tried to embrace her but she walked past him. She looked thin, weary in the man's hat that shrouded her hair. A loose jacket fell round her shoulders. Her face had the angular translucence of a sick youth's.

"I need money," she said grimly by way of greeting. "I need money for an abortion."

Alexei's face dropped. He didn't answer for a moment, allowed the fact to sink in. He tried to take her coat, but she shook her head.

"Coffee?" His lips formed round the single word with difficulty.

She shook her head and then, seeing his face, changed her mind, nodded. "I haven't got long." She paced the length and breadth of the living room restlessly, stopping to look out of the curtained windows, the first, the second, the third in an unconscious staccato rhythm.

He busied himself with the coffee. A refrain echoed in his head. "Whose was it? Whose was it?"

She took the coffee gratefully, sipped it quickly despite its heat.

At last he brought the words out. "Whose is it, Rosa?"

Only then did she look at him. "What do you want me to say, Alexei?" Her voice was tired. "Will you give me the money if I tell you it's yours or if I tell you it's not?"

"Tell me the truth." His tongue felt clumsy, dry. "I need to know."

She sighed, pulled her hat off. The red blaze tumbled round her face.

"If you know, that is?" a demon in him prodded her.

The jibe elicited an instant response. "Of course I know." She was adamant, the old Rosa.

She studied his face, lowered her eyes. "It's yours," she said and for emphasis counted on her fingers. "December, January, February and now March. It has to be done quickly."

He walked toward her with the curious swaying motion of a dreamer. "Have it, Rosa," he pleaded. She let him take her hand. "Have it. Please. Come back. Live with me."

She pressed his fingers. Heavy eyes. "That's kind of you, Alexei. But it's too late now. Too late." Her voice was weary, polite. It bore a weight of finality. She tried a smile which didn't succeed. "I wouldn't have come to you, but I need the money. I need it. Now. Right away."

He could feel her urgency. "Shall I come with you? To have it done?"

She shook her head vigorously. "That's not possible."

He went to find his checkbook, had the sense of a script being written in his presence with an ending over which he had no control. Like a bad dream moving inexorably to its end. He wrote out a check for a large sum, handed it to her.

She stood without looking at it. "Thank you." A shadow passed over her face and then she rushed into his arms. "Thank you, Alexei."

He held her, feeling her fear, a slight trembling, her body chill. "Are you being followed?" he asked.

She shrugged. "I don't know." She murmured something under her breath about the police, Milan, about not wanting to implicate him.

He suddenly remembered the break-in. That, too, could have been the police, looking for her traces. He didn't mention it, held her more tightly. "Are you sure, Rosa? Sure it can't be otherwise."

"Sure," she nodded, her face bleak.

He didn't know whether she had raised her face to be kissed or he had sought out her lips, but they met for a brief instant. And then she was gone, her hair folded back under her hat, another murmured thank you.

He had watched her from the window, a slight boyish figure, darting across the street, mingling with the morning crowds.

He had not seen Rosa again.

Alexei drained his second Campari, scanned the passersby in the Piazza di Spagna. He felt like an archaeologist digging for fossilized remains. Remains which would give him back Rosa. Give him an insight into the troubled culture which was his own, its extremes, its passions, its conflicts. Remains which crumbled into nothingness at his touch.

He couldn't revive the past, give it a different present. He rose. It was getting late. He was due back in Milan tomorrow. Due back in the apartment where Rosa's presence still roamed.

The road round Lago Maggiore winds through clusters of villas and ancient pines. At night, lights flicker like will-o'-the-wisps through the scented air. Shadows loom in a heavy stillness, broken only by an occasional cry, a bark, the rev of a motorbike, too loud in the awesome antique quiet.

The set of Alexei's features as he drove along the road to the family villa was stern. He was musing about his country. Its natural beauty so wonderfully tempered by human hands through the course of the centuries that this lake and its environs had been turned into a vast landscaped garden, nature and architecture at one. But now in this latter half of the twentieth century, there was strife in the land, guerrilla war between left and right. Thus far, it was an urban phenomenon. Milan, Rome, Bologna were all cities under occupation. Yet the countryside seemed untouched.

He was pleased that he had come here. Restlessness covered him in the Milan apartment. He had felt trapped, trapped between waiting and mourning in a space where there seemed nothing to fill his imagination except Rosa's absence. And when he went into the street, every corner gave rise to police, each one reminding him of the fate which inevitably awaited Rosa. He had needed to get away for the weekend, away too from prattling friends and telephones and invitations.

He pulled up in front of the villa and decided to take a walk before going in. The night air was chill. It braced him. He had walked here with Rosa in the brief days of their idyll. It was here that he had asked her to marry him. But she had loved her beliefs more than him. It was strange to think of it in that way, to pit oneself against a rival that didn't bear a human form. It made his own existence insubstantial. Yet, though he couldn't follow her into the world of her beliefs, it was the very fire of her convictions that he had first loved in her.

He wondered whether that fire was still with her, whether it was fanned by the life she was leading. He remembered the pallor, the tension in her face when they had last met. He worried, walked back toward the house.

As he reached the portico, he heard the crunch of glass underfoot. Odd. A window must have been broken somewhere. He hadn't alerted the caretaker of his visit, but he made a mental note to report it to him tomorrow. The man was getting old, only really saw to the house in the summer.

Alexei let himself in, switched on the hall lights, moved toward the sitting room. Suddenly arms grabbed him from behind, lifting him almost off the floor. He cried out, struggled. Saw the blur of a man's face before a blindfold obliterated it. A gag forced its way into his mouth. He retched, kicked, flailed his limbs. A thud landed behind his left ear and with it a wave of overarching pain. And then nothing.

He woke with an acute sense of disorientation. He couldn't move. He wanted to scream and couldn't scream. A nightmare, he thought.

Then he remembered. Realized his feet and arms were bound. The blindfold and gag still in place. He must be on a floor, a tile floor, cold, somewhere in the house. He listened. In the distance, from across the room, he heard voices whispering. He tuned his hearing.

"Old Gismondi will pay a lot for him."

"No, it's too tricky. We can't stay here. There may be others coming."

"It's too dangerous to move him. We're not prepared."

"I can get the van brought round. By tomorrow night."

"No. It'll wreck our other plans."

Then silence. In the silence, Alexei recognized the voice. A woman's voice. Rosa. He was torn between the need to call out to her and the recognition that she was complicit in his situation. How could she have allowed them to knock him out, to bind him? Did she know it was him? She must. What would they do to him?

The voices again.

"I still say we should take him with us. There's a lot in it."

"No. We're not cheap criminals. We follow plans."

She was defending him. Alexei's mind cleared a little. At least there was that.

"Go and get some sleep. I'll guard him. Go on. We leave in the morning, as planned."

Rosa's voice, authoritative. An indisputable order. He heard the shuffling of feet. And then nothing.

Alexei waited. His body cramped, his breathing constricted. In that interminable waiting, he at last realized that the Rosa he had known was dead to him. As dead as his aunt, as dead as Francesca in her cloister, as dead as the mother he had never known. Loss, black, despairing, filled him, greater than any fear. It bore none of the soft murkiness of self-pity. He didn't feel sorry for himself, felt no remorse. There was only that sense of loss, like a vast, dark vault, encasing him.

Into it Rosa's hushed voice crept.

"Alexei, Alexei, it's Rosa. If you can hear me, nod."

Alexei moved his heavy head.

"If you promise not to try to do anything rash, I'll take the blindfold off. Promise? The old Alexei's honor?"

He jerked his head. Up down, up down, scraping his ear on the floor.

There was a moment in which he could hear her hesitating and then slowly, nimbly, she removed the gag, the blindfold.

The dull, muted light of a torch. In it he searched for Rosa. Saw a raven head, short clipped hair. The purity of a face. Hers. Bared down to its essentials of bone and line. Her eyes flickered, green, greener. A trace of savage irony. "Your timing is appalling," she said to him, her voice flat. "Another day and we would have been out of here. I'm sorry they hit you."

"That's something, I guess," he murmured.

They looked at each other warily. He curled on the floor, bound, helpless. She, kneeling beside him, his jailer, his protector. Silence stretched into distance. Alexei stumbled into it, trying to cover miles.

"Are you all right, Rosa?"

Almost, she laughed. "That's an odd question coming from you." Her gaze lingered meaningfully on his bound limbs.

"You know what I mean."

"Always the same, Alexei." She shook her head slowly. "Always the personal first. You'll never understand. We're nothing." She snapped her fingers. "Here, gone. Specks of dust in history. What matters is greater than us. You. Me."

"Yet you won't let them take me. Kidnap me."

She shrugged. "It's not part of the plan," she said coldly.

"Is that all, Rosa?"

"That's the greater part of it." She met the insistence of his eyes, her own proud. "It would be complicated, messy. It's better when things are clean, straight." She swung her arm downward in a firm motion.

"Clean, straight," he murmured. "Without the complications of memory, of emotion. Without life."

"The life which is a privilege of your class," she came back swiftly, her voice hard.

"So many answers, Rosa. You always had so many answers," Alexei mused.

"And you always had too many questions. That, too, is a privilege."

They looked at each other through the thin beam of light, the distance between them growing.

"It's the last privilege I would want to lose," he said at last.

"I know, Alexei." There was a sudden glimmer of reminiscence in her face. Her voice grew softer.

And then, abruptly, she switched off the torch. Above them, Alexei heard a slight movement.

He felt her breath in his ear. "That's why you're so dangerous, Alexei," she whispered. He could feel her loosening the rope round his arms and feet and then swiftly replacing the blindfold. "Don't try to move till we're gone," she hissed. And then with another change of voice, she murmured, "Goodbye, Alexei. Thanks for the help. The past." Lips touched his. Lightly. Like the play of air. Then the gag. More firmly. Before he could speak.

A few moments later, there was movement in the hall, the click of the door, the muted rev of a bike, then another. And then nothing.

Alexei lay there. No longer waiting. He had a certain sense that he would never see Rosa again.

He was in Paris when he read the article which carried Rosa's name. A brief news piece in *Le Monde*: three members of the Red Brigade had been captured. It was June, the sky a clear blue in which the woolly clouds billowed playfully. He read the article again. Looked at that frivolous sky.

The next day he flew to Rome. He rang his lawyer, asked him to arrange permission for Alexei to see Rosa. There was a long pause. Then an incredulous voice asked, "Can you repeat that?"

Alexei repeated it.

"I don't think that's a good idea," his lawyer demurred.

"Do it," Alexei barked with Giangiacomo's tones. "Leave the reflections on good and bad to me."

By the time the permission came through a week later, it was too late. Rosa was dead. Dead by her own hand. Or was it? Some of the papers implied that she might have been helped, that her interrogators had been less than gentle.

In a sense Alexei was not surprised. He had spent the days trying to think himself into Rosa's skin. Rosa captured, deprived of her mobility, the freedom of her brisk energy. Rosa afraid, afraid of torture, afraid of talking, of implicating others. Rosa, her historical role complete, nothing to do but crumble into dust. Quickly, efficiently, cleanly, before the questions took over from the answers. Instantly and to maximum effect. Rosa, martyr to a cause. Santa Rosa.

Alexei felt cold. A cold the hot sun could not penetrate.

It had been inevitable. Sooner or later. They had both known it. Once the initial choice had been made, the rest had followed. And perhaps even before the choice had been made.

Yet he felt implicated, responsible. Why hadn't he been able to sway her, with his arguments if not with his person? He suspected it was because he, too, had been in love with her belief, its steady gaze into the distance, the pure whiff of its integrity which cut through the stale odors of cynicism and corruption. And yet he had not been able to share that faith, had merely longed for it as one longs for something one's reality cannot bear.

Yes, Alexei thought grimly, it was as if he, his friends, all of them, had willed the Rosas into existence to be the uncompromising guardians of a social faith they wished for.

And what if there was something wrong in the very origins of that longing, that desire? Where had centuries of belief, whatever its content, got them?

No, Alexei argued against himself, it was right, it was necessary. Otherwise nothing would ever change.

The arguments trailed him, chased him, unresolved. Throughout that long hot summer, they accompanied his mourning for the person Rosa had been. He began to read in areas he hadn't explored before, the history of the church, of religions. Texts on psychoanalysis. When the autumn leaves began to dry underfoot, he had a hot furious film in him. He wanted to make it quickly.

His intensity was transformed more rapidly than usual into a budget. Two generations of a single family. The wartime resisters and his own peers. The left's legacy. A dialogue. Through Rosa's eyes. He thought of calling it *Rosa x Two,* but wasn't sure. He wasn't sure of anything about the film except his need to make it. When it was finished, it caused a storm of debate in Italy.

Alexei could hardly bear to watch it. He felt empty, hollowed out, felt he didn't want to direct anymore.

Desultorily he picked up the strings of his life. Produced other people's films, spent time with Giangiacomo and conversely more time traveling. It all felt empty, directionless. He toyed with the idea of moving out of Italy, setting up a base elsewhere.

But his uncle was putting increasing pressure on him to spend more time in Milan. He wanted Alexei to be prepared to head the firm. "I'm getting old," he would mutter. "It's time you settled down. Gave me some *bambini.*"

To placate him, Alexei began to invite him out to dinner with women friends, an actress here, a designer or writer there. The next day, Giangiacomo would always begin tentatively, "I thought your friend last night was very nice ..." and would draw an idealized picture of the woman in question and the comforts of married life. Alexei would sit very still and try to imagine an existence with Elena or Marina or Giulietta and his sense of unreality would grow to disproportionate bounds. One day, his uncle raged, "You're spoiled. You've had too many women. I don't know what you're waiting for. Marriage is about families, continuity. Just choose a sensible woman who'll make a good mother and get on with it."

Alexei looked at him blankly. "And how do I know what a good mother is?"

"Bah." Giangiacomo scowled at him. "If you're not careful, I'll find one for you and that will be that."

"Perhaps that might be easier," Alexei laughed. But he stopped inviting his uncle to dinners with his women friends. Stopped going out very much himself. He realized with an occasional panic that he no longer particularly enjoyed making love. His imagination wasn't in it.

Instead, he threw himself into the business of Gismondi Enterprises. Not with passion, but with a kind of coldness he didn't recognize in himself. He split his time between the production company and the rest. That, at least, he thought, would keep his uncle at bay.

And he developed an interest in fine art. It had never been his favorite medium before, but now he grew enamored of it for precisely the reasons it had never moved him before. The lack of narrative, of movement beyond the single frame, gave him a kind of peace. He began to haunt the museums and galleries, to buy scores of art books. Each period fascinated him, the images like icons that could be returned to. Still, unmoving, always the same except for what one brought to them. He redecorated his apartment, filled it with pictures. Restlessly bought another in Rome.

It was during this time that he went to Rome to an exhibition entitled *Paris Between the Wars*. Ranged amidst Picasso's weeping women and Picabia's mechanical monsters, he saw an image he didn't know, a face that called out to him, childlike yet seductive, a woman's face mounted on an owl's feathered body. He glanced at the caption and then looked again: "Portrait of Sylvie Kowalska" by Michel St. Loup, Roussillon 1935.

That name, Sylvie Kowalska. It meant something to him. Alexei's mind sped through time, sifted, landed. That letter, all those years back, with the ring. During the kidnapping scare. A letter from a Sylvie Kowalska telling him she was his mother. How bizarre to find that name here. That face. Alexei tried to remember the faded image that had come with the letter, but his memory of it was blurred.

He stood in front of the picture for a long time. Those eyes. Was he dreaming it, or did they have the color of his own? He bought a catalogue, learned a little about Michel St. Loup, less about the sitter. He returned to the exhibition again the next day. And the next. Curiosity nipped at him. Bit. Who was this woman with the Polish name? Why had she written to him?

The face possessed him. Where there had been emptiness, Alexei was suddenly filled with a sense of mystery. No sooner was he back in Milan than he accosted Giangiacomo, told him of what he had seen, reminded him of the letter.

"You remember you said you were going to try and find out something about that woman. Did you?"

Giangiacomo looked at his son, noted the fire of an excitement there that had been lacking for some time. He grimaced. "You should be finding a wife, not chasing after ghosts."

"What did you find?" Alexei grew suspicious, prodded his uncle.

Giangiacomo shrugged. "You may not remember this. A journalist once came to interview you. When you were about thirteen."

Alexei tried to remember, had a fleeting memory of a woman who had watched his home movies with him. He nodded tentatively.

"Well, that journalist's real name was Sylvie Kowalska."

"Who is she?"

"All I found out was that she came from New York. Her married name was Jardine."

Alexei's imagination performed somersaults. So he had met the woman who claimed to be his mother. She had come to see him, sought him out. She wasn't just a crank letter writer. No, the woman in the painting couldn't be a mere crank. Of that he was certain. But then . . .

Alexei went back to the Palazzo with Giangiacomo. He rifled through his old room, found the letter, the ring, the photograph. He sat there for a long time staring at each in turn. He had never known a mother. What did the word mean? A point of origin. For him, a presence that existed only in absence, in lack. He looked at the faded photograph of the couple he had always considered his parents, stared again at the image of Sylvie Kowalska. He had a sudden awesome sense that he might not be who he thought he was. It produced in him a feeling of vertigo, but also a profound excitement. A desire to fill that lack.

A decade was closing. He had had no particular hopes of the next one. And now this. The signpost for a journey into the past.

The need to find out more about Sylvie Kowalska blotted out all else in him.

The very next day he went to an agency which specialized in tracing people.

PART IV

CHAPTER
TWENTY-FOUR

*I*n the early spring of 1980, Katherine Jardine was sitting in a restaurant on New York's East Side gazing restlessly from her watch to the menu and back again.

She was not, she consoled herself, alone in her restlessness. She found its echoes all around her. Time, after all, was running out. The century was growing old, speeding to its end. A new millennium was drawing closer. A millennium shrouded in the somber hues of science fiction. And as time ran out, each second became more precious. Everyone was in a hurry. To buy, to work, to achieve, to enjoy, before the old millennium wound down into extinction.

Just like her.

She tapped her foot and let her eyes trail down the menu yet again. A menu which bore the typeface and decorative fancies of an earlier period, like the prints and etchings on the wall. Here it was again, she thought. The visible signs of heritage, of tradition, to shore us up against the dying of the future. That was what the romance of roots was partly about, too, that search for points of origin— national, cultural, racial, personal. Histories, memories, to displace a life too difficult to live.

Katherine sighed, impatient at the direction of her thoughts, impatient too at Jacob's lateness.

It was unlike Jacob to be late and today of all days she had no patience for waiting. But he had insisted on lunch.

"Bring me a bottle of mineral water, please, Pierre," she signaled to the waiter.

"Right away, Ms. Jardine." He moved smoothly at her request and Katherine sat back in her chair. After all, she liked coming to Gerard's. The restaurant had become her regular lunchtime haunt when there were guests to entertain. The place calmed, soothed, as if it existed in its own timewarp far from the bustle of Manhattan.

Soothed perhaps a little too much, Katherine smiled wryly to herself. Pierre was having trouble rousing the man at the table opposite her from his reverie. It was the third time he had asked him if he was ready to order and still there was no response. Ah, there it was at last. The man ran his fingers through dark curling hair and with a slightly embarrassed manner acknowledged Pierre.

What had he been musing on so deeply, Katherine wondered a little idly. A lost love? A bankrupt business? It was an interesting face, craggy, slightly narrow, the forehead furrowed. A face with secrets. A good face for a portrait.

Suddenly eyes of a startling blue met hers with an unnerving intimacy, filled her with an uncanny sense that her thoughts were being read. Katherine looked away, reached for her drink, glanced again at her watch.

"I'm sorry, Kat." Jacob kissed her on both cheeks. "Couldn't get a cab. It's the rain. I know you're busy."

Katherine smiled, happy to see him now that he was here. "Yes, I have been. But it's good to see you."

"Next Thursday's the big day."

She nodded. "Thomas's collection ready for public eyes at last. You're going to come, aren't you?"

"Wouldn't miss it for the world. Not even for a psychoanalytic congress," he chuckled. "You've worked very hard." He looked at her benignly.

Yes, Katherine reflected. She had worked hard.

Transforming a private house into a public gallery had been more of a feat than she had imagined all those months ago when the matter of Thomas's legacy had finally been decided. There had been permissions to clear with officials; State and City administrators to argue with over funds for running costs; hundreds of lengthy applications to fill out in search of subsidies and endowments. To finance the initial work, she had used the money left over from the sale of her mother's Picasso. Part of that money had gone into the launch of her own gallery. She liked the idea of art subsidizing more art.

Then there had been the work of redecorating Thomas's house to make it suitable for its new use; the challenge of rehanging; of providing texts which illuminated a particular historical moment. All this, combined with the running of her own gallery, had involved resources of energy she was never altogether sure she had. But she loved the work, loved the sense of purpose it all gave her, the sense of working for an attainable end, the certain sense that Thomas would have been pleased with her.

"Yes, yes, I have," Katherine said aloud. "But when you see it, I think you'll agree that it's all been worth it."

"I haven't even the smattering of a doubt," Jacob applauded her.

"And Natalie's been an angel. Almost like a partner. We discuss everything. She has no reservations about telling me when she thinks one of the explanation boards or anything else is gobbledygook." Katherine laughed. "You have reason to be proud of your granddaughter."

"I am. Very." Jacob spread a little pâté on his toast and met Katherine's eyes. "It's Natalie I want to talk to you about, Kat." He suddenly switched to French. "You know I don't like to interfere, but for her sake . . ."

"What is it?" Katherine was instantly distressed.

Jacob avoided the vulnerability on her face, toyed with his food. "I think it's time you took her to see her grandmother, took her to Rome. Set a definite date."

"Oh, is that it? Princesse Mat's been getting at you," Katherine accused him.

"Kat, I think I've reached the ripe age where I'm capable of arriving at conclusions without consulting Mathilde." Jacob paused. "Natalie's been talking to me. It means a lot to her, you know, and she feels you don't listen, you always deflect her, make excuses. She's showed me the letters the Contessa has sent her."

"Letters?" Katherine looked at him sharply. "I thought there was only one."

She remembered the moment it had come all too well and the letter's every word. The envelope had arrived as always promptly on Natalie's birthday. Usually there was only a birthday card inside, a note in Italian which Katherine translated for Natalie. But this last year, the envelope had been plumper and when Natalie opened it, an airplane ticket had tumbled out. And the accompanying letter, this time, was in painstaking English. Natalie had read it herself before sharing its contents with Katherine.

"Dearest Natalie, It is my very greatest wish to see you again before it is too late. You are now old enough to travel to Rome on your own, even if your mother will not accompany you. I enclose an airline ticket which will permit you to do so. Please let me know the date of your arrival and all will be made ready for you. I await you with open arms. Your grandmother."

Natalie had met Katherine's eyes. "I'm going to go," she had said abruptly.

"Yes, hon, yes, of course." Katherine remembered how she had averted her face and procrastinated, changed the subject. Her daughter's look, at once challenging and accusing, troubled her. It was as if she had always known the depth of Katherine's resistance to her seeing her grandmother.

"You mean there has been more than one letter?" Katherine gazed at her father.

He shrugged, nodded. "I think Natalie has been corresponding with her grandmother with a degree of regularity."

Katherine's face fell. Natalie hadn't told her. There had been only that once, as far as Katherine knew. That first time, when Natalie had announced that she had written to the Contessa to say that she would be coming to Rome as soon as school holidays permitted.

"The summer is a good idea," Katherine remembered responding vaguely.

"Why not Christmas?" Natalie had asked stubbornly.

"Well, perhaps, we'll see." Katherine had changed the subject, as if it were a matter of no importance.

"I think, Kat"—Jacob's voice brought her back—"I think you are being just a little bit selfish about this. You are not considering Natalie. It seems to me you're so afraid of her identifying with her father, with his world, that you'll end up by achieving exactly the opposite. Sometimes what we most avoid takes us over by surprise. In the trade," he chuckled, "we call it the return of the repressed."

Katherine looked at him wildly. "It's not true."

"Isn't it, *ma petite?* Well then, take her to Rome. Let's set a date now. I don't think she particularly relishes the idea of traveling alone. It would be good for her to go with you. Good for both of you."

"No, I will not go to Italy. I will not set foot there again." Katherine didn't recognize the panic in the voice that welled up in her.

"That is not responsible of you, Kat. It is also a little bit cruel. You're trying to control Natalie too firmly. Think of the damage to her. A father denied her even in memory. Her fantasies may end up far stronger than any reality can ever be." Jacob looked at Katherine sadly. "But if those are your feelings, I will take Natalie myself."

Cruel. The word rebounded in Katherine's mind. She looked away blindly from Jacob. Saw the man from the table opposite staring at her with those blue eyes. Would he think her cruel, she wondered randomly. *Cruel.* It was the word she had always associated with her mother. Sylvie had been cruel to her. So cruel. She, Katherine, was not cruel to Natalie. They were friends. They shared everything.

Perhaps not everything, as Jacob made so clear. Did Natalie, as he said, consider her cruel? Had she done everything to avoid being like her mother, only in her daughter's eyes to emerge as her replica? Cold, unseeing, spiteful. No. She refused it.

A strange laugh rose in her. Oscar Wilde's comment sprang into her mind. "All women become like their mothers. That is their tragedy."

"I'm sorry, Kat. I did not mean to give you pain," Jacob said softly.

She forced herself to focus on him. "Let me think about it. After the opening. Next week. Let me think about it then."

Jacob took her hand. "I will remind you," he murmured, at once gentle and implacable.

Two days later, a new potential client who appeared in her appointment book as Alexei Gismondi came into Katherine's office. Katherine, glancing up from her telephone call, saw a tall, dark man with striking features. She remembered that face but couldn't quite place it. A corner of her mind bobbed through crowded streets, receptions, and then settled into a restaurant. Gerard's. The man from Gerard's.

He recognized her too. Her lips curled into a smile.

"Alexei Gismondi." She put down the telephone. "The man whose ears even a persistent New York waiter cannot penetrate." She stretched out her hand. She had had misgivings about this meeting with Mr. Gismondi, as she always did when confronted by a client with an Italian name. She had heard of this man, seen one of his films once, but no, she was certain now that she had never come across him during her days in Rome. She would have recalled that face, that slight air of diffidence, of world-weariness, which sat oddly with the startling directness of those blue eyes.

The pressure of his hand, his look, disquieted her. It was a sensation she had all but forgotten in relation to men. The old fear, always uncontrollable, returned. Perhaps he did know her, had known Carlo, was a witness to his activities, to her shame. For a brief moment, the scene in the catacombs the last time she had seen Carlo flashed through her mind. She forced it away.

"What can I do for you, Mr. Gismondi?" Katherine moved into smooth professional gear.

"I am interested in acquiring a portrait in your possession, a beautiful portrait of Sylvie Kowalska by Michel St. Loup. I came across it at an exhibition some months back," he said in careful English.

His words so surprised her that for a moment she was at a loss. She had been thinking too much about Sylvie since her lunch with her father and now to have this man come in out of the blue and ask to see her portrait was uncanny.

"That portrait is my own. It is not for sale," she said crisply.

Blue eyes surveyed her, persuaded her, felt as if they were seeing more than she wished to show. "I have a special admiration for St. Loup. Money is no object." His voice was warm.

Katherine defended herself. "Money is not my object either, Mr. Gismondi."

"Oh?" His face took on a supple irony. "I thought that in New York art and money were inseparable partners."

"I dare say," Katherine murmured. Her face grew hot. She didn't like that look, so bold, so intimate, judging her. "Sylvie Kowalska was my mother, Mr. Gismondi," she said emphatically. "One does not sell one's mother." It sounded to her own ears like an outburst.

Katherine struggled for her cool impersonal smile again. "But I could show you some other work, of course. We are not in the habit of turning away clients for whom money is no object." She mimicked his tone.

"Of course, I'm sorry. I did not know Sylvie Kowalska was your mother," he said reflectively. "How silly of me." He looked at her now, as if seeing her afresh, studying every angle of her face.

Katherine stirred uncomfortably. "How could you know, Mr. Gismondi? My mother and I do not look alike. And we certainly *never* had anything in common."

He smiled at that, a warm smile, open, friendly. Katherine felt herself drawn, despite herself. She averted her eyes, fumbled with some papers on her desk, signaling the end of the interview.

But he wouldn't go. "Well, even if you won't sell, I would dearly love to see that picture again. Perhaps you would allow me at least that?" His voice pursued her, gracious, warm, seductive, but with an undercurrent of amusement.

She was about to tell him that was impossible when Natalie raced in, excited, talking a mile a minute.

"I got an A in my dreaded math test, Mommy."

Katherine hugged her, smiled congratulations, forgot Alexei Gismondi, and then feeling those eyes, remembered. "I'm afraid my time is up, Mr. Gismondi. Can one of my assistants show you round?"

"I did so want to see that portrait of Sylvie Kowalska." He stood his ground. "I've come a long way for that sole purpose." His smile lingered, seduced, implacable in its purpose.

"Surely not with that *sole* purpose, Mr. Gismondi? A man with your schedule." She met him on it, laughed. The man had charm. If Sylvie's portrait had been here in the gallery she would have taken him to it instantly and let him look his fill.

And then Natalie took over, curious at the mention of her grandmother's name, smiling at the man, offering to take him home, making friends with him.

A man from Rome with her daughter. Katherine shuddered for a moment, tried to still her irrational fears. "You can hardly expect me to allow a stranger to go home with my daughter, Mr. Gismondi." She laughed brittlely. "This is New York, after all."

"Yes, no, of course."

Katherine watched his confusion, was startled as he produced passport and wallet and laid them on her desk as collateral against his safe return. There was something touching about his fierce determination to see the portrait. She felt herself relenting. "I shall ask my assistant, Joe, to take you round to the house. I would hate to see such rare dedication to a work of art disappointed." She returned his papers, felt the brush of his fingers, the warmth of his eyes as he thanked her.

And then they were gone. It was Katherine's turn to feel confused. What was it about this man that gave him the power to move her? That old fear of things Roman? His insistence on seeing Sylvie's portrait? She walked back to her desk, fingered the deep purple sprays of lilac in the white vase, breathed in the heavy fragrance of spring. Those once memorized lines floated into her mind:

> April is the cruellest month, breeding
> Lilacs out of the dead land, mixing
> Memory and desire, stirring
> Dull roots with spring rain.

Her own dull roots, she thought. She covered her face with her hands.

In the anonymity of a hotel restaurant, they sat facing each other across a starched white cloth. A little pool of intimacy gradually formed round their table as they talked. Katherine found herself saying things she had never uttered aloud before, fresh thoughts coalesced, sometimes surprising her. It was to do with the way Alexei listened, a particular intensity of listening, which made the words flow, unconstrained.

She told him the little that she knew about Michel St. Loup and her mother, the various portraits she had seen. "But you must meet my father. He knows far more. It was all before my time." Katherine smiled and then her brow furrowed. "My mother and I were never exactly close. She died when I was relatively young." She confronted those blue eyes. "She killed herself, you know."

Alexei took her hand, held it. "I didn't know," he said softly.

The pressure of his touch seeped through her, set up an ache she barely recognized. She had a fleeting vision of a tousled bed in a distant hotel room. She sat very still, held by his gaze.

He was the first to withdraw his hand. She missed its warmth. She looked away, shrugged, a little desolate. "It was all a very long time ago."

"Tell me about you," he urged her. "You don't bear your husband's name?"

"It's quite enough that I bore him a child." The words leapt out of her with an unexpected fury. Katherine moderated her tone. "I . . . I didn't like my husband very much. No, no, that's not quite true either." She played with her fork. She remembered that once, once she had loved Carlo, long ago, so long ago. That love had been buried, metamorphosed by its end into something else. But now, she recalled it. It confused her.

Alexei's eyes brought her back. They twinkled. "I don't think I would like to bear the force of your dislike," he said.

She looked at him. What she felt was something quite other than dislike.

They talked some more, little bursts and starts of self-revelation interspersed with the narrative of work and tastes. His questions probed subtly. She replied, asked him about himself too, but he was evasive, adept at turning back to her.

Over coffee she laughed. "And now I've told you everything and I still know almost nothing about you."

"There'll be another time." He met her on it.

"Are you in New York for long?" she asked fearing his answer.

"A little while." He was noncommittal.

They gazed at each other in silence. In that moment, Katherine had the sudden and distinct realization that she wanted him. It swept over her with an uncontrollable force. Made her turn away. Did he share it? He didn't say anything. Made no sign. She gulped her coffee too quickly. A voice rose in her, not her own, odd in its pitch.

"Perhaps you would like to come to the opening of the Sachs Collection in Boston next week? If you're here. If you have time."

"I'd like that," he said. "I'll try to make it."

Katherine stood. He wasn't going to ask her to stay. Why should he? They had only just met. It was the hotel that was doing it to her. A hotel like those other hotels in European capitals. But no, she forced herself to honesty. It wasn't just that. It was altogether different. He had been in her home, had been with Natalie, had crossed the threshold of her real world. And still she wanted him.

She stretched out her hand. "Thank you for a lovely evening," she said primly. "I'm sorry that I can't part with the Michel St. Loup. But you understand . . ."

"Of course, of course," he murmured, stood. "I shall see you home."

"There's no need," she demurred.

"I insist," he smiled. "I am an Italian, more or less."

They sat next to each other in the taxi. So close, Alexei thought, and yet untouching. They mustn't breach that distance. Of that he was certain. And yet the compulsion to hold her was so strong, that he had to keep his hands rigidly in his control lest they stray of their own accord.

What was he getting himself into? He hadn't bargained on any of this when he had left Italy in search of Katherine and Jacob Jardine. In search of Sylvie Kowalska.

He felt driven now, by a double compulsion. A compulsion to find out more about Sylvie and a desire to kiss her daughter, to make love to her. He wondered what she would be like in bed, this Katherine Jardine. It was a long time since he had felt this kind of interest in a woman.

The grim irony of it all made him laugh at himself wryly. There were no accidents in the psychic world. He had thought about her so much that there was an inevitability in the attraction, an inevitability in the fascination she held for him. An inevitability in his falling in love, he acknowledged it, with what was ultimately taboo.

He glanced covertly at her profile, at once vulnerable and so certain, so decided. Like her talk. In his imagination, he traced the creamy line of her throat, her shoulders above the dusky hue of her dress. She was beautiful. Achingly beautiful.

She turned to face him, her gray eyes shadowy, wild. Yes, she would be wild in bed too. Abandoned. Almost, he reached to touch her and then turned abruptly to look out of the window. He knew enough about women to recognize that she wanted him too. It made it even more difficult. He wasn't thinking straight.

And what if he was to say to her now, "Katherine, your mother once wrote to me telling me I was her son. It sounds ridiculous, I know. But I was born in Poland. And I never knew my mother and it's just possible . . ."

He could imagine the disbelief, the consternation in her face. The sense of vertigo, the betrayal, the feeling that history had cheated one. All those things he himself had felt. One didn't, one couldn't do that to people. Simply walk in and disrupt the accepted order of their lives.

And what made it worse was that she hadn't got on with her mother. Indeed despised her, that much had been evident in her words. It made it impossible even to explore the possibility with her that Sylvie might have had another child. He hadn't over dinner been able to bring himself to ask her, however indirectly, whether a rumor of that kind had circulated in the family.

No. If he wanted to find out more, it would have to be through Jacob Jardine. She had given him the cue. He could talk to him about Michel St. Loup. But Dr. Jardine was clever. Too clever for any easy ploys. That much he had realized all too clearly in that abortive interview he had had with him two days ago, when he had pretended to be in search of an analyst. Perhaps Katherine could ease his entry, make it seem less contrived. After all, it was possible to be looking for an analyst and also to be interested in a French painter of the 1930s. The two things did not necessarily make an equation in which the missing factor was duplicity.

The taxi bumped to a stop. They had arrived. Alexei helped Katherine out. That touch. He dropped her hand quickly.

"I hope you'll come to Boston," she said softly. "I'll have an invitation sent round to your hotel."

"I'll try," Alexei felt like an awkward schoolboy. "Thank you. Thank you for keeping me company."

He was gone. Katherine leaned on the door, surprised at the way her heart was racing. He hadn't kissed her. Hadn't even tried. She couldn't remember the last time a man had taken her home and she had felt even the ghost of that desire. And now . . . She laughed at herself. Laughed at her own disappointment. He was probably married. Attached. The thought suddenly presented itself to her. Of course. What a fool she was. Some men were faithful. Her disappointment deepened. Yet he hadn't felt married. Hadn't said anything to suggest it.

She tried to put him out of her mind, but as she slipped her clothes off, his presence came back to her with a little tremor. Perhaps, she forced herself to confront it, it was all to do with Carlo. The fact that Alexei was from Rome, Italian. It charged his atmosphere. And there had been too much of Carlo's ghost recently, what with her father and Natalie emphasizing his existence, or rather its lack. She tried to look at it coldly. No, she refused the thought. Alexei was nothing like Carlo. The shape of his intelligence, his sensitivity, the way he had listened.

Early the next afternoon, he rang her at the gallery.

"Alexei Gismondi." Amelia put her hand over the receiver. "Will you take it?"

Katherine nodded, stilled herself.

"Might you be free for a drink after work?" His voice was distant, punctilious.

"I'll just check my appointment book." Katherine went through the charade, knowing that she would cancel anything, even a date with Natalie. "About seven?"

"Fine." He paused, chuckled, sounding suddenly very close. "I thought I might have another try at persuading you to part with the St. Loup."

"You can try. But I don't think you'll get anywhere," Katherine said tartly, a little miffed at the direction of his intentions.

"I'm a determined man, Katherine." He laughed.

"And I'm a stubborn woman. Until seven then." She hung up.

"Who's not going to get anywhere?" Her friend Nora Harper looked at her curiously. "Got a new admirer?"

"It's not what you think, Nora." Katherine put her off. "It's about a canvas."

"Oh yes? Don't believe a word of it. You have a secretive look to you today, Katherine Jardine."

Katherine shrugged. "And you have too fertile an imagination. Now let's get back to work, shall we?"

Nora sighed and picked up the telephone at her desk.

Katherine watched her settle into another chatty conversation with yet another member of the press about the launch of the Thomas Sachs Collection. She had known Nora ever since her days at MOMA, when Nora had been married to one of the museum trustees, whom she had now divorced. A tall, curvaceous blonde with a taste for extravagant clothes and men, Nora was a friend without quite being an intimate. She knew everyone who was anyone in that world where art and high finance meet, and when she had offered to do the occasional PR job for Katherine, Katherine had accepted with alacrity. There could be no one better than Nora.

They had another kind of unspoken arrangement. If Katherine wanted to get rid of a man whose attentions were becoming a nuisance, but whom she couldn't afford to alienate, she called in Nora. A vivacious foil to Katherine's coolness, she would deflect the man's desires and assuage his ego. Katherine sometimes wondered what she did to these men. She suspected Nora had them for breakfast. But she seemed to need that breakfast, and there was always another man on the horizon.

Nora Harper was still there when Alexei arrived. And for once, as she introduced them, Katherine wished that her friend were slightly less seductive. It was a new feeling, this. It made her uncomfortable. As did seeing Alexei, now that he had occupied a space in her imagination. No other man had lodged himself there in quite that way since Carlo's death.

She avoided his eyes. Took in, instead, the dark open-necked shirt, the casual cut of the pale linen suit. Her voice sounded odd as she said his name.

"Alexei Gismondi?" Nora repeated it, smiled sweetly, looked up at him admiringly. "The director?"

Alexei nodded hesitantly.

"I *am* pleased to meet you. There's a film of yours playing on the

West Side, isn't there? I saw it last week. Wonderful," Nora breathed. She moved closer to him.

Alexei bowed slightly, signaling his thanks.

Katherine kicked herself. Why hadn't she known that? Nora was always in touch with everything. "Shall we go, Alexei?" she heard herself saying. "I mustn't be too late tonight. I fly to Boston early tomorrow morning."

"Yes, yes, of course." He murmured goodbye to Nora. And as he did so, Katherine suddenly felt ashamed. Perhaps he would prefer to carry on talking to her friend. She was behaving ridiculously.

"Would you like to join us for a drink, Nora?" she asked half-heartedly.

"Mmm," Nora responded with alacrity.

Alexei flashed her a strange look. "I'm sorry, Miss Harper," he said distinctly, "I don't want to be rude, but I think Katherine and I need to talk over some things alone."

Nora glanced questioningly at Katherine.

"Oh yes, I'd forgotten. Of course." Katherine smiled tremulously. "You'll lock up, Nora? I'll speak to you tomorrow."

Nora nodded. "But we'll see you in Boston, won't we, Mr. Gismondi?" She put an invitation into his hands.

Alexei smiled. Polite, formal. "Perhaps." He ushered Katherine out.

When they were in the street, he put his hand lightly on her shoulder. "For a moment there, I had just the tiniest suspicion that you might be avoiding me."

Katherine smiled. "Well, I don't want to be talked out of one of my pictures. I know how persuasive you Romans can be." The words as they tripped out of her staggered her. Was it really she who was referring to Carlo so lightly? She stiffened a little.

He looked at her oddly. "Don't worry. I know the difference between persuasion and coercion. I've had my lessons in female freedom."

She was intrigued. "Tell me. What kind of lessons?"

He didn't answer straight away. His face was taut, etched with melancholy.

They walked, their steps in tune, oblivious to the Manhattan bustle. Each caught up in private thoughts, yet intensely aware of the other's presence. Katherine pointed out a wine bar. "Shall we go in here? It's not too noisy."

He laughed suddenly. "So you can hear me persuade you."

"Perhaps that too." She met him on it. "But first you'll have to tell me about those lessons."

He looked at her seriously as they sat down at a corner table of the mezzanine, away from the crowd. "It was an attempted joke. It's nothing."

She felt she wanted to touch his face, wipe away the sadness. "Tell me anyway," she said softly.

Alexei shrugged, sipped his wine reflectively. "I was thinking of a woman friend who once pointed out to me in no uncertain terms how a man's persuasion can take on the oppressiveness of tyranny for a woman."

"I see." Katherine thought about it, hesitated. "Is she a good friend, this woman?"

"She was more than a friend."

Katherine searched his face. "Was?" she asked a little urgently. She suddenly needed to know.

"She's dead now," he said flatly. "She committed suicide. In prison."

There. It was said now. He had said it aloud to another human being. Alexei studied her. Watched the gray eyes grow wide, the tremor at the corner of her lips. "Like your mother. She killed herself."

"I didn't love my mother." The words spilled out of her. "It's not the same." She didn't know why she said it to this stranger. "I didn't care. I had left home by then."

Alexei gazed at her. All at once, he saw the little girl in her. The hurt. The determination. He kept himself from taking her hand.

"Why did your mother do it?" he asked after a long moment.

Katherine shrugged. "I don't know. I didn't really know her. She wasn't well. She suffered from breakdowns."

Alexei tried to put together the picture Katherine's words conjured up with the face he had seen in the painting, in photographs. But Katherine's features blocked out Sylvie's. He was making her miserable. "I guess we never really know other people," he said. "Only fragments of them. The fragments which collide with us."

"I would like to know you," Katherine murmured, without a trace of coyness.

His eyes lit up. "You might not like what you find." He laughed.

She joined him, suddenly merry. "I'd have to take my chances." Her words astonished her. They were so out of character. But she felt light-headed. She smiled.

"Would you take me, could we go and see your film? Together? I haven't seen that one yet." As soon as she said it, she realized that it was what she wanted more than anything else, to sit with him in the dark, watching his imagination take shape on the screen.

Alexei demurred. "It's my first film. Old now. And I thought you had to get back."

Her face fell. "I could ring home," she said tentatively. "But only if you . . ."

"Of course we can go," he interrupted her.

They took a cab across town, arrived at the theater a few moments late and sat toward the back. Katherine watched the screen avidly. Southern Italy. Dark, brooding. An atmosphere of claustrophobia. Heavy. Oppressive. A young woman, her face sensitive, closed and then flickering into openness. Life. The images carefully framed in a wealth of sensuous detail.

She was riveted by the film's unfolding. Alexei had made this. Alexei, the man beside her. He had told this woman's story. He understood. Without thinking, she reached for his hand, and then aware of her gesture withdrew. He wrapped his arm around her. So warm. Katherine cried. Cried for the woman and herself.

"Thank you," she said to him when they were outside. "Thank you." It was all she could think of.

When the taxi pulled up at her door, she asked him, "Would you like to come in and look at the St. Loup again?"

He stopped her at the threshold, took her hand. "Katherine"— his voice was urgent—"I'm not reliable. You must understand that. I'm not reliable." Rosa had said that to him, he remembered. Rosa, so different from the woman who now smiled at him, returned the pressure of his fingers.

"My venerable father has led me to believe that no one is altogether reliable. Least of all oneself." Katherine had hoped for wryness, achieved only a huskiness.

He came in, watched her mutely as she put Doreen into a taxi, checked on a sleeping Natalie.

"And now, while I rustle up a snack, you can go and feast your eyes on Sylvie Kowalska." She laughed. "Don't bundle her under your arm and disappear though. I won't allow that."

Alexei in Katherine's study reflected that he must be mad. He looked at the portrait cursorily and then sat down in Katherine's reading chair. He would tell her. Go and tell her now. She was stronger than he had thought yesterday. He would tell her the story, his suspicions. Perhaps they were all nonsense. After all, he had so little to go on.

Sylvie's eyes called him back. He stared at the portrait. Glanced in a small ornate corner mirror. His eyes. Her eyes. Both trapped. He felt the picture was laughing at him as he walked down the stairs.

He could hear Katherine's footsteps in the living room. He paused at the door, watched her as if in slow motion. With his film-maker's eye, he saw her bend gracefully to deposit a tray on the low coffee table. Saw the length of her legs, the curve of her back, a pallor of bared nape as her hair tumbled forward. He could have stopped himself, but he didn't want to. Once, just once, to hold her in his arms. He reached her as she turned.

A kiss. A fleeting eternity. Body molded to body. Lips to lips. A hunger. A fragrance. Nothing else.

And then, in the distance, a cry, insistent. "Mommy."

Alexei released her. Their eyes met. A moment of recognition. Long, slender fingers traced the line of his cheek. Wonder. He felt hers, returned it. Beautiful. She was so beautiful.

Melancholy hovered over him. "I'll let myself out," he said. He thought, perhaps he hoped, she might restrain him, but Natalie's call sounded again louder.

Katherine's lips curled. "Boston. Yes?"

Alexei nodded. "And perhaps you might arrange for me to see some of the pictures in your father's collection? If it's no trouble?"

"No trouble at all." She gave him a lingering smile.

Jacob Jardine put a glass into Alexei's hand and looked at him quizzically. "And so we meet again, Mr. Gismondi?"

"Yes, I hope I'm not putting you out." Alexei leaned back in the armchair and let his eyes peruse the walls of Jacob's living room. "I had no idea when we first met that you were a friend of Michel St. Loup's and that Sylvie Kowalska was your wife." There, he had said it. And now he could look the man in the face. "I happened on his portrait of your wife, the one in Katherine's possession, at an exhibition in Rome. It's a superb painting. It made me want to see more."

"Ah yes, a fine picture." A shadow flickered over Jacob's face and then his features settled into their more habitual irony. "Yes, and like all fine pictures, perhaps, its origins were not altogether untroubled."

Alexei waited for him to continue, had to prod him. "I noticed a tear, perhaps a cut in the canvas, when I looked at it more closely the other day."

"You are very observant, Mr. Gismondi." Jacob glanced at him curiously. "My wife, you see, though she was not then quite my wife, was not altogether enamored of the portrait and made a little stab at destroying it." Jacob paused. The scene at Roussillon he had not thought of for so many years suddenly played itself before him with all its force. Sylvie's pain. The poignancy of it. His own anger. His confusion.

The young man's voice brought him back.

"If it's not indiscreet of me to ask, was St. Loup having an affair with Sylvie Kowalska at the time?"

Jacob shrugged. "I don't think so, no. But what is an affair? And how is one ever to know these things? Particularly with a woman like Sylvie. She was a very special being, the young Sylvie Kowalska." Jacob smiled. "As all these images of her testify." He waved his hand round the room. "I can only tell you that St. Loup denied the success of any affair with her." He chuckled. "But the portraits he did of her at that time were some of his best and certainly they drew on some of the more troubled bonds artists sometimes have with their models. Look around, Mr. Gismondi, please. Feel free."

Alexei strolled. "Yes, a beautiful woman, a very special woman." He turned back to Jacob. "I think I might have met her once," he said casually. "I'm not certain. I was very young. But I think it was her. She came to interview me for a book she was writing. Under a pen name." He tried to hide the eagerness with which he awaited Jacob's response.

Jacob rose, paced for a moment. "It's possible. She was working on a book when she died. I was never allowed to see any of it and she must have torn up what there was. Nothing was ever found amidst her papers."

"I'm sorry." Alexei sensed Jacob's distress. "I didn't mean to pry."

A short sharp laugh came from Jacob. "No, no. Don't worry, Mr. Gismondi. That's the way of things. What is art history for some is life for others. Come, let me show you. There are other paintings in my study.

"There." He switched on a light, then another. "Look your fill. It's one of the few pleasures of old age, you know. One becomes a repository of the century's history. The young come to see one. Ask innocent questions." He chuckled. "I even have some of my wife's own work here, though she was better at destroying it than courting recognition." He rummaged amidst some folders, placed one on the desk. "Do look. Who knows? You might find inspiration in them. I like them very much myself, though they are not to my daughter's taste."

Alexei strolled round the room examining paintings. He did not allow himself to approach too quickly the folder which beckoned to him. His pulse felt erratic. So many questions pressed on him. At last, just before he dipped into the folder, he tried another, keeping his tone as even as he could. "Your wife was Polish. I was born there too. It was one of the reasons, I believe, that she came to see me."

"Yes, yes, that could very well be," Jacob mused, leaned into his desk chair. "She spent very little time in Poland, left when she was still a child and only returned once for a matter of months just after the war." He cleared his throat. "But childhood is such a crucial time, as my profession has been at pains to note, that she was always preoccupied with things Polish." He paused, followed Alexei's gaze. "Her drawings have a certain something, don't you think?"

Alexei nodded. He couldn't trust his voice. Amongst Sylvie's fantastic bestiary, he had just stumbled on a sketch which he knew must be of himself—a boy, a boy in a room which could only be his, a room with a screen and projector. There was another drawing of this boy, and then amidst scorpions and unicorns and phoenixes and mermaids, an unusual sketch of a room with beds, a man in uniform, his face indistinguishable, but at the corner of the drawing, two words, *Makarov*, and *Lublin*.

Alexei almost dropped the cigarette he had just lit. Makarov. His father. Sylvie Kowalska and his father. He thought back rapidly. There was no way Sylvie could have discovered the name Makarov from his uncle. They had held it secret between them, a talisman of the past. No, Sylvie Kowalska had been with his father. She had been in Lublin, his birthplace. His imagination proliferated scenes, images, the possible trajectories of a romance leading to him. Now that he had the proof in his hands, he didn't know what to do with it.

"Yes, they are troubling images, are they not, Mr. Gismondi?" Jacob's voice reached him as if from a great distance.

Alexei nodded. "Very." He closed the folder, focused on Jacob Jardine. How could he ask this man who had opened his house to him, this man who looked at him with kindly eyes, if he knew of an illicit affair his wife might have had with a certain Ivan Makarov.

One couldn't do things like that. He imagined himself in Jacob's place, tasted the anger he would feel, the cold fingers of betrayal, the confusion at having to confront the living product of a secret infidelity. "Very," Alexei repeated slowly. "Perhaps you might let me look at them again some time. But now I've taken up quite enough of your time." He rose. "Thank you. Thank you very much."

"Oh it's nothing, Mr. Gismondi. A friend of my daughter's is always welcome." Jacob surveyed him and smiled. "I hope we'll see you in Boston. If you are a lover of art, then the Sachs Collection will interest you."

Alexei bowed.

The Thomas Sachs House thronged with people and life. Excitement and champagne bubbled. The thrill of seeing and being seen. Everyone was there. The Beacon Hill and Park Avenue dignitaries looking like a restrained tableau from *Vogue*. The Bucks County rich with their exuberant voices and equally exuberant diamonds. The city and state officials. Even the artists had come, some languorous, some dashing, some plainly bored. Had come out of homage to Katherine or out of curiosity. And the journalists and critics were there to report on it all with their cutting superiority or their tittle-tattle wit.

It was, Katherine thought, as she walked through what had been Thomas's spacious reception rooms, the study, the library, a success, an enormous success. She smiled, greeted people, accepted congratulations. Some of the visitors, she saw, were even looking at the collection, particularly the students and school groups to whom she had extended invitations. She thought of Thomas, hoped that he would have been pleased. She felt at once exhausted and jubilant.

There was only one person missing. One person she hadn't seen. An ache bolted through her, making her smile stiff. Alexei Gismondi. He wasn't there. She didn't have time to examine the lack which opened up in her in the midst of small talk and kisses. But it was there. Palpable.

By nine o'clock the rooms, as well as the champagne bottles, were beginning to empty. Replete with congratulations, Katherine strolled through the galleries to where she hoped she might find Jacob and Natalie. There they were in the study.

And there beside them was Alexei, tall, intent, listening to her father. Her pulse raced.

"Isn't it all too exciting, Mommy." Natalie saw her first. "And look who's arrived. It's Alexei. I introduced him to Gramps, but it seems

they've already met. Gramps has invited him to join us for dinner."
Natalie's tone was triumphant.

So there it was, Katherine thought. All neatly taken care of. Quite
out of her hands. She patted Natalie's shoulder. "That's wonderful,
hon."

Natalie stole a glance at her mother. "You're not upset, about
Alexei joining us?"

"No, why should I be, hon? I'm pleased." Katherine smiled,
embraced her father, paused for a moment before taking Alexei's
hand. "I'm so glad you could come," she said quietly. She was struck
again by the magnetic force of his dark good looks, that sense of a
textured past he gave off, of buried secrets. She was also suddenly
acutely aware of the way her trim new suit hugged her body.

"I've invited Mr. Gismondi to join us for dinner, Kat. It seems
that apart from his passion for St. Loup, he has an interest in psychoanalysis." Jacob turned to Alexei, laughed. "That won't please my
daughter, Mr. Gismondi. If you've spoken to her at all, you'll know
that she has an undying contempt for matters psychoanalytical. And
whatever we say, she will argue us under the table."

"Mommy doesn't argue, Gramps. She just looks at you disapprovingly," Natalie's clear voice burst in.

Katherine flushed. "There you have it, Alexei. All the family
secrets out on the table at once. It's common practice in New York
households."

The intense blue light of his eyes washed over her. "I'm certain
there are still a few secrets to discover."

Jacob chuckled. "Without secrets, I would be out of a job."

"What secrets?" Nora Harper came up to them.

"The naughty kind," Jacob teased her, greeted her.

Katherine watched her friend carefuly as she shook Alexei's hand.
She had forgotten she was meant to be joining them for dinner. She
drew Alexei's attention back to herself, asked him what he thought
of Thomas's collection. As she spoke, Katherine suddenly felt
absurdly young. She had no ready responses for this situation. She
met Alexei's eyes, held them, read their desire. Yes, it was there.
She felt its response in herself. And yet there they were in front of
her father, her daughter. And still that flame kindling between them.

By the time they reached the seafood restaurant in Boston's old
quarter, Jacob Jardine had reaffirmed the lightning assessment he
had made of Alexei the first time he had met him in his consulting

room. He approved of this young man who stood a good head taller than him, approved of him not only for himself but for his daughter. This Gismondi had both a directness and a refinement about him. And yes, something else, Jacob thought. He was not unlike Katherine. Too much energy kept under a tight leash.

He looked at his daughter. She was radiant tonight. Somehow altered. Perhaps the opening of Thomas's house would mark a change in her. Perhaps, he stole a look at Alexei, perhaps it was this young man. He should contrive to leave them together. Soon.

Despite Jacob's earlier warning, dinner arranged itself around the menu of psychoanalysis. The delicately spiced seafood cocktail was served with Freud and the importance of the father. With the lobster came the primacy of the mother for Melanie Klein. Chocolate mousse inspired an argument on Lacan, language and the symbolic sphere. Natalie piped up at one point, "I don't know what you're all talking about, but I know I think fathers are important, and Mommy thinks mothers are important and Gramps never stops talking, so he must be on the side of language.

Jacob burst into laughter. Katherine, upset, smoothed Natalie's hair back from her face with a caressing gesture. Natalie moved away from her. "What do you think, Alexei?"

"I'm not sure I'm quite old enough to know. Or maybe too old." He smiled at her. His gaze shifted to Katherine. "I'm sure your mother is very important."

Katherine's hands trembled. She excused herself from the table. Nora followed her. "So who's going to go off with the delicious Alexei? Is it you or me?" she asked as soon as the door of the powder room closed behind them.

Katherine looked at her in astonishment. "Why, I hadn't thought," she murmured. And then, she thrust away her customary evasions. "Me, I hope," she said.

Nora laughed a little coldly. "I never thought I'd hear you say it."

But when they got back to the table, they heard to their surprise that Alexei was leaving.

"I must catch the last plane back to New York, I'm afraid. I'm sorry. It's been a pleasure." He shook Jacob's hand, Natalie's, Nora's. He paused in front of Katherine, held those long slender fingers tensed within his. He read the pain, the confusion in her eyes. "I'm sorry," he murmured again. "I must go."

She averted her face. "In New York then," she murmured.

"Yes, yes. Yes, Katherine." He squeezed her hand, smiled sadly.

He shouldn't have come, he thought. It was getting worse. He had to go. To escape.

She returned his smile, watched him leave, aware only of his receding form and the longing which coursed through her.

The next evening, Katherine was back home in New York. She tucked Natalie in, wandered through the house, at a loss as to what to do. She couldn't settle to anything. What was happening to her? Almost, she picked up the phone to ring Alexei's hotel. But no, she couldn't. She wouldn't pursue him. How bizarre that her life should have turned topsy-turvy in the space of a mere two weeks. It was madness. Did she feel this way only because all the energy she had put into Thomas's house now had no channel? Yes, Katherine thought. That was part of it.

But not all of it. No. There had been that kiss.

She went to bed and tried to sleep. She wasn't sure if she dreamed or thought, but her life suddenly appeared to her as a long, coiling tunnel, pierced only by the occasional light. Sylvie, gigantic, monstrous, stood at one end pushing her, forcing her to enter it, to go underground. It was hard to breathe in the tunnel. Lianas clutched at her, mud clung to her feet. But now the tunnel was growing smaller, Katherine larger. She was too big for it. She stood close to its end. Yes, she could see it, see the end. Another few turns, another few feet. A blaze of light. Bright. Obliterating that shadowy coil. All she had to do was reach out, pull herself through. Squeeze.

She woke, dazed but smiling.

As she was coming out of the shower, she heard the bell. A messenger. A vast bouquet. Her heart sang. Alexei. It could only be from him. She buried her head in the proliferation of spring blooms, hummed to herself. It was all right. She would see him, see him tonight. She hugged the flowers to her, then unwrapped them carefully. A small box fell from the bouquet, and a note.

Katherine tore open the note. It was in Italian. Her hands trembled as she read. *"Mia cara,"* my darling, he said. Her eyes sped over the words. Then, her face grew pale.

He was gone. Gone back to Rome. Disappointment spread through her, so tangible that she could smell it in the room above the scent of the flowers.

The box. She had forgotten the small velvet box. She opened it clumsily. A ring. Finely crafted. An emerald in an antique setting of white gold. She stared. Felt herself grow cold. Sylvie's ring. No. It wasn't possible. She examined the band. Initials leapt out at her, untarnished by time. S.K. Her mother's ring. It dropped from her fingers. The ring Jacob had given her mother. The ring Katherine had been accused of stealing, time and again. The ring which had signaled her own unjust punishment, anger, shame, Sylvie's ring.

She looked at the ring for a long time.

How had Alexei Gismondi come to have Sylvie Kowalska's ring?

Why had he sent it to her and gone?

"Try to understand," his note had said. What was it that she was intended to understand?

He had come for Sylvie's portrait. She mustn't forget that. She herself was incidental. An aside. A moment's company in a foreign city. But he had sent her Sylvie's ring. The ring, she now dimly remembered, which had never been found amidst her mother's jewelry.

Sylvie's web. Her mother's web reaching out to trap her now after all these years.

Katherine sat there for she didn't know how long. She thought of Sylvie. Thought of Alexei. Sobs overtook her.

Then, with a sense of foreboding, she reached for the telephone. She dialed the number of Alexei's hotel.

"Mr. Gismondi has checked out," a cheerful voice told her.

"Has he left a forwarding address?" Katherine asked. Her hand was trembling.

"One moment please." The voice, ever cheerful, disappeared.

Katherine waited, her knuckles growing white around the telephone.

"He has returned to Rome." The woman awkwardly spelled out an address.

"Thank you," Katherine said bleakly.

A fist clutched at her entrails. She rose painfuly, looked out of the window at the quiet street. Then she went up to Natalie's room.

"Pack your bags, hon," Katherine said with seeming gaiety. "We're going on a trip. We're going to Rome."

Natalie looked at her as if an angel had suddenly materialized from a vaporous sky.

*R*ome. A blaze of light. Sculp-
tured fountains. Secret lanes. Majestic squares. Moldering fresco.
The breath of the past. And everywhere people, faces animated,
horns blaring.

And Natalie chattering. Chattering with unstoppable excitement.
Hugging her. Squeezing her hand. In love with Rome.

Katherine could no longer recapture the emotions that had kept
her away.

They checked in at the Villa Medici on the Piazza Trinità dei
Monti, ate in the resplendent rooftop restaurant, gazed at the city
spread before them.

Then Katherine positioned herself at the telephone. She took a
deep breath. Dialed the Contessa's number, asked for her, identified
herself. Waited an interminable moment before a crackling but still
familiar voice came to the telephone, heard the woman's rush of
elation, the insistence that they come straight away, the chauffeur
would be sent.

Katherine said they would drive down the next day. She gave
Natalie the receiver, watched her daughter's face. The shyness. Then
the pleasure. She wondered for the second time that day why it was
that she had stayed away for so long.

The next call was more difficult to make. Alexei. What would she say? What could she say in front of Natalie? She decided to wait until the evening.

They went for a walk instead, meandering down the Spanish Steps, through the maze of small streets which lay at their base. Without quite knowing how they had got there, Katherine realized they were passing in front of the club where she had last seen Carlo. She shivered involuntarily and then forced herself to look at it in the clear afternoon light. Look at herself too. In a gleaming window her reflection confronted her. No, not the Katherine of old. A frightened child, fearful of her desires, afraid to face them, afraid to face her dependency on the man who had aroused them, as terrified of his rejection as she was terrified of the need. Needing to control both and to be punished, abased by both. Trapped.

It was hard now to locate that Katherine anymore. When had she disappeared? Perhaps only gradually. Perhaps only and finally when she had decided to come here. To come back to Rome. To find a man she barely knew but sensed she needed to know, regardless of the consequences.

Katherine looked at her reflection. *Une femme d'un certain âge,* the French would say euphemistically. Not in her first youth, but formed. The sun gave her hair a copper glow. Deep-set eyes wide in a face more finely honed now. A pale peach dress which swayed and clung in the breeze. At her side a young girl, dark eyed, eager.

No. She was no longer the Katherine of a decade ago.

"This is where I last saw your father," Katherine found herself saying.

"What was he doing?" Natalie asked.

Katherine laughed. "He was enjoying himself. Gambling. At a roulette table." The words formed without too much difficulty.

"What did he look like?"

"A little wild. Attractive. Not unlike you." She paused. "I thought he was very handsome," she said with slow emphasis.

Natalie flashed her a quizzical look. "And so you made a beautiful couple," she said after a moment, in her best magazine reader's voice. "I'm glad you've come here with me, Mommy," she added.

"So am I." Katherine placed a hand on her daughter's shoulder. "Come, we'll go and see what the house looks like."

She brought Natalie to the house near the Capitol where she had spent her first years, pointed out in great detail the trajectory of her walks, told her about her first nannies. She also told her, as they ate ice cream in the Piazza Navona, how Carlo had idolized his little

Natalie, had eyes and ears and arms only for her. Natalie cried. As Katherine embraced her, she suddenly thought of Jacob, thought he might be just a little proud of her. She wondered, too, how it was that she who had been so attached to her own father could have denied Natalie's need for so long.

The Roman light had somehow simplified things, given them clear, hard edges. Rid memories, which stole up on one like vengeful shadows, of their force.

From the lobby of the hotel that evening, she rang the number she had found for Alexei Gismondi. A woman's voice. Katherine swallowed hard, took her courage in hand, asked for him. Learned that Signor Gismondi was not in Rome, would not be there for another day or two at least. She didn't leave a message. Couldn't bring herself to wait for a call that might not come.

The next day they drove the ninety kilometers to the Palazzo Buonaterra. Natalie, now, was in a tizzy of nerves. "What will I say to her? I've never met a Contessa." She twisted the strands of her hair and looked beseechingly at Katherine.

Katherine laughed. "You've met a Principessa and you had no trouble finding words with her."

"But that's different," Natalie moaned.

Katherine stilled her, forced her to look at hills, trees, flowers, the blue Mediterranean in the distance. Natalie's anxiety obliterated her own. She felt calm. What was the Contessa but a lonely old woman who wanted to see her only granddaughter? Not an ogre, not Carlo's hungry, invasive shadow, a role that her own heated imagination had attributed to her.

And so it proved. The palazzo was as grand a baroque pile as it had ever been, the fountains and gardens as impressive as they had been of old. But the Contessa who inhabited them in the shelter of her countless servants was a small shrunken woman whose eyes filled with tears as soon as she spied Natalie.

"Che bella. Bellissima." She put her hands on Natalie's cheeks and kissed her. She kissed Katherine, too, but her gaze was only for her granddaughter. For her too the careful English, the long walk through every nook and cranny of the palazzo, which ended in a room the Contessa proudly designated as Natalie's, a room crammed with dolls and toys and books. As if the Contessa had amassed objects for every year of Natalie's life during which she had not been visited. For Natalie, too, the many-flavored *gelati* in the garden, the gamboling puppies.

It was as they were sitting, watching her play, that the Contessa said to Katherine, "Thank you for bringing her. Thank you." Her large bony nose quivered.

"I'm sorry I didn't do so sooner," Katherine murmured, ashamed.

The Contessa looked at her, a dark look from shrewd eyes. "You know, Katerina, I never had any illusions about my son's qualifications as a husband."

Katherine stared at her. So she had known, had suspected.

The Contessa hurried on. "The Buonaterra men . . . well . . ." She made a large, generous gesture with her hands. "But Carlo was a good son to me. And he loved Natalie. I only wish he could see her now. I still mourn him." Tears sprang to her eyes again. "I hope"— she pinioned Katherine with her gaze—"I hope you will let Natalie stay with me a little."

Before Katherine could respond, she called to Natalie in English. "Natalie, come. I would like to show you something. Perhaps your mother would like to see too."

They followed her inside, up the grand staircase, to a door on the first floor. The Contessa held herself straight, her stick a mere rhythmical punctuation. She led them into the library. Katherine remembered the room well, the heavy tomes which looked as if they had not been opened for hundreds of years, the high shuttered windows giving on to a breathtaking vista, its horizon the sea.

On the center table, carefully placed, lay four leatherbound folios. The Contessa urged them into chairs. She opened the first book. Photographs, sepia-tinted, from the turn of the century. She turned the pages slowly and as she turned, she told Natalie about the Buonaterras. Slow, lulling words, conjuring intrigue, power. Natalie sat, her eyes intent, her ears tuned. Katherine gazed at her. She began to see the magic taking over. The magic of history. That old, that other Europe. Began to see her daughter taken over.

She had a blinding urge to take Natalie's hand and flee. Run. Run, like she had all those years ago.

And then Natalie laughed. "He looks funny." Her nose crinkled as she pointed to a tiny uniformed man, stiff on horseback.

Katherine looked at her daughter in amazement. She sat back in her chair. Wonder dawned in her. She hadn't allowed for Natalie. Hadn't trusted her. She was her own person now. Another person. A separate person. Not Katherine.

Not me, Katherine marveled.

Another thick folio. Carlo. Carlo as a small boy with an elegant

Contessa. Now Natalie's attention was completely fixed. Katherine held her breath, watched image upon image of Carlo. Carlo at the seaside with tumbling dark curls. Carlo on his first pony. Carlo at twelve in his school uniform looking, she was not the only one to notice, a very great deal like Natalie.

And then—Katherine hadn't prepared herself sufficiently—there were the wedding photographs. Katherine, young, radiant, smiling blissfully in her fairy-tale dress. Carlo, darkly sensual, his arm on her shoulder. The two of them dancing, a sardonic lilt on his lips.

"A beautiful couple," Natalie murmured for Katherine's ears.

"Oh yes," the Contessa took her up. "The most beautiful couple." She smiled at Katherine.

Katherine averted her eyes, then returned to gaze. Gaze on Mathilde, Leo, Portia, Jacob. And more, more. Gaze on a plump baby Natalie in her father's arms. Carlo rapturous, flinging her in the air. Her first birthday. An idyllic family.

The story pictures didn't tell, Katherine thought.

And yet they did tell a story, a story she had forgotten. A story traduced by its ending.

Natalie saw only one of those stories. "Why don't *we* have these pictures?" she asked Katherine querulously.

She met her on it. "I'm sure we can have them now, hon. We'll get duplicates made."

"You promise?"

Katherine nodded.

Natalie beamed.

They stayed the night.

The next day after breakfast, and before they were due to leave, Katherine took Natalie for a stroll through the grounds to the little chapel.

"Will you take a picture of me here?" Natalie pressed her camera into Katherine's hands.

Katherine clicked, smiled at her. "Happy we came?"

Natalie nodded. She looked up at Katherine. "The Contessa has asked me to stay for a few days, a week. She says we'll go to the seashore." The question was poised on her face.

Katherine took a deep breath. "Do you want to stay, hon?"

"I'm not sure." Natalie considered, held her mother's eyes.

"If you want to, then it's fine by me." Katherine tried a smile, found it didn't sit too badly.

"Perhaps for a few days then. I can get to know her a bit. She's a strange old thing."

Katherine laughed. "It will make her very happy."

"And you? Would you stay?" Natalie asked.

Katherine shook her head. "I'd rather not. There are things I want to do in Rome. See some galleries. I'll come and collect you. Whenever you say the word."

Natalie looked at her shrewdly. "And see Signor Alexei Gismondi, I bet." She rolled the words off her lips with Italian aplomb.

Katherine flushed. "Perhaps that too."

"I think that's a great idea." Natalie giggled.

"As long as I have your blessing," Katherine murmured wryly.

She rang Alexei's number as soon as she got back to Rome. The same voice answered. No, Signor Gismondi was not in. Katherine's heart sank. He was expected back this evening, the voice continued. Around nine.

Katherine rang off. She had hours to kill. She showered, changed, put on a dress of boldly patterned black and white linen with a halter top, a short jacket. The jagged extremes of her mood. She was growing increasingly impatient. She had to see him. Had to know. What, she wasn't quite certain. Know about him. About Sylvie's ring.

She visited a few galleries. Was too late for the Palazzo Barberini where she had hoped to gaze on Raphael's "Fornarina," renew her acquaintance with Filippo Lippi. Instead she trod the stairs to the Capitol, looked out on the Forum, felt herself a tourist and yet not. The familiar grown unfamiliar. She walked some more, lost herself in a maze of streets, reemerged in the Piazza Navona, sat gratefully in a café overlooking Bernini's "Fountain of the Four Rivers." A church bell tolled eight. She could go back to the hotel now, ring Alexei again.

Katherine walked, glanced up at a street sign. Familiar. Whom had she known on this street?

Then she remembered. Alexei, it was Alexei's address. She had stumbled upon it. She quickened her pace, feeling uncomfortable, feeling like a spy. And then, as if her imagination had conjured him up, she saw him. There. Not a hundred feet from her. Getting out of a red sports car. Pale trousers, blue shirt, dark tousled hair, the hand, characteristically, pushing it back. The eyes, she could almost see the startling blue of his eyes.

She moved into the shelter of a half-columned doorway. Hid. She didn't want to be seen. Not like this. Not unannounced, as if she were stalking him.

There was a woman at the wheel of the car. Sleek shoulder-length hair. Red mouth. He blew her a kiss, waved.

Katherine waited, waited until the car had pulled away, until he had safely been swallowed up by a door. Then quickly, breathing a little fast, she retraced her steps, found a bar, ordered a drink. Ten minutes later, suddenly afraid he might go out again, she telephoned.

Alexei restlessly paced the length and width of the living room. She was here. Katherine Jardine was here in Rome. She would be here in this room with him in a few minutes. He had thought of little else but her since his return to Italy and now she was here. What would he say to her?

He had all but decided in these last days that his entire pursuit of Sylvie Kowalska was an aberration. An attempt to reconstruct a phantom past for himself so that the vacuum of the present might be filled. An escape, a tantalizing fugue into the romance of origins, to distract him from the void of a present he did not want to face.

He had pounced on the seductiveness of an image, the coincidence of the color of eyes, a Polish name, a letter from the buried past. Pounced on it as a distraction. A new door had been opened and in the very way that his favorite filmmaking dictum suggested, reality had entered through that door to violate his arrangements. Katherine had walked in. Real, alive, a figure of the present and perhaps the future. Not a shadowy phantom. Not another lost mother. He had told Jacob Jardine, partially in jest, that he suffered from a surfeit of absent mothers. There was no need for that suffering, that staring into the navel of history.

Over these last days, Alexei's desire, his desire for Katherine, had battled against those shadowy phantoms and blotted them out. She meant more to him than all that. He was ashamed of the way he had bolted from New York, fled to the safety of a refuge where he could think. Mull over the significance of the proof he had found, the proof that Sylvie Kowalska had known his father. And what of it, his reason had said, now that it had a new end, a future in view? His father had never been to France, couldn't have been in those latter days of the war. Jacob had told him that his wife had been in Poland only for a few months. So that was that. And as for Sylvie Kowalska's letter to him, he would never learn any more about her without disrupting too many lives. Let the past keep its secrets. More important things drew him now.

Katherine. That very morning he had woken thinking that he would return to New York very soon.

And now she was here.

He heard Gina opening the door to her, heard footsteps. And then she was there. Only the width of the room away from him. More beautiful than he had remembered her. Her color high as if she had been running. A slight air of worry about her features, like a forest creature sniffing the room for signals of danger.

He took her hands, held them. "Katherine, how wonderful." His eyes glowed. "A delicious surprise."

"I needed to come," she murmured, taking sustenance from his gaze. Yes, she thought, she had needed to. The current from him was almost too strong. She withdrew her hands. Looked around her. So this was where he lived. A large airy space, uncluttered. A minimum of objects, soft, rounded arches, blue-gray sofas, walls in a paler tinge, a fresco half unearthed from the plaster, white pyramidal lamps. An ascetic room, a space for contemplation.

She perched on the corner of a sofa. Took the proffered drink. He sat down opposite her, close, so close. She surveyed his face, looked away. Words came with difficulty.

"I had to know," she said. "I have to know."

"Know what?" Her face was shadowed, frightened. The vulnerability.

"About you." She lifted her gaze to him, hesitant, searching.

He kissed her. Words would only separate them. Confuse. They didn't need words. There had already been too many.

Her lips were soft, tentative. He lifted her to him, pressed her close, felt the curve and sway of her body, the resistance and then the little leap, the kindling, her hands in his hair. He forced her eyes to him. Secret. A little wild. He wanted those secrets, wanted to fan that wildness. Wanted her. He had not felt so certain about anything for a long time.

"Come, we shall know about each other." It was at once question and promise.

Katherine allowed him to lead her. Through an arch. A stretch of hall, another room, another hue of bluey gray. A vast white bed, naked, untouched, beneath a vaulted alcove. A bowl of flowers, red and creamy white, swaying frilled tulips. Her mind insisted on the detail as if in a dream. His fingers on her face, tracing the line of brow and cheek and neck. His eyes on her, the irises dark, fringed against the startling blue. Searching, exploring. A memory nipped at her and then vanished as arms enfolded her, lips roused. Sensation. A sea of sensation. Dream and his skin colliding. Warm. The imagined and the real in a wave of desire.

They tumbled on the bed. Cool sheets. Hands, limbs, eyes, lips, touching, holding, stroking. Dangerously searching. Nakedness beneath the skin. The world, memory, erased and heightened. Into him. Into her. The same and other. Known and unknown. The new.

Katherine felt but didn't think. Felt herself and not herself. Movements precipitating and echoing her pleasure. Tuned to her, Katherine, not any woman. Confirmed as herself, known and unknown. Wanting. Unashamed.

Alexei felt time stretching, opening out, unconstricted. Substantial. Not fugitive. In her. Warm waves lapping. Her eyes open on him. To him. Dilated. Urging, discovering. He kissed her moans, thrust deeper, deeper into time. A center opening out, enfolding, sheltering, pleasuring. A cry, a drowning, a together.

Afterward, he looked at her, his smile glowing, his hand caressing the line of hip and thigh.

"And now we know each other a little better."

"Only a little," Katherine mused, playful and earnest.

"You want to know more?" he teased.

She nodded.

"Oh, these modern women," he groaned in mock dismay.

She looked a little hurt.

"Silly." He rose, took a white robe from an invisible cupboard.

A tall man with bronzed limbs and startling eyes. Alexei, leaving her, moving from the room. The desolation his sudden distance caused surprised her. She buried her face in her arms, wanting to weep.

"Katherine?" He was back.

She lifted her face, tears glistening. Saw a tray, champagne. She smiled at her own silliness.

"Katherine." He was beside her at once, kissing her eyes, the tears, her lips. "Don't cry. I am glad. So glad you are here. With me."

She looked at him seriously. "But you left. Left me in New York?"

"Yes," he said simply. "Yes." He stroked the tumble of her hair.

He didn't want to explain. He held her again, that elegant body, somehow still dressed in its nudity. Her caress, hesitant, despite their earlier passion, as if he might not be there. Be there for her. Her sadness roused him. I'm here now, he said with his body, loving her, loving the tentativeness and then the hunger, kindling it, filling it.

Katherine wondered at his gentleness, a kind of physical courtesy, wondered at how it moved and fired her at once. Hadn't known that before. Hadn't known it was possible. For her. She wanted to cry, to cry out, I love you, don't leave me, don't leave me.

When it was over, she was suddenly afraid, afraid of her desire never to leave this room again. This whiteness and their clasped bodies. Afraid, too, of that other need, surfacing again, unforgotten, the need to know.

She took the glass he handed her, sipped, looked at him. "I still need to know," she murmured. "Need to know about your note. What is it that you wanted me to understand? Where did you get my mother's ring? Why did you send it to me?"

Alexei felt lost. The truth. What was the truth? "I think I'm beginning to fall in love with you, Katherine." His voice had a huskiness.

She stroked his face, smiled, smiled. "And me with you," she mouthed. They held each other's gaze. And then she lowered hers. "And the ring?" She laughed suddenly. "Did you find it in an antique shop? No. That's improbable. Sylvie would never have pawned it. And in any case, you wouldn't have known it was hers. Who gave it to you?"

She had preempted his alibi. He had had one ready. Yes, an antique shop, a coincidence of initials, a little find. But he couldn't lie to her. Not now. Not in front of that face, so open, so vulnerable.

"She gave it to me," Alexei said at last.

"She gave it to you," Katherine echoed softly. For some reason, jealousy bolted through her. "You knew her?"

Alexei shook his head. Then changing his mind, nodded. He would have to tell her. They would laugh over it, laugh at his own delusions. But he was afraid.

"I met Sylvie Kowalska once. She came to interview me."

"Interview you? For what? She never wrote. I didn't know she ever wrote." Katherine felt confused. She covered herself with the white sheet.

Alexei shrugged, rose, paced, then restlessly positioned himself in an armchair. He watched Katherine's face.

"I don't know what for. Some time later, a letter came from her. In 1968. With the ring." He took a deep breath and continued levelly: "In the letter she implied she was my mother."

"What?" Katherine sat bolt upright. A shudder rose in her spine.

Alexei's fear crystallized. She would hate him. Hate him because he might be tainted by the mother she hated. "It's nonsense of course. Completely incomprehensible. My own mother died at my birth. But last year, when I saw Sylvie Kowalska's portrait, the one in your house, I was intrigued. Why would the woman write to me? I was at a loose end. I came to New York, to find out more if I could. I found you instead." He took her hand. "She led me to *you*," he said urgently.

It wasn't enough. She needed to know more. "Sylvie died at the end of 1961." She looked away from him. Sylvie's web, still clutching at her after all these years. "Why didn't you tell me all this in New York?" She turned on him, accusing him.

"I don't know." He shook his head. "I don't know. I was confused. I thought it might be true. Something in it might be true." He laughed harshly. "Stupid. I thought you might be my sister. My half sister. Absurd. Ridiculous. But sometimes fantasies take hold of one. I was at a loose end." He talked on, trying to drown the look on her face with words. "That's why I didn't stay. Though I wanted to stay. Wanted you. Katherine?" His voice rose. She was getting up, pulling on her clothes. Brusquely. Harsh, painful gestures.

"Katherine," he murmured again.

She faced him, clothed now. Armored. "You *could* be my brother," she hissed, her face contorted. "Sylvie was always fucking around. Always. It would be like her, just like her. To spoil. To wound. Even after her death. To wreck. Everything. Anything I felt." She was crying, great heaving sobs. She raced from the room.

He caught up with her. Gripped her arm. "Where are you going?"

"Away." She struggled against him. "Away. I have to think. I'm going to phone Jacob." She was adamant.

"Katherine." He embraced her, held her. "It's a figment. A nonsense. Forget about it."

"I can't." The eyes she turned on him were wild, ringed with pain. "You didn't know her the way I did. It has the real Sylvie stamp. Manipulative. Cruel."

He held her still, tried to calm her. "Cruel? Why cruel? She couldn't have known I would meet you. It's not directed at you."

She wouldn't meet his eyes. "I'll phone Jacob," she said, pulling away from him.

"Why ring him?" Alexei's voice was harsh now. "Why cause pain? If he had known anything, he would have said so when I met him in New York."

That stopped her for a moment. He used it to make her sit down.

"But you told me you had taken your uncle's name, had been adopted by him. Jacob might not have recognized a new name."

"That's true," Alexei mumbled. It was worrying. She had taken the notion so much to heart. He should never have said anything. It was his own fault. He should have lied. She would go away now. He would never hold her in his arms again. The thought devastated him.

"You're upset, Katherine. You're not thinking clearly." He pinioned her with his eyes. "Have you ever heard stories in your family about a baby disappearing? About your mother having had another child? Has anybody ever mentioned a man called Ivan Makarov?"

She shook her head.

"Well then. There would have been hints, something. Forget about it. It's nonsense. I should never have said anything. I wouldn't have said anything, if I had realized how obsessed you were with your mother."

That hit too deep. Katherine's voice cracked. "Obsessed? If you had known her, then you would know that anything was possible for her." She stared at him, her face suddenly taking on the fixity of stone. "That's it. I knew there was something. You have her eyes."

"All right." He stood, angry now, handing her the telephone. "Ring your father. A man would know if his wife had carried a child for nine months and then that child had disappeared."

Katherine laughed strangely. "That's what you think. Even that. She could even have managed that. She could always pull the wool over Jacob's eyes."

There was hatred in her face. Pure, unadulterated. A passion. Alexei wanted to hold her, to protect her from it. He suddenly had an intuition of the child in her, the pain. He tried to take her in his arms.

"No," she cried out. And then more softly, "No. I have to find out, Alexei. I have to know. If we were to go on. If Natalie . . ." The tears rose to her eyes. "Goodbye." She turned away from him. "Goodbye." She looked back at him from the door, suddenly aware that she might never see him again.

Katherine never knew how she got back to the hotel, couldn't remember lying down on the bed. Her mind was a maze of dusty corridors, a labyrinth of dangerous intersecting paths which led nowhere. Laughter, cruel, pitiless, echoed through the halls. Somewhere at its center there was a beast, no, not a beast, a spider, huge, hairy, laughing, spinning as she ran.

She woke struggling against shadows, confused. Then the thought crystallized. Alexei. Her brother. No. She refused it now in the pale morning light. She hadn't made love to her brother. No. It wasn't possible.

But why, why then would Sylvie have written to him, sent him the ring? Jacob, she had to telephone Jacob. Katherine looked at her watch. It was the middle of the night in New York. She couldn't ring him now. And in any event what would she say to him? "Jacob, do you know whether Sylvie had an affair with a Russian called *Ivan Makarov?*"

No. She couldn't ask him that over the telephone. She would have to see him, be with him. And then, would he know? The laughter, spiteful, malicious, rang out at the back of her head. She tried to drown it.

Jacob would at least know when Sylvie had been in Poland. For how long. Stupid, she was stupid. She hadn't asked Alexei his age. She could find out. Go to Poland. Look up records. Were there records for those blighted war years? Did records tell the truth?

Questions, questions leading nowhere. Like madness, round and round. Katherine felt she was drowning. Wept.

When she finally rose, there was only one thought in her head. She would go home. Pick up Natalie and go home. Back to New York. She would forget about Alexei. Forget the whole thing. An aberration. She should never have come here. Would never come here again.

The tears blinded her as she flung her clothes and Natalie's into a bag.

The phone rang. Automatically she picked it up. "Katherine, *carissima,* I've been ringing all the hotels in Rome to find you. I'm coming over. Straight over. Wait for me."

Alexei. Her legs trembled. She sat down on the bed. "No, no don't." Her voice cracked. She hung up. She couldn't see him. She would fall into his arms again. No.

Katherine fled. Rented a car. Flung bags into it. Drove. Drove blindly. Away. Away. Toward Natalie.

She lost herself in a one-way system. Found herself heading in the wrong direction. Tried to correct her error. Another mistaken turn. What did it matter? She was away. No one was expecting her. She drove.

The road took over. The hypnotic rhythm of a motorway. Lulling her. Disconnected thoughts. Fragments of memory. She tried to reconstruct Sylvie's life. Alexei had said she would have known, would have heard something, overheard. Katherine probed, dug into the quarry of her childhood. She remembered nothing of Poland. How could she? And those early years in Paris? She tried to reimagine scenes, faces, words, heard, overheard.

Leo, she suddenly thought. Her brother. He might know. Eight years. Eight long years separated them. He had known about Violette, known long before she had. She would contact Leo as soon as she and Natalie were safely back in New York.

Katherine drove. Katherine dreamt. The texture of nightmare. When she looked up at one point consciously to read a road sign she found that she was heading for Pisa. She was a long way from Natalie. It didn't matter, she told herself. She was in no state to see her daughter. Tomorrow, tomorrow would do.

But she pulled up at the next motorway service area, drank three cups of coffee in rapid succession, crumbled a *panino* and telephoned Natalie. She was relieved to find that neither the Contessa nor Natalie were in, were on an expedition to the coast. Katherine left a message, said she would ring again tomorrow.

As she got back into the car, she realized that only a day had passed since she had last seen Natalie. One day. That was all it had taken to turn her life upside down. A hysterical laugh rose in her.

She drove. Oblivious to the sea, to the rise and fall of the hills. She was excavating the past, combing it for traces. The apartment in the Marais. Jacob, Sylvie, Leo, herself. Sometimes Jacques. More rarely Violette and . . .

Suddenly Katherine had a sense of destination. She put her foot down on the accelerator. Mat. Princesse Mathilde, who had known Sylvie from childhood. Mathilde. Her better mother.

CHAPTER
TWENTY-SIX

*P*rincesse Mathilde closed her well-thumbed volume of Madame de Sévigné's letters, removed her spectacles and relaxed into her garden chair. Beyond the house grounds, the lush meadows were dappled pink and purple with the frolic of wildflowers. And beyond that the mountains loomed, solid, steadfast with their caps of brilliant white against the clear sky.

If she had Madame de Sévigné's virtuoso pen, she would write a letter now to Violette. A letter evoking the rise and fall of landscape and emotions, a letter full of maternal solicitude. But the days of letters were past. Now everything was done by telephone. Instantaneous communication or its lack. Chatter without reflection.

Princesse Mathilde sighed, and then catching herself at it, smiled, a little wryly. Her life at one end seemed to extend back, way back into Madame de Sévigné's seventeenth century with its court intrigues and complex network of formal relations. A time of letters.

And now, now after the caldron of two world wars with their shocks and displacements, she was firmly in another world. A staccato world of jets and telephones and computers. A world grown smaller with speed, denser with information, all of it stored. Stored, not in the person, but on disk. Memory externalized.

A young woman had come to see her last week asking her to externalize her own memory. An enthusiastic young woman who wanted to write a biography of Princesse Mathilde. To interview her, read her letters, speak to family, to friends. The Princesse had looked at her in astonishment and then politely, but firmly, declined. She would keep her life to herself for the short time that it still might last. She didn't want to have to read it in another's words. Or have it served up, with all its intimacies, for public consumption. The proposition appalled her.

It also made her smile. The biographies of the future, she thought, would no longer have the dense texture of letters exchanged. They would be made up of a smattering of official correspondence and a long list of telephone bills. "From the telephone bill of June 1980, we can see that Princesse Mathilde spoke to her daughter only rarely that month. Did this signify a falling off of relations or . . ." Mathilde chuckled.

She wrote regularly only to Jacob now. Long detailed letters, full of musings, of books read, thoughts to be shared. He answered in kind. The correspondence had begun again when Katherine came to school in Switzerland and had continued over the years. A duplicate existence through the post. Sometimes she thought it was her real one. She still had a little rustle of excitement when she found one of his envelopes in the post, the black strokes of his firm hand. Like all those eternities ago.

Princesse Mathilde gazed up at the sky. A little gathering of clouds. She would go in now. The afternoon was growing cooler. She stood slowly. Old joints. No flexibility. It annoyed her.

She turned as she heard barking at the other end of the garden. The dogs. A visitor. She wasn't expecting anyone.

She saw a tall slender woman in white trousers.

"Katherine, *quelle surprise!*" Her face crinkled into smiles. "What a pleasure to see you like this. Without warning."

They kissed.

"I hope I'm not intruding."

"Not at all. Not at all. You're just in time for tea. I hope you're planning to stay the night. Where are you on your way to?

"Only to you."

The Princesse glanced at her curiously as they walked slowly toward the house. The girl looked strained, overwrought. With all her natural gifts, she had never had an easy time of it. That first marriage. Carlo's death. "And Natalie?" the Princesse asked. "Is she well?"

"You'll be pleased to hear that she's with her grandmother at this very moment."

"I am pleased," the Princesse said slowly. "But you? Is that why you look a little upset?"

Katherine didn't answer and Mathilde didn't press. She led her to the conservatory. "I see Cook already knows of your arrival," the Princesse observed approvingly. Two cups, a tray of cakes, the cane table with its lace cloth. Everything foreseen.

"You know you run the most efficient house in Europe." Katherine attempted a smile which didn't quite work.

The Princesse made small talk, congratulated Katherine on the Sachs Collection. Yes, Jacob had written to her about it. The letter had come only yesterday. She rambled on, aware that Katherine was only half listening, told her about this and that.

"And Violette?" Katherine was making a visible effort.

"Oh," the Princesse shrugged, laughed, "she's well enough by her own lights. She's running around with a younger man. Making her husband miserable. I'm sure she'll tell you all about it herself if you stay for a few days. She's coming up, the day after tomorrow."

Katherine said nothing. Mathilde wasn't even sure she had heard her. She was gazing at a bowl of tulips on a corner table.

Suddenly her voice came, low, urgent. "Mat, did Sylvie ever mention anyone to you by the name of Alexei Gismondi or perhaps Ivan Makarov?" Katherine stared at her with wild eyes.

The Princesse stirred her tea reflectively. So, the moment might have come, she thought. She had hoped it never would. "I'll have to think back," she said slowly. "My memory's not what it used to be. Particularly for names."

Katherine was playing restlessly with her napkin, crumpling it, straightening it, crumpling it again. The girl was distressed. Usually she presented a calm face to the world, so composed. The Princesse crumbled a piece of pastry. "Have some of this, Kat. It's delicious."

She shook her head.

"Gismondi, let's see. He's an Italian industrialist, isn't he?" Mathilde asked blandly.

"Yes, yes," Katherine urged her. "Did Sylvie ever mention him? Mention his son? His adopted son?" She faltered on the last.

Princesse Mathilde gazed into the distance, contemplated space. She looked back at Katherine. "Why do you want to know?"

"I need to know." Katherine's voice was harsh. She pushed back her chair so that it scraped the floor. She paced. Looked again at the bowl of tulips, fingered one, started to crush it, caught herself.

"I need to know." Her voice lilted. "Alexei Gismondi has told me he might be Sylvie's son." She stared at the Princesse.

Mathilde laughed loudly. To break the tension. "Did *she* tell him that?" She laughed again. "Sylvie was always so good at fabrication. A master storyteller." She paused beneath Katherine's gaze. "What does it matter, Katherine? She's dead. It's all so long in the past."

"It matters to me," Katherine said, her tone husky, almost inaudible.

Mathilde tried to laugh again. She couldn't in front of the urgency of that face. "Why, Katherine? How can it matter?" she asked softly.

"Because I'm in love with Alexei Gismondi," she said breathlessly. And then the tears came. Copious. A single desperate sob. She hid her face.

Princesse Mathilde rose slowly. She put her arms round Katherine. "Don't worry, my little one. I shall put my mind to it. We'll try and make it come right. Let's rest now, I need to think."

Mathilde saw Katherine to her old bedroom. Went heavily to her own. She sat in the window armchair and gazed out at the mountains. So it had come to this. Sylvie's reach beyond the grave. An impossible set of coincidences urged into motion by Sylvie. Mathilde had hoped the story would never have to be unearthed.

She remembered her last meeting with Sylvie. Forced herself to concentrate on it. Sylvie nervous, jumping up and down, filled with brittle excitement.

"I have seen him. I have seen my son."

"You've seen Leo?"

"No. Not Leo. My other son. My lost son. Alexei."

"What's this nonsense, Sylvie? What on earth are you talking about now?"

"It's not nonsense." Sylvie had looked at her triumphantly. She still remembered that look, the chill it had elicited in her.

"I have another son. I love him. I have found him. Katherine is not my daughter." The last had been uttered with a kind of contemptuous loathing. "I'll tell you. I'll tell you how it was."

And she had told her, in that shrill excited voice of hers. A fraught, confused tale of a Poland still at war, of babies exchanged. Of a woman called Hanka in Sylvie's parents' house, of a man, Makarov. A story which had left the Princesse reeling. She had thought to herself: She's making it up. A fabrication. A lie to excuse herself for her hatred of Katherine, of what she's done to the girl. She had said it to her, confronted her with it. "You've made all this up, Sylvie. It's a wish. A wish that Katherine weren't your daughter."

"I have no daughter." Sylvie had stared at her with those dazzling blue eyes. "I only have sons."

In that last look, the Princesse had half believed her.

She didn't want to believe her. Sylvie's story had breathed images she wished to forget. Images of children with frightened eyes, children torn from their parents, separated. Displaced. History's orphans. War. A war which had no place in the peacetime quiet of these Swiss Alps.

"Have you told Jacob?" Mathilde had asked softly.

Sylvie had shaken her head forcefully, the blonde hair flying. "He doesn't deserve to know."

"And the boy?"

Sylvie had looked a little dazed, had shaken her head again. More slowly. "No, no. Not yet," she had mumbled.

"So there's only me?"

A nod. "You're the only person in the world I trust."

The words, the Princesse thought, were uttered like a gambler's challenge.

Not long after that, Sylvie had killed herself.

Princesse Mathilde stared out of the window. After a moment she got up and went to the telephone. They would all have to be told now. All brought together. She sighed deeply. Jacob, how would he take it? And Katherine? Katherine already in such a state. And Leo? Leo, busy with more important things than these ashes of the past. And this man, this unknown, this Alexei? But there was nothing for it now. She would have to tell what she knew and only dimly believed.

Five days later, they were all gathered. All but one. Gathered in Princesse Mathilde's dining room. The telephones, the jets had their purposes, Mathilde thought. Jacob and Leo had flown at her bidding. Natalie was playing with the dogs outside in the grounds. Violette was here. And Katherine, pale with her waiting. The Princesse had refused to tell her anything more since that first encounter. The members of her audience, each with their separate knowledge of Sylvie and themselves, would have to determine the truth or fiction of what she related. Only Alexei was still to come. She had managed to reach him only yesterday.

They were sitting around the long walnut table in the dining room.

The afternoon light played over its polished surface catching reflections, throwing them back in fragmented form. Leo was talking, telling them of Salvador, of Guatemala, bruised tales of suffering in a world so different from this one, yet the same, made real by his quiet voice. Leo, the one she knew least well, his face darkened by years in the tropical sun, the bones evident beneath the skin. They were all engaged in his narrative. Yet beneath their attention, there was another current, a restless anticipation. A palpable waiting. She had not told them why she had brought them together. Had not even told Jacob. Jacob with his white mane, his eyes still piercing, in that face she now sometimes found it difficult to recognize. It was not the face she conjured up when she read his letters. The sensation must be the same for him. She smiled in his direction, a wistful smile, ruptured by Violette's restive voice.

"When are you going to tell us why we're here, Mat? I can't bear this waiting."

Princesse Mathilde looked at her daughter at the other end of the long table. Those mobile features, animated gestures. Herself and not herself. "Patience, my dear. You are old enough now for a little patience," she rebuked her gently.

The dining-room door opened. Alexei Gismondi was announced. The Princesse rose to greet him, looked. Her breath caught. Why did they all not see it? It was Jacob. Jacob as she had first known him. The same brooding, intelligent cast of the features. The set of the head. The thick curling hair. But eyes, eyes the dusky blue of Sylvie's. Or was it her fantasies speaking, resurrecting the Jacob she had loved? For a moment she felt dizzy. Then she braced herself, made the necessary introductions.

No, the others didn't see it. Jacob greeted the man curiously. "How good to see you again, Mr. Gismondi. Unexpected, here." She could see his mind working, the quick tread of it, but no ulterior recognition.

Perhaps she was imagining resemblance.

Violette, always alert to masculine charm, shook Alexei's hand lingeringly, threw a querying glance at her mother.

Leo stood tall, matter-of-fact. The Princesse looked for likeness. One so blond, uncomfortable in a suit which looked unworn. The other, dark, intent, noticing everything, but reserved, formal.

Only Katherine didn't stand, murmured an inaudible "Hello," averted her gaze. But his eyes now were only for her. Eyes ringed with pain.

And suddenly the Princesse felt it between them. The force of that ancient longing. Love, people called it. A dark obsessional force that obliterated the world and transformed it. The sickness of desire. It made her uncomfortable. She had forgotten its intensity. She remembered now, felt it stirring old bones. She took a deep breath, sat down.

Katherine was at her left. She placed Alexei in the empty chair at her right. Jacob faced her from the end of the table beneath the ornate tapestry which told biblical tales of gardens and expulsion. She took sustenance from its richness and from his eyes.

"I have called you together because I have a story to tell. A story that affects you all," she began slowly, poured herself a glass of water, sipped, looked at them each in turn. "It's a story shrouded in time. I cannot vouch for its truth. I don't know whether it can ever be verified. I can only relate it, more or less as it was related to me, by a woman who was known to all of you. Sylvie Jardine, or as she often insisted on calling herself, Sylvie Kowalska."

Princesse Mathilde paused. She could see the surprise in Jacob's face, the anxiety in Leo's, the relish in Violette's. Alexei's expression was more difficult to read—acute interest, apprehension and at the same time a wish not to know, a desire in sympathy with another, with Katherine, whose look was tortured, a child waiting helplessly for blows.

The Princesse continued. "Before she died, Sylvie came to see me. She was fraught. Overexcited. She had a secret to reveal. A wartime secret, a secret which reverberated with the confusions and shadows and distortions of that time. A story which it seems she had buried herself and only recently unearthed.

"The scene of the story is Poland and its outlines, I think, are only as clear as the tenuous borders of that troubled country." The Princesse allowed herself a little smile and found its echo only in Jacob.

"As some of you know, Sylvie returned to Poland in 1945. She was pregnant at the time. She gave birth to a child there. A child we had all always assumed was Katherine. The story Sylvie told me might lead us to assume that was not the case."

There was an audible gasp in the room. The Princesse rushed on, eager now for the end. "Sylvie told me that Katherine was not her child. Her child was a boy. She switched the babies at the clinic. The motivation was unclear to me, perhaps unclear to her. It had something to do with the death of her friend Caroline's daughter, something to do with the woman in the next bed, whom she felt sorry for and who was desperate for a boy. In any event, Sylvie claimed that she took the girl, Katherine, for her own. Left the boy to a couple called Makarov. The boy now, I believe, bears the name Alexei Gismondi."

All eyes turned on Alexei. There was a hush in the room, a silence tense with the unvoiced.

Katherine's thoughts reeled with the giddiness of vertigo. Not Sylvie's daughter. I am not Sylvie's daughter. I am not Jacob's daughter. That's why she hated me. But if I'm not their daughter, who am I?

She'll hate me now, Alexei worried. She'll hate me. I've robbed her of her parents.

Leo thought: Orphans. All this accursed history. Children are dying *now*. Being abandoned *now*. And we sit here excavating what no longer matters.

Oh, Sylvie, thought Violette. A surprise at every turn. Even after your death.

Jacob reflected, imagined Sylvie. Tasted Sylvie floating between the boundaries of reality and the tumult of her mind. Saw a scene in the hospital that was her home. The wished-for home that was always absent, always already gone. Dead, like her parents. Orphaned Sylvie, displaced but alive, seeking somehow to make reparations for her dead. Thought: I've been so stupid. True or not, it's the truth about Sylvie. A baby to give to Caroline. Herself to give to Caroline, her friend, mother and friend. She told me as much. And Caroline betrayed her by dying. Betrayed her in the way her parents had. Betrayal avenged in hatred for Katherine. And I didn't understand. I betrayed her. Sylvie.

Princesse Mathilde looked at them all. Tasted the silent seconds of reflection. It could be true. She had convinced herself of it in the telling of the tale. Remembered the dozens of displaced children who had moved like wraiths in this very room all those years ago. Recaptured the confusion, the horror, the heightened imaginations of war, the actions which couldn't be acted in the quiet ordinariness of the everyday.

Suddenly, from Jacob, there came a low whisper. "Sylvie's legacy. What less could we expect?"

His words were followed by general commotion. Katherine had turned ghostly white. She trembled, looked as if she were about to faint. Jacob moved toward her. Alexei was there before him, lifting her in his arms, brushing her cheek with his lips. Jacob poured a glass of water. Katherine drank, grasped his hand, held Alexei's.

"I'm not me," she whispered to them. "Not me. No one."

"You're still my daughter, Kat." Jacob was firm. "It's too late for me to begin to believe that biology takes precedence over history." He shook his head with a troubled reminiscence. But his voice held a note of awe. "Sylvie always did have a passion for the surreal. But *you* are still you."

"The you I love." Alexei's tone was insistent. "And whatever the truth, you are distinctly not my sister." His eyes spoke forcibly, burning into her, so that her cheeks caught flame.

Katherine looked from one to the other, from Alexei to Jacob and back. If he was Sylvie's son, she suddenly thought, then she could forgive Sylvie. Forgive her anything.

Jacob, watching Alexei, his arm around Katherine's shoulders, deliberated. Son or not, this was the right man for her. And she had had to come back to Europe to find him. That caldron of memories. That, too, was as it should be.

Leo after a moment came up to Alexei. He hesitated awkwardly, then smiled. "I'm not sure whether all this makes us brothers, but one way or another, we'll have to get to know each other better."

"And don't forget about big sister here." Violette, trying to dispel the tension, managed an impish laugh. "There you are, Jacob, two of each now."

He kissed her. "I've always been a decidedly fortunate man."

"Why are you fortunate, Gramps?" Natalie burst in on them, pink-cheeked, dogs in train.

"Me and you both, Nat." He bent to her.

Natalie raced into her mother's arms, looked boldly at Alexei. "Wasn't it good of me to leave you alone for so long in Rome?"

Suddenly Katherine smiled. A radiant face, glowing, transformed. "Yes, hon. You're an angel of a daughter. An angel to have left us alone." She glanced at Alexei, shy now as she remembered the warmth of his love.

Alexei kissed her. There. In front of everyone. Then he twirled Natalie round. The dogs barked excitedly.

"And now you come with me, Nat." Leo placed a commanding hand on the girl's shoulder. "We've a lot of serious catching up to do." He winked at Katherine and steered his niece away, urged Violette to join them.

Jacob looked after his son, pleased at his tact, proud as he always was, when he reflected on him, thought of the choices Leo had made, the direction of his life. A son worthy of his campaigning grandfather. And now, Jacob mused, he was faced with another son, an unknown, an adventure for his old age. He turned to Alexei, saw the protective arm around Katherine, the light in her eyes. Where to begin with this stranger? Jacob chuckled. The sting in the tail of Sylvie's scorpion, the creature she had left him on her deathbed, not so poisonous now, after all those years.

"Mathilde, I think all this calls for a bottle from your cellar. A very best bottle. Nineteen forty-five, if you can manage it."

She caught his humor. "I'll see what I can do. Two might be better than one."

Jacob, Alexei and Katherine strolled into the Princesse's salon, formed a little circle in the corner of the room. Jacob gestured them toward the sofa, positioned himself in an armchair. "And so, Alexei," he began, "you came to me looking for absent mothers . . ." Alexei nodded, embarrassed as he recalled his duplicity.

Jacob caught the question in Katherine's eye. "Oh yes, perhaps you don't know this. I first met Alexei when he came to my consulting room, posing as a prospective patient." Jacob laughed. "I kicked him out, told him he needed a philosopher, not an analyst."

Alexei felt the pressure of Katherine's hand, returned it, wanted to say it was her he needed, but he focused on Jacob. A new father. It was the last thing he had considered. He tasted the notion. It wasn't comfortable. He was perhaps too old for fathers. But he liked this man. "I couldn't very well come to you out of the blue and say I had reason to believe that your wife, that Sylvie, might have had an affair with my father. You see, her letter to me only stated that she was my mother, and so naturally, I assumed . . ."

Jacob laughed wryly. "Pure Sylvie. Men, lovers, husbands, they were always something of an irrelevance—necessary, but hardly crucial." Funny, he thought to himself, it no longer hurt him to think it.

"And then," Alexei continued, "when you showed me those drawings and I found myself, a Russian soldier, the name Makarov, the place, Lublin, amongst them, I thought there lay the proof. I fled." An involuntary shudder shook him. He lowered his eyes. "Because, you see, by that time I had met Katherine. Felt, well, felt things one doesn't feel for a sister." He put his arm around her, held her close, testing her presence.

"But you never suspected?" Katherine scrutinized Jacob.

He shook his head. "How could I? Sylvie, when I came to fetch her in Poland, presented me with this wonderful daughter, eh, my little Kat?" For a moment, his glance glowed over her, seeing that tiny fragile creature he had held in his arms, all those years ago in Krakow. He turned back to Alexei. "But what did Sylvie say to you?"

"Nothing. Or at least, as I remember it, nothing on the single occasion when I met her. There was only the letter. When it arrived, some time in '68, my uncle Giangiacomo and I thought it was simply another letter from a madwoman. We received quite a number at that time." He stopped himself. "I'm sorry, I didn't mean to imply . . ."

Jacob waved his apology away. "No, no, Sylvie was nothing if not extreme. Extravagant. Extraordinary. And troubled. Deeply troubled." He mulled it over. "That's why we loved her," he said softly. He gazed at Katherine, added, "And sometimes hated her."

Katherine met his eyes, saw Sylvie for the first time through them. A separate woman who was not her mother. And yet was. Two separate Sylvies blending into one. She took a long, deep breath. She suddenly felt free, unconstricted. And curious for the first time about that woman.

"What I don't understand is, if she wasn't my mother, why Sylvie never said, never implied anything?"

He shrugged. "We'll never know now. Perhaps she wasn't sure. Perhaps she didn't remember. Perhaps it was my fault. We all find ourselves in little traps sometimes. Traps made by the world, our families, ourselves. And Sylvie had a passion for secrets. For surprises." A twinkle lit his eyes. "But now, whatever the case, *ma petite Kat,* you will have to forgive this woman who was the only mother you ever knew, for good and for bad, eh? Forgive her because, if nothing else, she has brought you Alexei—in her own inimitable way."

Katherine looked from Alexei to Jacob and back. "I already have," she murmured. "I already have. But . . ."

"No, that's enough now." Jacob rose. "Mathilde will be waiting with those special bottles. And I want to celebrate with *all* my children." He put an arm around Katherine, another around Alexei, led them toward the others, already gathered, noted how, as soon as he released them, they reached for each other. He smiled to himself, moved toward Mathilde, took the proffered glass, noted the label on the bottle. Château Latour 1945. He saw Mathilde's air of feigned innocence.

"Sylvie's name during the war," Jacob whispered. "You remembered?"

That old air of secret amusement lit her face.

Jacob cleared his throat. There was laughter in the room, the rise and fall of excited voices. He drew everyone's attention, raised his glass. "I think a toast is in order. A toast to all the sons and daughters gathered here." He met their eyes one by one, little Natalie and Violette, Leo and Alexei and Katherine.

He drank deeply, a deep fragrant vintage, rich and mellow with age. He spoke again, his eyes sparkling. "A toast to mothers, as well. To Sylvie, for her wonderful legacy."

"To Sylvie." The room echoed with his words.

Jacob paused, turned to Mathilde. Carefully, he chose his words, "And to Mathilde, who has always known more than all of us; who has always, ever since the days of her Paris school, had a way with orphans." He chuckled, caught her smile. "And on top of it all, who has a very special genius for selecting her moments for revelation."

He took her hand, brought it to his lips.

Voices rose again.

Katherine thought, he has always loved Mathilde. And Sylvie. Both of them. My mother and not my mother. And me. Has loved me. Her daughter, his daughter and not their daughter. An orphan and not an orphan. Myself. Simply myself. Yes, *at last* myself. In love with this man. Alexei. She raised her glass to him. Touched him. I'm happy, she thought. So happy. Shyly she reached for his hand. "Alexei, I must ask Jacob just one more thing."

"Just one?" he teased her.

"At least one." Katherine smiled, tugged at Jacob's sleeve. "Jacob, who was Caroline? Why . . . ?"

"Off with you." Jacob shooed her away. "No more questions now. Take her away, Alexei. Yes, off with all you young ones." He gazed at them with mock ferocity. "Off with you. Leave the past to us." His eyes were bright as he took Mathilde's arm.

"Yes"—she leaned on him, smiled a mischievous smile—"*assez.* Leave memory to us. Go and concentrate on your desires."

Princesse Mathilde and Jacob walked slowly arm in arm into the garden. The setting sun clothed the mountain caps in palest pink. They strolled in quiet, made their way toward a wrought iron bench which gave out on the vista, sat silently for a moment and contemplated the rise and fall of the land.

"So all these years," Jacob mused, you've been the repository of our family memories. And you never spoke." He gave her a piercing glance.

Princesse Mathilde still gazed into the distance. Her voice when it came held a note of wonder. "Endless permutations on a family romance. The very essence of your trade." She smiled a slow wistful smile, turned to him. "And a storybook ending. Not every daughter gets to marry her father. He looks so like you."

"Then you think he *is* my son? You think it's true. Sylvie really did it. Her ultimate transgression?"

"Perhaps." She looked at him from twinkling eyes. "But what is truth?"

"Yes," Jacob echoed, "what's truth?" He surveyed the landscape, spoke almost as if to himself. "We search for it in the crucible of our memories, distort it with our fantasies, create pleasing fictions for ourselves, speculate . . ."

She laughed at him, at herself. That wry girlish laugh he remembered. "And what more have we to do, we old tattered coats upon our sticks, than to speculate. Eh, my old Dr. Jardine?" Her laughter embraced them.

"Yes." He put his arm gently round her shoulders. "And sit like Yeats's birds upon a golden bough 'to sing of what is past, or passing, or to come.' "

"Free from desire."

He nodded. "You understand, Mat. It's good to see you. Very good."

"Yes," she acknowledged him. "Yes, Jacob. It's very good to see you, my friend."